Solomon's Puzzle

a novel by
Loris Nebbia

Loris Nebbia

BLESSING HOUSE PRESS

ISBN-13: 978-0-9845164-0-7

Printed in the United States of America by United Book Press, Baltimore, Maryland

Cover Design and Photographs by Andrew and Valerie Vaché

ACKNOWLEDGEMENTS

Many heartfelt thanks to those who helped me while I was writing and who assisted in the production of this book: to my family, Karl, Eric, Care, Joe, Andrea, Val, Andrew, Karl, Joey, Jack, Clare and Cyrus for their wisdom, inspiration, steady encouragement and patience. To my early readers: Sherry, Andrea, Joe, Cindy, Jo-Ann, Walter, Stefanie, Karl, Teresa, Jada, Janice, Wendy, Elizabeth, Heather and Sam—your enthusiasm sustained me. Thanks to all who prayed for me and the project. Thanks to Eric for basketball expertise, to Karl for military and business details. Special thanks to the editing and production team at Blessing House Press: Kristen Intlekofer, editor, web design and construction—your wisdom and literary instincts were bright lights. I'm grateful for the generous time, heart and expertise you brought to the project. Care Nebbia, design and copy editor—your dedication, your ability to meet deadlines like nobody else, your tireless work and love of perfection let me sleep at night. Joe Nebbia, copy editor—thanks for your incomparable eye for detail and your cheerful work. Thanks to Val, who paved the way, then pushed me to finish and helped every step; your artistry and courage inspired me. Thanks to Andrew and Valerie Vaché for their creativity in design. Thanks to my friends in Annapolis, my colleagues and all my many dear students and their families at school who created a community worthy of celebration. And thanks to Karl especially for making all those perfect cups of tea.

to my husband,
Karl Nebbia,
the stalwart one who never doubted

&

to my father,
David Gosse,
whose absence bid me look up

Prologue

With his children gathered around him, Tom MacBride liked to describe his unusual birth by saying he was born in the belly of a great, silver beast as it winged its way west across the Atlantic. His parents had lived apart for nearly nine months while his jovial, soft-spoken father emigrated to Philadelphia to join an uncle's plumbing business and his mother waited at home in Jedburgh, Scotland. There she labored as a housekeeper in the elegant High Street homes, saving money with a staunch determination typical to her. She lived carefully and alone as she grew her unborn son on oatcakes with butter and bramble jam. Tom was later than expected, and his reluctance to be born chaffed his mother because she feared it raised questions about her faithfulness.

Her minuscule ration of patience rubbed away, she insisted on keeping the travel plans made before she had known a new life had begun within. On September first, Tom's mother—big-bellied and belligerent—boarded the plane bound for America. She silenced the flight attendants' worried inquires with her most frightening glare and said, "If I thought this child would be born any time in th' next *century*, do you think I'd be fool enough to get on this plane?" But born he was, in the next hour, a citizen of the skies. And when his father met Tom, still dewy, squinting and smelling of salt, he wept.

Tom grew, surviving his mother's harshness, cherishing his father's tender heart. He lived eagerly, married his first love, and his senses still came to attention when she moved past him. He had tried to live thoughtfully; his children—three teasing teenagers and an ambitious eleven-year-old—could meet his eyes and laugh with him at his quirks. He spent his days organizing competitions and coaching games as a high school athletic director, loving to see people work together, gathering armfuls of good friends. Tolerating those who annoyed him, always telling the truth, he had made only one enemy.

He remembered that enemy most keenly as September approached. When harvests ripened, fulfilling the deeply sown promises of spring and summer, and leaves turned bright before dying; when the school year stood poised to begin, and Tom celebrated the passing of another year of life, he paused for introspection. Tom MacBride regretted, as he had for sixteen years, that he had made an angry and dangerous enemy out of Max Hunter.

Their clashes could not strictly be defined as fist fights. Yet each had dealt injuries to Tom's back. He knew he could live with the resulting back pain, knew he could endure the inconvenience of legs that went numb, felt he deserved the frustration of having to resort more and more frequently to the help of a wheelchair. What Tom hoped he would not have to endure forever was the knowledge that he had so destructively failed another human being. His full-grown belief that God understood his agony told Tom that he would see Max again.

Tom knew that one more clash with Max would ruin his ability to walk. They had proven that they could not meet without violence—without the breaking of bones, the crushing of vertebrae, the remembrance of bitter anger. Yet Tom wanted one final opportunity to see Max, one last chance to keep an old and fervently sworn promise. He remembered that promise as his year began and prayed that he might fulfill it, though he expected it to cost him dearly.

BOOK ONE

Birds in the Air

1

That morning in August Ben Hunter sprinted from his father's quarters on the grounds of the U.S. Naval Academy. When he saw that his grandmother's car was gone, he stopped mid-stride; the heavy, morning air stuck to his face and pressed his shirt to his chest. Behind him, he heard his father's hard leather shoes slap their advance into the kitchen. Ben swung his backpack onto his shoulder. If he started now, he could jog the three miles to his new school and stay out of his father's car as he'd vowed to do each time he emerged from it alive.

His father opened the door. Ben straightened up. His hand went to the knot in his tie; he slid it up past the open top button. His brothers, Keith and Tim, ran out, their pace hollow and quick on the wooden stairs. Colonel Max Hunter, USMC, stood crisply uniformed and erect as an obelisk, impervious to criticism and suspicion. He flicked his wrist. "Get in the car."

Keith and Tim obeyed at a run, tossing their stuff into the back seat. Max stepped up so close to Ben that the medals on his chest scratched against Ben's shoulder and Ben could smell his minted breath.

"Get in, Ben." Max was an inch taller than Ben. His body, thick, firm, and only slightly overweight, showed an agility and confidence in the bearing of his dense shoulders that Ben could not help but acknowledge.

Ben's stomach tightened. "Gran said she was driving us." He glanced again at her empty parking space.

"Do you see Gran anywhere?" Max opened the passenger door for Ben, quickly rounded the front of the car and took the driver's seat. Ben shifted his backpack. When Max gunned the motor, Ben felt it in his stomach. "Ben. Now," Max said, his voice edged with irritation. "You don't want to be late."

Keith and Tim pressed their noses against the window and beckoned him with flapping hands; their unspoiled grins fell like boots on his glass vows. Ben slung his backpack onto the floor. He buckled his seat belt, wishing he had two. His father's mouthwash smelled too strong, his aftershave pungent as brass polish. Ben opened the sunroof an inch and the car lurched away from the curb.

"Did I say you could open that?" Ben glanced at him and saw Max wiggling his jaw back and forth the way he did when he was thinking about something else. "Air conditioning not enough for you, icicle man?"

"Aw, you know, I'm into fresh air, *sir*."

Max spoke into the mirror. "I think Ben's telling me I stink, boys."

"Ben would never say that," Keith vowed.

"That's right," Tim said. Ben turned to hush the unpredictable Tim, but too late. Tim said, brightly, "Ben knows better words for you than just stink."

"That's cold, Ben, nice and cold." Ben felt his father's glance, his eyes searching Ben's face the way they ought to be watching the road beyond the windshield. "You can find your own ride today after school."

"Yes, sir," Ben said, reminding himself that if he could survive forty-five days, he'd be sixteen. He imagined his own hands gripping the steering wheel of any junk car he could afford to buy.

The marine at the gate recognized Max and jerked to attention. Nodding, Max muttered his approval, "Damn good thing my marines don't salute like those navy slobs."

Maybe he's only his usual uptight self, Ben hoped, as Max swung the car in a wide left turn toward the city dock, Max glanced at a man jogging on the left. "Lots of folks out this morning," Max observed.

Try not to hit one, Ben urged silently. As Max drove, he studied the faces of people they passed. His father's peculiar habit, Ben had observed it for as long as he could remember. Today, Max gazed a bit too long at the faces. His elbow propped on the open window, Max stared as each driver approached, following the face until it snapped past his field of vision.

Fortunately, the light at Prince George Street stayed green because to Ben's dismay, Max did not look at it as he sailed through the intersection. Shaking his leg, drumming his fingers on the door handle, Ben glanced back to make sure his brothers wore their seat belts. He felt the car's direction shift slightly and looked to see Max's distracted expression. The left front bumper crossed the center line.

"Dad," he yelled, reaching for the steering wheel, "you're aiming for that car!" Knocking Ben's hand away, Max caught Ben in the mouth. A horn sounded. Max forced the steering wheel hard to the right, sending the Volvo rushing up over the curb where it smashed through a half wall that surrounded a café terrace.

Ben looked to the back seat, "You guys okay?"

They had bent double, covering their heads with their arms as Ben had taught them. "Did something happen?" Tim said.

"We crashed," Keith said.

His father sat back in the driver's seat, mouth open and slack, eyes stunned. The car roared and jerked, the wheels made a rubbing noise. Ben smelled coffee mingled with the scents of frying bacon and burning rubber. He tasted blood.

"Dad?"

"Damn."

"You okay?"

"Of course I'm okay."

"You might want to take your foot off the gas," Ben advised. His father blinked back to focus, moved his foot and gave Ben a withering look of correction as the car sputtered to silence. Disgusted, Ben turned to get out and found that his backpack was wedged against his knees so tightly he couldn't move. A woman rushed out of the café and marched toward them. Slim, white-haired and Ben guessed as old as his grandmother, she wore black trousers, a white tuxedo shirt and a determined, almost rough expression on her face. Her apron, the maroon color of the restaurant's siding, bore the same logo as the large MIDDLETON'S TAVERN sign that now hung askew over the wrecked terrace.

His father shoved hard on his door, forcing it open wide enough for him to squirm out. He turned to meet the woman and immediately stuck out his hand, which she ignored, bending to look in the back seat at the boys.

"Everyone okay?" she said.

"I think they're okay," Ben told her.

"We're just hiding," Tim said, peeking out from the crook of his elbow.

"It's okay to stop hiding," Ben said and both boys emerged, eyes wide, lips pressed together.

She opened the back door, and glancing at Max, introduced herself. "Lin Middleton," she said. "I own the place." She held Tim's backpack for him while he climbed out. Max smoothed the creases in his trousers, and when he looked up again, his composure suggested this sort of crisis happened every single day.

Then people came around. Two police cars careened to a stop. One police officer arrived on foot. Nudging his backpack along the back seat, Keith emerged and a stout, female officer bent to speak to the boys. Another came to Ben's side of the car. "You okay?" he asked, peering in above the crumbling window.

Ben nodded. The officer was fairly young with an animated, trusting face and keen blue eyes. His name-tag read *Smith*. Noticing that Ben read it, he said, "Call me Smitty."

"I'm gonna be late for school, Smitty. It's the first day, and I'm new."

"I'll get you there before you know it," Smitty said. "Your lip's busted open. Hurt much?"

"Not too bad."

"It's bleeding."

"Just a little. Hit the dashboard, I guess," Ben said, looking away.

"You'd better get out. The front of the car is pretty smashed up."

"I was waiting for them so I could move the seat back."

"Are you stuck?" Smitty yanked on the door getting it to open a crack. Ben popped the seat back, which loosened his backpack enough so he could pull it up onto his lap. Smitty took it from him, maneuvering it through the fragmented window. "You're going to have to climb out." Sirens wailed, approaching.

Another police officer poked his head in the driver's side window. "Legs okay? Can you move 'em?"

"I'm fine." His shins throbbed, but they were sound.

"You're a pretty big kid. Be hard to squeeze past the steering wheel with the front smashed like that."

Ben twisted around, thinking to escape as his brothers had.

"Climb out the sunroof," Smitty advised. "Can you do that?"

"If I can fit." Ben maneuvered until he could kneel. Outside the car, Ben's father spoke. In the voice that could convince healthy, sane, young men to shave their heads, to submit to tough discipline, and to offer their bright lives to the Marine Corps, in that booming, authoritative voice, Max described how an oncoming car had swerved into his lane forcing him to jump the curb and wreck Middleton's terrace. Somehow in tone and expression his father implied that crashing into Middleton's was the only courageous choice. Max said that the woman who drove the other car—the car that had fled—had obviously been distracted by a black Labrador romping in the front seat. Brilliant, Dad, Ben thought, blame it on a dog. His stomach tossed. Suddenly desperate to get out, he crouched below the sunroof. *Don't ask me what happened,* he warned silently, cranking it open with hard, rapid jerks.

Ben heard the whine of an ambulance then several short bursts of its strange horn as it parted the crowd and sidled up to the broken Volvo.

Sticking his head through the sunroof opening, Ben braced one foot on the dashboard. He found that if he slanted his shoulders, he could get them through one at a time. Then it was easy; pushing with one foot and lifting with his arms he emerged, sat on the edge of the sunroof and bent his knees one at a time to get his long legs out.

To Ben's keen humiliation, the crowd erupted in a roar of applause. People smiled and waved, the gold morning sunlight surrounding shoulders and faces with bright halos. In spite of his throbbing lip, he couldn't help but smile and give a quick, shy wave in response. Unbelievably, the crowd again applauded. He felt his nauseating disgust with his father recede.

"Welcome to Annapolis," Smitty said, arms raised as if to catch Ben. His face felt hot, then his vision went dizzy. Three paramedics joined

Smitty at the side of the car and all four raised their hands to help Ben as he scooted to the roof's edge. Eight hands around caught him as if he were a small child, supporting his weight with steady hands on his torso, his chest and under his arms. When he was down, they released him, patting him briskly like fond uncles or proud coaches.

"You okay?"

"Just need to get to school."

"I'll take you over as soon as the boys here check you out," Smitty said, clapping Ben on the shoulder. "CCS, right? Can tell by the uniform. Class of '89." He pointed to himself.

By the time Ben reached the ambulance, his brothers had been examined and pronounced sound. They called their good-byes to Ben as a police officer took one by each hand to walk them past the market and the dock to school. The paramedic examined Ben's lip and the inside of his mouth. He placed an ice pack on Ben's face and lingered, asking questions, probing Ben's neck and shoulders for injury.

"Come look at this," he said quietly to his partner. Smitty, too, leaned in to look as the paramedic tested Ben's eyes again with the flashlight. "The pupil's weird and it won't contract."

"That's nothing," Ben said, and reaching up, he rubbed his eye. "My contact must have gotten knocked off balance."

"Whoa."

"It looks weird when it's off center," Ben told them. "There's a fake pupil colored into the contact lens. My own pupil is shaped like a key-hole. It lets in too much light, so I have to wear this contact lens to see…like you do."

"You sure?"

"How could anybody make something like that up?" Ben gave a practiced laugh.

"Maybe we should take him in for a CT scan."

"I'm fine. I just need to get to school."

"Come on, guys, it's the first day of school," Smitty said. "He's already late."

While the paramedics listed head injury warning signs for Ben, Smitty interrupted Max's retelling of the sequence of the accident to say that he would drive Ben to school.

"I want to speak to him first," Max said. Excusing himself, he strode over the rubble on the terrace to where Ben waited at the back of the open ambulance deck. Seeing his father approach, Ben took the ice-pack from his lip and placed it down. He stood up straight, shifted his backpack to his shoulder and as the feeling rushed back to his lip, he carefully drew it in against his teeth to disguise the swelling he knew was inevitable.

Taking the back of Ben's neck in his hand, Max steered Ben away from those surrounding them. Ben shuddered. Max slid his hand along Ben's shoulders, pulling him close so he could speak in his ear. Ben stiffened, pulling away. But Max held firm, his fingers gripping hard into the tight muscle of Ben's shoulder.

"We'll talk later about what you did to cause this," Max said.

"What?"

"I'm covering for you in front of these people," his father said, his face so close that Ben could smell the faint fragrance of his breath, "but don't you *ever* reach over and yell the way you did. You hear me?" He dropped his arm, releasing his grip. Ben stepped back, a thousand retorts mounting furiously, begging to be spoken, dying at his throbbing lip.

Smitty chatted amiably as he inched his immaculate white patrol car through the crowded dock area, his elbow propped on the open window. At the traffic light at the summit of Main Street, Smitty slowed the car to a stop. "Turn around," he said. Smitty grinned, pointing behind him with his thumb. "Look back."

Ben turned to see the widening vista of Main Street slope down to the dock. The water in the harbor beyond lay still and smooth, glazed in a wide path with the hot sunlight that glowed above thin, gold-edged clouds. Seagulls coasted through the slanted, morning sunlight. This same clear light reflected from the harbor's white boats and gilded the scattered panes of glass in the quiet, brick storefronts that lined the street and burnished the brick streets to crimson. "That's Annapolis. That's my home-town. You got to *know* I like protecting this place. You *know* it." Ben nod-ded. Smitty turned the car to the right and glanced at Ben, eyes serious. "You're gonna like it here, kid."

"Yes, sir, I—I do like it."

"Been over to school yet?"

"Just for new student stuff. What did you think of it, when you went there?"

"I had a rough freshman year, but Coach MacBride reformed me. Shook some sense into my dumb head."

"How?"

"I dunno exactly," Smitty laughed. "Magic, I guess. But he tutored me and my twin brother in math and chemistry once we got serious about school. "

"A coach who knows math and chemistry?"

"Yep and we'd go to his house. I'd eat everything in sight while my brother studied. He's in med school now up at Hopkins. Ever need a good meal, go to the MacBrides'."

"Just go there when I'm hungry? Yeah, right."

"You met Coach MacBride yet?"

"Um, I met this short, bald coach with a white mustache."

"That's Bettinger. He's my old wrestling coach. MacBride is the athletic director. Coaches basketball and baseball. They say he saved a kid from drowning once."

"I wanted to meet the basketball coach, but Mrs. Poulard said he was taking his kid to college or something."

Smitty nodded. "You play basketball?"

"A little."

"Any good?"

"Sort of."

"Yep," Smitty said. "That's what my brother and I said about wrestling and we were state champions."

Ben suppressed a smile and looked out the window.

Smitty glanced at Ben. "Your dad mind me driving you?"

"He didn't have a choice, did he?"

Smitty slowed the car at the light on Bestgate Road. "Look, Ben, I know if you're the only witness against your father, he'll make you pay."

"Huh?" Ben said, stiffening.

"I know that split lip didn't come from you hitting the dashboard."

"You *know* that?" Ben felt his throat tightening.

"For one, you had your seatbelt on. And then, you're too tall. With little kids, they smash up their mouths. Somebody your height hits their head on the windshield."

"I don't think that happened."

"No wonder your dad lost control of the car if he's smacking you in the mouth while he's driving."

Ben said, "The light's green."

Smitty nodded and pulled forward. "It was a strange accident."

"Yeah."

"I hate to ask you this, kid. Is it possible he'd been drinking?"

"At seven in the morning?" Ben laughed to hide his memory of the second whiff he'd gotten of his father's breath—after the accident, that sickening smell overpowering the last traces of too much mouthwash. *I should never have let Keith and Tim get in the car with him.*

The worst thing about the silence resounding in the car as they drove down Bestgate Road was that Ben already respected Smitty, even liked him, and he thought his silence would be misunderstood. He searched for something to say that was neither a lie nor a betrayal. As Smitty slowed the car to turn into the school parking lot, Ben felt a new surge of anxiety.

"You have a great day, Ben. Tell Miz Poulard that Smitty drove you over after the accident. They won't give you any trouble about being late."

"Thanks for everything," Ben said as he left the car. He paused, both hands holding the door. "The other car was a silver-blue Jeep Cherokee. A dark-haired man was driving it. A white guy. His haircut might have been military."

Smitty nodded, meeting Ben's eyes. "I'll swing by after school to see if you need a ride."

Ben stopped and leaned in the window. "No, really—"

"Yeah, I'll be here."

Looking away, Ben said, "Thanks."

"One more thing, Ben. Was there a dog in the front seat?"

"It was weird," Ben laughed in a tense spurt. "I thought I saw a dog sitting up straight, wearing a seatbelt. But that couldn't be, could it? It's probably my imagination."

"You behave yourself," Smitty said, raising his hand in a farewell wave.

2

THE lobby of the school was not as empty as Ben imagined it would be at this late hour. He opened the door and saw the principal, Mrs. Poulard, shepherding students into the gym at the far side of the lobby. Mrs. Poulard was small and spry with short, chestnut hair and a rosy face. During his admission interview, she and Ben had spoken for thirty minutes on the reasons for Randy Johnson's amazing pitching, then another twenty about Tolkien's *The Hobbit*, after which she told Ben's grandmother that she couldn't possibly survive the school year without Ben.

From within the brightly lit recesses of the gym, someone using a microphone had begun to speak. Ben stepped into the lobby. The group that Mrs. Poulard urged into the gym was taller than average. They moved with a certain athletic distinction; this and their shoulder-bumping affinity made Ben wonder if they were the basketball team. He stared at faces trying to recognize them from the dozens of newspaper clippings his grandmother had given him about the school.

One of these boys, not quite as tall as Ben, with a dazzling and dimly familiar smile, said something to make Mrs. Poulard throw up her hands in laughter and move to shepherd another group of students. Smiling and calling out, the boy went to a man who rolled toward the gym doors in a sleek, sport wheelchair. The same boy slid a piece of notebook paper into his hand and patted the wheelchair-bound man on the back with it as he spoke to him, again flashing his winning grin. Exchanging significant glances, the group moved through the open double doors. As the man turned to follow, Ben saw that the boy had stuck the notebook paper onto the man's back. It hung like a sign. Ben squinted to read, WALK IT OFF, the standard encouragement given by coaches to their whining, mildly injured athletes. Ben gulped, struggling to keep from laughing. His mind raced: *Was the kid cruel…or daring? How would the man—who obviously couldn't walk—take it?*

"That's the basketball team," a female voice said, startling Ben. He turned to see a girl standing behind a table right next to him. Trying to take in her details in a polite glance, Ben noticed the light touching her face and her dark hair. A clear, honest expression showed in her bright brown eyes.

"The guys over there—the ones you're watching? They're the varsity basketball team."

"The whole team?" Ben asked, counting quickly. He dreaded his first inevitable contact with the team, wondering how he would ever break into that tight group.

"No, but the main ones."

"Did you see the paper they stuck on that guy's back?" Ben asked, still incredulous.

"He'll love it."

"He'll love *that*?" he asked, determined to show her what was dangerous about the joke.

She raised her eyebrows as if she thought he was a bit strange for questioning the sign's humor. "Coaches *say* that all the time."

"But he's…"

"He's in a wheelchair." Her tone changed, matching Ben's annoyance. "That's the *whole* point."

"I *understand* the joke," Ben said. "But does the man *deserve* to be made fun of?"

"Kind of."

"Maybe you don't like him," Ben said, "but considering his condition—" She laughed out loud, laughed *at* him. Ben said, "Whatever," and turned away.

"This is ridiculous. We haven't even *met* and we're already fighting."

Ben stared at the gym door. "I'd better get in there."

"Don't go away mad," she said, sticking out her hand. "I'm Bonnie Jean. You must be Bennett Hunter. Mrs. Poulard told me about you. She says you're an *incredibly good* basketball player."

"Ben," he said, automatically extending his hand. "My friends call me Ben."

Her hands were small and neat, but she shook hands with the trained confidence of a boy. "What do people who tick you off the minute they meet you get to call you?"

"Like you?" he said, watching the sparkle of life in those clear, dark eyes.

"Like me."

"Even my parents call me Ben." He smiled.

"Oh, Your lip! Is that blood?"

Ben tasted blood and drew his lip in toward his teeth.

"Yoo-hoo! Ben!" Mrs. Poulard surprised them, coming from the gym doors. She enveloped Ben in her friendly embrace. "I was afraid you'd changed your mind and gone over to Annapolis High."

"Do I need a note?"

"Just an explanation."

"We, um, we were in an accident this morning."

The principal held him at arms' length. "You weren't injured, I hope."

"Look at his lip," Bonnie Jean said. "It's bleeding."

"I'm fine."

"Do you need some ice?" Mrs. Poulard asked.

"I've had ice, thanks."

"You need more if—" She saw his forbidding expression and shut her mouth, but her eyes blazed their disagreement.

Mrs. Poulard looked from Ben to Bonnie Jean; her right eyebrow lifted. "I see you've met my faithful summer assistant, Bonnie Jean."

"Yes, ma'am."

"I can always count on Bonnie Jean to take care of new students until they find their niche."

"And I hoped I was something special to her."

Bonnie Jean shrugged, then leapt into a running dance step, her leading wrist and toe pointing toward the gym door.

"Another charmer!" the principal laughed. "I've got to go in there and speak to the troops. Warn them about the uniform code and violations." At this, she rolled her eyes. "It's a constant battle. You, however," she said to Ben, "look perfect. I should have asked *you* to model. Isn't he dreamy?" she added, calling to Bonnie Jean.

"I don't ever want to wake up," Bonnie Jean said, looking back over her shoulder.

Mrs. Poulard took Ben's arm at the elbow and pulled him after her through the lobby. "Jeannie, can you find Ben a seat? I've got to get in there."

Bonnie Jean stopped, twirled on her toes, her kilt whirling, and waited for Ben.

Mrs. Poulard hurried off.

"Do you want to sit with the basketball team?" Bonnie Jean asked Ben.

"Sure." She paused at the gym doors to scan the crowds of students in the bleachers. Ben followed her gaze, noting that students sat in the bleachers and in chairs placed in rows on a big tarp spread out to protect the gym floor. He waited for Bonnie Jean to speak, but she squinted at the bleachers. "Do you know the guys on the team?"

She said, "Sort of," in the exact same tone that Ben used when asked if he could play basketball. *Of course,* he thought, *she's so beautiful and she knows so much about the team—she's probably got a boyfriend who plays ball.*

"You know," Bonnie Jean said, "I don't see them."

"They were here before."

"Right, but…"

From the podium, Mrs. Poulard gave an enthusiastic welcome. The school paused together, bowing heads in silence as she prayed for the start of the school year. Ben knew a surge of hope at the tender practicality of her prayers. "…Cause them to succeed in all their endeavors…let them know we love them…let them know that you love them…" Ben knew a moment, just a moment of repose, and imagined the debris of the morning's trauma floating away from him.

While Mrs. Poulard reviewed the parking restrictions and the school-wide late homework policy, Bonnie Jean stood on tiptoe and scanned the crowded bleachers. "I just don't see them," she whispered, as Mrs. Poulard explained the uniform code and the penalties for breaking it. She announced that the soccer team would model the proper way to wear the boys' uniform. The team strutted out from the locker room wearing oxford cloth shirts with khaki or gray trousers. They looked polished, cocky.

Ben leaned toward Bonnie Jean. "Maybe the basketball team's going to model."

"No. Soccer team's modeling the boys' uniform and cheerleaders are modeling the girls'. Nothing's left."

"You're not a cheerleader?" Ben teased. Mrs. Poulard pointed out how the shirts were to be tucked in, and other finer points of neat, male dressing.

"My mother is against cheerleading," she said, lifting her chin defensively. "Women's lib and modesty and all. No cheerleading for me. I'm a ballet student."

"Which explains that little leap out there in the lobby."

"I adore ballet. It's mathematical."

"Unlike cheerleading, which is more…scientific."

Mrs. Poulard called the cheerleaders to come forward. Ben thought he heard a kind of a primal drumming and a strange, far-off wail like the gulls over the field.

"Exactly. Cheerleading is *biological,* if anything," Bonnie Jean said, her chin high, her arms folded defensively across her chest. She did not look at him, but Ben was pleased with her pose because it finally trapped the billows of that enormous shirt right against her body. Ben decided he would put Bonnie Jean on the defensive as often as possible.

"I suppose," she said, nostrils flaring, "being a basketball *star* and all— you think it's great the way cheerleaders fall all over you guys. Just wait a minute and you'll see them and if you want me to introduce you to them— of course I will."

"Me?" Ben whispered, "No, I think cheerleaders ought to be jailed."

"Ah!" she cried, too loudly, turning to grin at him, her arms thrown open. He was sure she would have flung her arms around him, but the back doors of the gym banged open. Five white seagulls, crying their wild call, flapped furious wings and flew toward the podium. The adults flinched, shielding their heads. The students erupted in the strangest sound—a delighted, shrieking gasp because just behind the seagulls, seven shirtless boys sprinted across the gym. Their only clothing was girls' uniform kilts fluttering recklessly in the dash. Their faces were hidden under hideous rubber masks—Clinton, Michael Jordan, Homer Simpson, a bull dog, a hockey mask, a gorilla and a bull.

Speechless, one elbow crooked above her head like a shield to the circling, crying gulls, Mrs. Poulard stood frozen on the riser several yards behind them. The man in the wheelchair moved toward the kilted boys who pranced in front of the students making exaggerated modeling movements. Arms raised against the possible onslaught of the gulls, the teachers flocked together while the students rocked with laughter. Mrs. Poulard's voice returned in a roar and she commanded silence. The models hesitated. The boy wearing the bull mask paused, whirled around, and flipping up his kilt, mooned the student body.

The entire population of the gym drew a long, stunned breath; the noises Ben had noticed moments earlier became clearly audible. Somewhere in the back of the gym, people screamed and thumped against something hard and immovable. Mrs. Poulard, eyes snapping, jaw set, stamped off the riser to follow the man in the wheelchair who rolled toward the back of the gym. The wicked WALK IT OFF sign flapped on the back of the chair like a warship's flag. The students' laughter exploded. A bell sounded.

The kilted boys dashed toward the lobby doors, ripping off their masks and kilts. The first two boys thrust them at Bonnie Jean. "I don't want these!" She juggled them as though lit on fire.

The boy in the bull's mask, sprinting madly, caught up with the others. He yanked off the mask just before reaching the lobby doors. His eyes met Ben's and he thrust the mask into Ben's hands. His bright grin returning, he dashed away. Bonnie Jean sank back against the wall and groaned.

3

SMITTY knew that there was only one person in Annapolis who made his dog wear a seatbelt and was surprised that Doug Davidson had not stopped after the accident. A navy reserve pilot and a photographer, Doug enjoyed friendship with every policeman in the county, photographing formal police events or using his private helicopter to help with search and rescue. Smitty pulled into the Taylor Avenue station to find Doug's Jeep and his black lab, Muffin, waiting by the front steps, tail wagging.

Doug paced the length of Smitty's office raking his hand through his short, black hair. In his early forties, he stood at medium height, was energetic and thickly muscled. Smitty's partner, Jacobs, at his computer, listened to Doug's ranting.

Doug greeted Smitty with a desperate handshake. "He crossed into my lane and I swerved to avoid him. Once I realized the guy had crashed, I u-turned at Gate Eight and Dougie's bug collection dumped all over Annie. She had hysterics—"

"One of the pins impaled her hand," Jacobs interrupted to tell Smitty.

"Sounds like you had your hands full," Smitty said. "Was Muffin behaving herself?"

"Sure. Muff was sitting there watching the road, seat belt on, like always. "

When Doug left, Jacobs asked about Ben.

"He saw a dog wearing a seatbelt in the front seat. He just didn't believe it."

"Okay," Jacobs said. "Let's go after this guy."

"We can't use the boy as a witness."

"It may come to that."

"We can't let it."

Shaking his head and scolding Ben in his slurred, Southern accent, Bettinger took Ben by the arm and led him toward the office, which stood behind a glass barricade on the right side of the lobby. "You'd better come, too," he said to Bonnie Jean.

"I didn't do *anything*," she said, tossing her head. "Those idiots shoved these masks in my hands."

Bettinger tolerated her outburst but shook his head. "I might have expected this from the wrestling team, but your dad is gonna tan some basketball hides."

"Your *dad*?" Ben whispered.

"He's the coach."

"*Your* dad is the *basket*ball coach?"

"And he's going to be *furious*."

"Wait here, you two, while I round up the other hooligans." Ben sank into one of the chairs in the front office, while Bonnie Jean recounted the entire incident to the secretaries behind the counter. Moments later, Bettinger ushered the team members into the office. The boys were still dressing, buttoning their shirts, tightening ties, fastening belts. Ben studied the faces and assessed their heights. Three boys were taller than he, one stood at least six feet seven inches tall, another just a fraction shorter, the third about six feet three inches. These three were laughing about how quickly Bettinger had nabbed them.

Four more guys stood together; three were thickly built and their scalps were so recently shaved that red nicks showed. One still wore only a kilt and clutched his rumpled uniform to his bare chest. With rapid, nervous gestures, the fourth scolded, "Joe told us to bring two sets of uniforms and leave one in the bathroom."

And then there was the boy who had shoved his mask into Ben's hands.

Ben witnessed a blatantly intimate glance between Bonnie Jean and this boy as he entered. Their eyes met. She whispered, "You're in so much trouble, Joe," and he flashed his grin at her. When this boy Joe smiled, his face had a disarming, off-center look. His teeth were noticeably white, his skin tan, and his eyes a bluish kind of gray. His hair, cut almost exactly like Ben's, was gold-brown. He was Ben's height and though he was thinner, his shoulders stretched tight the seams of his starched blue shirt. There was something compelling and substantial about him. Ben knew a moment of disappointment thinking, *Of course, the coach's daughter would be linked to the most confident guy on the team.*

Bettinger shooed them into Mrs. Poulard's office; Ben and Bonnie Jean were commanded to follow. Ben heard Joe teasing the pudgy team member. "Hey, Jason, I wonder how they recognized you."

"They figured I'd be with *you*, pretty boy."

The nervous boy said, "I can't believe Drew took his shirt off. I mean, was that stupid? You're the only black kid in the school."

"I've got news for you," Drew said, "my hands and legs are black, too."

"You should have covered them up."

"Did you forget your medicine again, Jon? Or are you just plain rude?" The boys laughed in a happy, collective burst then Drew added, "Anyways, like they wouldn't have recognized us. We knew we'd get caught."

"I didn't."

"Then you're an idiot."

When they were crowded into Mrs. Poulard's office, Drew noticed Ben. "Hey, who are you?"

Before Ben could speak, Bonnie Jean said, "He's the new member of the team. Ben Hunter."

There was a kind of buzzing confusion where they murmured things like "new kid," "military kid," through which Joe moved to meet Ben. He stuck out his hand. "I'm Joe. Good to meet you." They shook hands and Joe said, "Sorry to drag you into all this on your first day."

"That's okay," Ben grinned tightly, minding his lip. "First days are usually pretty boring. This one hasn't been."

He expected Joe's grin, but instead, Joe's grayish eyes intensified as he squinted at Ben. "Did you go here before? When we were smaller?"

"No," Ben said, patiently enduring Joe's scrutiny. "I was only in Annapolis for one day and that was when I was six."

"And?" Joe said, apparently understanding Ben's suggestion of importance. "What happened?"

"Nothing much. My father crashed the car off a bridge. And I saw a mermaid."

"Hey, do they really wear those shell tops or do they swim...naked?"

"I only saw her eyes," Ben said.

"*That's* a shame," Joe murmured. "I've always wondered about that."

"What's gonna happen? Are we in big trouble?"

"Nothing will happen to *you*. You were an innocent bystander. And besides, you're protected by the new kid rule."

"The *what*?"

"The new kid rule." Joe stretched his arms then grasped his hands behind his head, elbows out as if relaxing on the air itself. He grinned at Ben. "Aw, they never punish new kids here. They say, 'So what if he took hostages at gunpoint? He's got to make friends somehow. He's new!'" Joe squinted at Ben's face. "Not that, *you know*, that sick stuff is your style, because I see it isn't."

"No," Ben laughed. "But what will happen to the rest of you?"

"Probably give us detention or something. The punishments in this school are lame. No big deal."

"The birds were a nice touch."

Joe grinned, eyes sparkling. He took his hands from behind his head to gesture expressively. "I *know* it. *No one* expected them."

"Where did you get them?"

"Birds are easy to catch. But Mrs. Poulard will make me clean up after them."

"Your girlfriend seems more worried about what the *coach* will do."

"My girlfriend?" Joe repeated.

"Yeah. She seemed worried that the coach was going to come down really hard. What's the coach like?"

"He's...*you know*, a real human being. Pretty strict, but fair. Just don't sit in his desk chair or let him hear you swear. Plus, he hates lying. Yeah, he'll be mad, but wait...my *girlfriend* said this to you?"

"Yeah." Ben indicated Bonnie Jean, who stood beside Mrs. Poulard's desk, talking to Drew. Joe looked around the room and laughed. "You mean *Bonnie Jean*?"

"Yeah."

"Jeannie," he called sharply and waved her over to them. "Something else, isn't she?" Joe said, his eyes bright with fun.

"Spectacular," Ben admitted. "You're very lucky."

When Bonnie Jean was beside them, he put his arm around her shoulders.

"You're in so much trouble, you moron," she said, shrugging his arm off her shoulders. Ben's eyes widened.

"She's my sister." Laughing, Joe pointed at Ben's gaping expression.

"Your *sister*?"

"You're shocked, aren't you? That *my* brother could be such an idiot?"

"You don't look anything alike," Ben offered.

"That's because *he* was switched at birth."

Before Joe could spar, Mrs. Poulard opened the door. Several boys began to speak at once. She silenced them with a quick, severe motion of her hand. "I don't want to hear a single, sorry excuse. I'm doing all the talking." Taking her place behind her desk, she leaned toward them on stiffened arms. The boys were silent, respectful. Fearing he would be recognized and sent to class when he wanted badly to watch, Ben sat down in a chair at the back of the group.

"Let's see," Mrs. Poulard said. "Do I have everyone?" She found a pad of paper and a pen and began jotting down names. "This prank," she said, "is nothing to be proud of. You insulted the student body and you will repay them with work detentions. Friday and Sunday afternoons for the next four weeks. And boys," she leaned forward, "you'll be doing the most strenuous, unpleasant jobs that I can devise."

Joe stepped away from Ben, moving through the crowd.

"Really, Mrs. Poulard," he said. "It's my fault. Don't punish them for—"

"No, Joe. We've been through this before. They have to learn when they *shouldn't* follow you. Do you hear that, boys?" They nodded their heads at her. "And you!" she said to Joe. "You have to *think* before you lead your friends into—" She gestured with one hand toward the gym, searching for the right word. As she did so, the door opened. With the soft whirr of wheels over carpet, the man in the wheelchair entered the room, turned and shut the door behind him. Ben saw the WALK IT OFF sign still hung from the man's back.

"You must realize that you caused the cheerleaders unforgivable trauma by locking the door to the gym."

Ben observed suppressed smirks; Bonnie Jean whispered to Ben. "There's another door."

Mrs. Poulard noticed her. "Why are you here, Jeannie?" Ben slumped lower in his chair.

"I—um—"

Several teammates spoke as Drew said, "I gave her my mask when I ran out."

"She knew nothing about it," Paul insisted.

"She's totally innocent," Joe said.

The man in the wheelchair raised his eyebrows at her. Mrs. Poulard, with an expression meant to hide her amusement, dismissed Bonnie Jean. With a farewell glance at Ben, she closed the door softly behind her.

Mrs. Poulard continued, "The last thing I wish to say is that I am particularly distressed with Joe's behavior and I want you all to know that his father and I will carefully consider what to do with him." She gave Joe a look that must have stung, but Ben thought he saw a softening of compassion in her eyes that both pleased and bewildered him. "Do you have anything to add, Coach MacBride?"

At this, the crowd of boys parted. They turned to face the man in the wheelchair.

This is the coach? Ben stared. *How can a man coach basketball from a wheelchair?*

The coach wheeled up to the desk, giving the boys an inopportune glimpse of the WALK IT OFF sign he still displayed on his back and Ben's frantic questions succumbed to the complicated tension born suddenly around him. It was a tight moment; Ben held his breath, biting his lip hard, knowing that no one must laugh and that each boy badly wanted to bellow. Even Joe managed to suppress his incredible grin, though his eyes danced with such wild amusement that Ben was deeply relieved when the coach turned his back to the adjacent wall. The most delicious part of the whole moment was that the coach, maneuvering skillfully through the boys, had kept his back from Mrs. Poulard's view. The sign remained in place for future moments of delight. The boys—facing execution—clung to this secret thrill.

Coach MacBride met eyes for several uncomfortable seconds, until each boy lowered his eyes and shifted, standing with his hands clasped behind his back. Ben watched, feeling the secret joy in the room dissipate as poignantly as party balloons shrivel. MacBride was a tall man folded into his wheelchair; his solid shoulders strained the top button of his shirt, yet he held his forearms in an incongruously quiet way. His brown hands rested on his wheels, the clean calloused fingers still and relaxed. Short, dark hair shot with gray accentuated the angularity of his face—sharp, slightly crooked nose, strong chin and jaw line. His mouth was set so seriously, that Ben knew a moment of keen anxiety until he saw something in the man's eyes that said he understood his athletes' hopeful and wild hearts.

Coach MacBride said, "You boys know me well enough to understand how disturbed I am by your behavior. Not only did you disrupt the assembly, which Mrs. Poulard and many others had carefully planned for the benefit of the student body, but you showed your classmates a disturbing lack of respect."

Surprised by the eloquence of MacBride's speech—the rhythms and dignity of it seemed old world—Ben wondered if it was put on for Mrs. Poulard's sake, but the boys murmured, "Yes, sir," at his pause.

"Locking up your classmates. Do you know those girls were completely panicked?"

"There was another door," Jason said. "And it locks from the inside."

Palpable was the amusement that rippled, in absolute silence, through the team.

MacBride raised his eyebrows and pointed at Jason. "Don't even *try* to excuse yourself. When people panic they don't think rationally." The boys shifted uncomfortably, still keeping eye contact with MacBride. "Maybe you didn't mean to frighten them, but you've got to think ahead and anticipate how your actions are going to impact others. You are no longer children."

A bell buzzed, announcing a class change. No one moved. "Be dressed for exercise in the gym at three-oh-five." Ben felt the sobering impact of the implication they'd be running laps. They shuffled heavily toward the door. Ben stood up.

The coach said, "Joe, I want to see you in the gym."

Ben remembered that this man was Joe's father. Rapidly he compared them. The resemblance showed in the eyes, the slightly crooked slope of the nose, the shoulders.

"I've got class, Dad." Joe's expression was serious, slightly nervous.

"Right now, Joe."

Ben's stomach jumped. *He seemed calm and spoke intelligently; how angry is he?* Then, as the room emptied, both Mrs. Poulard and Coach MacBride noticed him.

"You've been sitting there this whole time!"

"Who's this?" MacBride asked, his eyes alive.

"How did you even get *in* here?" She rounded her desk and took his arm. "You've missed your first class on your first day!"

MacBride turned his chair to face Ben more squarely. "Have we met before?"

"This is the new boy I told you about," Mrs. Poulard said.

"You did?"

"Yes, remember? Ben. The basketball player."

Rapidly, MacBride's eyes studied Ben with the same squinted expression, the same intensity that Joe had, but in his scrutiny, Ben recognized the eye of a capable coach. He saw the questions recede from the man's face as MacBride took in the details of Ben's build and poise, speculating about his potential.

"Good to meet you, Ben," MacBride said. The coach wheeled up to him, initiating a handshake. Ben tried to give his strongest, most impressive handshake, but MacBride's grip proved sturdy, his warm, toughened hand meeting Ben's in size and strength. His eyes squinted at Ben's. "I'm Tom MacBride. Are you interested in playing ball this year?"

"Yes, sir."

"Good. Happy to hear it. What position did you play last year?"

"Point guard, but I'll play anything you need."

"We need a good point guard," Joe said. His father gave Joe a brief glance that Ben could not read, before turning his attention back to Ben. "How did you get mixed up in this? Do you know Joe from somewhere?"

"No, sir, I just—"

"On the way out, I gave him my mask," Joe said. Ben held the thing up.

"I'll take that," Mrs. Poulard said, snatching it away from Ben and hurrying past them to open the door for Tom. "Now hurry to class. Do you know where you're going?"

"Spanish, room 218."

She nodded, then bent to speak to Tom as they left the office.

"I'm in for it," Joe confided.

"What's he gonna do?" Ben asked Joe.

"Make me sorry," Joe said. Their eyes met and Ben saw a flicker of regret as clear and unsteady as a flame, making Joe's expressive eyes sober.

"You're already sorry," Ben offered.

"Take notes in Spanish for me," Joe said, as he turned and sprinted to catch up with his father. Ben watched them move abreast through the lobby, the insolent sign flapping on MacBride's back. At the gym doors, Joe looked back and seeing Ben, pointed surreptitiously to that wicked sign, a helpless grin flickering over his face. Joe quickly stepped ahead to open the heavy glass door for his father. He held the door, then let it swing shut behind him. Ben watched Joe sprint to his father's side.

4

BEN did not take notes in Spanish. The teacher, Señora Whispiefinch, energetic and white-haired, was competent and friendly, but spent the class period introducing procedures, the syllabus and the textbook. She spoke in Spanish then translated to English, explaining that as the weeks went on, they would converse only in *español*. Ben, who was somehow already fluent in Spanish, realized he should be in Spanish IV. No teacher had yet understood his language capacity and therefore did not quite believe it. But Ben, doubting that the next level course would prove challenging, decided he'd rather stay in a class with Joe and his teammates. He would have to be careful for the first two weeks while schedules could still be changed. He would have to hide how much he really knew.

So he listened while the teacher gave instructions in *español*, and when she spoke English, he worried about Joe, trying to imagine the exchange between father and son. He remembered Joe's anxious regret and Joe's description of his father. Ben wondered what strict but fair looked like. What did Joe mean—a real human being? But could Joe really say what he thought his father was like? What would he, Ben, say if asked what his father was like? Could he put what he knew into words—even with the resources of several different languages? So long had he been silenced, Ben doubted he could say what he thought. He'd laugh and duck the question. Thus ran Ben's mind as the teacher switched from Spanish to English. He grew sleepy, and aware, for the first time, of his aching shins and of an ir- ritated scratching inside his collar and wrists and around his waist. Pulling at his tie to loosen it, he yawned, tried not to yawn again, but did—widely, and more widely—opening his sore lip so much that it bled again.

Ben tried blotting it with his finger, but Mrs. Whispiefinch saw the blood. She asked if he'd like to be excused to the bathroom. He was so sleepy, he responded without being sure if she had spoken in English or *español*. But when he replied "*Sí*," she instructed him, in *español*, to take his backpack as the bell would soon ring. In his sleepiness, he hoisted it to his shoulder only then realizing he'd given himself away. Hoping she did not realize how much he knew, Ben glanced back at her.

In the boys' room, Joe MacBride stood at the corner sink, splashing cold water on his face. Ben went to the sink beside Joe and wet a paper towel with cold water. Joe glanced up, his face dripping, red blotches around his eyes.

"Hey," Ben said, blotting his lip, "you okay?"

"Yeah," Joe said, ducking his head down and splashing again.

"What happened?"

"I had to catch the birds again and let them free."

"That all?"

"No. Like I told you, he made me sorry."

"How?"

Joe laughed. "He's my dad. He knows how to get to me." Joe tapped a dripping finger on his chest, indicating his heart. "See—when we duct- taped the locker room door shut, I didn't realize the girls would actually be scared—Dad said they were. I have to take his word for it," he added, squinting hard. "And the whole disrespect thing. It didn't *seem* disrespect- ful when I was planning it. It never does."

Ben studied Joe's eyes. *A real human being*, he thought. "Yeah, I can see that," he said. Joe nodded, fully serious. Hoping to cheer him, Ben said, "How did you catch the birds?"

"Are you *kidding* me?" Joe said, his expression clearing. "Seagulls are *so easy* to catch. You just offer them food—anything, bits of bread—and then when they get close you throw something over them. A blanket or your coat. Whatever you got." He gave a half grin. "But Dad wasn't in the mood for fun so we just made a trail of crumbs that led them out the gym door."

"Was he freaked about the birds?"

Joe shrugged and rocked his hand to indicate slightly. "But it's okay," he said, grinning, straightening up, squaring his shoulders. "He hasn't found the gulls we put in his closet yet."

"It's *okay*—?"

"I put newspaper down on the floor and took all the uniforms out."

"But—"

"Yeah. Can you picture it when they fly out? Gaw! I'd love to see. Really! And after all this," Joe pointed at himself, "Dad's gonna *love* that I got in the last word. See he *loves* that I pull pranks, he just doesn't want anybody hurt or—now I find out—insulted."

"Are you *sure*?"

Joe thumped Ben's shoulder laughing again. "You sure I haven't met you before?" Joe said. "Maybe we met when you were here before. I've lived here all my life."

"I don't remember meeting a single kid that day," Ben said, blotting his lip.

"Only mermaids."

"I was six. Who knows? I probably imagined the whole thing."

"If you imagined it, you would have seen more than her eyes."

"True." The bell rang.

"Dang," Joe said, reaching for paper towels. "I *so* don't feel like going to school today."

"Maybe Coach'll find the sign on his back and get you out of another class. Or the mess in his closet."

They laughed, Ben holding the wet paper towel to his lip.

"What happened to you?" Joe asked.

"Split my lip."

"Sorry I missed *that* Spanish class."

"No. My dad smashed up the car this morning."

"Any more mermaids?"

Ben laughed, and trying not to smile, blotted his lip. "We crashed into Middleton's."

"No way!" As they walked down the hall to Math class, Joe introduced Ben to at least two dozen people whose faces and names mingled like dirt in water. He showed Ben where his locker was, and which water fountain had the "good" water. Then as the hall cleared, students draining into classrooms, he confided, "Dad was really upset about my mooning everybody. He thinks it's an insult to show people your naked rear."

"I guess mooning is meant to be an insult."

"But, what if your ass is beautiful?"

Pressing the paper towel to his lip, Ben laughed. "Then, I suppose it's a gift—"

"Ex*actly*."

"You didn't say *that* to him, did you?"

"It's true," Joe said, shrugging defensively. "Just think about it."

"But if he was mad anyway—"

"I just wanted to discuss the theory of mooning. But he wasn't in the mood. I *hate* making my dad mad. I mean it, there's *such* a fine line between making him really laugh and making him mad."

"Man," Ben said quiet as a vow, thinking, *I'd never push my dad like that. Never.*

"Anyway I wasn't *actually* naked. And at first I couldn't get him to believe that. I couldn't believe he thought I was lying. I never outright lie to him."

"You *looked* naked."

"See, that was the beauty of the prank." Joe stopped walking and swung his backpack around. "Wait a sec, Math's right in there. We've got a minute." Opening the zipper he reached in. "See, I was actually wearing these. I just *looked* naked." Joe held up a flesh-colored pair of spandex shorts. Across the seat, the letters CCS were painted. Joe thrust his hip out and tugged at the waistband of his boxers, pulling it up to show Ben the bright orange cloth with little Santas printed on it. "I was gonna just wear these underneath the kilt, but—" He shrugged. "Bonnie Jean tied them to the flagpole last year so everybody knows they're mine. Kinda hard to forget. Santa, orange." He squinched up his face and laughed. The second bell rang.

"Y'all should be seated by the time the second bell rings," the teacher said. She stood at the front of the class, smacking her open palm with an overhead pen. She was small and sturdy, with short, faded hair. They took their seats and Joe said, "hi," to the girls around them. "Leeza's so mad at you," one said, bending toward them. Ben noticed how her breasts nearly spilled out of her snug uniform shirt, the three open buttons revealing a bright red bra.

"Leeza your girlfriend?" Ben asked.

Joe nodded. "She's a cheerleader."

"No," Ben breathed.

"I bet she'll dump you," the girl added.

"Then maybe *we* can get back together," Joe grinned at her.

"Don't hold your breath."

"I have been," Joe murmured, his eyes intense.

She glanced at Ben. "Aren't you going to introduce us?"

"This is Ben, *Bonnie Jean's* friend." His hand swept toward the girls. "Tiffany and Michelle."

Ben said "hello," sat down and met Bonnie Jean's eyes to see what she thought of Joe's comment.

She made an amused face. "You survived Mrs. Poulard's office?"

"Joe's the one who caught it," Ben said.

Joe shrugged and set to work on the diagnostic test the teacher placed on their desks. When he finished, Ben saw Joe sitting back, eyes half closed, thinking. He glanced at Joe's paper and realized his assumption that the fun-loving Joe was a careless student was unfounded. Joe scribbled notes on the corner of his notebook describing the students around him. The small kid in front, who worked intently, shoulders hunched over, was nicknamed "Baby" because he was a ninth grade genius and was probably finishing the week's homework. Bonnie Jean was in tenth grade and had taken a summer course to qualify for this class; Victoria, to Ben's left, was smart and had a crush on Adam.

Dr. Deterding leaned over them. "Are you two finished?"

"Yes, ma'am," Joe said.

"Then *what* are y'all writing?"

"Just notes," Joe said, his grin winsome and helpless. "He's new. We've got lots to talk about."

She took their tests, pressed her finger to her lips and pointed to the homework assignment scrawled on the blackboard. Baby sat back, gave a sigh of satisfaction, and closed his book.

Captain Dain Strickland asked Smitty to stop by his office. The tall, deep-chested man had once played fullback for Annapolis High School, and had built a reputation on a lifetime of honest service to the city. When Strickland put down his cigar and crossed the room to shake his hand, Smitty knew something was up.

"Have a seat, Smitty. I know you want to go after this colonel, and I agree with you. Completely. But it's not gonna happen." He quieted Smitty's responsive growl by gesturing for him to stay seated. "Here's why. You were concerned with the kid—and you were right to get him to school. You didn't administer a sobriety test and I probably wouldn't have either at seven o'clock in the morning with the man playing the crowd like he was."

Smitty nodded, grinding his teeth. "There's more, isn't there?"

"Here it is," Strickland said, "Lin Middleton called to say she will not prosecute. She wants the whole thing to go away. Why do you think Lin won't prosecute?"

Smitty studied the grimy windows. "Some lawyer down the Pentagon called her. They want this colonel to work out. The one that just left—the guy involved in that stolen car ring—was an embarrassment. Lin Middleton gets a whole lot of business from them, so…"

"You're a smart kid, Smitty. Their argument is that nothing criminal was done. Why blow it up into a scandal?"

"Captain, sir, I'm telling you. This guy's trouble."

"He won't go away then, Smitty. Trouble never does."

5

THE small, pale yellow room that served as the athletic director's office looked as neat as an overcrowded, much-used room could look after housing seagulls for the morning. Nick Bettinger, ambling through the school as he always did during his free period, entered Tom's office. "Hey, Coach, how you doing?"

"Good," MacBride replied, from where he sat in the middle of the room, his wheelchair parked between his desk and the window. "Just trying to see if I can get my legs to work now that I've been off them all morning."

"Need a hand?" Bettinger came to his side.

"Sure, thanks, Nick." Tom leaned on his desk with one hand and gave Bettinger the other.

"What, were the old stumps numb this morning?"

"Couldn't move my right leg." Putting his weight on his left leg and leaning on Bettinger, Tom managed to get to his feet.

"How's that feel?"

"Still numb, but better. Let me see if I can walk to the window. I've got to teach next period."

"Switch with me, buddy. You can teach Bible sitting down." Bettinger released him and Tom stood, balancing for several seconds. "Easy, now. How's the leg?"

"Won't move right," Tom grunted. "But I want to stand for a few minutes and see if that helps."

"Sometimes that does the trick for you, doesn't it?"

Tom nodded. "I'd like to be able to move around for my P.E. class."

"Nothing's gonna happen on the first day anyway."

Tom looked at him. "You can say that after this morning?"

Bettinger chuckled. "We both knew Joe was gonna have a tough time without his brother here. I hope you weren't too hard on him."

"Too hard? I hope I was hard enough."

"Come on now, Tom. I've heard all your stories about when you were at the Naval Academy. You did some wild stuff."

"I want my sons to learn from me. I want them to be better than me."

"Aren't you asking a bit much?" Bettinger watched Tom drag his numb right leg in an attempt to step toward the window.

"I know I'm demanding, Nick," Tom said. "But I try to remember that we're made in the image of God. That speaks potential to me. That speaks possibilities."

"You've got a complicated theology, buddy."

Tom laughed.

"Are you sure it was the Holy Spirit came in your window that night at the Naval Academy?" Bettinger challenged him, referring to the oft-told story of Tom's conversion. "It sounds a little too idealistic to me."

Inching his left foot forward, Tom smiled, thinking back to his days at the Academy when his life had changed. Like Bettinger, he had been raised in a strict, God-fearing home that emphasized the fall of man and his resulting depraved nature. But his home had been more austere than Bettinger's because it sprang from the old Scots' strain, colored with the stubborn resolution natural to life in Scotland, shaped by the ever-present rod of correction that had been trusted in his ancestors' homes long before modern practices questioned its value. With this staunch tradition, Tom's mother had chastened him faithfully. But Tom's father had been a thinker with an imagination as vast and vivid as his heart was generous, and he had bred in Tom the discipline of hope.

When he entered the Academy at seventeen, he was all sharp edges, idealism and a cheerfully determined cockiness. The challenge of Academy life rocked his self image. Tom was not a detail person, and Academy life was *made* of details, one placed on the other like bricks in a wall. Did he know the lunch menu, could he recite those inane rhymes, was he wearing the right uniform, were his shoes polished, was his room ordered and shining? And it went on. But as he succeeded, working hard against all that was easy-going and generous and natural to him, his confidence materialized. And then, faith surprised him—riches from an unknown uncle.

One night in his second year he sat alone in his darkened room, staring out the screenless windows, listening to the drumming, late-summer song of the cicadas. He had an intense sensation that God was beckoning him. It was as if God's hand stirred the damp air, sending a summons to him on a soft, rain-scented breeze. He found it irresistible.

An idea of the Almighty began to form in his soul as if he had actually had a glimpse of God. Tom told his kids it happened to him that way because Scots "saw" the unseeable. His faith, this seminal understanding and the love for God those things inspired in him, translated into a Christianity that was best expressed in simple, homey ways of giving to those around him whose needs he suddenly saw. He sought to express—in practical ways, always in practical ways—what he saw of God's heart.

"Who ever heard of faith coming to a man on the summer breeze?" Bettinger teased him, knowing Tom's story well. "Heck, there's no breeze in the summer in Annapolis. Air's as thick as pea soup."

"That proves it was supernatural. That proves the existence of wonderful possibilities."

"You sound like Peter Pan," Bettinger shook his head. "Better be realistic than hope too much, Tom."

Achieving a sort of balance, Tom touched the windowsill for support and grinned at Bettinger. "You see what I mean, Nick, you're one of the kindest people I know. If you didn't have hope, you'd never take the lost boys you do and form them into winning wrestlers. Your actions speak louder than your words."

"I refuse to fight with a man who can't even walk," Bettinger grunted. Noting Tom's unsteadiness, Bettinger pushed the wheelchair over to the window behind his friend, and in doing so, his right hand crinkled a piece of paper attached to the back. Examining it, he saw the persistent WALK IT OFF sign and hurriedly glanced to see if Tom had seen. But Tom, frowning, concentrated to maintain his balance on a leg without feeling. Grinning, Bettinger maneuvered the wheelchair to where Tom could not see the back, then he locked the wheels.

When Bettinger left, Tom tried stamping his right leg, willing it to move, but it would not obey. The problem with his legs, which fluctuated in intensity, had developed from too many back injuries. Doctors considered the numbness in his legs an abnormal, but comparatively trivial result. He had broken his back as a young man in the Marine Corps—fresh out of the Naval Academy and newly married—in an accident so unusual and severe that doctors were certain of lifetime paralysis. Defying their prognosis, he recovered feeling and function, but two subsequent back injuries, both due to unavoidable strain to the weakened area, had been further devastating. The first had forced his resignation from the Marine Corps, and the second had resulted in back surgery to fuse disintegrating vertebrae.

His legs had been unreliable since then.

The doctors said he should either be fully paralyzed or pain-free, but he lived hovering between the two states. When his back was bad, as it was today, his hips and his right leg burned deep at the center until the pain seared away all feeling and responsiveness in the leg, leaving him with a limb that was more like a charred wooden post than a live thing. The first time it had happened, he refused to give in, and dragged his right leg behind him, until the strain on his circulatory system caused him to pass out. When he woke up, he couldn't see. Two days of rest restored his sight, but he had been sufficiently chastised. Now, he used the wheelchair when necessary, praying to submit to its humbling discipline.

On his best days his back ached a little, and oddly, on those days he felt best if he were moving—walking, running laps with his athletes, standing, working—anything but sitting. But on days like this when his right leg refused to come back to life, he regretted most consciously his inability to make life conform to his vision of it. Accepting that he would not be on his feet for the boys' P.E. class, he lowered himself into his waiting wheelchair, aware, painfully aware, that if his will alone could make him walk, he would be now sprinting across the gym.

On the other side of the gym, waiting for the second bell to ring, the boys stood together like tufts of grass. It sounded as Tom approached, and his students climbed into the bleachers to sit. Tom glanced at the roster for the first time, noting that there were twenty-five students and that they belonged to all four high school classes. Looking up at the group, he saw several young boys sitting together at the top of the bleachers. These must be the freshman, he thought, pausing to count the number of ninth grad-ers on the roster. The rest of the boys sat in clumps, the sophomores all near his nephew Flip Davidson, the older boys sitting in a line on the first bench. Joe sat next to the new boy, who nervously rocked his left ankle back and forth.

As was his custom on the first day, Tom opened with a joke. Pleased to see his students laughing, Tom watched the tension flee from the new boy's face as he laughed aloud. His features warmed with vitality. Tom felt a strange, incomprehensible burst of recognition. His tan skin, the eye color and the way he moved his head struck Tom as familiar. But he hadn't time to contemplate this; soon the boys' laughter subsided. Tom called out the roll, speaking to each boy briefly.

"Liam Adamos," he said to the tenth grader, first on the list. "I heard you made the soccer team."

"Jeff Birch," Tom called. "We've missed you at home, Jeff. Better stop by tonight. Mrs. MacBride is worried about you."

"Okay, I'll be there."

The new boy's back straightened and he turned to peer questioningly at Jeff. Tom spoke to his nephew, and next, to Sedo Gustafson.

The next name he saw on his roster was, *Hunter, Bennett W.* Tom's heart jumped. Disbelieving, he read it again silently. "Bennett Hunter?" he heard his own voice go squeaky and he dropped his clipboard. It seemed to float out of his hands and clatter endlessly against some distant floor. Tom made no motion to retrieve it. He couldn't; his limbs were limp and tingling and he was ineffably grateful that he sat in his wheelchair. He would have fallen over if he hadn't been. He didn't know how long he sat there, gaping at the kid, his heart thumping, while twenty-four other boys fidgeted and whispered and Joe's face squinched up, questioning at him.

Could this name belong to the new boy beside Joe with the wise eyes? Was this why the boy inexplicably stood out from his peers? Tom's mouth went dry; he remembered that the new boy's name was Ben. Could it be him? "*Bennett* Hunter?" he whispered, disbelieving the name as he heard it hit the silence in the gym, disbelieving it as much as the kid's presence in Annapolis.

"Yes, sir," the new boy said, grinning shyly, his bright, irresistible personality flickering out at Tom as he stood up, stepped forward and picked up the fallen clipboard. "That's me. You can call me Ben."

Tom stared at the tall, healthy embodiment of silent memories, of late-night whispered prayers that stood before him. Ben handed Tom the clipboard and Tom's nauseating disbelief washed away under a hot surge of affection. He marveled silently over Ben's striking appearance, noting the flexibility of his movements, the athletic grace of his stance, those hungry, contemplative eyes, the smile that was, at once, stubborn and earnest.

"You're new," he said inanely.

"Yes, sir," said Ben, eager and somewhat amused by his befuddlement.

"You met him this morning," Joe said from the bleachers.

"I remember, Joe. I remember. Where did you move from?"

"Quantico, sir."

"Your dad in the Marine Corps?"

"Yes, sir."

Though aware of the growing impatience of his class, Tom had to speak. "You know, Ben, I believe I knew your parents. Is your father's name Max? Max Hunter?"

"That's him," Ben said, his expression going blank.

Tom noted this with conflicting alarm and an enormous, guilty satisfaction.

"Are you a friend of his?" Ben asked, his voice gone brisk.

"I...knew him in the Marine Corps," Tom said, carefully, squinting at Ben. "We were in the same company in Quantico at TBS." Ben's expression cleared slightly. Tom said, "But your *mother* was a dear friend of my wife and mine."

"My mother?" Surprise flickered across Ben's guarded expression.

"Yes," Tom said, watching Ben carefully. He stuck out his hand again and taking Ben's hand, clasped it firmly in both of his. "I'm so happy to see you here. You are welcome, most profoundly welcome."

6

WHEN Ben walked into the lobby at the end of the school day, Smitty stood at the office door.

"Hey," Smitty greeted him, clapping him on the shoulder. "You had a good day, I can tell by the look on your face." At Smitty's words, Ben realized what a great day he'd had. Gran had been right about this school.

"The basketball team is meeting now," Ben told Smitty.

"Yeah, Miz Poulard told me all about that."

"I was going to stay," Ben said.

"Good. Good for you."

"Joe told me he can give me a ride home, so you don't need to worry."

Walking Ben to the gym, Smitty made him promise to call him if he needed anything. "I'll be watching out for you," he promised, as Ben sprinted across the gym to the locker room.

The boys' locker room was distinguishable from others in Ben's experience by its crisp Lysol scent. The team members were changing and to Ben's relief, they greeted him with the casual ease of long acquaintance.

Tom's voice sounded from the end of the locker row. "You've got five minutes." Ben could see Tom's feet and a crescent of his wheels.

"Smells awfully clean in here," Ben said to Joe as he opened the locker assigned to him during P.E. class.

"Not for long," Joe said, and with a barely perceptible nod of his head indicated two boys who had entered the room. Ben busied himself with removing his shoes and noted that the boys were essentially the same size, but one entered with more éclat. His hair was reddish-brown, his face freckled and his eyes a piercing black. He stood with his shoulders thrown back. The other boy stood slightly behind, shoulders hunched.

"What's going on here?" the bolder boy asked.

"Hey, Oliver," Tom's voice sounded from beyond the lockers. "Hey, Knox."

"You know it's illegal to practice before October," he challenged.

"Behold our point guard Oliver Saunders—we call him The Colonel—and his best friend Knox," Joe whispered. Ben wished he could see Tom's face.

"We missed you both during summer rec league," Tom said.

"I played with the Truxton Park league. I needed the challenge."

Ben whispered to Joe, "What a jerk."

"Just wait," Joe promised. "It'll get better."

"Good for you," Tom said to Oliver and Ben could not detect sarcasm in his voice.

"Yeah it was good, it was real good."

"Glad to hear it. No doubt you've learned some moves you can teach us."

"Not really," Oliver said.

"But you *did* find the challenge you were seeking, I hope."

"Nah. I was my team's leading rebounder. I scored at least 30 a game."

Tom said, "How 'bout you, Knox? I saw your name a few times in the stats."

"Yeah, I was with Ollie."

"Get much playing time?"

"Sure," Knox said, his voice tight. He studied his shoes.

"And why wasn't I notified of this practice, Coach?" Oliver said.

"It's not a practice," Ben said, loudly. "It's because of the prank."

"Who are *you*?" Oliver demanded.

Tom wheeled into view. The steadiness in his eyes surprised Ben. "Ollie and Knox, this is the newest member of our team, Ben Hunter."

Ben reached past Joe to offer his hand. "Hey, good to meet you," he said, his voice loud and clear as he shook first Knox's hand. He offered his hand to Oliver, who hesitated.

"Doesn't he even have to *try out*?" Oliver asked Tom, his voice going high. Tom studied Oliver silently. "I know what's happening here," Oliver said, pointing at Ben. "You've already had tryouts and I wasn't notified."

Paul groaned audibly.

"You're already a team member, Ollie," Tom said, his voice quiet. "You don't need to try out."

"You running with us, Ben?" Joe asked loudly, stripping off his shirt.

"Yeah." Ben put his shoes and socks in the locker.

"We don't have to run, do we, Coach?" Knox asked. "I've got to get to work."

"Of course not. You weren't involved in the prank."

Louder still, Joe said, "You know, Ben, you don't have to run with us."

"I run every day anyway," Ben said, loosening his tie. "Ah! What's that?" He felt something small and hard tumbling across his shoulders and running down his back. Fingers tugging at the buttons, Ben got his shirt and undershirt off quickly. Tiny jagged balls of glass fell to the floor and scattered.

"What the—"

"Watch out, it looks like glass."

"Glass?" Jon yelled, jumping up onto the bench between locker rows.

"Aw, come on, Jon. You're ten feet away."

"Everybody stay where you are," Tom commanded. "I'll get the broom."

"We didn't know anything about the prank," Oliver said, his voice loud and insistent.

"You can be grateful for that, Ollie," Tom said, his voice still booming as he wheeled to the back of the room.

"Where'd glass come from?" Scott said.

"Look, it's all over."

Tom rounded the corner of the row, a whisk broom and dust pan in hand. Ben moved to take the broom from Tom. "It's my fault, I'll get it."

"But nobody tells us anything," Oliver said.

"I give you my word, I'll keep you informed, boys," Tom said to them quickly, speaking over his shoulder. He held the broom and dust pan close to his chest, his gesture preventing Ben from taking them. "Your feet are bare, Ben. Get up on the bench. All of you, up on the bench." The others stepped up immediately, but Ben hesitated, eyeing the broom and the coach's legs. "I can sweep, son," Tom told him, "I just can't walk."

"But it's my fault."

"Now that you're on the team, you'll have to get used to the way I do things," Tom gestured toward the other team members towering above them on the bench. "Come on, now." Ben stepped up.

"Where did glass come from?" Paul asked.

Miserable with inaction, Ben watched Tom sweep.

"Inside Ben's shirt, I think," Joe said.

"Yeah. It fell out when I took my shirt off."

"He was in an accident this morning," Joe told them and immediately Ben was asked about the crash, the damage to the car and Middleton's. Tom swept the glass bits into a pile about the size of a small pancake. "All clear."

Ben stepped down and Tom said, "Sit down."

Thinking he was in trouble, Ben opened his mouth to protest, but Tom's implacable expression convinced him; he sat down, realizing then that bits of glass had fallen inside his boxers.

"You were in an accident this morning?" Tom wheeled closer.

"Yes, sir."

"Is that how you split your lip?"

Ben exhaled, shrinking from the question.

"The car windows break?"

Ben squinted, trying to remember if the windshield broke. "Actually, yes, sir, the passenger side where I was sitting."

"Apparently, you've been carrying the glass around in your clothes. You've got scratches all around your neck. Look at this, Joe." Tom gestured. Joe, team following, stepped close and peered at Ben.

"And look at his wrists."

Turning his wrists over, Ben noted batches of red slits and felt the same sharp scratching inside his waistband and along his seat. He shifted, making it worse.

Tom said, "Nothing looks too deep, but you're gonna be sore."

"I think I already am."

Bending over him, Paul said, "Look, there's some in his hair."

Tom told Ben to bend his head forward. Carefully, he moved the hair at the top of Ben's head and caught the pieces that fell. "You'd better get in the shower. Wash all that out."

"I was going to run with the team."

"First you should get this glass off your skin, Ben. It won't come off by running."

"No," Joe said, smirking and glancing from face to face, "but you could *walk* it off."

At the burst of laughter, Tom, puzzled, scanned the grinning faces.

Oliver's voice entered like the buzz of a mosquito. "You've got something on the back of your wheelchair, Coach."

"Not, now, Ollie," Tom glanced briefly over his shoulder. Oliver turned abruptly, thumped Knox's shoulder, turned him toward the door and left. Tom spoke again to Ben. "Besides," Tom said, "You don't deserve their punishment."

"He was holding the masks," Paul said.

Tom made a dismissive noise.

"I run every day, anyhow," Ben said.

"Wouldn't you know it?" Jon said. "Look at him."

"I suppose you lift, too," Scott mumbled.

"That explains how cut he is," Drew said.

"Buff."

"Makes me look skinny," Scott whined.

"Makes me look invisible," Joe said.

"Just look at him." And his team collectively stepped backward, examining Ben with the kind of satisfied admiration in their eyes that said they claimed him as their own champion. Fully embarrassed, Ben knew a moment of intense emotion. Had they any idea what their acceptance meant to him? He met Tom's eyes, and the only thing he could think to say was, "I think it's in my shorts too."

At this, they gave a collective shout commanding Ben to get into the showers. Paul turned on the water, Scott found him a bar of soap and Tom got a clean towel from the stack kept in the locker room and put it in Ben's hands as the others carried him to the brightly lit row of showers along the outside wall of the room where they left him.

When the door closed behind them, the locker room was silent beyond the steady patter of the shower. Shivering, Ben stepped under the hot water and closed his eyes. He let the water flood over him, picking out loosened pieces of glass from his hair, wincing as the soap seared each cut. Without the others' energy around him, he knew a feeble kind of weariness and flicked the water temperature to cold to combat it.

Minutes later, wrapped in his towel, he went through the deserted locker room, his damp feet sticking lightly to the floor. On the bench in front of his locker, he found worn, clean boxers, gym shorts, and socks. Beside them stood a tall plastic tumbler filled with ice water. Ben took it and drank greedily, dressed quickly and hurried out to join his team.

Ben walked down the alley between the brick wall and the backs of the houses on Porter Road. Entering the house from the ground floor, he stopped at the laundry room and started his glass-littered clothes to wash. He bounded the stairs two at a time, eager to tell his grandmother about the success of his day. In the kitchen, Donna Hunter sat at the small round table, filling out forms.

"Hey, Mom," Ben said, going to the sink for a drink of water. He briefly considered telling her how much he liked the school, but the immediate panic igniting in his stomach at the thought of confiding in her reminded him of her skill at ruining any good thing.

"You're much later than I expected."

"Sorry," Ben said. He looked in two cabinets before finding a large glass. "The basketball team had a meeting."

"I thought practice didn't start until October or November."

"It doesn't, officially, but we're going to be meeting to run and keep in shape and stuff."

"I can tell this is going to be very inconvenient."

"Sorry." Ben went to the freezer for ice. He counted six glass mugs standing in a row, chilling. One of Ben's chores included chilling his father's beer mugs. To be safe, Ben kept six at a time waiting in the freezer.

"So I can't depend on you to watch your brothers in the afternoons." Ben scooped his own glass full of ice. "I suppose I've got to arrange for after care."

"You and Dad want me to try for a basketball scholarship. I've got to be involved with the team, Mom."

"If you want to go to college, you'll need a scholarship. We simply can't pay for it."

"Where is everybody?" Back at the sink, Ben filled his glass with water.

"Your brothers are playing with the neighbors."

"Where's Gran?"

Donna gathered up her forms and stood up. She barely reached Ben's shoulder and looked thin and fragile in her bright orange T-shirt and shorts. Her arms were spare, her wrists minuscule and yet she slapped the forms she held down on the table with a surprisingly loud snap. "She argued with your father late last night."

Ben made a disgusted, knowing noise.

"She left this morning before you boys got up."

"This morning? But we were *calling* her this morning."

"Yes, and woke me up, thank you very much."

"We thought she was *here*. Why didn't Dad say something?"

"I don't suppose it was any of your business." Ben opened his mouth to argue, then thinking better of it, put his glass of ice water to his lips and drank deeply. Donna stepped closer to him. "I don't want you giving your father a hard time about Gran leaving." Still drinking, Ben widened his eyes in amazed protest. He gave his father a hard time about *nothing*. He knew better.

Donna shook her finger at Ben, but her hair, which was carefully combed into a smooth helmet, did not move. "Your father is under a great deal of stress and he doesn't need any more from you. He's beginning a new and terribly important job. His future in the Marine Corps depends on it."

"He says that same thing at every new duty station."

"You have no idea what it's like to live under the constant threat of utter rejection."

Ben took a piece of ice into his mouth and looked directly into her light, hazel eyes. Eye contact typically made Donna angry, but there were times when Ben had to look, had to see if she understood him at all. And as always when he looked, he saw that though her words bit and tore, there was a baffling restraint in her demeanor that suggested an entire volume of unspoken invective. Now her face and neck had gone red above her shirt so glaring orange Ben wished his eye defect were color blindness. He turned away from her to refill his glass. Paying meticulous attention to the water splashing against the ice, he hoped to sound casual when he changed the subject.

"I met an old friend of yours today, Mom."

"That's doubtful."

"No, I did. My basketball coach said he and his wife were dear friends of yours."

"A coach and his wife?"

"Yes, ma'am. It's weird. He's in a wheelchair and he still coaches."

"I don't know anyone in a wheelchair."

Ben sipped his water, thinking it odd that a woman who had been a registered nurse all of her adult life—a navy nurse for ten of those years—would not know *any*one in a wheelchair. "Maybe a former patient," he suggested lightly.

"Good nurses don't make friends with their patients."

"His name is Tom MacBride."

From the sink he heard her sharp intake of breath, and a chill went up his spine. "I don't know his wife's name," Ben added hastily trying to dilute her shock.

"Tom MacBride…in a wheelchair?"

"Yes ma'am."

"Was he seriously hurt?"

"I don't know. He seems fine." Ben turned a few inches so that he could see her out of the corner of his eye. He pretended to study his water glass, giving her quick glances. She sank down into her chair at the kitchen table, and folded her tiny hands in a final manner. Her mouth, bright with glossy lipstick, quivered slightly. "Wasn't he in a wheelchair when you knew him?"

"No, oh, no. And he *works* at your school?"

"Yes, ma'am, and his kids, Joe and Bonnie Jean, are nice, too."

Donna lifted her chin. "But to say we were *dear friends* is an… exaggeration."

"But you knew them, right?"

Staring at her hands, she spoke vaguely as if thinking aloud. "I knew both he and his wife when I was stationed in Annapolis years ago. Tom and I worked together here at the Academy."

"I didn't know you were stationed here."

"It was before you—it—" she broke off. She took a deliberate breath, and as if making a decision said, "Ben, when you see him again, you are to tell him this, exactly this." Her eyes narrowed in careful planning. "Tell Tom—I mean, Mr. MacBride—that I am flattered that he remembers me so kindly, but we are all very different people now." She looked prim, satisfied.

Thinking that he would never say anything like that to his coach, Ben said, gently, hopefully, "He was really nice about it, Mom. He mentioned Dad, too."

In a swift motion, Donna left her chair, turned for him and grabbed his wrist. Ben flinched, caught his breath and forced himself to steady, knowing she would fly into a fury if he wrenched free his arm. Her fingers tightened, the slick pink nails pressing against his skin, raw from the broken car windows. "Look, you," she hissed, suddenly fierce. "You caused enough trouble today with that accident."

"Me?"

Her nails rasped on his sore skin. He flinched, involuntarily pulling back. She tightened her grip. "Yes. Your father told me how you grabbed the wheel and sent the car crashing up over the curb."

"No."

"Your father is upset *enough* about your behavior this morning. Do *not* mention this—this *MacBride* nonsense—to your father. He can't *stand* Tom MacBride and I don't blame him for it."

Ben forced his arm to relax in her grip, hoping the lack of resistance would cause her to release him. "But why?" he said, pleasantly, lightly, trying to cajole her to reason. "He's so nice."

She dug her nails into his wrist, shouting, "You mention him again, and I promise you, Ben Hunter, you'll be out of that school before you can cry for help." Ben pulled away and she yanked at his arm, scraping raw tunnels on the skin as she tried to pull him toward her. She raised her other hand to slap his face, but Ben reared back, out of her range. She swung at him, missing by inches, and swung again.

He wrenched his arm free as she shouted, "You do as I say." Her shouting masked the sound of his father's steps on the back stairs and when Ben heard Max, right behind him, it was too late. Max grabbed Ben from behind, trapping Ben's arms to his side.

"You trying to slap him?" Max asked, his voice so congenial it was nearly jolly. Max thrust his own large powerful body up flush against Ben, forcing him to bend down toward Donna. Revolted, shuddering, Ben struggled wildly. Max leaned heavily on him; his solid body pressed against the full length of Ben's back, his knees thrust into the backs of Ben's thighs. Max's cheek, rough with the day's growth of whiskers, rubbed Ben's ear. Ben smelled an unmistakable sweetness on his father's breath. "There," Max murmured "He's low enough for you to slap him."

"You do as I say," she repeated. Donna slapped Ben's face; his sore lip opened and blood came. Donna turned away. Ben held still, held his breath, fearing the press of his father's body. His father released him and Ben stumbled forward, his left hand stopping his fall. Max laughed and slapped Ben's rear with his fabric uniform hat. Ben bolted up the stairs, reaching the bathroom on the second floor before he vomited.

7

BY bedtime, Tom MacBride could hobble on his left leg by dragging his right leg. He had pulled himself up the stairs and had even managed to turn the covers down for his wife, Laurie, who read now, in their bed leaning against several flouncy white pillows. All those pillows, as light and high as summer clouds behind her, with another tucked under her smooth, bare knees gave her the appearance of being well-insulated. Unsuspecting of Tom's burden, she wiggled her toes under the flower-colored quilt folded at the end of the bed. Tom wondered if he should try to keep the news about Ben from her until after the baby was born. He sat on the edge of the bed near Laurie's feet, holding the sole of his shoe in place until the glue he'd applied to it set.

"Why not buy a new pair, Tom?" Laurie said, without glancing up.

"I can make these do."

Laurie looked young and vibrant in her advanced pregnancy. Her dark eyes were liquid and bright as they skimmed over the printed forms in her folder, one finger on the line she read. Her hair, just as dark, was cut short and its loose curls shone in the dim, evening lamplight. She wore a scant, cotton nightgown, sleeveless and edged with lace; the flush across her high cheekbones spoke of her health and the time she undoubtedly spent in her garden after work. But Tom worried. The pregnancy had been utterly unplanned and Laurie was not the type to quit work just because she was forty-two and pregnant.

"Are you too warm?" Tom asked.

"I'm fine," she said, glancing up from her reading.

"Don't want your feet to swell," he said, patting her ankles.

"They're fine," she said, wiggling her toes as casually as if they were thrust into beach sand.

She evidently sensed no danger, though Tom had agonized, since his fourth period class, about the best way to tell Laurie. At dinner, Joe and Bonnie Jean had talked incessantly about the new boy. Tom knew, watching Ben and Joe fall, incredibly, into the rare step of lasting friendship that Joe would bring Ben home before too long. Laurie must be prepared for the sight of him, but Tom thought that she looked too happy and sound to disturb.

"You know, I'm not sure I should hire another employee." She closed the folder she had been reading. "This woman has experience. She won a prize at the Lancaster quilt show and she wants to bake for the café, but I have a feeling she'll be short with the customers."

"You need at least two more employees. If she doesn't work out, you can let her go."

"*You* wouldn't fire her. You'd try to fix her."

"Your standards for shop-keeping are worth upholding."

"I actually think she made a face when she tried the shortbread."

"Laurie," he laughed, "there's not a soul alive who would sneer at your shortbread."

"Okay, I'll hire her and if she turns out to be a problem, I'll call you in for help." She smiled with confidence. "If she can start this week, I'll be ready for the baby. Especially with the first day of school over without trauma."

"Hardly without trauma."

"Joe has always been hungry for your attention."

"He got a feast of it today."

"And the new boy. Isn't it good of our children to reach out to a stranger?"

"Yes, it is."

"What's your impression of him, Tom? The new boy—what's his name again?"

"Ben." Tom took a deep breath. "He's likable."

"You must have noticed more than that."

"Let's see…he's polite." Tom studied the sole of his shoe, noting how very worth saving it was, barely worn.

"Father in the military?"

"As most of our new kids are," Tom said, glancing at her, awaiting a flicker of recognition.

"And?"

"And so, his manners are impeccable, but it's more than that, he seems to know instinctively how to get along with people. There's a kind of observant look in his eyes. Borders on searching, his expression does at times."

"And you think he'll make the basketball team?"

"No doubt about it. I can tell by the way he walks. He's a natural athlete."

"What does that mean specifically?"

"I haven't seen him handle the ball yet. I've got to check him out on that, but he's fast; he's got incredible stamina," he said, telling *himself* that he was trying to paint a vivid picture of Ben for her, but the imperative to tell the truth was like a gun thrust into his back making him uncomfortable with his equivocation. He swallowed hard. "Today when he ran with the team, he came a little late, made up the missed laps and was still done first."

"And Jeannie kept saying how handsome he is," Laurie said. "She makes him sound like something out of a teenage girl's imagination."

"No, he's quite real and quite strikingly handsome."

"Really?" Laurie peered at Tom.

"Yes," Tom said with a finality that he hoped would alert his wife.

"He's *that* handsome?"

"Yes, he is."

"As handsome as Joe?" she teased, disbelieving.

"Yes."

"Come on, Tom, you never say *anyone* is as handsome as Joe."

"This boy is. Just as handsome. Just exactly as handsome."

"Tom?"

"It's him, Laurie."

"Him?" she squinched up her face.

"Him."

He watched her eyes widen with realization, heard her breathe. Her hands went protectively to her middle. "Are you sure?"

"His name is Bennett Hunter." Tom shook his head, still stunned, still disbelieving. "Ben is his nickname."

"No," Laurie said. "It can't be. There must be a million Hunters in this country."

"I spoke to him. I told him we were good friends with his mother."

"And?"

"And nothing. It's him."

"But what did he say when you told him we were old friends?"

"He looked pretty confused by then. I was so stunned to see him, I think I acted like a senile, old dolt."

"You said *good friends* to him?"

"I may have said *dear* friends."

"And he didn't respond to that?"

"The entire gym class was listening to us."

"Maybe it's not him, then." Laurie reached for his hand. He covered her hand with both of his.

"No, it is him. I asked him if his father's name was Max Hunter."

"So, then." Laurie took a deep, slow breath.

"Listen, I've thought about this and it's possible—no, it's probable—that Max never mentioned us. It's perfectly understandable."

Laurie's glance flashed anger. "Not to me."

"Not everyone has your generous heart," Tom said, humbly. Moving closer to her, Tom took her in his arms and was dismayed to find that she trembled.

Laurie said, "You should have brought him home to dinner."

"What?"

"Tomorrow."

"Laurie, we've got to take it easy."

"I can't imagine why."

"For one thing, you're about to give birth."

"That has nothing to do with this."

"For another thing, we don't know anything about his situation."

"What's to know? The kids said he was great."

Tom nodded, gulping down a deep breath of air. "He is great. As far as I can see he's a nice kid."

"Then what is the problem?"

"Laurie. We can't go barging in. We can't disrupt his life. We must show restraint."

"*You* can be restrained," she said, releasing his hand. "When I see him I'm going to grab him and hug him and never let him go." She fought tears and lost. Her head dropped against his shoulder and she clutched at his arms with both her strong, neat hands.

Tom spoke softly. "We've got to befriend him the way we would any kid. We have to be careful and see what happens. We don't want to do any damage."

"I don't see how I could."

"We have to be invited into his life. We can't demand a relationship with him. We have no rights, you know. No legal rights."

"So you've said before."

"I'm as sorry as you are that it's true."

"Your promise," she said. "You have that."

"That is between Max and me. We can't use *that* to force Ben into a relationship with us."

"You talk like we're horrible ogres. Half the high school practically lives over here."

Tom twirled one of her curls around his fingers. "You know I'm right."

She sat back against the pillow, snatching away at her tears. "The worst part of being pregnant is the inability to avoid crying."

"Here, I have something for you." He grinned at her hopefully, then stretched across the bed and grabbed his briefcase. From it he took a large folder. "I brought home as much of his academic record as I dared sneak out," he said, giving a short, embarrassed laugh. With an eager gasp, she took it from him. "There are pictures, too. I read as much as I could squeeze in today."

Laurie balanced the folder against her knees and flipped it open, catching her breath at the sight of Ben's first grade picture. "Tom, look, that thoughtful expression."

"When you meet him, you'll see why we've got to be careful."

"Is it thoughtful or is he worried?" Laurie said, considering the picture.

"That's why I say what I do. By all indications, he's pretty bright, but there's defensiveness, too. You'll have the same impression, that he should be treated with the utmost courtesy—intellectual respect, really—and gentleness." He meant to assure her of their decision, but she was lost to him, devouring the information in the folder with the kind of rapt concentration peculiar to her. Tom fell silent, realizing he was speaking cautionary words to his own astonished heart.

Rising Sun

8

Ben woke with the sun, feeling fully aware and apprehensive. Once outside, he eased the door shut in silence and inhaled the heavy, moist air with the relish of one long captive.

His backpack and gym bag on one arm, his uniform on the other, he jogged to Lejeune Hall, the huge swimming complex at the end of Porter Road, and hurried around the side of the natatorium to the men's locker room door. Now the eastern sky lightened over the Severn River beyond the swim center and Ben glanced around. There was no one. He thumped the door with his fist, caught it as it opened, and slipped in. With its harsh chlorine scent, the dark, empty building seemed as familiar and distant as a childhood home. There had been a swim center at every marine or navy base he'd known, and Max frequented them as some haunted men visit bars.

Ben saw the door that led to the pool and turned his back to it, enduring the shudder that passed through him always at the thought of the swimming pool and the diving tanks lying smooth and silent beyond. Remembering when he was small and swam nearly every day, Ben recalled the sensation of diving into the cool water. He remembered the thrill of falling, the chill and froth of the plunge beneath. Then he was gliding; he was weightless, no need to breathe, fast as a fish. The memory, briefly compelling, now left him seasick. But this time, teeth clenched, Ben clung to the images.

Why had his father forced him to quit swimming? Bright, tumbled images flooded his senses: countless pools on Saturdays with his father, splashing, racing, his own careless giggles. When he was young, Ben thought, he had loved swimming and he had loved his father.

He hung his school uniform in an empty locker close to the toilets. Stretching conscientiously, Ben thought about his lifelong presumption that Max had made him quit swimming because of his eye. It was the same year, when he was twelve, that his parents had insisted he wear a specially made contact lens to cover his keyhole-shaped pupil. Their exact instructions said he was never to be seen outside his bedroom without the contact lens.

Ben had grieved over this proclamation as much as he did about the loss of swimming. Ben had liked his eye. His friends thought it was cool; it had been useful for scaring girls. In the dark, he could see better than anybody, and sometimes in daylight, he saw quick, darting shapes and the slightest changes in facial expressions. But best of all, in the bright sunshine, ordinary things took on shimmery halos. All this was to be no more, and instead Ben understood the cold, slimy reality of his parents' displeasure with how he had been made.

Ben told himself that Max was afraid he'd lose the lens in the water, so he forbid Ben to swim. But he realized that this assumption couldn't be true; it didn't explain Max's implacable anger. It seemed to Ben that his father's anger toward him had begun that time Max hit him in the swimming pool bathroom, but forcing Ben to hide his eye was the most violent thing Max had ever done to him in years of escalating, baffling violence. Ben shook himself to action. Quickly, he left the building the same silent way he'd entered, the door open only for seconds. It was time to run and gather his morning portion of peace.

As he jogged across the green lawns, dew-drenched, Ben breathed in the damp morning air hungrily. This heavy Annapolis warmth was Ben's favorite running weather. He ran along the rocky sea wall, gazing out at the still, silvered water of the Severn, memorizing the peculiar marshy-salt smell of the river, and watching the rising sun spread a shimmering path across water that looked thick enough to support his weight.

He was warming up, his legs rousing to life, but he kept his pace slow and even as he ran past the docked sailboats, amused by their bold names—*Intrepid, Dauntless, Audacious*—thinking that the Academy was an odd place, celebrating such qualities, yet demanding uniform and unquestioning obedience. Relishing that dependable feeling of well-being that running inevitably brought him, Ben gave himself to it, sprinting in a long diagonal line across a silent parking lot and through the spindly legs of the bleachers that surrounded the track stadium. As soon as his feet touched the cinders, he pushed and ran hard, pumping with his arms, his feet scattering gravel, his heart soaring to flame in his chest. He circled the track once, and when he felt the rising sun glance upon his head and shoulders, he spun off and sprinted hard again.

Ben traced the perimeter of the Academy grounds along Hospital Point, the great, rectangular field that jutted into the Severn. Ben ran at the river's edge, his eyes watching the current, all the time keeping just ahead of the sunlight's burn on his shoulders. He turned at the end of the field and ran up a hill, past the hospital and into the cemetery, dark with the fragrant shade of pine trees. When he emerged the sun lay in bright possession of the entire Yard. *What would I see,* Ben thought as he paused to survey the sun's realm, *if I could see the way I used to?*

Breath coming hard, he sped past the still sleeping academic buildings, along the brick paths leading to the chapel that presided over the Yard in the splendid command of silence. The rising sun touched the eastern edge of the chapel's high, weathered dome and lit its rare blue windows. Ben jogged closer to the chapel, shaking his arms in a peculiar motion that helped him get his breath. Peering into the chapel, squinting to see high inside the arch of the dome, he stared at the lights that flickered and glowed there like burning, yellow stars—a little, indoor heaven hovering in the dark blue air of the dome. His breath came easier, the thought filling him with the very sense of wonder and safety he sought when he ran. He walked the rest of the way to Lejeune Hall, glancing back at the blue windows, clinging to his inspiration; he'd spent his strength and in a mystery that intrigued him daily, recaptured his composure and his motivation.

9

"THANKS for picking me up," Ben said, as he slid into the passenger seat of Joe's MG. A rich fragrance met him and his mouth watered in response. "It smells like a bakery in here."

Joe started forward, easing the noisy car into the morning traffic, setting the plastic, red-veined eyeball that hung from his keys swinging wildly. "Yeah, I have to stop by Mom's store with these rolls." Joe pointed over his shoulder to indicate the bulging paper bags sitting on the back seat. "She had to leave before they were done."

"She works at a bakery?" Ben murmured, swallowing hard.

"No, she owns a quilt store and she's got a little café in it—for shoppers."

"Oh," Ben said, staring at the unblinking eyeball swinging from Joe's key chain.

"What, are you hungry?"

"Who, me?" His stomach was louder than the MG.

"Reach back there and get one," Joe commanded.

"No, I—"

"You'd better. I can't drive with your stomach making that noise."

Ben glanced back at them. "Are they...how much do they cost?"

Joe made an angry noise. "Look. It's simple. If you don't take one, I'll beat you up."

"You couldn't beat me up," Ben laughed. "But thanks, I'm beyond hungry." As he unrolled the top of the bag, the warm, yeasty fragrance intensified. He groaned involuntarily and raised the soft, warm roll to his lips. The crust was brisk, but not hard and dusted lightly with flour. The inside, warm and light and yellow, fulfilled the promise of fragrance and heat.

"Get another," Joe commanded. "Mom would feed you if she were here. She'd insist." By the time Joe pulled his car to a stop in front of a neat little house set on the corner of a shady street, Ben had eaten five rolls. "This is it," Joe said, leaving the car and indicating that Ben should come with him.

Though the shop's cedar siding had grayed with age, the bright red shutters and pale gray front porch looked newly painted and clean in the sunlight. Surrounding the porch perimeter, roses bloomed in a tumbling profusion of golden color. The scent of the roses reached for them, drowning the fragrance of the rolls. Ben knew a moment of apprehension. "So many of those flowers."

"That's because they've been there forever, they survive anything. One time, Pete dumped a pot of boiling water on them and they still grew back." Grabbing the bags from the back seat, Joe thrust one of them into Ben's arms and took the others. Joe led the way up the sidewalk to the porch, wide and deep, which lay in a pool of misty morning sunlight that dazzled the panes of glass in the bowed display window. Ben hung back.

"Come on," Joe said, "we'll see what other food she's got inside."

The shop was awake, the upstairs windows streaked with sunlight, the front door ajar, and a faded quilt hung from the porch railing. Along the front porch, those overgrown rosebushes tumbled, their canes arched and laden with blooms in white and butter yellow and bold, clear gold. A sullen breeze moved the reluctant morning air with the flowers' spicy scent. Ben hesitated; the scent stopping him like a hand on his chest. In the farthest edges of his field of vision, he saw something rushing toward him. Startled, he looked to his right and noticed a banner hung from the porch that flickered with the movement of the fragrant breeze. An intricate design in bright colors displayed what Ben assumed was the store's name, EIGHT HANDS AROUND.

Ben stopped walking, suddenly nervous, more than nervous. He stared at the porch, determined to figure out what alarmed him. It was just a house with a front porch; the roses were just stupid flowers, not in the least alarming. He blamed his shakiness on yesterday's violence, the accident, his parents' attack.

"Oh, good, she's here," Joe said over his shoulder. "Come on. Don't be shy. She's gonna love you."

At the top step, Ben saw her through the window. There, behind those splashes of color that Ben realized were quilts and bolts of fabric, she approached, holding a pair of scissors and a long, bright yellow measuring tape. She was dark-haired, like Bonnie Jean, with the same set of the shoulders. The crisp collar of her white shirt drew attention to her face, with prominent cheekbones, large expressive eyes and a straight nose. Her short hair, glossy, curling, moved slightly as she did and round diamonds in her ear lobes caught the sunlight like quivering beads of water. She moved toward the window and Ben saw the shape of her advanced pregnancy in her low belly rounded against the cloth of the neat, white shirt. This sight provoked a tender concern that rose unbidden in him. It was always so with Ben when he noticed a woman in the later stages of pregnancy, but the response seemed particularly sharp that warm August morning, his own belly stuffed with bread this woman had made with her own hands.

As she peered over the quilt display, bending forward to stretch out a length of the yellow tape, she saw them. Her head and shoulders came into the shadowy light of the bay window. Her eyes were dark and liquid, as brown as her daughter's, but careful, without that clear readability that so interested Ben in Bonnie Jean's eyes. She saw Joe first; her eyes warmed with recognition, her smile quick and eager as a child thrilled.

When she saw Ben, she stopped moving completely. Their eyes met, and Ben saw an intense emotion that he could not define. He stared, nearly frantic that she would move or blink before he defined what he'd seen. But she didn't move; she stayed, leaning both hands on the quilt display in the window, looking out at him, her expression at once questioning and knowing. Ben's face burned; he looked down, studying the shape of her neat hands that gripped the scissors tightly and he found that her expression had been seared into his consciousness, troubling, familiar, and incomprehensible.

She was beside him on the porch before he could move.

"This is Ben, Mom."

"Ben." She was smiling, her eyes alight. Her hands were empty now and she held them out to him.

Ben did not know what to do, so he thrust the bag of rolls into her outstretched hands. Deprived of their warmth, he shivered despite the muggy summer air. "I—I ate several of your rolls on the way over, Mrs. MacBride," he told her, carefully avoiding her eyes.

"Several?"

"Yes, ma'am. They smelled so good, I couldn't resist."

"That's quite a compliment. Thank you," she said, her voice sounded so happy that Ben dared to glance at her face. There he saw again, that baffling look in her eyes. For a moment, Ben thought that if he had not been tall and so shy, she would have hugged him.

Joe shook his head at Ben's discomfort. "Mom, I'm gonna raid the fridge for our lunch. Okay?"

"I already made a lunch up for you. There's more than enough for Ben. But get him some orange juice."

"Okay," Joe said and took all three bags past his mother into the store. They were alone on the porch.

"Those rolls really were great," Ben said.

"I'm happy you liked them, Ben."

There was no doubting her sincerity; there was so much of it. Acceptance flowed from her expressive face, welcoming him, and her rounded pregnant body suggested trust and wealth and generosity. But Ben didn't understand from where this palpable emotion, strong and full-grown, had come. The people he lived with every day never approached this level of warm, outgoing feeling for him. What if his parents had once felt this way for him and some quirk in his personality—his irritating perfectionism or his tendency toward contemplation—had destroyed it? Even Gran, whom he knew loved him deeply, tempered her expression of that love with her preposterous gestures in defense of his father. Yet, standing there on Laurie MacBride's porch, his stomach pleasantly full with her fresh rolls, his senses awakened by the strangely provocative scent of the roses guarding the porch, Ben knew that she wanted badly to embrace him or more accurately, to take his face in her hands and kiss his face!

She seemed to sense his bewilderment and reluctantly stepped back a bit, folding her arms across her chest and resting them on her enormous belly. "Joe and Tom and Bonnie Jean told me all about you last night at dinner."

"No way," he murmured.

"Ben, I'm not exaggerating when I say that's *all* we talked about. Jeannie described you perfectly."

"She did?"

"Yes," Laurie said, staring up into Ben's eyes with an expression of such eager happiness that for a moment, Ben doubted he was awake. "Bonnie Jean was upset that you got involved in Joe's prank. She blames herself for involving you."

"But, that's okay," Ben said, "I got to meet everybody."

"That's *exactly* what I thought," Laurie said, still staring at Ben with concentration fit to memorize his details.

"Joe makes class fun. I just pretty much followed him around all day."

"You like our school?"

"I love it."

"Jeannie says you're taking French and Spanish along with everything else. Are you one of those people who just has an instinct about grammar and structure?"

"Yes, ma'am. It makes sense to me. I see how it all fits together," he murmured, peering at her, seeing that she understood somehow. He decided to describe his ability a little more fully. "And once I hear a word, I…I don't seem to be able to forget it."

"Is it when you hear it, or when you read it?"

Ben thought about this, chewing his sore lower lip. "Either, really."

She nodded again and looked so proud of him that he glanced away.

"Ben, I just don't know how to tell you how welcome you are to us. Tom was so pleased to meet you."

Joe emerged from the colorful shadows of the store holding a bag and a bottle of orange juice.

"Oh, you found lunch so quickly," Laurie said.

"And the rest of Ben's breakfast." He thrust the bottle of juice at Ben.

"Thank you," Ben said.

"Joe, get him a glass of ice and he can drink it here, before school," Laurie said.

"Mom," Joe said, "we've got to go."

"You're probably thirsty, Ben. All those rolls."

"Mom, we'll be late." Joe bounced his key chain's plastic eyeball against his palm.

She ignored him. "Or how about a cappuccino?"

"Mom, are you okay?"

"You've already *had* breakfast. I'm talking to Ben."

"Yeah, I know," Joe laughed. "You're hyper. You're scaring him. Dad said you'd get really hyper right before the baby comes. If you get any more hyper—"

"I'm fine." She glanced at her son. "It could be another two weeks."

"Two weeks?" Ben said. "And you're still working?"

"I have a lot to do before the baby comes."

"She never stops working," Joe said. "Dad's been asking her to slow down."

"He's one to talk," Laurie sniffed.

"*He's* not pregnant," Joe scolded. He draped an arm around her shoulders and kissed the top of her head.

"You'll be late for school," Laurie said, swatting at Joe's backside.

Joe swerved, grinning, and started down the steps. "Yeah, right, whatever you say, Mom."

"I hope everything goes well with the baby," Ben said. "It was nice to meet you."

"Come on, Ben. We'll be late."

But Laurie took Ben's hand, stopping him. "Come by anytime, Ben. You're welcome anytime."

"Come on, Mom," Joe said, "you're embarrassing him."

She dropped his hand and gave him a gracious, apologetic smile. "I hope that's not true."

Wanting to reassure her, Ben turned back to face her. "It's okay."

She gave a self-reproaching laugh. "I just wanted you to know I am absolutely thrilled to know you're here in Annapolis. Your mother was once my dearest friend in all the world, Ben."

"No kidding, Mom," Joe said softly, coming back to the steps.

Ben looked at Laurie, searching her deep brown eyes now so frankly open to him, wondering how it could be true that this lively, generous woman could have any enjoyable rapport with his mother.

"Yes, ma'am," Ben said gently. He was concerned for her condition, remembering how fragile and unhappy Donna had been while waiting for his brothers' births. How could he tell Laurie MacBride that his mother did not want to renew the friendship? "Mr. MacBride mentioned that to me yesterday when I met him. And I—" he swallowed hard, pleading with his eyes that she be strong. "I told Mom last night about it and she said... um...she said to say hello."

Laurie's eyes flashed wide open as if in astonished relief. For one brief moment, she looked confused, then her cheeks went bright pink. "She said...?"

Ben peered at her, afraid he'd hurt her badly. Meeting her eyes, he said, gently, "She said she was flattered to be remembered kindly."

"Go on," Laurie said. She was strong again, Ben sensed, courageous deep in her core and savvy. Perhaps in the years, she had forgotten his mother's ways.

"She said—Mrs. MacBride, you remember that she's kind of stiff and formal, right?"

Laurie nodded. "What did she say?"

"She said to tell you that you are all very different people now, but thank you for thinking of her."

Laurie met his eyes; the confusion was gone. Replacing it, Ben saw that some troubling question had been answered. He thought he might have been right to be honest, except for the keen sense of self-reproach he saw in Laurie's frown.

"That makes sense," Laurie said with finality.

"It does?"

"We'd better go, Mom," Joe said gently.

"I'm sorry," Ben said.

"No, don't be!" Her smile was sad, resigned, and her eyes were so bright they looked sharp. "Please tell Donna that I send my warmest wishes to her."

"I'll do that, Mrs. MacBride," Ben said, and impulsively, he bent to hug her. She was warm and soft and smelled of the kitchen. She held onto him for one intense moment, her warm cheek against his, her hand and arm firm on his shoulders, the other circling his back, her touch passing that vital, electric emotion deep into him.

10

"INTERESTING lecture, sir."

Max Hunter felt a burst of pride for his students, impeccably uniformed, as they placed their neat papers one by one on the corner of his desk. They were history majors, eager to study military strategies and one by one they thanked him for his lecture on the battle of Saratoga and the gentleman general, Johnny Burgoyne. He checked his posture, noting that his trousers were still sharply creased, and pulled in his thickening middle.

"Have a nice afternoon, sir."

Max shook his head slightly; his reluctance to come to Annapolis now bewildered him. *I can't believe that bastard Tom MacBride graduated from a great place like this. Must have been some kind of fluke*, Max thought. The students he taught seemed nothing like the man Max remembered. *MacBride didn't fit in the Marine Corps either*, Max reminded himself. *But nobody could knock the Corps just because MacBride had been an officer.*

Max appreciated the concept of the military academy. A professional place that did not tolerate slovenly dress, drug abuse, or insolent manners, it was rigorous, offered sports at every level of competition, and it cost nothing. When he was alone, Max walked to the sunlit windows that lined the back of the classroom and stood, his hands clasped at the back of his waist, surveying his domain. From this room in Chauvenet Hall, he could see the young athletes training on the track and on the closely mown, green lawns that stretched out to the banks of the Severn where sailing teams raced toward the low bridge west.

He pictured Ben running along the edge of the field that shimmered now in the late afternoon sun. His assistant, Nels Lindquist, had told Max that he'd seen Ben running this morning when he was out for his own pre-dawn exercise. "Ben was about a hundred yards ahead of me the whole time, running like a hungry cheetah. I couldn't catch him." That was Ben, fast, silent, and successfully evasive. This bit of covert information pleased Max immensely, because he felt certain it meant that Ben liked the Academy; he was comfortable and had already learned his way around.

Max took a deep breath and exhaled slowly, thinking that perhaps he could relax. Ben had not protested his grandmother's early departure, nor had he mentioned yesterday's car accident. Over the years Max had, with only three or four exceptions, found Ben compliant and easy to direct. He never missed a day of school, completed all his homework, earned only A's. When he wasn't reading, doing his chores, or entertaining his brothers, he was playing ball or running. Ben was quiet, never moody, always neat and clean, and incredibly, never sick. But sometimes, when Ben was still and unaware of Max's presence—when the boy was reading or standing by the kitchen sink watching his glass fill with water—Max sensed a discontent as palpable as thunder. In those moments, he feared that as he skimmed effortlessly over Ben's glass-like adolescence, in truth, he was navigating a measureless fjord, the depths of which moved in icy currents far beyond his perception.

Standing at the window Max glanced at the Severn River and tried to remember the last time he was certain he knew what was best for Ben. After one of Ben's rare instances of temper at age twelve, Max insisted that the boy play basketball. With a powerful instinct, he'd known it was the best thing for Ben. When the idea came to Max, the season was well in progress; nevertheless, he secured Ben's place on the best team he could find. The following summer he paid for two camps. By the end of the summer when Ben was twelve, Ben understood basketball and had an uncanny sense of his belonging to the sport. He excelled; not only that, Ben showed an inner motivation to train and practice that occluded Max's involvement. Basketball, which Max had forced Ben to play, had become Ben's private world. Ben neither needed—nor in his cool, polite way, tolerated—Max's involvement.

But after being at the Naval Academy for only two days, Max found his vision for Ben renewed. He decided that Ben must attend college here.

The sound of someone clearing his throat interrupted Max's thoughts. He turned around to see Major Nels Lindquist. Medium height, trim, muscular and impeccably groomed down to his tan Scandinavian skin and the glass eye that was a precise match to his own, Lindquist had become a friend over the past twelve years. They had been stationed together at three of the four last duty stations.

"Yes, Major," Max said, his voice brisk, but not unfriendly. He could tell by Lindquist's expression that something was up.

"I wanted to catch you before you left the building, Colonel, sir," Lindquist said. "The supe wants to see you ASAP."

"His office is in…?" Max broke off, hoping Lindquist would fill in the information he had forgotten.

"He's asked that you walk over to his house."

"Did he say what's up?"

"He did not, sir."

The house, a sprawling white mansion, stood in the midst of clipped gardens, to the side of the chapel at the end of Porter Road. The officers, who lived on Captain's Row along with Max, joked that Admiral Charles Johnson could see right into their bedroom windows. Max straightened his posture and squared his shoulders. He knew men like Johnson and he knew how to impress them.

Removing his reading glasses, Johnson rose from behind his enormous mahogany desk to greet Max, offering his thin hand in a grip so surprisingly hard that Max made certain his nervousness did not show on his face.

"How is your family adjusting to the move? I know it was sudden." Johnson gestured toward a leather club chair. Max obeyed, hating to sit because it wrinkled his trousers. Johnson also sat, placing his palms flat on a file that lay open on his desk.

"Very well, sir," Max said. "My wife started at the Medical Center in town this week."

Johnson nodded as if he knew this information. "And your sons? You have three, don't you? How is their adjustment progressing?"

"Outstanding, sir. No problems, sir. There never are."

"Yes," Johnson smiled. "The two younger ones attend Green Street Elementary. That is, incidentally, where Mrs. Johnson teaches. She teaches morning kindergarten only. She tells me the boys are in first grade and third. She was disappointed not to be teaching one of them, I can assure you."

"Yes, sir, that is a loss. For them."

"And the older boy?"

"He's doing exceptionally well, sir. Outstanding."

Johnson reached for his reading glasses and settled them on his nose. He turned his attention to the file spread open before him and traced the upturned page with one slim finger. "The older one is...he'd be nearly sixteen."

That's my personnel file, Max shuddered, unable to reply or swallow.

"Sixteen can be a tough age, Max. Very tough. Do you remember being sixteen?" He did not wait for Max to reply. "I do. I remember it clearly." Johnson's bright brown eyes wandered over the room, as if he were seeing his memories displayed around him. His eyes rested on the windows briefly. "I also remember when my son was sixteen. He's grown now. But you knew that, Max." He waited for Max to reply.

"Yes, sir, your son," Max could not remember the first thing about the kid, but he kept his eyes confidently on the admiral's face, focusing on the man's thin arched eyebrows, ready to meet his eyes if necessary.

"He went to your alma mater, Princeton, and he's become a physician."

"Pardon me, sir, I did not go to Princeton."

"Didn't you?" Johnson glanced down. "Oh, I'm sorry. That wasn't you."

"Princeton is an excellent school, sir." Max said quickly, wondering how much personal information was kept in his personnel file.

"My point was that when he was sixteen, my boy gave me a fit."

"I'm sorry to hear that, sir."

"He liked to test my limits. I made it my mission to make him understand my limits and why I made those limits. What do you think of that?"

"Sir, I—"

"I had to do *something*, Max. I really did. Here he was, *my son*, president of the junior class, honor society, varsity athlete, and he skipped school. I found him and some of his friends roaring drunk in my *own* living room." Johnson leaned forward and eyed Max as if Max surely understood and would make a profound or at least sympathetic remark.

But Max, thinking of his own personnel file open beneath the admiral's gaze, knew only the paralysis of a misunderstood underling. "Sir," he managed to say, "boys try things. It's natural."

"Yes, it's natural. I couldn't let him think I'd tolerate that *natural* tendency, could I?" Johnson paused, and the silence demanded that Max drag his concentration from the shock of his open personnel file. "Do you, for instance, tolerate the *natural* tendency of your marines to sleep until noon?"

Woodenly, Max murmured, "No, sir."

"Of course not." Johnson leaned forward. "I knew I had to demonstrate my displeasure. When he sobered up, I paddled him." Max was startled; he met Johnson's eyes. "How do you think my son felt about that, Colonel?"

Max thrust his chin out. "Sir, I don't believe in corporal punishment."

"Don't you?"

"No, sir. And, Ben has never needed it. He's a good kid. He won't be any trouble."

"Oh, you've misunderstood me, Max," Johnson said, throwing his hands up and giving an amused laugh. "Completely. Let's back up a minute and you tell me why you think I asked you to stop by."

Stop by? Max thought, *The message was ASAP.* Max swallowed hard. "Sir, when I am in command, I like to meet with my officers to make sure we're on the same page and can work together efficiently."

"Well said, Colonel. And you're right. A good commander seeks to form a consensus. That is the way I like to lead. We must all be on the same page...but it is *my* page."

"Sir, I admire what you've done here. I'm totally supportive of all the changes you've made."

"Good. I'm glad to hear it. We have a special position here at USNA," he said. "We have the opportunity to influence young lives—lives that will lead our armed forces and our nation. It is quite an honor."

"I sense that honor. I embrace it."

"Yet you were reluctant to come to Annapolis."

"Yes, sir," Max said watching Johnson's expression. "I was. But I immediately saw my error."

"Good." The admiral studied Max, his gaze keen. "But let's understand what made you uncomfortable in the first place." Max knew he was expected to speak but, unwilling to explain a lifetime of prejudice inspired by that bastard Tom MacBride's behavior, swallowed audibly. To Max's silence, Johnson applied the adage, "Just tell me the truth."

Max felt himself flush, feeling as if he were in high school, standing in a dripping Speedo before an angry swim coach. "Sir, I know you are an Academy grad."

"I'm sure your attitude has nothing to do with me. Speak freely."

"When I was a young marine, sir, I got the wrong impression about the Academy."

"From a graduate?"

"Yes, sir."

"Was he a poor marine? Lax? Slovenly?"

"No, sir." Max remembered MacBride in those days, straight as an arrow, an eager athlete to whom professionalism came easily. Rather, it was his personality, his baffling attractiveness that enraged Max. "I can't explain it. It was too long ago."

"You're referring to the young man with whom you had the violent altercation in Quantico?" Johnson tapped the personnel file. A chill shook Max; his stomach went leaden. He pictured the obstacle course in Quantico on that misty September dawn and felt again the sickening swing of that rope thirty feet above the ground, the initial thrill of hate for MacBride.

"Max, surely you know that the incident that nearly ended your career is recorded here in your personnel file."

Max remembered scrambling onto the log ladder and looking down thirty feet into upturned angry faces. "I was cleared of those charges, sir."

"Indeed," the admiral said, his gaze unblinking, his lips pressed in a disappointed frown. "But I must have an answer to my question, Max. Was this the same person?"

Max met the admiral's gaze. "Yes, sir."

Johnson sat back and gripped the arms of his chair. "An incident, early in your career, colored your view of the United States Naval Academy for twenty years?"

"Officially, there was no incident. The charges were dropped."

"I detest legal maneuvering, Max. Answer my question."

"Sir, to answer your original question, yes, that individual colored my view. However, I see how that was unfair of me."

"True," Johnson said, "that's obvious. But as your superior, I want you truly strong and healthy. I want to perform a little psychological surgery here."

"Sir—"

The Admiral held up his hand. Max's ears burned. Johnson spoke quietly. "Did you know that this man served on the honor board here, for three years, when he was a midshipman? He was trusted implicitly by his peers and by his superiors."

"I'm not surprised, sir," Max said, thinking, *MacBride always comes out smelling like a rose.*

Johnson raised his eyebrows at Max. "I noticed it when I worked with Tom."

"Pardon, sir?"

"Yes, I knew Tom MacBride well. I served as his company officer here at US-NA for those three years he served on the honor board. You see, Max, I trained the man."

The injustice of the situation frenzied Max and he wanted to shout aloud the unbelievable, unforgivable things MacBride had done to him. Instead Max made himself murmur, "I never meant to insult *you*, Admiral Johnson," so smoothly he felt the oil on his tongue when he licked his lips.

"Colonel Hunter, in the most important ways, *that* marine represented the very best training of this institution. He was the model of integrity. I can give you plenty of examples even after all these years. And just as important to this discussion, he understood teamwork. Do you? Do you understand what teamwork means?"

"Sir, those charges were *dropped*."

"Yes, I know. The charges were dropped, Max, *not* because the legal team concluded such action inevitable, but because the marine involved, Tom MacBride, *insisted* the charges be dropped."

Max's jaw went slack.

"You did not know that, did you?"

He tried to speak, but could not so much as blink.

"Despite the testimony of eyewitnesses, the marine in question said that *he* was there—closest to you and he—" Johnson flipped back several pages in the file. "He said, and I quote, 'Lieutenant Hunter was inches from my face. We were eye to eye. I would know if it was intentional. It was an accident.' That's what he said. That's why the charges were dropped."

Max wanted to spit. "No one told me that, sir."

"The reason MacBride's testimony was believed was, of course, because of his training and reputation. His word was to be trusted, you understand."

"I only knew the charges were dropped."

"MacBride's statement said that it would be a disservice to the Marine Corps to divide two officers with continued strife and controversy. This was a man who understood teamwork. Yet you, Colonel, were so sure you couldn't condescend to work with us that you squawked like a wet baby about being given the honor of serving as head Marine here."

"I regret my misjudgment of the Naval Academy, sir."

"Certainly not helpful to my mission," Johnson said, frowning. "Max, the way you do your job includes much more than just the quality of the lectures you give, or the organization you bring to the English and History Department. But you know that. The Marine Corps tells me you are their most valued recruiter."

"Yes, sir."

The admiral smiled. "Good, then I don't have to tell you what I told my son that day I found him drunk in my living room. I don't have to tell you that the way you conduct yourself every minute of every day is visible to your peers, those you are leading, and the community around you."

"Sir, I understand what you expect of me and I've committed myself to live up to those standards, for the sake of the Academy, the Marine Corps, and the United States."

"I would believe that, Max, if I hadn't I received a phone call from the city police yesterday morning about the damage done to Middleton's Tavern."

Max blanched. "I told Mrs. Middleton I would pay for the damages since the other car left the scene of the accident."

"That's good public relations. But I'm concerned because the police suspected you were not fully alert."

"The sun was in my eyes, sir."

"The sun. Really?"

"Yes, sir."

"That part of Market Street is in the shade at seven-fifteen, Max. I know. I walk my wife to work nearly every day. Unfortunately for us all, yesterday, I was attending the monthly prayer breakfast."

Max swallowed.

"The police officer said he suspects you had been drinking and he regrets not asking you to take a breath test. Imagine if that had happened. One of *my* officers asked to take a breath test at seven-fifteen right smack in the middle of downtown Annapolis."

Max opened his mouth to protest, but the admiral raised a forbidding hand and stared at him, his eyes as pitiless as stone. Panic slid deep down into Max's belly.

Johnson brought his hand down slowly and placed it flat on Max's open personnel file. "Then I thought about my son, drunk at age sixteen, and how I took him up to my room and, big as he was, paddled his behind until he understood me. I thought about my son, and I wondered, how *exactly* do I paddle a Marine Corps colonel?"

Max flushed so violently, the skin on the bottoms of his feet burned.

His voice harsh, Johnson said, "There is no way to prove you were drinking or not. I do not want you to say one word in your own defense."

Max knew the pause meant he was to respond positively, but he could not speak.

"The fact that you so quickly gained the town's sympathy tells me that you understand the vital importance of public relations." Max nodded with dizzy enthusiasm. "And, frankly, I can*not* believe that a Marine

Corps colonel could possibly be drinking before eight. But as far as I'm concerned, if the police *suspect* you, *you're guilty*. There will be no legal maneuvering in my command. Do you understand me?" Admiral Johnson rose from his chair.

"Yes, sir." Max followed, his T-shirt and trousers stuck to his sweating skin, the muscles in his calves twitching.

Max hurried to the natatorium and swam twelve hard laps, but his hands did not stop shaking until he took a frosted mug from his kitchen freezer. He sipped his beer, slowly, moderately, trying to sort out the admiral's meaning, trying to figure out how the police might have gotten the idea that he was drunk, trying to absorb the stunning words Johnson had quoted from his private file. But his mind's eye stared at the remembered sight of Tom MacBride flat on his back, thirty feet below his own safe perch on the top of Quantico's Tower of Terror, and his hands shook again.

11

BEN opened the door to the back stair, which led all the way to the basement where he had left his backpack. The stairwell was narrow and dark, and he moved down it, slowly, his hand on the rail, keeping silent. When he was two steps above the first floor landing, he paused and stared at the line of light beneath the door that opened directly onto the kitchen. A shadow shifted and he heard water splash and the creak of the floor. His instincts told him to jump and sprint down the steps out and away, but he hesitated, thinking of Keith and Tim waiting for him upstairs.

The door opened and light spilled onto the landing until Max stepped forward making the bright dim. Ben watched his father strain to focus and he realized his instincts had been right again. Had he jumped and sprinted, he could have been out the basement door by the time his father could see in the dark.

Max gave a short derisive snort. "What are you doing sneaking down the stairs in the dark?"

"I didn't notice it *was* dark, sir," Ben said.

"Don't you have your contact in?" Max demanded.

"I can still see pretty well in the dark." Max took a step toward him. Ben said quickly, "I've got to get my backpack and get started on my homework."

Max made a motion toward the kitchen. "Step in a minute."

"Keith and Tim are waiting for me."

"Your only acceptable response is 'yes, sir.' You know that."

"Yes, sir," Ben said.

"Dinner's ready anyhow. They'll be down here in a minute. Come here."

"Yes, sir," Ben said, but his legs were wooden, uncooperative, and he stumbled as he entered the kitchen. His father patted Ben's backside and Ben's stomach leapt, igniting an anger so furious that Ben wanted to fight.

"You're looking good," Max said.

"*Yes, sir.*" The weapon at hand became suddenly obvious.

Max stared at Ben in an appreciative, thoughtful way, nodding his head. "Been working out?"

"Yes, *sir*," Ben said.

"Good. I'm proud of you."

"*Yes*, sir."

Max peered at him, slightly confused. "I'm trying to talk to you here."

"Yes, sir," Ben said, making his tone serious, attentive.

"The classes tough for you?"

Ben waited, putting on a confused expression "Yes, sir."

"You think you'll be able to handle it though? You always do."

Feigning introspection, Ben said, "Yes, sir," slowly.

"Your last school was too damn easy. Do you know they wanted to put you in AP Spanish as a freshman? What a joke." Max leaned toward Ben, his smile knowing. He took Ben's elbow in hand and squeezed.

Ben felt the anger in flames behind his eyes. He kept his face composed and said, mildly in Spanish, "*Sí, Señor.*"

Max gave a tense laugh; Ben knew he was growing tired of being confused, but so far, no forecast of violence. "Mom said you're working out with the team. You think you'll be able to work with this coach?"

"Yes, sir," Ben said, immediately regretting his answer. *Caught in my own trap,* Ben thought, his mother's warnings sounding in his head.

Max looked at him sharply. "You like this coach?"

Knowing that he must abandon his facetious cloak, Ben feigned a worried expression. "He's tough. He seems fair…but he's too strict. Military strict. I think he was in the army or something."

Max laughed and went back to the stairway door. "The army is not the military, Ben. The army is the Boy Scouts." He stuck his head and shoulders into the stairwell and bellowed for Keith and Tim.

"Maybe it was the Navy Seals," Ben lied with deft speed. "The guys say he's a *maniac* during the season."

Max nodded, knowingly. "That sounds like the Seals. They're halfway decent."

"I just hope I can keep up; they've got some talent already."

"Have a seat, son." Max indicated the small, square table. For the first time, Ben noticed that it was set for dinner. In the middle stood a bowl with pale chunks of lettuce mixed with carrot slivers. Across the top, wedges of hard-boiled eggs were strewn. Ben sighed deeply. His father had begun another diet. The meat Ben craved would not be seen on the table for months.

"Sit, I said."

He heard Keith and Tim thundering down the stairs. Max came behind Ben and began to massage his shoulders. Ben fought his rising gorge.

His brothers burst through the door and when they saw their father standing behind Ben, in a position of fatherly care and friendliness, they beamed with happiness. Max indicated, with a nod of his head, that they should sit down and help themselves to the salad. They obeyed eagerly, glancing at each other with shining eyes. He heard Max chuckle, pleasure emanating like heat waves. Ben, alone, sat in misery.

"I'm glad we had this little talk," Max said, bending down to speak in Ben's ear. Ben watched his brothers' faces, seeing in their joy that if things were peaceful and good between him and Max, their everyday world would be a vacation. Ben swallowed hard, unable to respond with his flip, covert "Yes, sir." Keith would hear the derision in his tone and his moment of happiness would die.

Ben wondered that his father could not sense his miserable fury mounting within like a thunderhead. But Max was saying something about this being a great duty station, about this marking a new time for their family, and Keith and Tim were gobbling up his words like the starved boys they were.

Max explained that they'd have lots of company because his chief duty here was recruiting the most dynamic midshipmen to choose service in the USMC. Ben glanced at the rooms beyond, at the museum-like façade his grandmother, a curator, had created to help Max promote the Marine Corps. Gran painted the foyer and living room what she called a "welcoming gold." She chose cranberry for the adjoining dining room, thus employing the Marine Corps colors. Above the built-in china cabinet, Gran commissioned a local artist to inscribe in oversized gold calligraphy the Marine Corps motto, SEMPER FI.

Gran completed her tribute with memorabilia borrowed from the Academy museum. Rather than leave the china cabinet empty, Gran displayed officers' hats worn during the Corps' two-hundred-year history. Smaller pieces from Max's artillery shell collection stood on both fireplace mantels, drawing attention to a bronze bust of Thomas Jefferson. Grand paintings of marine battles decorated the entrance hall, and beyond.

"I want you to work hard, Ben—do whatever it takes to earn an appointment here to the Naval Academy."

Tim protested, "But, you said this was a stupid place."

"I was wrong about that," Max said. "This is a great place. I want Ben to go to college here," Max told them, all the while, kneading Ben's shoulders, his big, determined knuckles grinding to bone.

"Can't Ben stay home?" Keith said holding the salad bowl up. Max took his seat and held his hands out for the salad.

"It's two years away, Keith," Ben said. He took a small portion, hoping he could choke that much down. "Don't worry about it."

"No," Max said, looking at Ben with stern direction in his eyes, "you've got to start right away, Ben."

Ben started to reply, then stuffed a hunk of lettuce into his mouth.

"What you need to do, Ben, is work for that coach. Impress him."

Ben sensed an advantage. His instincts told him to play it out slowly. "I don't know, Dad. That's going to mean a big time commitment from me."

"You have to be willing to give your time and your energy."

"Yes, sir, but to impress him—I mean this guy has incredible standards."

"Good. That will mean something."

"Yes, sir, but, I mean, to *meet* his standards, let alone try to *impress* him."

"You've got to show him you're the best. You're going to need strong recommendations. They don't admit mediocre players."

Ben took a small bite and chewed slowly. Since he had been thirteen, his father had been talking about Duke and Michigan—Division I scholarships, and how to get into the NBA. Navy did indeed admit mediocre players; there was little chance to earn an NBA spot with Navy's service commitment at graduation. All this forgotten? Ben saw in whatever hidden event had changed his father's mind, some sort of ironic boon for him. He began to feel less sick and managed to swallow his mouthful of lettuce. "Dad," he said, keeping his face worried, "how would you suggest I go about getting the kind of recommendation I need?"

Chewing so eagerly they could hear each crash of his molars, Max nodded. "You do like I do in the Corps. You're there early, you stay late, and in between, you work your ass off."

"I'll do that, but will that be enough?"

"You're talented, he'll see that as long as he doesn't have to look past a big attitude. I want you there, ready to work, every time the team does anything."

"Yes, sir," Ben said. His hand shook as he stabbed another chunk of lettuce, realizing that he had just been commanded by his father to do exactly what was in his heart to do, what he needed to do.

"You said this guy has a reputation for being fair?"

"Yes, sir, but Dad," Ben said, laying his fork down to emphasize his concern, "are grades important for getting into the Academy?"

"Your grades won't be a problem," Max said, his mouth full. "Never are."

"This place is tough, and the other guys say that the practice schedule is really demanding."

"Good. You'll be there. The most enthusiastic guy on the team."

"Some days, I may need to go straight to the library from practice. Or stay for extra help. Just to make sure my grades stay high."

"Whatever you have to do, Ben, you do it. You hear?"

"Yes, sir," Ben said. He took his water glass and drank deeply; he did not trust his voice now to hide his relief.

Max sat back, narrowed his eyes, and watching Ben drink said, "I'll make an appointment for you to talk to Admiral Johnson about getting in. He'll give you some useful tips."

"Isn't he too busy for that?"

"He's not busy at all," Tim said, brightly, holding his empty plate with both hands. "He walks his mommy to work at our school every day. He told Keith and me that this morning."

"It's his *wife*, Tim," Max snapped.

"Every day?" Ben asked softly, examining his father with renewed interest. Max concentrated on pouring his beer into the glass, tipping it, foam swirling seductively.

"He said Keith and me could walk with them."

"Keith and I," Ben corrected, getting up. "That sounds like a good plan." He knew he had to escape the kitchen before his father drained that beer glass. Max was angry now, exposed in Tim's revelation, his mask of benevolent fatherhood fading to transparency. *So*, Ben thought as he slid his plate into the dishwasher, *the admiral knows about the accident. Dad's in trouble and he wants to use me to get back in the admiral's good graces.*

"I've got to start my homework," Ben said at the door to the stairs. In the basement, he put his gym clothes into the dryer, found his backpack, and started upstairs. As he neared his room, his stomach begged for more and he regretted that he hadn't negotiated for the food he needed in that rare moment of power. But Ben was cheered; even his hunger was a sign of well-being. And he was not alone in this. At eight o'clock, Tim came into Ben's room. "We're still hungry. Should we go get cereal from the kitchen?"

"No, I'll get you something," Ben said, emptying the entire contents of his backpack onto the floor. "Wait here."

Thrusting his wallet into his backpack, he slid it onto one shoulder, opened his window, and climbed out into the tree branches that brushed the roof below. "Don't tell," he warned Tim. "Cover for me."

Ben moved swiftly through the tree limbs. He jogged down the alley, toward the superintendent's house, smiling to himself at the thought of the admiral walking his wife to school every day, keeping an eye out for Keith and Tim. *What a smooth system*, Ben thought, *the boss' wife works at the school where his men send their families.*

Across from the admiral's house in Dahlgren Hall, a small restaurant stayed open late. Ben bought several hamburgers, fries, and three milk-shakes, then packed them with reams of paper napkins into his backpack. Keith and Tim waited at his window, eyes wide, mouths parted in expectation. At the first whiff of the food, they stifled squeals of delight, their hands to their mouths as they jumped up and down on their toes. With Ben's door locked, the three brothers sat on the floor and feasted in a hush, aware that the rare sense of peace and safety they shared surrounded them like a thin, blue eggshell.

12

AFTER dinner, in the deepening twilight, Max changed into a freshly pressed uniform before he left his quarters to walk. He passed Dahlgren Hall, looking festive, fully lit and alive with socializing midshipmen. With a sudden, physical pang, he missed the "real" Marine Corps. The early days of his career, when he was involved with the oversight of men training to defend their country, he had known an absorption, an exhausting fascination with his work that his years as a senior officer—an administrator, an advertisement—had only served to magnify.

He was trained as an artillery officer, and looking back at his entire career, had spent very little time, comparatively, performing that duty. But during those early years, despite his personal problems, his career had been satisfying. It was the memory of those years that made him such a damn good recruiter.

Max walked slowly, trying to evaluate his career in light of the awful information Johnson had given him. *MacBride demanded the charges be dropped?* It sickened him. He saw that he had been living and succeeding in the Corps because of MacBride's word, because of MacBride's...what was it? His need to look like the good guy? His smarmy way of kissing ass? Max's fury surged through his bowels as he realized this truth: he had proceeded through his career, believing he had a clean slate, believing that he had been exonerated of those ridiculous charges, and instead, every superior officer he'd served under had read MacBride's statement in his personnel file and had known that Max had been spared a court martial merely because of a self-righteous man's gesture.

He spat on the ground.

The lights burning in Bancroft Hall attracted him. Bancroft Hall would be alive with the cheerful energy that defined midshipmen and he was here in Annapolis to talk to midshipmen. Max turned on his heel and entered a door on the ground level. He whisked his cover off and straightened his back.

He passed the darkened and locked bookstore where mids were given their textbooks, opened the door to the stairwell, and started up toward the first deck of the first wing of Bancroft Hall. Its eight wings, numbered ship-like with even numbers on the port side, odd on the starboard, extended from a center dome, like the arms of a huge, resting spider. "Mother B," as it was called by those who dwelt there, housed all 4,000 mids, along with a mess hall big enough to feed them at one sitting, barber shops, a laundry, a small department-like store called the "midstore," a small chapel, a ballroom, staff offices, and in the basement, a rifle range where Navy's rifle and pistol team practiced.

Being around young people distracted Max. He knew this, and accepted it as a benefit of his job. His primary function at the Academy was to influence men and women to select the Marine Corps. His success in two tours of recruiting duty had been a factor in his assignment to the Academy. For the last ten years, the number of midshipmen who entered the Marine Corps upon graduation had declined. The Commandant expected Max to fix this.

Since he'd arrived, Max had studied the files of mids who had expressed an interest in the Corps. He'd made it a point to meet those who had been there for summer duty training the new plebes. Tonight, he looked for these familiar faces. It was some consolation knowing that these people—still innocent of the politics and the personnel file—did not know that his success in the Corps was based on MacBride's sick benevolence. He wanted to spit again.

Max greeted mids as he passed their rooms, using their first names when he knew them, reading their last names from their doors when he did not. They were evening busy—chatting, showering, making coffee, standing in gym clothes barefoot in the passageway.

He stopped at a room where a female mid busily sorted her laundry. Sitting on her desk was a male friend, dressed only in gym shorts. Max could feel the electricity between them.

He knocked on the open door. "Women do all the work in this life, I swear to God." Before they could move to attention, Max said, "At ease."

"Hey, Colonel Hunter," the male said, sitting up straight.

Max stepped in. The room felt jungle-hot. The window was open, but the air stood still. "We met last week, Brian," Max said, extending his hand.

The mid stood up, giving Max a strong handshake. "Midshipman Brian Corrigan, first class, sir. I'm in fourteenth company." Max turned to the room's occupant, trying to think where he'd seen her before. She was compact and muscular, her pretty face intense with energy. "You're a gymnast," he said, remembering. "I read an article about you in last week's *Trident*. You have my admiration."

"Thank you, Colonel Hunter," she said, taking his hand and grasping firmly. "Mary Natale. I'm a firstie in fourteenth, too."

"They won't let us be roommates, though," Brian said.

"I wonder why," Max quipped. Her hand was tiny and hot in his hand. In a few years, Max imagined, her muscular thighs would be heavy, but not now.

Aloud Max said, "You two engaged, or what?"

"Mary doesn't see the point in it," Brian frowned. "We'd be separated by our careers."

"That's another good thing about the Marine Corps," Max said. "There are fewer bases and fewer assignment possibilities. You're more likely to be stationed together. The Marine Corps tries to accommodate families."

"Is that true?" Mary said.

"Of course it is," Max said, folding his arms over his chest and meeting her gaze. "I married a Navy nurse. Her career is very important to her. She's not one of those stay-at-homes who run the wives' clubs." His audience laughed appreciatively. "We met at Twentynine Palms, and when it was time for her to be transferred, the Navy was totally unsympathetic. The Marine Corps found a billet for me at the same base. Good position, too. Kept me on the fast track."

"Where'd they send you?"

"Hawaii. Camp Smith."

"Oh, rotten duty," Brian groaned. Max could see his mind working, desire glazing his eyes. Max knew he was imagining Mary in her bikini, on the beach. He could picture it, too.

"Great duty for newlyweds," he said, moving toward the door, knowing it was time to go. "We were there for thirty glorious months. Then I was transferred to Monterey, for graduate school."

"That's what Brian wants to do," Mary sighed.

"Think about it," Max said, pausing at the door, "in the Marine Corps, you really *can* have it all. Family, career, adventure, more education. You name it."

"See you, Colonel Hunter."

Nice looking girl, Max thought. But there was something MacBridish about that Brian, something in the palpable emotion he felt for that girl. Though it wasn't necessarily Max's responsibility to screen candidates for the Marine Corps—he was only to recruit—Max wondered if this couple would fit in. Being too much in love did not work well in the Corps; you needed a more comfortable relationship based on compatibility and just enough lust. He had learned this lesson the hard way.

When he met Donna, she had just been transferred from duty in Annapolis. He was a captain, a platoon commander, stationed in the California desert. During a routine live-fire display, his mechanized ammo carrier hit a gully, jolting him and two others into the air. Max was injured with both legs broken.

Donna was a nurse on staff at the naval hospital. During the first week, he was only vaguely aware of her presence—a whiff of perfume, long fingernails. But, as his pain subsided, he noticed her. She was just a "butter bars," a second lieutenant, fairly new to the navy, her manner careful. Her beauty was generic, Californian, cute. Her pregnancy had just begun to show in breasts swollen too large for her small frame and in the hard, low bulge of belly. She wore no wedding ring.

"Are you married?" he asked her one morning after a thorough, briskly arousing sponge bath she'd given him.

"I was married," she said, shrugging, her dark eyes sad, "when I became pregnant."

Oozing sympathy Max nodded. "What happened? The baby scare him off?"

"Captain Hunter, I've got to shave you. It won't work if you keep talking."

"Okay," Max said, and touched her chin. "I promise, I'll be quiet if you'll talk to me. I'm so lonely in here, I'm ready to go crazy. What happened with your husband?"

She lathered up his face with menthol shaving cream, so generously that it dropped in clumps onto his chest. She wiped it up with her finger and shrugged. "He was a resident at the hospital where I was stationed. We were only married eight weeks when he left me."

"Did he know you were pregnant?"

"Yes."

"He felt trapped."

She sighed deeply, and gave Max a disgusted, resigned look, her shoulders drooping. "That's exactly what everybody said, even my parents. Of course they were also upset because Roger was from Thailand. They said a biracial marriage would never work anyway."

"Why get married anyway? It's overrated."

"We *were* in love. At least I thought we were. Both our parents objected to our dating and when we started to get serious, they got frantic." Donna paused to concentrate on shaving Max's upper lip. "The MacBrides were the only ones who disagreed."

"What did you say?"

"Hold still!" She held his chin firmly. "This couple I knew in Annapolis where I was stationed. I worked with him at the Academy." She pressed her lips together and took a deep breath. "They ran this coffee house out in town. We all would go there after work and talk about stuff."

"What did you say their name was? This couple."

"MacBride. Roger wanted me to move in with him, but I was raised in the church; we went to the MacBrides for counseling. Actually, *I* did. He was happy for us, but you know, being religious, thought we ought to get married, not just live together." She shrugged. "Gossip is a problem at the hospital. Nurses get reputations real fast."

"That's ridiculous!" Max wiggled, trying to sit up straighter.

"Hold still," she whispered. "Okay?"

She looked so *broken*, her lip quivering, her eyes full of tears, Max knew an urge to hold and comfort her. He touched her shoulder. "I'm sorry, it's just that I know a guy in Annapolis by that name," he said. "Tom MacBride. Tall guy, very popular."

"That's him," Donna's eyes going wide.

"He turned the only girl I ever loved against me," Max said, his own voice trembling.

"Tom? How?"

"Same kind of thing as what happened to you. Long discussions late at night about what was right and what was wrong. About life and God's will and crap. One thing leads to another. That's the way he operates."

"Oh, I'm sorry," Donna said, blushing so quickly that Max guessed he'd described her counseling sessions with Tom precisely. After a tense pause, Donna said, "Some of the girls said you were married."

"I'm not married."

Three days later they were lovers. She made it clear that she liked him. She talked to him. She sneaked beer into his room every night. She bought pizza and cheese steaks to replace the predictable hospital food. After hearing through the hospital grapevine that he liked blondes, Donna lightened her hair.

She switched to night duty, and asked him to avoid letting the day nurse give him his sponge bath. That night, when the lights were out and he was supposed to be asleep, she washed him. The water felt hot and silky and briskly scented.

At first, Donna politely, or professionally—he could never decide which—ignored his hard throbbing response to the bath. "You're awful good with that sponge," he said to her, gesturing at the evidence.

"You deserve to be treated right."

"So do you." He pulled her into his arms and up on the bed. Her breath was quick and moist on his neck. It was fast for both of them. He hadn't been interested in sex since he returned from the Mediterranean and had very little. Donna had to be on top—both his legs were in casts—and afterwards, she started to cry, and then her tears wet his neck and his chest. He didn't mind her hot tears on him. They were the cement of this new relationship, flowing from wounds so like his own, inflicted by Tom MacBride.

He decided to stay with Donna. He had sworn off beautiful women; she was pretty enough. Max's fascination centered on the fact that Donna had come away from a connection with Tom MacBride *pregnant*. Her needy, deserted state intrigued him to the point of obsession. He saw it as his chance to set everything right in heaven and on earth. He would take care of this woman. He would prove that he could love faithfully, selflessly, and completely. He would prove that he was everything Tom MacBride was not.

13

FRIDAY morning Ben waited for Joe. From where he stood, Ben could look back over USNA's brick wall to see his bedroom window, the lamp on his desk just visible. Joe had said to hang his boxers out the window any day he was not going; and Ben agreed without telling Joe he would not be absent as long as he could still crawl.

The town around him waited in waking sunlight for the day to begin with quiet, empty streets wet and black from an early rain. Ben watched for Joe's car, looking all the way down Market Street. The water in the harbor lay smooth and silver below a low, lavender sky heavy with the anticipation of a tropical storm creeping up the coast. Middleton's stood in the shade of taller buildings, its broken parts bandaged with the scaffolding of repair. Joe's battered car appeared. It raced through the sunlit harbor, approaching swiftly, its rumble audible from the moment it passed the damaged restaurant.

Joe's hatchback stuttered impatiently as he eased it next to the curb. Rust had eaten patches of the car's body around the wheels and along the back chrome bumper. The windows were rolled down so that Ben could reach into the passenger side and open the door using the inside handle. The outside handle was rusted immobile. Ben popped the latch and pulled the door open, wincing at the reluctant squawk the hinges made. He stuffed his backpack into the back and climbed into the low seat in a motion that was more like lying down.

"You've got to come to dinner," Joe said. "It's Dad's birthday."

"Isn't that just for family?"

"You don't know what it's like at my house," Joe laughed.

"I'm not sure I can."

"The food will be amazing." Joe licked his lips. Ben glanced up when Joe missed his usual turn onto College Avenue.

"I'm going the other way," he said. "Mom said, if you're watching your brothers just bring them."

"Are you *serious*?"

"Yeah. She really wants you to come. We'll sit them in front of some video games."

Ben laughed at Joe's easy generosity, then remembered his mother's warning. Keith and Tim would repeat Coach MacBride's name. "No," he said slowly, "that wouldn't work out."

"What's wrong? They couldn't be any more annoying than my little brother." Joe glanced sidelong at Ben. "When did you say you can get your license?"

"October fourteenth. I've got a Virginia learner's permit. I have to get a Maryland one."

"I'll take you to the MVA after school. Band practice will be canceled because of this weather," Joe said, glancing in his rear-view mirror. Joe flipped his blinker manually, up, down, up, down, and pulled the car up to the curb. "Here, you drive," he said, and yanking the emergency brake so hard it squawked, switched off the car and got out.

"What?"

"Yeah. You drive. This is a great car to drive," Joe said, leaning down to see Ben. "Your whole self is screaming for some freedom. When you drive this car—it's magic. You feel like you own the whole world." Joe dropped his keys into Ben's palm, the plastic eyeball wiggling against his fingers.

Ben felt comfortable immediately in the low, shabby driver's seat and understood what Joe meant. The engine chugged and sputtered, sounding through the rust holes in the floor. "This thing's a wreck," Ben said, grinning.

"Yeah, isn't it great?" Joe beamed. Ben inched the car forward trying out the clutch. Finally at a long break in the traffic, Ben moved forward, the car rumbling beneath him, onto the bridge across College Creek. The water beyond lay still as glass reflecting the pale, pinkish sky with a cool shimmer that belied the day's warmth. At the light, he nodded to Joe's directions, curving left around the corner, accelerating along the long slow bend beyond.

"Remember where we are? Mom's store is coming up," Joe said as Ben drove through several blocks of small cottages that housed stores.

"On the corner, right?" But the store looked so different as to be barely recognizable. The porch was empty, bare of quilts. The door was shut, the windows blank and sightless. Ben was assaulted by a strange lurching emotion that was more a sensation—harsh, unbidden, revolting. "I've been here before," he said aloud.

"Yeah, two days ago," Joe said, adding, "uh…the light's red."

Ben saw how quickly he was moving to the light, blaring red just ahead. He stomped on the brake; the car lurched, stalled, and stopped.

"Sorry. Shoot."

"You need the clutch to start it."

Waiting to turn left, Ben stared at the store, his heart still pounding. "It looks different."

"Huh?" Joe said, turning to look. "Oh, it's not open yet. Light's green." This time, he moved the car forward without stalling. He stole one more glance at the store as he turned. "You said it's been there a while. You said, 'forever.'"

"Oh, yeah," Joe said. "I guess she's had the shop for…Tommy was little and Dad had just had back surgery…maybe ten years? Before that, when we were little kids, Mom and Dad ran this soup kitchen there. Rising Sun they called it, but while Mom was cooking they kept the chairs upside-down on the tables and we kids pretended we lived on the ocean floor and were caught in seaweed. At night, it was a poetry-reading, free food and coffee kind of hang out. As Dad says, 'For the poor and the poor in spirit.'"

"Soup kitchen? They actually had soup for people?"

"Yeah. They wanted a place in Annapolis where anyone could come for free soup and bread. My mom still loves to make things in huge pots. I guess it's a good thing at our house."

"What happened to it?"

"Keep going straight, yeah, all the way to that stop sign way up there. I know they *had* to close it, 'cause Dad still mopes about it once in a while, but I'm not exactly sure why."

"Your dad is hard to figure out. He was a marine, then he ran a coffee house. It's just not something you think of a marine doing."

"True. And I think he was still in the Marine Corps stationed here when they started it. I'm bad with dates. Pete knows that stuff. He remembers everything. He remembers his second birthday."

"Why did your dad get out?"

"He actually got a medical discharge. Like his back's been a problem all along. He broke his back when I was a baby and I think after that they made him get out."

"He actually broke his back?"

"Yeah. It's a miracle he can walk at all."

Ben had yet to see Tom walk. He had seen him standing one day after school when he was on his way into the locker room. Bettinger was with him and Tom looked as if he were balancing on stilts, arms outstretched, legs in a stiff, unnatural stance. Ben had quickly looked away and ducked into the locker room; he found this vulnerability in his coach baffling and too poignant for his comfort.

"I know you haven't seen him walk," Joe said, "he's been in the wheel-chair all week, but really, the wheelchair is a pretty recent thing. When I was a baby they did this surgery and he was okay for awhile. Working to fix the coffee house or something re-injured it. Hell, I can't keep it all straight. I can't remember exactly which back injury did what to him."

"He's had that many?"

"Yeah. Three, I think. But he's up today…"

"You were right about this car," Ben worked the clutch, smoothly eased the car around the curve of the school driveway. "You have to wrestle with the steering wheel."

"Yeah, I love it."

Ben parked and, getting out, flipped Joe's keys over the top of the car to him; Joe caught them, holding them as he always did with the plastic eyeball clutched in his palm, keys swinging below. As they grabbed their backpacks, Tom pulled up behind them in his car.

"Hey, men."

"Hey, Dad."

"Morning, Coach," Ben said, "Happy Birthday."

"Thanks," Tom smiled.

"Ben's coming for dinner tonight."

"Good," Tom said. "That will make the evening."

"If I wouldn't be imposing."

"Imposing?" Tom and Joe laughed, naturally and in unison, and said, "No." Then Tom added, in the intriguing old-world courtesy that sometimes marked his speech, "We'd be pleased to have you join us." Ben shifted his backpack, feeling awkward.

Tom smiled. "I've been meaning to ask you, Ben, what did your dad say when you told him I was your new basketball coach?"

Ben straightened his back, shifting his backpack again. "I didn't have much chance to talk to my dad yet this week," he said, studying the door handle of Tom's car. "He's busy with his new job."

"What *is* his job?"

"He's the Marine Corps representative and the Director of English and History."

"How does he like it?"

"He's totally impressed with the Academy. Before we got here, he had nothing good to say about it. He did *not* want to come here. I mean, he *really* didn't." Ben stopped. He'd said far too much.

Tom's face looked so concerned, eyebrows drawn together, mouth in a deep frown, that Ben instantly feared in the same uncanny way that Joe knew things, Tom knew all about what kept Ben awake at night. Ben set his jaw and willed his own expression to become impenetrable. But if Tom did know, he said nothing. After squinting and frowning at Ben for an agonizing thirty seconds, his expression inexplicably softened. And he looked away to gaze absently at the MG.

"You enjoy driving my old junker?" Tom said.

"It's mine now," Joe teased, swinging his keys with happy insouciance. "It's awesome to drive."

"Are you—? No, you're not sixteen yet."

"No, sir. Not for six weeks."

"But he's got a permit," Joe said easily, his face calm, eyes clear and unshadowed as he hefted his backpack onto his shoulder.

"I'm not sure of the exact rule," Tom said, "but I think you're only allowed to drive with someone who's been driving for a year. It may be more strict than that. It may be that the other driver has to be twenty-one."

"I think it's six months," Joe said, "and I've been driving that long."

"Your birthday is the end of May," Tom said, grinning slightly and leaning out the window. He counted on his fingers. "June, July, August. That's three months, Joseph."

"Oops," Joe laughed.

"Joe, the privilege of driving includes the responsibility of obeying the law. You don't ignore laws because you have a reason."

"No, Dad, but this was a case of civil disobedience. Like Thoreau. Ben *needed* to drive this morning. I mean it. It was a spiritual thing. And it's a man's *moral* responsibility—"

"Joe."

"Yes, sir," Ben said loudly enough for both of them. He shot Joe a warning glance.

"Okay, Dad, but we don't know what the rule is...for sure."

"You find out what the rule is, laddie, and you keep to it."

"Yes, sir," they said, echoing each other, seconds apart.

14

THE weather worsened with the day. Swollen gray clouds wept over the school, driven on a wind that blew in erratic, powerful blasts.

The lights wavered and blinked. The air was electric with the students' hope that school would be canceled due to the coming storm. But to this electricity in the air, Ben responded with a quieting of his soul; he was oriented in time and space and could begin to make clear observations about his surroundings.

CCS was somehow different than his other schools. Many of the teachers seemed to have known their students in family or in church or in neighborhoods since they were small. The second day in Bible class, Bettinger grabbed a thickset kid in a headlock and rubbed his knuckles on the kid's just-shaved scalp, shiny and bare as Bettinger's own bald head. "Your mother told me you were going to shave your head, you little idiot. But I didn't believe her." His voice was a growl. "What, are you trying to look like your all-powerful wrestling coach?"

"No," the kid joked, "I'm trying to look like my ancient and decrepit Sunday school teacher."

When Bettinger released him, roaring with laughter, Ben knew that he had stepped into a conversation that had begun long ago, that had long since grown rich and familiar. Yet, he had never been more warmly welcomed.

That day, as they squeezed into the bleachers for the daily chapel service, the sounds of the building winds pounded against the high windows and on the roof of the gym. The proximity of the seating surprised Ben; so crowded were the bleachers that their shoulders touched. No one seemed uncomfortable with this, but instead took advantage of the human walls their bodies built to share the candy and sodas they'd sneaked in or to crouch unseen and finish overdue homework. Chapel had its peculiar magic—no matter how tightly wound Joe was, how hyper Jon seemed, how disgruntled Scott acted, or how bored Adam vowed he felt, when they sank into their seats, they almost sighed in relief. As a group of girls took seats in front of them, a small, black-haired girl with dark, flashing eyes stopped and looked at Joe expectantly.

"We're friends again, right, Leeza?" Joe said.

"Just friends. Always and forever," she said, eyes bright. She whirled around and sat down and glanced over her shoulder as if to check on Joe's reaction. Joe leaned forward and said, "Don't worry about me. Tiffany and I are getting back together." With this, he glanced at Tiffany who had just arrived and stood out of Leeza's field of vision.

"Don't bet on it, lover boy. Tiffany's got her eye on the new guy."

Tiffany's eyes narrowed and her hands went to her hips in a gesture that made her blouse gape just enough to pique the attention of the boys in that row. Jon whispered to Ben, "Please Lord, let that button pop off."

"Um, Leeza," Joe said, tapping her shoulder briskly, "meet Ben, the new kid."

"Hi," Ben said.

"Oops." Leeza's smile went charming and she fell back onto Joe's knees offering to shake Ben's hand in a gesture at odds with the girl's careless words. "Don't tell Tiffany I told you that."

"I won't have to," Ben said with a grin, "she's standing right here."

"Oops again," Leeza said, wincing. She met Joe's eyes and giggled. Tiffany tried to smile sweetly at Ben, but gave up when her blush mounted to crimson. She shoved Leeza's shoulder to make her move over. Tiffany sat down and the two girls whispered furiously at each other. Several times Leeza glanced back at Joe. Jon leaned across Ben's knees toward Joe. "Looks like you are definitely back in business, buddy."

Joe shrugged. "She was just embarrassed."

"Yeah," Jon agreed. "Leeza's most affectionate after she's made a big mistake."

"You've dated her?"

"Aw," Jon said, "Most of us have known each other since second grade."

Ben straightened his back and scanned the room for Bonnie Jean. He found her in the group of instrumentalists and singers in the center of the gym where she stood tuning a violin. Ben noticed how brown her arms were and that her thick hair was caught at the back of her neck into a heavy knot that slipped and unwound when she moved. The tentative sounds of tuning were muffled by the noise of sudden rain on the metal roof. The group gathered around microphones and the school rose to their feet and began to sing.

Ben watched Bonnie Jean, awed by her whole body absorption in the music. She fiddled with a swift grace that made Ben's heart skip. Carrying the melodies they sang, the expression in her face and eyes looked intense and alive. Beside him, around him, the voices of his new friends lifted, hearts and spirits opening like thirsty flowers; but Ben's own voice caught in his throat. He listened to the words and waited for his own soul to catch up.

The music changed and Drew moved from guitar to piano. Bonnie Jean held her violin at her side and stepped closer to the microphone to sing. The power of her voice startled him. As she warmed to the song, the school hushed and her rich voice, brimful of clear, strong emotion, moved the crowd to an uplifting of heart. All around him the tide of voices rushed to join Bonnie Jean; Ben had the impression that a strong burst of life flowed through all those open hearts. He wanted to join them. Voices rose, but the awe Ben felt weakened him and he was speechless.

Ben could hear her voice above the others and he knew a thrill of warmth that he would remember all his life. He could not sing; he could not move, but her strength came to him and for an instant, his heart soared. In some mysterious way she seemed to sense the connection and glanced again at him at the song's last note. And once more as she placed her violin in its case and took her seat to the right with the musicians, she met his eyes.

Tiffany followed Bonnie Jean's glances and seeing Ben, made an alarmed face, stiffened her shoulders, and faced front. Paul and Jon snickered at this, and Jon whispered to Ben, "Women are like orange juice. Most of them are watered down, but Bonnie Jean is woman concentrate. Watch out."

Paul whispered from behind. "She's never been much impressed with any of us. We're like brothers."

"What about Tiffany?" Ben asked.

"Many have tried, many have fallen," Jon said, sadly.

When they sat down, Joe squinted at Ben in the careful way he had when he was quiet. Joe gave a small, content smile and bumped Ben's shoulder lightly with his own. When Tom went to the podium, now limping slightly, Ben found that his soul felt as his body did after a good long run—shaky, but ready.

After a brief prayer, Tom lifted his head to speak, and a murmur of expectation rode over the crowd. Tom began, "You know, many people, including me, have spoken to you about obeying God and obeying your parents. But you are not children now, and the world is no longer simple for you. Today, I'm going to ask you to begin to make some sophisticated distinctions about what it means to obey. I'll begin with a story about when I was but a wee lad, in first grade; I got myself in trouble lurking school one day."

The crowd relaxed, grins and words of assent whisking through the crowd. "You see, my parents emigrated here from Scotland, and I had been carefully taught the Scottish ways at home. I had a bit of a brogue then."

Groans and laughter erupted from the crowd. "Then?" Drew shouted.

"This is not a brogue," Tom said, then uttered another sentence so thick with Scots dialect that the crowd roared appreciatively.

"Naturally, I was inordinately proud of my Scottish heritage. It was March seventeenth, Saint Patrick's Day—my teacher had mistakenly said that the Scottish and the Irish celebrated the day. As any Scot knows, there is a world of difference between a Scot and an Irishman. Saint Paddy means no more to us than the Queen of England means to you. And I explained this to my teacher in a way that she found utterly disrespectful. I'm sure I wasn't *actually* disrespectful, you know me too well for that."

The students groaned. "But she perceived my good intentions that way. For punishment, she kept me after school." As if choreographed, the rain beat on the roof, drawing an awed, worried response from the audience. "So, I was faced with walking home all alone."

Ben studied Tom's posture and movements, accustoming himself to the sight of Tom standing and walking. Ben saw deeply ingrained physical confidence. It made no sense for a man with undependable legs. There seemed to be an element of Joe's intensity, Ben thought, but there was also something content in Tom. Ben tried to imagine Tom making a fist, tried to imagine him with his torso thrust forward, his face distorted as he screamed at an athlete and remembered how quietly Tom had corrected Oliver in the locker room on the first day of school. That day Ben had seen something determined, something generous in Tom's expression. It was visible again as he spoke to the student body.

"On the walk home I was terrorized by ghosts and monsters and robbers. They were there every day, but of course they never bothered the crowd of us kids. But I was six years old, guilty of annoying my teacher and very much alone.

"At one point, I had to walk through an underpass. These were tunnels built for the sidewalks at certain places in town where the railroad tracks crossed above. When we traveled as a pack of kids, we ran through the underpass screaming, which never failed to scare those lurking monsters and ghosts. We never saw them when we were together, but many of us had seen them when we were alone.

"I did not feel up to a confrontation with a ghost. Remember, I had just been unfairly disciplined and I was smarting from that. And I was terrified to reach home. You see, my dad promised me that if ever I were punished at school, I would feel the sting of his switch on my backside."

Ben shifted uncomfortably. Joe glanced at him, his smile amused, relaxed.

"Thinking I would prefer a monster to my dad's switch, I tried to walk through that underpass without taking the precaution of scaring away the monsters. You see, as much as I loved to misbehave," Tom said, scanning the audience, and pausing to meet Joe's eyes. "I loved my dad more and I hated to disappoint him."

Joe chuckled as if he were hearing a favorite bedtime story.

Ben leaned close to Joe's ear. "He loved him even though he whipped him?"

"Sure," Joe laughed. "Gramps was great—like Santa, but a year-round friend."

"I crept through the underpass. It always smelled like rain in there and it was always wet, so going down there was like going into a long, dark cave. I kept my hand on the cold metal hand rail. Icy drips fell from the ceiling. 'Monster snot,' we used to call it and it always seemed to fall right on my scalp, or find its way right inside the collar of my shirt and run down my back." Tom shivered. "I was walking slowly, very slowly, when I heard footsteps behind me. I knew the robbers had come out of hiding and were following me.

"Next, I heard the monster's breathing, and when I saw the ghost moving in the shadow I decided I preferred my father's loving discipline to the unknown horrors of these villains who wanted to devour me. I started screaming, and ran so fast, I could still hear my own voice echoing in the tunnel when I was a hundred feet down the sidewalk on the other side."

"That's my favorite line," Jon said.

"Could that actually happen?" Scott said, emerging from his math homework.

Tom continued, "Finally, I came to the place where I had to cross the road."

Joe sat forward in anticipation, leaning his elbows on his knees. His face came between Tiffany's and Leeza's heads; he playfully nudged them each with his nose. Leeza whispered, "He's always so good."

"My parents had trained me well to look in both directions and wait until I could see no cars before I crossed. I stood at the edge of the curb, and looked one way, then the other."

Tom demonstrated this, coming forward, and looking first toward one side of the gym, then scanning the crowd and studying the freshmen who sat crowded by the stage.

"Several cars passed quickly and I kept looking. First one direction, then the next. This part of the road was particularly flat and I could see a car coming from a long way off. And remember my parents said, 'Wait until you see *no* car, then cross.' I could see a car always, coming in one direction or the other—from a far distance, sure. I could have crossed the road and back fifty times before the car reached me, but I could see it and with a switch already poised to greet me at home, I was not about to add disobedience to my troubles."

The audience breathed in a kind of satisfied anticipation.

"I stayed there, watching car after car approach from the distance. The sun was sinking fast and I grew cold and hungry. It began to drizzle freezing little drops of rain and still the cars kept coming, one always visible on the distant horizon. My stomach gnawed on itself and my nose—which was much smaller then—went numb from the cold rain. I gave up, in complete despair, unable to cross, unwilling to disobey, and sat down on the curb and cried."

In unison, the students uttered a sympathetic groan.

"Then I heard his voice. 'Tommy!' I looked up and he was there, my dad. He picked me up and opened his coat and wrapped it around me. He carried me home."

Murmurs of appreciation rose from the audience.

"You can see that as a child, I was unable to understand what true obedience meant. I was unable to distinguish between the literal meaning of the commandment—don't cross if you can see a car—and the intent of the commandment. I was frozen, unable to act at all. The rules your parents, your teachers, your society give are meant to teach you something deeper. The rule is *not* what you are to learn. The rule points deeper to the *truth* you are to learn. Think about it."

Whispers moved through the crowd and the wind howled above them.

"Are there any questions?"

"Did he whip you anyway?"

"Aye, he did," Tom said. His use of the Scots vernacular gave Ben a vivid and unexpected picture of Tom as a young child, raised in that strict, old fashioned home. "He gave me dinner and warmed me up and when I was settled down, he took me aside." Tom paused, peering at faces, "I was desperate and cried out, 'But I was defending Scotland!' And he said, 'Y' dinna defend someone you love by bein' rude.' The rest is history. I learned to be polite whenever possible."

"Was he really ticked off?" a freshman called out, giggling.

"He wasn't angry at all," Tom said, "but he considered it his duty to teach me right from wrong."

Ben swallowed hard, his eyes stung as if strained by the picture Tom had painted in this strangely lit world of the chapel where a beautiful girl sang in a voice he needed badly and the wild hearts of boys like him were comforted beneath a storm gathering strength outside their thin walls. Ben was a stranger who wanted suddenly and forcefully to enter. But the barriers separating him from this world were secret and dangerous and Ben suspected he could not pay the cost. *Don't ask me to obey my father*, he vowed silently. *I won't do it. I can't.*

"Any more questions?" Beside Ben, Joe's arm went up. "Joe?"

"What if you've got a bad parent?"

Everyone laughed.

"What do you mean by bad, Joe?"

"Like he asks you to steal or something."

"Good question. If you feel your parent is wrong, you must examine your heart. Are your parents' demands inconvenient, or unreasonable or immoral? An unreasonable parent still deserves your respect. You can try to discuss the matter with them. Things that stretch you or make you uncomfortable, like practicing hard or turning your papers in on time may feel annoying, but deserve your compliance. Unlike the little boy in the story, you have the reasoning powers to consider these things."

Scott raised his hand. "Coach, like, I'm making this totally up because I have a lot of respect for my dad. I mean he went to Vietnam and he fought in the Cold War and stuff. He's a good guy, but let's say you've got a dad who's a real jerk. Then what?"

"I'm not sure what you mean by 'a jerk.'"

"Like a *jerk*, Coach. Like, let's say he's selling crack out behind the bowling alley and you know about it. How do you deal with him?"

"Though he's made a terrible mistake and you may absolutely disagree with his behavior, you still love him and owe him respect. We almost can't help loving our parents. And I say that's a good thing considering some of our faults."

The students chuckled, Joe and Bonnie Jean smiling widely. But Ben found it difficult to swallow wondering if there were anyone else in this room who no longer loved his father, who strained daily to love his mother? He glanced around, seeing mainly quiet faces and a few with pained expressions.

Michelle, from Ben's math class, raised her hand. "But Mr. MacBride, if a parent is involved in things like that—aren't they likely to *ask* their kids to do wrong?"

Tom nodded. "If what your parent asks of you is clearly wrong you have to realize that your parents' authority over you is God given. That means they must answer to God. Your parents gave you life, but they did not create you. Your ultimate responsibility is to obey God."

"Hey, Dad," Joe said, "Just remember that the next time you want me to walk on my knees and say I'm ten so I can get in the movies for less."

Above the roar of laughter, Tom said, "You're dismissed."

15

AS they left the gym, Joe glanced at Ben and said, "I was kidding. About the movies."

"I know," Ben murmured as they walked amid the current of students crossing the lobby.

"Then what?"

"Nothing."

"No, there *is* something. I thought I asked your question for you. So tell me."

"Joe, think about it. Maybe your dad was *so* determined to obey—I mean, that was pretty extreme, but still—maybe he felt he had to behave perfectly because he was terrified of getting a beating."

"I don't think it was actually a *beating*, Ben," Joe said, frowning.

"What's the difference?" Ben demanded.

"Violence, I think." Joe opened his hand in a gesture that showed his confidence, but his quick look at Ben showed careful thought.

"Huh? Wait. That's happened to you?"

Joe made a face. "What? Are you kidding?"

Ben stopped walking, feeling sick. "How can you not hate him?"

"At the time, I'm not happy with him," Joe said with a slight, crooked grin, "but, I mean, *I'm* the one who did the wrong thing." Joe shrugged as if honesty were easy and everyday. "He's trying to teach me."

"He could *talk* to you about it."

"He does *now*, but that hasn't always worked. You don't know me."

"If you tell the truth—"

"Hey. I *always* tell the truth—mostly always."

"—you're scared of him."

"In a way, I guess," Joe shrugged. "I hate to disappoint him. And he's got power over me. You know. He can make my life miserable. Take away the phone, the car. And deep down, I want his respect. Now that you bring it up, I'm afraid of pushing him so far I lose that."

"That's pretty complex, Joe," Ben said, quietly.

"What are we talking about here?" Paul said, knocking into Joe's shoulder with his elbow.

"If we're afraid of our fathers," Joe said as they started again down the hall.

"Heck," Paul said, "I'm scared of my father."

"Paul's dad is bigger than he is," Joe said, "but he's a real softie."

"Man, he can be totally unreasonable about stuff. Just like Coach was saying."

"Like those earrings you got at the beach?" Joe teased.

"Yeah," Paul said. "He told me he was going to close his eyes and if he ever saw those earrings again, he'd sit on me 'til I made them disappear. I flushed 'em down the toilet. I knew he meant it."

Ben and Joe laughed as they took their seats in Bible class. Mr. Bettinger couldn't hear from his left ear. Each day, students scrambled to seats on the right side of the room so, they could whisper unobserved. Arriving at the bell, Paul and Joe and Ben had to sit in the hearing section. Ben settled back and tried to listen, but all the week's words and images ran through his head with the steady relentless beating of the rain on the windows. Finally, Ben wrote to Joe on the corner of his page. *You're not afraid of your father*, he wrote. *Neither is Paul.*

How do you know this, oh wise one? Joe wrote back. Ben drew a question mark, and Joe responded with the word, *Liar.*

You're basically comfortable with him. Even Paul trusts his father. He knew his father meant what he said…that's a kind of trust. You say "afraid," you mean "trust and respect."

Joe wrote, *Is being afraid why you don't push your dad?*

In the distinct languages of their separate worlds, afraid meant such different things that the comparison brought a derisive laugh up inside Ben. *Not the way you defined the word.*

Explain.

Again, that bitter inner laugh. Could Joe, in his uncanny way, hear it? Ben touched his pencil to the paper and in a vivid and astonishing flash remembered a night when he was so small he still had his nighttime blanket. He saw the room again, vague and blue and shadowed with moonlight.

He had been lying in bed with his blanket, soft, but for a little curved ridge of stitches on one side. Watching the moon rise in his window, he rubbed this ridge between his thumb and forefinger and rubbed his cheek against the blanket. His father wanted him to *say* something or *stop saying* something and he wouldn't. Ben tried to remember if he'd been spanked for his refusal, searched in his memory for an experience that would match the tone and description of Tom's, searched for something Joe might have experienced…but there was nothing like that there, only the sense of the room spinning as it always did when he was terrified, when his parents' emotions slipped completely from his control—and again, that ripping sensation deep in his stomach. He believed that night was the first time he'd felt it.

"Ben," Mr. Bettinger said, "You okay?"

"Yes, sir."

"You sure?"

"It's kind of hot in here, sir."

"Go get a drink of water, kid. You'd better go with him, MacBride. He's green enough I think he's likely to keel over in a dead faint."

In the hall, Joe said, "You're not standing up straight. You look like you're going to puke."

"Yeah."

At the water fountain, Ben gulped barely stopping to breathe. Joe stood by, one shoulder against the wall, watching Ben drink. Behind Joe, Tom came out of the library. "What's up, men? Why aren't you in class?"

Ben jumped. "Easy," Joe whispered to Ben. He looked at his father over his shoulder. "Come on. Are you *everywhere*, Dad?"

"That's a nice welcome," Tom said, coming up to Joe.

"There's trouble in the opening assembly and you show up," Joe said. "You're in the parking lot when I get here. Then we get out of class for, like, five *seconds* and there you are."

"I work here," Tom said, humbly. He came a bit closer to Joe and patted his shoulder.

"I wish I led a normal life."

Ben stood up, backed up and quickly took in the details of Tom standing and walking. His stance, the easy athletic bearing, which Ben saw in just those few steps, told him Tom was fit and strong, and had once been a formidable athlete. Ben had not figured him to be that tall, had not anticipated the sense of authority and certainty in the vantage of the man's height. His waist was neither slim, nor as thick as Max's, but solid and muscled. And the breadth of Tom's shoulders looked powerful enough to intimidate even a confident man. Ben knew two things at once: every day he spent in the wheelchair frustrated the athlete in Tom; yet Tom had something inside him that gave him the ability to endure the mounting pressure to move his body at will. Ben suddenly knew that this powerful restraint was what Max was most afraid of in Tom. He looked away, stared at the water fountain.

"You don't have to stop drinking," Joe said, making a face at Ben.

"What's up?" Tom said.

"Mr. Bettinger let us out to get a drink. He thought Ben was gonna puke."

Tom's eyes became immediately observant. "Are you okay?"

"Just weird or something."

"I hope you didn't hit your head in that car accident."

"No. I'm fine."

"Better get back to class then."

"But Dad, Ben wants to know if you hated Gramps for paddling you."

Ben felt sick again, but Tom squinted at Ben; he folded his arms across his chest and leaned back a little. "I never hated him. He was a kind man. But he was old fashioned and he took my discipline seriously. And, honestly, I liked that. He was solid and dependable. I could always predict his reactions to my behavior. No, I respected him."

Ben stared at Tom trying to decide if Tom's comfortable approachability were the miracle it seemed or if the extraordinary thing about this man was really a slick and polished ability to hide a wound like Ben's.

"How about your mom?" Joe said, making a knowing face.

Tom put his arm around Joe's shoulder. "That's another story."

"We have time," Joe grinned.

"Come on," Tom said, motioning with his head for Ben to follow. "I'll walk you to class." They walked slowly, waiting for Ben who lagged behind. Joe trailed his fingers along the row of lockers making a blunt, stuttering sound. "Dad doesn't like to say negative things about people," Joe explained looking back at Ben. "He won't tell you that his mother—my own grannie—doesn't like me."

"In her defense," Tom said, "it's not that simple."

"She says I remind her of Dad." Joe grinned over his shoulder at Ben.

Tom sighed. "If she doesn't like you, Joe, that doesn't say much for her. Right, Ben?"

"I hadn't thought about it that way," Ben murmured. He kept a few steps behind, silent, pensive, hungrily taking in the details of Tom MacBride walking with his arm around his son. It made Ben's eyes blur.

"Ben Hunter! Just the person I was looking for." All three turned toward the voice to see the school secretary walking briskly toward them. "I was hoping to catch you before class let out. Here's a message from your father's office." She thrust a folded paper into Ben's hand, said hello to Tom, and rushed off to deliver another message.

Tom and Joe waited for him by the classroom door. "What's the note say?"

"I have an appointment on base today at four o'clock. That means no MVA."

"Dad can take you to the MVA and I'll go to your appointment and pretend I'm you." Shaking his head, Tom's hand went to the classroom door handle, one finger to his lips to shush them.

"Hey, Dad," Joe whispered as Tom yanked the door open, "want to run in there with us and moon everybody?"

The lights wavered and smiling, the boys ducked back into Bettinger's lively classroom.

Mother's Dream

16

"It doesn't make any sense," Joe said as he sped away from the MVA that afternoon. Above them, clouds raced low and gray on a hot wind.

"Tell me about it," Ben murmured, his jaw clenched so tight it hurt.

"They're being ridiculous about the birth certificate. You've got a learner's permit from Virginia. Why not just let you transfer to Maryland?" Ben shook his head. "And," Joe said, "I don't see why your military ID doesn't count."

"Now I'll have to get my father involved."

"If he's too busy, I'll drive you back over here tomorrow. Just get—"

"You don't understand. I don't *have* a birth certificate."

"Huh?" Glancing at Ben, Joe swerved slightly on the wet road. "You have to send away for it?"

"No. I don't *have* one."

"How'd you get the Virginia permit?"

"Every time I need a birth certificate—like to join a team or go to camp or anything—my dad has to show them a letter from his commanding officer that says who I am."

"Can you find the last letter?" Joe asked.

"I don't know," Ben said. "I've *never* understood why there's no birth certificate and why a *letter* works—I could *forge* a letter. I mean, what does the commanding officer know about who I am and when I was born?"

"Let's do it. Let's write a letter and try it tomorrow." Joe squinted at Ben, his grin playful, convincing. "It's worth a try. What could go wrong?"

Ben rolled his eyes and smiled. "Yeah, that sounds like a pretty flawless plan. Except they might call the *police* if we get caught with a forged letter."

"They'll just hand us over to our dads," Joe said, with a dismissive gesture, "What does he usually do when you try stuff?"

"He never knows. I never get caught."

"Looks like *I'd* better take lessons from *you*."

"Come on, Joe, nobody's got it better than you."

Admiral Johnson met them at the door, his hand outstretched to greet them. "Welcome, boys. You are right on time for your appointment." He took Ben's hand. "It's good to see you again." He covered Ben's hand with his other. "How are you after that bizarre accident?"

"I'm fine, sir. Thanks for asking."

"And your brothers?"

"They weren't hurt at all."

"My wife was walking to school—you know she teaches at the elementary school over yonder. She actually saw the accident. She thought your lip was cut."

Ben wondered if she could possibly have seen the blow that split his lip. Their eyes met. Too late, Ben remembered to cloak the meaning in his eyes. "I'm okay now."

"Odd how it all happened," Johnson said, peering at Ben.

The sharpness of the man's scrutiny alarmed Ben; his response, so long practiced, worked like a reflex. His expression calmed into an impassive mask. "I'm grateful no one was hurt," Ben said in the most quiet, concerned way he could, hoping the admiral would not see the shame he could not explain.

The admiral nodded. "You certainly are a good-looking young man, I must say. You look nothing like your father," he joked, grinning at Joe who thought Johnson's comment was funny and laughed out loud. "Admiral Johnson, sir," Ben said, roused from his reverie by Joe's laughter. "This is my friend, Joe MacBride. He drove me over here."

"MacBride?" Johnson turned to Joe with a surprising eagerness, grasped his hand and clapped Joe's shoulder with his other hand. "Tell me you're Tom MacBride's son. Nothing would make me happier."

"I'm Tom MacBride's son," Joe said, hands out in a gesture of mock surrender.

"I know Tom from way back. Yes I do. My, it is *good* to see *you*. Especially here with this young man. Why, this changes everything." He turned and called loudly, "Claire! I've got a surprise for you!"

He took Joe's shoulders in hand again and studied him. "You know, you're quite a bit like him, Joe. I was his company officer for three years when he was here. I saw him graduate. He was one of my favorites."

"Are you the Charlie Johnson he calls Bulldog Johnson?"

"That's what all my mids called me. What did he tell you about me, son?"

"He told us you got that nickname because you were so fierce."

"I'm so fierce even my pillow's afraid of me."

"He told us about when he and his friends carried one of the cannons from the Yard into your office—"

"Filled it with popcorn. That's Tom. Always in trouble for pranks, but an exemplary officer in every way."

Claire Johnson walked through the foyer. "Were you calling for me, Charlie?" Johnson turned Joe to face his wife.

"Claire, this is Tom MacBride's son."

Mrs. Johnson shook Joe's hand warmly. "I was just telling the Garden Club about that prayer meeting your father used to run. We kept flowers in the little chapel for them. It's so good to meet you."

"His name is Joe."

She nodded, squeezing his hand. "Your father was quite a hero, Joe. You know he saved a drowning child once."

"They know about that!" Johnson nodded at Joe, then Ben.

Joe and Ben met eyes. Johnson squinted at them, his eyes now questioning. "Don't you?"

The boys shook their heads; Joe said, "No details."

Johnson cleared his throat. "That prayer meeting Claire mentioned? You see, the son of the company officer for the twenty-first company was sick with leukemia. When Tom heard the boy was expected to die, he organized a group to pray twenty-four hours a day. And the child got well. Yes, he did. He's grown now. Just won some kind of art commission for a building in Atlanta."

"I never heard that story, either," Joe said.

"'Do your good deeds in secret,' Tom always said, didn't he, Claire?"

With a smile and nod, Claire said, "Please remember me to your parents," and took her leave.

"Come in, we'll have a seat in here," Johnson said, leading the way across the foyer into his plush, orderly office. "Claire was kind enough to prepare a snack for us." He led them to his desk and poured two glasses of lemonade from a frosted pitcher. He handed one to Ben, meeting Ben's eyes and smiling when Ben thanked him politely.

"Are your parents well?" Johnson gave Joe the other glass.

"Yes, sir. My mom owns a quilt store in West Annapolis so she's busy with that, and my dad runs the athletic department at CCS, our school." He gestured to include Ben. "He coaches basketball and baseball."

"Yes, I knew that. I've called your father a few times since May when I started here. Haven't seen him face to face, though." Johnson stared from Joe to Ben, back to Joe. "In the same school. Tom MacBride's school. What do you know," Johnson gestured toward the two soft leather chairs that stood near his desk. "Have a seat, boys," he said, moving with a quick agility around the desk to his own chair. He showed them a large platter holding cookies, fresh fruit, cheese slices and crackers. "Help yourselves. I raised two teenagers and I know how hungry you are this time of day."

Joe took a napkin and filled it with fruit slices, quickly made three sandwiches out of cheese and crackers. Ben took a cookie and an orange segment, sure he could eat neither.

"Ben, how do you like your new school?" Johnson asked, taking his seat.

"I love it, sir. Everyone is so friendly."

"When we moved from place to place, my son was always worried over making the soccer team. Got him sick to his stomach."

"Ben will make the team," Joe said. "We need him."

"You play on the basketball team, Joe?"

"They had to let me on," Joe said. "My dad's the coach."

"Yes, you're your father's son," Johnson laughed. "I can see him all through you."

"Dad's thrilled to get Ben," Joe said. "He knows a good athlete when he sees one."

"Do you feel the same, Ben? Do you feel confident you can work with this coach?"

"Yes, sir, I do," Ben said, sensing the seriousness in Johnson's question.

"Eat, boys," he said magnanimously, and leaned back in his chair, emanating pleasure as if they were *his* athletes standing on the Olympic platform bowing their heads for their medals. "I can't tell you what good it does to see you both here together. Tom MacBride's son and Max Hunter's son—friends at the same school. Remarkable."

Joe stopped eating; the boys glanced at each other and sat up straight.

"Why remarkable?"

Johnson raised his eyebrows at them. "The two men did have some conflicts."

"We don't know anything specific," Joe prompted.

"Joe, I'm trying to remember the last time I had a good, long visit with your parents. Been a long while. I think it must have been at a New Year's Eve party at that coffeehouse they used to run. Too bad that had to close." Johnson glanced at Ben.

"That's where my mom's quilt store is now."

"Ah," Johnson said, acknowledging the comment though his eyes were distant, peering at a memory. "Of course we've seen each other briefly now and then, spoken on the phone, Christmas cards, but I do think back fondly on that New Year's. I was in town for the funeral of a friend. I went over there for some hot soup and a little comfort. That was when I met your mother, Ben. Charming woman."

"*My* mother?"

"Yes."

"She did say she was stationed here once."

"What? No, she was visiting the MacBrides as I recall."

"Oh."

"You get your good looks from her, Ben. My, she looked lovely that night. I remember her so clearly. And so thoughtful. Tom and I had the most interesting conversation with her. Your father was not there, of course. I didn't meet him until this month."

Ben caught the admiral's derision and was not sure what to do or say. *Does he know what's happened to screw up my parents?* Aloud he said, "What year was this?"

"Let's see. Joe, your mother was pregnant. Yes, that's it. The only other child was a little boy, talkin' up a storm."

"My older brother, Pete, came out quoting Shakespeare."

"Ha! I guess it was you Laurie was carrying. That's right. January nineteen-eighty. I should have known that right away."

"So, my dad wasn't there because he was in the Mediterranean," Ben said.

Johnson considered Ben's statement, again studying Ben much longer than manners allowed. Finally he waved his hand. "I have his file here." He pulled a file from his desk drawer and flipped it open. "Your father was stationed at Camp Lejeune, Ben. His battery was not deployed until the summer. Of course that makes sense. Your birthday is coming up, isn't it?"

"Yes, sir. October fourteenth."

"Ah, yes," Johnson counted on his fingers. "Or how could you have been conceived?"

Ben's eyes met Joe's in a smirking, sideways glance.

"This is a problem our men in uniform face all the time. Deployments usually last six months. That means the father can be home for the baby's conception *or* his birth. Naturally, we dads *want* to be home for the baby's birth, but we are absolutely indispensable for conception, now aren't we?" He sat back and smiled at Ben.

"My dad was away when I was born," Ben said.

"Yes," Johnson said, as he again studied Ben so obviously and carefully that Ben grew embarrassed. "Not hungry, Ben?"

"Uh, no, sir. I'm sorry."

"No, *I'm* sorry. An athlete your age who isn't hungry? I suppose your father scared you sick about being polite when you came here."

"Sir, I know how important your opinion is to my father."

"You just put that worry aside. Getting to know a fine boy like you can only do your father credit."

"I hope so, sir. Dad said you wanted to see me about maybe going here. To the Naval Academy."

"What do you think about that, Ben? Answer honestly."

"I really like it here and I'd like to look into it."

"That's terrific. I know you play basketball."

"He plays baseball, too," Joe said and popped another cookie into his mouth.

"And how are your grades?"

"They're fine, sir."

Joe rolled his eyes at the admiral and grinned. "I bet you've never even gotten an A minus."

"But my last school was super easy. That's why my grandmother wanted me to go to CCS. She said their academic program was more challenging."

Leaning forward Johnson said, "Joe, you would be an excellent candidate."

"My dad went here," Joe grinned. "I don't want to turn out like him." When Johnson laughed, Joe added, "I just came with Ben because we went to the MVA. We're going to my house to hang out."

"Please consider it a serious option, Joe." Johnson glanced with a satisfied expression at Joe, so that Ben thought their interview was nearly over, but Johnson turned to look at Ben and his expression changed completely. Ben's stomach leapt. "I want you to think of my home as a kind of oasis for you, Ben. You're welcome here anytime. After all, we're neighbors. Let me help you—both of you—with your applications. I'm most interested in your personal success."

"Thank you. I really appreciate that, sir."

"Hey," Joe said. "Tell Admiral Johnson."

Alarmed, Ben looked at Joe.

"Tell him."

"Yes, tell me," the admiral said, folding his hands on the edge of his desk and leaning forward.

"About the permit. Your learner's permit."

Ben hesitated; the admiral held out his hand as a way to invite Ben's confidence. "I have a permit from Virginia, but without my birth certificate, I can't get one for Maryland."

Johnson waited, not yet comprehending.

Joe said, "He doesn't have a birth certificate."

"What happened to it? Lost in the move from Quantico?"

"I never had one."

"That shouldn't be," Johnson said, rubbing his chin again, staring at Ben.

"His dad always gets a letter from his commanding officer to say who Ben is and his age. That's how he got the Virginia permit."

"A letter?" Johnson said, pushing back in his chair. "I never heard of such shenanigans. What the h—hoo-hah good would a letter do?"

Joe shrugged.

"I'd be happy to write a letter, but there must be a more permanent solution." He stood up, folded his arms over his chest and hunched forward. He began to walk toward the windows. "Even babies born overseas have birth certificates. There must be one somewhere." Johnson turned at the carpet's edge and walked back toward them. "Or there must be a way of getting a substitute. An official document. The boy can't go through life begging for letters."

Ben and Joe shared a hopeful glance while Johnson paced, thinking.

"I was thinking my driver's license would become that."

Johnson nodded, listening. "What's the reason for this mix-up?" he muttered, without looking at them.

"There was a snow storm in northern New Jersey when I was born. It messed up the electricity and—"

"An early blizzard. Highly unusual."

"Yes, sir. A freak storm," Ben said. "I've seen newspaper articles that my grandmother saved."

"The article about you?"

"No sir, there's not one specifically about me, just the storm. The electricity went out at the hospital and somehow the records got lost, I think."

Johnson clasped his hands behind his back and, pacing, studied the rim of the room. "That doesn't make sense."

"Another thing that may have caused it, sir," Ben said, his voice uncertain as he revealed his private explanation. "My mom was probably really sick afterwards."

"Yes, she was. And no wonder," Johnson murmured, his eyes now studying the path he'd made on the plush carpet.

"Okay, so I'm right about that," Ben said; he watched Johnson pace. "I thought so because she was totally bad off after my brothers were born. She was so weak that Gran and I had to feed her with a spoon."

"What?" Johnson stood still.

"Mom would be embarrassed if she knew I told you that. But I thought if she was even *half* that bad after I was born, maybe she forgot to fill out the forms."

The admiral's head jerked up; he squinted at Ben, studying him. Johnson's starkly knowing expression lasted only an instant.

Bewildered by the admiral's expression, Ben held still, enduring the slimy sense of shame that bathed him when he was forced to describe his baffling home life.

"Did you say earlier, that your *grandmother* thought your school in Quantico was too easy for you?"

"Yes, sir," Ben said. "She found out about CCS and told my parents."

"And your parents looked into the school and liked it. They approved?"

"I guess."

"You sound anything but convinced. This is important."

Not sure he understood the intent of the question, Ben hesitated. "You see, sir, when we move, it's busy, so my grandmother finds out where things are and stuff."

"Yes, yes," Johnson waved his hand. "Your grandmother does all the initial pokin' around. But when your father visited the school with you and met your teachers and your coaches, and *saw Tom* again, he agreed it was the right place for you?"

"Admiral Johnson, sir, I think they just took Gran's word for it."

"Has your father visited the school?"

"No, sir." Ben could see the situation through Johnson's eyes. Johnson was a careful administrator, an insightful one. He searched out the reasons for problems. Meeting Ben was a step in analyzing his father's behavior, especially after he crashed into Middleton's. Max's neglect in visiting CCS showed a carelessness that was not only antithetical to Johnson's method, it showed his disinterested managerial style. Only Ben knew that Max's disinterest was made of desperate stuff. His father experienced noticeable relief when his responsibility for Ben was shouldered by another. Ben's ability to take care of himself was the one point of true affection he knew toward Ben.

Johnson rubbed his forehead and squeezed the bridge of his nose between his thumb and forefinger. "Major Lindquist can notarize the letter. Can you meet me at his office at nine tomorrow morning?"

"Yes, I can. Thank you, sir."

"I don't see what good a letter can do," Johnson said. "But it will take time to look into the other matter. You can be sure I'll look into it."

"Please, no, you don't have to—"

"You cannot apply to the U.S. Naval Academy without a birth certificate. You must get this matter settled. You have your life to live."

Ben got to his feet. "I'll be at your office at nine."

Johnson rounded his desk and took Ben's hand in both of his. "It's been a pleasure speaking with you." Looking into Ben's eyes he said, "You've got a true friend in Joe. See to it that you don't let any nonsense separate you."

"I won't, sir."

"You can trust a MacBride," Johnson said.

17

JOE sped his car onto the Eastport Bridge over gray, swollen waters, frantic and wind-flecked. Brooding above, the clouds deepened from gray to dark green and black. Ben could feel the surge of the wind, the mounting of the storm; he breathed in the brackish, rising scent of the river and wished for his journal.

They drove past the city limits, past small, well-kept houses and gray strip malls to a rural road winding toward the glimpses of shimmering water on the horizon. Joe turned suddenly and Ben saw a white, two-story house with gabled windows and bright green shutters. Joe raced the car on a long, curved gravel driveway, stopping hard before a building that looked like a barn. It stood at an angle to the back of the house; on one side, near the driveway, a large concrete slab capped with a basketball net waited for them.

"Basketballs are in the garage. Come on. I'll show you. Try not to trip over my dad's junk," Joe said as he unlatched the iron clasp. "It used to be a barn, now Dad uses it for fixing stuff. And for the trampoline." With both hands, Joe grasped the door's edge and pulled; it swung wide, wobbling as it opened. The smells of wood sap and oil and sawdust made a pungent blend; the air was warm and faintly dusty.

In the instant that it took his eyes to focus, Ben followed Joe's voice. "He fixes stuff like what?"

"Stuff. Anything. I swear, he can fix anything. He even patches basketballs," Joe said, his voice moving farther away.

Ben could see the shape of Joe's head and shoulders moving quickly into the dark room. Ben noticed first the big, round trampoline, blue as a swimming pool, in the center of the room. Around it, lining the walls of the barn, were work areas, shelves, two wide tables all crowded with garden tools, boxes and old toys. Like the space in Tom's office by the gym, there was an attempt at order: Tom's tools hung on the wall's peg board; wooden things like picture frames and chairs hung from the ceiling; broken crockery, bicycle tires and a toaster stood in a line on one of the tables. Above the table, a basketball stood still, as if caught in flight. Looking closer, Ben saw that a large vice, grips stretched wide and padded with a thick towel, held the ball. It was attached to an air pump.

"See?" Joe said, his voice amused.

"He's fixing this ball?" Ben said, going to the captured ball and touching the slim brown patches that contrasted like bandages against the ball's skin.

"Trying to," Joe said, smirking. "Come on, I'll show you the apple attic." Joe motioned for Ben to follow him beyond the work area toward the stairs, which led to a loft above the trampoline. As he went up the stairs, Ben glanced down, still fascinated with the basketball.

"He holds the ball in the vice—the towel's there so he won't cause more tears—and he pumps in air," Joe explained. "When he hears a leak, he patches it."

"Amazing." They had reached the top of the stairs; the air hugged close and hot.

"My father will do anything to save a few pesos."

"But can he fix basketball *players*?" Ben laughed, but it sounded tight and weak.

Moving past stacks of boxes and empty bushel baskets to the widest section of the loft. Three cot mattresses, rolled and tied, cushioned the wall beneath the window that showed a thick-branched apple tree beyond, stirring in the wind. A pile of tightly rolled sleeping bags filled one corner, stacked beside a camping stove, lanterns and empty backpacks. Unlatching the curious wooden sliding windows in the slope of the roof, Joe said, "Good question."

Ben helped Joe shove the wooden slats apart. Damp gusts of air skirled past the open windows. Joe leaned out the wide window and again Ben followed. Heat rose from the roof with the smell of melting tar, but coursing over that, the wind carried past them the fragrance of late summer, apples and grass and rain. They put their faces into the damp wind and stared up at the building gray clouds, at the tossing trees on the horizon. "He hasn't been able to fix Oliver," Joe said.

"Yeah, what's *with* Oliver?" Ben said. "He shoved into me in the hall today. I swear it was on purpose."

"He's such a jerk."

"Is he any good?"

"Yeah, he's good, but he's not worth the trouble. He thinks Dad ought to be more impressed with his talent. And Dad *is*, but he makes Ollie share the ball, and he won't let Ollie mouth off or throw chairs and stuff."

"Throw chairs?"

"Yeah, last year Ollie got mad when a ref called him for traveling and he picked up the assistant coach's chair and *threw* it."

"What a punk."

"Dad was off the bench so fast. When he's mad, he can move *so* fast. He told Oliver if he picked up the chair and apologized to the ref he could get off with only a three-game suspension. If not, he was off the team."

"And?"

"Ollie apologized, grudgingly. I *never* would have been allowed to get away with something like that. *Never*. Dad knows his behavior is out of control, but he doesn't want to push him over the edge."

Ben hesitated before saying, "I kind of got the impression your dad doesn't like Oliver."

"But he'll never come out and say that. He refuses to say anything negative about people." Joe laughed. "Dad's so weird. I mean, he's too careful with people. But Jeannie, that girl's got guts. She went right up to Ollie after the game and told him he was the biggest, spoiled baby she'd ever seen. It was beautiful. "

"Ha! I can picture that."

"Bonnie Jean is the bluntest person I know."

"Does Oliver like her? Bonnie Jean?"

"No. He's going out with Morgan. That quiet girl in our math class.

But I've seen him flirting with Tiffany all week. Morgan puts up with so much crap from him."

"Tiffany is—"

"The one who tried to flirt with you in chapel."

"The girl with—"

"The perfect breasts."

"They *are* huge, but—" Embarrassed, Ben directed the conversation away from himself. "So, Ollie is after Tiffany's boobs?"

"I've got news for him. She doesn't let anybody touch them. I know. In eighth grade, I went out with her for six months and God knows I tried," Joe said dreamily. "Man, I was obsessed. She'd come over here so I could help her study math—what a joke." Joe pointed to a thicket at the far side of the meadow below. "I'd try to get her to make out back there, behind those trees. One day, she stormed up to the house and complained to Dad about the pressure I was putting on her." Joe shrugged, looking sheepish. "I was being a jerk. We're pretty good friends now."

"Is it rough having everyone know your dad?"

"It's annoying," Joe agreed, "But most of the time, I deserve it. Like that time…you were gonna tell me why Tiffany isn't perfect."

"Other girls are prettier. Like Victoria. Or your sister." Ben said, seriously, missing the teasing lilt in Joe's voice. "Bonnie Jean's not showy, but, I mean essentially—"

"I've never heard you quite so articulate. Try Spanish."

"Um," Ben said, thinking, aware on some level that Joe was teasing, but fascinated by the challenge to describe her. "I don't know how to say it. You just feel like you can connect with her because she's not hiding what she thinks. And I love her expressions. Her face shows so much."

"Yeah, yeah," Joe grinned, "but let's get serious, here. I think you have a chance with her."

"Why's that?"

"She doesn't scare you. Like before math when she was telling everyone that weird dream she had about finding her evil twin."

"That was *so* funny. She made this terrifying face and changed her voice when the twin was talking. I could picture the entire dream."

"Everyone else blew her off. You were into it."

"Yeah."

"You're farther gone than I suspected."

Ben clamped his mouth shut, afraid he'd revealed too much. Joe bumped his shoulder. "Hey, you know," he said, his voice barely audible above the sound of the wind in the trees, "my brother and I always talked up here. Except he's taller than you so he kind of hangs out. It looks *ridiculous*." Ben felt his embarrassment ebb in the steady euphony that was Joe's voice. "When we were in trouble or just wanted to escape, Pete and

I would climb this apple tree and go into the attic through this window. Come on, I'll show you." Joe hoisted himself up onto the open ledge and scooted out onto the slanted roof. Ben followed, the roof shingles so hot they felt soft under his feet.

"Man," Joe said, "Pete's only been away three weeks and it feels like seven years."

Busy in her kitchen with preparations for Tom's birthday dinner, Laurie MacBride heard the roar of the old MG in the driveway and looked up. Through the window, she watched the car come into view and saw that Joe had brought a friend. Suspecting, hoping it was Ben, Laurie stepped closer, her heartbeat quickening. Ben's bright blond head emerged from the car and her breath caught. "I should have known back then," she reproached herself, "when I saw that hair color."

As he walked with Joe to the garage, Laurie noted Ben's height, his slim, muscular build with that familiar, athletic stance, that natural agility that she had always so admired. Her heart swelled with an awed kind of pride, and she shook her head in amazement. Who would have believed that Joe and this child could have become fast friends?

She turned back to the fresh greens she was washing at the kitchen sink, thinking, *Who would ever have believed that Donna Boswell would have married Max Hunter?* It was just this skepticism that had made her doubt herself when she saw them together—intimately and bizarrely together—with Ben, a bright, incongruous shadow shining from behind them on the night after Donna had won her lawsuit against Tom.

Laurie shook her head again, thinking how strange life was, as she plunged a colander full of fresh salad greens under the cold, running water. She shivered with delight at the cool water on her puffy fingers and would have liked to climb in the sink and plunge her whole puffed, pregnant self into that chilling water and shake the sense of heaviness that doubled with the remembrance of Donna's lawsuit and all that came of it.

Back when Rising Sun was thriving, Tom had encouraged Donna to marry the man she loved. The resulting pregnancy had weakened Donna's body to the point that her doctor concluded she could bear no other children. Someone had to pay, so said the lawyers and doctors. Her husband had fled. Because Donna's lawyers proved through the notes Donna took in counseling sessions that Tom had convinced her to marry, had "applied undue pressure," the court required Tom to pay for Donna's disappointed spirit and damaged body.

The night he lost the lawsuit, Tom had been so broken that he had gone to bed when the children had. Laurie left them sleeping and drove to Rising Sun to continue her preparations for the next day's soup dinner. Earlier that day, Laurie had sprayed both old ovens with cleaner and her first task was to wipe them out. She knelt between the open doors and sopped up bubbled residue with old rags. The fumes stung her nose and drew water to her burning eyes. She worked rapidly, holding her breath, turning to the side to breathe when she was forced to do so. In her haste she pushed some of the cleaning fluid across her knee and onto the floor. She hurried to the front room for more newspapers to absorb the caustic, dripping ooze of the oven cleaner.

Remembering that she was lightheaded and bleary-eyed from the fumes, Laurie had, for ten years, mistrusted her memory of what happened when she reached toward the stack of papers. She remembered seeing the stack and misjudging its distance from her hand and she stumbled. She was still reaching for the papers when some angry force hit the house with a sharp, cracking boom.

It was an expansive sound, brutal and terrifying, bigger than the house, resounding immediately against her chest. The impact jolted her to her knees. She scraped her palms and forearms on the floor. Tiny blue lights popped at the fuse box in the corner—and then darkness. Plaster fell all round her in chunks. Dust swirled, illuminated by the headlights of the car that had broken the front wall and stuck into the room where the display window now stood.

Laurie remembered crawling toward the light, approaching the beams from the side, willing her eyes to focus. In the car a woman screamed, her voice, her face familiar. Laurie choked with recognition. An accusing thought soured her mind, *But why, Donna? You won the lawsuit.*

She hurried closer, anger propelling her to ask the question aloud, to demand an answer. Inches from the intruding car, she stopped, unable to move or scream, unable to breathe. *I must be dreaming. It's the fumes or I've hit my head.*

Donna was in the car with the *wrong* man.

Her swimming eyes peered into Max Hunter's face and when she saw the bright, golden head of a child emerge above the back seat, his blue eyes wide and terrified in the dimming light, she tried to speak to him, tried to comfort him. She reached out both hands for him, but the car scraped away in desperate recoil and her vision went black.

When she revived, hospitalized with a concussion, her lungs scalded from the cleaning fumes, Laurie distrusted what she'd seen in the swirling, chaotic darkness of the crash. Knowing the sharpness of her bitterness, she did not tell the police that the same woman who had just won the lawsuit against her husband had rammed a titanic car into the building where the offending coffee house thrived. She told herself that it had been a bizarre, if symbolic, hallucination. Laurie suspected her anger had put Donna's face in that car beside her husband's sole and relentless enemy—Max Hunter—of all people.

Nor did she mention her suspicion to Tom, having discredited it as sour grapes. At first, Tom was frantic, trying to care for her and their family as he began to rebuild Rising Sun. His damaged back revolted at the constant, straining work.

During this time, Laurie needed all of her vitality to look after her children and nurse her broken husband back to strength. She told herself then and for years afterwards that it was the shock and the darkness that made the woman in the car look like Donna and the man next to her look like Max. In loyal and heartfelt defense of her husband, her troubled mind had coupled together the two people who had hurt Tom. They were symbols to her of Tom's pain, of friendship gone bad.

It followed that it was merely her imagination, influenced by the memories the lawsuit raised, that created a child so like what she imagined Ben would be to pop up from behind the back seat. But he had looked so real…and the terror she'd seen in his eyes haunted her on still, hot nights. Those times, unable to sleep, she rose from bed and pondered the shape and color of his eyes while she moved her needle through the layers of her quilt, rocking up and down, up and down to the rhythm of her whispered and solitary prayers.

It was from this wreckage, this sense of turmoil and uncertainty, that Laurie conceived her sewing store. While Tom rested in his hospital bed after the surgery meant to repair his back, she sat with him and stitched a colorful quilt for Tommy. The motion of the needle through the fabric as it joined the soft layers soothed her nerves and provided the concentration needed to shape her plans. "People need something to do," she told Tom as he grieved over his lost dream, over those he perceived to be going hungry without the provision of the coffee house on the corner. "Rising Sun was a beginning. I want to give people a place to help them create beauty. This will feed their spirits."

And so, they laid Rising Sun to rest, and with it Laurie buried her suspicions of Donna and Max. That is, until Joe brought Ben to Rising Sun's rebuilt, quilt-filled front porch two days ago. She told Tom, that night, that she had made a terrible mistake. Ben's description of his mother, the words of hers he quoted, revealed the impossible truth that Max and Donna were indeed married. It shook Tom profoundly to think that Max Hunter had been behind Donna's vicious lawsuit; Laurie woke at midnight to find him doing pull-ups on the bar he'd put in his closet. The only thought that comforted them was that this revelation brought some explanation for Donna's behavior. They both had suspected from the beginning that she, who had once been so dear to them, was incapable of devising that bitter lawsuit alone.

Two nights ago, after she told him what she had truly seen those long years before, Tom insisted that they hope Max had changed. After all, Tom reasoned, they had met Ben, loved him on sight, recognized his keen intelligence and his manners, noted that his accomplishments were the kind seen in carefully raised children. Tom insisted that they believe Max had risen to the challenge of raising Ben. They must give Max another chance, Tom said, for Ben's sake.

But Laurie felt thrust back in time, anxious to begin tasks left undone. Now she knew that there had been a small golden-haired boy in the backseat of the car that night. Laurie had seen Ben that terrible day in the darkness and dusty confusion of the crumbling coffee house and Laurie could once again feel the powerful instinct that had made her reach out her arms toward him, despite the law and the cold-hearted rulings of the court, despite convention, despite the gulf that separated them.

Ben was here in her backyard. Her fingers waited with the restlessness of a craftsman kept from her art. *What did he know? What had he been told? What did he remember?* Laurie intended to find out; he would not slip from her arms this time.

18

"YOU know what *that* is," Joe said with a grin, pointing to the basketball court as he led the way to a stone path dotted in leaps toward the house. Gardens colored the back of the house on both sides of the kitchen door, and the colors—vibrant purple chives, shades of pink carnations, white and yellow lilies—seemed to emanate their own light in the stormy afternoon darkness. Dripping from the day of fitful rain, the bent plants swayed heavily at the wind's gusts. Again, the overpowering scent of roses met Ben, underscored with the tang of blue-green herbs.

Opening the door, Joe called, "We're home, Mom."

"Hello," he heard her call from within. For just an instant when Ben stood poised to cross the threshold, the garden's scent mingled with the spicy, rich smell of cooking, he knew a moment of sensory exhilaration. He hung back, wishing to hover there, but Joe pulled him into the kitchen.

He saw everything at once in a grasp of clarity that he remembered all his life. There was food everywhere. On the counter stood five freshly baked loaves, golden and steaming slightly. Muffins had been tumbled from their pans onto a rack. Two lemon meringue pies stood as high as gilt-edged summer clouds. Bunches of flowers and herbs filled the sink, and on the drain board beside, a glass bowl held salad greens so crisp they rose in a leafy mound above the rim. Dark red tomatoes, peppers gold and green, carrots and cucumbers lay scattered, washed and dripping, on a worn wooden board. On the stove beside a plump, roasted turkey breast, steam rose from a pot that was as big as an armful.

"Mama?" Joe called.

"I'll be right there," sounded from within.

An open brick hearth filled with flame-colored geraniums formed the wall at the far end of the kitchen. The mantle displayed photographs clustered around a blue and white teapot. A corner cupboard held piles of plates and cups, in a jumble of white and orange and blue. Centered in front of the hearth was a long table set for dinner with bright blue dishes, gleaming silverware and butter-yellow napkins.

Ben stared open-mouthed at this foreign world, unable to form a single word.

Joe said apologetically, "It's my dad's birthday."

I should go, Ben thought, feeling sickeningly out of place despite a sudden, sharp hunger.

Mrs. MacBride entered from the room beyond carrying a bowl overflowing with creamy yellow roses, which she stood in the center of the table. "Hi, boys," she said. "I'm so glad you came, Ben."

Joe said, "Haven't you overdone it a bit, Mom?"

"I took the afternoon off," she said briskly, as if that explained the miracle of the food.

"Yeah, but *Mom*."

"You must be hungry, Ben," she said. Coming to him and taking his elbow, she guided him to the cabinet above the sink, went on her tiptoes and took a plate down for him. "Help yourself." She made a sweeping gesture that indicated he could choose from all he saw around him, but Ben could not so much as swallow. Ben searched for what to say. In the three languages he knew, not a single word arose in his mind that could describe the bounty he saw before him.

"What would you like?"

"Everything."

This made Laurie laugh with delight and she touched Ben's arm in an affectionate kind of rub. "Everything but the pies. They're for dessert tonight."

Ben held his plate, unsure of what to do. Joe said, "Can I cut this turkey and make sandwiches?"

"Slice up half of it and put what you don't use in the fridge," Laurie said. "I want to use the rest for turkey salad."

"Man, it's cold in here, Mom. What did you do, turn the air conditioning down to zero?"

"Oops! Don't tell Dad," she said as she hurried from the room.

"Get the mayo out of the fridge," Joe commanded. Ben found that he could obey instructions, but was stunned again motionless by the sight of the refrigerator contents. An orange Jell-O salad, potato salad, broccoli salad, a bowl filled with raspberries, a huge bowl of marinating steaks, a plate of deviled eggs and a dish of curling pink shrimp crowded the shelves. "And get some bread that's already sliced. I'm starving."

"There," Laurie said, coming back to the kitchen. "I always turn the temperature way down when I cook," she laughed self-consciously. "It makes Tom nervous when he thinks of the electric bill. He tends to be frugal." She joined Ben at the open refrigerator. "Sometimes when I'm really hot, I open the door and just stand here," she said, again laughing at herself. "Doesn't the cold air just feel delicious?"

"Yes, ma'am," Ben said. *Was he imagining it? Or did she want to hug him?* He looked down at her. She smiled at him, her happiness palpable as sunlight.

"Now, what do you see that you want?"

"Joe wants me to get the mayonnaise and bread."

"Why don't you sit down, Mom? We'll make you a sandwich, too."

"No, I want to make sure Ben has what he needs."

"Please sit down, Mrs. MacBride." Ben said taking the mayonnaise and bread from her. "I'm used to taking care of myself."

"You mean you cook for yourself?"

"Mom, most people do," Joe said. "Put your feet up. Aren't you supposed to put your feet up in the afternoon?"

"Just for an hour. I'm fine." She went to the sink and took a tomato in hand.

"How's the baby doing?" Joe asked.

"Quiet today. Kind of settling down."

"That's good, isn't it?"

"Good, yes, but I've got so much to do before the baby comes. Here's some tomato slices for your sandwiches," she said. Ben took these from her and carried them to Joe. "Make sure you put enough turkey on for Ben."

"What about enough turkey for Joe?" Joe said.

"You're well nourished. Ben has to cook for himself."

"Look at him," Joe protested. "He weighs twenty pounds more than me."

Though Laurie laughed, Ben felt he had to say something conciliatory, so he offered, "It's great you're still up and around. My mother had to stay in bed for months before."

Laurie's eyes went bright and alert. "Before what?" She faltered, her expression, even the sound of her voice, had gone tight.

"Before my brothers were born. I guess it was the same with me. I don't remember that far back." Ben paused waiting to see if his feeble joke would dilute the tension suddenly presiding.

"To when you were born?" Laurie peered at him; her eyes looked hard and bright.

"It was a joke, Mom."

"Oh, wait," she said, comprehension dawning in her eyes. "You have younger siblings?"

"Yes, ma'am. Two brothers. Keith is eight and Tim is six."

"Two? Two boys?" Laurie said, exhaling the words like a contented sigh. "That's *wonderful*. The last I heard from Donna," she said, looking at Ben in a way that said she understood the awkwardness of the broken friendship, "she was *sure* she couldn't have any more children. I'm so happy things worked out for her." Her expression turned purposeful. "How do you like Annapolis?"

"I like it." He took his sandwich from Joe and was swept by a wave of hunger. "I love seeing the water every day and the bridges."

Laurie nodded. "What about the rest of your family? How are they adjusting to the move?"

Ben considered how to word his answer. "Dad's enthusiastic about the Academy."

"That's a switch," Laurie said, immediately embarrassed, realizing she'd said too much.

Ben and Joe glanced at each other. Joe said, "We know you were friends with Ben's parents…"

"Oh, you might as well know I actually dated your father. In high school."

"No," Ben breathed.

"You're kidding, right?" Joe said.

"For nearly two years."

"Two *years*," Joe and Ben said together, staring at each other.

"I was terribly in love with him."

"*My* dad?" Ben put his sandwich down and stared at her. "What did you see in him?"

"Oh, I don't know. He moved to Hillside in high school, so he was the new boy, unfamiliar, always brooding. Intense and possessive. As a teenager, I found those things irresistible."

"He's still intense," Ben said.

"It's funny remembering how when Max was intense about something—which was almost always—he'd walk leaning forward, like this." Laurie tried to demonstrate this, holding onto the sink for balance. "I always thought he was looking for some body of water to dive into so he could go really fast. He was much faster in the water and he always seemed to resent having to walk to get places." Laurie laughed, the cheerful lilt so careless and obvious in her voice that Ben joined her.

"That is how he walks," Ben said, staring at her.

"Why did you break up?"

"He fell in love with someone else," Laurie said, "and broke my heart."

"Ben's mother?"

"Yes."

Ben's heart sank. "I'm so sorry, Mrs. MacBride."

"It's long since healed, my darling."

"Really?"

"Yes," she said, meeting his eyes with such honesty and confidence that Ben believed her. "And remember, I loved your mother, too. She was my dearest friend." Ben looked away. "So having you here—right here in my very own kitchen—is an absolute thrill for me. I've wondered about you so often over the years."

His hand unsteady, chest hot, Ben put his plate aside and glanced at Joe for a cue. Joe was shaking his head in a gentle, indulgent manner, his eyes clear and free of any mocking note. "I don't know what to say, Mrs. MacBride."

"You don't have to say anything. Just know that you are welcome to me."

It's true, Ben thought, *I can feel it.* The way that she wanted him right here in her home surrounded Ben so palpably he thought he could wrap up in it and sleep well. She came to him and rubbed her hand along his shoulders.

19

THE sound of a car door jarred Ben's thoughts.

"Oops!" Laurie said. "Tom's home." She hurried to her chair at the end of the table by the window and reached for a basket kept beneath. From it she pulled out a pillow and lowered herself into the chair, putting the pillow on the bench beside to cushion her legs. She took a large, colorful rectangle caught in a wooden hoop in hand. "Joe, could you get me a half-filled glass of water, so it looks like I've been sitting down?"

Joe got up and put his plate in the dishwasher. "Mom, as soon as he walks in here, he'll know you've been on your feet all day." He grabbed an apple from the bowl on the counter and threw it, aiming low, to the left of Ben's shoulder; Ben fumbled, nearly dropping it. "I got you," Joe sang out triumphantly, as he went to the sink and filled a glass. This he took to his mother. Joe held up his hands to catch the apple, and Ben, with a glance at the door, flung it back to Joe.

"I just want the truth to dawn on him slowly," she grinned.

The back door swung open and Tom entered, carrying several bulging bags of groceries. He paused at the threshold and said, "Hello, everyone. It is I." With an expectant grin, he looked at each of them.

"Happy Birthday, darling," Laurie said, demurely, from her corner.

Joe whizzed the apple past his father to Ben who caught it and held it.

Joe held out his hands to catch it again, but Ben grimaced in protest and held onto the apple.

"Let me guess, Laurie," Tom said, looking around the room. "While you were sitting there, resting, with your feet up as your doctor ordered, an army of little men came in, turned the temperature down to zero degrees and prepared all this food." He crossed the room to a door in the wall opposite the kitchen table. This he nudged open with his foot. Going into the room behind it, he clunked the grocery bags down.

"Actually," Laurie said when he emerged, "it was four men and a boy, but the boy was very fast."

Tom laughed. "Haven't you overdone it a bit, my love?"

"You've bought more food for your over-stocked pantry and you ask me about overdoing?"

"Just some Pringles for Jeff."

"Five bags of Pringles for Jeff?" Joe teased.

"And a few other things. All this only cost me eleven dollars and seventy-three cents."

"Tom, you should encourage Jeff to eat healthy food."

"I do, but Pringles make him happy."

As he went to kiss Laurie's upturned face he said, "Just tell me *please* that you were not the one who was out on the garage roof and left the sliders open."

"Of course not," she said, "I haven't been up there since last week."

Tom laughed again.

"That was us," Joe said, taking a step toward the back door.

"I sent Tommy up to close them," Tom said. "You want to watch that. Especially in this weather."

"Sorry, Dad." Tom faked a jab at Joe's abdomen. Joe caught his hand and Tom pulled Joe toward him, trapped him in a headlock and ground his knuckles on Joe's back between his shoulder blades. Bellowing in laughing protest, Joe squirmed and got away. Ben held still, absorbing the details of their interaction, so hungry to join in that his mouth watered.

"Hey, Ben." Tom said. "What are you guys doing?"

"Playing catch with that apple," Joe said. "But Ben refuses to throw it now that you're home."

"I knew he was smart from the moment I saw him," Tom said, passing behind Ben to go to the room where he'd left the groceries. He patted Ben's shoulder lightly. "Good to see you here, Ben."

"Come on, Ben, throw it," Joe taunted, backing up across the kitchen.

Ben winced. "Let's go outside." But Joe grabbed another apple and threw it at Ben. Ben flipped the one he held into his right hand and caught the second. Joe fired a third at him; Ben juggled the other two, catching the third.

"Stop." Ben said. "If I miss it's going to hit your mother or something."

"You'd better throw one back," Joe said, taking another in hand.

Quick as a blink, Ben threw one to Joe. Surprised by its speed, Joe missed it. The back door opened and the apple smashed into the forehead of a boy, knocking him down. The apple dropped on the floor and split in half. Tumbling the apples he held onto the table, Ben rushed to the boy. Joe reached him first and helped him up. He was quick and slim as a wire, with bright brown eyes, the shape of his face and the set of his mouth all Tom's. He came up roaring, wrested his arms out of Joe's grasp and lunged at Ben, swinging with both fists clenched. Tom came between them. With one arm, he pushed Ben back and with the other, he wrapped both arms around the boy. "Easy, Tommy."

"He hit me on purpose!"

"Hey, hey, hey. Settle down. It was an accident."

"It was not," Tommy yelled, struggling against Tom's grasp, wiggling up and down so strenuously that he knocked his head into Tom's lip.

"Ah!"

"Tommy," Laurie scolded. "You've hurt your father."

"And made your mother get up from her seat," Tom added.

"Mom never sits down unless you're home." He shoved at Tom's arms to loosen their grasp.

Tom lifted Tommy up and turning the boy to face him, set him firmly on both feet. "You'd better rethink that last comment, son," Tom said, his voice a severe and convincing law. Tommy met his father's eyes. Ben heard his own breath catch.

Tommy stopped struggling and whispered, "I'm sorry, Mama," his voice breaking.

"That's right. You keep your temper. I'm in pain too, thanks to where your head hit my lip. You don't see me having a temper fit, do you?"

His lip quivering, an angry flush coloring his brown face, Tommy said, "You okay, Dad?"

"I'll just walk it off," Tom said, with a wry smile at Joe.

Joe laughed.

"It's not funny," Tommy growled.

"I'm not laughing at you, turkey. Here's some ice," Joe said offering a clump of ice in a wet cloth. "Sorry about that, Tommy," Joe said. "I thought I had it, then it dropped."

"It's not your fault. *He* threw it," Tommy snapped, his eyes spilling tears.

"I'm sorry," Ben said. "I am *so* sorry."

"Yeah, *right*. You *meant* it." Tommy's voice broke with a furious sob.

"That is enough," Tom said grasping Tommy's shoulders.

Ben's hand went out in a reflexive, protective movement. Laurie prevented him, her hand gently on his arm. "It's okay," she whispered.

"You come over here," Tom said, steering him to the bench, "where I can talk to you."

Tom took Tommy onto his knees. He pressed the ice pack to Tommy's head. The boy fought his tears, biting his lip hard. "I can't have you behaving like that," Tom said. "You're hurt and you can cry for being hurt. But you must stop this nastiness right now." Laurie sat at Tommy's back, rubbing her hand across his shoulders.

Cushioned between his parents, Tommy lost his bravado. "My head hurts," Tommy said, wiping his tears furiously on his father's shirt. "He threw it hard."

As clearly as if he'd grown up in that crowded, fragrant kitchen, Ben saw the shape and definition of Tom's fatherhood. He understood the nature of Tom's instruction, his purpose so seriously taken it was sacred. Ben knew that if Tommy had not abandoned his temper, Tom would have taken swift action. Recognizing the quality of Tom's passion, Ben felt uneasy. His gut stormed; his spirit tossed between a ravenous need for such purposed, thoughtful fathering and an aversion to any child suffering punishment at a father's will.

The contrast to his own father hurt bitterly. Dewar's Black Label determined Max's interaction with his sons, not a standard more dearly held. "He's going to have a big lump on his head," Ben mourned, his voice a choked whisper.

"Let's hope it does him some good," Joe whispered back.

"Don't," Ben said, miserably.

"To hit that hard, he must have been aiming for me," Tommy whispered, glancing at Ben.

"He really wasn't, Tommy," Laurie said. "He was throwing it to Joe."

"Can't aim."

"That may be but that's nothing to fight over."

"You don't understand," Tommy mumbled. "If I give in, on *anything*, they think I'm a wuss."

Tom met Ben's eyes and winked, offering a reassurance that Ben was too miserable to accept. "Joe, why don't you and Ben put those groceries away for me," he said, "while Mama and I talk some sense into this child."

As Ben followed Joe to the dim room off the kitchen, he heard Tom say, "You're ashamed because you got in the way of a speeding apple. This is foolish, Tommy."

"How old is he?" Ben asked, when they were behind the door.

"Eleven. But he thinks he's thirty."

"He's small for his age, isn't he?" He followed Joe into a crowded room. "Keith is eight and he's that big."

"That's why he's such a defensive maniac. Over here," Joe said, scooting around the washing machine and dryer that stood together directly inside the door.

"Does your dad always act like that?"

"Like what?"

"Tommy on his lap and everything. That was…" Ben's voice trailed off as he noticed how much food was stored in the room. Above the washer and dryer, and to the left, sturdy rows of shelves were crowded with more than thirty cereal boxes, packages of crackers, salted, unsalted, buttered and plain popcorn. Pretzels, bags of rice cakes, bundles of gum and bags of candy were piled up like sandbags to stay the flood. "What's all this?"

"Food."

"Food?" Ben murmured, staring.

"To eat," Joe said, glancing sideways at Ben from where he piled canisters of Pringles onto an old bookshelf stuffed to overflowing with baking supplies. Cans of baking powder stood in a stiff regiment beside a tumult of bags filled with chocolate chips. One shelf held ten jars of peanut butter beside cylinders of raisins. On the shelf beneath stood jars of tomatoes, bags of smooth white almonds, crowds of cherries, applesauce, jams colored like jewels.

"This isn't normal," Ben said, pointing toward his right where metal shelving racks held more.

Joe laughed and dragged another grocery bag past those racks and Ben followed. There was more! A narrow passageway of shelves holding cookbooks, colored pencils, rolls of tape, and a variety of hardback theology and philosophy books. This led them into an inner room crammed full of more food.

"This used to be the coal bin," Joe explained. "Dad made it into a pantry."

"This is scary, Joe." The volume defied the imagination. Here, jars of juice and dark brown honey, bottles of syrup, and golden jugs of olive oil caught the light from a small window above. Dozens of cans filled the next shelves. Ben noticed every possible tomato product, black olives, green olives, relish—ten *kinds* of relish—more pickles than Ben dreamed existed, catsup, mustard. Beneath these full shelves stood huge, round bins marked FLOUR and SUGAR and RICE. In the corner were cases of soda and a huge cardboard box that overflowed with chips and pretzels. "Holy shit," Ben said. "I've never seen so much food."

Grinning, Joe said, "Dad uses coupons and buys stuff only when it's on sale. If we want something and it's not on sale we have to wait."

"How could you want anything?"

"It happens," Joe said. He gave Ben two bags and steered him to the shelves at the end of the wall, where rows of deodorant, toothbrushes, school supplies, boxes of Band-Aids, soap and polish for every part of the body and every room in the house stood in abundant and cluttered order. Ben unpacked the bags, adding to stacks of notebook paper, filling the already crowded coffee can with the mechanical pencils he'd seen Joe use at school, supplementing the pile of Chapstick tubes and the clusters of suntan lotion. He glanced at Joe, who stuffed boxes of tea bags into the narrow space above the rows of coffee cans, and felt his emptiness deeper than hunger.

"Last year," Joe said coming up beside him, "when Tommy learned about tariffs, he made up a list of stuff that Dad wasn't allowed to buy until we used some of it. It made Dad so miserable. He gave away so much more than usual." They heard Tom call them.

When they emerged, Tom patted the bench next to him indicating that Ben should sit beside him. Reluctantly, Ben complied. He peered under the bundle of ice that Tom still held on Tommy's head to see the boy's face.

"I'm really sorry," Ben said. "I know that hurt you."

"It was going about ninety miles an hour," Tommy said, squinting hard at Ben. "I'm sure you didn't mean to throw it *that* hard, right *at me*—"

His father thumped his thigh lightly. Laurie scolded, "Tommy!"

"I really didn't," Ben said, shaking his head sadly. "I was *trying* to hit Joe."

Tommy looked at Joe, considered the idea, and laughed. "How'd you get it to drop like that?"

"That's my sinker."

"If you teach me," He stuck out his hand. "I'll forget all about this."

"There's a trick. I'll show you how I do it." Ben shook with him.

"Okay," Tommy said with the finality of the goal-oriented. "Let's go."

"After dinner," Laurie said. "I want to keep ice on his head."

Tom nudged Tommy off his knee, moving Tommy's own hand to hold the ice to his forehead. "That apple was smokin', Tommy. Now it's apple-*sauce*. You could learn something from Ben." He left them and Ben demonstrated the arm movement. Laurie got up and returned to her vegetables at the sink. Joe plunked down on the bench on the other side of Tommy and took a bite out of one of the apples Ben had dumped on the table.

Tom emerged a few minutes later wearing a T-shirt, gym shorts and socks. Ben stared at him, expecting his legs to be wasted muscle, the picture of disuse. But Tom looked normal and when he sat on the bench to put on his athletic shoes, Ben saw that Tom had noticed his worried glance and had accepted Ben's curiosity with a kind of amused tolerance. Ben had the feeling that if he had wanted to poke Tom's knees to see if they were sound or if the reflexes worked, Tom would have allowed it. But Ben was embarrassed and studied his own knuckles.

"Don't think I can whip you, do you?" Tom said with a sideways look.

"Sir, I—"

"You ready for a little hoop action? Little two on one? I'll bet you and Joe *together* can't beat me."

"Me, too," Tommy said. "I'm coming, too."

"No, you're not," Laurie said. "Not yet."

"Come out as soon as your mother lets you, Tommy," Tom said, eyeing Ben. "By then, Ben and Joe will need your help."

"I hate to prove my coach wrong," Ben said, his embarrassment dissipating as he caught Tom's excitement to play ball, sensed Tom's love of sport, his competitive nature rising as he yanked the ties of his shoes tight.

"You try to prove me wrong, son, and you'll find out who you're playing against."

"Playing against an old man," Joe said, holding the kitchen door open for Tom to follow Ben out.

"First to twenty-one by two," Tom said, stepping onto the concrete slab that served as their basketball court. "There's two of you, so I get the ball first."

"Not fair," Joe said, moving into position beneath the basket to guard Tom, but Ben moved to the side, and when Tom lifted the ball to begin his dribble, Ben reached beneath the ball, poked it up and free, caught it with his right hand and tossed it in a loop over his head to Joe. "Hey," Tom said, lunging sideways toward Joe, knocking his shot off. Ben jumped for the rebound, hooked it in with one hand. "That's two," they said in unison, grinning, and Joe put the ball into Tom's hands.

"I forgot to mention," Tom said, dribbling the ball to the edge of the court, "no stealing. That one doesn't count."

"Oh, there's stealing," Joe said, coming toward his father, hands extended, forcing Tom to move. "There's stealing." Seeing Ben to his left, Tom went right. Ben followed him, circling around behind Tom and staying to Tom's right while Joe occupied him, talking to him, thrusting his hands in Tom's face. The moment Tom moved, shifting his footing to shoot, Ben put his hand underneath the ball, tipped it up away from Tom, grabbed it and dribbled fast as a flood out to the foul line and shot, scoring from there. Tom and Joe exchanged glances.

"Four, zip. Your ball, Coach," Ben said, eyes wide and pleased.

"Come here and guard me." Crouching low, Tom dribbled, and Ben, guarding him, forced him around the court. As they played with the ball, Ben sensed the man's steadiness, glowed under his generous scrutiny, identified with his determination to win; Ben knew Tom was a good coach. He slapped at the ball, pretending to steal it. Tom gave Ben his shoulder, thrusting him away. "You're good," Tom said, panting, "but not good enough." He faked right and whirled left, rising up to shoot. Ben knocked it away again into Joe's hands. Joe took it to the foul line and passed it to Ben who jumped. Mid-air, he saw Bonnie Jean, walking down the driveway, her arm around the waist of a tall, slim, good-looking boy. They were laughing, obviously close friends. His shot wobbled around the rim and out.

Tom took the rebound easily. "You look like you saw a ghost," he teased. Dribbling out to the foul line, Tom saw the couple also. His dribble slowed as he stared.

Joe easily took the ball from him, and whispered to Ben, "My brother, Pete. Just in time." Ben knew physical relief. Joe dribbled three steps and shot, making the basket. "Six, zip, Dad," Joe laughed, but Tom had left the court and jogged, his limp noticeable again, down the driveway. They met at the corner of the house and Tom grabbed the boy, inches taller than himself, into a big embrace that was at once ferocious and tender.

"Happy Birthday, Dad."

"Everything all right?" Tom said, stepping back, his hands on the boy's shoulders. "You're not unhappy there, are you?"

"No, I love it. I couldn't miss your birthday. I got a ride from a girl in my dorm. Who's the ace?" Peter said, indicating Ben who stood at the edge of the court, basketball under his arm.

Tom took Peter to the court. "Ben Hunter. My oldest son, Pete."

They shook hands; Ben sensed Pete's strength of character, saw genuine friendliness in the expression of his dark brown eyes. His features were strong and straight, his hair longish and curly. He looked nothing like his father and Joe.

"Is this the same Ben you've been telling me about, Jeannie?" Peter asked.

"That's him," she said, her face a mask of impish delight.

"Hey, Jeannie," Ben said, noticing without staring at her brown legs, the hint of sunburn on her cheeks, how her knit shorts showed those sleek, tight curves.

"Where you been?" Joe asked.

"Band practice. Where were *you*? Adam and Paul had to cover for you."

"I thought they'd cancel because of the weather. There's a hurricane out there." He gestured eastward.

"Don't you check before you miss practice?" Tom said.

"Dad, honestly," Joe said, "Mrs. Miller never knows who's there or not. And if she does, she blames everything on Paul."

"That's not the point," Tom said.

"How was practice?" Ben asked to shift the conversation's focus.

"Hot. I nearly melted. All the boys had their shirts off. It's just not fair."

"Jeannie, I don't even want to hear you thinking that way," Tom warned.

"Don't worry, Dad, I'll leave the public nudity to Joe."

"Yeah, man. What's all this I hear about your prank?" Pete asked. The brothers shook hands, then embraced.

"Man, it's good to see you, Pete. I missed you."

"You'd better go in and say hello to your mother."

Peter laughed. "She was in on it. I got home at one-thirty and went to get Bonnie Jean at school. I tried to surprise you there, but they said you went to the grocery store." He looked at Ben, who was still holding the basketball under his arm. "Hey, let's play ball. Looks like you need my help, Dad."

Pete and Bonnie Jean joined their father's team. Bonnie Jean was graceful, quick and distracting. Peter scored once. Next round, Jeff and Drew arrived and joined them. Bonnie Jean muttered something about being outnumbered and skipped away into the house. A minute later, Jason jogged onto the court. Pete bragged that he and Tom alone together could easily beat all the others and in the next few minutes Ben regretted that he wouldn't be playing with this athlete at school. His love of the game, his clean style and formidable skill mirrored Ben's goals for himself. In his good-natured way, Peter proved a staunch competitor. From the back door, Bonnie Jean called something out about the grill. Tommy burst out of the kitchen and jumped on Peter's back, joining as an adversary to both sides, claiming he was playing an all-defense game. It had begun to rain again, first in fitful spurts, but when Tom left the game briefly to put the steaks on the grill, more steadily.

They quit when the steaks were nearly done. Joe dragged out a hose and turned it on his head until the cold water ran over his body in sheets. They took turns and while they were cooling off; Peter sent Tommy into the house for a towel. The boys shared this, rubbing it over their heads and whisking off the bits of wet grass stuck to their feet before they trooped through the kitchen to get dry clothes from the laundry room. Crowded in there beside the shelves of food, they changed. Joe gathered up the soggy clothes and threw them into the dryer. "Don't forget to change back before you leave," he called out as Drew left the room, a glimpse of orange boxer shorts showing above his gym shorts, "you're wearing my favorite boxers."

20

BEN stood beside the pantry door, watching the action, waiting for someone to tell him where to sit. While Tom and Laurie brought the food to the table, the extra guests got plates from the corner cupboard, searched in the drawer for forks and knives and took places along the benches on either side of the table. Bonnie Jean and Peter brought more glasses to the table; Joe passed around napkins. Tommy struggled to carry a large tub of ice. Ben went to help him and found himself swept into the activity. Everyone seemed to know where to sit, and their movement to the table carried Ben there, too.

Tom tried to establish an order for passing the food, but Peter was describing his classes and the people he met in an animated way while Jeff teased Tommy and Drew told Jason and Bonnie Jean about how his grandfather had gotten a fish hook stuck in his scalp. Bonnie Jean made sympathetic or agonizing faces in response, rousing bursts of laughter from anyone who looked up to observe. Smiling slightly, Tom gave up his attempt at order and heaped food on his plate, then on Tommy's, before he passed each bowl to Peter.

Peter expressed his delight by repeating, "Wow," and shaking his head in wonder as each dish was passed to him. Ben was grateful for the audible expression of his own wonder, but he dared take only a little. Joe passed a small salad bowl to him, full of bright greens, tossed with dark red tomatoes, peppers, and purple, yellow and orange flowers. Ben took it from him using both hands, careful with it, with the treasure of it. He looked around the table. They were all watching him, smiling as people do at children opening presents. He felt his hunger keenly and with it the odd and compelling notion that he was wanted. In the panic of disbelief, Ben glanced to Laurie and to Tom and saw echoes of the same welcome defined in the expression around their eyes. He looked down, breathed in the fragrance of the food, unable to accept that he was really awake.

The table quieted and Tom held out his hands. Peter took one of Tom's hands and Jeff the other; they all joined hands and Tom bowed his head. Ben's shyness flushed hot in his throat and his ears pounded so that he heard Tom's simple thanksgiving prayer the way a child hears night noises from beneath his pillow.

For just a moment, a hush came upon the table and everyone took a soft breath. Somehow in unison, they all knew to break hands. Conversations began anew and Ben lifted his eyes and caught Bonnie Jean watching him. Her expression, as it had been on the first day of school when he noticed the fresh bloom of her tan skin, was lively and interested, her eyes entirely unguarded and full of affection. She looked away, her dark eyes glancing at her mother and Joe.

"What are you looking for," Joe asked her, with a quick glance at Ben, "the salt and pepper?"

"Huh?" She studied her salad. "Yes. Where is it?"

"Which one do you want?" Jeff said.

"The pepper."

"Right in front of you," Tommy said, picking them up from where they stood between she and Ben and thunking them down beside her water glass.

"What's wrong, Jeannie?" Joe said, slowly, his voice teasing. "You seem upset."

"It's nothing."

"Did you have a good day, darling?" Laurie asked.

"Except for math," she said, almost brutally. "I got an awful grade on my math test."

"What went wrong?" Tom asked.

"I don't know. I just don't get this stuff. I told you I couldn't skip ahead."

"You got a ninety," Joe said. "That's not awful."

"You got a hundred and so did he—so did Ben."

"We had this last year," Joe and Ben said at once.

"I'd pay cold, hard cash to get a ninety on anything," Jeff said.

"It's hopeless," she said.

"It is not hopeless," her father said.

"Not for you, Jeannie," her mother said.

"In fact, I'd eat seventeen worms to get an *eighty-five* on anything," Jeff added.

"Jeff," Tom said, "you earn good grades by studying, not by stunts."

"I thought I understood it. I even checked my answers three times."

"But, Jeannie," Ben said, "it means you understood ninety percent of what she asked." He wanted her to look at him, but her eyes came up no further than the top of the potato salad that stood between them on the table.

Jeff said, "How much do I have to eat before I can have my Pringles?"

"Steak, a vegetable, and your salad," Laurie said.

"Are rolls vegetables?"

"No, but the jam is," Drew said.

"Just to be honest, Jeannie, I don't see how you missed the ones you did," Joe scolded, "Dr. D. told us what was going to be on the test. She showed us how to do those problems yesterday."

"That should be enough for you," Laurie said.

"When Dr. D. made Ben solve the example on the board," Joe said, "that was your chance to make sure you got it."

"Ben at the board—bet she couldn't concentrate."

Bonnie Jean raised hostile eyes to Jeff. "That is *so* not true."

"She asked a couple of questions," Ben said quickly, "so she must have been paying attention."

"Oh, I wouldn't be too sure," Jeff smirked.

"No, listen," Ben spoke quickly. "I've noticed when you start a word problem, you freeze up and start drawing flowers."

"Flowers?" her father said, "You're drawing flowers in class?"

"It helps me concentrate."

"Evidently not enough," Joe said.

She looked up, her eyes guarded, annoyed. "How do you know I'm drawing flowers? You look at my paper during the test?"

"No," Ben said, laughing a little, enjoying her defensiveness. "But when I'm done, I turn my paper over and you know, kind of look around. The flowers caught my attention."

"It must be nice to be so darn smart you get done before everyone else."

"Yeah," Joe said. "Poor Bonnie Jean. Good thing Ben doesn't sit next to you. He'd be tempted to cheat during the test, you poor math-handi-capped girl."

Ben said, "No, think about it. With word problems, you have to recognize basic patterns. The real challenge is to turn the words into mathematical symbols. If you're going to draw when you're stuck, why not draw a representation of the problem? Once you do that, you can forget about the words and solve it just like a normal equation."

"Oh," she said.

"She gets it," Peter said.

"Yeah, I can do that."

"Anyway," Drew said, "If I could sing the way you do, Bonnie Jean, I wouldn't worry about math."

"Maybe not as much, anyway," Jason said.

"Oh, that's right," Laurie said, "How did your solo go in chapel?"

"Okay. Not as good as you heard me rehearse it, Mama."

"It was beautiful, Laurie," Tom said.

"Oh, I wish I had canceled that worthless class and come."

"You really didn't miss much, Mrs. MacBride," Jeff teased, "It was kind of squeaky."

"That's what everyone was saying at the middle school," Tommy said, grinning. "That it was squeaky."

"It's all over campus," Joe said, "Squeaky little math-handicapped girl."

"I'm the only girl in the world with a hundred stinkin' brothers."

"I thought it was beautiful," Ben said, and she met his eyes for one happy moment.

21

AS they took their plates to the sink, Tom and Laurie announced that they were going for a walk. And though the rest of the guests wandered away, saying they were going downstairs to play video games, the MacBrides began the kitchen clean-up. Ben stayed to help.

Joe was scrubbing a spot on the stove top when Pete said, "Head's up, Joe," and tossed an apple at him. Joe glanced up, caught it, said, "Jeannie," and tossed it to Bonnie Jean, who threw it to Tommy.

Tommy flung it at Ben. "Is that how you do it?"

"As soon as we're done cleaning up, I'll show you outside," Ben said, pitching it back to Tommy in a quick, clean arc that the boy caught easily.

"Hey, good catch," Ben said.

Tommy hurled the apple at Ben.

"Not so hard," Joe warned.

"You're allowed to throw things in the house?" Ben bounced the apple from hand to hand; it was so smooth and hard that it made a crisp slap when he caught it.

"Sure," Joe said, "but in this game, we go age order. You're the newbie, so you have to throw it back to Pete."

Hurrying through their tasks, they kept the apple in the air and Ben discovered that the game was complicated. Age order could not be broken, you could hold the apple no longer than five seconds. You tried to choose chores that gave you a throwing or catching advantage so that no one wanted to shake out the tablecloth and replace it, because that required two hands and several changes of location. Abandoning a chore for more than ten seconds meant you were skipped for the next turn.

Peter remained unruffled when he dropped the apple because Tommy distracted him with a noise that sounded like a jet splitting the sound barrier, but Joe scolded Tommy, his eyes flashing. Bonnie Jean threw equally well with her right and left hand. Tommy was a wild man who held others to the rule with an authoritative severity, but refused to comply, resorting to hiding under the table to cause Bonnie Jean to hold the apple for longer than five seconds, or trying to distract his brothers so that they would miss their catch.

Somehow, in the midst of the chaos, Joe was keeping score. Suspiciously, everyone agreed, Joe led, followed by Bonnie Jean and Tommy who were tied. Peter's one fumble had dropped him to just above Ben, who did not yet understand the scoring system and hoped it would all come clear as he played. They were nearly finished with the kitchen chores, when Ben, who was sweeping the floor, caught Tommy's pitch and swiftly threw the apple to Peter who was helping Bonnie Jean replace the tablecloth.

"A hornet!" Tommy squealed, pointing. Startled, Peter leapt away and missed the apple, which zoomed past his shoulder and hit the teapot, knocking it off the mantle. Peter reached for it, but it bounced on the table edge and smashed on the hearth.

A rush of warm humid air surrounded Ben and in that fleeting second, Ben realized that the door had opened behind him. He turned to flee, his speed immediate and desperate; he smashed into Tom, his mouth and chin striking Tom's shoulder as his weight forced Tom back into the doorjamb. Blindly, Ben sensed his direction and spun left to go. Tom's hand caught Ben's wrist, stopping him in a stinging and inexorable grasp that frightened him to his core.

"Whoa, son."

Ben struggled; Tom held on, his arm going around Ben's shoulder. "Hey, settle down." Tom said. "No need to run."

"I'll pay for it. I'll replace it. Let me go."

"No, you'll stay."

"Please, Coach. Let me go."

"I will not." Something steady in the man's voice stopped Ben. He realized the frantic cowardice of his behavior and, humiliated, could not look up and meet Tom's eyes as he knew Tom wanted. Tom took Ben's shoulders in his hands and turned Ben to face him. He spoke quietly. "It's just a piece of clay. I won't let you run from us over a piece of clay."

"It's not just a piece of clay to Mrs. MacBride."

"She'll feel the same way I do."

"Here she comes, Dad."

"Now," Tom said, still grasping Ben's shoulders, still bending forward slightly, speaking to Ben's bowed head. "You can tell her honestly what happened."

"No, I can't."

"You can do this, Ben. You reach down deep and pull up your courage and face this." His voice dropped to a whisper. "I promise you, she will not reject you."

Ben looked up and found in Tom's expression a confidence so bright it was fierce.

Laurie rounded the back of the garage slowly, a bunch of herbs in one hand, the other holding her low, round belly. The wind gusted at her back, filling her shirt, ruffling her hair. Tom's children gathered behind Ben a living, breathing support.

"Stick your lip out so it looks more swollen," Joe advised.

"It really wasn't your fault, Ben," Bonnie Jean said.

"I'll tell her. It's my fault too," Peter said. "I missed the catch."

"And mine," Tommy added in a gruff voice. "I distracted Pete on purpose."

"Ben needs to say it first," Tom said.

"What's wrong?" Laurie demanded when she saw them.

"Laurie, something's happened."

"What? Is everyone all right?" She quickly scanned the faces. "Your lip, Ben."

"He smashed into my shoulder."

"What is going on here? Tom, I've told you not to wrestle with these children."

Ben straightened his back. "Mrs. MacBride, I—"

"Is it bleeding?"

"No, Mrs. MacBride, *please*."

"Listen to him, Laurie." Tom's arm went around Ben's shoulder again. "Steady, now."

"I broke your teapot. The one on the mantle. "

For a moment, the silent tension of held breath.

"Katie's teapot?" Laurie asked Tom. He nodded. "I don't believe it," Laurie whispered.

All her children spoke at once. "We were playing the clean-up game—"

"Peter missed it."

"It was my fault. I yelled—"

Ben cut in. "I'll get another one." Laurie shook her head. "I'll find one exactly the same. You won't even remember that I—"

"I know you didn't mean it," she said and indicated by gesture and movement that they were to enter the kitchen. Her family followed her cue and Laurie took Ben by the arm and brought him into the kitchen where she made him sit on the bench. Tom sat down next to him, stretching his arm out on the table behind Ben in a gesture of support.

"Please, Mrs. MacBride. I'll look for one just like it," Ben said. "I won't quit until I find one."

"Mama, let him try," Bonnie Jean said. "We'll all pitch in to pay for it."

Laurie shook her head. "It can't be replaced."

"Listen, Mrs. MacBride. My grandmother knows how to get old stuff. She deals in antiques and—"

"No." She stood over Ben, bending to see him closely over her bulging stomach. She touched his face lightly with her fingertips at the corner of his jaw, tipping his face up to her. "Let me see how badly hurt you are."

"It's *noth*ing."

"Come on, now." She cradled his jaw in her hand, her touch careful. "Let me see inside your lip." Her touch capable and insistent, he looked up and opened his mouth.

"You lip is all bruised. It's purple in there. And swollen." A look of intense pain blanched her features. She shuddered, breathed deeply. "Oh, this is terrible." She moved the ice pack toward his lip, but he prevented it, raising his hand, ducking his face away.

"I can't let you take care of me when I destroyed something you obviously love so much."

Laurie gave up trying to place the ice pack and let her arms drop.

"What makes you think I loved that teapot so much?"

"I just know it," Ben said, meeting her eyes, thinking, trying to explain. "It was the place in the room that your eyes went to. And you had it surrounded by family pictures. I know you love your family, so…" he faltered, his voice shaking, and the terror that had driven him to run revived inside, shaking his stomach.

"I loved the teapot because your mother gave it to me," she said, her eyes bright and direct. "I loved it because she was lost to me. And you with her. But now you're here. Do you really think I could care more for a bit of clay than for you? Yes, I loved it, but let's face it: there's no comparison."

He opened his mouth to protest, but found he couldn't. Instead he lifted his chin. She touched the ice pack to his lip. Their eyes met again in a moment of deep understanding.

"Mrs. MacBride," Ben said, the hope in his voice muffled by the ice pack, "maybe now that we're living here, you and Mom can get reacquainted."

"Ben," Laurie said, her voice sounding slightly offended, insistent, even impatient.

He searched her face, trying to understand. *Why do I feel like she's warning me not to lie?*

"Ben, I'm talking about *your mother*."

Ben nodded, ashamed. "You're right. She wouldn't be into that." He faltered, further ashamed of his disloyalty. "I guess she's changed a lot since you were friends with her."

Laurie's expression clouded painfully again. She reached for the back of the chair and held it. She glanced at her children, who stood close and silent and still. She looked at Tom, her expression pleading. Tom sat forward and again encircled Ben's shoulders with one arm. "Ben, you don't need to apologize for your parents."

"Coach—"

"No, let me finish. It's just that there have been disagreements between your parents and us, Ben, ugly disagreements that ruined our friendships. We don't want that to happen with you. Not over a teapot…or anything else."

For some reason, they wanted him. Though Ben did not understand the logic of this, he knew it was true: he could feel it as keenly as he could feel the intense cold from the ice that had penetrated his lip just enough to make it ache. Laurie saw the confused pain in his eyes. She touched his jaw right behind his ear. "Does it hurt?"

"Yes, ma'am."

"The ice will help." Again, a shudder passed through her composure and her expression ignited in anger. "Though it is a shame you were hurt," her voice tightened abruptly.

"You okay, Mom?" Joe asked, just as Bonnie Jean said, "Mama?"

"I'm just wondering," she said as she shot Tom an angry look, "why the first time this child is in our home, he's injured?"

"You're not blaming Dad, are you, Mom?" Peter asked.

"Laurie," Tom said. "It was an accident."

"But how did you manage to smash his lip, Tom?"

"I don't go around smashing lips, Laurie. My shoulder just happened to be in his way."

"I ran into *him*, Mrs. MacBride," Ben said.

The others agreed, all talking at once.

"And anyway, my lip was pretty cut up earlier in the week when—um—at the accident. I bet the bruises are from that." Her eyes softened again, brightening with tears and she nodded. Ben laughed self-consciously and said, "I'll bet Tom's shoulder's pretty bruised."

"You call him Tom?" Peter laughed. "Tom? To his face? You're all right."

"He thinks he's immune to my wrath just because he's hurt." Tom said, bumping Ben's shoulder with his own. "Here, Laurie, look at my shoulder. See if Ben's right." Tom stretched open the neck of his T-shirt.

"It looks like you bit him!" Tommy yelled.

"You'll be all right," Laurie said coolly.

"Yeah," Joe said, "just walk it off, Dad."

"Hey, you," Tom said, grabbing Joe in a headlock. Joe grabbed his father around his waist and pretended to thrust his shoulders into Tom's chest.

"Tom, don't," Laurie said. "Not today."

"I won't hurt him, just soften him up a little," Tom said, pounding on Joe's back with his flat palm, making a hollow booming sound. "He needs it."

Joe struggled to get away, laughing loud and high. He snuck his fingers up into Tom's armpit and poked. Tom jumped, yelping, but held on, pounding Joe's back.

Tommy threw himself at his father's legs, knocking Joe and Tom back into the kitchen door.

"Tom," Laurie warned.

Drew and Jason and Jeff came upstairs, delighted with the fray, ready to join, but Laurie cut in firmly. "Time for dessert," she said, "Now or never." She began giving directions: Peter was to get the dessert plates, Jeff, the candles, Drew should look for some vanilla ice cream in the downstairs freezer, and in moments the group was moving like a team. Bonnie Jean made coffee, Tommy and Jeff stuck as many candles as they could into the lemon meringue pie, Joe set out a jug of milk; Peter filled a pitcher with ice water, while Laurie set out glasses and mugs.

Tom disappeared into his pantry and emerged with a paper bag, a dust pan and whisk broom. He motioned for Ben to come around the backside of the table, and together they squatted to clean up the teapot's rubble. The bustle going on around them, above them, as they crouched there gave Ben a feeling of privacy. Tom's amused, content expression invited Ben to voice his questions. "Hey, Coach," Ben said.

"What, Ben?"

"Um…let's just say…what would you have done to Joe if *he* had broken the teapot?"

Tom glanced at Ben, read the intent of the question and swung into play as easily as if Ben had been probing this way all his life. "Was Joe angry when he threw the apple?"

"Let's say no, he wasn't," Ben said.

"I'd tell him shake it off, clean it up, and replace it."

"Then why can't I replace it?"

"Mrs. MacBride wanted you to know how important you are to us."

"Joe's important to you."

"Absolutely. But you know, Ben, I probably never would have thought of it this way if you hadn't broken it—but it's almost as if the teapot was holding your place. It was something we had from your mother. Now that you're here, we don't need it the same way. Any teapot will do to make tea, but we don't need reminders now that you're here. I think that's it."

Ben's hand closed over the perfectly circular base of the teapot.

"Careful," Tom said, "it's sharp."

Ben recognized the distinctive, back-slanted handwriting in which *Laurie* was written in red crayon on the white porcelain. It resembled his own. "Did Mrs. MacBride write this?" Ben asked.

"No, your mother did. She bought it for Laurie."

He hadn't noted this likeness before, this readable connection to his formal, distant mother. *Were there other unmistakable things that linked them?* "Can I keep this?"

"If you want."

Ben slid it into his pocket. Tom handed him the whisk broom so he could sweep the corner of the hearth Tom could not reach. "Coach, if Joe *had* been angry when he threw the apple, what would you have done?"

"Why was he angry?"

"Why does that matter?"

Tom made a gesture to say the answer was obvious. "I can't work with a kid I don't understand."

"Oh." Ben had expected an answer as melting and sweet as a small, round mint. But Tom, he saw, for all his humor and generosity, played for keeps.

Tom squinted at Ben. "First I'd have to find out why Joe was angry. If we couldn't talk about it, I'd wait it out," Tom said, still squinting at Ben.

"If he can't talk—I mean if he refuses to talk—how do you find stuff out?"

"Sometimes it's obvious why a kid—I mean *Joe*—is angry. You know, he flubbed a test, had a bad day at school—some event. If it isn't obvious, I'd hang around with him, I guess. Help him with his chores, do some fun stuff with him, hoping to win his confidence or hoping I'd understand just by being with him."

"Okay," Ben said. "What else?"

"I'd have to see if his anger was just."

"He still shouldn't smash things even if his anger is justified."

"True, I'd have to correct Joe about that…"

"Yeah, I thought so. I thought you'd think that."

"You're one step ahead of me, son. You win this round."

Though Tom smiled, Ben nodded seriously. He understood the tacit explanation, the promise implicit in their conversation, and he understood that he and Tom would play this game again, many times again, until Ben's hunger, his need to know how a father loved, was satisfied. He felt far too full for dessert.

Laurie squeezed behind Ben and Tom to place forks around the hearth side of the table, putting one hand on the edge of the hutch as if to steady herself.

"What should we do with these fragments, Laurie?"

"Oh, I don't know."

"Pitch them?"

"Maybe I can use them for drainage in those clay pots."

"Okay. Ben can put them in the garage for you."

Laurie said, "No," her tone gone firm, distant, troubled.

Tom said, "I'll tell him exactly where to find the bag."

But Laurie thrust the forks she held onto the table in a jumbled pile. "This won't work." Her tone was so strained that the room went quiet, all motion stopped. Ben assumed that the reality of the broken teapot had hit her. He froze, crouched there on the floor, dreading the ugly fury of rejection.

"What?" Tom said, getting up, pushing up with both hands flat on the bench. "What won't work?"

"I thought I had time to serve dessert, but the contractions keep coming every two minutes."

"What contractions?" Tom said, stepping over Ben. He was beside her in one stride, his arm around her waist. "When did this start?"

"A while ago."

"A while ago meaning *what*?" Tom said.

"You mean for the baby?" Ben said, coming alive, getting up.

"No wonder you've been acting so weird," Joe said, entering.

"Wait a second. *How* long ago?" Tom demanded.

"Since dinner."

"I'll get your bag, Mama," Bonnie Jean said. "Where is it?"

"I haven't packed it yet. But the baby's bag is ready."

"I'll pack it," Bonnie Jean said, rushing from the room.

"I can't wait. I've got to go now."

"I'll take Mom in the van," Tom said. "You kids come over in my car once Jeannie's got the bag together."

"Do I have to come, Coach?" Jason said. "I—"

"Drew and I will stay here and clean up," Jeff offered.

Tom turned his attention to Laurie. "Can you walk?"

"If we hurry."

"Scoot out ahead of us," Tom commanded Ben. But Laurie stopped Ben at the end of the table, touching his elbow. "Come with the other children to the hospital?"

"I wouldn't miss it," Ben said.

"I wanted you to have your dessert."

"No, I'm full. I'm so full."

She nodded at him, her eyes bright with tears. "I've got to go," she murmured, distracted. But she paused to kiss Joe and Tommy and Peter on her way out the door. "Tell Jeannie I need my make-up, my pillow, and something to quilt."

"Don't worry, we'll get everything," Peter said.

"Here's another one," Laurie said quietly. Tom and Laurie drew together to endure the contraction, his arm around her back, her arm around his waist as she leaned on him for support.

"Breathe, my love," Tom coached in a whisper, and Laurie breathed deliberately, her face quiet, concentrating. When she relaxed, they began toward the door again. "You kids hurry," Tom called over his shoulder. "The baby will be here within the hour."

22

"REMEMBER that close call with Tommy," Tom said, as he helped Laurie into the car. She suffered another contraction and he squatted beside her to help her endure. "After Tommy you promised me you'd tell me earlier the next time," Tom said, starting the car.

"I didn't think we'd have any more babies," she said.

"So you were merely pacifying me," Tom shook his head; turning to back out of the driveway, he glanced over to smile at her. "You okay?"

"Tom, he doesn't know anything about his mother."

"I knew that was what you were fishing for. That's why you stayed around, wasn't it?"

"We have to tell him."

"Let's concentrate on this baby right now."

"I can't until everything is settled with Ben."

"Laurie, please. *Everything* may *never* be settled with Ben."

"Tom, you promised."

Tom drew a long breath and glanced at his determined wife. "Think about it, Laurie—" She held up her hand to stop him and bowed her head, both her quick, neat hands going to hold her belly. "Remember to breathe, Laurie, don't hold your breath." She nodded, enduring. Tom accelerated, thinking that the contractions were coming far too quickly.

"Hurry," she said when it ended.

"Don't worry. I've delivered babies before, ma'am," he said grinning, but his eyes were serious, remembering other such dangerous moments and when he looked at Laurie, he saw the same memory mirrored in his wife's dark eyes.

"Something about you," she said, "brings babies quickly. Human Pitocin."

"You're just as vigorous as a girl, that's all."

"You can't humor me out of intending to tell Ben."

"We have to win his confidence first. Think about it. If he knows nothing—really nothing—"

"As it seems."

"If that's true, it must mean he's been intentionally deceived all his life. If we tell him, what will that do to his family life? To find out from people who are really strangers—we've known him less than one week—that his parents have lied to him." Tom came to a hard stop at the curb outside the emergency room entrance to the city hospital. "We're here."

"I would think you, of all people, Tom MacBride, would be concerned with the truth."

"I'm concerned with the boy. As you are," Tom said firmly, not allowing himself to say that he dreaded the inevitable confrontation with Max Hunter. "Is that another contraction?"

By the way she gripped his hand, Tom knew the moment when the baby's head crowned and Tom understood her intensity. He could feel that and her surprising exhilaration. But he was a man; he knew no physical pain as she did now, and stood apart from her shuddering concentration that brought to his thumping heart a mixture of pity and deep respect. He wanted to pull closer to her, somehow to touch and know her inexplicable connection to life.

In a rush of life, the baby was born.

"A girl!"

A short while later, the baby examined, tested, and wrapped in a flannel blanket with a white knit cap on her round, dark head, she was given to Laurie, who took her in trembling arms and nestled her to her breast.

"Such dark hair. Oh, what a beautiful face."

"Cara," Laurie breathed.

A hush settled over the room and Tom took several heated blankets and bundled them over Laurie's knees and across her lap. Eyes squeezed shut, the baby nursed eagerly. They delighted in her, memorizing the newborn, salt smell of her, the silken feel of her fine, dark hair, the way her little ears lay flat, the way her fingers curled around Tom's.

"Should I run and tell your children?" the nurse asked quietly. "They're right outside the door listening."

Tom and Laurie laughed. "Tell them they can see her in a few minutes."

When Laurie was settled in her room, a pediatric nurse took the baby for further tests and a bath. Her children stayed with her, but Tom, not wanting the baby to be alone, followed Cara to the nursery. He was permitted to watch if he promised not to interfere. They warned that the baby might cry, but he convinced them to let her hold his finger, and so attached by his daughter's tight grip, he witnessed Cara's first bath. When she was clean, weighed and measured, and placed beneath golden warming lights, she clung to Tom's finger in an inexorable grip that captured Tom's heart.

"I'm sorry," a brisk voice sounded in the quiet nursery, scraping across the soft, sleeping sounds of babies. "Parents are not allowed inside the newborn nursery, sir."

He looked across the room and recognized Donna Boswell by her peculiar tense posture. Beyond that, her looks had changed considerably in the last fifteen years. When she attended Rising Sun, her hair had been much darker, always a little messy, but now she glowed with yellow blond hair, which had been precisely cut and glued strictly in place. Her make-up and brightly painted fingernails were noticeable even at his distance and her slight figure seemed muscular. It took her a moment longer to recognize him and when she did, he unbent himself from cooing to Cara, stood as straight as he could with his forefinger captured in the baby's hand, and smiled. "Hello, Donna," he said, hoping he sounded merely friendly, hoping that neither anger, nor bitterness, nor the pity he felt sounded in his voice.

"Tom MacBride?" she said crossing the room, looking as brisk as the veteran nurse that she had become. "What are you doing here?"

"Laurie just gave birth to our beautiful, little daughter." Tom indicated the baby that clutched his finger, but Donna did not so much as glance at her.

"At her age?"

Tom smiled. "I can see you're in charge here and I've broken a rule. Sorry about that. I didn't want to miss anything."

Flattered by his notice of her position, Donna's face relaxed in a smile that was more vulnerable and shy than pleased. Tom read her name tag, and stared at the new surname *Hunter*. To stop the bittersweet rush of pity, he spoke quickly. "Wow, the *head* nurse," he said. "Congratulations, Donna. I'm happy for you."

"Are you?"

"*Of course* I am."

"I suppose it's beneath you to hold a grudge against me."

"For the lawsuit? You did what you felt was right. I choose to respect that. You won; I respect the court's judgment, as you know."

"I was told that you would never comply, but—"

Tom recognized Max Hunter's opinion of him in her remark. He sensed it was meant to attack his integrity and said, "You know me better than that, Donna. You knew I would meet my responsibilities. Whatever they shaped up to be. We all answer to God, ultimately."

She looked around to see if they were alone. "I have two sons of my own, now, Tom," she whispered, her throat flushing bright red.

Tom pressed his lips together and nodded. "Donna, I'm so happy for you."

"I don't know how you can mean that."

"I *do* mean it."

"But it proves you were right."

"It proves only that God has blessed you."

"Does it?"

"Of course. Laurie will be thrilled to see you, Donna."

She looked up, tears in her eyes. "Tom, it would be a mistake for you to try to contact Max."

"I thought since Ben was enrolled in my school, that Max might be ready to talk things out."

She shook her head.

"I have things I've got to talk to him about, Donna. I've tried—"

"You need to stay away from him."

"It's been years—"

"Time won't help with this."

"I think it will help to discuss what really happened with Ben."

"The only thing that will help is if you ignore Ben and act as if we don't exist."

Tom squinted, considering whether to tell her about the promise he'd made about Ben, wondering if she could understand—*really* understand—things like loyalty and duty and the kind of heartfelt commitment that remains alive despite circumstances and lawsuits and years rushing past over feelings as hard as stone. If she did understand, would it make a difference? Or was pacifying Max Hunter ever and again his wife's main task?

"The last thing we need right now is *you*, trying to meddle," she added with a severity that chilled Tom.

"Me? Meddle?" Tom said, forcing a smile.

She shrugged, her face grave and unapologetic. "You've been known to in the past."

"Remember, Donna, it was you who taught me to care for my own children *first*, before worrying about other people's problems."

She took this as flattery, again blushing pink. "Oh, yes. I suppose that was me."

"Thank you for that," Tom said, trying to squelch the emotion in his voice. "And thanks for letting me stay with my baby girl," Tom said. "You see, I learned my lesson well."

As Donna hurried away, she said to the nurse approaching Cara's bassinet, "He can stay. But no others."

23

JOE and Ben left Laurie's room a few minutes after Tom did to find Laurie "a good, hot cup of tea." They passed a shadowed corridor that led to the newborn nursery. At the end of it, Tom stood half-bent over Cara's bassinet.

"Look, there's Dad," Joe said, laughing at Tom's absurd half-bent position.

"Uh-oh." Ben said, backing into the shadow at the corner. "That's my mother he's talking to. She works here."

"Let's go see," Joe said, starting down the corridor.

"No," Ben whispered.

"Why? We might find out what they were mad about. Or something interesting."

"No."

"Look, Dad made her smile." Joe said.

In the dim light, Ben could see more clearly and noticed her vulnerability. The emotion in Donna's expression showed in her brief, tentative smile. Keeping to the shadows, Joe crept closer. Afraid of what Joe would do, Ben grabbed Joe's arm at the elbow. "No closer," he whispered. "She won't be happy to see me." Joe stopped, his back straightening with a quick agility that indicated his alarm. He turned to Ben eyes alert.

"I ditched my brothers to hang out with you guys, and now I show up at her work. She won't think hanging out at a hospital is a good reason for leaving my responsibilities."

Joe's eyes swept over Ben once as if he would find a more plausible explanation in Ben's posture or stature. Ashamed of his evasion, Ben shoved his hands into his pockets, deciding to allow Joe's scrutiny. When their eyes met, Joe said, "Let's go find Mom that cup of tea."

When Joe asked at the main desk if there was somewhere they could get their mother, who had just had a baby, a cup of tea, the nurse was so delighted that she took them back to the small kitchen where she gave them free reign. Joe opened the floodgates of his charm, insisting that they make the tea exactly as his mother liked it. He couldn't use the microwave; Joe explained that his mother had taught him to bring the water to a full rolling boil and boil it not a moment longer. The nurses—first one, then another, and a third—were so impressed with his consideration that they managed to find him a tray, a pink mug, and a china teapot, which Ben scrubbed clean in the little sink.

"Your mother sure is lucky to have sons like you," one nurse purred as Joe demonstrated the way he'd been taught to pour the boiling water directly onto the tea bags to release the most flavor.

"She's pretty much crazy about us," Joe said with a glance that told Ben that he must not correct her. But Joe had no need to worry. Ben would never break the subtle spell that bound him now in this fragile fantasy, in this living mirror of his fervent, late-night prayers. He knew how to pretend.

"I know which one of you is the extrovert, but which one is older? Twins always have one of each."

"How did you guess we were twins?" Joe's eyes were bright with amusement.

"I knew the moment I saw you."

Joe grinned, "I'm older though Ben is, you know, better looking and bigger."

"Just as good looking," she corrected, "not better."

"Our grade point averages are almost identical," Ben said, "but mine is slightly higher."

"Don't worry," she said, patting Joe's shoulder, "with your personality."

"I'll carry the tray," Ben said, "since I'm the stronger one."

"I'll lead the way," Joe said, "if one of you kind ladies will point me in the right direction." He laughed, helpless and merry at once. Joe called out his thanks, but all fond smiles, they hushed him, reminding him of his whereabouts and the hour.

Peter met them at the door. "Where have you been? I sent Jeannie and Tommy to find you two."

In the small, square room the lights were dimmed. Laurie, sitting in the bed, looked frail. She shivered despite the layers of white blankets over her and around her shoulders. Ben's heart burned in panic. "Boys," she murmured, smiling faintly, eyes brightening. She held out one hand. "What a welcome sight."

"Us or the tea?" Joe teased.

"Both, of course."

Ben placed the tray down on the rolling table beside the bed. "It's hot. We just made it."

"Bring it closer so I can reach, please," Laurie said, her voice happy, but strained.

"I'll pour it, Mrs. MacBride."

"Can you? Oh, thank you."

"Put in lots of sugar and cream," Pete directed. "She's pretty shaky."

Ben nodded, working carefully, despite the urgency he felt. He took the steaming mug to Laurie and she held it in both hands. "Thank you, Ben," she said. She sipped, drank deeply. "Perfect."

"Are you feeling all right?" Ben said.

"Blissful." She drank from her cup again and sighed. "I'm going to drink an entire bucket of tea."

"Mrs. MacBride," Ben said, "You would have been proud of Joe. He charmed his way to getting this pot of tea."

"I always said you could talk the spots off a leopard," Laurie smiled at Joe. "Joe has *always* gotten his way because of his personality."

"He hasn't *always* gotten his way," Peter teased.

Ben took Laurie's empty mug from her, handed it to Peter, who refilled it, adding a teaspoon of sugar, a generous dollop of cream. "No, not always," Ben agreed with a grin at Joe.

"I have the feeling you boys are talking about something you shouldn't be," Laurie said, taking the mug from Peter. She scanned their faces, took another grateful drink. "Oh, I know, you're talking about his awful behavior around Tiffany. Joe, I'd think you'd feel some shame for that."

"I do feel shame. You have no idea."

Laurie shook her head, her smile and her sleepy eyes knowing. "I want my boys to be noble."

"Yes, ma'am," Joe said with a reflexive kind of sincerity that showed the subject was familiar.

"What do you think could be keeping Dad and the baby?" Peter asked.

"Don't they have to test her and fingerprint her?"

"Fingerprint?" Laurie said through a wide yawn.

"For the birth certificate," Ben said.

"They take footprints."

"And they make the birth certificate from that?"

"There's a hospital birth certificate with footprints. Then somebody—I forget who—brings state forms so her name is spelled right. They send you the official one a few weeks later."

Ben observed Laurie closely. Though her eyes closed frequently, her color had improved, her trembling seemed gone. She looked tired, but well and happy. He would have liked to touch her arm to make sure the trembling had fled.

His mother had been so sick after Keith had been born; even worse after Tim. Still and staring as a statue, Donna had shown no emotion but irritation at Gran's clumsy attempts to help. Though Gran could arrange anything, she could not manage people well, and around those who felt ill and were inexplicably sad, Gran became downright bumbling. *There's a difference between lifeless and tired,* Ben told himself as sudden tears stung his eyes. *She's sturdy; she'll be all right.*

But the same protective urge that had driven him to care tirelessly for Donna rose up in him again. Here in the dimly lit hospital room, Peter sank into the armchair beside his mother's bed and Joe hoisted himself up onto the deep windowsill. The setting sun reached trembling orange fingers through the swift gray clouds and threw Joe's shadow across the room and onto the floor in a wide and unsteady splash.

Now the possibilities of danger rose to flood Ben's mind. What if Laurie was not as well as she seemed? Maybe there was something he had not anticipated in his absorption with this family. He saw the light change in the hallway and knew that someone would enter the room. He wondered how he would explain himself if Donna came in. This, he remembered, was her domain.

Laurie yawned, her hand to her lips, her sleepy eyes a quick mirror for the faint light that reached to her bed from beneath the steely clouds. A deep voice sounded, "The nurse said my twin sons brought you a pot of tea, Laurie," Tom said, pushing the sleeping Cara in a clear plastic bassinet. "Which twin sons would that be?" Tom said, looking at Joe who jumped down from the windowsill immediately and started toward Tom. Leaving his chair, Peter came to stand beside Joe.

"Ha! I told the nurses Ben and me were twins."

"Ben and I," Tom corrected

Ben waited behind them. But what was the danger here, unless…unless Tom would be angry about Joe's joke? "The nurse really started it," Ben said. "She insinuated that we were twins and Joe just went along with it."

"Uh-huh," Tom said, "I bet." The brothers approached Tom with the eagerness of puppies and peered into the bassinet. Tom's hand went to Peter's shoulder, which he rubbed with a friendly kind of enthusiasm as the three of them peered at the new baby.

"So little."

"So pretty."

"How are you feeling, my love?" Tom asked Laurie.

No danger here, Ben thought. Deep inside, though, something hurt Ben.

"Wonderful. Just sleepy. Can you bring the baby over?"

"She looks like you, Mom," Peter said.

"She's perfect," Tom said, carefully guiding the bassinet.

"Can you believe we used to be that small?" Joe said.

"Did they," Laurie yawned, "weigh her, Tom?"

"She's seven pounds, five ounces. Nineteen inches."

"Oh, perfect," Laurie said, enamored. "And bigger than all you boys, except…" She yawned widely again, "you know, Ben."

"How can you tell how big Ben was?"

"Nine pounds. Around that," Laurie said. Tom wheeled Cara close to her mother, Peter and Joe following.

"What," Joe laughed, "are you guessing that from how muscular he is now?"

"I feel like the richest woman in the world," Laurie said. They gathered close to admire Cara, who slept with her eyes tightly shut. Ben inched closer, but hung back, troubled by the closeness of his memories pounding in his consciousness, demanding attention. So clearly he remembered the night that Donna brought Tim home from the hospital. He had spent that night awake beside her bed on the floor, miserable and stiff with tension.

Bonnie Jean and Tommy burst into the room. Tommy said, "Mama, we told the people at the cafeteria all about you and they were closing, but they gave us this sandwich and all this cheesecake and this great fruit salad for free."

"Oh, good, I'm so hungry." Laurie said, rousing.

"Kids," Tom said, "You have never seen an appetite as fierce as your mother's when she's nursing a baby. Puts a grown man to shame."

"Can I hold her?" Bonnie Jean said, going to the bassinet. "If you don't think I'll wake her."

"If we keep her bundled up in her blanket, you can probably each hold her while I enjoy this meal. Sorry for eating in front of you." Laurie added, with a shrug.

"That means she's not going to share," Tom teased. They decided they would take turns from oldest to youngest. Tommy insisted that Ben wait until last since he was technically newer than Tommy. Bonnie Jean, nearly frantic to hold the baby, occupied herself with taking pictures dancing on tiptoe to reach her desired angle. Peter was in no hurry, speaking in a hopeful and somehow uncertain voice.

Joe seemed nervous as Peter handed Cara to him, but he drew her close to his chest and Ben saw the same solemn expression Joe had during chapel now glow in his friend's eyes. "Wow," he whispered. "I see why you two keep having babies." Bonnie Jean took several pictures quickly and Ben was sure she'd captured the changes in Joe's emotions. When Joe finally consented to relinquish the baby, Bonnie Jean thrust the camera into Peter's hands and held her sturdy, graceful arms out for Cara. She drew the baby close, looked down at her quiet, sleeping face, and gave a gasp. The tears came so hard that they fell on Cara's cheek. "Daddy," she pleaded. Tom took the baby from her. Laurie put her food aside with a reluctant parting sigh that was comic in its honesty and took Bonnie Jean into her arms. "What's wrong?"

"Mama, I was so worried about you."

"You shouldn't have been," Laurie stroked her daughter's long, silky hair and rocked her slightly. "For me it's natural to do."

Tom placed the baby carefully into Tommy's arms and stayed with him, hovering, arms extended.

"I've wanted a sister for all my life," Bonnie Jean told her mother, still sobbing.

"We are going to enjoy her so much," Laurie said.

"Look," Tommy said, "I think she likes me." Cara had opened her eyes and regarded Tommy with calm interest. Bonnie Jean sat up and wiped her eyes.

"Quick, Pete, get that," Bonnie Jean commanded. Peter aimed the camera, and Bonnie Jean corrected him. "No, the light's all wrong."

"Here, you do it," Peter said, handing the camera to her.

Her eyelashes still bright with tears, Bonnie Jean stood on the chair so that she could capture both Tommy and Cara's faces just so. "Hi," Tommy said, his friendly voice confident. "My room is right next to yours, so I can hear if you cry. Okay?"

"She blinked," Peter said. "I think she's hears us."

"Oh, definitely," Laurie said. "Babies understand so much."

"They recognize voices and scents," Tom said.

Tom took Cara and laid her in Ben's arm, placing her round head in the crook of his elbow. She gazed up at him with dark, knowing eyes. Her scent was salty, but sweet, not brisk, and when he touched the dark fringe of her hair, it felt as soft as a breath. He was aware of Bonnie Jean's concentration on him, heard the repeated clicking of her camera and knew by the flush he felt in his throat that he was turning red. Cara made a noise that sounded like a mew. Ben looked up. She whimpered, drew a deep breath, and cried.

"Look what you did now, Ben," Tommy laughed. "First my head, next the teapot—"

Bonnie Jean reached for her baby sister. "Let me try," she said. She lifted the baby out of his arms and sang a few notes. Cara's cry dissipated like thin, shimmering bubbles. "Sweetest little baby...don't know what to call her, but she's mighty like a rose…"

Laurie said, "She recognizes your voice. She's been listening to you sing for months now."

"Do you think so?" Bonnie Jean asked, turning to her mother, eyes alight with joy.

"Someone should get a picture," Ben advised.

"You do it," Tommy gave Ben the camera and was insistent. Ben chose his spot so that the tinted light from the clearing sky beyond and the warm glow from the single incandescent bulb above Laurie's bed fell on the girls' faces.

"Pete," Tom whispered. "I want you to take Tommy and the others home. Tommy needs to get to bed. I want to stay here with your mother."

"But Dad," Tommy protested.

"It's getting late, son," Tom said.

"But—" he glanced warily at Peter and Joe. "We're right at the end of the book."

"We can read tomorrow."

"Can't you read to me while Jeannie's putting the baby to sleep?" Tommy said, glancing quickly at his mother for support, then at Bonnie Jean and the baby. "I brought my book."

"You did?" Tommy squatted down and searched into Laurie's bag. He pulled out a worn brown book, the binding rubbed, the corners buckled. "Look at that," Tom said, glancing at Laurie, who smiled, shifted over and patted the empty spot beside her on the bed. "Are you sure you'll be comfortable if we crowd onto your bed?"

"Perfectly sure."

Tom sat beside her stretching an arm around her shoulders. Tommy squeezed onto the bed's edge. "Where were we?"

"Right when Telemachos is coming to the shelter." Tommy said.

"I'll hold the book for you," Laurie said, taking it from him and moving into the shelter of Tom's arm so she could rest her head on his shoulder.

> "At this time
> the clamorous dogs came fawning around Telemachos, nor did
> they bark at him as he came, and great Odysseus noticed
> that the dogs were fawning; above them he heard the loud noise
> of footsteps.
> Immediately he spoke in winged words to Eumaios:
> 'Eumaios, someone is on his way here who is truly
> one of yours, or else well known, since the dogs are not
> barking—'"

"Do you think Telemachos will figure out it's him, Dad?"

"Remember, he's disguised as a beggar. Are you comfortable, Laurie?"

"Oh, yes. Look how Jeannie's quieted the baby." Ben saw that Joe and Peter had settled on the window ledge and that both wore the same contented look on their faces. Jeannie hummed as she walked the baby. Ben, feeling awkward in the deepening comfort of the family, stood in the middle of the room, hoping no one would notice that he didn't belong, had nothing to do, and didn't know where to sit. But he feared moving and breaking the spell. Ben, who had imagined such a family, who had dreamed of them and described them in desperate prayers to a God he hoped could hear, knew the rare and fragile magic of the moment. With his entire hungry soul, he devoured this incarnation of his prayers. Tommy's eyes rested on Ben now, asking for his consent. To reassure Tommy, Ben said, "I can't remember what happens next."

Then Joe commanded, "Come over here and sit, Ben. You're blocking my view."

He lifted up to fill the space the brothers had made beside Joe. There was room to sit, but their shoulders collided; Ben and Peter leaned forward, Joe leaned back. "Go ahead," Peter said.

"It's okay, Dad," Tommy said, then yawned, wriggling closer to his father. "Nobody minds."

> "His whole word had not been spoken when his beloved
> son stood in the forecourt. Amazed the swineherd started
> up, and the vessels, where he had been busily mixing
> bright wine, fell from his hand…"

Tom's voice was a bit too loud as all military men's voices become, but it was distinguished by the way it resounded with interest, and by the startling lack of defensiveness that Ben often heard screaming below the surface when violent men were unguarded as Tom was now. Tommy sighed and leaned his head back on Tom's shoulder. *No, the danger here is different,* Ben thought, holding up against the aching inside that pulsed now with rising power.

Ben thought about his mother warning him about Tom MacBride. In the deepening beauty and closeness of the evening he realized that she had been right about the danger. If he had heeded her, his heart would not have been captured. It was too late now. He was caught and suffering an aching desire he would never escape. *The home I have is no good. And now I won't be able to stand it again. This is what I want, this is exactly what I want, and I've got no right to it.*

Bonnie Jean sang soft syllables of unformed words, her voice a clear and delicious accompaniment to the rhythm of the poetry. Ben watched her, drinking in the lilt of her voice, the loving intensity of her gaze. He noted the details of her slim, graceful frame—the sunburn that brushed her cheeks, the crest of her forehead, and the curve of her arms where she held the quieted baby so tight to the swell of her body. She seemed to know he was watching her and glanced up at him. He tried to tell her, wordlessly, that he thought she was beautiful, and from the way her eyes brightened, he hoped she understood. She turned back to the baby, bending her head close so that her glossy braid fell forward. He watched her, fascinated; he watched them all and he drank deeply.

"...He came up to meet his master
and kissed his head, and kissed too his beautiful shining
eyes, and both his hands and the swelling tear fell from him."

He had been afraid that if Laurie had faltered, had drawn inward, the shining welcome the MacBrides had given him, which he recognized to be extraordinary and now essential to him would have slipped through his fingers.

So he understood, as Bonnie Jean sang to her baby sister, and as his coach read aloud to his quieted children while his wife leaned against his shoulder, that like the mermaid he'd imagined that first trip to Annapolis reaching for him, welcoming arms had been opened to him. He became aware that Laurie was watching him and he looked up. Her eyes, above the book she held, looked so like the mermaid's eyes, dark and concerned and bright with eager love, that he wondered if he had seen the future that first day in Annapolis. No wonder his father had fled the crash like one terrified of the flame-licked chasm of hell yawning wide and wider at his heels and had determined never to return to this enchanting city of bridges and bright water. Ben, whose heart, whose inner citizenship, had been captured with one glance of those bright, liquid eyes, would never be satisfied with Max Hunter's dry, angry world again.

Complications

24

"Major Lindquist," Johnson said, stepping toward him and extending his hand to give his renowned handshake. "Thank you for meeting me on a Saturday morning. I hope it didn't inconvenience your lovely wife."

"Admiral," Lindquist said, grinning good-naturedly, "I get up every morning at oh-dark-thirty to run. It's practically lunchtime for me."

The admiral nodded. "If we can step into your office," he said, motioning with a sweep of his arm. After closing the door behind them, Johnson went to Lindquist's desk, opened his briefcase, and extracted a stiff folder from which he took a formal letter. "This matter concerns Ben Hunter, Colonel Hunter's son."

"Sure, I know Ben. He looked after our boys when Colonel Hunter and I were at Quantico together. He's a great kid."

"He came to see me about applying for admission to the Academy, and he revealed to me his frustration over the fact that he has no birth certificate."

"Peculiar," Lindquist said.

"He asked for a letter confirming the facts of his birth so he can get his driver's license. Ben claims this letter has been written for him at each duty station as he's needed it to play ball—and I imagine whenever the need to prove his age arises."

"I didn't know that was an option for military kids."

"Why would it be?" Johnson said, eyebrows raised. "Nevertheless, I'm inclined to believe Ben. I don't see what he would have to gain by lying about something like this." Johnson held out a typewritten page crowned with his official letterhead. "I'd like it notarized."

Lindquist took the letter, politely keeping his gaze away from it.

With his right hand Johnson made a directive gesture. "You'll want to read it before you put your seal on it."

Lindquist read quickly, peered at the admiral in disbelief, then read again.

"Speak freely, Major Lindquist."

"I'm not sure I should," Lindquist said, looking up to check the admiral's expression.

"You're known as a straight shooter, Major. We don't know each other well, but your character and loyalty have been commended to me. Please speak freely."

"Yes, sir. Thank you, sir. It's just that I've known Max—Colonel Hunter—for over twelve years."

"That's precisely why I asked you to help me. I knew, as his friend, you would handle this information with appropriate sensitivity."

"But sir, I've never heard this story." Lindquist stared at the letter. "Not from Max or Ben."

"I'm surprised to learn that," Johnson said, his expression searching. "I thought everyone knew."

"Had *you* heard this before?"

"The navy's a little world, Major Lindquist, cunningly connected." Admiral Johnson scrutinized Lindquist for a moment, then reached for his briefcase. "I confirmed the facts that I remembered by consulting Max's personnel file." Johnson lifted a fat file from his briefcase.

"But that's official," Lindquist said, eyes going wide.

"Indeed," Johnson nodded and opened the file on Lindquist's desk. "There is documentation to support what you just read. Here," he said, flipping pages. He turned the file toward Lindquist and showed him where to read, then turned to another page, then another. "What concerns us here, is that his commanding officer allowed Hunter special leave from duty in the Med because Ben's mother was so ill right after he was born that the doctors feared she would die—"

"Right. This says he was ordered home. Refused to go? I don't understand."

Johnson shrugged. "Whatever his reasoning, the important thing is that the dates, the baby, the place of birth, the mother's illness—all are confirmed by those orders. Ben says that his mother's illness is the reason he does not have a birth certificate."

"Hm."

"The other events must have affected Max's duty and his presence on the ship, so they, too, were documented in subsequent pages by his commanding officer. Perhaps the turmoil described there in Max's fitness report is why the required papers were never filed."

Lindquist shook his head. "How does a marine survive with fitness reports like that? The man's a full colonel."

"What they told me when Headquarters Marine Corps sent him here to USNA was that after his appalling *early* fitness reports, Max's detailer shipped him to Twentynine Palms to try to get him to resign. Unfortunately, he was injured there due to the fault of the Marine Corps. As compensation, they sent him on to recruiting duty in Hawaii. Colonel Hunter turned out to be the best recruiter the United States Marine Corps has ever reared."

"He's good, that's the truth."

"I don't doubt it," Johnson agreed. "But as I said, Major, I brought this file to show documentation of the dates. And it all matches up neatly. This was nearly sixteen years ago. Ben is ready to turn sixteen next month."

"Yes, sir," Lindquist said, troubled. He unlocked his desk drawer to get his official seal and he adjusted the date.

"You are troubled by this, Major. I regret the necessity of involving you."

Lindquist nodded, pressing his lips together. "Colonel Hunter is my commanding officer, sir, but he is also my friend. I see what's written and I don't know what to think."

"Time will tell, Major. Perhaps there is a reasonable explanation. I hope Max will give me that explanation when I stop by his house this morning to let him know I've given the letter to Ben." Johnson glanced at his watch and said, "I expect Ben here in one minute."

"Yes, sir." Lindquist moved the letter into the seal and pressed. He signed it, turned it toward Admiral Johnson for his signature, folded it crisply in thirds, and placed it in an envelope. This he signed across the seal.

Max ascended the curving marble stair in Sampson Hall slowly, his left hand gripping the broad brass banister. He had fallen asleep on the sofa waiting up for Donna and Ben and had slept a numbing and torturous sleep, unable to rest, unable to rouse. His neck was stiff; his head pounded behind his ears and along the hairline of his brow. As he went down the long, dim, thickly carpeted hall past professors' offices, he heard a door click shut and familiar voices.

Walking together, conversing with an ease that surprised Max, the superintendent of the Naval Academy and Max's own assistant, Major Nels Lindquist, crossed the sunny open center of the department Max ruled.

When they saw him, discomfort flickered across Lindquist's face, the glance of his glass eye momentarily askew, but Admiral Johnson smiled his polished, professional smile and quickened his pace to stride over to Max. He offered his hand for shaking.

"Max. I'm glad we ran into you. I was just about to walk over to your house."

Max nodded his greeting to Lindquist, who straightened his back and nodded in return. "Major Lindquist's not in trouble again, is he, sir?"

Johnson laughed with appropriate amusement, but his eyes looked hard. "Nothing like that."

In the awkward pause that hung between them, the admiral indicated by the slight nod of his head and the gesture of his hand that he wanted

Max to walk back out the way he had just come. "You don't mind, Colonel," Johnson said, his voice brisk, his blue eyes resolute, "do you?" Max conceded, following Johnson's quick stride with the sinking knowledge that Johnson's strategy seemed well formed while Max was still uncertain of so much as the battleground.

All the way down the curving stairs, Lindquist and Johnson made small talk about the navy soccer team, but Max kept his trembling hand on the wide, flat brass rail. What could have happened to make things even worse since his last tense meeting with Johnson?

Ben had met with the admiral.

But Max knew he could count on Ben to behave; Ben invariably behaved. Then Max remembered the accident and feared that *if* the admiral had extracted Ben's version from him, it had not coincided with his own. His fear rose so violently that his pounding head spun and he tasted the sour tossing of his stomach.

Max hurried to open the door. He held it for the admiral and indicated with a brisk head motion that Lindquist should move through also. Johnson descended the two steps to the brick walkway with the light agility of a young Olympian, replacing his cover as he went. Max, knees stiff with anxiety, followed with the speed and grace of his aged, overweight mother. "What can I do for you, sir?" Max asked.

"Do for me? Why, nothing," he said. "I met with your son yesterday, as you know. I wanted to tell you about it."

"Yes, sir. I hope Ben was on time and used his manners." They began walking rapidly in the manner of military men who may not run in uniform. Lindquist led the way, three steps ahead of his senior officers, head bent slightly forward, clearly trying to stay on the edge of any conversation.

"Max, when I tell you I was impressed with Ben, I want you to know that I don't say that often." One of Ben's staunchest champions, Lindquist slowed and turned toward the conversation. Johnson stopped walking.

"I'm happy to know that, sir," Max said, standing still before the admiral.

"He reminds me so much of his mother."

"Yes, sir. Donna gets all the credit." Max could not tell if his reply carried the calm, lighthearted tone he intended, because blood pounded in his ears.

Johnson lay his hand on Max's arm. "I meant your first wife, Max."

Repulsed, Max pulled away; the admiral's action was taboo in the military community, his comment a swift shot in the gut. Unmoved by Max's turmoil, Johnson continued, "I met her once when—"

"I will not discuss this with you," Max snorted.

Johnson eyed him with a cold steadiness that made Max sweat. "Colonel Hunter, I think you'd like to rephrase that remark."

Fighting to regain his composure, Max breathed deeply and reached for a tolerant tone, but his anger resounded loudly. "Sir, I am not accustomed to being asked personal questions by my superior officer. It's not done in the Marine Corps. There's a professional code that allows us to keep our family lives private—as they should be."

"As I explained yesterday, Colonel Hunter," the admiral smiled, not in acquiescence, but in some kind of icy determination that Max found menacing. "Your family life is *not* private at the Naval Academy. I think this conversation is necessary to you doing your job here. No, I think it is vital. Why such a reaction? There's no shame attached to being remarried, Colonel."

"Sir, we were married a very short, unhappy time. Nothing but pain ever came from it. We were discussing your meeting with Ben and *this* has nothing to do with Ben."

"But Ben is her *child*," Johnson said.

"Pardon me, sir," Max said, his molars crashing together with the quaking of his jaw. "But you're mistaken. *Donna* is Ben's mother. She always has been."

"I don't understand," Johnson said.

"With all due respect, sir, there's nothing *to* understand."

"But what happened to the infant?"

"Sir?" Max said, his face wooden, except for the muscle beside his eye that quivered.

"Your infant son—I read the newspaper article about him."

"Newspaper article?"

"I was stationed in Charleston at the time. It was in the *Tribune*, Colonel Hunter. Naturally, I assumed Ben was the baby boy in the article. The dates are right. Did you not know it made news? Incredible story and you were named the father. In the paper. In print."

Max forced his whirling vision to focus so he could get his bearings and think. They were standing on the sidewalk in front of the superintendent's house. Max didn't even remember how they had gotten there. His buddy Nels Lindquist stood stiffly, just behind this pompous, interfering admiral's right shoulder. *Lindquist didn't know, before a minute ago, that I was married before. What is Johnson's problem?* Aloud in the most bitter voice he could manage, Max whispered, "No, sir. That was not Ben. The boy you read about did not survive."

"I understood that he *did* survive. That he *survived* is what made it news."

Though blood pounded in his ears and throat, Max found a strange detachment that allowed him to assess his situation. He saw Johnson—untouched, completely impervious in his rank—so determined, because of one silly driving incident, to ruin him. He noticed how perfectly still

Lindquist stood, how his tense posture revealed his uneasiness, his un-asked questions. He could not afford to lose Lindquist as an ally, nor could he allow this continual disdain from Admiral Johnson.

"Initially," Max said, his voice bold. "You read *initial* reports."

"You are claiming the child died?"

Max came to a close approximation of attention, back straight, shoulders thrust back, arms at his side. For the first time in two days, he met Admiral Johnson's eyes. The situation demanded it. Deliberately and slowly, courage resounding in his voice, "Yes, sir."

"When?" Johnson demanded.

"He lived just a few days."

"How did he die?"

"Brain damage. It was a mercy."

The admiral passed his hand over his eyes. "Do you know what you are saying, Colonel? Your assertion is totally contrary to what I read in—"

"Her elderly parents were not interested in continuing press coverage. You read one article. That's not the whole story. Money can buy silence."

Slowly, enunciating each word, Johnson said, "Are you sure you're telling me the truth, Colonel Hunter?" Then, almost pleading, "It's not too late to revise your statement."

"Admiral, it's merely hard to believe because it's so horrible. A horrible ending to a painful relationship."

"You have my most profound sympathy, Colonel Hunter." Max moved to salute, but the Admiral shook his head, saying, "Now that I think of what I put in that letter…"

"Letter, sir?"

"Ben explained that you always obtain a letter from your command-ing officer that substitutes for a birth certificate. I wrote the letter, Major Lindquist notarized and sealed it, and we gave it to him this morning at nine."

Max looked from one officer to the other. "What does the letter say?"

"Ben asked me to write a letter verifying who he is, when he was born, et cetera. I checked the dates against information in your personnel file, but now that I think of what you're saying—they don't match up. Your marriage date to Donna, for instance. Ben is nearly sixteen."

Max was practiced in fielding this question and he feigned an embar-rassed laugh. "Sometimes that happens, sir," Max said, pausing to allow the admiral to give a knowing boys-will-be-boys kind of response. But his superior officer gave none; instead he peered at Max with eyes too cold and fierce to register a warm and binding thing like camaraderie over sex-ual misdeeds.

This reaction from a navy man? Max thought. *Maybe Johnson really is the religious fanatic people say he is.* "Sir, Donna, was, um, not free to marry. She was in the middle of a messy divorce."

"Ah, forgive me. I understand now. Ben is *Donna's* son, but not yours."

"Ben is *my son*. My *flesh* and *blood*. You can tell just looking at us."

Johnson looked at Max, unconvinced. "Are telling me that in the same year of your life—the same month—you fathered two different sons by two different women?"

"No, sir. My first wife and I were separated," Max said, with conviction, glancing at Lindquist, hoping for sympathy. "The child who died was not mine."

"Do you know what you're saying?"

"*This* is precisely why I don't discuss the past. I've made it my business to shield her reputation. I'd rather you thought badly of me than know the truth about her. Why ruin the reputation of someone who can't defend herself?"

"I wish I had known of your noble motives before now," Johnson drawled.

"I don't know why she behaved the way she did. I can't explain it except that men were crazy about her. *You'd* met her. Everyone who knew her liked her…or loved her," Max said, slowly, meeting the admiral's eyes again with a look that was outright challenge.

"As you say."

"I'm not perfect either," Max said, giving the broken sigh of a man who has come to terms with his faults. "Of course, I regret *my* behavior now that I see how it might hurt Ben. I've always believed that Ben doesn't need to know he was conceived out of wedlock. It wasn't his fault. The courts were slow and we couldn't wait. Let the blame—the embarrassment—fall on my shoulders, not his."

"The blame absolutely falls on your shoulders."

"Agreed. Let's drop it."

"No. However much I dislike continuing this discussion, I *did* write that letter, which I now realize is invalid and unnecessary."

"Personnel files are not *personal* files," Max said, swallowing his sneer to add, "*sir*."

"Max, you must stop hiding Ben's birth certificate from him just so he won't find out he was conceived out of wedlock. Give the boy his birth certificate, for God's sake. Stop imposing on your colleagues to write letters! This masquerade is voodoo."

"No, sir, I'm not hiding anything," Max said, vehemently. "He has no birth certificate."

"After all you've said, how can that *be*, Colonel?"

"Some mix-up at the hospital because of a—"

"A snowstorm?" Johnson asked, eyebrows raised.

"Wait," Max said, catching himself. Forcing his voice to be casually annoyed, added, "Just some clerical error. Inexcusable, really. It's been such a hassle for Ben."

Johnson glanced at his watch. "I suppose, by now, Ben has used the letter I gave him and has obtained his learner's permit. All on so-called false information taken from official files and given at my hand. My apologies, Major Lindquist. Good day, gentlemen." He returned their salutes, turned on his heel, and took his front steps two at a time.

"He's an odd duck," Max said, grinning at Lindquist.

"He means well," Lindquist said.

"So, Nels, now you know my deep dark secrets."

"Hey," Lindquist said, shrugging, avoiding his eyes.

"I'd better try to find Ben," Max said.

"Good luck with that," Lindquist said. He saluted crisply, and turned to go.

25

MAX forced himself to stroll down Porter Road to his quarters. He stepped inside and bellowed for Ben. The house was silent. Donna would sleep until noon; Keith and Tim were probably upstairs watching videos.

Mounting the stairs, Max went straight to his large walk-in closet. With his uniforms, he kept the bulk of his artillery shell collection; his mother would only allow a few of the shells to be displayed in the decor she designed. The shells stood in the four corners of the closet, stiff, silent sentinels. He hid things behind them.

Max went first to the near right corner where he had an open bottle of Jack Daniels. He took a burning swig from it, then turned to the left corner, which hid the safe. Rocking the large shell from side to side, Max walked it over and lifted out a small square safe. This he balanced on the tips of the crowd of shells while he took another swig before attempting the combination—an unforgettable number, his wedding anniversary.

He fumbled it, tried again, fumbled again.

Hands shaking, he put his bottle down on the floor. Then, parting the hanging trousers, he sat down and leaned against the wall, letting the trousers close in front of him so that only his legs extended straight out. He settled the safe on his thighs and took his bottle in both hands. He licked the mouth, savoring the fragrance, the sweet sting of flavor, before he sipped again.

In the middle of the next try at the combination, he realized he was using the wrong wedding date. His hands went into convulsions and he cursed Admiral Johnson aloud for awakening that painful memory. Should he have foreseen this complication? No, never would he have anticipated an overreacting, interfering CO like Johnson. "Something about Annapolis," he muttered, "they breed this type of man here." *Think*, he told himself, taking a drink. *Donna's and my anniversary.*

He knew the month was November, because it was two weeks after the baby died. He turned the dial on the safe to eleven. His casts were removed on Halloween. He remembered all the jokes about losing his mummy costume. How could he remember crap like that and not remember a simple sequence of numbers? *Johnson rattled my nerves*, he told himself and took another brief sip to jog his memory.

Max had moved into Donna's apartment a month earlier when he was discharged from the hospital. He needed her; he admitted this. Not only did the casts on his legs mean he could barely take care of himself, but the sexual relationship they began in the hospital helped him. Her need for him pleased him. The notion that she had come from Tom MacBride brokenhearted and pregnant attracted him. Max thought that caring for Donna would somehow make up for all that had happened. Neither of them mentioned marriage. And when he found out later that her baby was not Tom's, when he had *proof*, they were too deeply involved for him to leave.

The first month they lived together they spent in glorious sexual discovery. Though Max, with both legs in casts, was immobile, Donna proved as eager as her behavior in the hospital had suggested.

Max found himself growing fascinated by Donna's pregnant body, he liked to stare and touch. Every time he ran his hand over her bulging stomach a thrill stirred his heart. But in Donna's bed, inevitable comparisons to Katie arose, unbidden and irresistible. Had Katie looked like this when she was pregnant? Did those tiny breasts of hers swell this big? He missed Katie's beauty, the feel of her skin, the familiarity of gesture and taste formed of years together. He remembered their shared dreams and the consuming love he'd had for Katie—the strongest emotion of his life—but told himself that lovemaking with Katie had been all passion and an unquenchable desire.

Though he might never be enchanted with Donna, she was easy to understand and he could manage her. And when in her shy way, Donna initiated sex by joking, "practice makes perfect," Max decided he preferred Donna's raw need to Katie's physical confidence.

Halloween, the day his casts were removed, they celebrated by going out to dinner at a crowded family restaurant full of costumed children. Later, during lovemaking, the baby kicked. Max felt it thump his belly, and emotion erupted within him. He lost his momentum.

"What happened?" Donna asked, as he rolled off her, turning his back to her.

"The baby kicked."

"So?"

He waved her away with his hand.

"Don't turn away from me," she said, her voice injured. But Max was weeping and couldn't face her. Donna came up close to his back and held him from behind. "You didn't do anything wrong," she said factually, nurse-like. "It doesn't hurt the baby."

He turned to her and wept in her arms. "Tell me again," he said when he could speak.

"What?"

"What you said."

"You didn't do anything wrong," she soothed him. "See? It didn't hurt him." She took his hand and placed it on her belly. The baby kicked a series of quick thumps against his fingers, then a big lump rolled across his palm.

"That's probably his butt," Donna said.

"Oh, my God," Max said, overcome. He flopped back on the pillow. "You can feel the kid's backside in there."

He was embarrassed, then, for his ignorance and his uncontrolled emotion. Donna covered him with the sheet, pulling it tightly around his back as if to shield him, and she aroused him as he'd taught her to do, until they shuddered together in the fulfillment of their joined bodies and hearts.

That night as Donna slept in his arms, Max lay awake, thinking of Katie, of the pregnancy she'd borne alone, of how he'd turned his back on her, and his remorse mingled bitterly with self-justification. *Any husband would have done the same*, he told himself in the long darkness. But in those quiet hours after lovemaking, as Donna's child stirred against his side, Max fell in love with it. Out of his bitter indignation arose the sweetest strain of love he'd ever tasted. His second chance. He anticipated the child's next softened movement, vowing in his heart to take care of it, and of Donna. He fell asleep waiting for the child to move again.

Donna's screams awakened him.

"It's just a dream," he murmured, reaching for her, trying to open his eyes, sore and swollen from before.

"No!" she screamed. "The baby!"

He switched on the light. Blood drenched the sheets between them, pulsed from her body with every heartbeat.

"It's okay," he said, reaching for the phone.

"No. Something's wrong. Help me, Max."

"I'm calling an ambulance."

"Too late," she gasped.

Max shouted their address to the operator, watching Donna shudder with pain. He crouched next to her. He didn't know what to do.

She sank into the pillow, eyelids fluttering.

"Don't faint on me now, babe," he said, taking her shoulders, fearing her imminent death. "You've got to tell me what to do." Her eyes rolled, her breathing increased to feeble, rapid gasps at air.

Max's mind raced. *Got to stop this bleeding.* Donna made a sharp, choking sound. Something slid out of her body. He heard a faint noise. And then he saw it, tangled in a wiggling, bluish cord, arms and legs moving, mouth open, gasping for breath.

"The baby," he whispered to Donna, his voice a mix of horror and wonder. He slid his hand beneath it. "It's a little girl," he said. Donna was crying somewhere in the background, her sobs shivery and distant. An ambulance wailed at the far edges of his awareness.

The baby's head was smaller than a tennis ball, her body so tiny her heels touched the top of his wrist, her wide-open eyes inky and knowing. Her skin was the dusky purple of twilight. Her blue lips trembled, begging for breath.

"She can't breathe very well," he said to Donna. Max wiped the gook from her face with the sheet, clearing out her nose. There were tiny gagging sounds in her throat. He bent close and pressed his lips over her nose and mouth. Her skin was warm and damp, her facial bones as fragile as china. He blew carefully into her mouth.

There was pounding at the door. Max clutched the baby to his chest and sped to open it; the live, blue cord hung over his arm; the placenta dangled on the end, swinging, scattering blood.

Paramedics ran for the bedroom. Others came to him, to examine the child resting in his hand. Her breathing had stopped. Her eyes begged him for help. But they took her from him. Her tiny doll-like arms bounced as the paramedic sprinted to the ambulance. Two minutes later, they wheeled Donna out.

Donna never saw the baby. She had no memory of the small, wide-eyed daughter who spent her life in Max's hand. Max still dreamt of her, resting in his hand, begging for breath, a child, a nameless person he would always love. She would have been fourteen years old on November first.

Max wiped his eyes. He shook his head to clear it. He squinted to focus in the closet's muffled light. Unable to see the dial of the safe, he put his bottle down and parted the hanging trousers that hid him. "Eleven," he said, his fingers on the dial. "Let's see, two weeks...fourteen plus one." He turned the dial to fifteen, then counted the years, spun the dial, and it opened.

Beneath the jewelry boxes, at the bottom of the pile of papers, Max found the envelope with *Letter from the CO* written across the front. Inside he found Ben's birth certificate, the stiff waxy paper crinkled with a notarized seal. He slid the envelope into his chest pocket, replaced the safe, and hid the bottle of Jack. He took the back door, hoping no one would see him on his way to the car; he'd wrinkled his trousers by sitting on the floor with that heavy thing on his lap.

26

OUTSIDE the MVA, Ben slumped against the brick wall in defeat. "This is what my father does all the time. I can't believe they wouldn't even *look* at the letter."

"We'll think of something."

Ben stiffened, coming away from the wall to stand straight up. His arms dropped to his sides. "Oh, no," he said, staring towards the parking lot. "My day just got worse."

Joe followed Ben's gaze to see a tall, squarely built marine approaching with strides so determined, his footsteps resounded across the diminishing distance. "Your dad?"

"The one and only."

"How did he find us?"

"I don't know, but if you're smart, you'll run away now."

"No," Joe said.

"Am I in time?" Colonel Hunter called when he was ten feet away. His face was bright red and although he smiled, his entire frame suggested that he was tensely loaded, ready to spring.

"Dad, this is my friend, Joe," Ben said. "Colonel Hunter, my father."

"Joe," Max said, gripping Joe's hand and shaking it briskly. "So, where is it?" he asked, eyes bright and hard on Ben.

"I didn't get my learner's permit. They wouldn't accept the letter."

"Why *not*? Did you open the letter?"

"No, sir. Major Lindquist told me to give it to them unopened. So I—"

"Okay. Good. Where is it?"

"The letter?"

"Yes, dammit, Ben, the *letter*. Give me the letter."

Ben looked down at his left hand that held his loose papers and the smooth, unopened envelope. Max lunged at him and snatched them from his grasp. "I'll take care of this," he said, panting slightly. "You'll have your permit in no time."

"But Dad—"

"Don't argue with me. I said I'd take care of it."

"Colonel Hunter, sir," Joe said. "You should know that the woman at the counter wouldn't even consider the letter."

"You leave it to me," he said, winking at Joe. "In fact," he said, clapping Joe hard on the shoulder. "You can go on your way."

"Dad—"

Glaring at Ben, Max said, "This kind of thing takes an experienced negotiator."

"I don't mind hanging around," Joe said with pointed informality. "I'd like to see what happens."

Colonel Hunter shot Joe a disdainful look, his upper lip curling into a sneer. "No need for that, Ben," he said, turning to Ben and motioning with a thrust of his head toward Joe. "Say good-bye to your friend."

"Thanks, Joe," Ben said stiffly, politely, "for picking me up this morning. I really appreciate it."

"I don't mind staying."

"Look," Max said to Joe, his smile losing all its power to convince. "We're in a hurry here."

"Dad," Ben pleaded under his breath.

Max stepped close to Ben, trapping Ben's toes under his shoes. "I'm a busy man and I came all the way out here to help you out—"

"Hey, you know what?" Joe said, stepping close, into the Colonel's field of vision. "I've got to go." Max backed off. "*Great* to meet you, Colonel Hunter."

"See ya, Joe," Ben managed to say.

"Call me," Joe said as he jogged backwards away from them, "if you want to come over and study for that chemistry quiz."

Max poked his finger into Ben's chest, pushing him up against the wall. Max could not see that Joe watched as he continued, crablike, across the parking lot. Ben felt hot with shame. "I'm gonna be nice to you and forget your snotty behavior. I'll take this stuff and get your permit for you. You shouldn't have tried it without me."

"No, sir."

Max's finger pressed on Ben's sternum. "You'll have to run to the car and get my checkbook. I left it in the glove compartment. You know you got to pay for a permit, right? Good thing I showed up."

Behind Max, Joe mimed a kick aimed at Max's backside. Ben covered his mouth with his hand for an instant to show Joe he had seen and dared not laugh. With a grin, Joe waved, turned, and sprinted across the parking lot to his MG.

"You ready to take the test?" Max asked.

"I'm ready," Ben said, without the slightest hint of a smile.

After twenty minutes of searching his father's faultlessly neat car for the checkbook, Ben gave up. He decided it would be better to face his father in the crowded MVA building than out in the far reaches of the parking lot. His empty stomach sour, he jogged back to the building. Ben saw him coming away from the series of booths at the far back of the room. He strode toward Ben, head thrown back, a smug smile creasing his face.

Squaring his shoulders Ben said, "I can't find your checkbook."

"I had it in my pocket the whole time," Max said, waving his hand. "When I realized, I didn't want to get out of line to get you." He showed the completed form to Ben and pointed to a four-digit number circled at the top. "You're in, kid. After you take the test, you can get your picture made."

"But—"

"It just took a little charm and they put the forms through, no problem."

"You're kidding."

"You should never doubt your old dad," Max said, his voice slightly unctuous. "The clerk over there told me she thought you and your friend were up to no good. Kids could just write anything in a letter. You need a respectable adult with you."

Leaving the MVA, Max would not allow Ben to drive, so he sat buckled up in the front seat, his brand new permit shining unused in his hand. Max narrated every action he took to move the car in a voice booming with tense authority. Ben felt conspicuous with the bright red Miata's convertible top down, the hot, midday light flooding the car. *It doesn't matter*, he told himself. *I've got it now. I'm almost there.* To distract himself, Ben stared at his permit, tipping it so that it reflected like glass in the sunlight.

"Put that damn thing away. You're flashing it in my eyes."

"Sorry," Ben said, and slipped it into his pocket with his journal. Max ranted about license points, speed traps, and red light cameras. Ben kept silent, watching as his father crossed Rowe Boulevard. He tried not to show his interest when they passed Laurie's store, but noted the IT'S A GIRL sign hung from the porch. Sensations from the evening flooded his consciousness. He felt sudden, fierce hunger. His discontent begged from deep within and he shifted restlessly in his seat.

Ben felt his father's mood shift as if Max could sense the danger in Ben's volatile longing.

"What's with you?" Max demanded.

"Nothing, sir." His voice betrayed him.

Max lurched the car over to the curb and cut the engine. "You think you can drive? Fine." He got out of the car, slammed the door, and rushed to Ben's door before Ben understood. Max motioned with his head. "Go ahead." He flipped the keys. Ben caught them and, senses wary, took the driver's seat. Ben started the car, adjusted the mirrors, and waited to merge. He pulled into the lane with smooth caution, breathing deliberately, concentrating.

Max's voice came, an irritating scrape, unreasonable with emotion. "Ben, you were way out of line today. If I were the kind of father who punished, I'd beat the crap out of you and ground you for a month."

Ben kept his eyes on the road.

"I don't want you bothering Admiral Johnson anymore. You hear me?"

"What do you mean, sir?"

"Don't be a smart ass. You know what I mean. You stay away from him. Admiral Johnson doesn't have time to be your buddy. Got it?"

Slowly executing the right turn, Ben saw the low bridge that crossed College Creek ahead. Ben straightened his back, glancing swiftly to catch the glaze of midday sun on the water ahead.

"But—but I was *commanded* by *you* to go over and see him. You were the one who set up the appointment."

Jerking his hand back hard, Max hit Ben's face; Ben swerved the car far into the other lane and wrenched it back. "You watch it," Max growled as the passing car leaned angrily on the horn.

"You almost made me hit that car!"

"Yeah?" Max said. In the corner of his vision, Ben saw his father move. Max came up out of the seat; his foot hit Ben's right knee. Max thrust his foot down onto Ben's, forcing the accelerator to the floor. The tires screeched; the car leapt, rushing to speed.

Ben couldn't keep the car in the lane. It roared up the bridge, tires crossing, weaving, recrossing the double yellow line, the back end like a fish in flight. Max pressed harder. Ben's vision sharpened; cars approached. His desperate eyes sought the mirror; one car far behind. He kicked at his father's ankle, stomped down on the brake, and forced the steering wheel right, toward the gleaming water beneath the bridge. Screeching, the car ran up over the curb, rushed over the sidewalk at the foot of the bridge, and stalled. The bumper rammed into the grassy slope beside the boathouse at the back of St. John's College. Ben leapt out, stumbled away; astonished eyes accusing his father.

"Help me out," Max commanded. "I'm stuck on this gear shift thing. Come here."

Ben shook his head, staring open mouthed, words failing him, his heart so wild, breath felt like fire. Glaring at Ben, Max tumbled into the driver's seat and out. Ben moved back into the slick grass. He spun left to run. Max grabbed Ben's waistband, pulled him back around, hit him clumsily, his fingers jabbing Ben's face. Ben slipped, fell and slid. He rolled into a crouch, shielding his stomach, hiding his face.

"That's right, that's right," he heard his father taunt him.

A car door slammed. "Is there a problem here?" The voice sounded brisk and official. Ben peeked up to see a police officer striding toward them.

"No, sir." His father's voice was smooth and polished. "My son is sick to his stomach. I shouldn't have let him drive. I knew he wasn't up to it. He tried to pull over and misjudged the curb. Went right up over it."

"I thought I saw you take a swing at him," the police officer said.

"No, sir. He's disoriented. He was out drinking with his buddies last night and he's got a helluva hangover. Didn't want him throwing up in my car. I was steering him away, so he'd throw up in the grass."

"Is this man your father?" the officer asked, bending toward Ben.

"Yes, sir," Ben whispered, choking.

"You okay?"

"No, sir," Ben said.

"You gonna throw up?"

"Probably," Ben murmured, keeping his face hidden.

The officer stood up. "I'm going to leave him in your hands," he said to Max. "But you need to straighten him out."

"I intend to do that, sir."

Max stood by Ben until the police car was out of sight. He touched Ben's hip with the toe of his shoe. "What are you doing down there, *crying*? For God's sake, *crying*?"

Ben held still—so furious he knew if he moved, he *would* get sick. *This is disgusting. Other people don't live this way.* He pictured Tom holding the makeshift ice pack on Tommy's head.

Max bent down and grabbed Ben's elbow. "Get in the car."

Ben wrenched his arm free, crouching tight and low. "No."

"If I have to force you, you're gonna be hurting a lot worse," Max said poking at Ben's hip with the point of his shoe. "Now do as I say."

"I'm gonna be sick," Ben whispered.

"The police officer is gone now," Max laughed. "You don't have to keep pretending."

"I'm not. Leave me alone. I'll walk."

"I'll be waiting at home for you, and when you get there, I'll beat you senseless."

Ben knew this wasn't true. He knew that if he delayed, his father would go home, drink some—a little or a lot—and forget. Max forgot what he did; he forgot his threats, forgot Ben's discipline. If he dealt Ben blows in the guise of correction, they came as surprises, given in fury, provoked by the wind or the gleam of the sun on the water, by a vague, passing fragrance as swift and elusive as a threatening emotion flickering across Ben's features. But if he got back in the car *now,* if he obeyed as he had always been forced to do—*No, I won't be trapped in the car with that brutal idiot. Not now. Not ever again.* Shivering violently in the muggy August heat, he hugged his knees tightly, keeping his face hidden.

"God, you look like a scared rabbit," his father murmured. He kicked Ben's hip with the heel of his shoe, sending Ben sprawling into the muddy grass. Ben rolled to his knees immediately, protecting his soft places, so that the second kick struck his shoulder and ear.

"You're too damn muddy to ride in my car. Walk home."

When Ben heard the hard shoes slap the concrete sidewalk, he breathed again. When the car roared to life, when it scraped and bumped off the sidewalk, he squelched tears of relief. But he didn't look up until he heard the Miata gaining speed down the street. Refusing to allow himself the luxury of a single tear, he stood up and began to run. He would turn down College Avenue and run away from the Naval Academy. He'd run to the MacBrides and tell them what happened.

In a moment, he was going fast and feeling some power. His ear and his lip throbbed, but he was gaining speed, and he could ignore the pain in the other places. Quickly, he approached College Avenue, his path to freedom. He could breathe deeply and felt life come back to him.

He looked up just before it happened. Speeding along the next block toward the Maryland Avenue intersection, his father seemed oblivious to the red light and sped relentlessly toward a car stopped there. Ben called out. His father swerved hard to the left, smashing through a wrought iron fence and into a towering tree.

27

THE next thing Ben knew, he was holding his father's left hand and trying to soothe him. Sirens wailed, approaching. "It's okay, Dad. It's okay."

"Ben?"

"It's okay, Dad. You're gonna be all right."

"Where's your mother?"

"She's home, Dad. She wasn't with us."

Max began to groan in pitiful, emotional pleas that quickly deteriorated to throaty sobs. "Get me out of here, Ben."

"The ambulance is coming, Dad."

There were people around, asking him questions. Ben said, "He's hurt. He's trapped. See?" And for the first time, Ben took in the details of the wreck. Just beside him, the left front wheel of the car sunk into a brick-rimmed lily pond. Dozens of big goldfish swarmed, gasping open-mouthed at the tire. The back of the Miata hung on the tips of the iron fence. The right side of the car, crumpled like tin foil by the impact of the tree, had been shoved up into the crushed passenger seat; Max was pinned between it and the steering wheel. Ben's stomach gave a wild lurch. "Hold on, Dad. They'll get you out. They're here."

With a calm efficiency the paramedics moved to check Max's vital signs, asked where he was hurting and began to pry the crushed car away from him. "Who are you?" they asked Ben.

"I'm his son."

"How did you get out of the car?"

"I was—back there—"

"Don't believe him. When I hit, he was thrown loose," Max said, his voice gone shallow.

"Don't faint, Dad," Ben pleaded.

"It hurts me," Max moaned. "Oh, it hurts me."

"You're going to have to let go of his hand, son," one paramedic said, "so we can get him loose."

"But *he's* holding onto *me*."

"Sir, let your son go. We're going to take care of you now."

"No," Max wailed. "I need him. I can't lose him, I can't."

Ben's emotions rose in a tumult of confusion. How could he pity this man? But his pity was forceful and real and completely beyond the valid dictates of his clean, hot anger. Ben was ashamed of himself; his pity repulsed him. This swirl of conflicting emotions always made Ben sick to his stomach. He gulped, wild to flee, and pushed at Max's grasping fingers.

"Let me talk to him, for a sec," Max pleaded.

"Make it quick."

"Come close, Ben," his father whispered. Stomach heaving, Ben obeyed, moving in close enough to smell the sweet stench of his father's breath. "Don't tell on me, Ben. I'm in enough trouble already. Johnson will ruin me. I'll be out of a job, my retirement. Please, Ben."

"Dad," Ben warned, "don't."

"I won't be able to afford your school."

Ben groaned, pulling his hand free. The paramedic took this as a cue and came close again.

With his free hand, Max grabbed Ben around the back of the neck and kept him close, nose to nose, his grip biting and inexorable, his brown eyes pleading, "Promise me, Ben, please."

"Tell him what he wants to hear, kid. We need to get him out of there."

"Ben," his father pleaded, sliding his hand down Ben's shoulder to grip his arm.

"Okay, Dad. You win."

The paramedic moved between them, blocking Max's view of Ben. "Sir, you've got to let go of your son so we can get you out of there."

"Ben," Max pleaded as they pulled Ben back and away from him.

"It's okay, sir," the paramedic soothed him. Prying Max's fingers loose of their grip on Ben's arm, he freed Ben. Ben stumbled backward into the same policeman who had stopped at the bridge.

"Oh, it's you," he heard himself say.

"I just left you two down the road. Couldn't of been five minutes ago. What happened?"

"I don't know," Ben said, noticing that his right forearm gushed dark red blood from a three-inch slice. "When he saw the red light, it was too late. He was going to crash into a car, so he swerved." Ben dug in his pocket and found a crumbled wad of paper. He pressed this to his gash, a tissue against the flow of Niagara.

"Are you sure you weren't driving?"

"Me?" Ben said. "No. I wasn't driving."

The officer took Ben's uninjured arm. "Look, I'm gonna give you a breath test. If you were driving in your condition—there's gonna be trouble."

"Look at the car," Ben pleaded. "He's trapped in the driver's seat. If I'd been driving, that would be *me* in there."

"He's right, Mitch," the other officer said. "And look at the passenger seat. It's a miracle you got out alive. How *did* you get out?"

"I didn't. I mean, I wasn't *with* him."

"You were with him five minutes ago."

"The dad says he was thrown out," the second officer said. "You've got mud all over you. Your ear is bleeding, too. You probably hit your head. Do you know what day it is?"

"He was confused before the wreck," the first officer said. "These two were stopped a few minutes ago by College Creek. The dad says this little hot dog had been drinking and was sick. He's still too smashed to know what happened."

"Okay, give him a breath test, so we know if he's a credible witness, but there's no way he was driving."

"But wait—"

The officer grabbed Ben's arm, fingers pressing hard into his bicep, and led him away. Max called for him, his voice weak and hysterical. "Now breathe into this." Ben obeyed, his eyes keen, anger beginning to melt his numbing shock. His arm throbbed; he grew dizzy. "My arm's bleeding all over, officer."

"Hmm, that's funny. Nothing. It shows nothing."

"It's *not* funny," Ben snapped. "I wasn't drunk this morning *or* last night. This just proves it."

"I don't get this," the officer said, staring at the results as if they might change.

"I told you. I didn't even have one drink. Do you have something I can stop this bleeding with? It's getting everywhere."

"Then what was happening out there by the bridge? Your dad said you were hung over."

"He was beating me up," Ben snarled. "That's what was happening."

"You expect me to believe that?"

"No," Ben said, giving a cynical laugh. "Not any more than I expect you to believe my arm is bleeding."

"Hey, watch your tone of voice with me."

"Why don't you try your stupid test on my dad? He's the one driving."

"You'd better shut your mouth, kid."

His partner came over quickly. "What's going on?"

"Test is absolutely negative. No evidence of alcohol at all."

"Why are you shouting at the kid, then? For God's sake, look at his arm."

"He's got a smart mouth. He needs to learn some respect."

"I'll take over," the other said, pulling a napkin out of his pocket and thrusting it into Ben's hand. "Here. Apply some pressure to that. We keep forgetting you were in the accident, too. Can you walk? I'll take you over to the ambulance."

"No, I'm fine. I wasn't in the accident. I told you."

"Come on, now. You're gonna need stitches." With a firm hand at the small of Ben's back the officer steered him toward the ambulance.

"Is Smitty on duty?" Ben asked.

"You know Smitty?"

"Yeah. He was there when my dad crashed into Middleton's last week."

"That's the same colonel?" the officer said.

"Ask Smitty. You ask Smitty about him." Then, he shut his mouth firmly, his slimy promise snaring him.

At the back of the ambulance, they bound up Ben's wounded arm before they examined him. When the paramedics asked, he did not explain the bruises that were coming up purple on his lip and chin or the weird, muddy cut on his ear.

Ben did not again say the words, "He was hitting me." This he could no longer do. The moment, a moment of brave abandon he had been yearning for since he was twelve, had come and passed. He'd spat out the truth only to be mocked.

Oh, he had threatened to tell before and his mother had confidently predicted the officer's reaction. *No one would ever believe you,* she assured him, trapping him in the twisted covenant to which he now, again, did shameful, public homage. So he perpetuated the lie by his silence, his acquiescence, by keeping an ill-wrought promise he'd given his crying father.

Loathing himself, Ben squatted beside the ambulance, wishing he could at least cry as he heard his father doing several yards away. He could neither cry, nor tell the truth. So, he endured, seething, furious, all his sore places pounding.

Two tow trucks tugged at the wreckage of his father's car to free it from the crumpled iron fence as the ambulance took Ben and Max down Maryland

Avenue toward the hospital. Max's right arm was bent above the wrist and there was a purple bulge near the elbow. He whimpered through tears, sweating and tossing his head. Ben sat beside his father in the ambulance and, once again, his father gripped Ben's hand; all the while an irreverent wish scampered through Ben's weary, shamed soul with the bright caprice of an imp. *If only Dad's punching arm is as badly broken as it looks.*

At the hospital, medical people wheeled Max away. In the process of being admitted, the nurses found out that Ben and his father belonged to the Donna Hunter who worked upstairs in the NICU. When she didn't answer their attempts to reach her at home, they treated Ben with solicitous, though not particularly speedy, care. Weary of waiting to have his arm stitched, he asked the nurse for a bottle of peroxide and he blotted the bloodstains out of his shorts and socks. An hour and thirty minutes passed. The peroxide dried on his shorts and socks leaving vague brown rims of stain. Ben drank from the sink in the room, cupping his hand to bring the cold water to his mouth. He was trying to loosen the dried blood and caked dirt from his legs with a shredding wad of wet tissue when a young doctor came into the curtained area, shot Ben's arm full of Novocain, and sewed up his gash. He was told to wait there until the nurse came to get him for a CT scan.

Ben slipped into the restroom where he washed the rest of the dirt and blood off his body. Hoping to fade into the tumultuous background of the ill and injured and that way avoid the unnecessary CT scan, he decided to sit in the waiting area.

He shifted uncomfortably in the hard plastic chair and felt his journal in his pocket. He took it out and, leaning his right elbow on the arm of the chair, he crooked his arm around the journal to shield the words from easy view. He began to write, recording everything that had been said and done in the car from the moment they left the MVA. And though his hand shook and he felt sick again, he described his father's behavior in courageous and vivid prose, in paragraphs decorated with details: the throbbing in his lip and ear, the angle of the car, the smashed up passenger seat, the dripping blood, the policeman's blind prejudice. Ben's last sentence recorded the repulsive promise his father had extracted from him. Shaking his stiff, cramped hand, he looked up, but went dizzy, unable to focus. It felt as if the walls of his stomach were stuck together. He glanced at his watch. He'd been writing for three hours.

Man, where is Dad? What could be taking this long? Flexing his cramped left hand, Ben wondered with an irreverent glee if they'd had to amputate his father's punching arm. Shoving his journal back into his pocket, he told himself he ought to find out.

28

"BEN?"

He looked up. Tom MacBride stood before him, carrying a bright quilt over his shoulder, an armful of white tulips, and a huge wicker basket stuffed with food.

"Hey, Coach."

"What are you doing here, Ben? Are you all right?"

"My dad was in a car accident."

"Just your Dad? You look pretty rough."

"No, I'm okay. I just—uh—I just cut my arm trying to help him when he was stuck in the car."

"But your face is bruised."

"Oh." Ben said. "Yeah."

Tom sat down next to him. He put the basket on the floor and set the tulips carefully beside it. "Bruises all around your mouth. Funny bruises. And your ear," Tom said, squinting at Ben. "What happened?"

As he drew his breath to lie, Ben's stomach started to shake. "Dad was going down Prince George Street and he didn't notice the light was red. To keep from smashing into a car there, he swerved and the Miata ended up across an iron fence."

"A red Miata?" Tom said, turning more fully toward Ben. "I was behind a tow-truck pulling a smashed Miata earlier. You know, of all things, I noticed the SEMPER FI sticker on the back bumper and I thought, that couldn't be Max's car..." Then, as if he suddenly understood, he sat back to focus more clearly. He peered at Ben, his blue eyes squinted and keen. "Ben, how did you survive that crash? The passenger seat looked completely smashed."

"Coach," Ben said, stalling for time. *What can I say without breaking my promise that isn't a lie or partly a lie?* Something about Tom's protective expression said he was liable to pull Ben close and embrace him. Ben's stomach growled; he shook his head, incapable of further expression.

"Let me take you home. You can get some rest."

"No, Coach, thanks." His shaking spread from his hands up through his body and down to his knees; he was aware Tom saw. "I've got to stay here with Dad."

"Why? You're not doing him any good, and you don't look well yourself. Have they examined you?"

"Yes. I'm fine." Ben lifted his arm to show the official bandage.

"Your color's lost. You look beat."

"I am beat," Ben whispered, looking away. "But I've got to stay."

"It's cold in here," Tom said, standing up and taking the quilt from over his shoulder. He shook it out, its colors flowed in a unity of pattern like undulating waves.

"Get up. I'm gonna put this around you."

"Coach—"

"Come on. Get up." He took Ben's elbow and pulled him up, then wrapped the quilt around him like a cloak.

"Thank you," Ben said, settling back into the chair, hugging the quilt up close to his neck, holding it tightly closed. But his trembling seemed to double. Tom put his arm around Ben and rubbed his shoulder briskly to warm him. Ben held still, not allowing himself to wince or draw back as Tom's hand passed over the sore place on his shoulder again, then again. *He doesn't know my shoulder's hurt and I can't tell him. If I bring up the accident again, he'll ask questions and I don't want to lie to him.* But he began to feel warmer, and Tom's hand ceased hurting him so much and finally lay still on his shoulder, providing an unfamiliar warming comfort that Ben hungrily tried to memorize.

"If Joe were here right now," Ben murmured.

"Joe wouldn't *be* here right now," Tom said. "Joe would be home in bed, which is where *you* ought to be." Then he sat up straight and took his arm from Ben's shoulder to wave to the nurse who had admitted Max and Ben. "Margie! Margie Wilcox!" She shut the door to the treatment area and shifted the large plastic bag she carried onto her crooked arm.

"Tom? Hey, congratulations. I stopped in to see Laurie on my break."

"Thanks. Isn't the baby a beauty?"

"Just perfect. What are you doing sitting here?" she asked as she approached. "Oh, there you are, Ben. Is Ben one of your students?"

"He's on my basketball team. How are you, Margie? How's Bill doing?"

"In love, thank you very much. A girl in his organic chemistry class."

"Tell him I say hello. Hey, Margie, do you think it's okay if I take Ben home? He's tired and pretty hungry."

"You've been seen, haven't you?"

"Yes ma'am," Ben said, thrusting his stitched arm out of the quilt folds to satisfy her question without technically lying.

"Good," she said, stepping close. "Look, your father's really upset."

Ben stiffened. She was going to ask him to go in there. He was going to have to hold his hand again and pity him. "I'm sorry to hear that, ma'am." Tom rested his hand at the back of Ben's neck. Ben tried to feel its warmth through the layers of the quilt, but he had turned cold again and felt only the weight steady on his neck.

"We had to cut his uniform shirt off him," she said, "because we didn't want to move his arm."

"Oh," Ben said, his heart leaping.

"The x-rays show that his arm is badly broken. Both bones."

"Oh, wow," Ben said, bowing his head to hide the sweet relief that coursed through him.

Margie said, "He was so worried about his shirt—I guess because of the medals—I thought I'd bring you his things. There's a letter in the bag, too. He's worried about losing it. I'm sure it will ease his mind to know you have everything."

To take the bag from her, Ben had to completely open the quilt and reach out his arms. The chill set him shaking immediately. He put the bag on the floor and tried to bundle up again. Tom helped him, wrapping the quilt around him as if he were a child. "Did they put a cast on?"

"Eventually. He's heavily sedated while we're waiting for the orthopedist. It will be awhile."

"How long?"

"Maybe a couple more hours."

"No, I mean, how long will he have to wear a cast?"

"That depends on how it heals, but my guess would be at least six weeks."

"Wow, six weeks," Ben said, so happy, he wanted to giggle. He shivered in delight. Tom patted his shoulder thinking to reassure him.

"Do you have any idea where your mother could be?" the nurse asked, leaning close as if telling a secret. "We've been calling."

"She usually goes to the gym in the afternoons. She may have gone to the Commissary after that."

"I'll keep trying to reach her."

"If it's okay with you then, Margie," Tom said, "I'll drive Ben home."

The nurse nodded. "It may be better if someone tells his mother in person. People hate to get calls from the hospital."

"Help me take these things up to Laurie first, Ben. She's expecting me."

"That'd be great," Ben said.

In Laurie's room, the curtains were open and the low, evening sun threw a red-orange glow across floor. Ben let the quilt slip from his shoulders, then quickly folded it in fourths. Laurie did not see them enter. She stood beside Cara's bassinette, whispering to the baby. Dressed in pink pajamas and a bright red bathrobe, she looked round and rosy. Tom made no comment, just crossed the room and presented his wife with the flowers and a tender kiss on the lips.

"Oh, my favorites," she whispered. "Thank you."

"And look who I brought."

"Ben!" She started toward him, and he met her in the middle of the room. She kissed his cheek, hugging him with awkward tenderness while holding the tulips in one arm. "What's happened to you?" she said, holding him at arms' length to look at him.

He looked down. "My dad was in an accident. I had to get a few stitches, too." He raised his bandaged arm in explanation.

Laurie touched his face with tender concern. "Are you all right?"

"My father's a lot worse. He broke his arm pretty badly."

"Ooh," Laurie winced.

"He's a terrible driver," Ben added.

"Yes, I know that about him." Cara had begun to cry. Laurie turned toward her, but Tom scooped her up and her cry quickly unwound to a whimper.

"Are you hungry, Ben?" She stood the tulips in the water pitcher, paused a moment as if to command their poise and when she stepped back, they fell into a full and graceful arc as elegantly as if they rested in a crystal vase.

"He's been here waiting for Max. His stomach sounds like it's fighting a battle."

"The food is dreadful here," Laurie said. "Pull that chair up to the bed and we'll share."

"No, really, Mrs. MacBride, I couldn't."

"You will," Tom commanded. Tom's tone was a hand pushing down on his shoulder and Ben sank into the chair. Laurie had begun to unpack the basket, taking out three fat turkey salad sandwiches. Ben's mouth watered. "And," Tom said, his voice gone to teasing, "you'll enjoy it."

"Yes, sir," Ben said, weakly.

There was a thermos of steaming soup with tiny meatballs, pasta and vegetables, a container of fruit salad, and a box of richly fragrant chocolate cookies. Laurie divided the soup into two cups, opened the package of sandwiches and moved it within Ben's reach. Sharing the table, they ate hungrily, comrades in complete sympathy. "This soup is the best stuff I've ever eaten," Ben murmured, holding his cup out for a refill.

"I've never been so hungry in my life," Laurie agreed.

Tom walked with Cara, whispering to her. As he filled his stomach, Ben heard snatches of Tom's words. "Tomorrow when you come home, sugar pie, I'm going to plant a pear tree in your honor."

"He's in love," Laurie explained between bites.

Tom sang to Cara, sang a happy, little lullaby during which the baby lay content against his shoulder. Ben and Laurie ate without stopping, their spoons clinking in unison.

"Want some more?"

"No, thank you." He met her eyes, which had the same bright welcome, the same expression that only yesterday had so badly startled him. Now, her loving expression felt familiar to him, anticipated. "I'm full."

When Tom fell silent, Cara cried, but Ben stretched and yawned. "She's hungry," Laurie explained as she and Ben moved the tray aside. Smiling into his wife's eyes, Tom lay the baby in Laurie's arms. Cara cried shrilly.

Tom said, "Ben." But Ben was watching Laurie with the baby, noting her calm competence, her happiness both deep and vibrant. "Ben," Tom repeated, his voice louder, commanding again. "Look at me a minute. I want to tell you something important." Ben lifted his eyes to Tom expectantly. "I'm going to go jog over to City Dock Café and get Laurie a cup of tea, and when Pete and Joe get here they'll take you home."

"If you say so, Coach."

Tom bent to kiss Laurie and then Cara. Ben realized that while Tom had diverted his attention, Laurie had put Cara to her breast, both now hidden in the folds of a soft pink blanket. Ben yawned again. Laurie said, "Put your head down and close your eyes for a few minutes."

"I'm so tired," Ben agreed, resting his head on his arms, folded on the bed. He fought to keep his eyes open, wanting to remember the tenderness, the homey practicality of the moment between mother and baby, but Laurie touched his head with the tips of her fingers, somehow invoking sleep. Soon the baby's muffled sounds blended with the touch of Laurie's fingertips. His eyes closed. He felt time passing in a quiet, blanketed way. In his sleep, he noticed the rich, sweet scent of the milk and thought he was back at his grandmother's house, in the big guest bedroom where he always slept when he was there. In his dream vision, he was lying on his back on the bed in the guest room, looking up past the ceiling, past the attic at a bright blue sky. His back was cold, icy cold as if wet, and he heard a baby crying in the distance, crying with a mounting passion that was part grief, part anger.

The next thing he heard was the crinkle of a plastic bag that he knew was somehow important. He felt the damp, night air, then heard the rumble of Joe's MG. Streetlights flickered rapidly past his closed eyelids. Joe muttered about something spilling. Peter asked if Ben knew how many medals were supposed to be in the bag. Ben could picture them in rows on his father's chest, but he was too sleepy to count.

Once at home up in his room, Keith and Tim asked where to put their father's medals. "Top drawer," Ben heard himself say, "Don't mix them up or he'll have my ass."

"We know, Ben."

He tried to get his eyes open, but they refused; he fell back on the stiff, perfectly made bed.

"Put the letter on his dresser," Ben murmured. "Throw out the uniform shirt. Don't let Dad see it cut up."

"What letter?" Keith said. "There's no letter, Ben."

"The letter's with the medals," Ben said. "The nurse said so."

As he left, Keith insisted that Tim lock Ben's bedroom door. "He'll be safe."

Ben tried to sit up and tell them that it was okay, that they could leave the door unlocked, even open. He'd been given six weeks.

29

WHEN Ben returned from the basketball team's Sunday detention, he intended to sneak up to his room using the narrow servant's staircase that wound up through the house past the kitchen. But he came upon Donna in the basement, carrying a basket of clean laundry. With a courtesy that was deeply bred, Ben asked to carry the basket for her.

"You're responsible for your own laundry," she said as he took the basket from her.

"Yes, ma'am, I know. How's Dad doing?"

"He's awake and he needs to talk to you. Take that up to the boys' room and come straight back down to him."

Ben walked slowly back downstairs. He stopped in the kitchen for a drink of ice water. Once his thirst was satisfied, he refilled the glass and took it with him, his feet reluctant, into the living room. But after taking one look at his deeply medicated father seated on the sofa with his arm elevated on several neat, flat pillows, Ben relaxed. He put his glass beside a photograph of Max as a slim, smiling lieutenant in a slanted silver picture frame that stood on the edge of the glass coffee table.

"Hey, Dad."

"I need you to help me upstairs in a few minutes, Ben. I want to watch the rest of the Giants' game."

"Sure."

"I'm just down here because Lindquist came to see me."

"That was nice."

"He got pictures of the Miata so I can send them to the insurance agency."

"Can it be fixed?" Ben asked.

Max attempted a shrug, to indicate that he didn't know. "It's unbelievable for you to have gotten out of there alive." Tears flooded his father's eyes.

"Dad, it's okay," Ben said quickly, quietly. "I wasn't *in* the car, remember?"

"I know," Max gave a bitter laugh. "I was going to say you were driving, but by the looks of the wreck, no one would believe that. So, I'm stuck holding the bag."

Ben stiffened at the icy feeling in his own live veins. He stared at his father in stark comprehension. He could feel his own expression freeze and all the compassion he'd felt for Max's injuries harden. Ben knew Max noted the change, because hate flickered like hungry flames in his father's brown eyes. It was a look that anticipated Ben's betrayal and stood ready to condemn him for it. Taking a deep, measured breath, Ben forced his composure to become again inscrutable and stared at the smiling facsimile of his father in the picture frame. *Am I not supposed to react to the fact that he wants me to take the blame for his screw-up behavior?*

"That's a *shame*, Dad," Ben murmured.

"Ben." Max spat out his name. Ben refused to lift his eyes, though he knew that was what his father expected. Max wanted Ben's eyes so that he could threaten Ben silently against the imminent betrayal he sensed. Anger flushed up Ben's neck to the tips of his hairline and his cheeks burned with an unreasonable and uncontrollable shame. He stared at the glass of ice water weeping drops of condensation beside the photograph of his father's youth. "Tell me you what you did with the letter. And I want the truth."

"Letter?" Ben wondered when the photograph had been taken and where. Max was dressed in his camouflage uniform and stood in an open, green field.

"Don't play dumb, Ben. The *letter* with my uniform shirt. What did you do with it? I need it back."

"You mean the letter from Admiral Johnson?" In the photograph, Max's cover was pushed back from his forehead, in a jaunty, careless way he would never tolerate now. Grinning, he held a rifle on his hip.

"Where is it?"

"I told Keith to put it on your dresser."

"It's not *on* my dresser. Keith says he never saw a letter. Mom looked all through the trash, which was very unpleasant for her. Now, where is it?"

"I don't know, *sir*," Ben said. He had never actually seen his father smile the way the photograph showed.

"Ben. Look at me when you answer me."

Without moving his eyes, Ben murmured, "I am looking at you."

His father made an angry grunt and Ben saw that he was trying to get up, but fell back on the sofa pillows. Ben took the silver frame in his hands and finally met his father's eyes. "This used to be in my room when I was little," he said. "I remember it."

"Listen, mister. You were given a bag with my uniform shirt and my medals. The letter was in there, *too*. You were given an important responsibility."

Angling the frame so the glass caught the slanting afternoon sunlight, Ben explained himself. "The nurse gave me the bag when I was sitting there waiting for you. When I got home, I was really tired. I told Keith to put the medals away, put the letter on your dresser, and throw the shirt away. I didn't open the bag. I didn't even look in it."

"*Where* is the letter?"

"The last time I saw it was when you took it from me outside the MVA."

The doorbell rang. From the dining room, Donna gasped. Ben got up, stood the photograph on the coffee table, and went to the foyer. He could see Admiral Johnson's profile and the top of his wife's head. "Mom," Ben called. "It's Admiral and Mrs. Johnson."

"You remember what you promised me, young man," Max said.

"I remember."

Ben opened the front door. "Hello. Please come in," he said and extended his hand to the admiral.

"You look like you've been out in the sun, not in a car accident."

"Yeah. I'm sorry I'm so grubby. The basketball team did some service at school today, and I just got back," he said, as he shook Mrs. Johnson's hand.

"How are you doing? We were so concerned when we heard about the accident."

"I'm fine, thank you, ma'am. Dad's the one who got hurt. Would you like to come in and see him? He's resting on the sofa in the living room."

"Yes, of course," Mrs. Johnson said, looking around.

Admiral Johnson clapped Ben on the shoulder, and pulled him close to speak to him in a loud whisper. "Service at school on a Sunday afternoon? Sounds like a work detention to me. What did you guys do?"

"We played a really awesome prank."

"Was it worth the punishment?" Johnson said, grinning at Ben, his hand clasping his shoulder tightly.

"Absolutely." Ben leaned close to confide in Johnson. "And when we were done working, there was *food*. I mean it. Root beer floats, too."

"That's what I'm talking about," Johnson laughed.

His mother stood, teetering on the edge of the thick area rug, wringing her hands. "May I take your cover for you, Admiral Johnson?"

"Yes, thank you," he said with a genuine smile. "How are you holding up, Donna?"

"Oh, I—I—that is, *Max* is in a great deal of pain."

With solicitous concern, Johnson turned to Max. "I simply cannot believe it. I had just been speaking with you that very morning and to think…it's terrible."

"Thank you for stopping in, Admiral. Pardon my not standing."

"Nonsense, I wouldn't allow it."

In the awkward silence that followed, Ben waited for his mother to make the Johnsons comfortable. Finally, he said, "Would you like to sit down?"

"Oh, yes, thank you very much, Ben." Claire Johnson chose a dainty chair and surprisingly, Johnson took a seat on the sofa beside Max. He sat back and stretched his arm on the back of the sofa. A shudder of discomfort passed over Max's face. Ben kept his enjoyment from showing.

"Your fingers look mighty swollen there, Max. You're going to have to take it real easy for a few days."

"He'll be much better tomorrow," Donna insisted.

"Sit down, Ben, join us," Johnson said.

"He really shouldn't sit on the living room furniture in his work clothes," Donna said. "Go on and shower and change, Ben."

"Yes, ma'am."

"Oh, but we wanted to see how Ben was feeling," Johnson protested. "I understand it was a miracle that you survived. Thrown from the car, were you, Ben? I know there's been a lot of rejoicing going on in the Hunter household since yesterday!" Johnson said.

"It's a blessing," Claire said, "that you weren't killed."

"Thrown from the car and no broken bones, no concussion. I'm telling everyone I know what great things God has done for you, young man."

Aware of the tension in the room, Johnson glanced from Ben to Donna, and then to Max, whose expression had darkened. Any composure Ben had enjoyed in the newfound safety of his father's broken arm evaporated and his stomach began its shaking. He *had* to say something. He couldn't let the admiral go on praising God for something that hadn't happened. But he couldn't say, *Dad and I fought. He was hitting me. I wouldn't get back in the car with him.* Johnson looked at Ben expectantly. Ben felt his color rise. He swallowed hard. "I wasn't in the accident, sir," he said, his voice betraying his turmoil.

"What's this?" Johnson said, surveying Max and Donna's tense, frightened faces.

"I...um..."

"This all happened on the way back from the MVA, didn't it?"

"Yes, sir," Ben said.

"But you were with your father."

Ben swallowed hard again. He felt his father's eyes scald him, waiting for the betrayal he deserved. He heard Donna's tense, shallow breaths. "I...um, missed my morning run, so I asked Dad to drop me off at the corner, so I could run home."

"What corner?"

"I mean, at the bottom of the bridge. Right by St. John's boathouse."

"That wouldn't give you much of a run, Ben. Round the corner and home."

"No, sir, but I was going to just go in Gate Three and then circle around to Hospital Point," Ben thought frantically for convincing details. "If I run the entire perimeter of Farragut Field, it's a pretty good workout. Then, if I'm still going strong, I backtrack and go up the hill and through the cemetery."

Holding out his hands in the protest of the confused, Johnson glanced from face to face. "But the police reports say that you were thrown clear. There was concern about head trauma. I read the report," he said, looking at Max for an explanation.

"It was pretty hectic at the scene of the accident. Dad was stuck and—"

"It's never too hectic for the truth, young man."

Ben stood stiffly, tightening all his muscles against the violent shaking in his stomach. "I tried to tell the paramedics the truth," Ben said bitterly. "But they wouldn't believe me."

"Why not?" Admiral said.

"I'm not very convincing, I guess," Ben murmured.

"On the contrary," Johnson said, his eyes for an instant startlingly like Tom MacBride's. "You are very convincing." Ben saw how deeply the admiral despised lying, so deeply that he could—and did—recognize even a slick, practiced liar like Ben. Ben looked away, miserable in the realization that he'd just thrown away the respect of an honorable man for the sake of his appalling father. He wanted to run away, felt the thrust of speed in his legs and fingertips.

"Can I get you something to drink?" Donna asked, her voice a timid squeak.

"Yes, please. I'd like a tall glass of ice water," the admiral said, still staring at Ben.

"And you, Claire? I just made a fresh pot of coffee."

"That would be lovely. Can I help?"

"I can do it," Donna said.

"I'll help you, Mom," Ben said. "Then, I'd better change."

He followed Donna into the kitchen, feeling the admiral's eyes on him as he walked away, feeling as foolish and vulnerable as if he were naked. The swinging door swished shut behind them and Ben rushed to the sink, turned on the cold faucet, and splashed his burning face.

"I don't want you going back in there," Donna hissed. "They're asking too many questions."

"Don't worry," Ben vowed as he lifted handfuls of cold water to his face. "I'm getting out of here."

"What about your brothers? They haven't seen much of you in the last few days. Have you forgotten about them?"

Ben wrenched the faucet handle closed. "They're your children, not mine."

"You have responsibilities here, young man."

"Yeah?" Ben said. "Yeah, my responsibility is to lie to keep the most dangerous drunk driver in the country on the road. I've taken care of that for today."

"Shut up," she hissed. "They'll hear you. They can't know about that. We'll lose everything."

"You would have lost *me*, Mom, if I had been in that car. Have you thought about that?"

"You weren't in the car and you're obviously fine. Your father is the one who's hurt and who is in grave danger of losing everything he's worked for."

"He's *dangerous,* Mom. He's *messed up*. We've got to *do* something."

"We *are* doing something. We're taking care of each other. That's why I need you to stay quiet and stay home and help out with your brothers."

"No," Ben said, going for the back door. "It's enough that I just lied to the admiral to protect Dad. I'm going for a run."

Breathing hard, too thirsty to think, Ben stared at the traffic. *Where am I?* A cramp began in the arch of his right foot. He bent over, his head pressed to his knees. He began again, carelessly jogging across the highway, half-hoping to be struck by a car in the vague color of descending twilight. Going slowly now, his leg muscles hot and numb, his feet throbbing, he jogged the long way back. Stopping frequently to rest, Ben found these pauses benefited him less and less. As he approached the Severn River, his strength flagged. Thinking it would be easier to run on grass, he swerved toward a circular, granite memorial on the north shore of the river, but he stumbled and fell. Knowing he was seriously dehydrated and in trouble, he sprawled on the grass gasping for breath, his leg muscles twitching in hard cramps.

He couldn't close his eyes, gritty as they were and too dry. Before him lay the river, silver in twilight beneath a pale, gray sky streaked with steel-colored clouds. He fixed his eyes on the chapel prominent against the horizon, its blue windows opaque in the pale gold light of the sunken sun. Trying to focus on it, Ben felt his consciousness fading; he saw darkness puddle at the edges of his vision until the clear and hollow notes of "Taps" sounded across the water announcing sunset to the brigade of midshipmen, echoing across the river to Ben.

"Hey, kid, you okay?"

The cold, moist nose of a big, black dog touched his cheek. The runner bent beside his dog. "Do you need me to call an ambulance?"

"No," Ben whispered.

"Muffin, come on. Leave him alone." Despite the man's commands, the dog licked Ben's face, ear, and neck. "You been running?"

"Sir."

"Here, take a drink." The man squirted water from a bottle into Ben's mouth. "How far did you run?" When Ben didn't answer, he lifted Ben's head and forced him to drink. "Where's your water bottle?"

Ben shook his head.

"You run a lot?"

Ben nodded.

"You ought to know to carry a water bottle. Drink some more."

Together, man and dog coaxed Ben into a sitting position. Once Ben was upright, the man dribbled the entire bottle of water into Ben's mouth, while his dog washed Ben's ear and neck and injured arm.

"Let me take you home. My Jeep's parked just up there at the overlook."

"No, I'm okay. Thanks."

"It's no trouble."

"I'm okay now. I live right over there," Ben pointed.

"Military kid?"

"Yes, sir."

The man stared intently at Ben, started to speak, and then as if he thought better of it, shook his head. He swallowed hard, then said, "I'll drive you home. Least I can do."

"No, sir. I can walk home. I'd rather."

"Let's see you get up, then."

With the dog nosing the back of Ben's knees, he stood. He breathed deeply, stroked the dog's silky black head in thanks and then smiled at the man to show his confidence. "Thanks for helping me out."

"Make sure you never run without water," he said. "It's too hot here in the summer." Clapping Ben's shoulder, he turned and whistled for the dog, who gave Ben one final good-bye kiss, tail wagging wildly, before she followed.

30

BEN began walking, stretching as he went. Before him, the silver blue bay met the sky in a rising mist that blurred their boundary. From the edge of the water, the moon rose. Its immensity and translucent coral color suggested a frailty far too porous to hold the reflection of the hot, yellow daylight that was now quickly sinking away. Limping, moving inch by inch up to the crest of the bridge, Ben watched the moon climb through the mist into the thickening sky; it grew as white and unyielding as a clean, round stone.

By the time he reached the south bank of the river, his strength had returned. He began to jog. Ben cursed his resilient body that belied the frailty he felt now, alone in the world, alone with his secret, alone with his burden and his lies. He healed rapidly, keeping no visible record of the trauma he faced. Those who glanced at Ben saw the tan skin on which bruises seemed to melt away. People who saw him assumed that his speed, his coordination, his active body, meant that everything was good. And he had learned to respond to the rosy, naive outlook of others with a performance that reflected their belief in his well-being. Ben knew that this was why no one suspected his despair, why no one would ever believe his assertions about his father. Ben did not look like the starving, betrayed son of a brutal man.

He slowed his pace as he came to the end of the little bridge where his father had pulled over the day before. He went into the grass looking for evidence of their conflict. It seemed to Ben that even if his wildly healthy body could not do so, the homely earth should keep a record of wrongs. But the grass had grown lush, thick and bright green. So, the earth, too, conspired to keep his father's secret.

Ben ran away. The moon stayed above him, growing more golden as the sky darkened to blue and deeper blue. He began to grow thirsty again and ran harder. As he neared a residential street, Ben realized he had been running toward the MacBrides' house.

After taking a long drink from the garden hose left to dribble water at the foot of a sapling newly planted, Ben turned toward the house, anxiety cresting within like an ocean wave. Light from the kitchen window spilled out on the garden's glossy leaves and touched the tips of the shuttered buds of flowers, reaching toward the hollow where Ben stood in the shadows and looked in.

There in the kitchen, Tom stood at the sink pouring water into a stout, brown teapot. Steam billowed up touching Tom's shoulders and chin. Tommy sat at the kitchen table, eating an apple with a magazine spread flat before him. Tom moved toward the table, ruffling Tommy's hair as he reached past him and picked up the sugar bowl. He placed this, along with the teapot, down on a brightly painted tray.

Ben heard Bonnie Jean singing before he saw her step into the kitchen. Carrying the baby bundled in a pink blanket, she came close to her father, turning so Tom could see the baby's face. Ben could also see Cara's peaceful, sleeping face and Bonnie Jean's face glowing with a kind of triumph. Tom touched the back of Bonnie Jean's neck, bringing her toward him and he kissed her forehead. Ben backed deeper into the shadows.

Tom filled a glass with ice water and placed it on the tray. He opened the refrigerator and bent to look in. A car entered the driveway, the path of its headlights striking the front of the garage and missing Ben by inches. Peter entered the kitchen, his backpack on his shoulder, his duffle bag in one hand. Joe followed him, empty-handed, face sober. Peter hugged Tommy first, then Joe, and though he hugged Bonnie Jean carefully, Cara stirred and cried. Tom embraced Peter hard, but released him in a rushed way and clapped his shoulder several times. They all walked to the door together and standing in a kind of a huddle on the threshold, called out final good-byes, Cara's cries joining in bright, loud notes.

Something inside Ben told him to step forward, to make his silent and miserable presence known to them, but he could not. The car backed away, and they went inside. Shivering now, Ben watched as Tom took the tray to places in the house beyond Ben's ability to see.

Lights glowed from the upstairs windows. Which was Joe's? Where was Jeannie? Was the basement already full of needy boys? Staying in the shadows, he moved along the perimeter of the yard, watching the house and praying for the courage to approach the back door. The light from the kitchen fell on the sidewalk in approach. Stepping toward it, Ben saw a sign on the back door: MACBRIDES ONLY TONIGHT, written above a quick, deft illustration of a mother holding an infant. Ben tried to get his breath, but it caught.

Of course, it made sense. Mrs. MacBride and the baby needed quiet. This dismissal was out of consideration for her. He squelched his disappointment, telling himself to think of an alternate plan. He couldn't go home; he couldn't go in. He wanted to find a place to hide and sleep.

Standing in the shadow near the garage, the sudden warm breeze brought him the scent of ripening apples; the touch of the day's hot sun lingered on them in the gathering darkness. Ben's stomach growled and he bolted through the streak of kitchen light that separated him from the garage to the apple tree behind it. Ben climbed the tree, ignoring his shaking muscles and following his nose to a cluster of apples just above, close to the garage roof.

Thinking that he'd use the window to the loft as a foothold, he wiggled the heavy wooden shutters open. Ben saw into the shadowy, moonlit loft. Though it had been empty the day before, waist-high mounds of apples in baskets crowded the room. Their collective sun-warmed smell bid him welcome. Ben looked around the loft to see that the thin, bare mattress still lay beside the railing. Ben went to it, sat down, and ate an apple. He took off his shoes and socks to free his throbbing feet, lay back on the mattress, and closed his eyes. He wished for sleep.

Bright with moonlight, the loft lay too warm from the heat of the day and Ben's thirst kept him at the unsteady edge of wakefulness. A breeze, tinged with the provocative scent of apples, tickled his skin. He opened his eyes, studied the moon framed by the open window. It was a golden lantern now, the color of candle flame. The sky was dark blue and the moon cast its gold upon the scattered clouds. *My parents have no idea where I am*, he thought, swept with a kind of shabby contentment. *At least I'm safe, even if I'm not comfortable and I can't sleep.* He shut his eyes again to concentrate on the hush of the fragrant breeze in the apple tree. Ben almost believed the soft rushing of the wind in the leaves would put him to sleep, thirsty and stiff though he was. He let it surround him and he had the pleasant, heady sensation of being lifted up. Abruptly, the sound in the tree changed; limbs shook hard and scraped against the side of the garage. Ben sat up, blank with fear. Then, Joe's head appeared above the windowsill.

"I knew it was you."

"How?"

"I saw the apple tree shaking and none of the other trees were moving much." Joe climbed in. "I had to wait until I could sneak out without anyone seeing me." Slowly Ben got to his feet, his muscles stiff and protesting. "Why didn't you come in?"

"The sign said not to."

"What are you doing here, anyway? Everything okay?"

"I was running and I—"

"You staying the night?"

"I hadn't thought that far ahead."

"Let's sleep out on the porch. It's cooler, and we can get some food for you on the way."

"Your dad doesn't want company tonight."

"He won't care if it's you. He just doesn't want the basement full of guys playing video games and making a lot of noise."

"He'll probably feel like he has to call my parents and let them know I'm here."

"So, we'll call. We have a phone."

"No, I don't want to call." Trying to sound casual, he added, "It's a hassle."

"Okay," Joe said, regarding him seriously. "Don't worry about it. I'll handle it."

"How?"

"Watch and see. Come on."

Joe led the way down the stairs and through the garage. Seeing Tom walking the length of the kitchen with the baby on his shoulder, Ben hesitated at the door. "I'll wait out here."

Joe opened the door. "Dad. Ben's here. He was out running. He's afraid to come in because of the sign."

"Tell him to come in. And shut the door. You're letting bugs in."

Joe came back out. "You heard him."

"I can't ask him to make an exception for me."

"Don't be stupid. Of course you can." Reaching past him to open the door, Joe nudged Ben's shoulder, which made Ben trip forward, and then Joe gave a quick, practiced shove with his fingertips at the small of Ben's back, sending Ben stumbling into the kitchen.

"Hey, Ben," Tom said.

"I don't want to impose."

"No problem. You're always welcome. Laurie would agree, but she's just gone to sleep."

"We're gonna spend the night on the porch," Joe said. "It's all arranged."

"Sounds good to me," Tom said but his gaze focused on Ben and his expression grew thoughtful.

Ben stood in the middle of the kitchen. Aware of his bare feet, his dirty, sweaty body, his noisy, demanding stomach, he feared Tom's response. To distract attention from himself he said, "How's the baby doing?"

She slept on her father's shoulder, cuddled in her pink blanket. Her black lashes lay on smooth cheeks and her tiny pink mouth opened slightly with each sighed breath.

"Perfect, happy, and finally asleep," Tom whispered, rubbing his cheek against her silky black hair. "You were out running? Don't you wear reflective clothes when you run in the dark?"

"Oh," Ben said, glancing down. "I forgot."

"That's an important precaution."

"I—normally—I—"

"You look like you've had quite a workout."

"No, sir. I'm fine. I just dropped in to…" He felt Joe bristle beside him and realized that if he made it seem as if this were a spontaneous visit, Tom would make him call home.

"I invited him yesterday." The three of them looked at each other, waiting for someone to speak. Joe said, "I'm going to get the sleeping bags and stuff." He dashed off into the house.

"Would you like something to eat, Ben?"

"Just a glass of water, please."

"Help yourself," Tom said. Ben filled a glass with cool water and drank, painfully aware that as Tom walked the length of the kitchen with his new baby daughter, he was studying Ben. Ben filled the glass and drank again. He wanted to dunk his head under the faucet and wash away the dried sweat that itched his forehead and the back of his neck.

"How far did you run?"

"Not far," Ben said, drinking again.

"You didn't just run from home to here. You left way before dark and you've had a major workout. I think you're downright dehydrated."

Holding an armful of pillows and quilts, Joe rushed down the stairs at the far side of the room beyond the kitchen. He ran to the front of the house and out the door, slamming it behind him. "I always drink a lot," Ben told Tom, speaking loudly, in a tardy and futile effort to cover the sound of the slammed door. "I like ice water. My dad says it runs in my veins."

Cara stirred and whimpered on her father's shoulder. Tom swayed gently and rubbed his cheek on Cara's head to soothe her. "So, where did you run?" he said, softly.

"Up," Ben gulped, "Ritchie Highway. Not far at all."

"How's your dad?"

Ben's mind went still. He glanced at Tom's expression without meeting his eyes, trying to remember which version of the truth he'd told Tom. Joe came striding through the large family room beyond the kitchen, holding a couple of towels. He ducked into the laundry room and emerged with gym shorts and t-shirts. Ben exhaled in relief.

"Your dad," Tom prompted. "How's he feeling?"

"He's in a lot of pain, but he's home from the hospital now. Thanks for asking, Coach."

Tom nodded at Ben, his eyes squinted, his right hand still now on Cara's back.

"Ready?" Ben said, turning to Joe.

"Yeah."

His father said, "Joe, you've got to be careful not to slam doors. Okay? Mama needs quiet."

"Sorry, Dad. Come on, Ben, let's go." Joe nudged Ben's shoulder with his own, urging him toward the back door.

"Did you get in trouble at home, Ben?" Tom said, turning slightly to stay in Ben's field of vision.

"What?" Ben asked, feigning ignorance, his heart sinking.

"At home," Tom said gently. "Things kind of tense at home because of the accident?"

"No. I just was bored and—"

"You should call your mom and tell her you'll be here tonight."

"It's okay, Coach," Ben said, his throat closing. "I told her where I was going when I left."

"How is that possible? I thought you dropped in."

"I invited him, Dad," Joe said, stepping between Tom and Ben, intercepting Tom's intent gaze. "He just doesn't believe he's really welcome."

"I see," Tom said, stepping toward the sink so that he could again make eye contact with Ben. "So your parents know you're here for the night?"

"Yes, sir," Ben lied.

"And they don't mind?"

"Why would they mind?"

"Hey, Dad," Joe said, pulling Ben toward the back door, "Can you keep Jeannie away from the back of the house? We're gonna hose off by the basketball court and then change in the garage."

"Will do," Tom said. He turned away and walked deep into the house, patting Cara's back in a soft, slow rhythm.

"He's ticked," Ben said, once they were well beyond the shut door.

"Yeah," Joe agreed.

"I didn't really mean to run that far or for that long. I just kind of… ran."

"How far did you go?"

"There was a gas station with students doing a car wash."

"Oh. Jones Station Road. That's about ten miles. Wow."

"Yeah. How did he know that?"

"It's weird how he knows things." Joe shook his head. "How are you still walking?"

"I'm pretty tired."

Crossing the basketball court, Joe fixed the hose onto a hook on the back wall of the garage and stripped down to his boxers. "It's okay," he told Ben, gesturing toward the dense stand of trees beyond them. "The neighbors are way down by the water. No one's going to pay attention to us." Joe twisted the faucet and stood under the flow of rushing water. "Ah, it's cool, perfect." The water sheeted over Joe, splashing from his shoulders and head, rushing into his shorts, pushing them down low on his hips. "I usually soap up everywhere, then at the last minute, drop my boxers. Don't want to tempt fate."

"This from the man who mooned the entire school."

Joe stepped aside so Ben could share the water. Ben stepped under the cool flow and shivered with physical delight as the water sheeted over him. Looking up at the candlelit moon, he noticed the scent of the water, the tartness of apples, the spice of flowers and herbs growing secretly in the starlight—and he breathed in deeply.

"Remember, I only made it *look* like I mooned the school. I was fully covered."

"Another technicality?"

They soaped up, laughing, remembering the prank. Finally Joe wiggled out of his shorts and stood spread eagle to the moon, laughing. Ben, shy about being naked outside, watched the patches of window light as he rinsed away the soap, but his soaking boxers nearly slid off. Joe sprinted back into the shadows to get the towels. He threw one at Ben who stretched to grab it before it landed in a foaming puddle. Joe's face went serious and Ben saw that Joe had noticed the big, purple bruise on his hip. Ben pulled the towel tight around his waist.

"You know, Ben," Joe said casually as he grabbed the pile of dry clothes he'd brought outside, "it's not worth it to lie to Dad about stuff like you did tonight."

Ben forced a laugh. "This from you?"

"You saw he was ticked. That's why," Joe said, meeting Ben's eyes, holding steady while Ben wavered, pressing his lips together. "Why not just tell him?"

"Tell him what?"

Shrugging, Joe took the hose from the hook and sprayed the soapy residue into the grass. Joe pointed the nozzle at Ben's feet. "Pick up those wet clothes and grab those towels." Avoiding the spray that now felt too cold, Ben began to retrieve the stuff scattered all over the basketball court. Joe turned off the water, straightened up and spoke quietly to Ben. "Tell him the truth."

"What's the *truth*, Joe?" Ben asked.

"You were mad at your parents, and went for a run."

"It's not that simple."

"Simpler than lying."

"Shut up," Ben flared. "What makes you think there's anything to tell?"

"For one thing, the way your dad acted like a royal, flaming *asshole* yesterday at the MVA."

"Hey, I don't owe you or your dad anything." Ben looked around for somewhere to dump the wet towels so he could dash away. "Take these," he thrust them at Joe. "I'm outta here."

"Hey," Joe grabbed his arm. "You're right." Ben looked back, surprised. Joe held out dry boxers, the orange ones he called his favorites. "Here," he grinned at Ben, his expression goofy, embarrassed. He bumped Ben's shoulder with his own. "You *don't* owe us anything."

"No kidding," Ben said, softening, turning his back to step into the boxers.

"Except...it's weird," Joe said, shivering as he pulled on shorts. "I mean, here we are, *instant friends*. That doesn't happen. And it was just what I needed with Pete gone. After he left tonight, I was so glad to see the apple tree shaking." Joe bumped Ben's shoulder again. "So damn glad."

Joe led the way past the flower gardens radiant in the moonlight, through the damp grass to the side of the house that Ben had not yet seen. Here, the front porch wrapped around to its end and two porch swings, piled with pillows and sleeping bags, hung parallel, spaced far enough apart for swinging.

"Why do you say it's not worth it to lie to him?"

"Because. Isn't it obvious? It breaks things between people."

"That's sort of extreme, isn't it?"

"No," Joe said, belligerent in his intensity. "You were uncomfortable around Dad for the first time. You wanted to get out of the kitchen and get away from him. And a minute ago from me."

"People need space...or privacy."

"I don't think you're right," Joe said, leading the way up the porch steps and across the smooth wooden floor slick with moonlight. Joe lit three yellowy candles—to keep the bugs away, he explained. Opening his sleeping bag, Joe tossed his pillow to the end of one swing and flopped down. As Ben imitated his friend's actions, Joe murmured, "We want to be understood. We want people close to us who get it."

"Sometimes it's necessary to lie." Ben said, getting onto the swing. Beneath him it swayed lightly. He settled back and his stiff, spent body gave an aching sort of physical sigh.

"Look," Joe said. On a small, low table between them stood a brightly painted tray laden with food.

"What's this?" Ben's mouth watered and his stomach came loudly back to life.

"It's Dad."

"How do you know?"

"Oatcakes." There were two full plates on the tray with slightly different contents, but both had several homey, round, brown cakes slathered thickly with butter. "He thinks oats heal everything. He makes us oatmeal for breakfast every morning."

"He makes you breakfast?"

"Yeah. We have to have a bowl of oatmeal, then we can eat anything else we want. It drives me crazy."

"But he makes you breakfast."

"Oh, wait," Joe said, "this is Jeannie's touch." Joe lit the candle that stood in the center of the tray and gave Ben a paper napkin with his name written on it in curling expansive script. Drawn on the napkin was a sketch of Joe and Ben showering on the basketball court, clouds of spray and soap bubbles covering all but bare feet and bare shoulders, and smiling faces.

Ben laughed out loud. Joe said, "This is her way of telling us she knew we were out there and Dad wouldn't let her near us," and gave Ben his plate. Beside the oatcakes lay chunks of dark red watermelon, a mound of cheese slices, carrot and celery sticks, three devilled eggs, small round tomatoes, and five fudgy cookies.

Joe showed Ben his napkin. In Bonnie Jean's writing it said, *Dad says to tell Ben to eat his oatcakes first. And sleep well.* The illustration showed them both, heads on pillows, eyes shut in deep sleep, dreaming a joint dream of a big, round basketball. Ben said, "Witty."

They ate eagerly. "I guess your dad isn't too mad at me if he gave me all this food."

"You don't get it at all," Joe said, shaking his head.

"I do get it. This was an incredible gesture. It proves he's okay with me."

"He's your coach. It's like a dad. He wants you healthy and well-fed and—"

"So I can win for him?"

"No, you idiot. It's not cold like that."

Ben reached for his glass of water. Joe had taken the swing closest to the end of the porch so that behind Joe there was only porch railing and beyond that the wide, grassy meadow bright with the full moon's white light. Ben tried to understand Joe, tried to define the singular outlook of this boy who bathed and slept outside beneath the starlit blessing of his generous father.

"Okay," Joe said, propping up on one elbow, the movement swaying the swing. "Like today. Grannie came over to see the new baby. You have to understand that my grannie is really a bitch. She hates me. Like last year for Christmas, she gave Pete *golf lessons* and she gave me a new rake because I broke hers doing *her* lawn."

"That's harsh."

"Yeah, no kidding. So, she came to see the baby and I had to drive her home because Dad was busy with everything. All the way home, she picked on my driving. Like gasping when she saw a light turn yellow and grabbing onto the sides of the seat when I turned."

"Were you driving the MG?"

"No. Mom's van. It rides as smooth as water. And when we got to her house, I'm *required* to walk her into the house, because if she falls and breaks something, she'll end up living over *here*, which none of us wants. Once we get inside, she makes me do chores. I'm changing the light bulbs she can't reach and the whole time, she's after me—why's my skin broken out, don't break her step ladder, how to unscrew a light bulb—but I just ignored her. She keeps picking on me. Not only can't I drive, but I'm too skinny. And then she says I wouldn't need that ladder if I were nice and tall like Peter."

"Uh-oh."

"Yeah," Joe said. "Can you believe it? I shouted, 'Shut up. Shut the hell up.'"

"Sucks."

"So, I get home and Dad's waiting for me." Joe took a deep breath and Ben saw he was upset by the way he pressed his lips together. "Grannie called him, of course. He says to me, 'Just tell me what happened, son.' I considered lying to him, I really did, because he knows Grannie, and I could easily paint it out to be totally her fault."

"It sounds like it was pretty much her fault."

"But I know he doesn't want me to speak to her like that and besides, no matter who we're talking to, he has this *thing* about *language*—especially when you curse because you've lost your temper. He thinks that's *below* us or something." Joe lay back, arms folded beneath his head.

"What happened?"

"I thought I could get away with telling him part of the truth because once he heard how she'd been needling me, you know. But I couldn't break things between us. Things have been going so well. Dad and I had this great summer and everyone's been so happy about Cara...I knew Mom wanted it to be a really special day. So I just said, 'Dad. I'm ashamed to admit it, but she pushed my buttons and I was extremely rude to her.' I told him what I said word for word."

"What happened?"

"He explained again, at *length*—I thought I'd have to shave before he got done—how he wants me to behave. And as if that's not enough punishment, I have to go over there tomorrow and work for her. Labor Day. A day off from school and I've got to get up early and spend it with that grouchy old witch. And you can spell witch any way you want."

Laughing, Ben said, "Was he mad?"

"No, he understands, but I still have to behave." Joe flipped over onto his stomach and pressed his chin into his pillow. His emotion showed in his eyes and in the set of his mouth. "And he said if I speak to Grannie that way again, he'll whip my ass."

"He said that?"

"He said, 'butt.'"

Ben wanted to ask Joe what exactly Tom meant, but he only had the courage to say, "I'll come with you tomorrow. To your grannie's."

"What? Okay. That'll be great."

The boys lay back and fell silent. The heavy lemon of the candles blanketed the porch, and over it flowed the clean, delicate fragrance of the garden. The candle flames winked and flickered, inviting sleep. Sometime later, when he heard the front door open behind him, Ben's instincts told him to rouse, to get awake and aware, but he was far too tired and too full of good food to respond. Opening his eyes a wary slit, he saw Tom come between the two swinging beds and sit down on the edge of Joe's. Feeling embarrassed for his lies, he pretended sleep, keeping still and deliberately taking slow, deep breaths.

"Hey," Joe said, his voice husky with sleep. "You'll break the chains."

Laughing softly, Tom leaned closer to Joe and whispered, "Is Ben asleep?"

"I think so," Joe said. "He hasn't said anything for the last half hour."

"He looks asleep," Tom whispered.

"That food was great. The oatcakes were a nice touch," Joe said. "He ate half of mine."

"That's what I figured. I brought an article about Huck Finn I've been saving. I'd hate for Ben to miss it." Ben opened his eyes a slit to see Tom slide his glasses onto his nose.

"Read it," Joe commanded. "We'll quiz him in the morning."

Sitting beside Joe, the candlelight flickering in the slant of his glasses, Tom read in a whisper. Ben lay still in the darkness and a memory rose up inside him. With the abrupt certainty that is both sensory and emotional, he remembered that he had once loved his father. He remembered lying on his back in the grass with his father next to him, and he had been somehow weakened by an intense feeling of love and admiration.

The picture of the moment began to focus in Ben's mind, the details of sunshine and clover, the shape of the ball he held under his arm, the way his father breathed. What came next, what always came next, was a falling feeling as frightening as the truth and as irresistible as the pull toward sleep.

He clamped his teeth together to stop the shaking that erupted within. If Ben had loved Max once, he did not love him now. *I will never love him again. Never.* There was something terrifying about loving his father, something more costly than enduring his abuse, and Ben could not allow it. Instead, he listened as Tom read to his son, listened and watched through squinted eyes, imagining how to describe the faintly flickering peace that bridged the space between this father and son; he watched, wishing for his journal.

Ben saw Joe's eyes close and Ben felt himself grow drowsy. The last thing he saw was Tom bending to kiss the top of Joe's head. Tom blew out the candle on the tray, lifted it, and when he passed Ben on his way back into the front door, he touched Ben's shoulder briefly and said, "Sleep well."

31

THEY awoke at the same moment. Around them, birds peeped in the tentative white sunlight. "I've got an awesome idea," Joe said, swinging his legs over the side of the bed. "Let's take the canoe over to Grannie's."

Though Tom was not to be seen, in the kitchen oatmeal waited for them in a big pot. A box of Band-Aids stood on the kitchen table. "Those must be for you," Joe said as he wrote a note telling his father his plans.

Carrying the oars and a large canvas bag of supplies, they made their way through wet meadow grass toward the water, the sun already hot on their shoulders. The canoe was chained to a tree. Joe whirled the combination lock to loosen it and together they flipped it over. Inside, a complicated contraption made of wood and chicken wire was tied to the rear seat. Using his bare hands, Joe cleaned out the spider webs and searched for bugs lurking in the corners. "Can you swim?" he asked Ben.

"Like a fish."

"Good. We have to take the life jackets. If we see a patrol boat, we'll have to put them on. Otherwise, I don't wear mine."

Hoisting the canoe up onto their shoulders, they carried it down the slope to the water's edge and gently lay its bow in the water, leaving the stern on the pebble beach. Joe stripped off his shirt and shoes; Ben did too. From the bag of supplies he brought, Joe emptied frozen chicken necks out onto the canoe's middle seat and spread them out, Ben supposed, to defrost them. "For crabs," he told Ben.

They shoved off, climbing in when the canoe was afloat. They worked well together and in a moment, the canoe was gliding away from the shoreline into the smooth, brown water. "We'll check the crab pots on the way. Grannie will be pleased if we bring her crabs. I'm going to head toward that floater with the red stripe. That's our crab trap."

They slowed beside the floater, which was simply an empty milk jug painted with a thick red stripe around the middle. Joe grabbed the rope and pulled up a complicated wire cage. Inside a large blue crab clattered against the wires. Reaching in to avoid the moving pincers, Joe took it out, held it up for Ben to see, pointing to the shell markings on the underside that identified it as a male. He put it into the wire bucket that was chained to his seat. Ben saw now that the bucket was made to prevent the crab from escaping. Joe dropped the whole thing into the water beside the canoe. He cut up one of the chicken necks, baited the trap anew, and submerged it.

The next trap was empty, but the one beyond held two. Joe put one into his bucket, and looked closely at the other's belly. Showing Ben the marking, he said, "This female hasn't had eggs. They only have eggs once, so we've got to give this one her chance." On his open palm, Joe lowered it gently into the water. "Oh, I can see more down there. Look." When Ben shielded his eyes from the bright slanting sun, he found he could see the bottom of the river below, the sand and the waving green water plants, but not the crabs. "Trust me, they're there," Joe said and tied a piece of chicken neck onto a string and gave it to Ben. "Toss it in over there and let it just rest on the bottom."

The canoe drifted on the current and Joe put in his oar to create a brief hesitation. "Now, when you feel the line jerk, pull the string up very gently. He's holding on with his pincers, and he'll let go if you pull too fast." In a moment, it came and Ben, nerves alert, drew the string in with a slow concentration that belied his inexperience. He felt something nudge his hip. Joe said, "The net is right by you. Guide your crab over close to the side and as soon as you can, lean over and scoop him up with the net." The maneuver proved delicate, but Ben succeeded and Joe was triumphant as he took the outraged crab from Ben. "A big fat one! On your first try!" They established this as their routine: Joe emptied the traps and reset them, while Ben fished for blue crabs still free and hungry on the river bottom.

So they glided over the quiet, smooth-watered river gathering excited blue crabs from its depths while the rising morning sun gilded their faces and chests and arms. At the confluence of a larger creek, Joe whispered to

Ben. "Let's go in there," Joe indicated a shallow, marshy cove to their left. Joe steered in a long slow arc, bringing them to the middle of the cove.

They drifted, the water making small, lapping noises against the canoe, the crabs clattering in the partly submerged pot. Joe held his oar across his knees now, and studied the trees at the shoreline. Ben felt Joe's weight shift slightly, then Joe whispered, "There."

He pointed to the shore, to the trunk of a tree that had fallen and lay gray with age, sun-baked and smooth with the wear of the water and the wind. Behind it, a tall gray bird with a white head, a black crest and a neck curved like question mark, walked on thin, stilted legs. It touched its beak to the log, then paused, looked around, and took a few more steps.

"Blue heron," Joe said. "Let's get closer. Don't let your oar splash."

The boys slid their oars into the water and moved the boat with slow, silent strokes. When the bird saw them, it became still and Joe held his oar mid-stroke, whispering, "She's seen us." The heron, its feathers the odd, windy blue of the bay, took a step and in a single graceful motion, spread her wings and mounted the breeze, flying twelve feet further around the shore of the cove. They followed her, marveling at the grace in those wide, arched wings, the effortlessness of her flight. She grew tired of the game and with a squawk, mounted high, circling the cove, flying above them so they could see the slim gray body between the enormous graceful spread of the wings and then the wing shadow fleeing across the water so near them. She landed out of reach, nearly out of sight, at the top of the tallest tree at the edge of the cove.

Detours into the coves became part of their routine. Joe pointed out osprey nests—messy mounds of sticks perched precariously high. They watched an osprey—as sturdy and bright as the heron is gray and graceful—dive for fish, its wings spread to show the striking white underneath. Once they reached the pristine dock, they secured the boat to the dock pile and pulled on shirts and shoes. Joe was grinning broadly when they started up toward the cluster of houses at the crest of the hill with their catch of crabs.

Grannie came out the back door and, with her fists on her hips, watched them approach. She was as thin and small as a girl. She kept her hair, white as wisps of gauze, twisted back and up. Her blue eyes squinted in the sunlight and her expression, set in a determined way, made her lips look as thin and bloodless as a steel sword.

When nearly face to face, she said to Joe, "You've come to apologize and to pay your penalty."

"Yes, ma'am. I do apologize. And Grannie. This is my friend Ben."

"It's nice to meet you, Mrs. MacBride," Ben said. Grannie sized him up with such a keen and eager eye that Ben felt sure she was about to pinch him like she would a tomato. "Just the kinda boy I like t' see. Not scrawny," she said with a derisive glance at Joe.

"Uh, Grannie," Joe said, "We brought you some crabs."

"And what you're doin' leaving them out here in the heat to spoil, I don't know." Snatching the crabs from Joe, she muttered some instructions about mowing the lawn. "And don't think bringin' a friend wi' ye will lessen your work."

The boys fell to their work, sharing the tasks like brothers, completing the to-do list Grannie gave them. When the lawn was manicured, the walks swept clean, her antagonism toward Joe seemed to increase. She criticized the way he trimmed the grass around the mailbox, saying he'd ruined it. Joe threw down his shovel and walked away. Ben hurried to the curb and said he'd finish the task.

Working quietly, Ben marveled that Tom MacBride had sprung from such a woman. When they said goodbye, exactly at twelve, the pre-appointed limit, Ben had no difficulty being sincerely pleasant to Grannie. She had given him hope. The thought that Tom had become the man he was—despite his bitter mother—gave Ben a happiness so buoyant he felt like laughing out loud.

"What the *hell* are *you* so happy about?" Joe grumbled, as they went toward the canoe.

"You kept yourself out of trouble."

"I couldn't have done it without you. You saw how she treats me."

"It's unbe*liev*able."

"I don't think my dad knows how bad it is. She didn't even feed us," Joe complained as they shoved off. "Can you imagine if my dad was running that punishment? There'd have been some kind of food."

"Yeah, but your parents are different."

"They're what should be."

Joe's expectation that he would be treated with generosity contrasted sharply with Ben's guarded outlook. Joe, expecting to be treated like a prince, would always be affronted by meanness; Ben, hoping to escape abuse, would always be delighted by kindness. "We've got those apples you put in the bag," Ben said.

"Oh, yeah." Joe dug into the canvas bag and came up with muffins, slightly squashed, and the apples. "Good thing the canoe was in the shade." As they paddled toward home, they ate and talked, gathering crabs from traps set that morning and rocking on the wakes of the boats that sped past them toward the open waters of the Chesapeake.

"Where's Ben?" Max asked as Donna propped up his arm on several pillows. After a long night, cushioned by plenty of painkillers, Max intended to rest until the admiral's annual barbecue that afternoon.

"The last I heard, he went running," Donna said. "He's become obsessed with being in shape for basketball season. He spent yesterday morning with the team. It's too much."

"Let him go. He's got to work hard if he's going to earn an appointment to the Academy."

"You don't know what you're saying," Donna murmured.

"What do you mean by that?" The phone rang, and Max jumped at its shrill bleat.

"I need him to help me with Keith and Tim," Donna said as she went to answer it, and Max knew that she was hiding something from him. Donna's attitude toward Ben was odd. She depended on him more closely than she depended on Max, but theirs had always been a difficult relationship, and if Max were honest, the blame had to fall on Ben. Donna—chilly, self-possessed feline that she was—had sincerely tried in the beginning, but Ben's heart was colder than a knife in the back.

Donna came back to the living room with a stricken look tightening her face. "What's wrong with you?" Max demanded.

"That was Admiral Johnson on the phone."

Levering himself up higher on the sofa with his one good arm, Max said, "And?"

"He says you're to stay home and rest today."

"Did you tell him I'm feeling fine?"

"He said that was brave of you, but he thought it would be the best thing for you to stay home and rest. He said consider it a direct order."

Max exhaled, making an explosive sound. "Did he sound angry?"

"I think he knows."

"What could he know? He's just a control freak." But Max knew he was being punished. Banishing him from a required social event was a subtle humiliation.

"Maybe Ben is over there," Donna whispered, her fear a dark mask.

"What is Ben gonna do, drop by the admiral's house after his morning run?" Max said.

Donna said nothing, but the way she stared at Max disturbed him.

"What aren't you telling me?"

"Don't be silly. Nothing."

"When's the last time you saw Ben?" Donna froze, eyes widened; she opened her mouth to speak, but didn't. "Donna," Max warned.

"Yesterday. He had a temper tantrum and went out for a run."

"Did you see him last night? Did he come home?"

"I don't know."

"You don't *know* if he was home all night?"

"Did your mother know where you were every minute when you were almost sixteen?"

Max swallowed hard. "Here's what you're gonna do. You take the boys over to the barbecue at Johnson's house. You pour on the charm and find out if Ben's been there. Maybe he's still there. Try to find out what Johnson knows or thinks he knows. If Ben is there, send him home to me."

"And if he's not there?"

"If he's not there, and he hasn't been there, then we don't have anything to worry about."

32

ALONE in the house with his pounding heart, Max tried to clarify his problems so he could devise a strategy. He knew Johnson was punishing him. He knew he was expected to bear this with a stoic demeanor. He had to find out how deep Johnson's anger ran, or if Johnson knew the extent of his lies.

Max had always run with a group that proclaimed that the real, tough officers—the ones everyone respected and admired—were expected to get drunk now and then. Among this crowd, his drinking while driving would be considered foolish in a winking, boys-will-be-boys kind of way. But dishonesty—especially under direct confrontation—was a crime that really could not be blamed on manliness, on the wild and priceless thrust of testosterone.

The sound of his heartbeat thundered in the empty house. Unable to stand it any longer, Max struggled to his feet, going toward the back door that opened onto a little concrete porch and down steps to the sidewalk.

Why beat myself up over a few necessary lies? Max thought as he wandered slowly down the parking alley that ran along the brick wall separating them from downtown Annapolis. He went in the opposite direction of the admiral's house. *There's no way Johnson has the documentation to prove I'm lying.*

As always, his deceptions centered on Ben's existence. Max walked across the road toward Lejeune Hall, remembering Donna's despondency when she was released from the hospital several weeks after her daughter died. The doctor had advised Donna never to become pregnant again. She took a leave of absence from work and sat on the sofa all day, watching a succession of soap operas and drinking Slim-Fast.

He opened the door to the swimming facility smiling benignly at those he passed on his way down the hall. Max had been consumed with Donna's recovery. He brought her flowers, tried to tempt her back to health with elegant meals at the best restaurants, made promises of gifts and vacations. He wanted someone to pay for her anguish. In his heart, he blamed Tom MacBride, and wanted him to take responsibility for the existence of the child who died. After several weeks of expensive, long-distance inquiries, he found a team of lawyers in Annapolis who agreed to take his case.

Donna had responded negatively. "Roger and I had intense feelings for each other. We can't sue someone for counseling us to get married. We were going to live together, anyway."

"That would have been better and you know it. Roger obviously didn't want to get married."

"Roger *did* want to get married. His parents were against it and so were mine."

"He had doubts or he wouldn't have run away."

"Do you think I forced him?"

"No, I think MacBride forced him." He had reason to suspect MacBride's motives, bitter reasons, and remembering these propelled Max to walk quickly, to hurry to the room that housed the pools so he could relax in the familiar warm, damp air. Once there, he tried to breathe in deeply, but anxiety pounded his blood. Even when he had been trying to convince Donna about Tom's dangerous influence, even then he had not been able to speak his real suspicions about Tom; he had still never voiced them to a living human being.

Standing beside the lap pool watching swimmers, he remembered Donna's response, the way she'd turned her face away from him that day to hide a flood of tears. "None of this has anything to do with the fact that I'll never have children."

"Look, Donna, this pregnancy never should have happened. The people who caused it ought to pay. And since no one knows where Roger is, we've got to sue Tom."

She didn't answer, but wept into her hands. Max wanted to go to her, but hesitated. He remembered his first wife, tall and sleek and golden, weeping for a child on their bed in Camp Lejeune. Like a discredited goddess, defeated but self-possessed, she never allowed him to touch her when she was weeping for the child she wanted so badly. She feigned independence, claiming it was her problem, her icy vehemence communicating how deeply she blamed him.

But Donna huddled before him, a small, pitiful woman, dark roots showing where her bleached hair parted and fell to hide her face, her frail, bony shoulders convulsing. *Donna will never be as strong as Katie*, he thought as his eyes filled, blurring his visual memory of his first love, a woman who had never needed him. He took Donna in his arms, his heart overflowing with the pity that Katie had refused to accept, and he wept with Donna, his own tears coming from a place years beyond their recent coupling. *Why did you run away from me, Katie? I would have loved you like this.*

Now Max stood by the pool, remembering, feeling his loss as acutely as if it had happened that morning. Then his thirst distracted him; he felt so thirsty that his throat stung, the cast on his arm so heavy that his shoulder and neck and back ached. He could be weightless in the pool, he could forget…He looked up helplessly, weak with emotion. For a moment, Max Hunter thought he might pass out. The cool blue water and sharp chlorine scent of the pool reproached him for Katie's flight from him. A torrent of memories rushed at him like a crosscurrent at his knees. He fled the room, forcing his mind to return to Donna, to return to how he had given Donna back her motherhood, to how he had atoned.

As he held Donna that day and soothed her, Max knew that Donna's grief would win the lawsuit for them. His instincts compelled him to win her confidence, to convince her of his sympathy. Max knew he must give Donna something that would fill her emptiness, something that showed he understood, something that would win her loyalty.

He told Donna about Ben.

Painful to relate, Max chose the story's details carefully, avoiding the fears about Tom and Katie that he dared not face. They were up all night. Again and again Donna asked about Tom's crimes. "But if it was *really* none of Tom's business," she asked, "why did he take you to court?"

"He was interfering. He thinks he knows best and he decided I could not parent my own kid according to *his* standards. He had nothing to go on. The judge laughed in his face." By sunrise, Donna was convinced that Tom MacBride, with his compelling ministry in a shabby coffeehouse in Annapolis, had a destructive pied piper kind of power, and that the lawsuit Max proposed would stop him from doing further harm.

Max was unsure how Donna would view his connection to Ben. He expected her to be furious with him for hiding the fact that he was responsible for a young boy, but she seized the news with the blissful fervor of one who had just discovered a misplaced bank account grown fat in the addition of lost years.

"He's legally yours?" she questioned, squeezing his hand in both of her small cold ones, the sharp fingernails digging in.

"According to the law, there was never any question of that," Max told her. "We were still married."

He and Donna made plans to get married, to buy a house and prepare a room for Ben. After their wedding, Max flew to New Jersey to visit his mother and break the news that Ben was coming to live with him.

It was his first lesson in recruiting. He had seen Ben before, the last time when the boy was a year old, but when he drove up the street to his mother's home and the sturdy toddler pointed at the car and ran for the driveway, Max experienced his first affection for the boy.

Ben waited on the sidewalk, blond as the morning sun, his blue-eyed gaze steady and contemplative. "Daddy," he stated, when Max climbed out of the low, rented sports car. Ben looked healthy, his skin tan, hair a bright crown. He was perfectly proportioned, athletic in stance with his hands on hips, his feet apart. Max bent down and Ben stepped close, arms out to hug. He smelled fresh and sweet.

"Hi, Daddy," Ben said, "I wait for you all morning."

Max allowed Ben to kiss his cheek, but taught him to shake hands. "Men shake hands with each other," he said.

"No," Ben said. "One kiss each cheek."

"With me you shake hands, Ben."

"I'm Bennett, Daddy. Not...*Ben*."

"I'll call you 'Ben,' and you call me 'Dad.'"

Max greeted his mother, whose manner was cool and suspicious. "He knew me," Max whispered to her, showing happiness.

"Of course he did," Ella replied. "I keep a picture of both of his parents right by his bed."

Max held his tongue, knowing an argument would not work in his favor.

Ella and he had coffee on the porch. Ben drank ice water. "His favorite," Ella explained with a shrug. It worried Max, as did the boy's calm, serious manner. Ben listened and watched him as he told Ella about Donna and their new house and the room they'd fixed up for Ben.

"I knew that's what you were after," Ella said, pulling out a cigarette.

"You've done enough, Mom," Max said, keeping the urgency out of his voice. "I've taken advantage of your kindness long enough."

"Don't be silly. I adore this child."

Max put his coffee cup down, realizing he'd have to convince the boy. "I brought you a present, Ben."

"Where?" Ben said, looking around.

"In the car," Max said, rising to his feet. Ben ran ahead. Max opened the trunk and pulled out a plastic bat and a wiffle ball. For the next hour, he played ball with Ben and learned that the boy possessed both superb coordination and an extensive vocabulary.

"Be very careful near Gran's flowers," he warned as Max backed up toward them. "They're delicate."

"Where'd you learn a word like that?" Max laughed, tossing the ball up high. Ben ran forward, getting under it. He nearly caught it.

"I drop it."

"Try again," Max said, holding his hands out for the ball. Ben scooped it off the grass and tossed it to him. "Delicate," Max repeated, tossing the wiffle ball again, up in a high arc. "What does delicate mean, Ben?"

"You can break it," Ben said, watching the ball, centering himself under it, "so you hold your hands like this." He cupped his hands, reaching for the ball and caught it easily.

"Nice hands," Max cried. Max had to grab him and hug him. They wrestled on the grass, Ben screaming with delight.

When Ben lay beside him, spent from tickling and laughter, Max asked, "You want to come live with me and your new mommy?"

"Where my mama go?" the boy said, sitting up, watching Max's face for an answer.

Max stared at the bright April sky. Soft clouds raced beyond the colored treetops. "You'll like this new mommy," Max said, keeping his voice steady. "She's real sad right now. She's not strong like Gran. She's...delicate. She needs a little boy to make her happy and strong."

"She delicate?"

Max looked Ben in the eye. "Very delicate, Ben." He cupped his hands.

"Okay, Dad," Ben said. Max knew that he had brought this thoughtful child to the first important decision of his life. A pride as strong and sweet as love filled his heart.

So, wielding his own gift of persuasion, he had acquired a son, a gifted son, an athletic son with a passion for words, a son who was motivated to self-denial by the thought of easing other people's struggles.

Max stopped at the double doors. He took the handle and peered through the glass. Lost in his memories, he'd walked to the far side of the building. Max flushed with shame, hoping no one important had seen him wandering around thinking. *Damn it, what am I doing here?*

33

LATE that afternoon, Ben left the MacBrides' with a bag of food too heavy to carry in one arm. As he was walking up the alley behind his house he caught sight of his brothers dashing toward him. He put the bag down and bent, arms open to receive them in a big hug. Tim ran into his arms and then climbed onto Ben's back, while Keith pounded Tim's shoulder.

"You guys are wound up," Ben said, extracting himself from Tim's wild affection.

"Tighter than a thumb," Tim beamed.

"A drum," Keith explained. "That's what Mrs. Johnson said we were."

"I'll run this food up to my room, then we'll go over to the playground behind the hospital."

The boys ran ahead of him to the playground. Full, contented, well exercised and slightly sunburned, Ben walked lazily, contemplating the gold of the late afternoon sun on the perfect green lawns of the Yard. Inventing games, challenging them in races, pushing them on swings, he exhausted his brothers at the playground. Finally, they made their way home after the sun had set and the moon rose above the chapel dome. They were hurried on their way by hungry mosquitoes who ruled the still, warm evening with their busy and familiar relentlessness. Coming around the side of the tennis courts they saw that the house lay in darkness. Ben stopped, a sudden apprehension holding him.

"Let's go back to Admiral Johnson's house," Tim said. "He said to bring you back there." Tim pointed down the street to the superintendent's house that sprawled on the corner in front of the Academy chapel. The sounds of a party could be heard dimly, and lights burned in the formal gardens and on the porches.

Keith stood as straight and tall as he could, commanding Ben's attention. "He said, 'I would very much like to see Ben today.'"

Ben couldn't face the admiral, whose questions were far too perceptive. He would only have to lie again; he would have to lie every time he spoke to the admiral now and Ben was sick of this sharp, twisted skill of his.

"Is Mom still at the party?" Keith asked, wringing his hands and glancing toward the sounds and lights at the superintendent's house.

"Maybe," Ben whispered. "The real question is, where's Dad? Isn't he with her?"

Keith shook his head. "He stayed home."

Signaling silence by laying his finger on his lips, Ben led the boys up the back stairs and listened at the kitchen door. The rooms beyond were dark and still. Ben pushed the swinging door out, and they stepped into the kitchen. "I'm just going to get some cups and stuff," he said, crossing the kitchen quickly. Tim followed right at his heels, but to Keith he whispered, "You stay there and hold the door open." When he had the things in hand, he turned back and saw his father sleeping on the living room sofa.

Max lay on his stomach, his knees bent, feet over the arm of the sofa. His broken arm dangled over the side, the pure white cast the brightest thing in the dark room. Ben, who could see best in the dark, saw the grotesque, painful swelling of his father's fingers. He had broken his own arm once and he knew that to sleep through the relentless, pounding pain of broken bone and swelling fingers, serious anesthesia was required. He glanced around the kitchen for evidence and saw that the whiskey cupboard above the refrigerator had been left slightly ajar. "Shit," Ben said under his breath.

"There's Dad," Tim said, pointing.

Ben put the cups into Tim's hands and whispered instructions. "You guys go upstairs and take your baths. When you're clean you can get some food out of that bag in my room."

Determined to spare them the sight of their incapacitated father, an experience that always shook Ben to his depths, Ben waited to take action until he heard their footsteps reach the next landing. "Dad?" Ben whispered as he approached, expecting no response. Up close the fingers looked like fat, purple sausages, the skin shiny and tight. "Dad," Ben said, shaking him. "You've got to sit up." But there was no way to rouse him. He considered leaving him there, but he knew that if Donna came home and found Max in this position, she would become hysterical and the blame would fall on him.

There was nothing to do but to try to sit his father up. Though his stomach protested in a violent lurch, Ben forced himself to get down on his knees and then carefully slid in close to his father. The smell was there, the stench of scotch on his father's breath that elicited a frightened response in Ben so fierce his bowels turned to water and adrenaline burned down his arms to his fingers. Nose to nose with his father, Ben pressed in on the cushions of the sofa, and thrust his shoulder under his father's, into Max's armpit, and slid his shaking and reluctant left hand across his father's chest. Pushing with his knees and feet, he levered the torpid, slumped body of his father to an upright position. He pushed Max against the back of the sofa, and quickly—struggling not to vomit—he propped up the broken arm and piled pillows from the sofa and chairs on Max's lap and chest to anchor him into position. Then he dashed to the kitchen sink, his stomach shuddering in revulsion, and heaved.

When he could, he forced himself to look into the living room. Max had not moved. He let his brothers come down to the kitchen, but he made them sit at the kitchen table with their backs to the living room. Using a chair, he propped open the swinging door that separated the kitchen from the rest of the house and sat where he could still keep an eye on the sporadic, reflexive twitches of his torpid father.

Keith and Tim ate and chattered. Ben played with them, read to them, and helped them with their homework. When they grew sleepy, he put them to bed. Alone in the kitchen, the only sounds the uneven gusts of his father's breathing from the darkened room beyond and the faint buzz of the florescent light above the kitchen sink, Ben took out his journal and wrote.

As he recorded the truth about Admiral Johnson's visit and the details of his own desperate flight up Ritchie Highway and back to the MacBrides, Ben recognized a feeling of power similar to the knowledge that came to him when his jump shot left his hands. He could do this, he could do this well, and as often happened on the basketball court he knew a sensation of shimmering heat along his shoulders, the back of his neck, and the top of his head.

This sensation heightened Ben's perceptions and he looked around expectantly. When he was alone, writing in the semi-dark, Ben often felt this strange burning assurance as if light itself traced from his pen.

Unexpectedly, like a phone call that startled him awake, he remembered a time when he was young and small. He was in his bedroom. There was a big double window and though his father had pulled the shade, he could still see the moonlight, white and insistent, behind it. He was crying, frightened; his father was shouting at his grandmother. Moments before, he'd heard her solid frame slam against his bedroom door. She was crying, too, begging his father to be reasonable. Ben knew they were fighting about a thing in Ben's room.

This thing—rectangular, silvery and slanted, resting on his night table—caught the drift of the moonlight, thin and silvery and Ben stared at it as the voice of his father intensified outside the door. He took the glinting thing from his night table and carried it in both hands to the door. Elbowing the door open, Ben held it up to his father. He remembered saying something that made his father take the thing and smash it to the floor. Max ground the hard black heel of his shiny uniform shoe into it. Ben distinctly remembered the harsh, gritty sound of broken glass, and a shudder passed over him.

Ben put his pen down and stood up. He went to the sink and took a glass for water. As he filled it, he wondered if other people had an imagination like his. As a small child, he must have tried to explain his father's behavior by seeing meaning in the moonlight and creating conscientious mermaids, by dreaming of the perfect family, of one decent coach. He drank the water slowly, acutely aware that he was alone. He allowed his glance to roam into the dim living room and onto his father's snoring form. And oddly, when he moved to refill his glass, light from the front porch caught in the glass of the framed photograph of his father that he'd seen on the coffee table the day before. In the semi-dark room, its slant reflected like the brightest mirror. Ben took a step forward. His father and grandmother had been fighting over a picture frame.

34

"HAS anyone seen my wallet?" Tom said, coming to his office door.

"Not me," Joe said from his place with the others in the short wide hall between the locker rooms. They had abandoned their lunchtime football game because the heat on the field rose in visible, sticky waves and bees hovered like angry fans. Jeff had been stung twice and now sat with an icepack pressed to his swelling chin.

"None of us make a habit of snooping in your office," Jon grinned.

Tom turned back to his office and Joe said, "Okay, where were we? I've got him every day to and from school. Paul's going to take him for that hour after Driver's Ed class ends and before band practice finishes."

"But you're in *band*, Paul," Ben protested. "You're the *drum major*."

"I can sneak away," he said, stretching his long legs out so that his feet nearly reached the opposite wall of the hallway. "Mrs. Miller'll never miss me."

"Okay," Joe laughed. "We'll take turns sneaking out of band."

"There's got to be another way."

"You need to be ready to drive by your birthday," Joe said and every boy in the circle gave his assent.

"I told you not to teach Ben to drive," Tom said from his doorway. "It's illegal."

The boys exchanged glances but Joe looked up to meet his father's eyes. "No," he said. "You told me to *find out* if it was legal."

"Did you?"

"No, I haven't had the chance."

"You were at the MVA on Saturday. *With Ben.*"

"But I was busy, meaning…I forgot." Joe grinned at Tom, his dimple showing.

"That was your chance," Tom said. "And if I see Ben driving your car before October fourteenth, I'll whip both your tails." Coming out of his office, he pointed first at Joe, and then at Ben. "That goes for you, too, Paul." He limped down the hall past Paul, ruffling his hand over Paul's buzz cut hair as he went by. "And don't leave your lunch trash."

"This makes it interesting," Jon said.

"Yep, he just raised the stakes," Paul chuckled.

"Exactly what does Coach mean by that?" Ben said.

"What do you think?" Joe said, writing on the schedule.

"If he *sees* Joe," Paul said. "The key is to not let him see."

"Yeah," Joe agreed. "We need to fit driving time in on Saturdays."

"Wait a minute," Ben said.

"Look, you *need* to drive," Joe said.

"You can't just ignore what he said," Ben said.

"We could skip some of the band bus rides and drive to the competitions. That would add hours."

"But the bus rides are the most fun."

"I know," Joe said, chewing the end of his pencil.

"Do you think he'd actually do anything to Ben?" Jon said.

"He's not going to find out," Joe said.

"Ben's not his own kid," Jeff said, extending his arm to squeeze the water from his melting ice pack into a soda can. "But I'd bet my ass he'll find out."

"You've got a good six months left of the new kid rule," Paul said.

"That's not the point. Not the *whole* point anyway," Ben said, getting frustrated.

"The most that could happen to you is a call home," Adam said.

"Let's just forget it," Ben said.

Paul said, "We get in deep shit if a teacher calls."

"A call home is nothing," Jon said. "Just convince your parents the teacher hates you. They get mad at the teacher. Works every time."

"I can't do that, so we're *not* doing this."

"I think we can get around him on this," Joe said.

"No, Joe. What about you not wanting to break things between you and your dad? Remember telling me that? This will do that."

Putting the schedule down, Joe met Ben's eyes. His ears went bright red and he pressed his mouth together. The bell rang. They got to their feet and, without hurrying, picked up their trash.

Before band practice, Joe and Ben went to Tom's office. "Can we come in, Dad?"

"Of course," Tom said, looking up briefly. He stood before the carton labeled LOST AND FOUND separating items into categories—gym clothes, books, sweatshirts—which stood in shabby piles, like ruined towers, around the box. With an audible sigh, Joe sank down on the cot beneath the window. Ben sat beside him. "What's up, men?"

"Dad, I've got to tell you something and you're not going to like it."

Tom turned to them, a single mud-caked baseball cleat in his hand. "Go ahead."

"I fully intended to defy you and take Ben out driving."

"I'm sorry to hear that."

"Wait. It gets worse. I was making an entire schedule…for others to follow."

Tom put the cleat back into the box and took a step to cross the small office. He sat on the edge of his desk and gave Joe his full attention. "I need some kind of explanation."

"I want Ben to drive and I had a feeling I could push you on this. I wanted to see if you'd let this slide."

Tom folded his arms over his chest. "But you know me, Joe. You already know."

"True. But you're different around Ben."

Tom squinted at Ben, his eyes worried. Keenly embarrassed, Ben moved one hand to his stomach in a vain attempt to quiet the tremor that had begun inside.

"Is that your stomach?" Joe laughed.

"Shut up," Ben whispered.

Tom's attention went back to Joe. "I'm different around Ben?"

"It just happened. You had this really stern face and you looked at Ben and kind of, I don't know…smiled or something." Joe turned to Ben. "You saw it, Ben, didn't you?"

"Maybe I should go," Ben murmured, but Joe thumped Ben's knee with his fist and shook his head.

"I want the same things for Ben as I do for you. If I have a tender spot in my heart for Ben, it has nothing to do with you, Joe. Ben can never take your place."

Joe shifted uncomfortably. "Dad, I'm *not* asking *that*. I just want to know why."

Tom stood up.

"I'll wait outside," Ben said.

"No," Tom said. He traced his steps to the far wall and back three times while Joe waited and Ben endured the earthquake in his stomach. "Because I knew Ben's parents years ago—" Tom faced them, his expression mirroring Ben's embarrassment. "I suppose Joe's right. The past makes a difference. I didn't know it showed."

"It shows," Joe prompted.

"I don't know what to say except that I was very fond of your mother, Ben. She was a dear friend. But your dad—" He stopped abruptly and Ben was sure that Tom wanted to say more. Instead, his face got a grieved expression. "Has he said anything about your coming over to our house?"

"No, sir," Ben said, truthfully enough.

"I've got to talk to him," Tom said, staring intently out the window over the boys' heads.

"Right now," Ben said, keeping his voice from showing his alarm, "probably isn't a good time. He's on a lot of pain medication and he's pretty upset about the accident."

"But see," Joe said, sitting up straight. "That's why Ben needs our help. His dad has been in two accidents in the past week. That's drastic, Dad. He's not the person to teach Ben to drive."

Tom winced. "Joe, I don't feel comfortable criticizing Ben's father. Or making plans to compensate—"

"I'm just being practical."

Ben found Tom's discomfort in criticizing his father interesting. Yet his expertise at prevarication made this an easy situation for Ben. He could ask for the help he needed without breaking his promise to his parents. The trick of the game was to emphasize certain facets of the truth and stay silent about others. And he, Ben Hunter, was a skilled player. He glanced at Joe and then spoke to Tom. "Even if my dad *hadn't* had two accidents in one week, he'd be too busy to teach me how to drive. Being head marine and all. With his broken arm, there's no way."

"How about Donna?"

Ben knew there was no way she would, voluntarily, spend one unnecessary minute with him. "No," Ben said, feigning calm acceptance. "She works at night and sleeps during the day. When she's awake, she's got my brothers. It wouldn't work out."

Tom paced the length of the room and back. Joe and Ben watched him. Finally, Joe said, "So, Dad, I was thinking, since this is an unusual situation, you could give me special permission to teach Ben to drive."

"Here's what we'll do," Tom said. "You practice basic skills with Ben *in* the school parking lot *when* it's empty. Away from cars and people. Okay?"

"Sure."

"And if you're willing to get up early, Ben, I'll take you out on Saturday mornings. Do you run on Saturdays?"

"I run every day."

"Then get up, run over, and we'll drive. Then you have the rest of your Saturday free. How does that sound?"

"Great. *Thank* you," Ben said, getting up. Tom gripped Ben's hand tightly.

"Are you proud of me for coming to you?" Joe said as he offered to shake hands.

"I am," Tom said, taking Joe's hand in the same eager manner, but pulling him into a tight hug. Joe made an "oof" sound just to be funny, and Tom said to Ben, "Make sure you tell your father what our plan is, okay?"

Ben stared at them; his mouth shut tight. *No. There's no way.*

"That way he can relax. One less thing to think about while he's recovering."

"Coach, it's okay. My parents…they're comfortable with me taking care of myself."

"I think it would be courteous to let them know. Do that for me, okay? And tell your dad, I wish him a speedy recovery."

"Yes, sir," Ben said. He felt his throat flush with the pointed knowledge that he'd just urged Joe to tell Tom the truth but could no more live by that standard than he could fly.

35

JEFF slipped into Tom's office as Joe and Ben left. "I hate to interrupt this tender moment," Jeff grinned, "but can I talk to you, Coach?"

"Sure, Jeff."

Jeff dug into his pocket and pulled out a couple of rumpled pieces of notebook paper. "It's about this." He gave the papers to Tom and wandered around to the desk, where he picked up a box of paper clips and bounced it against his open palm. "I'm supposed to get you or my mom to sign it. And Mom's not up to that now."

The heading of one paper read *Homework #4, Jeff Birch,* in the most miniscule handwriting imaginable. Beside this, a large zero was drawn in red ink. "Jeff," Tom said softly, shaking his head. The next paper with the heading *Quiz, Unit 2*, showed the numbers one through twenty lined against the margin with only two right answers.

"I guessed on those two." Jeff sank down on the cot.

"Ouch."

"She says I've already got an F. I've got to pass this year, Coach. If I have to take the same class three years in a row, I don't think Harvard will let me in." He pretended disinterest by hooking paper clips end to end.

"No," Tom grinned. "They might not like that." He studied the quiz again for a moment. "What happened, Jeffrey?"

"I have no place to study. I can't study at home and I can't study at your house."

"You most certainly *can* study at our house."

"Uh-uh," Jeff said. "Video games. When I'm there, I have to play them."

"That's easily solved."

Jeff was quiet for a minute, before brightening. "By the way, when I was looking for that *Goonies* game we played all through eighth grade—I found a twenty-dollar bill stuck in the case, so I put it in your wallet. But, Coach, your wallet was so stuffed I could barely fit it in. You shouldn't carry so much cash around. It could get stolen."

"Where was my wallet?"

"You left it in the laundry room when you were playing basketball with Ben. You leave it everywhere. I was gonna tell you, but then all this stuff happened, like the baby was born."

"Thanks, Jeff." He knew the wallet couldn't still be there because he'd bought food and flowers and gas since the baby had been born.

"I thought about keeping the money, but I don't think it was mine."

"That shows a commendable strength of character."

"Could you tell Mrs. Bernadotte about that? And about how I found your wallet today?" Jeff pointed to the file cabinet beside the window. Behind a trophy lay Tom's overstuffed wallet. "You always put it there when you're getting in your wheelchair. Only that trophy's usually standing up."

Tom righted the trophy and took his wallet, checking to see that the important papers and pictures were there before sliding it into his back pocket. "Thanks, Jeff."

"That must be worth you sticking up for me to Mrs. B."

"I'll talk to her but she's not grading you on character."

"I didn't learn *anything* last year."

"I'd be happy to help you study. I'll give you a quiet place, help you make flash cards and quiz you. But I don't know French."

"Ben does. He got a hundred percent on this quiz. Jeannie only got an eighty-three."

"I'm sure Ben would be happy to help you. Jeannie, too."

Jeff shook his head and added another paper clip to his swinging chain that now reached the floor. "Ben won't help me."

"You're just feeling bad because of your grade compared to his."

"No. He's jealous 'cuz Jeannie and I've been friends for so long."

Tom leaned against the edge of his desk. "Ben has no special feelings for Jeannie."

"Are you kidding, Coach? Have you seen him look at her? He's got it real bad."

"That can't be," Tom said vaguely, staring at Jeff's string of paper clips that he now had made into a complicated loop.

"You're worried Ben'll turn out like his father."

"Where did you get an idea like that?" Tom said, embarrassed.

Jeff shrugged. "When I was standing out there, I heard you talking. You don't like that guy."

"Listening like that isn't polite, Jeff."

"Admit it. You don't like him."

"You should have made your presence known or backed out of earshot."

"Face it, Coach, you depend on my knowing stuff."

"Not at the expense of your integrity."

"Okay, I'm sorry, Coach, but I'm telling you, Ben—"

"Would be *glad* to help you with French. I'll talk to him. I'll make it happen."

"Tell him I'm no threat between he and Jeannie, so he won't beat me up."

"Between *him* and Jeannie. And I won't tell him that because the whole thing is irrelevant. Not to mention made up. Now go on your way. I'll see you tonight."

Jeff went to put the paper clips, hopelessly entangled, back into the box.

"Hey. Take those paper clips with you and get them apart."

"Can't I leave them here 'til my next little visit?" Jeff said, putting them back on Tom's desk. "Taking them apart'll give me something to do."

"Better than having you hang around for the next hour messing more stuff up."

"You know you love me," Jeff pleaded, standing at the door grinning.

"*You* know it," Tom said, and managed a smile, despite the fear that had dropped on his chest like a boulder.

"There's one more thing," Jeff said. "I don't have a French book."

"What about the one from last year?"

"Do you really think I would have *failed* if I had a book?"

"You went without a book *all* last year?"

"I knew I was going to fail anyway."

"Jeff. This is ridiculous. Go to the office and buy a book."

"I would, Coach, but I needed the money for gas and I was extra hungry at lunch—"

Tom took out his wallet and gave Jeff two twenty-dollar bills. "Put the receipt in my office mailbox. When do you get paid next?"

"Thanks, Coach. Next Friday."

"You can work the debt off at five dollars an hour. There's plenty to do here and at home."

"That's below minimum wage."

"Get out of here."

"I hate to hit you up for money and then run," Jeff prompted.

"Just so you keep running, I don't care," Tom grinned at him.

Jeff left laughing, but Tom went to his desk and sank down in his chair. If his disdain for Max was this obvious to a kid! After all the soul wrestling, his progress in forgiving Max had been scant. The proof was obvious: he was stalling because Ben was becoming part of the family without him having to say a word to Max. And Tom had hoped to wait until Ben trusted them so that the ensuing conflict with Max would not destroy the boy.

He'd waited *years*, promising himself and God that when the opportunity came, he'd seize it with zeal and compassion. Max Hunter was finally within reach, just down the street at the Naval Academy! Max could no longer return letters unopened or hide behind lawyers. Tom could walk up to Max's front door and say what he'd promised to say. But he hadn't done it.

Tom squinted at nothing while he tried to think of what he should do first. He found a pencil and from the bottom drawer got out a clean pad of lined paper. He chewed on the pencil until his teeth hurt and somehow the pain brought clear his questions. What if Max had changed? What if he had matured and no longer deserved Tom's contempt?

But the things that Tom had to say to Max pounded against his conscience. Tapping his pencil on his desk, Tom steeled himself. *It's your duty. You promised. You've been praying for the chance to fulfill this promise. You've got to put Ben and what's right above your own comfort.*

This he told himself, though he knew much more than his comfort stood at stake. *Laurie gave birth just two days ago. I can't risk a back injury at least until she's gotten her strength back.* Another violent confrontation with Max would, at the very least, rob him of the use of his legs.

The last time he had seen Max Hunter face to face, Tom had not been able to land one decent punch, but Max's relentless blows forced Tom backwards over the low, open door of his MG. It broke his back. Max preyed upon Tom's love, used his dearly held principles against him.

Max's defense—unfair, even *unconscionable*—was also impenetrable. Tom had been beaten because he refused to strike back.

Later, when he recovered enough to walk and sit stiffly in his back brace, he tried to fight for Ben through the legal system, but every lawyer he spoke with told him that the scrap of paper on which Tom *himself* had scrawled the dictated, fragmented desires of a frightened woman would never stand up in court. They had all scorned his evidence and refused him. Tom had never won any type of disagreement with Max Hunter. He had always been beaten—soundly, painfully beaten.

Facing facts brought out the Scots' practicality in Tom. He began a list of necessary preparations:

> Lawyer—update will and discuss situation.
> Insurance—extra life and disability insurance for Cara's sake.
> Family—write a letter to each of the kids. Include Ben to explain.

But when he wrote down Laurie's name, a despair, deep and shameful, covered him and for just a moment he doubted his ability to do the right thing, to correct his failures of so long ago. Surely it would benefit them *all*, his many children, and certainly Laurie, if he were alive and mobile, his spine only as damaged as it was now. They had learned to live with that. Surely it would be better to have him alive and tarnished than to have him sacrifice their security for the sake of his stubborn and demanding integrity. Wasn't he raising up his principles to be god if he put them above his family's needs?

With a knock on his open door, Joan Poulard stepped in. "Tom, I've asked around. No one has seen your wallet."

"I found it," he said, drawing it out of his pocket to show her. "Evidently I leave it all over the place."

"That's a relief. I was worried it had been stolen."

"How much do you know about the new boy, Joan? What did you think of his parents when he enrolled?"

"I didn't meet them. Just the grandmother."

"Was an older man with her? White hair? Tan face?"

"No, the grandmother enrolled him. She's evidently paying the tuition. She said his parents were busy moving in and getting settled in new jobs. But they must be nice people to have raised a kid like Ben."

"You've *never* met the parents? They didn't come to orientation either?"

"No, the grandmother was there then, too. Why?"

Tom took his chewed-up pencil and tossed it into the small tin trash pail at the side of his desk. Absently he reached for another and tapped it on the desk in a quick, slightly maddening rhythm. "Listen, Joan, I have to tell you something about my past because it may end up having a big impact on the school. And if you want me to, I'm prepared to resign."

"What?" Joan said, her eyes going round as the moon. She sank down on the cot beneath the window.

"That can't be comfortable for you. Sit here," Tom said, getting up.

"No. Don't get off the subject, just tell me."

"Ben's father and I," Tom began, "have a long and violent history."

"Tom, you're pulling my leg," she said, tossing her head back and laughing loudly.

"No. I'm not. We began fighting when we were twenty-two years old. He…uh…somewhat indirectly is the reason I had to get out of the Marine Corps."

"I thought you were discharged because of your back."

"I was."

"Was Ben's father the doctor? Did he insist on the medical discharge?"

"In his own way," Tom shrugged and covered his mouth with his hand, the realization of Max's destructive power in his life washing over him. His hand shook. For an instant it seemed as if it were not the loving will of the God he served, but Max Hunter's vengeful actions that governed his life. He was sitting here, in this shabby little coach's office, taking care of kids like Jeff because Max Hunter had eliminated his Marine Corps career, had ripped away Rising Sun's financial base with a vicious lawsuit before smashing his car into the side of the building—twin blows from which neither Tom's back nor the simple, kindhearted ministry of Rising Sun had been able to recover.

"Tom?"

He swallowed hard. "It was in a fistfight with Ben's father that I broke my back."

"What happened?"

"To make a long story short, we argued, he hit me, and I landed funny. It broke my back." Tom rubbed his face, thinking that he had been blessed immeasurably by his life as a coach. *Max meant it for evil, but God turned it to good*, he told himself. Yet fear gripped his heart.

"Take a deep breath, Tom."

"Joan, I know things about Ben's father, and therefore indirectly about Ben, that are going to have to come out."

"Like the fact that he broke your back? You think Ben should know that?"

Tom squirmed in his chair like a freshman asked to rat out his classmate. "I'm trying to decide how much to say. I know much of this in strict confidence."

"Is this going to break up your marriage?" she asked.

"No. Not that."

"So, Laurie knows everything?"

"Yes," Tom said quickly, then grimaced and said, "Nearly everything."

Joan Poulard stood up. From a deeply ingrained courtesy, Tom also rose immediately. She smiled at him. "My door is open when you figure out how much you can say."

"It may involve the courts. It has before."

"Have you broken the law, Tom?"

Tom thought a minute, sat back down. "It's complicated and I'm not guiltless."

"What an answer!" She shook her head. "Keep me posted. You know I stand behind you as your boss and as your friend. There's no way I'm letting you go because of the sins of your youth."

"Thanks," Tom murmured. He chewed the pencil, but this time felt no pain.

BOOK TWO

Apple Tree
Little Low Heaven
Cross and Crown
Grandmother's Choice

Apple Tree

1

On those rare fall evenings when Tom did not have a game to watch, a faculty meeting to endure, errands to run for his wife, his children or his mother, he drove from work to the Naval Academy. After chatting with the marine on guard, he circled the perimeter of the Yard, and window open, elbow out, he went through the shaded cemetery, past the obstacle course, and around the far edges of Mother B. He drank in the familiar details of stately buildings still standing, of midshipmen younger every year, of the subtle, unforgettable color of the Severn. He parked in front of the chapel, went in and knelt in prayer for as long as his back could tolerate. Leaving the chapel by the side entrance, he walked past the superintendent's house to Captain's Row and Max Hunter's residence.

No one was ever home.

Hunter's name and rank were blazoned on the front step riser, but not once in those weeks did anyone answer the door. He considered leaving Max a note, but constrained by the conditions of his promise that he *tell* Max, he did not. Showing up at Max's office did not seem fair.

That chilly evening in late September as the sun sank behind the chapel changing its blue windows to the watery color of the bay, he walked back to his car. He felt cold and disappointed in himself. He folded his arms across his chest, ducked his head to his chin, and because his midshipman training *still* kept him from breaking into a run on Academy grounds, he quickened his pace, walking rapidly.

"Is that Tom MacBride walking right past my front door without so much as a friendly hello?"

Startled, Tom came to a sort of civilian attention and looked up to see his old friend, Charlie Johnson, standing on the sidewalk.

"If it isn't old Bulldog Charlie Johnson," Tom said, striding forward to take the admiral's hand, but Johnson embraced him briskly, his warmth obvious in his grin and his eyes.

"It is good to see you, Tom. Come on in. Say hello to Claire. You can stay for a long overdue visit." Charlie put his arm around Tom and urged him up the front steps. "I don't know how many times I've said to Claire since we've been back, 'Got to call Tom MacBride. Got to see how he's doing.'"

Claire Johnson had prepared tea for Charlie and she was placing a silver tray on the admiral's desk when Charlie shut the front door behind them. Claire listened to Tom's description of his children as she admired the photographs he carried in his wallet, but soon left the two men alone in the spacious, book-lined study. Johnson poured strong, dark tea, and with a sweeping gesture of hospitality, told Tom to help himself. Tom had taken one gulp of his tea when the admiral said, "How's it been having Max Hunter's son in your school?"

"Ben is a terrific kid. He's easy to love."

"Yes. He and your son Joe came over one day. Good-looking boy you've got there. Plus he's got his mother's brains."

Tom laughed. "Joe wouldn't hear of applying to the Academy until *you* recommended it." The gingerbread was warm and fragrant. Tom took a large piece and poured the steaming lemon sauce over it.

"Has Ben said anything about that visit?"

Tom shrugged. "He seemed as positive about it as Joe was. Good gingerbread. Tell Claire I said so." He scooped up another forkful.

Johnson nodded. He wasn't eating, but held his mug in the palm of his large, thin hand. "I thought I'd made some inroads with Ben that day. Naturally, I took to him right away. He is so like his mother, it's uncanny. The eyes, the coloring, the sharp, questioning mind beneath that cool composure. Fascinating."

Tom nodded, his heart sinking, his promises stirring with the quick, demanding vitality of life. He put his fork back down on the plate and the rich piece of cake fell off into a puddle of lemon sauce.

"Naturally, I mentioned his mother to Ben," Johnson said. "It seemed the decent thing to do. I think it may have turned him off to me, though."

"Why do you say that?"

"When he was here, I was sure I'd won his confidence. But the next day I provided him with a letter that certified his date and place of birth, all that. He told me that he needed this for his driver's license. I confirmed what I knew," Johnson tapped his chest over his heart, "with info from his father's personnel file. Ben claims he gets one of these letters at every duty station, though I don't believe a word of it."

"Something about a missing birth certificate," Tom said. "I don't understand how that could be."

"It makes absolutely no sense to me. I contacted the New Jersey Board of Records, but they refused to help me because I'm not a relative. Tom, did *you* ever see a birth certificate?"

Tom rubbed his face, "No. I do remember filling out the form you need to *get* a birth certificate, but we didn't finish it. There was a question about his name, so…maybe it was never sent in."

"Didn't you have something written down about his name?"

"I think that was in her diary. The note I have is about other things. I never have given it to Max." Tom studied his hands, studied the glint of the cool, white artificial light on the warm gold of his wedding ring.

Johnson put his mug down and scooted his chair a little closer to Tom. With a gentle fist, he thumped Tom's knee. "I do believe that's what you were doing over here today, Tom MacBride. You were looking for Max Hunter."

"Charlie, I'm hoping there's something in what I have to say to him that will mend things."

"I don't see how that's possible. To the contrary."

"I don't see the logic of it either, but deep inside me something says that if I do what I promised, all will be right."

"Does Ben seem to trust you right now?" Johnson asked.

"Who knows? I've been taking him out driving Saturday mornings. He changes the subject when I bring up his family."

"After I gave him that letter, I expected to hear from him again."

"What did you put in it?"

"Everything."

Tom swallowed hard. "Ah," he said when he could speak.

"If that was a shock to him or an offense…"

"Laurie and I think he knows nothing at all—"

"That's what *I* thought—I was sure of it at that first meeting," Johnson interrupted. "It tore me up."

"Then again, sometimes I think he's been trained to be silent about it. He says he gets one of these letters at every duty station—think about the implications of that. If he's seen even *one* of these letters and has been taught to be silent—"

"Right. He'd have to avoid me. Because, you see, Tom, I expected him to come straight back to see me about it. That way we'd get the whole ugly truth out in the open without you being involved. That was my strongest motive in providing such a detailed letter. But that was the day Max crashed and busted his arm. Since the accident, Ben will not so much as look me in the eye. He's guarded to the point of being guilty. Something's gone wrong."

"Maybe he did read it and Max told him it was all lies."

"Is there any possibility that Ben is not the child we think he is?"

"No. Why?"

Johnson leaned forward. "Max insists it's so."

"It's him," Tom said. "No doubt in my mind."

"Max claims Ben is his son by Donna from a premarital association."

"No."

"If Max told him the letter was a lie and that Ben was conceived years before their marriage, the boy might be ashamed to discuss it all."

Tom gave a frustrated shrug. "How do I bring it up? Do I say, 'Ben, how much do you know about your parents' marriage?'"

"No, you can't do that. You've got to get him to open up to you."

"I'm working on it."

"There's no better man for the job. In the meantime, I've got to find out what's wrong with Max. The man has some problems, Tom."

Tom groaned. "Don't tell me that, Charlie."

"You were hoping he'd changed?" Johnson laughed.

"I've been on my knees about it every day for nearly sixteen years."

"Have you heard any more from her parents?"

"No."

"So, they never regretted their decision."

"I don't know how that's possible," Tom sighed. "But we did hear that they live in Switzerland."

"How about Max's parents?"

"What are you planning, Charlie?"

"I just want to know the lay of the land. Are Max's parents interested in Ben?"

"Max's father passed away. His mother refuses any contact with Laurie and me. And we've tried everything."

"I know you have, Tom."

"Last time I knocked on her door, she called the police."

"You've done all you can to right the past. That part of this war is over. If you go over there, Tom, knock on Hunter's door and open old wounds, you'll lose Ben again."

"He knows I'm in town. I'm his kid's coach. He's probably waiting for me to make the first gesture toward peace."

"No, he's not, Tom. He's thinking that you don't want to risk your health, your reputation or your family life and you're going to stay out of it."

"I don't care about my reputation. I care about Ben and keeping my promise."

"Tom, you know I believe in keeping promises, but it's because of Max's behavior that you had to make that promise to Katie. We have to be strategic, sensible. If you confront Max with what you promised, I *guarantee* you, Max is gonna turn the heat up at home and Ben is gonna slip through your fingers like melting butter."

"I have a feeling it will lance his anger."

"Tom, think back to what happened when you tried to tell Max before."

"You know what I think about that day. I failed. But I've been given another chance—"

"You told me how Max behaved."

"Charlie, in his defense...I mean, *think* about it." Johnson raised both eyebrows, unconvinced. Tom went on. "Anyway, time has gone on. He can*not* behave that way now. Not at his age, not here with all his responsibilities."

"He used Ben against you that day."

Tom winced, remembering Ben's frantic cries, Laurie's voice from inside the house shouting into the telephone, Ella Hunter's shameless, open-armed begging. He shut his eyes and a shudder ran through his body. Johnson reached over and patted Tom's shoulder. "I'm uneasy because I don't understand why Max put Ben in my school and hasn't tried to contact me. I don't know how to read it."

"It *is* odd that Ben is in your school. It might mean that Max has come to terms with your part in Ben's life, but Ben seemed to indicate that Max hadn't yet visited the school. Ben's grandmother enrolled him."

"But Max must know I'm there. *Donna* knows. I saw her at the hospital the night Cara was born."

"And how was she?"

"She told me not to contact Max. Told me bluntly."

"And you're ignoring this warning?" Johnson extended both hands in a gesture indicating the obvious logic. "She lives with him. She ought to know."

"If he's still angry at me, if he's still a messed up maniac, then the past is still an issue."

"Tom, I *hope* Max knows you're the athletic director at his kid's school. To me, his knowing would speak well of his attitude. But I doubt he does."

"But I've asked Ben many times to say hello for me. Besides, everyone knows me, Charlie! I'm constantly quoted in the prep school sports section. Come on. He's *got* to know."

"Maybe," Johnson shrugged. "As you used to say, yours is the only MacBride in the phone book."

"Actually, I'm not in the phone book anymore. My principal's recommendation."

"Hmmm."

"He's probably sitting at his kitchen table telling Donna, 'If Tom wants to talk, *he'll* call *me.*'"

"No, he knows *you* want to talk. That's the way you left things. You made every possible effort to speak to him—you even went to court. He's the one who refused. I wouldn't push it. I really wouldn't."

"I heard some authority in your voice just now."

"You are no longer under my command," Johnson said.

"And if I *were*?"

His eyes sad, "I would order you to stay away from him. I would order you to initiate no contact, and if he contacted you, I would order you to agree to no meeting unless I or another big, strong witness was there."

"You're not so big and strong, Charlie. *I* could beat you up, and that's not saying much."

Johnson laughed but his hand went again to Tom's shoulder. "If he showed up at your house, I'd order you to lock the doors and hide in the bathtub. Rather you faced a tornado than Max Hunter, Tom."

"You're ordering me to behave like a coward. And you despise cowards," Tom grinned. "You're worried about my back."

"I'm worried about a lot of things. Your pretty wife having to do without you is one."

"How about if I go see him and just refuse to fight him?"

"You tried that. You refused to strike back, that's why he beat you so badly." Johnson paused before adding more quietly, "He never beat you because he was stronger than you. Max Hunter beat you every time because he has no conscience. He'll do anything to win. That's why I don't want you to seek him out. I won't have you hurt on my watch, Tom. Uh-uh."

2

"HISTORY," Max Hunter told his students as he finished his lecture, "is a matter of perspective." He glanced around his clean classroom, alight with the late-day reflection off the wide, silver Severn beyond the big windows at the back of the room. Standing at a simple podium, Max rested his heavy cast on the rim. His shoulder ached from the weight of the cast. As his students recorded his words into their neat notebooks with a diligence that thrilled his military officer's ordered and commanding soul, he glanced down to see that he had touched on the points in his plan. Teaching was definitely the easiest job the Marine Corps had ever asked him to do. "Ask yourself as you research, 'What does this storyteller have at stake?' When you answer that question, you can define your source's bias." He glanced at his watch and though the bell had not yet rung, he added, "Class dismissed."

They grabbed their things and stood, except for Midshipman Campbell, a tall, athletic female who lingered daily after class with questions.

Max watched through the glass door, left slightly ajar, until the last fleeing mid was well out of earshot. She walked toward him from the back of the class; he studied her body. Nearly six feet tall, she had just the kind of young body he liked best except that her buttocks looked flatter than a chain-smoking redneck's. Female runners never had any ass.

"I'm thinking you've asked every possible question about your assignment," he said, leaning to sit on the edge of his desk and grinning at her. "What *else* can I do for you today? Your name's Lindsay, isn't it?"

As soon as he'd spoken, he saw Ben at the classroom door. Ben had raised his fist to knock but, seeing Max, reading the body language, the facial expressions, dropped his fist. Max knew he understood.

"Ben," Max barked.

Midshipman Campbell startled, came to attention. Max waved Ben in. "Ben." He strode to the door and swung it wide. He grabbed Ben's forearm and pulled him into the room. The bell rang.

"I thought class went until four o'clock," Ben said, glancing quickly at the clock on the wall, his expression going polite and wholly unreadable.

"Ben, this is Midshipman Campbell. This is my son, Ben Hunter."

Max wondered about Ben's reaction beneath his polished and impenetrable mask. However uncomfortable, Ben looked vibrant. He was sweating slightly, tan and lean, his face more confident, his jaw somehow stronger, his blue eyes keener than Max remembered. Max realized that he had not seen Ben in three weeks and the last time he saw him was just a glimpse of Ben's back—backpack slung on one shoulder—as he rounded the corner of the alley on his way to catch his ride to school.

Now Midshipman Campbell appraised Ben, and Max saw his son through her eyes. Ben had obviously been running and running hard, and his exercised breathing accentuated his features and his athleticism. Dressed in gym clothes, his bare arms and legs looked ready and graceful; his white T-shirt and dark shorts clung damply to his body revealing the shape and breadth of his fine, tight muscle. *He might be inexperienced and way too uptight for a son of mine but he looks like a young god,* Max thought, recognizing the powerful and palpable effect Ben had on Midshipman Campbell.

"It's nice to meet you, Ben," she said, extending her hand. "I guess I can see a *little* of your father in you." Ben shook her hand in the strong, polite way that had become his habit. Campbell stared at him, a smile playing at her lips. "You look like you've been out running. I hope you didn't get too...hot."

"No, I'm not overheated," Ben said, his jaw tense. "Ice water runs in my veins, right Dad?"

"Now, Ben," Max said weakly, his face reddening with the consciousness of his own softened belly and broadened ass.

"I don't know," Campbell said, looking with playful intent at Ben, "I think there's some fire in your eyes."

"No fire here. The Colonel is fire. I'm ice," Ben said with polished aplomb. "I'm also in a hurry. I ran over here from school to get these forms signed. Do you mind, Dad?"

"Huh? Sure," Max said.

Ben took a folded form out of an envelope and flipped it open. Holding it at arm's length to read it, Max stepped to the desk. He rooted in a drawer for a pen. Ben followed him. "Sign where it says parent or guardian. Right next to Mom's signature."

"What's this for?"

"One of them is for permission to play basketball. The other says I'm covered by your insurance." Max quickly signed the basketball form, but he tried to read the other form quickly, panic rising in him as he searched for any evidence that Ben had read Admiral Johnson's letter about his birth.

"You need a birth certificate for this team?"

"No, sir. Coach says he doesn't need one."

Max stared stupidly at the form. Since the day of the accident, he and Donna had searched for Admiral Johnson's letter and the missing birth certificate. *What if Ben had read the letter? What if he'd found the birth certificate.* "You don't need the normal letter? Because…?"

"Coach says school records are fine. For once, we don't have to hassle."

"Great." Max knew the school records were safe, but he stared at Ben to try to see if he were lying.

Ben whispered, "Mom and I filled the forms out, Dad. Gran's paying the extra insurance. All you have to do is sign."

Max hesitated, glancing back nervously at Midshipman Campbell. Questions dashed through his mind. *Why do I never see you? Are you ready to take your driving test? How do you like driving? Who's been teaching you? Did Johnson's letter give you this newfound confidence? What do you know about who you are?* He could ask none of them—not even the most benign—in front of this desirable midshipman. He swallowed audibly.

"Dad? Can you sign okay with your cast on?"

"My arm is fully healed," Max said, quick to defend his prowess. "The cast comes off any day." He signed the form.

"Thank you, sir," Ben said, giving them each a brisk, knowing smile. He moved swiftly to the door. "Gotta go," he said. "Be late for practice."

"Will you be home tonight?" Max heard himself blurt out as Ben fled.

"Late," Ben called from the end of the passage, turning around as he jogged, his expression direct, the keen blue of his eyes noticeable from the distance between them. Then he turned on his heel and was gone.

Max did not have to look at Campbell to know that her attitude toward him had changed forever. She stared at the empty hall, her expression altered, bereft.

Max busied himself at his podium gathering papers. Keeping his voice even, disinterested, he said, "You're dismissed, Campbell."

Her sweet reply, "Yes, sir, Colonel," told him that she'd not wait for him after class again.

Max shoved his lecture notes into his slim briefcase and took a great deal of time to erase the blackboard. He walked out of Chauvenet Hall alone.

Along the brick walks that dissected the chapel green, Max strode toward Sampson Hall where his office was housed. Though he knew a mild pleasure at the thought that his uniform still looked sharp this late in the afternoon, his usual preoccupation with his military bearing could not erase the astonishment he felt after Ben's visit to his classroom. Looking for faces like Ben's, he scanned the groups of saluting midshipmen. No one looked as healthy or strong; not one midshipman in crowd after crowd had so much as a grain of Ben's beauty. Max's heart thumped and ached. The boy was amazing. Max wanted Ben beside him, across the table from him, across the lawn waiting with a baseball glove poised to catch. Ben was his, hard won, and Max wanted him.

Crowded with midshipmen, Sampson Hall reeked with the acrid smell of boysweat. He had heard it said, by someone who knew this kind of thing, that at one day old, an infant human or animal could identify his mother's scent. The reverse ought to be true, he thought. Parents should instinctively know their kids. As boy after athletic boy rushed past Max, he wondered if he knew anything about Ben. What kind of music did he like? What was his favorite food? Ben liked to drink ice water, this Max knew, but no kid could get to look that robust on ice water alone. When had Ben become so *interesting*?

Before he reached the top of the curling staircase, an eager lieutenant met Max. "Mrs. Baird sent me to find you, sir," he said breathlessly, though he'd only walked down the hall from the department offices.

His secretary took good care of him, Max noted. Some things were still right in the world. "What's up, Lieutenant?"

"Your appointment with Admiral Johnson, sir. He called to see if you could meet him at sixteen-fifteen instead of sixteen-thirty. It's sixteen-oh-eight now. You're to go to his home, not his office."

"His home?"

"I'll take your things back to your office for you, sir."

"I'll take this with me, thank you, Lieutenant." Max turned and left him standing there sputtering. Johnson. Damn. He'd forgotten.

Johnson introduced Max to a marine lawyer named William Kuhn, who looked around thirty years old. Impeccably groomed, handsome, his expression was intelligent, serious, and professional. Why a lawyer? For the second time that day, Max felt blindsided.

"Major Kuhn is here to explain your legal situation and to advise us both," Johnson said, motioning for Max to take one of three chairs drawn together around a bare coffee table at the deep end of Johnson's office where tall windows looked over an expansive garden stretching toward the Academy wall.

As they took their seats, Major Kuhn took out a manila folder and held it on his knee. "Colonel, while you've been recovering, the admiral and I have been negotiating with the city of Annapolis to reconcile the grievances that have risen from the driving problems you've had. Both sides desire to gain certain advantages from this situation."

"Both sides? Me and who else?" Max said.

"By both sides," Johnson said, "we mean USNA and the city of Annapolis. You are the subject of the disagreement."

"We've reached what the admiral and I think is a satisfactory agreement for all. Including you, of course, Colonel. In the end, this will benefit you."

"The last thing I knew, Admiral, you told me to take it easy until my arm healed. Despite that invitation to relax, I've been doing an exemplary job. I've reorganized the summer Bulldog program and I—"

Johnson bent over to brush a speck of lint off his gleaming black shoe. He looked up and met Max's eyes. "Major Kuhn has been defending you with vigor to one and all. There's no need to react defensively." Abruptly, he stood up, straightened his chair out, and walked to the window. Gazing out, folding his arms over his narrow chest, he said, "Come straight to the point, Will."

"It is in the best interest of the Naval Academy, the United States Navy, the Marine Corps, and your career, I might add," said Major Kuhn without emotion, "that you surrender your driver's license to the admiral and myself and provide a written statement with your intent to refrain from driving under any and all circumstances for the next year."

"What? Are you kidding?"

"Absolutely not," Kuhn said.

"Have I been arrested and don't know about it? Or is this some kind of kangaroo court?"

"That's enough, Max," Johnson said, looking over his shoulder at Max. "We had a choice to make. We could allow the police to pursue arresting you for the accident when you broke your arm—"

"On what charge?"

"Thanks to the negotiations, the police never made a formal charge. But they believed that you were going far too fast. There is evidence that you were driving recklessly. A case could be built against you. Your career is at stake here, and a great deal more than that."

With a cautious look at Max, Kuhn said, "Remember, the police have several witnesses, so if we refused to negotiate and they were forced to use the evidence available to them, we knew we'd be unhappy with the outcome. An arrest and public trial are not in our best interest. So we volunteered to put some serious restraints on your behavior."

"It sounds like I've been tried and convicted."

"No," Johnson said with strained patience, turning now his back to the window. "We don't want you to be tried because you surely *will* be convicted. You were clearly at fault in both accidents."

Looking embarrassed, Kuhn said, "The witnesses are reliable. And there are rumors that you'd been drinking."

"That's insane," Max sputtered, stars popping in the periphery of his vision. "You've got to find out who's spreading these lies!"

Kuhn shook his head. "We don't address things that way. We look at the evidence and we come up with a compromise. The fact is, you caused two serious, highly visible accidents. There are witnesses who could do you and, by association, USNA, great damage. We have to avoid a public trial."

"And that is why," Johnson added, speaking slowly as he left the window and returned to stand behind his chair, "you are taking a voluntary break from driving—until this whole thing blows over and no one remembers if it was a marine colonel or a teenager or a little old lady who wrecked two structures in historical Annapolis in one week."

"What do I gain out of this?"

"You have an opportunity to continue your term as the command marine and you have the opportunity to avoid a court martial," Kuhn said.

"Court martial?" Max hollered, getting to his feet so fast the chair skittered and fell. "You've gone too far! I want to fight these charges. There's no way I was drunk."

"No," Johnson said, bending to right the chair. He came upright, his face inches from Max's, his eyes furious. "You will not fight them. You will sit down." Max glared at him. "Sit down," Johnson said, quietly, his voice terrible; Max sat. "You will submit to our proposal and thereby avoid the kind of investigation that will dirty the reputation of the Naval Academy. I've had enough trouble with marine colonels already, Max. I want no more. Tomorrow morning, I want a signed promise stating that you'll not drive for a full year, beginning today."

3

THE "O" Club was fairly empty; only two tables were seated with wispy-haired, retired couples. Three bachelor ensigns, who roomed upstairs, leaned on the bar. The emptiness emphasized the declined elegance of the place. Faded, dirty curtains, spotted carpet, stucco walls stained from years of cigarette smoke and bored conversation in a room that was high-ceilinged, richly wooded and chandeliered as if expecting to serve important crowds. By the time he was seated, Max was feeling pretty miserable. His commanding officer was treating him like a child, and as far as he could see, his control over Ben seemed to have evaporated. There was the look of imminent betrayal in Ben's bright blue eyes, and his behavior was baffling—rarely at home, quieter than ever. And those two accidents—if Ben hadn't been there, they would not have happened.

Max sat where he could watch the door and see when Patty Edwards arrived. Since he'd run into her at the credit union, he'd been looking for a reason to call her. Johnson's ultimatum meant he needed a lawyer and Patty would prove a competent and sympathetic advocate.

He ordered dinner for two, a bottle of Patty's favorite wine and a drink for himself. He took his drink slowly, pondering a weird statement Ben had made that afternoon. "Ice water runs in my veins, right Dad?" It was something Max often thought about Ben, had described Ben that way to Donna. But it was unlikely that he had said that *to* Ben—except for one time, and then Ben had been young, surely too young to remember...

When he first took Ben to California and home to Donna, Ella came too, insisting the shock of separation from home would damage Ben. "Hasn't this poor child been through enough?" she demanded, her face close to Max's, her cigarette breath choking him.

Donna and Ella disagreed about most things. Ben clung to Ella and to the things she had taught him. The first six months with Ben ached with tension. Max and Donna had not been prepared for Ben's intelligence or for his stubborn loyalty to Katie. Donna was clumsy with Ben, so desperate was she for him to love her. Ben's attitude toward her was careful and patronizing. After six months, he tolerated her presence, would allow her to read to him, but when she tried to take over his care, he asked questions that inflamed Donna's impatience, robbed her confidence.

If Donna put him to bed at night, Ben asked her, "Where my mama go?"

When Donna wheedled, "I'm your mama, now." Ben told her that she was only "the new mommy."

And if that wasn't bad enough, every night Ben took the photograph of Katie that Ella stood on Ben's night table, kissed it, and said, "Mama," in warm, loving tones. The ritual repulsed Max. He insisted Ben stop. Ben refused, fists on his hips, saying, "That's Mama." A weeklong battle ensued—emotional, reasonless battle as can occur with a three-year-old.

Now in the "O" Club Max remembered when he had decided to wipe out Ben's fond memory of Katie and keep her forever a secret. The idea came to him when the house was quiet and Max heard Ben crying in his bed. His mind was feverous with the thought; he was sickened, tossing in bed with memories threatening to focus and accuse him, until he remembered those awful notes in her diary and he realized he had a right to this strategy. Unease withered within him and a mission formed. He rose, dressed as if for work, and went to Ben. Like tonight, the moon was nearly full and lit Ben's bedroom like a blue twilight. His hair was spun gold threads, static against the pillow, reaching toward the moon. Ben turned away from Max.

"Want a drink of water, pal?"

"No, thank you, Dad," Ben said.

Max sat on the edge of the bed. Ben scooted away, hugging his ridiculous baby blanket to his chin. He wiped his nose on the edge of it, his lip trembling. Watching him, Max knew that like Katie, Ben would never cry in front of him. Ben fixed his eyes on the moon and bit his lip. The moonlight unnaturally brightened his eyes, pouring into the empty, widened left pupil. "Do you know my mama?" he asked Max, staring at the moon.

Max could have enjoyed Ben's innocence if the situation had not been so desperate. He stood up, went quickly to the window, and yanked down the shade. "I know your new mommy. That's all." Max came to the bedside and squatted, placing himself at Ben's eye level. "Understand?"

"Where my mama go?" Ben asked, his eyes searching and empty.

Max straightened his shoulders, "I told you. That hurts Mommy. You stop saying that."

"But where is she? You came. I wait a long time."

"Look, you're hurting Mommy when you say that. I'll spank you the next time you say that. You hear me?"

"What means that?" he said, rising on one elbow. Intrigued though he was by a new word, he did not miss the weight of Max's threat. "Does spank hurt?"

"Hell," Max swore, getting up, thinking, *Enough of this semantics crap. No wonder you're so hard to handle.* He told Ben, "Worse than your earaches."

"I cry this night. You spank here," he pointed to his chest, lip trembling convulsively. The child's depth frightened Max, infuriated him; Max feared he would be impossible to control and stepped toward him wanting to grab him and shake him. Max had wanted to hurt him.

Ben pulled his baby blanket over his head, scrunching his sturdy little body into a tight question mark. His little toes, showing beyond the edge of the quilt, were curled so tight they went white.

"Then quit saying that. Don't ever say it again. Stop hurting Mommy."

Outside Ben's room, Max met Ella, wringing her hands. "How is he?" she said.

"This is your fault, Mom…teaching him to kiss her picture. That is so sick."

"I taught him to kiss *your* picture, Max. That's why he recognized you when you finally visited him." Ella folded her arms under her enormous breasts.

"I'm trying to form a new family here. You're supposed to help me. I want him to forget her."

"You can't ask the child to forget his own mother."

Max threw his arms open, "Where is his mother?" he shouted, thrusting his face close to Ella's.

"Please, Max."

"No. Let's face facts. This whole mess is Katie's fault."

"He's your child, too."

"That's debatable."

Ella stepped back, her hand going to her throat. "Max, stop—"

Max focused his eyes on the "O" Club door. *Where is Patty?* He drained his glass. Back then, he remembered, with Donna's happiness and his new marriage at stake, with Ben's brilliant mind to evade and his diamond will to crush, he knew that winning the battle with his mother was key. Looking back he could congratulate himself on handling the two of them with the required force. Yes, he had forced his mother to acquiesce.

Catching the waitress' attention, Max touched his empty glass and remembered shouting at his mother, rising to his full height, pushing his forefinger against the base of her throat, which backed her up against the wall. "I have taken this child in despite his mother's appalling behavior. Do you recognize that? We've got to pick up the pieces and build a new family here. That child has got to learn to love Donna. There's no turning back. Do you understand that?"

"I do. Of course I do. I was there, remember? Max, you're hurting me," Ella said, her voice croaky under his finger. "Be patient. Donna's hard to get to know. She's weak and nervous and she's...so *cold*."

"Ben is the cold one. Ben is solid ice. I've got to thaw him out before it's too late."

Ella tried to push his hand away. She cried hoarsely. "He keeps things in, that's all."

"He is so much like her it scares me. I am going to make sure Ben doesn't turn out like Katie. We're done talking about her. It's the only way. That way we're equal, Katie and me."

Ben's door opened and he stood there, eyes wide, holding Katie's picture in both fists, his blanket over his right shoulder. "Gran, is this Katie?"

Max grabbed the frame, threw it on the floor and ground his heel into the glass. "Get out of here, Mom. Get out of my house."

"No," Ella cried. "You *can't* send me away. Think of Ben."

"Out!"

Ben whimpered beneath them.

"No! He's hurt."

"He's hurt? What about me?"

Ella tried to grab Ben, but Max blocked her, stepping on her feet, shoving her backward. Even now, he remembered his desperation and though he found himself looking around to see if anyone noticed his flash of discomfort, he knew as surely as he had in that moment that his behavior had been justified. Ben had to be won over, his adamant will absolutely broken. "He's bleeding, for God's sake," Ella pleaded.

"You want to stay? You never mention her again. Never again. That's the deal. Either you promise me or you'll never see this child again."

At the emergency room, Ben had to be sedated before he would let them see his gashed hands. Max took this as a sign of victory, silently rejoicing that his son's cold-as-steel composure had been tempered. Ben shook in deep, violent tremors of hysteria as if *he* had been shattered.

The washcloths Ella had pressed on the wounds were soaked with blood, but Ben clutched them, still grasping his baby blanket also with two fingers of each hand, holding it like a shield. Any attempt to take the blanket, any suggestion that the nurse look at the bleeding hands, escalated his screaming and shaking. So when the nurse murmured that they would have to sedate Ben, Max took the necessary action. He ripped the blanket away, and catching Ben in that moment of surprise, grabbed both the boy's wrists and spread his arms out, holding them down on the table and leaning his chest down heavily on Ben's torso to quell him.

Two nurses caught his kicking feet and the doctor injected something powerful into Ben's little thigh. Ten seconds later, he lay tense but still beneath Max.

"You can ease up," the nurse told him, "but hold his wrists."

Max lifted up, his hands gripping hard Ben's wrists. Ben met Max's eyes briefly, then looked up; his knowing, contemplative expression returned as he stared at the ceiling with the absent focus of a learned man trying to remember an obscure point of a text. Max moved his head to try to catch Ben's eyes, but Ben refused and Max had the oddest sensation that Ben was drifting away. Panicky, he glanced at Ben's bloody right hand and saw the doctor calmly repairing. "Ben?" he called to his son.

Ben's stare remained fixed. Desperate to get his attention, Max went forehead to forehead with Ben, and watched his son's blue eyes shut deliberately.

"Is he okay?" he asked the nurse, glancing sideways.

"He's heavily sedated and he's been through a lot."

"Is his heart still beating?"

"Do you need to sit down, sir?"

"No, I—"

"You should be able to feel his heartbeat," one nurse said.

But Max could not. He stood up abruptly. "I think I've smothered him."

"Nonsense," the nurse said. "But he's calm. You can let go of his wrists and sit down yourself."

They got him a chair and Max sat at the top end of the bed. He held Ben's unmoving head with both hands, chattering to him, reassuring him. When Ben's hands were stitched and bandaged, Donna and Ella came into the room. The sight of his mother lit Max's fury anew and he left Ben's side, picked up the bloody baby blanket, thrust it into her hands, and hissed in her ear, "Get rid of this. I want it gone. Forever."

Before he would sign the discharge papers, the doctor tried to get Ben to speak by asking him how he cut his hands. Normally so articulate, Ben repeated, "Ice. On the ice. On the solid ice…" The doctor scolded Max and Donna for allowing Ben to stay up so late. He gave them pamphlets on children's sleeping habits and on making the home a safe place for a child. As if Donna had not been humiliated enough, he recommended a child psychiatrist if Ben's speech did not return to normal.

Ben did not speak for three days. He sat where they put him, hugging his knees, eyes wide, looking out the window or studying the ceiling. He avoided looking at Ella and did not voluntarily approach her. He ate only what they required, didn't play, cry or smile. On the third evening, Ben approached Donna on tiptoe and whispered in her ear. "I'm cold without my blanket."

"Your blanket is all gone," Donna said. Ben studied her. He nodded, biting his trembling lip. "We gave it to a baby. You're a big boy now."

Ben nodded. "Are big boys always cold?"

Donna went to her room and found a sweatshirt she had been saving for him. She helped him put it on. Ben sniffed the sleeve. "This smells like you, Mom," he said.

"I hope that's okay with you," Donna huffed.

Ben reached up and patted her cheek with his bandaged hand. "Don't be scared, Mom. I be careful." He turned toward Max, "I 'member what you told me when you bringed me that ball." Ben cupped his hands, the bandaging puffing oddly as if he were holding a snowball. "I 'member delicate."

Katie was never mentioned again.

Max saw Patty stride across the carpet just as the waitress placed their salads on the table. He stood to pull out her chair. Not even when they were lovers years ago had she been beautiful, but Max liked her confident, athletic bearing and her hard ass. She called herself "raisin-chested," and was unusually tall. Her hair was too curly to be stylish, but it was a pretty, bright brown color; free still of dulling gray and her eyes were large and pale green.

They kissed, pressing cheeks. She took her chair gracefully and exclaimed over the salad. "A salad, how perfect." Max winced at the sound of her raspy voice.

"I ordered you a New York strip steak, medium rare. And a bottle of Pinot Grigio." He lifted the bottle from the ice bucket to show her.

"My favorite. You are a doll."

"Supposed to drink red with beef, you rebel you."

"You know me."

Max leaned toward her, smiling, "I swear to God, Patty, your voice gets deeper every time I see you. You promised me you'd quit smoking years ago."

"You promised me you'd quit drinking," she said, eyeing his half-empty glass of scotch.

"I hate smoking, but you have no real objection to drinking."

"Too much wilts a good erection, I've heard."

"Not mine," he smiled warmly. They sat for a minute, looking at each other, smiles tracing fond, sensual memories. He reached across the table for her hand and squeezed it. "You've been awfully good to me over the years," he said.

"My pleasure." Her voice was huskier still. "A pleasure I wouldn't mind continuing to experience."

"Don't you think Donna would mind?" Max laughed.

"Funny, you never ask if *I* mind about Donna—or anyone else. I know there've been others."

"You're not the jealous type."

"I'm not the maternal type, either," she said, "which is why we broke up after we met up in Greece that time."

"That is *not* why. And we didn't break up. My ship sailed." Patty raised an eyebrow. Max continued, "And anyway, I don't need a mother. I've got one. I don't like maternal women. In fact, I can't stand them. Big breasts are repulsive. I like little ones like yours."

"Max, you are turning me on big time."

Max shrugged, took a big drink, and smiled. "I mean it, Patty. You've got a great body."

"So, did you ask me here to seduce me?"

"First, I need legal advice."

"Somebody suing over the accident?" She pointed her lettuce-speared fork at his cast.

He shifted in the chair to lean closer to her. "Johnson is freaking out about my accidents. He—"

"Admiral Charles Johnson, I assume."

"Yeah. The supe."

"Spotless reputation, Max. He's a stickler for getting naughty officers to behave. That's why he's here."

"I know that, Patty." The waitress brought their steaks, juicy and steaming.

"Delicious," Patty croaked, pushing her salad dish aside.

Max twirled his plate so the steak was closer to his left hand. "So, Johnson and this hotshot lawyer told me today that I had to voluntarily surrender my license and give them a written promise—by tomorrow—that I wouldn't drive for a year."

"Were you charged with DUI?"

"They didn't even take a sobriety test the first time. I can't remember the second time. I don't think so, because one of the cops vouched for me. He'd seen me a few minutes before giving Ben hell for his wise-ass mouth."

"Ben is—?" she said, her tough voice sounding tender.

"Yeah. He's the one," Max said, nodding, glancing up hastily to see if there was accusation or sympathy in her eyes. But Patty had never judged him and he relaxed to see that this also hadn't changed. She reached for his hand and squeezed it hard. For the first time since they had met again, Max's fond memories felt like urgent desire. He wondered if he could get away with the kind of hot affair he and Patty always had—right under Johnson's nose.

"You were giving Ben hell *while* you were driving?"

"No. I stopped right off the bridge. By the St. John's boathouse. The cop pulled up. He could see Ben was out of control. Then, at the accident he told everybody he'd just spoken to me and I was lucid then."

"Maybe they did a blood test once you were in the hospital."

"I don't know. I was so out of it." Max watched her chewing and thinking, her green eyes half-closed. "Can they make me give up my license?"

"What is their rationale?"

"To avoid prosecution or a lawsuit. They made a deal with somebody."

"You do need a lawyer, my darling."

"So, you'll take me on?"

"What a question."

"I need you, Patty, I'm desperate."

Patty chuckled. "What's the lawyer's name?"

"William Kuhn, Major USMC."

"I know Will. He's top notch."

"Great."

"They must have something on you, Max."

Patty took a black mobile phone from her bag, found Will's number, and dialed. Patty warned Max not to speak. She didn't want Will to know he was within earshot.

"Hey, Will? Patty Edwards. Sorry to call you at home. How's the family?" Patty nodded, listening. "Will, Max Hunter has consulted me about this paper you want him to sign."

"Compose and sign. I understand, Will. I stand corrected." She rolled her eyes at Max. "I understand it is in his best interest but—" she listened. "Yes, I realize that the Marine Corps has officially assigned you to his case, but Colonel Hunter doesn't understand—" Listening, she looked absently at Max, her gaze drifting. "Is there evidence?" Her eyebrows went up. "I see." She reached for Max's hand. "I'm interested in Colonel Hunter's well-being, I can assure you." She folded her phone closed.

"What did he say?"

"You're going to have to turn in your driver's license. My darling colonel, there are witnesses for both accidents. The witness for the second says you were speeding. The police are giving Admiral Johnson one chance to keep you from having another accident. He figures the only way to do that is to make sure you don't drive."

"Pisses me off."

"I'll drive you anywhere you want to go for the next year."

"Isn't there anything you can do, Patty?"

"I can help you write the statement."

"My place or yours?"

"Yours has children in it," she said.

"Right. I forgot."

4

OVER the top of the computer he was using at Nimitz Library, Ben saw the Officer of the Day enter the silent study room. In the middle of an IM conversation with Bonnie Jean, Ben hoped he would not be noticed. But man by man, the OD strode through the room, repeating in his command-level whisper that they were closing the room for a security check. Ben said good-bye, promising to find another computer if he could.

"Plebes are supposed to be in by now," The OD said when he reached Ben.

"Sir, I'm a dependent," Ben said, thrusting his hand into his backpack for his ID. This he showed to the officer.

He glanced at Ben. "How do you explain the military haircut, huh?"

Ben stared at him, letting his incredulity show. Rare was the military brat allowed to grow his hair.

"Thought I saw you trip over your feet yesterday when Second Company lost the parade."

"No, sir. That wasn't me." Ben sensed trouble and shoved his journal and his chemistry book into his backpack.

"You know, some plebes keep their dependent IDs and try to get away with stuff."

Ben stood up. Slinging his backpack over his right shoulder, he said, "Sir. I'll be sixteen in two days. I have a military *haircut* because my *father* is a career military officer. And, sir, I *never* trip over my own feet. In fact, I never trip at all." He turned and, knowing the man would continue to hound him, left.

When he opened the basement door, he heard Keith's step on the kitchen stairs, scurrying frantically. "I was watching for you from upstairs—"

"Dad home?"

"No."

"What's the matter, then?"

"Tim's stomach hurts bad."

Racing up the stairs with Keith at his heels, he found his brother thrashing in bed, groaning. "He was fine when I put him to bed," he murmured, half to himself, half to Keith. "What's wrong, buddy?"

"Hurts," Tim moaned.

Ben lay his hand on Tim's forehead. "Man, you've got a fever."

"I was crying for you, Ben."

"I'm here now, Timmy. Show me where it hurts."

Tim pointed, and as if on cue, went wide-eyed and vomited.

"No," Ben groaned, grabbing Tim and hauling him to the bathroom. "Try to hold on, Tim. Try to—"

Ben held Tim's head over the bowl. Swaying slightly and looking ashen, Keith stood at the bathroom door, careful to keep his feet out of the puddle across the threshold.

"Go get me a big glass of ice water," Ben commanded, just to get him out of the room.

Keith managed to stay away until Ben was carrying Tim back to their room. "What do I do with this?" he asked, his voice funny and strained.

Looking around for somewhere to put Tim while he cleaned up his bed, Ben said, "Put it on the desk." He put Tim on an old bean bag chair and told him to lie still.

"On the desk?" Keith asked.

"Yes," Ben said, glancing at him. Keith's lip trembled. "Are you sick, too?" Ben said, grabbing the corner of Tim's sheet and flipping it loose.

"I don't know."

Ben bundled the whole mess into the sheets, put the bundle out into the hall and went to Keith. Ben squatted down to him. "What's wrong?"

"I was scared without you."

"I'm sorry, Keith. I thought you guys were asleep."

"Where did you go?"

"Just to the library."

Keith clung to Ben; his tears wet Ben's shoulder. "What do I do if something happens when you're not here?"

Ben held him close, patting his back, thinking. "Hey, I know what," he said, remembering Keith's love of gadgets. "I'll get us cell phones so you can call me, okay?"

"And you'll run home?"

"Yeah. Sure. Unless I'm at a basketball game. And then you can call Major Lindquist."

"Or Mrs. Johnson. She said we could."

"Yeah. Either one if I can't get home."

While Ben put fresh sheets on Tim's bed, he urged Keith to tell him step by step what had happened—how Tim woke up, what each one said, and by the time Tim was settled again in bed, Keith was quieted. Tim closed his eyes and Ben gave Keith his watch and told him to time how long it took for Ben to get the bathroom cleaned. Keith stood at the bedroom door, so he could keep the semi-conscious Tim informed about Ben's progress. With two trips down to the basement to put the soiled stuff in the laundry and to locate the bleach, Ben had things clean and antiseptic-smelling in less than twenty minutes. Keith was jubilant and willing to go to bed.

Ben got the phone from the kitchen and, sitting on Keith's bed, called his grandmother.

"Bennett, what a lovely surprise."

"How are you, Gran?"

"I was going to phone you this weekend. I have been looking around for cars for you. Your birthday is nearly here."

"That's really nice of you, Gran."

"I don't know what you're interested in, but I found a wonderful classic Fiat."

"I don't know if I can afford that, Gran. I've only saved three thousand. And I need other stuff, too."

"This belongs to a friend of mine. I think I can negotiate a deal. This is a wonderful old car. Convertible, nice leather seats."

Dad'll just take it over and wreck it, Ben thought, but said politely, "What color?"

"A beautiful tan."

And then he had a flash of brilliance. *Dad can't wreck a car that he's too embarrassed to drive.* "I need a pink car."

"Pardon?"

"I need it to be pink, Gran. The kind of car—even the quality—isn't as important as that. I'll get a cheaper one and use the rest of my money to get it painted, if I have to."

"But why?"

"I can't explain, Gran, but trust me. It's important."

"Won't you regret it?"

"No."

"I'll see what I can find."

"Listen, Gran, I need something else. And I don't mind using my savings, I just thought you might know the best kind."

"What?"

"I need cell phones for Keith and me. I was at the library tonight and Tim got sick and it scared Keith. If I have a cell phone, they can reach me."

"Where are your parents?"

"Mom's at work."

"And your dad?"

"I'm not sure, Gran."

"The boys can call him—"

"Gran, I think this would be best for them. You know?"

If his grandmother did know, she didn't say. She talked to Keith and then gave Ben advice about how to care for Tim. This Ben took with polite disinterest. Though well-meaning and genuinely concerned, his grandmother was not competent with sick people the way she was with the other details of life. And Ben knew that cell phones would be in the mail tomorrow morning by ten—eleven at the latest. Ben read to Keith and he fell asleep, leaving Ben to the dark and the quiet.

He made space on his brothers' little desk, found his journal, and settled down to write and to watch Tim. In the austere moonlight, Ben could see that his journal's brown leather cover had become scuffed and worn in the last weeks with Ben's continual need to write in it. He opened it, glancing through the pages.

As Ben flipped through, reading the initial entries—short, pained descriptions of his father's violence—he realized that he had filled fifty pages since he had recorded the details of the accident that broke his father's arm. Ben's journal entries had always been as stark and astonishing as the white moonlight that now illumined the room. The journal existed beyond his father's jurisdiction, beyond the code of secrets and lies by which he lived. In those pages and only in those pages did Ben tell the truth. And he told it with the passion and exuberance of one long denied.

But in the last few weeks, his worn little book had become the place where he recorded his assimilation into his school—triumphs in class, joining the marching band crew, the amazing growth of friendships. And here, Ben wrestled with Tom's ideas, Tom's way of doing things. His recent entries included an analysis of his own lying complicity. Yet, the more pages he turned as he sat there watching Tim, sipping his ice water and noting the way the moonlight stretched like a dispassionate spotlight across the desk, Ben realized that it had also become a sensory, spiritual record of these weeks free from his father's violence.

Tim stirred and Ben went to him, removing the cold, wet cloth to feel Tim's forehead. "Are you okay?"

"Mom home?"

"Not yet."

When Tim released his hand, Ben went back to his journal and found his latest description of Joe's struggle to obey his father. Ben had been describing interesting things that happened between Joe and Tom—the easy banter of teasing counsel, scolding, rehearsal of rules and expectations, hugs, words of praise—through which Ben tried to define a decent relationship with a father, or at least what he wanted.

He and Joe were undeniably different. Joe's achievement in school was a breezy thing. He was smart, did his work, and was always on time. But where Ben achieved through meticulous, nearly paranoid preparation, Joe compensated with buckets of charm. Ben made sure he knew every obscure point. If Joe missed such a question, he finagled the points with a disarming grin, a cunning argument and shameless begging. All of this he enjoyed immensely, especially when he related the stories of his success to his chagrinned but doting parents.

Ben wrote, *Joe celebrates his sonship. He explores its length, depth and breadth. He guards his sonship.* Ben looked at the entry written after last week's chapel service and he saw in his narrative the satisfaction his friend Joe got from testing his father. Ben suspected that the testing he'd seen over and over in Joe did feed some hungry thing in him. Now, in the moonlit space at the bottom of the page, Ben expressed his worry: *Tom's determination seems so much more powerful than anger.*

Below him, the door slammed shut. It was as if Ben felt the vibrations three floors up, so immediate and chilling was the tremor that erupted in his stomach. He glanced at his watch, thinking, *This late, that loud, he's gotta be so drunk.* But then he heard his father laugh, followed by a woman laughing as if into her cupped hand. He heard them whispering and then the door shut. His father's footsteps sounded on the stairs. Ben closed his journal and slipped it in his backpack. He went out onto the landing and leaned over the banister, watching his father's staggering approach, waiting. "Smells funny in here," Max said, looking around as if lost. "Am I home or—"

"Tim's sick, Dad," Ben said, knowing they were magic words. Max looked up at him, peering through squinted eyes, trying to focus.

"Ben? I need to see you. I mean it. I miss you so bad. I hardly know you anymore."

Ben steeled himself, hanging onto his defense. "Tim's sick. He's been throwing up." Max stood on the second floor landing with one foot on the stair that led up to the boys' floor. "Did you hear me? Tim's been puking all night. That's what you smell. Throw up. Lots of it."

"No, I smell swimming pools. Did Tim throw up in the pool?"

Ben cursed silently. *Used too much bleach.*

"All over the bed, the floor, and the bathroom."

"Here?"

Behind him Tim thrashed on the bed. "Uh-oh," Ben said. "Stay there, Dad, he's about to puke again."

Ben dashed to the bed, grabbed Tim, and made it to the bathroom in time. The sounds of Tim's suffering drove Max back down the stairs, and as Ben held Tim's burning head, he hoped his father would fall asleep before he remembered, again, his sons on the third floor of his home.

By the time he heard Donna at the kitchen door, Tim had kept some Kool-Aid down for an hour and now slept. Knees to his chin, Ben sat at Tim's bedside, a blanket wrapped around him, trembling from exhaustion, fighting to stay awake. His mother's step was as silent as a cat's, yet Ben could trace her approach. Her scrubs scraped as she stole closer, and the scent of hospital coffee floated before her like a sensory banner. He sat very still in the long cast of moonlight on the floor, wondering as he heard her bedroom door close a floor below them if she ever checked on Keith and Tim when she came home, wondering why he had not once thought of calling her at work to tell her about Tim.

At five-thirty, the sound of his father in the shower startled Ben awake. When he reached up to touch Tim's forehead, he found that the cloth had slipped off and Tim felt warm, live…normal. Ben stood and stretched. Keith still slept, his slim body curled in a tight ball. Ben went to his own room, packed his backpack, got his school and practice clothes together, put his weekend things in his gym bag. It was Friday. He wasn't coming home tonight. He pictured himself falling asleep on the swinging bed on the MacBride's porch, his friends in their own perches talking in low whispers all around. It was six o'clock. Ben dressed, brushed his teeth, shoved his toothbrush and a towel into his bag. Before he had to meet Joe at seven, he had time for a short run and a quick shower at Lejeune Hall where he now kept shampoo, soap and a razor.

His father left, Ben supposed, to get a hot breakfast at Dahlgren Hall. If he were not mean drunk, Max never slept long and then awoke to a ravenous stomach. Ben was on the stairs when he heard Keith groan. He stopped still.

Practiced as he was, Ben got Keith to the bathroom in time, but Keith's stomach was empty and he merely retched in agony. It was twenty minutes to seven by the time Ben got him back in bed, cool cloth on forehead.

He showered quickly, leaving the bathroom door open. He skipped his shave, pulled on his clothes, grabbed his stuff, went down to his parents' bedroom. Knocking, he called, "Mom?"

"I'm sleeping. I worked all night."

Ben called through the door. "Tim was sick all night, throwing up. Now Keith's got it." There was no answer. "Mom. Mom?"

He put his stuff by the stairs and went into his parents' bedroom. Crouching by her bedside, he shook her shoulder. "Wake up, Mom. Keith is sick."

She rolled onto her back and pushed him away. "Go see what he needs."

"I have to go to school."

"I need my rest."

"Mom. Come *on*. Keith needs you."

"He's eight years old. He'll be fine."

"*Mom*. I'll call Mrs. Johnson if you don't wake up." He counted to seven.

Her eyes snapped open, fully awake and angry. "How dare you."

"I've been up all night and I'm going to school."

She sat up, keeping her little knees together, putting her small feet down toes first. She rubbed her eyes and stretched. Ben relaxed, rocked back on his haunches to prepare to stand. Her hand shot out and she grabbed his wrist, digging in her fingernails.

"Let go," he snapped, wrenching his arm away.

She leapt to her feet, slammed the door shut and flattened herself against it. "I don't know who the hell you think you are. You live here and eat our food and never contribute to this family in any way. Where are you all the time?"

"Mom. I'll be late."

"Where do you go when you don't come home at night?"

"Nowhere. Let me by."

"You'd better not be going to Tom MacBride's house. Are you? I warned you about him."

Ben stared at her, trying to anticipate what would happen if he picked her up and put her out of his way. She was so little, and no match for his strength or agility. But she was quick and mean and he feared the repercussions so irrationally that he scanned the room for another way out. He could go out the window onto the front porch roof and jump down to the sidewalk.

"That's where you're going, isn't it? After I forbid you."

"Mom. Calm down. All my friends get together on weekends and we stay at different people's houses." This was partially true because one Friday night, they had all crashed at Paul and Adam Ridout's house.

"Are you sleeping at Tom MacBride's house? Tell me the truth if you want to get to school. Tell me."

"Come on! Keith is *sick*! If you don't get up there, he'll probably throw up all over the bed."

"I don't think so. Those dry heaves he had show his stomach's empty."

"You *heard* him and you didn't come upstairs?"

She raised her hand up. "Are you sleeping at the MacBrides'?"

"Only once," Ben lied.

Her lips parted in relief. "Don't stay over anymore. Don't even *go* inside. And don't ever be alone with Tom. You hear me? I don't want you getting comfortable with them."

"Okay, Mom." He felt himself redden with his lie. "Let me by."

"I need to know where you go after school. I demand to know."

"You *can't* count on me to be here in the afternoons. What the *heck*, Mom. I help them with their homework and put them to bed every night during the week. Dad never does it. Basketball starts soon, so I'll be even busier. I've got to be involved at school if I expect to get the kind of money I need for college. Extracurricular activities count in scholarships."

As she considered this, Ben lied, "Admiral Johnson told me that if I want to get in the Academy like Dad *wants*, I need at least one extracurricular activity each season. I have basketball in winter and baseball in spring, so I just needed something for fall. That's why I'm running for band."

"Is this a rock band?" she said. "Because you don't know anything about music."

"It's a *marching* band. Like the Drum and Bugle Corps. I'm like an errand boy. I run stuff to different parts of the field of competition to make their performance successful."

"I have no idea what you're talking about."

"You could come see a competition," Ben said. "Most parents do."

She sniffed, dismissing the notion. But she was calmer. Ben glanced at her alarm clock. Joe would be there in one minute. He was hoping to grab an apple before he left. She put her hand on the doorknob. Hope leapt inside him. But then she said, "Dad wants to know if you have a girlfriend."

"What does he care?"

"Your father says no boy your age stays out unless he's getting sex of some kind or the other."

"He doesn't know me."

She moved so the doorknob was hidden at the small of her back. "Your father told me to tell you that you need to use condoms. If you don't know how—"

"Get out of my way, Mom," Ben said, reaching for her shoulder. She swatted his hand away, swinging her arms, nails poised to scratch. "You'd better not be involved with Tom MacBride's daughter," she screamed. "Tom will ruin your life over this kind of thing. I'm warning you."

"He only says nice things about you."

"What about your *father*? Does he only say nice things about your *father*? Did he tell you about what happened at Quantico? Or about the fight? Or the accident?"

"No. What happened?" Ben said quietly, thoughts going deep. "What accident?"

"He'll tell you things. That's part of his style. He's seductive."

"What are you *talking* about?"

"Tell me. Are you having sex with Tom's daughter?"

"What is *wrong* with you?" Ben shouted. He tried to move her aside, but she grabbed the doorknob behind her back and hung on as if daring him to use force.

Ben turned and raced to the window beside her dresser. Frantically, he twisted the latch and slammed it open. She was after him and grabbed his arm. Twisting away, he bolted out the door. Grabbing his stuff with one hand, he jumped down the steps three at a time, ran out the front door, down the alley, and out the gate. Joe's MG stood at the curb, sputtering.

5

SEVEN kids from school ate dinner at the MacBrides' house that night, five boys and two girls joined the MacBride family. Laurie served them spaghetti with meatballs and sausage, an enormous leafy salad, and loaves of crisp-crusted bread.

"What's wrong, Jeff?" Tom asked. "You've eaten your entire salad without one complaint."

"Nothing," Jeff said, head lowered, staring at his plate.

"Aw, come on," Bonnie Jean nudged him with her elbow.

"He's matured," suggested Victoria, "and decided to put something besides salt and fat in his stomach."

"Not likely," Drew laughed.

"Something must be wrong, Jeff," Laurie said. "You haven't said a word."

Bonnie Jean put her arm around his shoulder and tilted her head toward him. Jeff leaned toward her until their heads touched. Bonnie Jean squeezed his shoulder. "You can tell us. We're practically family."

"Nothing...only...just...my dad came home last night."

"Oh," said Joe.

Ben looked up to see his friends glance at one another. Michelle looked alarmed. Even the oblivious Scott stopped eating for a moment.

"My brother let him in because he looked so sick."

"Oh, no," came from Laurie and Bonnie Jean at once.

"My mom was so mad when she came home. But what could we do?" Jeff said, finally looking up to Tom. "His new wife kicked him out because his liver is acting up and—" Jeff looked down the table to Laurie. "You know what that means." Ben swallowed hard.

"I'm so sorry," Laurie spoke for them all.

"Hey, man, that's rough," Joe said.

"Here, take some more salad," Drew said, holding it for him.

"Thank you," said Jeff, grabbing the tongs and heaping his bowl full again. "I hope this helps."

"I don't see how *that* will help," Tommy said.

"Does your stomach hurt?" Tom said.

"No. I—I figured I'd shape up and try to do what you and Mrs. Mac are always telling me and then maybe God would see and help me out."

"I don't think it works that way, son."

"God's love is a gift," Laurie said. "It isn't earned."

"Then why are you always emphasizing obedience?" Ben heard himself speak his thoughts aloud.

Everyone was silent for a long moment before Adam put his fork down and backed Ben up. "It's true. You're always saying obey God and our parents."

"And teachers," Bonnie Jean said. "And the law. We hear it all the time."

Ben said, "Mr. Bettinger said the other day that there's a promise that goes with the command. 'Honor your father and mother and it will go well with you.' Isn't that conditional love?"

"Right," Jeff said. "That's what I'm thinking."

"But Dad isn't Jeff's real dad. So obeying Dad doesn't count," Tommy said.

"Jeff is probably thinking of Tom and I as substitutes."

"Surrogates," Michelle added.

"I'm glad you brought that up," Tommy said, "because I have a problem with that idea. Just because you think somebody is something, doesn't make it real."

Tom opened his mouth to speak and then shut it. All around the table, they turned to Tommy. Victoria said, "What have you been feeding this kid, Mrs. Mac? He's gotten so deep."

"What do you mean, Tommy?" his mother asked him.

"Like if Bonnie Jean just thought in her head—I think Scott is my husband—"

"That would never happen!" Bonnie Jean sniffed.

"No, Jeannie, it's a for instance," Tommy said, sitting up straighter. "If she thinks that, does that mean it's settled and they can stay together at night and scopulate?"

"No, you're right," Tom said. "It doesn't work that way."

"And the word is copulate," Joe corrected, his eyes sparkling; the others at the table exchanged glances.

"Next time use *yourself* for an example, Tommy," Bonnie Jean said, glaring at him. "That was way too personal."

"And cold," Adam drawled. "Makes it sound like a business deal."

"I disagree," Ben said. "Tommy had to choose a really unsettling example to show everybody how shocking an idea it is—if you *think* it, it's real. That's extreme—especially if applied to relationships."

"Yeah. Right, Ben," Tommy said, seriously pleased.

"Think about the implications. If we go back to what Jeff was saying, isn't that kind of a betrayal—just thinking or wishing you had other parents?"

"I can't help it," Jeff said quietly.

Jeannie hugged him again and Ben said. "I know it, man. Like, I don't think *you're* wrong at all. It's just the *idea* I'm trying to figure out."

"I think there is a difference," Laurie said. "Marriage begins with a public commitment to trust and care for each other," Laurie said. "Not just thinking about it. The decision is so distinct and important that we have a ceremony that marks the beginning. Parenthood is more vague. People become parents without a ceremony, without a public proclamation."

"You could *call* it a ceremony or at least a celebration," Joe grinned at his mom.

"My dear Joe, neither parenthood nor marriage is only about *scopulation*," Laurie said, her eyes twinkling.

"I don't see anything wrong with other parents stepping in," Adam said. "I mean—like Coach and Mrs. Mac have been second parents to Paul and I since forever."

"Paul and me," said Laurie.

"My point exactly."

"And the other way around," Paul agreed. "My dad would rip an earring out of Joe's ear quick as he would outta mine."

"And," Tom added, "there are bounds I would never cross with you two or with any child who is temporarily under my care."

"Like what?" Ben said.

"I can't arrange for medical care without a parent's permission. And morally—lots of things. I wouldn't counsel Paul or Adam to do anything that I knew was against their parents' wishes or even against their parents' taste."

"And you probably wouldn't punish them," Michelle said.

"Wait a minute, Coach." Paul said. "Remember when my folks were traveling and Pete 'n me—I mean Pete 'n I—set the meadow on fire?"

"But you know, Paul, I phoned your parents to ask them what they wanted us to do."

"Who's tougher?" Drew asked Paul. "Coach or your dad?"

"My dad is much bigger than Coach, but he's a softie. Coach is tenacious."

"Ooh," said Victoria. "Vocab word."

Ben shifted, at once uncomfortable and curious.

"What happened?" Michelle asked.

Paul said, "We were trying to start a fire with Adam's glasses. At first it didn't work, so we somehow got the bright idea of dousing some dry leaves with gas. Then it worked. Un*fortu*nately."

Tom said. "If it hadn't been for Laurie's quick thinking...I *still* hate to think what might have happened."

"I'm surprised Joe wasn't involved in that," Michelle said. "He's always fascinated with fire. When Mrs. Walker burns candles in class she's always telling him to get away."

"Could I have the spaghetti, please?" Scott said.

"Joe and I were stuck in the house with chicken pox," Adam said with a quick glance at Joe. "My glasses must've been stolen."

"Well, actually," Joe said.

Adam cleared his throat, glaring at Joe.

Joe shrugged at Adam. "Actually, Dad, I might have been responsible for the whole thing."

"Excuse me?" Tom said.

"Mrs. Mac, this is a *delicious* dinner," Adam said.

"It's been seven years," Joe said to Adam, "He can't do anything to us after seven years," then turned toward his father. "Adam and I—dared Pete and Paul to do it."

"You what?"

Ben put his fork down, looking quickly from Joe to Tom, but Laurie laughed out loud, tossing her head back, her voice a delighted musical note. Cara started in her swing at the sound.

Tom confronted Paul. "I *knew* you were lying to me. Remember? I said as much."

"Lying is a strong word, Coach. I merely held my counsel," Paul shrugged. "What were you going to do to them? Adam had a fever and Joe had those itchy things all over his self."

"Someday, Joe," Laurie said, "you'll have a son just as mischievous as you."

"So, back to Ben's question," Bonnie Jean said.

"How about Scott's question?" Scott said.

"What was that, sweetie?" Laurie said.

"Could someone pass the spaghetti?"

Ben picked up the bowl and, holding it with both hands, said, "So, you're saying if the parents don't consent there is a kind of betrayal there," Ben said. "Here's the problem. Isn't the father-son relationship a kind of picture of the Christian's relationship with God?"

"Whoa," said Adam. "Now we're getting somewhere."

"But what if it isn't?" Victoria asked softly, with a glance at Jeff.

Ben said, "If it's *supposed* to be, then wouldn't looking to other parents be the everyday metaphor for the idolatry the Bible describes as heinous?"

"Could someone please pass the salad again?" Jeff said. They went silent as one man, all eyes going to Jeff. "Man," he murmured, shaking his head, eyes bright with tears. "I'm glad I'm not smart. I just want God to notice me."

The table went silent until Ben said, "I'm sorry, man."

"Pass the salad and I'll forget about it."

"Wouldn't you rather have some Pringles, darling?" Laurie said.

"If it's okay with you and Coach."

"I'll get them," Tommy said, sliding off his stool and dashing into the pantry. He put the tube of Pringles on Jeff's plate. "You can have the whole thing."

"You know," Joe said. "Seriously, Jeff. I read, just last night, about a man who had cirrhosis of the liver and he refused to—"

Jeff looked up and glanced quickly at Ben. Joe's nod was barely perceptible. "He refused to take care of himself. But his daughter had been reading all this stuff about prayer for the sick and she got her friends together and prayed for her dad every morning, and six months later, his doctor said he had eighty percent of his liver functioning normally. So, I mean, we could—"

"Right," Bonnie Jean said. "We'll pray for Jeff's dad and see what happens."

"We could try," Jeff said doubtfully, and popped a Pringle into his mouth.

"Let's pray before we leave the table. Let's all join together right now. Does anybody else have anything?" Tom asked, but each one shook his head around the table, determined that this be Jeff's moment. Together they bowed their heads.

Bonnie Jean said, "Lord, you're known for healing people and fixing up their lives. Please touch Mr. Birch. Heal his liver. Make it like new."

"Lord, we ask that you would also heal Ray's soul and mind," Tom prayed. "Make whole and clean all the hurt places that bother him so deeply. Show him your love and comfort."

"Help Jeff's mom to cope," Michelle murmured. "And keep her safe."

Drew said, "Lord God Almighty, show Jeff that you *see* his situation, that you have *noticed* him."

When Laurie was praying for Jeff's peace of mind, Ben heard Jeff sniff and looked up. Tears ran from the end of his nose and splashed onto his hand. Ben stomach lurched in sympathy. They sat, heads bowed in silence but for the sound of Jeff's sniffing, and then there was the scrape of Tom's chair on the floor and the muffled sound of movement and Ben saw Tom take Jeff into his arms. Normally when he stood by himself, Jeff's wiry, athletic stance distracted notice from his small stature, but in Tom's arms he looked like a child and there his sniffing broke into sobs. Tom somehow walked him away from the table and into the room beyond. Ben heard a door shut. Around the table his friends' faces shone with hope and together they left their seats to help clean up.

6

IN the cool, bright October evening, they played outside until the moon rose high above the apple attic. They tied toy basketball hoops to facing railings of the apple attic loft and competed, boys against girls, using the trampoline's bounce to help them score. The Ridouts—afraid of heights—served as spotters, while the rest of them bounced and crashed into each other, soared into the warm attic air, shrieking with carefree laughter. Hot and breathless from three games of trampoline basketball, they took turns in the canoe or swam in the river and Ben worried about Jeff's absence.

Ben asked Joe, "What's taking so long with Jeff in your dad's study?"

"Jeff's gotta cry it out on Dad's shoulder," Joe said, looking at Ben, his eyes showing a kind tolerance that Ben had come to value. "Then Dad's got to put him back together."

Paul draped a massive arm around Ben and said, "He'll be out soon." They were filling childhood water guns when Jeff joined them, eyes puffy. But once the water fight began and he managed to squirt Bonnie Jean in the forehead, Jeff's laughter returned; Ben relaxed.

Soaked through, the girls went in to change clothes, claiming they had to learn some music for a choir performance. Through the open living room windows along the front porch, the boys heard them at the piano practice a single line of music between long intervals of whispers and shrieks of laughter. Dripping wet and chilled, the boys crowded into the laundry room, stuffed their wet clothes into the dryer, and borrowed boxers and T-shirts from the pile of clean laundry.

Back in the kitchen, Laurie served them hot apple crisp, ice cream melting atop, after which the boys claimed the porch for the night. Jeff requested the hammock, so Drew hung it for him and Ben was given one of the hanging beds. Joe took the other. Drew, Paul and Adam dragged the cot mattresses and sleeping bags out of the apple attic and made beds on the porch floor using the wicker settee pillows for padding. Laurie lit the citronella torches and told them to move indoors if it got too cold, but they were happy there; not even a blizzard would have sent them up to Joe's room.

Crowded on the two swinging beds, they played poker. They made sure Jeff won the most—seventeen dollars; Ben was sure Jeff had not noticed Joe's slick dealing. Once in their own beds, they talked in low whispers, made plans for tomorrow's band bus ride, and laughed a lot until Tom came to the front door and told them to quiet down. So they muffled their hilarious happiness in cupped hands, in the corner of a sleeping bag or a big, white pillow shoved down on a friend's irrepressible guffaw.

Sleep took them one by one and when Adam and, last of all, Joe, fell silent, Ben lay on his back and in the quiet came the full force of his exhaustion. Alone, he felt his stiff back; his knees ached and his thirst was acute. He considered going into the kitchen for ice water, but his mother's insane demands came back to his mind and with it the entire bizarre conversation and the guilty questions that haunted his yearning.

Her warning echoed in his brain—don't go in the MacBride's house, don't spend the night inside, *don't, don't, DON'T!* He thought of Keith and wondered if he slept or still lay sick, alone and frightened. Around him, his friends breathed quietly, above him the stars kept silent vigil and the moon stood above the garage, as pure and unconcerned as ever. He stretched and tried to get comfortable, reminding himself that this was his favorite place in the world, this outside bed, this swaying perch in a bedroom without walls, surrounded by his sleeping friends in a cool garden scented fresh and ripe. Last night he had longed for this place, had imagined every detail, but now, his demons hissed in his ears and he could not forget his mother's weird and insistent command.

When did I learn to obey them? And why should I? Ben obeyed his parents if doing so kept him safe from their notice and abuse. But his new, infinitely dear friends lived by this code. Had they agreed at dinner that wishing for new parents was the betrayal he feared it was? Or would his friends justify his desires if they knew his parents? Tom seemed to think God cared if he disobeyed his parents. Did that mean he was in danger now, transgressing somehow, transgressing all evening as he had feasted and played and laughed? Should he obey if it made no sense? What if obeying meant lying, as it often did for Ben? Ben remembered most bitterly how his father required him to lie to Admiral Johnson—to *the police*—to protect him. What, then? Ben turned over onto his stomach. *Why is Mom afraid of Tom? Where does she get her crazy ideas? Why do they think that stuff about me?* His back hurt, his knees ached all the way down to his ankles. He turned over again.

"What's wrong with you?" Joe demanded sleepily. "Sick or something?"

"Just thirsty."

"Go in and get water. You're keeping me awake." Joe flopped over, deeply asleep in a second. With quiet caution, Ben scooted to the edge of his bed and let himself down to the porch. The slick porch floor was chilled with the cool of the autumn night. He climbed past the sleeping boys and picked his way in the moonlight along the fragrant gardens to the back door. A low light burned above the stove, and it wasn't until he had stepped inside that he saw Laurie there, walking Cara.

"I'm sorry I startled you," she whispered. "The baby's fussy and I don't want her to wake Tom up, so I'm walking her down here."

"Is she okay?"

"Busy day. She may still be hungry."

Aware that he was clothed only in boxers and that he had intruded on her assumed privacy, he stood still. Laurie was barefoot, her bright red robe showed the collar of shimmery white pajamas beneath. Cara whimpered and nuzzled her mother's shoulder, moving her tiny body restlessly beneath the fluffy blanket flung over her. His mother's wild words nagged him and a slow burning panic lit the edges of his composure.

"What brings you inside? Still hungry?"

"No ma'am. Dinner was awesome. I was just hoping to get a drink of ice water. Joe said—"

"Could you get me one, too? I've been dying of thirst, but I was afraid if I took Cara near the freezer the cold would wake her up completely."

"Sure," Ben said, happy to comply. Laurie drained the glass and held it out for a refill. This she took to the rocking chair and settled down there. Ben stood by the sink and drank an entire glass rapidly, then, like Laurie, refilled it, sat down on the bench facing her. He leaned his elbows on the table, his head in his hands. The fresh, lively connection he always felt to Laurie MacBride coursed through him now and he breathed deeply, relieved somehow. *Mom is so wrong,* he thought. *It's nice here.* Cara whimpered more urgently, as Laurie drank again.

"Do you mind if I feed the baby?"

 Ben said. "Do you want me to leave?"

"Never."

Laurie could put Cara to her breast without the onlooker having opportunity for embarrassment, and somehow that night the sounds of Cara's contentment cleared his mind. He felt his demons quiet—chased away in a kitchen so full of good sense. "You don't mind feeding her yourself?"

"Mind? No. I can't stand the way formula smells. Like throw up."

Ben remembered Tim, and in the darkness confided, "My brother was sick last night throwing up. Mom was at work."

"Poor thing. He wanted her."

"I've been taking care of him since he was born, a lot of the time. So he's used to me. But when I was trying to fall asleep on the porch, I kind of felt bad for having so much fun over here when my brothers are home. I probably should have gone home."

240

"Do you want Tom to take you home, Ben?"

"They've got to be asleep by now. I just hope my mom's okay with me not being there."

"But when they're sick, she'd want to be there herself," Laurie said. "And she'd want you to have time here with your friends."

Ben knew that Laurie was thinking the best of Donna and he watched her face to see if she'd suddenly remember what his mother was really like. But she was concentrating on Cara, whose body relaxed beneath the cloak of the blanket. Her head fell back and she burped. Laurie laughed and smiled at Ben. With sudden force, he wanted to confide in her, to express all that was wronged inside and he heard himself say, "How can you always think the best of people?"

He saw that his tone alarmed her; she said, "What do you mean?"

"My parents think I'm doing stuff—"

"Like what?"

"But I'm not—"

"Drugs?"

"I don't know, probably."

"Why would they think that?"

"I don't know."

"Did they say what they think you're doing?" Ben shifted uncomfortably and hid his face, his hand across his brow. "Have they actually accused you?" He laughed a little into his hands, wondering what she would say if she knew. "But just looking into your eyes, anyone could tell—"

"She thinks the worst because I haven't been at home much and I'm happy." Laurie reached for his hand and covered his with hers.

"Did you explain to her that all the kids stay over each other's houses?"

"It's mainly *your* house, Mrs. MacBride. Everyone stays here."

"Did you tell her, though?"

"I couldn't reason with her."

"Maybe she was tired and not thinking clearly." Laurie held his hand tightly, her kind, dark eyes the brightest thing in the room. "Her children were sick and she worked all night. She was just upset."

"Was she like this when you knew her before, Mrs. MacBride? Did she get worried about stuff and get extreme?"

Laurie was quiet. Her eyes swept over him slowly; he saw her thinking. She met his eyes and said, "Yes. Donna's always been that way."

"Did she believe lies about you? Is that why your friendship is broken?"

"That's what it was, Ben."

"What was it about?"

"I don't know if she'd be comfortable with you knowing."

"It might help me."

241

"It was before you came into her life, Ben. It really has nothing to do with you."

"She doesn't trust Tom."

"She doesn't trust *you*, though you deserve it. It's not her nature to trust."

"Yeah," Ben said, drawing in a deep breath. It was a good answer, true and satisfying. Quietly, he confided in her. "Do I stay home and try to convince her I'm good? Or do I skip out like I'm doing tonight? I don't mind helping but I also see other moms who work and take care of their families. Like now. It's not Joe or Bonnie Jean up feeding Cara."

"I think you are unnerved by having to care for your brother all night."

"No, it's not that," Ben said. "I want to be good. I try. Even though I'm not doing the stuff they think I am, I'm still not good enough. I know I'm not."

"You're tired and upset, Ben."

"No. Listen. At school they're always talking about sin and depravity and stuff like that. And I don't really *get* that—I don't really have a *grasp* of what that means, Mrs. MacBride, but I do know that I don't really measure up to Tom's standards—not his standards for Joe."

"How so?"

"If I were Tom's son, he'd be disappointed in me for different reasons than my parents are."

"Neither of us could ever be disappointed in you," she whispered, her voice full of conviction, her neat little hand squeezing his tightly.

From deep inside, Ben chuckled sadly at her passionate, misplaced loyalty to him. "Real reasons, not ones like my mom comes up with. Believe me. You'd be disappointed."

"Everyone has faults, is that what you mean?"

"Worse than faults…like, for instance, Mrs. MacBride, I'll tell you, but don't tell Tom—it's easy for me to lie. *Really* easy."

"You're right. Neither Tom nor I want you to lie."

Ben shook his head, closing his eyes. "There's so much Tom wouldn't approve of."

"I wouldn't approve of what?" Tom said, coming into the dark kitchen. Ben startled, sat up, yanked his hand away from Laurie. Tom crossed behind the table and bent to kiss Laurie's head. "It's cold up there without you, my love."

"I didn't want to wake you."

"Baby asleep?" he said.

"Getting there," Laurie said. "I had such a busy day, I think she was hungry."

"You've got to take a few rests and a nap," Tom said to her, his voice serious.

"I had enough milk, just not enough time to let her nurse leisurely."

"Still. I think I'll take over the laundry like I did after Tommy was born. And speaking of that…" He left the room and came back with a basket full of jumbled, clean clothes.

"No. Tom, I appreciate the offer, but I don't like the way you do the laundry."

"I'll do it exactly the way you want." He began folding the T-shirts and tossed one to Ben. "Just for a few months, Laurie. You need the help."

"It's almost basketball season."

"Talk some sense into her, Ben," he pleaded.

"He's right, Mrs. MacBride," Ben said, before shrugging into the clean T-shirt still warm from the dryer. "I'll help when I'm here. I'm neater than Tom by nature."

Laurie laughed at this. "Okay. Tom can do it and you can make sure he's doing it right."

"Good job, Ben," Tom said, patting Ben's back briskly. "I want you here all the time to win my arguments for me."

Ben laughed a little; Tom continued to fold the laundry, making neat rolls of the shirts and socks. It had the oddest effect on Ben. The panic in his nervous stomach dissipated. When Laurie again reached to pat his wrist, he did not shrink away.

"Why are you still up?"

Laurie said, "Last night, he had to take care of his little brother, who was throwing up."

"I finally fell asleep sitting by Tim's bed." Now Ben felt sleep coming to him, his eyes watered when he yawned, and yawned again.

"Ben was just saying how he's realizing that he can't always live up to his own high standards, or yours."

"That's a good place to be in life," Tom said. "We all have broken places; most of us just won't admit it."

Ben put his head back down on his arm and said to Tom, just as if he were *not* Ben the outsider, but Joe, "Can you fix me?"

Tom laughed at this and patted Ben's shoulder. Ben closed his eyes and listened to the room's soft sounds and he began to feel weightless and content. He hovered in a twilight sleep, warm, and for the first time in twenty-four hours, quenched of thirst. Ben heard them talking about him as he drifted toward sleep. "Look at him," Laurie said to Tom.

"We knew there'd be nobody like him," Tom said. "And what an amazing thinker."

"He needs us, Tom," Laurie confided. "He's struggling."

"He's seeking."

"Things must not be good at home," Laurie said.

"I think he was interested in the *ideas* Jeff's dilemma raised. He's so bright."

"It's more than that, Tom," Laurie said and in whispers that Ben caught in wisps, Laurie related Ben's worries about his brothers for a moment, but then the bright tones returned to their voices and they talked about what he might grow up to be like, what he might do when he was a man and Ben felt so safe he let sleep take him. He felt Laurie's hand on his shoulder and Tom's hand on his back as Tom said, "Come on, stand up, now."

Ben tried to say something as Tom walked him through the dark house, the quiet, snug house that had been forbidden to him for its danger. The screen door squeaked open and Ben stepped on the chilled porch boards, felt the frosty autumn air around his ankles awaken him just enough so that at Tom's urging, Ben roused to hoist himself onto his swinging bed. Tom zipped the sleeping bag all the way up. He heard the screen door again and through sleep-swimming eyes saw Laurie cover each boy with her quilts. Lingering a moment over Jeff, she came last to Ben, and together she and Tom spread the last quilt over him, folding it close to his neck and then lifting his feet and tucking it tightly. "Goodnight, my darling child," she whispered, kissing him on the forehead, and Tom, too, bent and kissed Ben's head in the quiet darkness with only the silent, staring stars as witness.

Ben awoke with a thought fully formed in his mind. He leaned over and grabbed his backpack, found his journal, and took it up into his bed. Pulling the covers up over his head, he found a blank page and wrote:

> The MacBrides' world is one Mom could never comprehend. That's why she's afraid. She's afraid the way someone who had only seen light bulbs would be afraid of the sun. But I've felt the sun on my back and I want to stay here in its heat. I want to see it with my own eyes. I want to touch it, to swallow it, even if I have to change my sorry ways to earn the right.

He wrote the date, *October 14. My sixteenth birthday.*

Ben wondered if he had time to describe his evening there. He heard noisy birds hunting for food in Laurie's garden and splashing in the puddles that gathered from the boys' boisterous showers draining off the basketball court. Ben sat up. The sun had risen above the trees that bordered the meadow and lay in a warm patch on his legs. All his friends were awake, their beds abandoned. He smelled bacon and coffee. Ben knew a moment of utter contentment and stretched like a cat in the sun. He had slept dreamlessly and deeply; now his hunger was rampant.

As he moved to get up, flinging the covers aside, Tommy came out the front door, holding a towel, his bright brown eyes alight with mischief. "Mama says you're to get a quick shower because she's got to go to work in one hour."

"Okay," Ben said doubtfully.

"She has to make sure you have breakfast before she goes. You can shower upstairs if you want. All the girls are done."

"Thanks," Ben said. "I'll use the outdoor shower."

When his friends saw him coming, they quickly moved out of the way so Ben could get to the shower. They were acting weird; they dried off quickly, grinning so widely at him that Ben wondered if they were setting him up for some embarrassing joke. So he showered rapidly and, oddly enough, when he was toweling off, Jeff and Drew stood by the side of the court waiting for him. "You ready?"

"Go ahead without me," Ben said. "I really have to shave today." He turned to go into the garage, where he and Joe often shaved using a small, dim mirror hung over the sink Laurie used to pot her plants.

"No, you don't," Jeff said.

Ben just looked at him. Drew grabbed Ben's arm and pulled. "Come on. There's a little bathroom off the kitchen. You can shave in there after breakfast."

When he opened the door a crowd of people shouted "Happy Birthday!" Ben stepped back, his heart pounding. But his friends overwhelmed his shock and pulled him into the room, an arm around his shoulder, an affectionate punch in the arm. Laurie hugged and kissed him. Bonnie Jean delighted him with one of her tight, sturdy hugs around his neck; Tom hugged him, then Joe and Adam together, and finally Tommy. And then he saw the table.

The miracle of food was not to be believed. Laurie urged them to sit down quickly and begin while the food was hot. They feasted on fresh fruit salad, crisp hot bacon, steaming browned sausages, scrambled eggs, and Laurie's high, light scones.

"Here's your present," Tommy said, holding a box out to him.

Inside Ben found a school varsity jacket with his name embroidered on the left chest. He lifted it out and stared at it. "But I—"

"We all pitched in," Drew said.

"—I haven't made the team yet."

This made them all laugh as if at a merry, if secret, joke.

"It was Coach's idea," Adam said, "so that's a pretty good sign."

Ben looked around at the table, at the eyes shining with acceptance.

"It's getting cool out," Tom said, shrugging. "All the guys will be wearing theirs, so—" he broke off.

"Thank you. Thank you all so much."

"When you've had all you want," Tom said with a gesture at the table, "I'm taking you over to the MVA to get your license."

7

THE next Thursday morning, Bonnie Jean missed both math and French. During lunch, Michelle told Joe that she was in the stairwell crying but wouldn't say why. Ben and Joe left the crowd that ate in the hallway between the locker rooms and went toward the stairs. As they came through the gym doors, Mrs. Campbell stopped Joe with a question about his English test. Joe signaled to Ben to go on alone and Ben found Bonnie Jean in the stairwell, her head on her knees, her hair flung forward, her shoulders shaking with sobs.

"Hey," Ben said, sitting down next to her. He kept his voice calm, but inside he was frightened. "What happened? Are you okay?"

"I know I'm overreacting. I just can't help it." She picked up her head and looked at him. Red blotches swelled around her swimming eyes. Her lips were puffy and a tear rolled down the side of her nose.

"Man," Ben said, sympathetically, "what *is* it?"

"I have to have an operation. I bet you're brave when it comes to doctors and stuff, but I'm not. I'm afraid of needles. Terrified."

"It's not like you to be afraid of stuff, Jeannie."

"I am, though."

"It must be the only thing you are afraid of."

"Except for Ursula in *The Little Mermaid*."

Ben laughed. "Do you want to borrow my sleeve to wipe your eyes?" he said, offering his arm.

"No. Thanks. I've got my blankie." She thrust her hand into her backpack and pulled out a ragged cloth about the size of a newspaper. "My baby blanket. I stuffed it in here this morning in case I needed it at the doctor's." She blotted her face with it. "Are you afraid of needles?"

"No, but lots of things," he said. "Too many to list."

"Like?"

"Abuse of power is the main one, I guess."

"You're so much deeper than us MacBrides. We're afraid of stupid, weenie things. Peter's afraid of spiders and Joe's afraid of clowns."

"Clowns? That is lame."

"People can avoid clowns. I can't avoid this."

"What's the operation for? Do you mind me asking?"

"I have a huge, horrible mole they have to take off."

"Huge *and* horrible? That's rough."

"I can *almost* believe you understand, except how *could* you?" she said, hiding her face in her hands. "You're perfect. You're brilliant and here I am—a moley B plus student sobbing my eyes out."

"I'm not perfect, Jeannie. You just can't see what's wrong with me."

She looked up again. "I honestly can't, except you seem a little lonely."

"Besides that," Ben confided, smiling a little and shaking his head at her apt understatement, "my eye is deformed. I hide it every day."

She searched his face, her expression gone worried, sympathetic. "Which eye?"

Ben pointed. "I wear a contact lens. Specially made. The pupil cuts into the blue part. Instead of being round, like yours, like my other eye, it's got a big cut in it that makes it look like a keyhole. It can't be fixed, only hidden."

"Does it cause problems?"

"They say so. They say it was letting in way too much light."

"But you don't agree?"

Ben shrugged, embarrassed. "I see differently—I think I see more without my contact. But either way, I have a blind spot." Ben pointed to a slim sector above his head. "My other eye compensates, but—"

"How does that work with basketball?"

Ben met her eyes. "I work extra hard to make up for it so no one will ever guess."

"I see," she said softly, inched closer to him and patted his shoulder.

"Yeah," Ben said.

Impulsively she hugged him. "You are so sweet. You told me all that personal stuff just to make me feel better."

He melted into her embrace nuzzling her cheek, breathing in her fresh, live fragrance. "Don't tell anybody," he whispered.

"I won't. And I *do* feel better. But I think I made *you* feel worse." She pulled away a little. "Do you want to share my blankie?" she teased, eyes sparkling now. "It helps."

He smiled and took the corner of it between his fingers. The cloth was so silky, it felt like warm water. "I used to have one of these," he said. "It had a little ridge on it that I rubbed. It did help back then."

"Where is it?"

He laughed. "Who knows?"

"My dad put mine away in the apple attic with my baby things and I snuck it back out and I'm keeping it in my bag today. I need it." Her eyes filled again. She bumped his elbow with hers. "I guess it bothers you to have to hide your eye."

"Yeah. A little. But if you have your mole removed, you won't have to hide it."

"I can't really always hide it anyway. It's on my upper thigh and like when I wear a bathing suit or short shorts—shoot, everybody's seen it. Look." She moved her kilt and pulled the spandex shorts beneath away from her skin. The mole, smaller than a quarter and dark brown, marked the high outside of her right thigh.

"It's kind of cute."

"They said when I get old, it will probably grow big ugly hairs."

"That won't be good."

"So, it's off with her mole."

"Will it leave a scar?"

"That's the worst," she said, her voice unsteady again. "Plastic surgery for the scar. Maybe twice. More needles." She shivered.

"It'll be okay," he said. Ben touched her knee and then in an instinctive impulse, covered the mole with his hand. He looked at her, his affection for her rising in him: a warm and inexorable flood. He leaned toward her, knowing she also wanted to kiss.

Later, when he was alone, pacing in the principal's outer office, Ben could understand how the moment must have looked to Mr. Bettinger when he came through the doors into the stairwell. There he was, alone with this beautiful girl, his hand beneath her skirt, his lips just about to touch hers—they had been dazed at Bettinger's interruption. But reality struck hard when Bettinger grabbed Ben's elbow and pulled him away from Bonnie Jean, off the stairs, and to his feet bellowing orders that he go straight to the office. Now Ben wondered if he was going to throw up. The torture of knowing she was being reprimanded when the incident was entirely his fault was acute. He stood and went to the office door and knocked. Mrs. Poulard opened and put her finger on her lips. "She's talking to her mother on the phone," she whispered.

Ben winced. "It wasn't her fault. It was—"

"She's explained it all."

Bonnie Jean saw Ben and turned toward him. She gave a wobbly smile. "Thanks, Mom. I gotta go."

"Are you okay?" he said, standing just inside the door beside Mrs. Poulard.

"Better now."

"I'm so sorry, Bonnie Jean."

"No. I'm sorry. I got you into this."

Mrs. Poulard stepped forward. "I think the important thing is to recognize that you have the beginnings of a great friendship. In school, certain gestures, based on the most pure and noble emotions, are just not a good idea."

"Yes, ma'am."

"You'd better get to class, Bonnie Jean. I need to talk to Ben."

When Bonnie Jean had shut the door, Mrs. Poulard invited him to sit down. "Bonnie Jean explained that you were merely comforting her and I can buy that, Ben," she said, evenly. "But in the future at school, you'll have to think of a different way to comfort her."

"I wasn't really doing all that much thinking at the moment."

"No, I imagine not."

"I can't believe I messed up so bad. I'm usually so good."

"I generally tell boys to touch a girl only on the hand, briefly, or lightly on the shoulder. Kissing is not for school hours."

"We didn't actually kiss," Ben said, miserably.

"Through no fault of your own, I understand."

"No, ma'am. You're right."

"You were overwhelmed with the moment."

"How can I fix this?"

"I think you should have a serious discussion with Bonnie Jean," she said, smiling fondly at him. "Don't assume she's got everything resolved in her mind. Women seldom do."

"Okay."

"I commonly call parents in situations like this—" she looked down at a small white card.

"Listen, Mrs. Poulard," Ben said quickly. "My mom works at night, and she sleeps during the day, so it would be really bad if you called her and woke her up."

"It is probably a better idea to talk to a boy's father when he's been kissing at school."

Ben felt shock like a blow to the head; his stomach tossed. "He's really busy with his new job. He's under a lot of pressure—" He felt himself blush hearing himself spout off his mother's rote excuse for coddling his father. But what could he say? If the principal called with the news that Ben had tried to kiss a girl at school, Max would be disappointed that Ben hadn't seduced her in the locker room. Ben would suffer only his father's mocking; that he could manage. But he didn't want Mrs. Poulard to mention Bonnie Jean's last name.

"Actually," Mrs. Poulard said slowly, studying his face, "I don't have a home number or an office number for your father. You must know them."

"Yes, ma'am," Ben said. He took a deep breath to fight his panic.

"Home first," she said. Ben began truthfully and then thought to change the last digit. He did this also for his father's work number. The dirty feeling that came after he'd lied to someone he respected fell on him.

"But I was thinking, Ben," she said, writing on the white card. "I'd rather you talked to Mr. MacBride about this."

"Pardon?"

"I normally call parents to inform them of official punishment. Or if the student is uncooperative. You've been very humble and truthful."

Ben winced. He'd lied *unnecessarily*. He'd sold off another piece of his integrity and she was softening anyway. She raised her eyebrows questioning him, and though he wanted to come clean, a phone call to his father meant he'd lose everything he loved here. "You called *Mrs.* MacBride for Bonnie Jean. Couldn't I talk to her instead?"

"I called Laurie to help calm Jeannie down. No, you've got to talk to Coach MacBride so things stay clear between you two."

"Right," Ben said, wincing.

"He's been off campus this afternoon at a county scheduling meeting, but he's due back any minute."

"Great."

"Tom's a good guy; you'll be okay. And I'll be sure to talk to him first."

"How will he be in this situation?"

"Tom's strict but fair."

"I've heard that before."

"Now you'll get to experience it."

"Lucky me," Ben said.

8

WHEN Ben opened the locker room door that afternoon, his friends and teammates, in various stages of dress, stood straight up and applauded him. Ben smiled despite his building anxiety and when, at Jon's count of three, they bowed down as if in obeisance to him, he had to laugh. Then they were all around him.

"Man, you've done what none of us dared to do."

"The unattainable."

"How close were your lips?"

"Nothing happened, really," Ben smiled.

"In *your* book, nothing. In the history of *this* school—everything."

"Man, you are *in* business."

"We are exceedingly proud of you," Paul said, grabbing Ben in a bear hug.

"I still have to face Coach," Ben said, his misery returning. "I just looked for him in his office. And on the first day of practice."

But his friends refused to let him despair. "He got Bonnie Jean out of Madrigals," Drew said. "So that's good. She's already talked to him."

"Yeah, cause she's got him wrapped around her finger. Isn't that true, Joe?"

"Absolutely," Joe said, joining them in the locker room and elbowing his way past Adam and Drew. He met Ben's eyes and punched his shoulder. "Jeannie told me everything," Joe said, swinging his hefty backpack to the floor. "You've got nothing to worry about."

"Yeah, Coach'll be fair to you. Everything will be fine."

"I don't want justice," Ben said miserably. "I want mercy."

"He's good at mercy," Joe said.

The locker room door opened. The boys fell silent as in one caught breath.

Oliver stood by the door until it shut. He glanced around and leveled his eyes at Ben, "I'm surprised to see *you* here."

"Here I am," Ben said, sounding calm and nonchalant.

"My dad expects you to be suspended at *least*."

"Your dad?" Ben said. "Is he—does he work here, too?"

"Here?" Oliver laughed at Ben. He went to his locker facing Joe's, separated by the wooden bench on which Scott now reclined. Oliver turned his back on Joe and Ben to take his lock in hand. "He works for a think tank in D.C."

"What'd you do," Drew challenged, "call him up and rat Ben out? You don't even know what happened."

"He said to tell you that the Bible carefully warns us that '...fornicators and adulterers God will judge.'"

"What?" Ben said.

"Don't you know your Bible?" Oliver asked.

"Where's it say in the Bible that you can make out with your girlfriend and feel her up?" Joe said to Oliver.

"Yeah, Ollie. Practice what you preach," Adam warned.

"Only her nice little tits. I only enjoy *them* when we make out," Oliver said, bending into his locker to get his shoes.

"You son of a bitch creep," Joe hissed, his fists tightening. Adam put one big hand on Joe's shoulder.

"Calm down, MacBride," Oliver said without looking up from the shoes he held. "Anything *above the waist* is approved for the dating relationship. It says so in Proverbs."

"That's so full of crap," Paul said.

"Right," Scott said, sitting up. "Even *I* know that's not true."

"It says, 'Be satisfied with her breasts.' That proves it." Oliver's voice echoed into his open locker.

"Does the line before or after define who 'her' is?" Ben said. "Because I—"

"See?" Oliver stood up and spun around, his clenched fist by his side. "That proves he doesn't know his Bible."

"You're right, Ben. It's not a manual for dating." Joe said, taking a step toward Oliver. "That passage talks about 'the *wife* of your *youth*.'"

"Get off my back, MacBride." Oliver turned back to his locker. "*I* didn't have my hand up some girl's skirt."

"Shut up," Joe said. "It wasn't like that."

"Were you there?" Oliver said.

"*I* was there," Ben said. "So shut up."

"My father's calling Miz Poulard. My parents are sick of unchurched kids like Ben getting away with this immoral behavior."

Ben looked to Joe for a translation. Joe rolled his eyes, grabbed Ollie's shoulder, forcing him to turn and face them. "If you weren't my teammate, I'd beat the crap out of you, Ollie, I mean it."

"Teammate or not," Jon exploded. "He's mine." He lunged at Oliver, but Adam caught Jon, his massive arms around Jon's chest, and he pulled Jon back, whispering, "Not this way, man. You know better. You don't hit your teammate."

Paul stepped between Jon and Oliver. "Ben's one of us, Ollie. You'd better not try to get him in trouble."

The locker room door opened again. The boys stiffened, stepped apart. Tom held the door open with one hand. His eyes went over the boys. He stepped in and shut the door. "What's going on, men?"

They composed themselves, cloaking the tension in silent, impassive expressions, shoulders gone slack, hands open now; they met eyes, avoiding a single glance at Oliver. Tom waited. No one spoke; no one looked at him. "You ought to be dressed. It's nearly three-thirty."

"Yes, sir," Adam said to his gym socks. "Sorry about that. Let's get going, guys." The boys turned as one man toward their lockers to dress.

Tom waded into the crowd of them, his step the only sound above the boys' closed mouth breathing. "Does someone want to tell me what's going on?"

"Nothing, sir," Joe said.

Tom waited. He glanced at Ben for some clue and, seeing the boy's misery, touched Ben's shoulder with a cupped hand. "Mrs. Poulard said you were looking for me. Can you stay for a couple minutes after practice to talk?"

"Yes, sir," Ben said, his voice a tight cramp.

"Okay. Good. Do your best in practice. Then we'll talk."

"Coach, I'll try."

The silence fell again. Tom looked down the row to Jon, who flicked his eyes at Oliver. "Ollie, what's going on with you?"

The locker room door opened again, and Knox entered. He stopped short, looking around at his silent teammates. "Uh, sorry I'm late, Coach."

"Don't let it happen again."

"Yes, sir." Knox pushed past them to reach his locker and fumbled with the lock. He shot Oliver a questioning glance.

Ollie cleared his throat. "Actually, Coach, Joe wasn't quite truthful when he said nothing's wrong. Just a minute ago he called me—excuse my French but I'm quoting Joe—he said, 'a *son* of a *bitch*.'"

"Joe? Is this true? You spoke to your teammate that way?"

Joe straightened up and met his father's questioning gaze. "Yes, sir. Actually, I called him a son of a bitch *creep*."

"I hate to hear that trash come out of your mouth, son," Tom winced.

"It causes me physical pain."

"I'm sorry."

"Are you?"

"You know I am, Dad."

"Why would you use such demeaning language toward your teammate? Especially when you know how I feel about it. You're not cruel. I know you."

Joe swallowed hard, pressed his lips together and shot Ben a warning glance, met Adam's eyes with the same message, then looked back to his father and said, quietly, slowly, "I don't have an excuse, Dad. Just my 'stinkin' humanity' as Gramps used to say."

"We'll have to do something about that," Tom said, his eyes lingering on Joe's eyes for a moment as if he were reading Joe while assuring Joe how adamant was his determination. No one moved or spoke. "You owe Ollie an apology."

"I know that, Dad," Joe said, his eyes just as determined as Tom's. He turned to Oliver. "I've no excuse to offer you, Ollie, only my sincere apology. I was wrong to say that to a teammate and I'm sorry." He stuck out his hand.

"Okay, good," Oliver said, and let Joe take his hand.

"Joe, you can run ten laps around the soccer field and join us when you're done. We'll talk more about this tonight at home."

Ben opened his mouth to speak but Joe glared a warning at him, so Adam said, "Coach, sir, I called Ollie an effing jerk."

"What?"

"Sorry, Coach."

"I told him to go to hell," Paul said.

"You, Paul?"

"I'm not perfect, Coach."

"I don't believe this."

"Sorry, Coach," Paul said, convincingly.

"I told him to screw himself," Scott said. "Twice."

"All right, that's enough," Tom said. "How many of you are going to claim to be involved in this?"

One by one, giving first a warning glance to Ben, every player except Knox and Ben raised his hand.

"Knox?" Tom asked.

"Remember? I came in late, Coach."

"And you, Ben? You weren't involved in this cussing fest?"

Ben cast one pleading glance at Drew who stood right behind Tom. Drew shook his head and mouthed the word no. Ben said, "I wanted to, Coach, but I've gotten in enough trouble already today. So I restrained myself."

"I see," Tom said. "Okay. Forget the laps, Joe. You each apologize to Oliver and then everybody runs twenty suicides."

One by one they filed past Oliver, offering an apology and a few words about teamwork with the handshake. Ducking his head, Knox left the room. When he was alone with Oliver and Tom, Ben extended his hand to Oliver. "I apologize for wanting to cuss you out. Doesn't the Bible say something about thinking a thing is as bad as doing it?"

Oliver shrugged. "Something like that."

"You can run the drill until I get there, Ben," Tom said, taking the whistle from around his neck and tossing it to him.

When they were alone, Tom said to Oliver, "Tell me what might have provoked such animosity from an entire team of good kids."

"No one is good, sir," Oliver said. "Bible says, '*All* have sinned.'"

"Ollie, I want to hear what *you* did to provoke your loyal teammates to such anger."

"Joe was the only one who let foul communication come out of his mouth. The others were lying to you."

"Think about your *own* conduct a little more carefully, son. What did *you* do to irritate your team members?"

"I told you, they were just defending Joe."

"We're talking about *you* here. Your teammates are trusting you to admit your fault, as they have."

"Joe is—not the good kid you think he is," Oliver said. "I was just changing my clothes and Joe said, 'Get out of the way,' and he swore. I only told you because I want him to get help—" Oliver swallowed deliberately. "Maybe you shouldn't let your kids hang out with someone like Ben."

Tom took a deep breath and exhaled slowly. "I'm looking forward to a great basketball season this year, Ollie. For that to happen, the team has to work as one unit. Ben is going to be part of that unit. You've got to find a way to get along with the other guys."

"Me? What about *them*?"

"I'm speaking to you. You know I will speak to them."

During the layup drill, Ben's eyes were opened to Oliver. The team split into two groups, lined up at center court, and advanced one by one to the basket. After his attempt at the layup, the player stood by to rebound, dribbled to the end of the line, and tossed the ball to the teammate waiting for his turn. Each group had three balls.

Ollie had managed to stay behind or beside Ben. Now Ben took his shot, Drew handled his rebound and sprinted off. Ben watched Oliver approach. He was right-handed and dribbled skillfully; his hands were disproportionately large and he cupped the ball, dumping it over. Ben thought it was a pretty slow way to dribble and wondered if he could go faster.

Ollie's layup was also good. He was light on his feet, had a good eye, but Ben saw immediately that there was nothing smooth about his play; he was aggressive and highly confident. The layup wobbled on the rim and shot off threatening to go out of bounds. Ben saw by the look on Ollie's face that he had been unable to cure his tendency to overshoot in this way that made rebounding so difficult. But Ben jumped, grabbed it with his left hand and came down easily. He dribbled twice before he sensed Ollie beside him and, surprised, looked up to see the intent in his eyes just before Ollie's hand hit Ben's bicep and his hip swung into Ben's. Ben skidded across the wood floor, crashing into the tumble of band instrument cases left out. Helping the sophomores with their layups, Tom's back was to him. He turned at the sound of the crash.

"What happened?"

"I must have slipped on the floor."

"You okay?"

"Yes, sir," Ben lied, knowing his upper thigh rubbed raw from the floor burn.

"Clean up the floor before someone gets hurt," Tom instructed. "There are towels in my office. Drew. You know where they are."

The drill continued, the boys muttering their disgust to Ollie as they passed him on the court. When Drew returned, Ben took the towel from him, checked to make sure his skid hadn't left a trail of sweat, and when he saw Tom concentrating with a younger player, jogged up to Oliver. "Try something like that again and I'll knock you on your ass."

The hot shower after practice was to Ben the single most rewarding physical benefit of playing basketball. He stood under the wobbling stream of steaming water, leaning his forehead on the tile wall, shielding his paper cup of cool water by holding it under his chin. The water trickled onto his shoulders, coursed down his back, stinging the palm-sized raspberry on his leg. "What's with the water pressure?" he heard Paul complain beside him. Ben put the paper cup to his lips and slurped in satisfying sips of water. His back was scalded and he had to turn around. He stuck his head under the shower and lifted his cup, draining it. Slowly he became aware of the others around him, the smell of soap rising with the steam, the slap of bare feet on the wet tile, of exhausted groans, and the distant, choking sound of Scott puking in the adjacent bathroom sink. Above him, the water slowed to a trickle. He stood directly beneath rubbing the soapy residue out of his hair.

"Please don't let me throw up," he heard Adam whisper in prayer beside him. "Please, not today, not tomorrow, not never."

He turned off the dripping shower and grabbed his towel. Beside him Joe stood naked, rubbing his towel vigorously over his hair, grumbling about the water pressure. Paul came over to them, his towel tight around his waist.

"That was rough," Ben said.

"Shower or practice?" Joe complained.

"Tomorrow'll be worse," Paul promised.

"We won't start with suicides tomorrow," Joe said. "I hope."

"I think you should tell him tonight what really happened," Ben said to Joe.

"I didn't see you run over there and snitch when Ollie shoved you."

"I'm new. It's different."

Adam joined them, toweling off, and then Drew, already dressed except for shoes. Oliver and Knox had left right after practice, without showering. Most of the sophomores were still too shy to shower in front of them and were pulling on their clothes over sweaty bodies. Scott was quiet now, resting on the bench. The locker room was all theirs.

"No," Joe said, his eyes tired, his mouth still pressed and swollen. "I'm not telling him," Joe said.

"What will he do to you?" Ben asked, his voice unsteady.

"I don't know. Nothing, I hope."

"He said you'd have to discuss it more at home."

"Yeah, but it was just one little cuss, and not one of the bad ones."

"What are the bad ones?" Ben asked.

Joe considered Ben a minute as if intrigued. "Why don't you know stuff like this?" he said with a laugh.

Ben shrugged. "Be serious, Joe."

Still watching Ben closely, Joe said, "He *might* whip me, I guess, but I don't think so."

"You've got to tell him, then," Ben said. "Ollie deserves it and it will save you."

"Why are you so afraid of a whipping?" Joe said. "It's no big deal."

"It's violent," Ben confided.

"I told you," Paul said. "It's just a few quick swats on your ass. Just stings. I only hated it because I know my dad was so disappointed with me."

Ben looked to Adam for confirmation.

"It's kind of cold and just," Adam shrugged. "From what I remember. Been a long time."

Drew said, "I just get the look and she holds out her hand and I got to give her my car keys and my cell phone. I'd personally rather have a few little whacks on my super hard ass. It gets it the hell over with."

Joe laughed. "I think Dad knows something's up from the way you guys covered my ass."

"If you're right," Ben said, "and he knows something's up, then tell him."

"No." Joe gestured toward the doorway. "I'm not telling Dad what Ollie said. And neither are *you* guys. If he whips me for my language, okay. I can handle that. If he takes away my car or whatever, I can live through that, too. But we're *not telling* and here's why. First, Ollie's our teammate. He may treat us like crap, but we can't reciprocate. We've got to show him how it's done. I honestly believe you should 'do unto others.' So that's how we have to live." They bent closer, forming a sort of huddle. Jon was with them now, and the three unshowered sophomores, Justin, Austin, and Flip. "And then, there's this. Ollie's quoting the Bible right and left, but *we* are going to live it. You understand me? This is important. This is the difference between people like Ollie who are all talk, and us who really mean it. We believe this stuff and it's not the kind of stuff you go throwing in people's faces or twisting for your own pleasure. It's important. It's life-and-death shit. We're taught to turn the other cheek, and that's what I'm doing."

"Maybe literally," Adam said.

Joe laughed at this. "We know God requires us to take responsibility for our own actions, and that's what we're going to do. You with me?"

Nods of heads and murmurs of assent rumbled through the crowd. But Ben said, "But these guys all lied to Tom about what they said. How does that fit in?"

"Shit," Joe said. "Shit and a half. I forgot about that."

"It wasn't really a lie," Jon said, "because the way I looked at it is just a matter of timing. I used the opportunity to cuss Ollie out right in front of Coach. It was happening in the present, I just said it happened in the past because I wanted to cuss him out both times."

The boys laughed together.

"And God is outside of time, so we're off the hook," Adam joked.

They laughed again, but Joe said, "No. Ben's right."

The locker room door squeaked open. The boys fell silent, except for Adam who whispered, "Dear Lord, please don't ever let him fix that squeak."

Tom held the door open and leaned in. "Ben still here?" The boys straightened up and faced Tom.

"Right here, Coach."

"You about ready to talk to me, Ben?"

"I've just got to put my shoes on, Coach."

"I'll be in my office," Tom said. "By the way, men," he said. "For the rest of the week, I'm going to increase your suicides by five a day. I mean this as punishment, and I hope you'll take it to heart."

"Punishment for…?" Jon said, in mock innocence, though Adam elbowed him.

"You know what for. For what you did and did not say. And don't bother coming to confess to me. I'm not changing my mind." He shut the door.

"Is there some kind of listening device in here?" Adam asked. "I mean how does he *always* know?"

"It was obvious, guys," Joe said, his arm briefly around Paul. "And thanks."

9

BEN walked into Tom's office for his very own opportunity to find out what it meant that Tom was strict but fair. Practice and his scalding shower had given him the muscle-numbing exhaustion that substituted for peace, but the slow tremor rumbled again in his stomach. When Tom saw Ben at the door, he invited him to come in, pulled his desk chair around to the front of the desk, and motioned toward the cot. "Have a seat, son," he said to Ben and when Ben sat down, Tom handed him a paper cup filled with ice water before settling into his desk chair and leaning forward toward Ben.

"You did a fine job in practice today, Ben."

"I wasn't really on top of things."

"A little distracted at times."

"Yeah. Sorry about that." Ben stared at the water cup.

"Drink that. I know you're thirsty."

"Very," Ben said, draining it at once.

"I suspect you were involved with whatever happened with Ollie."

"Me?"

"Yes."

"It's complicated, Coach."

"I know from the team's reaction that Joe must have been sorely provoked."

"He was."

"Want to tell me about it?"

"I do. But I promised Joe I wouldn't. Joe wants us to support Ollie. Treat him as we want to be treated."

"Does all this have anything to do with what happened this morning between you and Bonnie Jean?"

"I'm not sure. I can't always understand what Ollie's talking about."

An awkwardness separated them. Ben wanted to confide in Tom, feared Tom, even considered trading information for Tom's favor. Tom was studying Ben, looking worried. "How's Bonnie Jean? Were you able to calm her down, Coach?"

"Not really," Tom said. "But we had a good talk. Jeannie is generally cheerful, but once she starts crying, it is a storm of rather lengthy duration."

"I know I messed up. I don't know how to prove to you how sorry I am."

"Why don't you start by explaining your intentions."

Ben rattled the ice in his cup. "I was trying to comfort her. Did she tell you that?"

"Yes."

"And I don't know what happened. I don't know—when I saw her mole and I knew how upset she was about it, I just wanted it to seem like not such a bad thing, so I kind of covered it with my hand."

"I see."

"I wasn't thinking, Coach, but I know that's no excuse. But I wasn't trying to take advantage or touch her in a way that—um—it wasn't like that. But then, we were so close and—I don't know—I just had to kiss her. But that's when Bettinger ripped me away from her." To hide his emotion, Ben rattled the ice in his cup and lifted the cup to his lips letting the few melted drops trickle into his mouth.

"He means no harm, Ben."

"He was pretty scary. But if I think of it from his perspective, I—" Ben's hand had begun to shake so badly that he set his ice cup down on the floor. He looked to Tom, knowing himself to be now utterly inarticulate.

Tom said, "In general, I discourage dating in high school. You kids should go out as a group and have fun without getting too serious."

"But Coach—I want to spend time with her—I mean, she's so fun and great."

"I've taught my children to wait for a time in life when they are ready to make a deep, heartfelt commitment."

"I know that, Coach and I respect it. In fact, I think it's beautiful." Tom considered this, his eyes softening as they swept over Ben's tense form. "I promise you that I will always respect her. Today was a horrible start, but I promise I'll treat her exactly according to your standards. I won't mess up again."

Tom was quiet for a second, squinting, concerned. "Ben, there are a hundred reasons for you to treat Bonnie Jean strictly as a friend."

"This has to do with who my father is, doesn't it?" Ben said, his tone going tight and angry.

Tom swallowed hard and studied his hands. "In a way, yes."

"I'm nothing like him. I won't hurt her."

"Ben—it's *difficult* to explain."

"I know he hurt Mrs. MacBride. But you've got to give me a chance on my own."

"It's not that, Ben. Believe me."

"What is it, then?"

"You're going to have to trust me a *little*."

"Is this about what Oliver was saying—something about 'un-churched?' Because I can *go* to church."

Tom shook his head again. "This is not about the quality of your character. I think very highly of you in every way. So far."

"Then what?"

Tom said, "Look, what I'm about to say may sound sentimental and even…lame, and you may not see your need for it, but right now, Ben… Mrs. MacBride and I believe it is important for you to feel perfectly at home at our house—just like one of us. *Because* of—not in *spite* of—who your parents are."

Ben's eyes pulsed and stung. He strained to keep them focused. Tom was offering him what he had been longing for—praying to a silent heaven for as long as he could remember. He pictured his skinny twelve-year-old self sobbing into his pillow at night, praying for just such a family. His stomach tossed at the vivid memory, his ears burned.

"If you get romantically involved with Bonnie Jean and break up, you're going to feel awkward. You're going to stay away. I do not want that to happen."

"Coach," Ben urged. "If you let us date, I promise we won't break up."

"You can't guarantee that."

"It feels so right, Coach. I know it's right."

Tom winced, his discomfort obvious. "That's not what you need right now, son."

"So you want me to *trade* the privilege of dating Bonnie Jean for—as you say—being part of the family."

"Yes."

"Coach, I want both."

"Trust me. Be her friend. You'll be glad for it later." Tom's gaze was level and serious. "Honor my request for a few months longer, Ben. Can you do that? Get to know us all a little bit better. When you understand what Laurie and I—"

"You'll let me date her then?"

"We'll talk about it again soon, I hope."

Tom stood up and Ben followed, slowly, noting that his thigh muscles had tightened painfully while he sat. Tom extended his hand. Ben met his eyes and saw clearly there a kind of authority with which he was largely unfamiliar. It was as if Tom's handshake would seal their agreement, and the concerned, knowing look in his eyes told Ben that Tom was bearing the responsibility of the outcome; Ben had only to hang on and hope. Ben stared at Tom's extended hand, shoving his own hands in his pockets.

"So, what's the MacBride punishment for something like this?"

"Pardon?"

"Mrs. Poulard said talking to you was supposed to be my punishment."

"That is punishment, indeed," Tom laughed.

"Someone mentioned suspension."

"There's no need to punish you, son. I've given you some very clear instructions—some standards for how I want you to behave, and I'm going to be praying for you to be able to live up to those standards. That's fathering. That's what you need."

Fathering? Ben repeated Tom's words silently and glanced up at Tom who looked keenly embarrassed. His mind snapped with vague and vivid impressions, snatches of conversations, his mother's ranting, and for some reason, a clear vision of what Tom claimed was his mother's handwriting on the fragment from the bottom of Laurie's broken teapot. He wondered now where he'd put it.

Tom moved his extended hand palm up and finally Ben took it to shake hands, feeling the baffling and uncontrollable threat of tears for the second time in minutes. He felt a strange kind of anger at Tom, kind of a pushing anger that held no resentment.

His eyes squinted, his lips pressed together, Tom clapped Ben's upper arm as was his way with all his not-quite-sons. And then Tom said, "Hey, you're going to be okay," with a brisk kind of tenderness that Ben found somewhat fortifying. A tall, thick-looking, freckle-faced man stepped into his field of vision. Through the handshake, Ben felt tension and dislike enter Tom's concentration, and Tom released Ben's hand, turned slightly, and said, "John. Didn't expect to see you here."

"Came right over soon as Oliver called me. You and me need to have a talk. Right now about the morality of this team."

"Aren't you headed home for dinner? I know Laurie is expecting me."

"That can wait." The man stared at Ben.

"John, I want you to meet Bennett Hunter. Ben, this is Ollie's father, Mr. Saunders."

"They call me Colonel. Just like they do Oliver. My old grandmom always said we were descended from the guy that invented fried chicken. Get it? Colonel Saunders."

"Hello," Ben said politely and extended his hand.

But Mr. Saunders folded his arms over his chest and said, "You're the new hotshot basketball player."

"No, sir," Ben said. "You must be thinking of someone else. I'll be lucky to make the team."

"There you go," Saunders said. "Hate to have a cold bench." He

261

turned to Tom and said, "I need to discuss the little pervert who molested your daughter today."

"You are grossly misinformed, John. No one did anything of the sort! Step into my office before you say another word."

Ben's stomach lurched violently and he bolted from the room.

In the bathroom, Ben retched until his stomach ached and shuddered. When Joe approached on tiptoe with a cup of water, he was resting his forehead on the cool toilet bowl. "Is that man gone?" Ben murmured.

"No. Dad told him off, but Colonel Saunders is sermonizing up a storm right now. Dad doesn't want him to be able to get to you. So, as soon as you're ready, I'll sneak you out the back door and take you home." When they were in the MG, Ben lay his head back and closed his eyes.

"Was he rough on you?"

"Tom? No," Ben said. "But he doesn't want me to date Bonnie Jean."

"He just doesn't believe in dating in high school. So don't take it personally. He thinks you're great."

"That's hard to believe."

"All truly great things are hard to believe," Joe said.

"Will you be on IM tonight?" Ben asked as Joe pulled up to the curb to drop him off.

"If I can make it to the computer," Joe said. Ben blanched and Joe laughed at him, punching his arm. "I'm kidding, Ben. Yeah. I'll be there at ten. Mom and Dad go to bed then."

"Talk to you then. I need to talk to Jeannie, too."

"I'll make it happen, buddy," Joe said.

Ben nodded, shutting the door with what he felt was an enormous effort. He stood, trying to move his stiffened legs as Joe pulled away from the curb, the MG chugging wearily. He moved toward the gate, his thirst growing with every inch.

At home, Keith waited for him at the top of the stairs, cell phone in hand. "Gran has a car for you. You got to call her right back."

"She called on the cell phone?" Tim came running and threw himself against Ben's legs; Ben endured the pain, straining to stay upright. He patted Tim's shoulder. "Watch it, Tim, I'm real sore."

"Did Dad hit you already? You just camed home."

"No. Hush. From practice. What about Gran calling, Keith?"

"First she called Dad, then this one. She was scared to call on yours because you were at practice."

"Right. Because we're only calling during practice if it's an emergency."

"Keith told her that. So you gots to call her back."

Ben shuffled into his room, his brothers following. "You didn't tell

Mom and Dad about the cell phones, did you guys?"

"No," Keith said seriously.

"We kept it on buzz only."

Ben sat down slowly. Wincing, he eased his backpack onto his bed.

"Are you gonna be okay?"

"Yeah. I just need some rest."

"Do you want a drink of ice water? I'll go get you some."

"No, that's okay. Stay up here." Ben scrutinized their faces. "Did Dad actually say he was going to hit me?"

"No," Keith said. "But if you're sore, that's why, most the time."

Ben's eyes stung. He lay back on his bed and stared up at the ceiling, trying to gather his strength.

"Want me to call Gran?"

"Yeah."

Keith put the phone to Ben's ear. "Hey, Gran, it's me, Ben."

"You sound awful. What's wrong?"

"Tired from practice," Ben lied. "First practice."

"That's right. Listen, Ben. I was able to get that vintage Fiat for you for a price you can easily afford."

"How much?"

"You have three thousand in the bank, right? And I promised to match your savings. He's willing to let it go for four thousand. If I pay half as we agreed, that leaves you some cash."

"Why so little? Is it a piece of junk?"

"Indeed not!"

"Sorry Gran, it's just that I looked them up online and the restored ones start at fifteen thousand."

"It's in perfect running condition. It's better than new."

"Then…?"

"The owner has personal reasons for getting rid of it."

"Like?"

"So, it's a bargain. I think you should take it. If you don't like it, you can sell it and buy what you want."

"I'm sure I'll like it, Gran, it's just that I don't understand—"

"You're not going to find such good quality for so little money." Her voice was getting shrill, frustrated.

"Okay, Gran. If you think this is best, I'd love to have it."

"Good, I'm glad to hear it. And if you insist on going through with your pink idea, you can have it painted. You'll have enough cash left over for that."

"Yeah. I really need to have it painted."

"I'll look into making those arrangements."

"Thanks, Gran. Wait, hold on." He covered the phone with his hand

and lifted up slightly. "Quick, Keith, that's Dad on the stairs. Shut the door and lock it."

Keith rushed to obey. Ben went back to the phone. "I've got to go, Gran. Dad's coming upstairs. I'll call you later. Thanks for everything."

Max bellowed for Keith from the second floor landing. Ben stuffed the cell phone under his pillow and told Keith to be careful.

Ben heard Max ask if Ben wanted dinner. Keith came into his room. "What do I say?"

"Tell him I threw up after practice and I think I might throw up again."

When Keith came back with the happy news that their father had hurried away, Keith and Tim crowded onto Ben's bed to tell him about their day and to finish their homework. Ben's strength rallied and he wondered how stark his life must have been before his brothers came along.

10

TOO sore to run the next morning, Ben showered at home. He splashed his face with hot water as the basin filled. When he twisted the faucet closed, Ben heard his parents' voices. In the bathroom, floors below, their conversation carried up the exposed pipes in a rumbling whisper.

"He's changed towards me," his father complained. "He won't tell me anything."

Ben leaned in toward the mirror to spread shaving cream in a thin layer and listened carefully. *Dad wants to talk to me?*

"He's always been that way," his mother answered. "Since he cut his hands."

"Donna, why bring stuff up? Why do you always bring stuff up? And anyway, what did he have to tell us back then? This is teenage stuff. It's not rooted deep down somewhere."

Since I cut my hands? Ben put his razor down and stared at his palms. Visible on both were short, thin, raised lines. He remembered being younger and knowing these were scars, remembered staring at them when he finished his timed multiplication tests, wondering if they would ever disappear. But over the years he had forgotten to watch them. Now they were faint, easy to forget.

"I don't know why you're asking me," Donna said. "You know how he feels about me."

"He's been very good to you. I never saw a kid take such good care of anyone as he did when Keith was born. Tim too. He was devoted."

I didn't realize he even knew about that. He was away.

"What do you want to know?" Donna's voice was shrill. "I tried to ask him if he was sexually active, like you wanted me to, and he got angry."

Ben listened, staring in the mirror, shaving.

"All this about a car—and his license." Max's voice boomed up the pipes. "How did all this happen?"

"Do you really want to be involved in teaching him how to drive? That sounds stressful."

"It's too late. He's already got a license. But what about school? Does he like it? Do you know?"

"He must like it. He's always there." Ben swished the razor through the basin of hot water.

"He seems so cold and distant."

"That's who Ben is. What do you want from him, Max?"

Ben stared into the reflection of his own blue eyes. *They don't know me. At all.*

"I'm worried he found that letter, Donna. What if he did?" Ben hurried to finish shaving, suddenly sick of the conversation, wanting only to get away, get to school.

"What if he read it? His birth certificate? What then?"

"That birth certificate nonsense has been a nuisance all our lives. I'm sick of it."

"It doesn't matter if you're *sick* of it, Donna. It's the way things are."

"Okay, Max. If you want to talk about *the way things are,* then accept the fact that Ben's been cold and silent since day one. He's bright, he's strong; he'll be fine in life. He doesn't need us and he never has. *That's* the way things are."

"No, you're wrong, Donna. You're wrong."

Birth certificate? Ben thought. *What are they talking about—the letter from the CO? Do they always refer to that as my birth certificate?* Realizing the time, Ben went to his room and dressed quickly. He packed his gym bag with clean things—jeans, shirt, sweatshirt for later at Joe's house, his journal, and clothes for band tomorrow. Wondering why his father was so worried about Johnson's letter—it had been useless to him anyway—he took his alarm clock, as he did now every morning, reset it, and carried it to Keith's night stand. He touched Keith lightly on the top of the head and sighed. Friday. He'd lived through another week.

Creeping down the back stairs silently on burning leg muscles, Ben found he could not resist a sudden craving for orange juice. He peeked into the kitchen, and seeing it was empty, stepped in, crossed quickly to the cabinet, got a large glass, and went to the refrigerator to fill it. *One thing about Mom,* he thought, filling the glass. *She never scrimps on orange juice.* Standing at the open refrigerator, Ben drained the glass put it in the sink and turned to go out the back door. His father stopped him, grabbing Ben's pants, his fingers thrust inside the waistband.

"Ah!" Ben cried. He hadn't heard him. He whirled away, breaking his father's grip. "I'm in a hurry. My ride's waiting."

Max, shoes in one hand, was too close to him. "Just orange juice for breakfast? That's not enough for an athlete in training."

"I'm fine. My stomach," Ben lied, laying his hand flat on his stomach for emphasis.

"Threw up last night from practice? A lot of guys throw up?"

"Yeah, it was rough. I've got to go, Dad."

"Looks like you got all your earthly possessions in there. What're you doing? Running away from home?"

Ben looked away, looked at the clock. Joe was there, waiting. "It's just stuff I need," Ben murmured, feeling his betrayal.

"What's the matter, son?" Max asked, seeming genuine. "Something bothering you?"

"I—um—I overheard you and Mom this morning mention my birth certificate, sir."

"Overheard us?"

"Yes, sir. It was weird. I was shaving and for some reason, your voices were traveling up the pipes in the bathroom."

"Really?" Max asked, sounding interested, his face a furrow of calm, intellectual incredulity.

"I didn't mean to eavesdrop, but I had to finish shaving and I wondered what you meant about my birth certificate."

Max smiled in an indulgent, understanding way, but he stepped closer and said, "How often do you shave now?" He lifted his hand as if to touch Ben's cheek. Ben ducked away; the fog of hope vanished and he spun for the door, but Max leapt at him, grabbing his face, his chin, turning, then shoving Ben's head back into the corner beside the door, until it hit hard. Max thrust his left forearm across Ben's throat, shoving him back, trapping his backpack and gym bag behind him, pinning his arms down, forcing his body to arch out. "I would think a decent point guard could evade that move." Max leaned in, menacing.

"Dad," Ben blew the word out, but unable to inhale, the edges of his vision went black.

"Where's Johnson's letter, Ben?"

Ben shook his head, trying to breathe and answer.

Max bumped hard against Ben. Somehow rising taller, he thrust his knee between Ben's legs. "Answer me," Max commanded, moving his knee up just enough against Ben's thigh to make Ben sure of his threat. Ben stamped on Max's stocking foot, and in that moment of pain and surprise, brought his laden arms forward, his backpack and gym bag swinging out. His backpack hit Max in the right shoulder, knocking him back; Max sat down hard, shaking the house. The backpack fell into Max's lap. Ben bolted out the back door.

Sprinting so hard he saw blue flashes, forgetting how to breathe, his lungs on fire, Ben ran down the alley and flung himself around the corner at the wall. Joe's car sputtered by the curb.

Ben tried to compose himself as he opened the MG's door and got in; he hugged his gym bag to his chest to hide his gasping. He shut the door a little too hard. "Let's go. *Go. Drive.*"

"What's wrong?"

"Nothing."

"Right," Joe said, putting the car in gear. "I believe *that*."

"Go. Let's *go*."

"What happened?" Joe pulled away from the curb, edged into traffic, then glanced at Ben. "Did you guys argue?"

Ben turned around to look. "It's not like that."

"What are those marks on your face?"

"What?"

Joe flipped down the sun visor to reveal a small, grimy mirror. "Look."

Finger marks, red and angry, showed on Ben's jaw. "I don't know. I fell. I was late and had to run to catch you."

"Did he slap you? Because those look like finger marks."

"No," Ben said, his voice shaking. He shut his eyes and let his head rest back. "He didn't slap me."

"What did he do?"

"He's just—" Ben tried to breathe deeply but the air caught. "He's—annoying." His stuttering mind, feeling the sharp probe of Joe's questions, searched for a cloak, fumbled to create a distraction.

"Yeah," Joe said. "We can call it that."

"Shit. I left my backpack. I can't go to school without my backpack. My homework, my books. Just drop me off at the corner. I'll think of something and run over."

"No. You shouldn't go back right now."

The rumble of the MG hid Ben's ragged breathing. "I need my backpack."

"No, you don't."

"C'mon, Joe. I don't want to get in any more trouble."

"No trouble. This is now your lucky day."

"Right."

"I know you don't believe me because the day started out rough. But all that's changed."

Ben opened his eyes. Joe was grinning.

"Why are you dressed like that? Is it jeans day and I didn't know about it?"

"Nope. Guess again."

"I don't know. It's really Saturday?"

"Nope. We're going to Mom's shop where breakfast awaits us. We're gonna do a few chores for her, then drive to Philly to pick up Peter for his fall break." Joe laughed at Ben's incredulity.

"Your parents are sanctioning our skipping school?"

"I knew you hadn't listened to the news this morning."

"What's that got to do with it?"

"Yep. We're takin' a road trip, you and me, and if you ever calm down, Pete and I are gonna let you drive all the way home."

"Joe, I can't skip school."

"You forgot to ask *how* Pete and I were gonna let you drive all the way home."

"Huh?"

"After we IMed last night, I told my parents about your grandmother getting you a car and this morning Dad suggested Pete and me drive you up there to get it."

"What?"

"Yep. They said have a great time."

"But we have band tomorrow."

"If we leave at five or six in the morning, we'll be back in plenty of time. We don't have to be at band until three-thirty. Night performance at Glasgow. No problem."

"I told you, I can't skip school. How come your parents are okay with this?"

"You really ought to listen to the news in the morning, Ben." Joe laughed. "Remember how lame the showers were after practice? Turns out there's something broken in the water pump. No water anywhere so school is closed. Classes canceled. Band canceled and even more important, practice canceled."

Ben let out a whoop of joy that made Joe laugh again. "For the first time in my life," Ben said, "I actually think that God might be good."

"He *is* good," Joe said, grinning and punching Ben's shoulder. "And he wants *you* to have lots of fun."

Joe turned into a driveway on the far side of Laurie's store. Walking past the bay window that served as a drive-through, Ben could see into the store and the café in its back corner. The sun bright, the air clear with a cool, gusting wind, Joe led Ben to the front porch. Though the maple tree stood in a flame of color, roses bloomed profusely on the bushes at the front of the store and Ben's heart thudded the instant he smelled them. *Get control of yourself,* he counseled silently. *You don't want Mrs. MacBride to see you're upset.*

The store was awake. Quilts hung on the porch railings; a sign with the day's menu specials and sewing class schedule stood by the door. The handwriting was Bonnie Jean's, her witty sketches enlivening the mundane message. Ben smiled. This was the world he wanted. *I'm not going home. I'm never going back there.* Beside him the store's bright blue, white, and yellow banner flapped in the breeze.

"What's the name mean—Eight Hands Around?" Ben asked, staring at the pattern and colors, which pulled hard on his imagination.

"I'd tell you, but I don't want you to know how much I know about quilting. So ask Mom."

Ben laughed, relaxing a little, grateful for Joe. "Bonnie Jean told me you can pin a quilt together."

"Yep. I used to make money working for Mom when I was younger. Now Tommy does it. Good money, too," Joe said as they mounted the steps. "So, I already called Pete and he's up for it. You just have to call your grandmother and see if it's okay."

"They're here!" Bonnie Jean's voice sounded beyond the screen door. Ben pushed the horrors of his morning down and away and in a moment, she slammed the door open. Dressed in jeans and a fuzzy red turtleneck, the sleeves pushed up to her elbows, she smiled and threw open her arms. "Can you believe we have an entire day off?" Her eyes shone brighter than ever, her dark hair swung loose. As Ben stepped through the door, she grabbed him around the neck in her eager, sturdy hug. His hand went to her little waist. "You look really nice today, Jeannie."

She made a funny, appreciative face and Ben knew that if her mother were not walking toward them, if her father had not put those restrictions on them, if her brother were not inches away, they would be kissing with a wild happiness all their own. "Am I forgiven for yesterday?" he whispered.

"For being the sweetest, most understanding friend ever?" she whispered. "Never. I'll never forgive that."

"Mom," Joe protested as his mother hugged him. "You just saw me."

Then it was Ben's turn. "Ben!" When she hugged him, Ben wanted to cling to her, felt almost overpowered by the need to stay with her and tell her everything. He clamped down on himself, stuffing his need, swallowing hard, assuming a fake smile. Would she see through it?

Laurie touched his jaw lightly. "Did you hurt yourself?"

"Huh? I don't know," then looking around, eyes not focusing, "What smells so good?"

"I've started the soup for today and Jeannie's baking brownies. Did you set the timer?"

"Oops!" She dashed to the back of the store.

Relieved that they were sufficiently distracted from the brutal marks his father had left on his face, Ben pushed the attention further from himself. "What does the name mean—the name on the banner?"

"It's a quilt pattern symbolic of the old quilting bees. Four women would work on a quilt. One on each side. Two hands each. See? But in the store name, I mean it to suggest a cooperative effort. People working together. It's my philosophy."

Ben looked around. By the front porch near the bay window, there stood two armchairs surrounded by bookshelves and racks of patterns. Watching him, Laurie said, "We have to keep the fabric out of the sun, so we put the books and patterns there."

Bonnie Jean walked back toward them with a timer in her hand. "Let's show him around," she said, taking Ben by the elbow and dragging him forward.

Laurie explained that her most popular patterns and items were also sold as kits. Because most women are in a hurry, Laurie explained, they could stop by and grab a kit. If someone called ahead, Laurie made the kit up for them. "Something for everyone."

Joe said, "And they have classes in all this stuff. Mom has all her bases covered."

Ben looked around at the garden of colors. Laurie grouped them, she explained, by hue, but separated the hues with a section of complementing neutrals. The blues looked like an ocean, beside it bright whites, beyond that, the sunny yellows, and on around the room, bolts of fabric, shades of color, carefully wrought samples of quilted artistry.

Joe had gotten Cara out of her seat and held her against his shoulder. She bobbed her head against his neck, making him laugh. "I think she's looking for you, Mom."

"That's because you picked her up."

"But she looked so cute," Joe protested, nuzzling his cheek against her head.

"Here are the finished quilts," Laurie said, stopping in front of a case that reached to the ceiling. In it were folded white quilts dense with stitches and quilts made of one bright print with a curving edge that revealed a striped underside. "My French collection. The samples are here; we have more in the back." Ben picked up a small pillow. "Do you have a quilt on your bed, Ben?"

"Tom loaned me one that day at the hospital. Remember?"

"That one is so old. You can have a new one to take home with you. Any pattern or color."

"We were promised breakfast, Mom," Joe said, giving Ben's shoulder a shove that sent him stumbling toward the back of the shop. Eight tables were spaced around the coffee colored room, each with a red cloth and a bowl of golden roses. Centered on the back wall were shelves holding white cups, various teapots, and stacks of small plates. Beside this was the drive-through. Built into the wall beneath the window were shelves that held bags, wrapping materials, and thread; baskets of folded fabrics grouped by color; rulers and scissors. The left side of the café housed the stove, wall ovens and refrigerator. There was a work space and in front of that, a counter with stools, and nearest them at the edge of the café was a display counter with loaves of bread, mounds of chunky cookies and pastries.

"Did you make all this today?"

"No, that's what I meant about my business philosophy," Laurie laughed. "When the children were little, I wanted to be home with them. So, now I hire young mothers to cook and bake for the shop. They cook at home and bring me the finished product first thing in the morning."

"She pays her help a little too generously," Joe whispered, "according to my frugal Scots grannie." He leaned toward Ben so that Cara saw him and lifted her head and cooed at him.

"Hi, baby," Ben said, taking her finger.

"I hire women to make the samples and the ready made goods, too. The patterns and specifications and materials are given to them, but the labor is theirs. I make quite a profit on these things, so I can afford to pay my employees."

"I see what you mean about the store name."

"It has many wide implications," she said, looking carefully at him as if waiting for something.

11

BECAUSE he had been born and raised in Annapolis, Joe wondered at the deeply familiar sense that awoke in him when he approached Hillside, New Jersey. Slowing with traffic on Route 17, Joe glanced in the rearview mirror and noted the wary anger still smoldering in Ben's eyes as his friend stared out the window. "Do you recognize this?" Joe said to him.

"Sure," Ben said, his brooding thoughts holding him apart from the poignant excitement of homecoming beginning in Joe now with the sight of Champion Bowling Alley ahead on the right.

To Joe, it felt like waking up and realizing that it had grown light while he had been sleeping. And when he slowed to a stop at the traffic light beside the bowling alley, gaudy and faded, he immediately looked over his left shoulder and yes—there in the distance, across the acres of woods, up on a hill—he could see the back of his late grandparents' house just the same as it had always been, though they had been gone for years. Peter was looking, too, and he punched Joe softly on the shoulder. "How long's it been since we were here, Pete?"

"Grandma Davidson died when I was eight and a half, so ten years.

Hey, Joe, let's go down Franklin Turnpike," Pete said, as they came to an angled intersection. "I want to see if the celery farm is still there."

Joe took the left fork and Peter made him pull over to the curb so he could see the boggy fields there. Peter rolled down his window and breathed. "I remember this smell."

"How do you remember a smell?" Joe mocked. "I can't believe we have this town in common and this is the first time we've been here together."

"It might not be," Ben said. "Were you ever here for the Fourth of July?

"Yeah, when I was five," Peter said. "Fourth of July is fun here."

"I don't remember," Joe said. "How can you remember stuff?"

Peter shrugged. "I remember everything after my second birthday. I remember you home from the hospital, Joe."

"There's something wrong with you, Pete, I swear to God."

Ben directed Joe to turn at the light across from Brookside Elementary onto a street that took them up a steep hill.

"This'd be fun to sled down," Joe said.

"That's Gran's house," Ben said, indicating a driveway just before the crest of the hill. The driveway wound up another small incline past the extensive front lawn. The spacious stone mansion, slate roof glinting in the bright October sunlight, was set like a jewel atop the incline. An enormous maple tree dominated the front yard, its orange-gold leaves as bright as fire.

"Some house," Joe said.

"Park around back," Peter said, absently frowning.

By the time they were out of the car, Ella Hunter was crossing the concrete patio at the back of the house. White-haired and ruddy-cheeked, she was tall, hefty and sure-footed. Joe perceived her nervousness when she hugged Ben; her hands shook on his shoulders. But Ben's smile was genuine and he hugged her without caution, though his effort to put aside his private turmoil was obvious to Joe as Ben circled Joe's shoulders with his arm to introduce him, his voice somehow hopeful. "My new friends, Gran. Joe and Peter MacBride. You knew their mom, Laurie."

But Mrs. Hunter would not meet Joe's eyes, and her voice sounded tight and reluctant when she took Joe's hand in her damp one. "Small world." She glanced at Joe's face and then looked to Ben, dots of sweat appearing on her upper lip.

"It's nice to meet you, Mrs. Hunter," Peter said, taking her hand in both of his and sounding easily as warm and genuine as their father. Joe was concurrently irritated and relieved. Peter had learned, as Tom had, to mask his infallible perceptions in the interest of the person's comfort. And Peter put Ella Hunter at ease, though Joe could see by the look in his eyes that he was working on something that puzzled him. While Joe noted, with an unwilling aversion, the sterile gardens planted with clipped evergreens, the underlying mulch free of even one golden leaf, Peter and Ben walked ahead with Mrs. Hunter.

"We never see stone houses like this in Annapolis, you know," Joe heard him saying. And when she gave the standard answer about the ice age and the glacier leaving all its stones no farther south than Northern New Jersey, Peter sounded delighted with this stale information that he'd heard on every visit to this town and every time their own mother needed rocks for her southern garden.

Peter really scored points when he guessed that the house was one linked to the Underground Railroad. Mrs. Hunter grew animated as she told Peter the extent of her research into establishing the house's role in slaves' escape to the north, and led them first to her study, pausing to open the pocket doors that rolled back silently into the walls to reveal a lavishly furnished room that smelled of lemon. Joe wanted to be offered a drink and the bathroom, but Peter leafed through Mrs. Hunter's research, reading aloud the names of the people proven to have escaped through this house. Her countenance brightened with his interest and though Joe knew Peter's winning her confidence was a good thing, it was to Joe's dismay that Peter asked to see the door and the tunnel she'd discovered in the basement. Ben bumped Joe's shoulder with his own, giving a brief smile. Joe remembered Ben's frantic dash to his waiting car that morning and he squinted to find traces of the weird marks on Ben's face, but in the dim basement light he could not see them. In Ben's eyes there now remained only faint traces of anger as subtle and lingering as thin, blue trails of smoke.

So down they trouped, over a stairway that began with the familiar sinuous feel of wood underfoot but at five steps down became cool, curved stone. Though the basement's stone walls were damp, it smelled pleasantly of earth, and Joe saw that the floor was the packed dirt of an old cellar.

"Pretty cool growing up in a house that was part of the Underground Railroad," Joe said to Ben.

"He wasn't reared here," Mrs. Hunter corrected Joe, without glancing over her shoulder as she led the way through the cellar's dim light. "He visits."

"It feels like home, Gran," Ben said. "That's what Joe means."

Stooping slightly, warning them to watch their heads, Mrs. Hunter led them to a wooden doorway in the darkest part of the cellar. From a shelf beside the door, she took flashlights and distributed them. She turned an iron key in the lock.

"When the tunnel was in use," Ella explained, "this entrance was hidden by a false wall with pocket doors like the ones in my study. But the wall itself was covered with moss so that it looked like earth. Then in front of that, they had constructed these same shelves you see lining the walls on the west side of the cellar. They kept the wine and the preserved food over there, so that any soldiers inspecting the place would be attracted to that side of the room. Here were gardening tools and clay pots with some unpleasant-smelling herbs. The soldiers were repulsed from this area."

At her touch the door opened without a squeak. Peter remarked on this and Mrs. Hunter seemed pleased with his powers of observation. Ben said, "Gran keeps things running perfectly."

"I have help." She ducked below the doorjamb and led the way into the tunnel. The air felt dry and warmer than the cellar. Underfoot was earth, packed and swept to a soundless path. The walls of brick and timber had a brisk woody pungency.

"It feels good in here." He heard Peter voice the comment he was just about to say. "Not like a cellar at all."

"They tried to make it comfortable. People sometimes lived in here for days."

"I didn't realize that."

"There's an intriguing ventilation system. I'll show you the plans when we're back upstairs, if you're interested."

"Very much so," Peter said, with a glance and a wink back at Joe.

Joe couldn't help but smile at him. "Peter's going to be a history professor, you know, Mrs. Hunter."

"I'm not surprised." She grabbed Peter's wrist to make him thrust his flashlight into a dark hole in the side of the tunnel. The temperature had changed slightly; it felt cooler and the light from Peter's flashlight showed an ellipse-shaped area with narrow shelves that held several wooden boxes, their corners smoothed with age and polish, and a stack of sealed, plastic containers.

With a sweeping gesture she indicated the boxes on the berths. "These were sleeping bunks to hold the tunnel's guests. Shelves here in the wall for foodstuffs. I keep certain historical articles here that require a hermetically controlled environment. It's the perfect storage spot for a collector like me." She gave what Joe thought was a tense laugh.

"I didn't know you kept stuff down here, Gran."

"Now you do." Again that tense laugh.

But Peter said, "This is absolutely the coolest thing, Mrs. Hunter. I'd heard about these underground tunnels from my mom and my uncle but never expected to see one."

"Your grandparents' house was built after the war, so there wouldn't have been one. This tunnel leads to two others that are restored and capable of use."

"Wait," Joe said. "You knew our grandparents?"

"It's a small town. Everyone knows everyone." And with a contrite glance at Ben's raised eyebrows she examined first Joe's face, then Peter's. "They were a nice couple. Your mother, too, of course, lovely. At school with my Max."

Touching his grandmother's wrist, Ben said, "We know they dated in high school, Gran."

"That's hardly important now." She stepped back out into the main tunnel. Casting the light of her flashlight before her, she said, "The tunnel extends to a nearby house, with one narrow exit through his root cellar and another into the main house."

Gran paused atop the stairs and wiped her feet vigorously on the mat on the kitchen floor. "Make sure you get the dirt off your feet, boys."

Ben's grandmother seemed pleased with Peter's offer that he drive over to see the car she'd found for Ben. They were to go past their grandparents' old house to the edge of town. "Near the apple orchards?" Peter asked.

"Yes," Mrs. Hunter said, looking, Joe thought, a little worried. She was nervous as they drove, fidgeting with her purse until she finally opened it and took out a cigarette.

"Gran," Ben said softly to her. "They're not used to smoking."

"Of course!" she said too brightly, her hands shaking. "It helps me to hold it. I'm helplessly addicted."

Not even Peter could think of something charming to say and so they rode on in tense silence until Ben brought up the car. "Gran, you said on the phone that this car belongs to a friend who has to get rid of it, right?"

Tapping her cigarette on her purse clasp, she told them, "Don't mention that he's giving it to us at a good price. It's a matter of pride. Just thank him for it and we'll be on our way. I've worked out the cost with him."

"Did you take half from my account?" Ben asked.

Putting her unlit cigarette to her lips, she murmured. "We'll discuss that later, Ben."

Up the hill past their grandparents' old house, Peter turned left onto a narrow street, colored on that bright autumn afternoon with towering, dark evergreens and bright, bronzed oaks and maples. Peter said he remembered that it led to orchards. When apple trees came into view, still laden with red fruit, Ben and Joe congratulated him.

Ella said, "Your memory is startling."

"Hey, Gran—"

"Don't say 'hey,' Ben. It's slang and it's southern." She said absently, fishing around for something in her purse. She took out a small silver lighter.

"Yes, ma'am, but Gran. I need to ask you about my birth certificate."

"We've been over this before, Ben. And not today. You have guests." She lit her cigarette and inhaled, blowing smoke toward the crack in her open window.

"But Dad mentioned it today. Is there any way—while I'm up here—if

I can find out why I don't have one?"

"What do you mean he *mentioned* it?"

"Sometimes in the bathroom, you can hear people talking a couple of floors down—"

"You shouldn't eavesdrop. Your parents only have your best interest at heart." Ella Hunter stared straight ahead, puffing furiously on her cigarette.

"I had to finish shaving and the sound was just coming up the pipes. Dad said something about my birth certificate."

"You heard him wrong."

"I don't think I heard him wrong, I just didn't get exactly what he said. He talked about it as if it existed. Kind of."

"Ben, how vague can you get?" She flicked her cigarette out the window and rolled it all the way up. "And you know what happened to your birth certificate. Why beat a dead horse?"

"I don't know. I just thought from the way he said it…"

She gave Ben a sharp, correcting look and faced forward, indicating that the subject had dropped.

12

AT Mrs. Hunter's direction, Peter swung the car into a long driveway and slowed to stare at the white clapboard mansion, perfectly kept, the gleaming wooden door slightly open, the shutters, carved with apples, painted bright red. The front of the house and its trim gardens, neat pillared porch, brick steps and walkway lay in afternoon shadow, but the sun lit the back of the house and top edge of the roof and both brick chimneys. Beyond the house, orchards over rolling fields stood in the sunlight.

As they climbed out of the car, an elderly man, tall, leathery tan skin with a full head of bright white hair, walked down the front steps. His bearing was straight-backed and he did not smile; his deep brown eyes examined the boys with an unblinking intensity.

"This is—um—the *friend* I was telling you about," said Ella. Her glance at this friend was brief and apologetic before she commanded, "Go on, boys, introduce yourselves. I dropped a cigarette somewhere in here."

The old man offered Peter his hand. "You're Peter, the eldest," he said, with a slight smile, his eyes twinkling briefly at Joe.

"Peter MacBride, sir. This is my brother Joe."

"I am Gregen Bénet. You may call me Gregen." He turned to Joe and took his hand in a strong handshake, hand tough, thin, so calloused, his fingers scratched the back of Joe's hand. "I knew your mother when she was still Laurie Davidson. We were neighbors and dear friends. And her brother, Doug, of course."

"Uncle Doug," Joe said. "You know Uncle Doug?"

"I do." He smiled again at Joe, a stern, knowing smile, but Joe liked him immediately. "By trade I am a physician and I set his arm the time he broke it sledding." Peter and Joe nodded at each other, familiar with the story. "I'm happy to meet you both." His speech seemed shined up, with a hint of an accent Joe could not every word detect.

Bénet turned to Ben with a swift searching of the eyes in which Joe saw the flash of anger, the ache of hope. But the old man extended his hand to Ben in the same firm, masculine way. "Ben. I am happy to see you," he said, emphasizing each word of his greeting.

"It's nice to meet you, too, Mr. Bénet, sir."

Joe could tell that Ben was awaiting a comment about his own father's younger days, but Gregen Bénet merely stared into Ben's eyes, holding the handshake a bit too long, before he dropped Ben's hand and said, "Your grandmother tells me that you are a good student."

"I work hard, sir."

"That, coupled with your fine intellect, means you are at the top of your class. Certainly this is true."

"School has always been easy for me, Mr. Bénet, sir, and, um, Joe is just decimal points behind me."

"I got a ninety-one in keyboarding," Joe said with a shrug.

"Indeed?"

"I can *type*, Mr. Bénet. Don't get me wrong, but the teacher made me sit by...this girl. It was ninth grade and I'd always liked her."

"But of course, you couldn't concentrate."

"Couldn't. Didn't. Both."

"But other than this one course, you are also a fine student, Joe?"

Joe shrugged again. "I test well."

Bénet nodded approvingly at Joe. "I'm not surprised. And no doubt Peter, you are a scholar?"

"I love to read," Peter said.

"He never forgets anything he reads," Joe explained.

"Yes. You boys come from gifted people." He glanced over at Mrs. Hunter, and Joe followed his gaze to see her pacing on the far side of the car, puffing desperately at her cigarette. Bénet turned to Ben, his clear brown eyes—for just an instant—fervent. Quietly he said, "The part of Switzerland from which your people hail is known for razor-sharp intellects, all the athletic ability required to negotiate the Alps on foot, and a particular gift with language."

"I didn't know I *was* part Swiss."

"But you are. Swiss and Danish, in fact." They stared at each other, and watching them, squinting his eyes, Joe tried to define the apprehension between them. Something stood there, invisible and barbed, something that belied what Joe easily recognized with his eyes. In Gregen Bénét Joe saw a vague echo of Ben's shape, specifically the set of the shoulders, the length of backbone, the gesture of the arms.

"I thought my dad was Scottish, English descent. My mom is from California."

Bénet made a dismissive gesture. "Your grandmother Hunter herself is half Danish. Though I'm not surprised she never mentioned it. Her interest lies only in American history." He glanced at Joe and Peter. "The Scots have a gift for language, but also the sciences. And they bring to life a tenacity that cannot be equaled in the other European races. The Scot's tenacity in you, Ben, is cloaked, I would think, by your Scandinavian tendency to contemplation."

Ben smiled at him with his charming half-smile that invited Bénet to tell him more. Joe believed this expression of Ben's was part of what made him so appealing; people were convinced that Ben was eager—no, dying—to hear more. But now in Ben's eyes, Joe saw authentic hunger. He said, "Joe is slightly better at science than me."

"The nationalities all have their gifts, beautiful gifts, but heritage is handed to us. Good and bad together. Europeans' knowledge of this is centuries old. Their property or businesses and titles are given to them with all the privilege, trials and responsibilities that follow. People grow up in homes where their ancestors lived, made fortunes, lost fortunes, broke hearts, wrote books—where they lived and died. In America, people are isolated from these complexities. They do not consider the vast resources of heritage over which their will presides. I hope you understand me?"

"I think so, sir."

Bénet said, "I'm very pleased to see you again."

"Again, sir?"

Bénet glanced at Ben's grandmother. "Nearly ready, then, Ella?" he called before turning to Ben, his back now to Ella and saying quietly, "Various times when you were with your grandmother. You don't remember me? I'm not surprised. I did miss you the time Timothy was born."

He sniffed, his mouth going tight, and he looked around for Ben's grandmother. Nodding toward Ella Hunter as she ground her cigarette butt into the driveway, he said, "And since your grandmother is—um—now fortified, shall we look at the car?" Turning on his heel, Mr. Bénet led the boys on a neat brick path that circled the house past bright, elegant gardens of sculpted boxwood, underplanted with chrysanthemums, white and gold and rust-red now in bloom. His pace was quick with the same physical confidence Joe noted so often in Ben. Joe moved close to Ben and whispered. "What do you think?" Hearing this, Peter came close too, the three of them abreast for a moment on the walkway. "He's pretty cool."

"He seems nice," Ben said.

"Maybe he's a long lost relative."

"He would have said so," Ben said. "When he was talking about heritage."

Bénet waited for them in the sunshine at the back of the house, where the brick walk extended into a patio. When Ella caught up with them, Bénet led the way down three steps to a grassy lawn, and across the driveway to the detached double garage. He opened the right side garage door by pressing a series of buttons that also flooded the garage with light. Inside stood a gleaming Fiat Spider, tan-colored, with what appeared to be new tires. "If you like this, Ben, it's yours."

"It's amazing," Ben breathed.

"Come and see it up close."

Joe looked around the room. Beside the Fiat stood a shining silver Jaguar XL and beyond that, in the third car bay, an antique Fiat that was bright red, its convertible top folded back to reveal creamy leather seats. Joe's eyes met Peter's in eloquent astonishment.

Noting their interest, Bénet said, "The red Fiat is the first car I bought myself. I've maintained it, as you can see."

"Yes, sir," the MacBrides murmured in reverent unison.

Bénet led Ben around the newer Fiat, explaining in his too-perfect English that there had been only two owners of the car and that since acquiring it, he had restored it to perfect running condition. It had been driven only 27,000 miles, the tires were new, the seals around the windows and the entire convertible top including the roll bars were new.

Unable to restrain himself, Ben whispered, "But it must be worth so much more than I—"

"Ah," Bénet whispered, "I told your grandmother you would not be able to forgo discussion of price. She does not understand how men work. But it's not a concern, Ben."

Ben glanced at his grandmother to see her approaching the tool shelves. "Sir, I—"

"You must trust me that it is acceptable to take this from your grandmother and I."

Now it was Ben's turn to scrutinize. He stared at the old man who stood with both hands extended toward Ben in a bald pose of supplication. Gregen Bénet drew a deep breath, glanced at Ella Hunter, and said, "We did not pay—really *anything* for it, neither of us."

"It was given to *you*?"

Bénet said, "To paraphrase the owner, 'Take the useless thing, if you want it,'" He adopted a brusque, cruel tone in imitation.

"Bet he didn't say useless," Joe said.

"And to think I neglected to laud the Scot's acute perceptions," Bénet said.

Ben stared at him, trying to grasp what seemed like some sort of hint. "You mean it's a gift?"

"Yes."

"Gran doesn't want me to *know* it's a gift? But I read my bank statements," Ben whispered. "I would notice if the money was still there."

Bénet winced, pressing his lips together. "This is what I told her." With an expressive gesture as if to explain his efforts spent on the subject he said, "Fixing this car interested me."

"Was it wrecked up or something when you got it?" Joe asked.

"The car had been somewhat compromised by misuse. So, I placed one dollar in the owner's hand and took the car."

"There you go," Peter patted Ben's shoulder to encourage him. "It's in beautiful condition."

"Your grandmother and I have made it a hobby to restore it. And we have worked out the expense between us."

"But she can't spend so much on me. And, and you—I mean—I'm *grateful*, sir, but this is such an amazing gift. I don't mean to be impolite, but people don't just give each other a—a treasure like this, do they?" Ben looked to Joe and Peter for confirmation.

His keen, brown eyes narrowed, Bénet said, "But people do. Friendship itself is a treasure. I cannot explain further out of courtesy to your grandmother."

Ben saw that his grandmother lingered at the shelves on the far side of the Jaguar absorbed in studying an old, wood-handled saw. Wincing, he murmured, "You and Gran...?"

"No," Bénet said with emotion, his intonation suddenly nasal, foreign. "We are not lovers, your grandmother and I. We are old friends." Bénet looked directly into Ben's hurt and doubting eyes. "No, my child. Ease your mind." Bénet seemed to want to take Ben's shoulders in hand; his dark eyes had gone wide and he stood tensely awkward, finally folding his arms over his chest and trapping his brown hands. "You can believe me and trust that the bargain between your grandmother and me is pragmatic in your interest. That is all that is shocking about it. You know this word *pragmatic*, don't you?"

"Yes, sir."

"It's an old-fashioned word, but it applies here."

"I'm sorry for even thinking—"

"I warned your grandmother that we would have to say something," Gregen Bénet dismissed Ben's stammering with a wave of his hand. "Now come and sit in your car to see if it suits you."

The inside of the car was even more beautiful than the outside. Leather seats, shades darker than the outside, felt supple. Everything was clean. "I installed the air conditioning unit myself. It is highly efficient," Bénet said. "The CD player is used, I'm afraid, but I did inspect it closely and I can honestly say it is as good as new."

"It's terrific, sir. Thank you."

"Will you start it, Ben?"

The purr of the car brought Ella Hunter over to the side. "See, Ella?" Bénet said to her. "I installed that computer chip you found for me." He pointed to the dashboard where a digital display told the temperature and the direction of the car.

"That's wonderful, Gregen."

"You might say that this car has been our joint hobby, hasn't it Ella?" Bénet said. "We've been preparing it for the time that Ben could drive."

"But why for me?" Ben said.

"Why not? What better way for two old people to occupy themselves than to serve the young generation? And we've enjoyed doing it, haven't we, Ella?"

"It's an awesome car," Ben said, "I don't know how to thank you both."

"Take it for a drive," Bénet said, opening the passenger door for the MacBrides. Joe tipped up the front seat and climbed into the back. Peter followed and said, "Come with us, Mr. Bénet, sir."

"I would prefer if you could call me Gregen."

"Okay," Joe said, amiably. "Come with us, Gregen."

"That's better." Gregen looked to Ella for permission. She shrugged and nodded, thinking, Joe could tell, of another cigarette.

"While you wait for us, Ella, my dear," Gregen said as he ducked into the front seat. "Would you mind using the garage extension to ring up the kitchen? Tell them we'll be ready shortly—let's say twenty-five minutes— for refreshments on the terrace."

Out on the road, Ben relaxed a little; the car was a pleasure to drive. Aloud, Ben described its feel—the power of its pick-up, the smoothness of the transition, even the silent efficiency with which it ran—to Gregen's delight.

"It's so great," Ben said, turning back toward the house, but Gregen urged him to take a narrow fork.

"We have a few more minutes before we are expected. This road will take us around the back of the orchards to the house."

Ben drove slowly so he could glance at the orchard as Gregen explained the kinds of apples he grew and about the grant he had received from Cornell University to develop an earlier flowering type of Golden Delicious. There was a section of apples Gregen claimed to have been planted by Johnny Appleseed. "After we have some refreshments, I would like very much to show you some of the trees."

"How long is the grant for?" Joe said, "I guess it takes a while to know if you've made an improvement."

"I'm in my seventh year. I have three to go," Gregen said. "My best success has been achieved by using the older stock. More flavor, but the apples are too small for the modern market. This is my next goal."

The orchard road took them out to the main road where Ben turned right into Gregen's driveway. "Sir—

"Gregen," the old man interrupted. "Please feel free to call me by my given name. You used to do so, Ben."

"I did?"

"Yes. You don't remember?"

"No, sir, I don't, I'm sorry—"

"Gregen," he repeated, then laughed and patted Ben's shoulder. "Try to say it. I know it goes against your father's training."

"Um, speaking of my father," Ben said, his voice tight, choked. "Did you know my father when he went to high school here?"

Gregen hesitated, tapping one finger on his closed lips. "Naturally," Gregen said. "He was the champion swimmer, those years. Everyone in town *knew* him."

Ben eased the car into the garage and switched it off. Clearing his throat he met Gregen's eyes and said, "Gregen, I have to tell you before I take this car that I intend to paint it."

Bénet frowned. "Your grandmother mentioned that. She has made an appointment for you at a place on West Avenue in Annapolis."

"West Street," Joe corrected from the back seat.

"Of course. West Street. You're driving there directly to have it painted."

"I hope you won't mind the change in color."

Bénet looked uncomfortable. He opened the passenger door and as he got out, said, "The paint on this automobile is not new. I suspected you might want to choose your own color, so I have not repainted it in many years. But the paint is in good condition, so it will take the new color with ease."

Ben took the keys and got out of the car. "I guess I'm trying to ask if my painting it will *bother* you after all the work you put into it."

Across the car roof, Bénet studied Ben. "Tell me your reasoning."

Ben rounded the front of the car, approaching Bénet. "My father will never drive a pink car. So I want it pink."

"I feel only shame that this strategy did not occur to me." Bénet stood before Ben with an almost naked expression in his posture, chin tucked down, shoulders brought forward slightly, looking as ashamed as he professed. But in his strong, brown face, his liquid brown eyes burned with a stark intensity as he endured Ben's scrutiny, waiting for Ben to believe him. "Maybe when you are older and this time of your life has passed, you might paint it a strong red. One day I should like to see it red." Ben nodded, their agreement tacit. They shook hands, emotion showing in both their eyes, in the clenching of both jaws, the tensed stance.

13

ELLA Hunter had preceded them to the brick terrace and when they joined her there, she was directing a young woman, who held a stack of dishes, to place them on the small wooden table beneath the orange tree. Peter hurried to help this young woman and though she smiled at him, would not give him the stack of plates. Bénet thanked her, and as he was introducing her to them, glanced up toward the house and gave a little cry. Joe saw a tiny old woman in an odd, blue dress and white apron holding an enormous, heavily laden tray. She stood less than five feet tall, had wound her iron-gray hair into braided coils at the side of her wizened face.

Gregen sprinted toward the house.

"Marie, *non*," he cried as he bounded up the stairs and reached for the tray. But the old woman held firm and scolded him in rapid French. Ben ran up the steps; Joe followed, standing at the bottom of the steps.

"Ah, you understand," Bénet said softly to Ben.

"She says it is so heavy we *both* have to carry it," Ben said as he took the tray from her. "But she's carrying it all by herself!"

Speaking in French, Gregen introduced Ben to "Madame Marie Challant."

"*J'enchante, Madame.*"

Marie took Ben's face in her hands and pulling him down to her lips, kissed his cheeks in turn. "*Bienvenue, Benedetto, mon petit.*"

"No, Marie, Ben." Marie shook her finger at Gregen, scolding him again in a dialect Joe recognized but did not understand. Bénet raised his eyebrows in chagrin and explained, "Since my brother and I were infants, Marie has cared for us so she will not be corrected by me."

Marie made a cradle of her arms and spoke rapidly in French.

Ben seemed to understand. "*Nourrir* means nourish?"

"In spirit, yes. She was my wet nurse. Another old word from an old man. This was the custom in some families when I was young. The mother was not to be inconvenienced with feeding her own hungry infant."

Marie beamed at Ben and when she spoke it was as if she were giving a family recipe. Ben nodded and smiled at her. She directed him pointing to the table and those waiting.

Bénet smiled indulgently and said to her urgently in French, "Marie, please come sit and eat with us."

"*Non*," she said, her old face wrinkling, bright tears sparkling like diamonds in her eyes. She reached to touch Ben's shoulder with her fingertips, and he bent toward her. Her rough fingers touched his cheek. "*Faites attention*," she cautioned him, her voice and eyes tender.

When Ben replied softly in French, she caressed his face with her sturdy, gnarled hand. "*Mon chignon*," she murmured, tears coming fast, she spoke rapidly in French words Joe could not hear.

Bénet motioned to Ben to take the tray away, and he bent to the old woman, embracing her and guiding her back into the house, hushing her with whispered words.

Ben set the tray down and slid onto the bench with Joe and Peter with a cautious glance at his grandmother.

Joe nudged Ben's shoulder. "Did you get most of that?"

"She was worried I'd fall with the tray. I told her I never fall," Ben said.

But Joe saw his hands shaking and remembered his explanation that morning for the marks on his face. Now in the dimming afternoon light Joe saw the fading edges of the fingerprints. "No," Joe said. "You never fall."

Ella Hunter leaned forward from her seat on the other side of the table, taking a salad, a tart, a bowl of cream and a pitcher of juice from the tray. "Gregen employs a cook and an assistant. They are always students from some foreign land or another, trying to make it here in America. The elderly woman has been part of his household ever since she served as his governess, I believe."

"Is he a foreign prince or something?" Peter asked.

"Nothing so glamorous. He is a medical doctor and also taught at a university in Europe. He moved here in the sixties. He works all the time. How he keeps up with his medical practice and his cars I don't know. Never sleeps. His clinics and such work have made him a prominent citizen—always being asked to do this and that—though I can never get a straight answer out of him about whether he's actually taken American citizenship. He teaches in Europe, when he feels like it. He's got a good dose of the wanderlust as my father used to call it. Always traveling. He was the CEO for the International Medical Corps until he decided to plant a vineyard."

She turned in her chair and gestured. The boys saw that beyond the driveway and garage, stone steps led to a second yard, lined with terraced grapevines, ripe for harvest. "Apples, grapes—Gregen can get anything to grow. He's an artisan. All he touches turns to gold."

Gregen joined them carrying a large copper frying pan and a small ceramic block. He placed the block down and asked Ella to light the candle in its center. The frying pan fit atop and it contained a bubbling, golden potato dish. He turned to a small, free-standing ceramic fire place, lifted it, and brought it close. Taking a match, he lit the coals in its belly. Roaring to flame, they cast an intense and welcome heat on the terrace growing cooler in the fading afternoon.

"Marie is ninety-six years old," he told them, as he spooned out generous helpings of the potato dish.

"Why wouldn't she eat with us?" Ben asked.

"Please help yourselves to salad. The lettuce is grown in my greenhouse, the grapes are also mine." He glanced at Ella and said, mildly, "Marie is sturdy, but she tires easily and is highly emotional. She knows what she can handle."

"The food is delicious," Peter said.

"Are you warm enough, Ella, my dear?"

"Yes, thank you. "

"And you boys?"

"We're great," Peter said.

"You're very kind to feed us," Ella said. "The food is always so good here."

"I merely thought to save your grandmother from the expense of taking you out to dinner," he teased.

"Everything is homemade here," Ella said, "even the furniture. But there's really nothing wrong with buying things other people make, Gregen. If people didn't, you'd never sell your produce."

"True."

"My mom would love this table," Peter said, indicating the carved apple at the center and looking under to peer at the smoothed tree trunk used for its pedestal.

"An old folk craft. Marie taught me. The apple wood from the orchards comes in handy."

"You made this?"

"Yes. Do you like it, Ben?"

"I like everything here, Gregen," Ben said, at which his grandmother perceptibly ruffled. Quickly Ben added. "It's so smooth and detailed."

"Perhaps one summer when you are visiting your grandmother I can teach you."

"I'm coming, too," Peter said.

"Please. Plan on it. Marie will no doubt preside over my teaching. She is the expert. You see, Marie comes from the Italian Alps, the French part of Italy—the Savoy. A town called Aosta. This region of Italy is known for wood carvings. You may recognize her maiden name. It is Jaquerio." He waited for Peter and Joe to respond. "Does it sound similar to any of your family names? Perhaps in an odd way—phonetically."

Peter squinted. "I think that my grandmother's maiden name sounds something like it. Ackery has some of the same sounds."

"How do you remember this stuff?" Joe asked.

"A natural historian," Ella Hunter commented.

"Yes. Your mother's mother and Marie are distant cousins. The name Ackery was thought to sound an Americanized version of Jaquerio. Your grandmother's people changed it when they arrived here. Many people do that, though I cannot understand why. Your mother's family—the Italian part—come from Gressoney, near Marie's home. She asks to see you both when we are finished here."

"We'll need Ben to translate," Joe said, helping himself to more potatoes.

"Marie can manage a little English. She was educated in French schools. She and I speak mainly French, but when she is tired or wants only me to understand, she speaks to me in Italian and sometimes when she is upset, she mixes in words from her childhood patois. She was testing you, Ben."

"Marie is not your relative, then?" Peter asked.

"That is a complicated question, Peter. Here, eat some more salad, Ben. And more potatoes. That's good." Gregen turned to Peter, holding the salad bowl for him as he refilled his plate. "When Marie was a young girl, she defied her family and married a very handsome, wealthy young fool who was killed in a hillside skirmish. She was pregnant when he died and she blames her sorrow for the fact that the child was unhealthy at birth—and died sometime soon after. His family blamed her also and so she was left alone. My father was her attorney, and when he and his new bride became the surprised parents of twin boys, my family hired Marie as a wet nurse, as I explained to Ben. So, you see, Marie has been a mother to me." He glanced at Ella Hunter and then to Ben. "She has been a treasured part of my household my entire life—in many ways, much closer to me than the woman who I called, 'Mother.'"

"And such a good cook," Ella said with a stony frown.

"Indeed," Gregen said, nodding at his guest. Joe could not tell if he missed Ella's sour tone or if he was ignoring it. "I would very much like to show you the orchards," Gregen said. "Are you up to a short walk, Ella?"

"It's not a short walk, but I'd better come along."

The orchards lay behind the house down three more stone steps and they stretched over the hills for twenty acres, Gregen explained, shepherding them past the garage. Behind it, he showed them a small workshop, which opened with a computerized keypad.

"It is here that I practice my woodcraft," he said. Switching on the lights he took up a small wooden pear. "This is to be a reproduction of an eighteenth century tea caddy. Your grandmother, Ben, bet me a scandalous amount of money that I would not be able to pass it off to one of her antique dealers as authentic."

"This is so cool," Peter said.

"I'm blessed to have the time and resources for such creativity," Gregen said, leading them out again. Mrs. Hunter stepped downwind, drew out a cigarette and lit it. Gregen took Peter's elbow briefly and said, "Would you mind walking with Mrs. Hunter? I am concerned about her footing in the meadow and the orchard."

"I'd be happy to, sir."

"If you stay upwind, the smoke will not bother you, I hope."

"It smells just like your dad's workshop in here," Ben said.

"How interesting," Gregen said, "Your father has developed an interest in woodworking?"

Joe answered, "He doesn't actually *work* with wood the way you do. He fixes things in there. It's more a fix-it shop than for creativity. Mom's the creative one at our house—she can make something beautiful out of scraps—she's a whirlwind when she works. Dad mops up after everyone."

Gregen laughed. "Your powers of description are delightful, Joe."

He moved closer to Ben and Joe hung back a little. Gregen put his hand out in a halting way as if he wanted to put his arm around Ben's shoulders, but stopped. "Have you spent time at Joe's home, Ben?"

"Yes, sir," Ben said. "They've been great to me."

"I'm happy to hear it."

"There's tons of kids there. Coach put a trampoline in his garage that we use all the time. It's so fun over there. And Mrs. MacBride is an amazing cook. It's an unbelievable place," Ben said, turning to look at his host. "Kind of like here."

Again, Gregen's arm moved in an instinctual effort to embrace, to pull Ben close beside him, stopping midair. Joe hung back, sensing Gregen's desire for confidence with Ben. "And Mr. MacBride? Are you getting along well with him? I understand from your grandmother that he is your basketball coach."

Ben nodded. "He's great. Generous. All the kids at school love him. He's been great to me."

"Before I met Tom, I was told again and again that he was a most trustworthy man."

Ben glanced at Gregen. "That's cool. Who told you that?"

Seriously, eyes intent, Gregen said, "Do you find him trustworthy?"

"Yes. I think so. He's good to his wife. Really nice. And he understands stuff, which is great. He's just so different...from what I'm used to."

"In what way?"

"He enjoys his kids, so..." Ben frowned, thinking, "so there's never any tension about the stuff kids usually get in trouble for. You know, making noise or needing something or asking questions. But he's also got these strong principles. He wants his kids to be really honest. And he kind of

287

applies those standards to all of us who hang out at his house. So, like, we can play and goof around or bring up any topic. I mean *any* topic, that's okay with him, which is great, and we laugh a lot. But you just know that when you lie to him, he's—he's like disturbed deep inside about it."

"Have you lied to him?"

Ben stopped walking, glanced back at Joe and said, "Yes, sir." Even in the gathering twilight, Joe saw Ben redden.

"It's unreasonable to lie to a trustworthy man. Besides the moral repercussions." Ben stared at him, lips set. "You doubt me because I was constrained to respect your grandmother's confidence earlier about the car."

"I could tell you wanted to say more. Is that being honest?"

"I cannot betray her confidence."

"Sometimes, then, you excuse lying."

"There are times when a gentleman must be tactful in order to care for others," he said. "Tact expresses the truth in a kind way or at the right time."

Ben stared hard at Gregen, the way Joe had seen him do to Tom, his eyes intent on the face, then sweeping quickly over the man to read the gauge of gesture, the signal in stance.

Ella called from the edge of the orchard. "Gregen! What is taking you so long? I hope you're not telling that child all my shortcomings!"

"We'll be right there, Gran," Ben called to her, his face reddening. He looked back to Gregen, lips pressed together, eyes full of regret. "I think I may have been disrespectful to you just now, Mr. Bénet, sir."

"I will answer *any* question you ask me, my dear child," Gregen said, quietly, glancing at the determined Ella who stood, feet apart, arms akimbo, "with the truth."

Ben gulped.

"Though I am constrained by courtesy, I am *not* inclined to—nor *willing* to—hide anything from you. I will not evade your direct questions." Gregen leaned forward slightly.

Hesitating, casting a glance at his grandmother, who stood impatiently glaring at them from the edge of the orchard, Ben whispered, "Who told you Tom MacBride was trustworthy?"

Gregen's gaze was very bright. "Your *mother* told me this."

"My *mother*?" Ben gulped, voice barely audible.

"The Cornell trees, Gregen," Gran called, "which are they?"

"Yes," Gregen said to Ben. "Your mother trusted him implicitly."

"Gregen!"

"We must go to her," he said. "She is terribly anxious." They quickened their pace to reach them, Joe seeing the same ingrained courtesy in Gregen that he knew so well in his own father.

Ben stayed so close beside Gregen as he led them through the orchards among the trees, that their shoulders often bumped and though he hung right behind, Joe sensed the palpable emotion drawing them together, unnamed though it remained.

Gregen gave each of them a basket and instructed them to pick ripe apples as they passed by them. The smell of the sun-warmed apples lingered in the twilight and mixed with the musty pungency of the windfalls turned to spores underfoot and the scents of autumn leaves on the crisp, frosting air. They filled their baskets as Gregen taught Ben about the trees. His enthusiasm for the apple trees seemed compelling to Ben and Joe figured it was because there was something promising in Gregen's manner, something that suggested he was offering Ben a ring of keys to unlock treasures. It was only when they had turned back toward the house and had reached again the edge of the orchard and the steps leading up toward the house that Gregen spoke directly to either of the MacBrides. He laid his hand on Peter's back and said, "You do not remember this orchard? You visited here before your brother Joe was born."

"I have a dreamy kind of memory of making apple cider in an orchard. But the light was different, and there was a swing and some kind of a block or wall."

"We did make cider that day. In those years, I kept the press near the road." Gregen pointed and laughed. "And there, near the stone stairs was a swing that you enjoyed."

"There were privet hedges here then," Ella said. "We've got to get going, Gregen. No telling how long we'll be here if the boys all start remembering their childhoods."

"You're welcome to stay, Ella, my dear. I have nothing else I would rather do."

"I'm sure that's very kind of you, Gregen, but we had planned to leave around dark. The boys are leaving very early in the morning. They've got some activity or another."

"Yes, of course, Ella. Marching band competition tomorrow. You're right. Let's go back up to the house."

"Why was I here, sir?" Peter asked.

"Visiting, of course," Ella snapped. "It's a small town."

"Yes," Gregen said. "Your mother brought you over to visit. She wanted to show you off—her firstborn son. I must tell you that she was one of my favorites. And my wife loved her dearly. They were kindred spirits, my wife and your mother. We were good friends, like an old uncle would be with a special niece. My wife and I were blessed to be asked to read from the Holy Scriptures during your parents' wedding ceremony. Having lost touch with your mother has grieved me."

"For pity's sake, Gregen," Ella chided. "Not many physicians extend themselves the way you do to patients. No one expects you to keep in touch. It simply isn't done."

"I have my quirks," he replied to her, his face tight, his voice smoothed and unexpressive. He touched Peter's shoulder and said, "Let's hurry. You must say hello to Marie. She is no doubt up from her nap and waiting for us."

14

NOW aware of the chilly air, of the purple shadows that cloaked the terrace and gardens, they hurried toward the house while the sunset cast its bronze on the brick and the windowpanes in the back door. But as they approached, lanterns came to light along the pathway and by the time they reached the terrace it glowed with golden lamplight. Taking Ella's arm in a charming, conspiratorial way, Gregen said, "I promised Marie that the boys would stop in to see her before they left. Would it be satisfactory for you, Ella, if they did so now while you enjoy another cigarette? I can tell you are thinking of one."

"But Gregen," she said, warning him, Joe thought, with her eyes.

"She'll be fine," he nodded to her and ushered the boys into the house at a side door that led onto a glass sun porch.

In this spacious room, fragrant with flowering plants, Marie sat on a tiny settee, her feet on the ground. Gregen motioned to her to stay seated and brought the boys close for introductions. "Marie," he said, "May I present to you Laurie Davidson's sons, Joe and Peter. Madame Marie Challant." Peter and Joe offered to shake hands, but she opened her arms wide and each bent to hug her in turn.

"I will leave you for a few minutes," Gregen said.

Marie patted the settee beside her for Ben to sit and the MacBride boys found chairs and pulled them up close at Marie's urging. She took Ben's hand in her own and in a whisper asked if he spoke French. And so Ben translated for them Marie's happy memories of Laurie as a child. She was beautiful and smart, with sparkling dark eyes. She won art contests in town, the spelling bee. Many times she was in Marie's kitchen with her best friend to cook and sew.

"You are a lot like her," Joe said.

Ben translated and Marie was delighted. She reached for Joe's hand and patted it. Marie asked about Laurie's sewing business, and so Joe and Peter took turns describing the quilt shop, the café inside it, Laurie's creations, community activities and awards. Ben translated, his speech becoming more quick and sure, more inflected with perfect accent as he spoke. Ben surprised them by saying Marie had seen Laurie's picture on

Eight Hands Around's website and said that she looked *"enceinte."* Ben told about Cara's birth. She said that she wished to send the baby a gift. Joe scrawled out their address for her; she took it, folded it, placed it in her pocket and turned abruptly to Ben.

Tugging at his shirt, she asked Ben about it. Unsure what she meant, Ben looked to Joe and Peter for help.

"I don't think she's asking what it's made of, but why you're wearing it."

Marie beamed at Joe. She tugged at Ben's shirt and asked him a question. Ben said to Joe, "She wants to know if it comes off!"

"She wants you to take your shirt off."

Marie nodded, her iron gray curls bobbing. She held out her hands. "She wants you to give her your shirt, Ben." Joe said.

"I understand the *words*," Ben whispered, "but—"

Joe said, "Maybe she has a shirt for you and she wants to see if it's the right size."

Peter shrugged. "Makes sense."

Ben shrugged out of his shirt in the way he did, pulling at the collar and lifting it over his head. She frowned and tugged at the collar of his undershirt and so Ben knew he was to take it off, too. Glancing at his friends, Ben obeyed, shivering slightly. Marie folded both shirts. Her bright eyes grew brilliant with tears and her face softened as she reached up to caress Ben's face. Her rough, old fingers touched Ben's shoulder lightly. Ben strained to understand, sputtering to find words to ask. Marie's tears spilled over; she snatched at her white apron, bringing it to her eyes.

Joe said, softly, teasing, *"Moi aussi?"* his accent bad.

Marie laughed and Gregen returned to the room, a framed photograph in hand.

"Oh, no! Marie!" To the boys he said, "I do apologize for your embarrassment. This is a custom from Marie's village."

"Oh," Ben said.

"To Marie, this is an ancient and meaningful ritual. When a young man returned from a long absence, it was customary for the older women of the town to require a bath of him—to inspect him for disease and damage and scars and, of course, to recognize him before they cleaned him up. It was a formal way of breaking that tense feeling when someone has been away and everyone wonders if he has changed irreparably and will no longer be able to fit in. It was believed that the naked man cannot fake such things. In a minute, I fear she would have had your trousers off also, Ben. In the old days, the women checked everything."

Pete and Joe laughed.

"But she means well."

"Really, it's okay."

"I was just about to join him," Joe said.

"Joe loves getting naked," Peter joked.

Marie laughed, tears still wet on her cheeks. "*Je voudrais couvrir tu cœur.*"

"Cover?" Joe said.

Gregen and Marie nodded at Joe. "This step in the ritual is spiritual. The elders place their hands over the boy's heart to symbolize their protection and acceptance."

Ben glanced at Joe, and then took Marie's old hand and held it flush to his chest. She closed her eyes, concentrating. "She is counting—remembering your heartbeat," Gregen said.

Marie opened her eyes finally to command, "Gregen."

"May I touch your back, Ben?" the old man asked, his voice shaken for the first time that strange afternoon. "She is my mother and I'm afraid I must still obey her despite my advanced age and the conventions of my new home."

"My back?"

"I must cover your heart from the back to protect you from betrayal and surprise."

"Yes, sir. You may."

"My hand is cold, Maman."

She flipped her free hand in the air in a gesture of impatience. Gregen touched Ben's back with his fingertips, moved them just a little to the right and then laid his hand flat. Ben's eyes went once more to Joe's before he shut them. "Together we hold your heart and remember your heartbeat," Gregen said, his voice low and rough, "and find it strong and true. God's blessing and ours rest upon you now and always. Amen."

Tears now visible beneath his eyes, Gregen stepped away from Ben and bent hastily to take Ben's shirts from Marie's lap. But Marie opened her arms to Ben and clasped him to her, kissing his cheek and his neck behind his ear, her hands smoothing over his shoulders.

"Marie," he said, "the MacBride boys are astonished. You must stop."

She released Ben and threw up her hands in delight as if her life's work were, at last, complete. "Here are your shirts, Ben," Gregen said. "I thank you all three for indulging Marie. This was very important to her, though foreign to you." He smiled at Peter and Joe. "Your father, I know, would have responded as you have. He is a tender-hearted man," he whispered with approval. Joe nodded seriously.

Ben dressed, his lips pressed tightly together, eyes wide and watchful.

As if on cue, Mrs. Hunter called from outside for them. Ben stood up. "We'd better go."

Gregen walked them to the door. "I've taken the liberty of packing up a bag for each of you filled with our preserves and fruit drinks and wines to take home to your parents. I put them in your car, Ben."

"My car," Ben said.

"Your grandmother is waiting, not too patiently," Gregen said, gesturing for Peter to lead the way.

Marie grabbed Joe's hand, preventing him. "May I ask you one last favor, my dear boy?"

Joe drew back in surprise. "You speak English." Her eyes twinkled merrily at him. Joe said, "You can ask anything of me. I'll love you all of my life, Marie."

"Ah, I knew it! Will you look after Ben? Ben trusts you, I'm pleased. He must trust what he's seen here today."

Peter called Joe from the yard. Marie held his hand. Joe covered her hand with both of his, compelled by her tenderness, the familiarity of her spunky warmth. "I've got to go. I'm sorry. But can you tell me why?" Joe said. "Can you tell me what this is all about?"

She sniffed with disgust. "I am told that Ben must—reason it all out." Joe stooped to hug her before hurrying to answer Peter's call.

Gregen shook hands warmly with each of the boys. "Your visit has meant a great deal to me and to Marie. Thank you for indulging us."

"We had a great time, Gregen," Joe said.

"I enjoyed every minute. Thank you," said Peter.

"And you," he said to Ben, taking his hand. "Mr. MacBride can help you with basic maintenance of the car, but I do know the car well. Please phone me with larger questions." He pressed Ben's hand firmly, holding on.

"Thank you. I'll take good care of it. I promise you."

"I know you will, my dear boy. Read the owner's manual. I've put it in the glove box for you."

"I—I can't thank you enough."

"No, I thank you. Your kindness has been overwhelming."

"I hope to see you again, sir."

"And I you. But your grandmother is waiting." He released Ben's hand and turned away slightly, again visibly moved.

"Gregen," Ben said.

Gregen met his eyes again. "As soon as possible." Gregen opened the driver's side door for Ben, held it and shut it for him. Nimbly he rounded the front of the car and opened the door for Ella Hunter. When she was seated, he took her hand and kissed it. "Thank you for sharing your grandson with an old, childless man, Ella, my dear."

15

THAT night, moonlight fell on Joe's face and he dreamt some odd police force had caught him in the tunnel. He startled awake, unable to move, then heard Ben's pen scratching across the page of his journal. When he heard Ben shut the book, give a long sigh and lay back on his pillow, Joe whispered, "This bed is so comfortable, you'd think we could sleep."

"I'm not used to sleeping with a man," Ben teased.

"What are you writing?" Joe asked.

"Trying to describe—everything."

"Like?"

"Like how I wish Bonnie Jean was in bed with me and not her scrawny brother."

Joe laughed, then sat up. "Hey. Do you hear that?"

"Pete's breathing sounds bad."

Joe got out of bed, fumbled in Peter's backpack until he found his brother's inhaler. "Pete. Wake up. You need your medicine." Peter roused just long enough to inhale the metered dose, then flopped down, turned on his side with his face toward the window, and slept.

"Why is he wheezing like that?"

"Probably the cigarette smoke irritated his lungs. He has asthma."

"I've tried to get Gran to quit. Maybe we should go now. If this place is bothering him."

Trying to be tactful, Joe said, "We *could* leave a little earlier."

"Hey, Joe," Ben said.

"What?"

"Do you think I did the right thing, taking that car from him?"

"Yes. Why?"

"Something's weird about it."

"True that."

"Really weird. I mean, why couldn't he tell me stuff? Why did Gran want him to be quiet about how much the car cost? What he told me seemed okay, just really, really generous. Unless there's something creepy going on."

"I could see it if he was shy," Joe said, "but he isn't. He seemed to think giving it to you was almost expected. But maybe he was afraid you wouldn't take the car if you knew it was free."

"No, that was Gran. They've planned this for years. And all the time she's been telling me lies. 'Save for a car, and I'll match your savings. Save for a car and when you're sixteen, we'll go shopping for one.' Here she's got one being restored for me. It's either evasive or weird."

Joe hesitated a minute. He couldn't criticize Ben's grandmother to him, but in his gut he suspected her. She seemed so vulnerable to flattery, so shifty and condescending. "The car is great and Gregen seems like a great guy, don't you think? He's like the ideal grandfather."

Ben murmured, "I'm not sure." Joe could sense the confusion like waves of fever rising from Ben. "Your grandfather. Was he like that?"

"Yeah," Joe said. "Gramps was great like that. Fun, generous. He knew about everything. Everything you need to know, like how to build a snow fort or how to make invisible ink. Everything."

"How old were you when he died?"

"I dunno. Twelve."

"So you remember a lot about him."

"Yeah."

"Gregen asked if I remembered him, but I don't. And it's hard to believe he's been away *every* time we've visited Gran. I mean, wouldn't we have just dropped by one time or another? We were all here last June."

What do you remember from when you were little? Like around when Gregen was talking about."

"Nothing," Ben said quickly.

"C'mon," Joe said. Ben flipped onto his side, his back to Joe. "What's your earliest memory?"

"You know these questions are making you sound like a girl."

"Come on. Think back."

"The only thing I remember from being around here was playing catch with my dad on Gran's front lawn once. Other than that, just…a couple of books I liked and coloring at Gran's kitchen table. I had a box full of books and what she called quiet toys she kept under the table."

"Quiet toys?"

"She loves me and she's been good to me, but she's not a whole lot of fun," Ben murmured.

"Like matchbox cars or what?"

"No, a tape recorder and headphones."

"Cool."

"French," Ben said rising up on one elbow. "You know, those tapes were in French. *'Le chien est plus gros que le chat.'* Fat dogs and cats."

"That would explain how well you know French."

"It doesn't explain anything, Joe. Nothing."

"You mean about the car or—the other stuff?"

Ben looked at Joe, his eyes relieved, free of their keen edge for just a second. "See, I'm not sure what was happening. Was he trying to tell me something, do you think, Joe?"

"Yeah. I think so…hey, Ben?" Joe said, turning to face him. "Maybe you'll think I'm a girl for saying it, but—there was something there. I could see it when you were walking together. I could see a connection."

"What are you talking about?"

"It's hard to explain, but sometimes I see things. It's kind of an understood visual. Only lasts a second. Like the week before Mom told us she was pregnant with Cara? I saw it. Really fast one day when she walked by me, I saw her entire shape changed. And today when we were heading back up to the house there was one second where you two were standing on a hill way above the orchards and there was a sense of time. I don't know. It was weird."

Ben stared at Joe, unblinking.

Joe swallowed hard, feeling himself redden with this sudden disclosure. "That's why I think you're related."

"Then why didn't he say so? He said he was childless."

"Then there's the thing with Marie. They outright told Pete and me we were distant cousins, but it's *you* she zeroed in on. Either it's because you're a closer relative, or you were the one who was away somehow."

"Yeah," Ben said. "Or else it's just weird."

"No. It was a cool ritual. I mean, what a concept. Holding a heart, protecting from betrayal. Cool."

Remembering Ben said, "Covered. I felt covered. I guess. I don't know."

"You must be someone to them."

Ben lay on his back, arms folded over his chest, staring at the ceiling. "No." he said, shaking his head. "If I were so important to them, where have they been all this time?"

"There's more, I'm telling you," Joe said. "When we were leaving, Marie told me to watch out for you. Turns out she speaks English. She said you have to reason it out."

Ben turned his face to Joe. "Figure it out, like a puzzle? Why?"

"Dunno."

"They're playing with me. They bought me with the car and they're playing."

"It's not like that."

"You didn't hear this but Marie called me Katrine," Ben confided, his voice gone tight. "She whispered, '*Tu es Katrine.*' What's *that* about?"

"That means you're really a girl, switched at birth."

Ben gave a tense, reluctant snicker, then laughed out loud.

"I'm gonna call you Katrine from now on."

"Shut up," he laughed.

"Gregen carved you a magic penis out of one of those apple trees to change you over when you were born. You owe them your masculinity."

"Shut up. You're much more of a girl than I am. Shit. You've even got a dimple."

Joe was laughing loudly now, "And your balls are petrified apples. That's why he was looking at you so weird in the orchard like he was trying to get you to remember something—he wanted to see if your balls stirred to life from being back in the orchard of their birth."

Ben's laughter dissipated. "You saw that, too?"

"That's what I was trying to *tell* you." Joe nodded seriously. "It was the weirdest thing. Like he was trying to get to something in you or wake something up."

"I thought I was imagining it."

"No," Joe said.

They were silent, listening to Peter's quieted breathing.

"Want to go for a run?" Ben said, sitting up and swinging his legs off the bed.

"It's dark."

"Not for long."

"To Gregen's house?"

"Yeah."

Ben led the way, running to some surefooted inner rhythm as Joe struggled to stay no more than three yards behind on the sidewalks disrupted by gnarled tree roots as big as a man's leg. He stumbled once, coming down hard on the other side of a cement sidewalk slab pushed nearly perpendicular, but the next time he fell, hitting his palm, scraping his knee. Ben was beside him before he could get up.

"I'm okay," Joe said, brushing himself off. "I just tripped. The sidewalks are a mess."

Ben looked down, looked surprised as if seeing them for the first time. "Sorry. I see pretty well in the dark."

"I'll run in the street. Come on."

"Yeah," Ben said absently, starting in the street, along the curbside, leading again, but in a matter of minutes, he had stepped up again to the sidewalk. Joe watched him, watched the way he ran, eyes straight ahead, feet somehow nimble in a way that had to be intrinsic in his astounding awareness of his surroundings.

They smelled the apples before they saw Gregen's house, smelled the grapes touched with the scent of the chill falling dew that October morning, and slowed to a walk. Ben stopped and waited for Joe at the edge of Gregen's property, looking back once for him. And when Joe reached his side, Ben nudged Joe's shoulder with his own. "Look."

The house was quiet, but not dark. Side windows showed the light above the kitchen stove and then upstairs another light shone. The window was open and the breeze disturbed the net curtains enough so that, in flickered glimpses with the gusts of wind, the boys saw that Gregen sat in a large reddish chair beside a fireplace still aglow. His eyes were trained down as if reading.

"We should go knock."

Ben prevented Joe, his hand on Joe's wrist. "If we move past these trees, into his property, I bet motion detectors will set lights on."

"Don't you want to talk to him?" Joe heard Ben swallow.

"Why do I have to figure out a puzzle? Why not just tell me? That's playing. What am I—a mouse in a maze? Maybe he has a grant from Cornell to study the puzzle-solving abilities of Swiss-Danish boys and how they react to bizarre old people."

"Let's go ask him."

"No." Ben hesitated, breathing hard.

"Gregen said he'd answer any question you had."

"Think about it, Joe. If I go up to his door and ask him what he was trying to tell me and he says it's a puzzle I have to figure out, then I know the guy is playing with me—and what gives him the right to play with my mind? The car. The car gives him the right. Then I know he bought me with that car. That's sick. That creeps me out."

"I don't think so, Ben. I can tell—"

"What do *you* know about it, Joe?"

"I just—"

"The second option is that nothing's going on. What if I knock and ask what that whole ritual shit meant and he explains that Marie is almost one hundred and not right in the head and that's why she made me take my shirt off. Then he's ticked and wants to know what am I doing coming here in the middle of the night? Then I look like a fool in front of someone whose respect I want. And really I owe him respect, gratitude, and *what else* because he gave me a *car.*"

"You think too much—"

"Look. *You* have nothing to lose, Joe MacBride. You've already *got* everything and you're not putting anything at stake by going up there, so just shut up. I'm outta here."

"Wait—" Joe grabbed his arm at the elbow.

"I like Gregen. But I don't like what I'm feeling." He pulled his arm from Joe's grasp and sprinted away. Joe finally caught up to him at the corner of Gran's street, and as he pushed himself to get abreast of Ben, Joe fell immediately to a stumbling walk, bent double, holding his side. Ben stopped, came back to Joe, and bent down to him. Taking Joe's arm across his shoulder, he helped him stand up. "Sorry," he said. "I left you in the dust."

Panting, Joe tried to answer, but gave up.

Ben said, "Let's hurry and get out of here."

"Let's go home."

Peter was awake and suffering—sneezing, coughing and wheezing. They made Peter shower first, while Ben drove to the 7-11 and bought Benadryl, tissues, juice, bagels and a couple of things to get the smoke smell out of Joe's car. Peter dressed and waited outside while Joe and Ben showered and threw their stuff together.

At Ella Hunter's insistence, Joe helped Ben carry a wooden box from the garage to Ben's car. She wanted Ben to take it home with him, explaining that it had his grandfather Hunter's tools and things in it.

"There's dirt on the bottom of that box. Put this on the seat first," Gran commanded, coming from the house with a sheet. After some careful maneuvering the boys fit the box into the Fiat's backseat and bid Ella goodbye.

Joe decided that Peter should ride with Ben until he could get the smoke smell out of the MG, and so they set out. Peter fell asleep quickly under the medicine in Ben's warm, comfortable car. Joe drove with the windows down. He led the way driving and once they were on the Garden State Parkway, Ben sped up and drove next to him as often as he could.

It was sometime during the first hour on the Parkway that Joe looked over to see that Ben was enjoying his car. The tension and fear lingered in the way he pressed his lips together and the tight set of his shoulders, but there was something surprised and pleased in his eyes when he glanced over at Joe. Sighing deeply, Joe's own tension and sleepless night fought inside him. He had a sense that he'd only glimpsed a portion of the turmoil and confusion that roiled inside Ben.

Reaching to turn on the radio, he knocked over his bottle of orange juice and it rolled beneath the passenger seat. One hand on the wheel, Joe flipped the lever to move the seat back, and seeing the cap of the bottle, he stretched to reach. He couldn't quite grab it, and glancing away from the road to see exactly where it was, noticed one of Gran's cigarettes on the floor. Joe glanced at Ben. He shivered in the cool dampness of the autumn dawn. Keeping his eyes on the road as he stretched down, he snagged the cigarette with two fingers and brought it up into his hand.

Fingering it, rolling it along his scraped palm, Joe noted that it was only somewhat crushed, bent about a third of the way from the filter. His stomach tightened in pain and he remembered the last time he'd searched the Internet for information about this pain he suffered when stressed, he'd found an article in JAMA that said sometimes cigarettes helped.

He glanced at Ben again, noting that he looked calmer still and then slowly, deliberately, Joe sped up. Traffic was thickening, it would be harder for Ben to stay right beside him all the way home, he reasoned, and as soon as he'd lost him, maybe he'd try the cigarette.

Joe forced himself to think about other things, but his mind stuck on Gran and her odd ways. His suspicion of her swelled inside him. He told himself that his father would want him to put himself in Ella Hunter's shoes. Instead of judging her, he should try to understand. He fingered the cigarette, thinking, *Maybe they calm you down so much you don't care about what's right and wrong.*

Ben was two cars behind and traffic was swarming around them now. He opened the ashtray and pressed in the cigarette lighter.

The first puff was a little nauseating, but with the second drag, Joe could actually feel his intestines relax. He coughed a little, coughed again, took a deep drag on the cigarette, ignoring the burning in his lungs and allowing the drug to soothe his stomach. He began to enjoy it, sat back and relaxed, short puffs, long puffs until the cigarette was nearly finished. Abruptly his stomach turned. He looked up. Riding beside him was Ben's car keeping up with his considerable speed; Ben and Peter stared at him, Peter's window rolled down. Joe felt a lurch of nausea.

Peter shouted, "What the *hell* are you doing?"

Joe dropped the cigarette and, trying to reach it, swerved, burning his finger and going dull with nausea. His foot was heavy on the accelerator, the car gaining speed, rattling beneath him. As he pulled away from Ben and Peter, the distance between their cars widening, Joe heard the sickening blip-blip of a police siren behind him.

He swung the car onto the shoulder, scattering gravel as he came to a hard stop. He laid his head back against the seat and listened to the state trooper's boots crunch the gravel underfoot in approach.

Little Low Heaven

16

The band bus, turned toward home, was a kingdom apart. After a week of long outdoor practices, after the tension of the competition, the ride home had all the noisy joy of balloons released. That night, the three-hour bus ride began with a giddy celebration of their second-place finish. When the bus driver and chaperones demanded students take their seats, they settled into groups, tending to sit in the same places. Band rules required the boys to sit on the left side and girls on the right because the band director, who drove the equipment truck, earnestly expected restrained behavior in her absence. Joe's group claimed the back two rows on both sides of the bus. At night, in the dark cover of the back of the bus, they played their weekly poker game. That night Ben sat one row in front of his friends, close to the window, facing front. Tonight Jon sat beside him, chatting, not requiring an answer, and Ben found himself lost in thought about Gregen, Marie and about his new car, the keys to which he now fingered in his pocket, he knew he wanted Bonnie Jean's clear vision. He needed her beside him.

But she was his coach's daughter, forbidden to date, forbidden to date *him*, and right this moment she belonged to the entire band as she rallied the group to sing a few chapel songs. This brought everyone to the kind of settled peace that was beyond any bus driver's ability to command. When quiet sighs were heard, she highlighted the things that had happened in the day's competition.

In her uncanny ability to imitate anyone, she recounted the judges' complaint that the red plaid boxers of one of the baritones showed through his uniform. At this point, Scott stood up and bowed to the band. Adam made him pose and snapped Scott's picture with the disposable camera he carried to competitions.

They laughed about the Snickers bar that melted in Victoria's pocket, the way Mrs. Miller replaced the pad on Michelle's piccolo with a wad of gum and a Band-Aid, and about how she had borrowed a mouthpiece for Oliver's trumpet from another band.

Ben grew nervous when Bonnie Jean exaggerated Oliver's concern about the germs on the mouthpiece. She could look and speak like each of the boys, capturing the laconic, but somehow terrifying strength in Paul's voice when he commanded Oliver to use it and mirroring Oliver's prim refusals and inevitable surrender.

Ben dreaded Oliver's response, but the band roared with laughter in a collective shout that was almost thunder. Even the loyal Knox could not keep his face straight. In the end, the potency of their laughter irresistible, Ollie had to force a benign smile though Ben could see the turbulence of a tantrum building in the dull, sullen glint of his eyes.

So satisfied, the band members settled into their seats, pulling out pillows, fitting on headphones, leaning against each other to murmur confidences. The serious couples waited for the nodding of the chaperones' heads before they moved to take seats together, ignoring the whispered protests of those concerned with Mrs. Miller's rules. Ben leaned into the corner on a pillow he'd borrowed from Drew, his head against the window, where he watched, waiting to see what Bonnie Jean would do.

"You better go up there," Paul said.

"No," Ben said.

She stood alone, looking around.

"Hey, Jeannie," Joe called out, "Do you have cookies or any food from home?"

"Yeah."

"Can you bring it to us?"

Bonnie Jean did not reply, but ducked out of sight; she walked to the back, unsteady with the bus' movement. Jon scurried away from Ben's seat and squeezed in beside Scott.

"You owe me," Joe whispered to Ben.

"Forever in your debt," Ben replied.

Holding the bag by the corner, she swung it over the boys' heads to Joe's outstretched hands. "Wait," she said, before letting go of the bag. "You never *did* tell me what happened on the way home from New Jersey. You guys were acting all funny about it earlier." She looked from Joe to Ben, back to Joe. "Does it have anything to do with the fact that you're wearing about a gallon of Jon's vile cologne? Ugh. I can smell it from here."

"Not actually wearing it," Joe said. "It's just on my clothes."

"Have *you* been *smoking*, Joe?"

"Jeannie!" Joe said, mock surprise, eyes sparkling dully, perking up a little at the challenge of evading his sister.

"Do Mom and Dad know?"

"What do *you* think?"

"That is so dumb, Joe."

"Shut up. Don't you think I *know* that?" He shrugged. "I blew it, okay? I just *tried* it. Just one little cigarette."

"Yeah, he blew it. Ask him how much it cost him to smoke that one cigarette, Jeannie," Paul teased.

Jon answered, "Three hundred bucks. That is one *expensive* habit, my friend."

"He got a speeding ticket," Ben explained. "Pete caught him smoking, so Joe sped up. The state trooper was right behind him."

"You got pulled over for *speeding*? You know Mom will be even worse than Dad over this."

"I may wait to tell them," Joe said.

"I don't understand you, Joe," Ben said. "Your parents are great."

"They're *parents*, Ben. There's no way I'm up for their reaction."

"Well, *I'm* not telling them," Bonnie Jean said. "You have to."

Paul reasoned, "Might as well get it over with."

Ben watched Joe take in Paul's advice, wince, and groan. "Okay, okay. I've suffered enough today. Can't we just play poker now?"

As the boys went back to their game, Ben said to Bonnie Jean, "Don't go yet. Can you sit here a few minutes?" She hesitated, looking at Joe, but Ben saw that the boys had bent their heads low in feigned concentration on the game. "With me? For a few minutes?"

She glanced toward her friends at the front of the bus, then slid into the seat next to Ben. Once beside him, her shy hesitation evaporated. Smiling, she curled up on the seat, her knees close to Ben who said, "I was hoping we could talk. About Thursday and all."

Her eyes sparkled mischief. "After Thursday, after what happened, everyone thinks we're going to make out."

Ben said nothing, but looked at her in the flickering light of the moving bus. "Notice your brother is sitting right behind us."

"I've got so much on Joe, he's really no threat."

"Aside from him *telling*, which he wouldn't do, there's the privacy thing."

"Why is *that* important to *you*?" she said so casually that Ben, the brilliant test taker, understood her quest.

He laughed. "I don't know exactly *why*, Jeannie, it's just the way I want it."

"If we were alone?"

"Your dad wants us just friends. Remember?"

"We're *not* just friends, Ben. That's the truth. Sooner or later he's got to see what's here." With one deft hand, she drew an arch connecting them. "Something alive and good."

"Umm, I agree. But I want him to see in a way that's…that's like waking up late on Saturday morning. Not in a way that angers him. Anyway, it's deeper—what your dad wanted me to promise him."

"Nevermind Dad—after Thursday—I promised *myself*."

"Oh," Ben said, nodding, "you were testing me. I thought so."

"The privacy thing," she said. Sitting up straight, she gestured toward the front of the bus. "That's a huge issue here. Look at Ollie and Morgan. I don't get how they do that when everyone's watching."

Ben followed her gaze, knowing what he would see. His friends, disturbed by Oliver's callous behavior on previous bus rides, had discussed this problem. Now, Oliver lay back on the bus seat, feet on the floor in the aisle of the bus, and Morgan lay on top of him, holding his face with both hands kissing him. The blanket they meant to use for privacy had slipped to the floor.

"And look at them. Morgan told us he even—" Bonnie Jean glanced back at the boys playing poker, cupped her hand, leaned close, and whispered in his ear. Ben's breath caught and when she read his reaction, Bonnie Jean's eyes went wide and she covered her mouth, suddenly embarrassed at her candor. "Shoot, I always say too much."

"How honest you are," Ben whispered, "is one of the things I like best about you." He slouched in the seat and turned toward her so that they were nose to nose, smiling in embarrassment and newfound camaraderie. Neither spoke for a moment. Bonnie Jean's eyes were sparkling in the darkened bus and Ben knew she understood the wild nature of his desire as palpably as if her fingers measured the pulsing of his blood. He kept his eyes on her eyes, savoring the intensity of their building understanding.

"Mr. Bettinger's not on the bus somewhere, is he?" Ben said.

"That was awful when he pulled you away from me."

"I honestly thought I was losing my life."

"I'm so sorry about Thursday."

"Jeannie. It was *my* fault."

"Our *souls* were *touching*. Like now."

"Yeah, I know," he said, moving his left hand to touch her fingers. "I don't know how to explain this, and I don't know what you'll think of it, but…"

"Just say it."

"It's about your dad," It came out sounding tight and emotional. She was frowning, listening, her eyes unblinking. "It's not about basketball… There's stuff I have to figure out about him—like why he's different. How does he manage to treat people the way he does with that kind of deep down respect? I want to be that kind of man and I've got to figure out how he came to be that way." Her eyes searched his. "And I need to know why…"

She nodded, her eyes serious and sympathetic. "Why he loves you? Mom does, too."

Ben couldn't reply. Ashamed of betraying his parents by admitting his need for a father, knowing that his deepest secret lay bare to a girl whose respect he craved. To Ben, who lived in hiding like a leper in a cave covering his wounds and his passions, this disclosure felt like the sun's fire over his smooth body.

But she moved a little closer to him, resting her head on the back of the seat so that she caught his downcast gaze. She touched his temple so lightly it felt like a breath. And then she was hugging him in her fierce, sturdy way, arm tight around his neck, her smooth, hot cheek against his cool one.

"That's the other problem with you and me," he managed to say in her ear, his voice croaky and low. "I haven't been raised like you and Joe. There are things—"

"You need Dad to help with," she finished his thought, nodding decisively, her head against his.

"I may not end up being good enough for you, Jeannie. I may not be able to be fixed."

She moved away from him. "Maybe there are broken things about you. I can tell you're hurting and I know you're right about Dad. I complain about how strict he is and other stuff that bugs me, but…" she looked down.

"He's worth respecting, Jeannie, and that's something really valuable."

She hugged him again with both arms. He could have kissed her then. His entire self wanted to meet her in a kiss, to have just that much—that everything—for now. "Hey," he whispered, teasing, "the guys are watching us, so…"

She pulled away from him. "Are you happy with your car?"

Taking her cue, Ben described the car, Gregen's home and orchard, the meal, Marie's strange ritual. She asked questions and glanced back at the boys, who were loudly involved in the game. "Jeannie, so many weird things happened. By the end, Joe and I were really freaked out. Which may explain his smoking that cigarette."

She rolled her eyes impatiently. "What kind of weird things?"

"This guy Gregen seemed to know stuff about me and your family. Like your mom and Marie—"

"Oh, I've heard her talk about Marie."

"Really? They're distant cousins?"

"I forget."

"He knew the family names and he knew what nationality everyone was descended from and everything. He told me I was Swiss and Danish, which I didn't even know."

"Are you part French, too? Because you sure are good at it."

"That's another thing. Gregen and Marie spoke to me *in French*," Ben said, leaning toward her, "and I understood most of it."

"But you always do. That's nothing new."

"It was like I *expected* to speak French to them. It was freaky because—

I haven't told you this but—every Christmas and birthday, Gran gives me a stack of books wrapped in this fancy paper that my dad always makes fun of. So, I open them alone, one at a time, and read from the top of the stack down. There's always at least one book in French."

"That explains why you know so much French. Ben, you wreck every curve."

"Sorry," he said, thinking, worried.

"It sounds like your grandmother is trying to teach you French."

"Yeah, but she doesn't *speak* French. What I'm wondering is if this guy Gregen convinced her to give me those French books. He actually said Marie was testing me to see how much French I knew." He met her eyes and confided, "I can't help feeling he's playing with me. Like a science experiment."

"Your grandmother might have just been trying to improve your mind. Liz's grandmother is always sending her videos on science and philosophy. That's why Liz is so brilliant."

"I try to talk to Gran about them, but she never wants to. She claims she's not much of a reader and just thought I'd enjoy them. But she *insists*—and she doesn't insist on much of anything—when I'm done reading, she *insists* I write a page of what I liked about each book."

"It's like she's giving you homework," she said. "Did you get a stack for your birthday this year?"

"No. I got those cell phones." It was the first year that he could remember without a stack of books. "The ones from last Christmas kept me going 'til August."

"Are there inscriptions in them?"

"Huh?"

"In the front—like—'Here's hoping you get into Harvard. Love, Gran.'"

"No," Ben laughed. "Just a label with my name." Ben rested his head back on the seat and Bonnie Jean shifted, her knees pointing toward him, and shivered. "Cold?" She nodded and yawned. Ben scrounged for his jacket shoved behind the pillow and put it across her legs, then leaned back again. Resting her cheek on the back of the seat, she reached over and touched his forearm. He covered her hand with his. "The thing that's bothering me is that Gregen seemed to know me. He seemed to be a little possessive of me. He was even telling me how I should behave and asking about my grades. I just wonder if taking the car from him gives him this—I don't know—this *right* to tell me stuff like that."

"But the car was a gift."

"Maybe I was bought."

"But if he and your grandmother have been friends forever, that explains how he knows you. Old people always feel like they can tell you what to do and they always go on about the old country and how people were moral over there and stuff."

"I guess." They reasoned together as the bus bumped along and the poker game burned on like the embers of a slowing campfire behind them. Ben was amused to see her grow sleepy while she talked, and soon, her eyes closed and her head began to nod and her words no longer made sense. Finally, she slept, her cheek resting on his shoulder. Ben's confusion dimmed as he memorized the sunny scent of her hair, the grip of her hand on his arm, her steady breathing.

A half hour before home, as the bus rumbled down the long curves in the dark, unbroken part of the highway, even the boys playing poker grew quiet. Looking back he saw that Jon and Scott had fallen asleep. He heard Joe whisper to Adam. "We have to say something to Ollie. It's gone too far. Look." Now, looking front, Ben could see that some of the couples were still awake. Oliver and Morgan had switched positions and she lay on her back, her head toward the aisle, her pale blond hair hanging over the edge of the seat like phosphorescence in murky sea water. Oliver knelt on the floor beside her. From where he sat, Ben could see that her shirt was open, he could see the glow of moonlight on her bare, white skin. The whispering behind him grew fierce. The bus sped along and Ben heard rustling behind them. Joe said, "It's got to be now. The chaperones wake up when we slow down to exit." Bonnie Jean stirred beside him and sat up, rubbing her eyes. Ben saw that Joe was carrying Adam's disposable camera.

"What's going on?" Bonnie Jean murmured.

"Player patrol," Paul said. "About to strike."

"Go for it," Adam murmured.

Joe crept forward, aimed the camera. The flash paralyzed Oliver. Joe snapped another picture. "What?" Oliver yelled. "What?" Joe was thrown off balance when the bus slowed to make its turn onto the Bestgate exit; everyone woke as if an alarm had buzzed. He scrambled to his feet and bolted to the back of the bus as Oliver screamed, "MacBride! That better not have been you!" Oliver struggled to his feet and by the time he was roaring toward the back of the bus, Joe stood behind the gigantic Ridout brothers.

"Don't come any closer," Paul warned.

"I'm gonna kill you, MacBride. I swear."

"Serves you right," said Adam.

"You're disgusting," Joe said from his place of safety, his eyes just above the Ridout brothers' bulky shoulders.

"Yeah," Ben said. "I could see her bare chest all the way back here."

"Why don't you take a picture of *them*?" Oliver screamed, rocking sideways, reaching for a handhold as the bus turned into the school parking lot. "I'm sure your dad would be much more interested in that."

"I didn't do this for my dad, you idiot," Joe said. "We're sick of you treating Morgan like this."

"They were behaving," Paul said. "We kept an eye on them all night."

Adam stepped forward, crossing his arms in front of his chest. "You weren't. You're having sex in public, you horny little creep."

Morgan, crying hard, surrounded by a gaggle of girls, was calling him. Awakening chaperones were commanding silence, asking what was wrong.

"If you're a man," Joe said, "you'll go to her. Think how humiliated she feels knowing half the band saw you feeling her up."

"You're gonna regret this, MacBride," Oliver thundered as he muscled his way up the aisle.

There was some discussion about who should take the camera, and finally it was given to Adam on the basis of his sheer power. They agreed that the film would be developed first thing in the morning at the one-hour place in Bowie. Oliver would expect them to get it done locally.

"Should I get doubles?" Adam called to Joe as he and Paul headed for their truck.

"Triples," Joe said. "I'm taking him down."

17

BECAUSE the wooden box Gran had required him to take with him was wedged onto his knees, Ben struggled to reach his wallet in his back pocket so he could show the marine guard his military ID.

"What's in the box?" the young marine asked, holding Ben's ID and comparing it to Ben's face.

"Just old tools and stuff from my grandmother. We're just coming back from visiting her. I'd walk, sir," Ben said, "but this is really heavy. They're just going to drop me off."

"I'm not really supposed to let cars without DOD stickers drive in after dark," he said slowly. "So, if I don't see you two exit in a reasonable amount of time, I'm calling the MPs."

"Okay. Thank you. They won't be long," Ben said.

Ben directed Joe to drive around the back of the house and park in his mother's spot, explaining that she wouldn't be home from work until four. Ben and Joe had to carry the box together and Bonnie Jean led the way, opening the basement door for them. In an unspoken consensus, they went silently, the depth of the hour and their own exhaustion keeping them quiet. Once inside the basement, Ben whispered directions, taking them through the main area past the pungent laundry room to a window-less storage room beyond. Here he flipped on a light.

"Let's put it over there in the corner," he whispered, "next to those boxes of Christmas stuff."

They settled it on the floor and Ben turned to go.

"Aren't you going to look in it first?" Bonnie Jean said.

"Aw, there's nothing in there but some old tools of my grandfather's. Antique stuff. Probably not really worth anything," Ben muttered.

"Let's just look."

"We're working under a time limit here, Jeannie," Joe said. "I don't want MPs escorting my ass home."

"Just a peek," she begged. Kneeling down in front of it, she lifted the lid. The boys peered over her shoulders. The box was fitted with a tray that was a kind of a first shelf, but inside the box lid was a flat board with a lock.

"Do you have the key?" she asked Ben.

"It's probably in there with that other junk." The tray held a tire gauge, leather-bound maps most certainly long out of date, wrenches, a screwdriver, a large leather book stuffed with papers, a bundle of fountain pens bound together with a broad purple rubber band, and a book of matches. "See?" Ben said, "Old junk. You guys better go." But Bonnie Jean moved the book looking for the key. Ben's body went tense as if shot with a charge. "Wait."

There were footsteps above and the loud, careless whispers of the drunk. "Shit," he hissed and leapt across the room to slam off the light switch. For a few seconds, they stayed still, unable to see, captured by the sounds above. Ben found his focus and crossed the dark room to his friends; they stood together, Ben in the middle, hidden in the shadows. "You can't leave now. You've got to wait. Sorry. I'm so sorry."

His father's voice boomed recklessly above and when he opened the door to the back basement stairs, it roared down as if he were shouting at a basketball game. "I can't find the light switch," he laughed, obviously drunk.

Bonnie Jean whispered, "Shouldn't we say something just to be polite?" Ben shook his head.

A woman's voice answered. "I'll get it, Max." The light burst on and the three friends backed away from the brighter stream, keeping themselves in the darkest place. Bonnie Jean touched Ben's hand to say she now understood. Above them they heard the woman scold, "I can't believe you couldn't find that, handsome. You know, you're really only good at one thing."

"And aren't you glad about that?" he laughed, and then there were wet, exaggerated kissing noises. They clumped down the stairs while Ben and Joe and Bonnie Jean stood stiffly, shoulder to shoulder, breathing quick, nervous breaths. They heard them at the back door, heard them lean up against it. "Now," Max said gruffly, "the kids didn't bother us over here, did they?"

"I haven't been so happy since Greece," the woman croaked, her voice gruff and raspy.

"Yeah. I told you, Patty. You were wrong about kids. They go to bed early, my wife works late. Plenty of time to satisfy even you."

"Umm." There were bundled sounds of physical contact. Ben's stomach had begun to shake and he knew his friends could feel its thunder. Bonnie Jean reached for Ben's hand and Joe moved in closer, his shoulder pressing against Ben's.

"I'd better go, Max."

"Come back," he grunted. The door opened. The woman commanded Max to go up to bed and then the door shut. Ben heard his father rattle the doorknob. Shaking outwardly now, he waited, holding onto his friends, all of them fearing to breathe in the silence, listening to Max trace his shuffling, drunken steps back up the stairs. They could hear him stumble across the kitchen, through the first floor rooms and onto the carpeted main staircase. *Please don't let him collapse on the stairs. Please,* Ben prayed silently. When Ben heard the rumble of his father's crash onto his bed, he swallowed and tried to speak, but couldn't.

Joe said, "Come home with us," his voice thick, emotional.

"Please," Bonnie Jean said. "You don't belong here."

"I want to. But my brothers."

They held onto him, Bonnie Jean's arms going tight around his waist as Joe slid his arm protectively around Ben's shoulder. "Come tomorrow, then."

"Don't tell," Ben whispered. "Please."

His friends considered this. "But—"

"Your dad will never—" his voice broke. He struggled for strength. "He'll never trust me with you," he said looking at her and then turning to Joe, "with Bonnie Jean, if he knows."

"Ben," Joe said. "That's not it."

"Please," Ben begged.

"*You've* got to tell him, then," Joe insisted.

"You show me how," Ben said, his eyes meeting Joe's.

Slowing for the curve, Joe pointed to their home visible beyond. "The kitchen light's on. We can't let Dad see you've been crying," Joe said to his sister as he sniffed and drew his sleeve across his nose.

"Don't go home yet. Drive down to Heron Creek, 'til we get ourselves together."

Joe switched off his blinker and continued straight, passing their street. On the slim dirt road beside the water, he slowed and pulled the

MG to a stop in a place where the sea oats parted, showing the moonlit waters of the wide creek. Bonnie Jean rolled down her window and they sat there, heads back, breathing in the marshy, brackish scent. "That was horrible."

"What are we gonna do, Jeannie? We *never* should have promised him to keep that a secret."

"We had to."

"But can you *imagine*?"

"No."

"I feel like such a creep for how I treat Dad all the time."

"Me too. Is that why you were crying, Joe?"

"And Ben."

She turned her head toward the water and they listened to its soft lapping, watched the moon's calm, silver light shimmer. She reached for Joe's hand, and together they bowed their heads, "Heavenly Father," Joe prayed, "Please, Lord Jesus, help and show us what to do." Joe drew his breath in hard, fighting tears. "Please help Ben."

"Ben needs you, Lord. Please be with him tonight and comfort him."

In the dark they sat in silent communion, heads bowed, praying, listening to the water, to the breeze rustle the sea oats, and to the inner whisperings upon which both had been raised to rely.

Tom heard Joe cut the engine halfway down the driveway. He watched the dark shape coast to rest in its parking spot. But as soon as they stepped into the kitchen, Tom made his presence known. "You're more than an hour later than I expected," his voice taut with anxiety.

"Sorry, Dad," Joe said.

"We had to take Ben home," Bonnie Jean said.

"Didn't he get his car?"

"Before band we took it to have it painted."

"You might have called. I had no idea where you were."

"Sorry."

"What took you so long?"

Joe looked down. "First the guard gave us trouble and then we had to help Ben carry stuff in."

"Stuff?"

"Stuff his grandmother sent. It took awhile. Sorry."

"When you're going to be late, I need a phone call."

"I understand, Dad," Joe said. "And I apologize for being so inconsiderate. It won't happen again."

"Me, too, Dad. I promise I'll call."

"Okay then," Tom said. They stood together, the tension of silence dividing them. His children looked so alike when they were avoiding him, lips pressed tightly together, nostrils flared in determination, and Tom noticed how similar the shape of their lowered eyelids were. Finally he said, "The band did well. You guys were terrific."

"You and Mom leave right after the performance?'"

"I wanted to get Mom and Cara home before too late. How was the ride home?"

"Oh." Joe sighed. "Long."

"Did you sleep all the way home as usual, Bonnie Jean?"

"Not quite all the way."

"Pretty quiet on the bus? Everyone tired?"

"Oh, you know, Dad."

"Got Ben home safely, then? His parents waiting up for him?"

"No," Joe said, looking up at his father for the first time. "He's not as lucky as us."

Bonnie Jean went to Tom and hugged him fiercely. "We love you, Daddy."

"Really? Then call next time so I can get some sleep."

"We will. Sorry."

"You'd better get to bed. Church in the morning."

"Yes, sir," they said in unison, and Joe came to him and hugged him, clinging a minute; Tom felt the boy's emotion, felt it catch in Joe's throat. Tom noted the scent of the bay in their hair, but he said nothing. He had been watching and had seen the MG scoot past their street. His children were keeping secrets and they weren't very good at it.

18

HIS back throbbing as if it had been crushed, both legs stiff and numb, Tom hobbled to the sink to fill the coffee pot with fresh water. He wanted very much to see Peter, who had left a note saying that since his entire family had gone to the band competition, he went to visit a new friend from college who lived in Great Falls. Tom was hoping his eldest son would be home in time for breakfast and church.

But breakfast was quiet. Tommy had spent the night at a friend's house and would be meeting them at church. Cara slept in her mechanical swing; Joe and Bonnie Jean's pleasant but conspiratorial silence left Tom and Laurie to their worried thoughts.

Ben was waiting for them when they got home from church, his polite veneer polished to a distracting sheen. The teenagers ate little at lunch and spent the afternoon playing board games with Tommy, first Boggle, then Scrabble, and finally a marathon game of Risk; Tommy won round after round.

When Peter had still not arrived by three and the phone rang, Tom lunged for it; his legs like posts, refusing to follow, made him thunk into the wall.

"Hello?" His expression went serious as he listened. "Is he badly hurt?" Joe stood up and Laurie put down her quilting hoop. "That many? Any other injuries? We'll be right there."

"Peter," Laurie said weakly.

"No. Adam Ridout. He was at the Motophoto in Bowie and he looked out the window and saw his truck rolling toward the store. He ran out to stop it and got himself knocked down and pretty cut up. He had to get fifteen stitches over his right eye." Tom hoisted himself up to his feet. "I'm going over to the hospital. Joe, you and Ben come with me."

They heard a car on the driveway gravel. Peter got out of the car, swung his backpack onto his shoulder, and the MacBrides rushed out of the house to greet him.

"I thought you'd be home earlier," Laurie said.

"Sorry, Mom. They wanted me to go to church with them. Took forever," Peter said.

"Come with us over to the hospital," Tom said, putting his arm around Peter. "Adam Ridout's been injured."

Tom asked Peter the question that Joe and Ben, sitting in the back seat of the car, waited to hear. "Why didn't you call this morning? Mama and I got worried. We didn't even have a name or a phone number."

Peter chewed his bottom lip. "You know, it's weird how fast I got used to being away and not thinking about the fact that you'd be wondering where I was. When I'm at school you probably don't even wonder where I am."

"No, I still wonder," Tom said, "I think about you first thing in the morning and last thing at night. But I don't expect you home, so, you know, the tension doesn't build," Tom shrugged.

Peter reached his arm across the car to pat his father's back. "I'm sorry, Dad."

Joe leaned up and rested his arms and chin on the back of the front seat. "So, if you're done whipping Pete's rear," he said, grinning, "have either of you ever heard of the 'Above the Waist' doctrine?"

Tom groaned. "Has *that* resurfaced?"

Peter turned around to make eye contact with Ben and Joe. "Is that the one that says it's okay to do anything above the waist?"

"Not only okay, it says that it's *scriptural* to do anything above the *girl's* waist," Joe corrected. "It's God's provision for horny teenage boys."

Peter mouthed Ollie's name. Ben and Joe nodded. Peter smirked and shook his head.

Tom said, "Who's into that?"

"A bunch of kids," Joe said. "Do you think it could be God's provision, Dad?"

"No."

"Why not?"

"It's based on male desire, not clear interpretation of scripture. I think that's obvious. I'd like to have words with whoever is spreading it around. It puts girls in a situation no loving father would sanction. I don't know why a self-respecting young woman would put up with it."

"Maybe she likes it," Joe said. "Think about it." Tom turned his head to shoot Joe a warning glance. "When I was young," Tom lectured, "this ridiculous theory was running rampant in certain groups of religious people. I say now what I said then. It's meant to use women and that's not what sex should be about." He yanked hard on the emergency brake and the boys smirked at each other. "Got that, men?"

"Yes, sir," they said in unison.

"Don't forget it."

"What's going on?" Peter whispered to them when they all climbed out of the car and waited for Tom to get to his feet.

Quickly, Joe explained about the pictures. Peter shook his head in a way that made him look exactly like his father.

They squeezed to fit into the small, curtained area in the emergency room already crowded with the colossal Ridout family members. Adam relaxed on the bed, his feet extending ten inches off the end. A look of happy conspiracy passed between the boys as they greeted each other, shaking hands, asking about Adam's condition. Mr. Ridout stood as tall as Paul. His hair was an impressive crown of iron gray, his face tanned and his brown eyes merry. His body was massive with shoulders that dwarfed Tom's, with a thick torso and hands the size of catcher's mitts. Mrs. Ridout looked like a china doll beside him, slim and neat—the top of her head brushed her husband's bicep—but when she shook Ben's hand, her grip was so strong it hurt. They were friendly to Ben and welcomed him, reminding him to stop by their home anytime. Both Mr. and Mrs. Ridout embraced Joe and Peter, asking a dozen loving questions.

Ben and Tom squinted in sympathy at Adam's gruesome stitches. The cut traced his eyebrow and curved around the orbital bone. His lips were swollen and five stitches held his chin together.

"My poor Sugar Bear," Mrs. Ridout said, patting Adam's enormous shoulder.

"Aww, Sugar Bear," Joe teased. Adam shrugged and grinned contentedly.

"Any concussion?" Tom asked.

"Head's too hard," Mr. Ridout said. "Just like his papa." He knocked on his own forehead with his knuckles. "Made of solid wood."

"The doctor says he'll have to take it easy this week."

His words sounding slurred from the Novocain that numbed his chin, Adam said, "Mom, tell them what you did when the police called you saying I was hurt."

"It's so embarrassing." She laughed out loud. "I was in the middle of making my Sunday dinner and here Adam—"

"You mean Sugar Bear," Joe interrupted.

"That's right," she said, leaning over to kiss Adam's forehead. "Sugar Bear was nowhere to be found. I was already steaming because he'd skipped out early from church."

"Can't sneak out of church early when you're six feet, seven inches tall," Tom said.

"No," Mr. Ridout agreed. "And at our house, you don't want to miss half of church *and* Sunday dinner. Mom has her standards."

"Anyways," Mrs. Ridout said, "the man sounded just like you, Joe, so I figured you must be trying to get Adam out of trouble for skipping out early on church. I was real skeptical, but trying to play along and waiting for an opportunity to trip you up. When he said, 'Your son is okay, but his own truck knocked him down,' I said, 'Joe MacBride. That's the lamest excuse I've ever heard. At least make up something believable.' Then I slammed the phone down."

"Luckily," Mr. Ridout said, "the gentleman called us right back."

The parents withdrew to discuss Adam's injury and approaching basketball season. The boys crowded around Adam. "Way to take one for the team," Joe said, punching Adam's shoulder.

"I gave the pictures to Paul as soon as he got here."

From inside his shirt, Paul took the packet of pictures.

"They're on the bottom," Adam said. "Only one came out. But it's a good 'un."

Paul flipped through and brought the photograph to the top of the stack. The boys restrained their comments, eyes wide. The flash had worked in the dark bus, illuminating Oliver's surprised face, upturned to the camera, his right hand covering Morgan's exposed breast.

"Good, it doesn't show everything on her," Ben whispered.

"This is one valuable photograph," Paul said.

"I'll keep one," Joe whispered, sliding it into his shirt pocket. "Paul, you keep one, and Pete, you take the other back up to school with you," Joe said, handing the pictures to them. "When you guys get home, call. We'll figure out what we're going to do."

"What were you doing in Bowie, anyway, Adam?" Tom asked, turning toward the boys. "There's plenty of places to get your pictures developed around here."

Adam glanced at his father, then at Tom, then at Joe. He shrugged his shoulders and sighed in indolent nonchalance as if to say his behavior, if baffling, was inconsequential.

"Kids," his father said. "Don't think."

But Tom's keen glance went swiftly over the boys. "Did you get your pictures before you ran out there?"

"Yes, sir," Adam said. "They're pretty good, too."

"May I see?"

"Sure thing, Coach."

"Nice pictures," Tom said when he had looked at them all. "It was a good day." He searched the boys' faces again but they were standing together on the opposite side of Adam's bed and their faces wore the impenetrable masks of conspiracy. Tom's eyes lingered on Ben's and Ben felt himself begin to color, his throat flushing hot red with his newly acquired affliction—shame at lying.

"Why do you need triples?"

"You just never know, Coach," Paul said.

"Right," Tom said. "I just bet you don't."

He shook Mr. Ridout's hand, shook hands with Adam and Paul. "Let's go, MacBrides," he said. "We've got to take Ben home."

19

AS they drove home, the boys said little, speaking meaningfully only in their quick and silent glances. Ignoring Ben's invitation to drop him at the curb, Tom insisted that it would be rude and drove up to the marine guarding the gate. He rolled down his window at the marine's salute.

"Good evening, marine," Tom said. "You're lookin' sharp today."

"Thank you, sir. Have a good day, sir."

Tom followed Ben's directions to take him to the back of the house, but when Ben got out, Tom turned off the car and opened the door. It was slow getting his legs to move again and he finally had to lift the right leg at the knee and swing it out.

"Coach?" Ben said, his face blanched.

"I'm coming to the door with you."

"No."

"I don't feel honest just dropping you off without coming in to say hello. I wouldn't behave that way to any other old acquaintance, let alone the parents of one of my athletes."

"Coach, you can barely walk today."

"Give me a hand up. I'll be okay. This car is hard to get out of."

Ben cast a despairing glance at Joe. Both brothers got out of the car and came around to the other side.

"Want to lean on me, Dad?" Peter said.

"No," Tom said, leaning heavily on the car door as he struggled to sense his balance. "I'm fine."

"Obviously," Joe drawled.

Ben walked slowly with Tom, staying beside him, saying at least three times to Tom that his parents were probably not home. "Please, Coach. Be careful," he whispered.

"I've survived this long, Ben."

Ben heard footsteps in the kitchen—quick, scampering steps—which he knew belonged to his brothers. Knowing that Keith and Tim rarely came into the kitchen if their father was at home and awake, that they never *ran* through the kitchen if Max were around, gave Ben the courage to climb the steps.

Keith and Tim were hiding under the kitchen table. Overjoyed at seeing Ben, they threw themselves at him, nearly knocking him down.

"Are Mom and Dad home?"

"Nope," Tim said. "They goed out for shopping."

"Went," Ben said, relief spreading through him like a thrill. "You remember my friends, don't you guys?"

The boys nodded, eyes squinted in concentration. Then they began pulling on Ben's shirt. "Where you been, Ben? You been gone so long."

"I'm home now."

Tom limped past Laurie's garden to the kitchen door Joe held open for him "Want to tell me what you boys are up to?" Tom said.

"No, sir," Joe said. "We're doing the right thing. Trust me."

"Peter?"

"I just got home, Dad."

"Where's Ben?" Laurie said. Standing at the counter beside the sink, she held a round biscuit cutter above a circle of dough.

"We took him home," Peter said, going to her and putting his arm around her shoulders to hug her.

"Yeah, Mom," Joe said, his eyes dancing. "And you should have seen Dad. Here he can barely walk and he insists on going up to the door with Ben, just to be friendly. How could he confront Colonel Hunter in his condition today?"

"I don't believe this," Laurie said. "You went up to the door, Tom?"

"I felt it would be dishonest, like hiding, if I stayed in the car. If it were any other kid, any other dad or old acquaintance, I'd have gotten out and said hello."

"But it wasn't," Laurie said, shoving the biscuit cutter into the dough. "It's Max Hunter. You were foolish."

"Laurie, that's a little harsh," Tom said, coming up behind her and touching her waist.

"No. I'm serious. You need to stay away from him."

"I've got to talk to him."

"Tom. When your legs are bad, like they have been, you know what the doctor said...the tissues are swollen. If you're injured during one of these episodes, it is certain to cause more damage."

"I'm not going to be injured."

"How can you say that? You always are."

Tom looked at his sons, standing tall and straight, watching him. Joe munched on an apple, crunching loudly, his eyes alight with fascination. Peter was eating his way through a handful of cookies, his calm countenance marred by creased eyebrows.

"It's been a long time. He's got to have outgrown—"

"Tom," Laurie said. "You know better."

"He *is* kind of big," Joe said.

Laurie said. "You've met him?"

"At the MVA. The day Ben got his permit. His dad met us there. What a jerk. He made me leave and he stepped on Ben's toes."

"Stepped on his toes?" Peter said, squinching up his face.

"That's a standard military intimidation technique," Tom said.

"It was mean," Joe said. "He's a little taller than me and Ben, but real padded. For a marine."

"Yeah," Peter murmured under his breath to Joe. "Nothing like those tight-assed marines."

"Like Dad," Joe agreed.

"I may not be able to walk, boys, but I can hear well," Tom said.

"You do have a lovely, muscular rear end," Laurie said, reflectively, without glancing up. "I'd hate to see it turn to flab from sitting in a *wheelchair* the rest of your life."

Tommy came into the kitchen holding a football and two neon-bright frisbees. "What's going on?"

"Dad's in trouble."

"Anybody want to play this new game I made up?" Tommy said.

"In a minute," Peter said. "We want to watch Mom whup up on Dad."

"We're just having a discussion," Tom said, "about the fact that I'm in better shape than Max Hunter. That ought to make you feel better, Laurie."

"You intend to fight him, don't you, Tom?"

"I intend to *speak* to him and if I must—"

"Nope," Laurie said, flipping the last biscuit onto the pan. "You're going *nowhere* near him."

Tom glanced at his boys. Tommy tossed his football up and caught it. "I made a promise. It's time to fulfill it."

"No, Tom," Laurie said, putting her pan of biscuits into the oven. Wiping her hands on her apron, she turned toward Tom. "That's all past. Forget it."

"I can't. I promised."

"And you tried to fulfill that promise. It doesn't matter anymore."

"A promise is a promise."

"Not at the expense of your health—or worse."

"That's exactly what a promise *means*, Laurie."

"Oh, for pity's sake." She whisked off her apron and flung it into the sink. "I'm going outside for a breath of fresh air," she announced to the boys. "Somebody keep an eye on those biscuits."

It took Tom an embarrassingly long time to get to the back door. Laurie, angry, fuming, walked along the herb garden on the side of the garage, ripping out the tall weeds.

"You know I've been praying for an opportunity to keep that promise."

"That was a stupid thing to pray, Tom MacBride," she said, but she allowed him to take her into his arms. She said, "If anything *else* happened to you—"

He held Laurie close, keenly aware of her strengths. She was supple and beautiful, made of strong stuff. The mother of so many, creative, practical, energetic, she had made him a rich man, had seen how to put their shattered life together more than once. He admired her with all of his heart, felt vulnerable to her.

"Don't forget me," she said. "In the pursuit of your principles, don't forget me again." Tom knew his boys were watching him, standing at the kitchen door and staring unabashedly at him as he was presented with the opportunity to bow to their mother out of compassion and respect. He held her, thinking, whispering comfort to her, knowing that they—none of them, not even Laurie—knew how deeply sworn that promise had been. Only Tom had been there and Tom knew he had to fulfill it and beg his family for understanding.

20

THOUGH there were only three practices that week, Mrs. Miller would not allow Adam to play his tuba, sure that his eye would pop the stitches and burst out of the socket. This made band practice the perfect time for negotiations. While Paul and Joe fulfilled the tuba squad's responsibilities, Adam loped along in his languid way with messages to Morgan and Oliver, who finally agreed to meet with them at the base of the hill when the band took a water break.

But Morgan intercepted them on the way. They stood together, a half-circle of big men and Jon facing her, and she burst into tears.

"What's wrong with you? Why are you doing this to us?"

"We don't mean it against you, Morgan," Joe said.

"It's Oliver," Paul said.

"Ollie is taking advantage of you and we want it stopped."

"But he's not. It's *not* his fault. I love him," she sobbed into her hands. Tiffany and Johannah ran to them from across the field, came up behind Morgan and embraced her, patting her back and arms, trying to soothe her. They glared at the boys. Joe murmured "Hey," to them both.

"Does he love you?" Ben said.

"What are *you* doing here? You don't know any of us," Johannah said.

"You don't have to be rude," Jon said.

"After watching Ollie on Saturday night," Ben said, "I know there's something wrong with a guy who would treat his girlfriend that way."

"I bet you know *all* about girlfriends," Tiffany sneered. "I bet you're the expert."

"C'mon, Tiff," Joe said.

"And you're one to talk," Tiffany said. "After eighth grade."

"I've changed, Tiffany," Joe said, holding up both hands in a gesture of surrender. "I regret what I did. You know that. Everybody in the whole school knows that."

"My sex life is none of your business," Morgan sobbed. Her friends wrapped their arms around her, trying to pull her away from the boys.

"I don't want it to be my business," Joe said. "But we could *see* what you guys were doing."

"They can't get any time alone with their parents around," Tiffany whispered to the boys. "The bus is the only place—"

"I thought you believed in abstinence," Joe said to Tiffany, angry now.

"Maybe I just didn't want to do anything with *you*. For God's sake, Joe. You had zits all over your nose."

Joe pressed his lips together. Ben bumped his shoulder and said quietly, "Don't let her get to you, man."

Joe shook his head. "This isn't about us."

"There's no us," Tiffany said.

"Right," Joe said. "So quit bringing it up."

"Back to the point. Oliver's the jerk now," Paul said.

"And the bus is *not* the place," Adam said.

"You don't understand," Morgan begged. "If you guys had Oliver's strong sex drive, you'd understand."

"Hey, that's insulting," Jon said.

"Oh, come on," Joe said. "That's absurd. Does he tell you that stuff?"

"It's true," Johannah insisted, her eyes wide. "I dated him last year. It's true. He can't help it."

Adam, Joe, Paul, and Ben glanced at each other.

"He *needs* sexual activity," Morgan said. "He actually feels pain in his—his *testicles*," she said primly, "if he doesn't."

"That's bullshit," Ben said. "That's the cheapest line in the world."

"You ought to know," Johannah squeaked.

"Lay off Ben," Adam said. "He's right. We all know that's bullshit."

"We can't stand by and watch Ollie use you this way, Morgan," Joe said. "So tell superman he's got to talk to us himself."

Morgan, her friends following, ran across the field to a clump of trees at the far corner. The boys saw Oliver step out from behind the trees to meet her. Though she stood too far from them to hear her words, her wild gesturing seemed to propel Oliver into motion and he came across the field toward them, leaning forward, stomping his feet, his face nearly purple with rage. "This is none of your business."

Adam stepped closer to Oliver. "You made it our business. Now shut up and listen."

Joe took an envelope out of his pocket and handed it to Oliver. "Open it."

Inside was a color copy of the photograph. Oliver went ashen, his freckles marking his cheeks like spots of ink. "Here's what you're going to do," said Joe. "On the band bus this week, you're going to apologize to Morgan for treating her this way. You don't have to be specific. I don't want her further shamed. Write out your apology and Paul will fix it. Next, you stop this. When you're in school, on the bus, at parties, anywhere that's public, you keep your hands off Morgan."

"You can't make me do anything."

"Any slip up or any rumor of a slip up and I send these copies out. One goes to Morgan's dad, one goes to Mrs. Poulard, and one goes to your dad. And remember, I made copies like that one."

"You don't have the balls," Oliver said.

Paul said, "It takes balls to do the right thing, Ollie. Try it."

"I'm telling Coach MacBride about this. Teammates are supposed to stick together."

"If you weren't our teammate, your ass would be toasting over hot coals right now in Mrs. Poulard's office," Adam said.

"My dad'll get your dad fired. He'll stop this."

"Go ahead, Ollie," Joe said. "You just go ahead and tell."

Oliver pushed through the Ridout brothers and stomped up the sloping hill to the school. They watched him go across the field to where Mrs. Miller stood. Humbly, head hanging down, he spoke to her.

"Uh-oh," Jon said, "he's making up some whopper to tell Mrs. Miller."

"Yep," Paul said, "here she comes. After us for who knows what." The band director marched toward them, leaning forward, her furious expression evident even at a distance.

"Quick," Joe said to Paul, "Give Adam your tuba." Paul hoisted it up from where he had rested it on the grass. As Joe dug his keys out of his pocket he told Adam, "Now get ready to give a few long blasts, that part from the first movement."

"You can't fool her into thinking we're practicing," Jon said, reaching for his trumpet anyway.

Joe ripped the dangling plastic eyeball off his key chain and shoved it into Adam's huge hand. "Go for it, Adam," Joe said.

Grinning, Adam turned away from the boys, waiting for Mrs. Miller to get closer. When she reached the base of the hill, he blasted a few loud notes on his brother's tuba, let out a primal scream, covering his wounded eye. Paul grabbed the tuba as it fell and the boys all screamed in shock and horror. Adam took off running toward Mrs. Miller, holding his eye, crying, "No! No! You were right, Mrs. Miller! You were right!"

She stood straight for a second, then dashed toward Adam at a frantic pace, arms outstretched to him. "Call an ambulance," she screamed. "Someone's got to have a cell phone! Call nine-one-one!"

"My eyeball, my eyeball," Adam screamed. "I blew on my tuba and it popped out. Just like you said!"

She was beside him in a moment, both little hands on his massive biceps. "Come on, let me see. Adam, sweetie, let me see."

Adam took his hand from his eye and dropped the plastic eyeball into her palm. She screamed and dropped it, then stood stunned for several long seconds watching it bounce and roll in the grass while the boys around her shrieked with laughter. Her mouth opened. Her mouth shut. She pointed up at Adam's grinning face. "That was the cruelest possible joke. Never in all my years! Never!" The boys saw that she was going to cry.

Immediately they surrounded her, offering honeyed apologies, though their glee still shone in their eyes. She would have none of their penitence and, wiping away tears, waved them away with a promise of detentions and worse. As she stomped away, they heard her vow, "I don't need this grief. They don't pay me enough for this."

"I don't care what happens to us," Jon said. "That was so worth it."

"You are honestly a genius, Joe," Paul said.

"Let's hope so," Joe said. They were still laughing when they took their places with the assembled band, the innocent members baffled by Mrs. Miller's fury. When Adam tried to take his place in the formation she simply pointed at him and then pointed to the instrument cart, which meant he was not allowed on the field. Oliver tried to speak, raising his hand and calling out that he had something to share, but Mrs. Miller silenced him and the boys grinned at each other, pleased that they had fooled Mrs. Miller into thinking Oliver was part of the prank. By the end of practice, the story had been whispered all through the ranks and Ben noticed the admiring glances directed toward Joe. He wondered why Joe seemed to be oblivious to these; Joe looked distracted, though he did smile a little when Adam brought Mrs. Miller a bunch of wild flowers and went down on one knee to present them to her, before kissing her dusty work boots.

At dinner, Laurie asked, "How was band?"

"Fine," Joe and Bonnie Jean said, simultaneously, careful not to look at each other.

"Too bad about band practice this week," Peter said. "The team needs you."

"Yeah," Joe said, watching the gravy fill the holes he made with his fork in the mashed potatoes.

"We can work with the JV and the sophomores on Wednesday and Friday. We'll have the entire team two days this week," Tom said. "Glad you're willing to help while you're home, Peter."

Joe nodded without looking up. Bonnie Jean chased a pea around her plate.

"Heard lots of laughing in the locker room after practice," Tom said. "Did you have fun today?"

Joe and Bonnie Jean shrugged. "You know," Joe said. "Same ol', same ol'."

"Do you really have to be there?" Tommy asked.

"No," Joe said, glancing at him.

"We never do anything," Bonnie Jean said. "This time of the season. The guys could all go, 'cept for Oliver, 'cause he's got a trumpet solo."

"I promised Mrs. Miller could have you Monday, Wednesday and Friday," Tom said. "The last competition is important to the band."

"But imagine practice without Oliver," Joe said, glancing briefly at his father, meeting his eyes for the first time in a couple of days. Tom held his glance, eyes careful.

"How are things going with Oliver?" Laurie asked.

"Aw, you know," Joe said.

"Are you feeling okay, Joe?" his mother said. "You haven't eaten much."

Joe met her eyes briefly. "I'm fine, Mama."

"Really?"

"Don't worry, Mama."

"Too bad Ben's not here," Tommy said. "He could change the subject for you, Joe."

"Yeah," Joe said and smiled. "Ben's good at that."

21

TOWARD the end of English class, last of the day, Ben noticed that Jon, who sat beside him, was squirming and twitching at random intervals. The normally cheerful Mrs. Campbell rushed to list the ways she required them to fix their papers due tomorrow. Leaning back slightly Ben saw that Adam Ridout sat forward, his gigantic forearms extending nearly to the chair in front occupied by Jon. Adam barely had to move to reach Jon and with a stoic expression on his face, his eyes fixed on Mrs. Campbell, he poked Jon's ribs. Jon reached behind him with slow caution and the next time Adam poked him, he grabbed Adam's finger and twisted it. Adam shrieked, a ridiculous high gasp of pain. Jon released Adam's finger and sat perfectly still.

"Whatever is the matter, Adam?"

"Nothing, Mrs. Campbell, sorry."

"People don't *shriek* when nothing's wrong."

"Oh, well, my paper needs *so much* work."

"Don't let it happen again." She returned to preaching about the paper's thesis when Adam poked Jon three times rapidly. Holding himself still despite the tickling, Jon moved his hand back and with a skillful lurch backward caught Adam's finger. Silent this time, Adam struggled to get away, but everyone around him saw and the giggling was audible.

Mrs. Campell said, "Adam Ridout. Let go of Jon's hand. What are you doing? Grabbing someone during lecture? You see me after class." Her eyes flashed her indignation and while she was staring Jon and Adam down, Joe scribbled a note to Ben on the corner of his notebook.

I hope Dad's thinking we should concentrate on offense today. Without moving his head, Ben chewed his pencil for a moment before answering.

Ben wrote Tom's favorite saying, *Defense is money in the bank.*

We've been doing defense forever. I'm running that corner trap in my sleep.

I bet we do rebound drills. He knew Joe hated rebound drills and he wished he could grin at him. *Get the rebound and score.*

Shit, Joe wrote. *Shit, shit, and double shit.*

Mrs. Campbell, stepping back to glance at her notes, said, "What's the last thing you wrote, Joe?"

Joe sat up straight, his eyes immediately wide. "Pardon me, ma'am?"

"I want the class to hear how you expressed the idea of a thesis. What did you write down? I saw you writing."

"I...uh...thesis is the..." Joe looked down at his paper to make it seem as if he were reading. "It's the statement in the first paragraph that explains why your paper is important." Joe looked up, frowning slightly, his discomfort showing.

"Please read your thesis to us, Joe."

Joe flipped back pages in his notes, glanced at the clock, looked around the room and said, "Okay...'Because Dimmesdale fails to find personal growth in his seven-year determination to punish his hidden sin, he subtly proclaims Hawthorne's distrust of the Transcendentalist's commitment to self-reliance.'"

"Good. Excellent. And you have research and quotes to help prove that?" she said. When Joe nodded, she looked at Ben. "How can he improve it?"

Ben leaned over to look at Joe's notebook. "I think Joe needs an adjective to describe what he calls the 'seven-year determination.' Like solitary or silent or self-imposed. Yeah," Ben said, glancing at Joe, his eyes merry. "Dimmesdale's solitary, silent, seven-year determination—"

"Po-etic," Adam said, his voice approaching shriek as Jon again caught and twisted his finger.

"Can I use that word for word?" Joe asked.

Ben nodded. "By saying what *kind of struggle*," Ben paused, glancing at Joe, his eyes bright, "Joe will have defined the basic failure in the philosophy, which the adjective he chooses will...*illuminate*."

"Illuminate?" Joe muttered, "I'll illuminate you."

"Don't tell me you're feeling a bit vulnerable, Joe," Mrs. Campbell said as the bell rang. Over the class's laughter, the teacher told Joe that his thesis was excellent, but she wanted to see him and Ben after class.

"I know you were writing notes," she said to Ben and Joe, before pointing at Jon and Adam. "But first you two."

"I didn't do *anything*, Mrs. Campbell," Jon said. "Adam is always picking on me."

"Adam. You are so much bigger than him."

Adam was outraged. "He grabbed my finger!"

"You did have your hand behind you, Jon," Mrs. Campbell said, considering them.

Indignant, Jon's voice went high. "That's because he was *poking* me! Here—I'll show you." Jon lunged at Adam like a small puppy throwing himself at a bear, fingers extended. Adam ducked, shielding himself as if from wild bullets, crying, "Stop! Ow!" Adam crouched forward, holding one hand out to stave off the attack; doubled over, he was taller than Jon. "Help!"

"Any more poking," Mrs. Campbell said, "and you've got detentions." But they could still hear her laughing when the door shut behind them.

"Once again, Joe MacBride and friends escape unscathed," Adam said, as Ben and Joe emerged from the classroom. Adam draped his right arm onto Jon and his left across Joe's shoulders, reaching all the way to the middle of Ben's back.

"Nobody can touch me at this school," Joe said, with a huge, contented sigh.

"Yeah," Adam said, "I'm feeling mighty good. I disrupted class, got away without a detention, and we got our first big game tomorrow, men."

Jon said, "First game means Coach is gonna be a maniac today."

"Joe says only offense today."

"Good. If I have to practice any more free throws, I'll free throw up," Jon said.

"Free throws are offense, aren't they?" Adam said.

"Yes, stupid," Joe said, swatting Jon's head, "They're scoring."

"So," Ben said, thinking out loud. "We'll go over that anticipation thing he's big on—"

"Yeah, and tell me this, new kid, how'd you get to be so freakin' good at free throws?" Jon said, reaching around Adam to poke at Ben, who dodged the assault.

"Practice," Ben grinned.

"How'd you get to be so freakin' good at everything?" Joe said. "How did you listen to my thesis—which was really complex—listen to it one time and come up with all that stuff. What *the hell* was that?"

"Shh!" Adam said. "Coach is comin' out the office door, man."

"Shit," Joe whispered, going wide-eyed to see his father there, at the office door, holding the door open, but talking to someone just inside so that his face was turned from them. His friends laughed out loud at him; Adam shoved Joe into Ben while Jon shrieked, "If you coulda seen your face."

Adam said, "But really, Joe, your language gets so bad during basketball. I'm genuinely shocked."

"It's the old testosterone surging," Joe grinned at them.

"Now you sound like Oliver," Jon said.

"Take that back or I'll poke you to a bloody pulp."

Practice in Tom MacBride's gym had proven to be satisfying and fun for Ben. The initial four days, Tom worked them so hard that anybody not dedicated to playing hard and loving it would quit. He told the boys trying out, "If you survive past Friday, you're mine; you can't quit. So if you're gonna quit, do it by Friday afternoon." Legend had it that Tom hadn't had to cut a kid for the past nine years, though at the mention of this statistic, Joe and Peter laughed, calling it an exaggeration. Rumor or not, Ben watched the four kids he knew would never make ball players struggle and, one by one, stop by Tom's office after practice to break the news to him in private.

But those days were past, and the team was set, excited and getting ready. The reason for this was that Tom was organized, he emphasized the basics, and he approached basketball with an analytical intelligence akin to Ben's own. Tom actually wrote a schedule for each practice, which he kept on an index card folded over the waistband of his gym shorts. The holes in game plans that usually frustrated Ben, the weaknesses in skill that dragged a team down, Tom saw and worked with strenuous method to address. He pushed them in a fast-paced, demanding practice schedule so that playing a scrimmage was a relief.

And best of all, Tom never blew up. He liked basketball, came to practice in an energetic mood, and if they worked as hard as he demanded, he was smiling when he left. He loved the strategies, the energy and the competition. "Basketball is war," he liked to say, eyes alight with something more intense than determination, "each play's a battle to be won." He loved displays of talent and nodded in approval anytime they took a credible shot. Sure, he didn't want them throwing the shot away, or giving a premature heave at the basket that had nothing to do with instinct, but he wanted them taking the kinds of risks that Ben loved taking. This is what Ben liked about Tom's intelligent practicality. "You can't score unless you take a shot," Tom said at least ten times each practice.

Oliver was the only dark blot with his bragging and his sullen resistance to Tom's coaching. Now with the deadline Joe had set, Ben saw the anger building in Oliver's eyes.

That afternoon began as it always did with stretches in the gym.

"Remember that time Noah got pulled over on Bestgate," Scott said, one foot behind the other, hands clasped behind his back, "and the cop let him off with a warning."

"And *how* does that help Joe, exactly?" Jon said. "He already *got* the ticket."

Knox offered, "I went to court this summer for a speeding ticket and the judge took the points away. Your dad's letter really helped. The judge went to school with your dad or something."

"*Everybody's* been to school with my dad," Joe murmured.

"The judge was nice about it. Mentioned him saving that drowning kid and everything."

"I don't think he was actually drowning," Joe said.

"Not what I heard," said Flip. "My dad told me the kid was drowning *and* he had a broken back—"

Joe shot a warning glance at his cousin. "You know my dad doesn't want us exaggerating about stuff like this."

"Who says I'm exaggerating?"

"When Unca Doug gets here to help with practice, I'll ask him. Okay?"

"Anyway," Knox sighed, "I appreciated it. Your dad's help this summer."

A brief, awkward silence stretched between them as the boys recognized Knox's effort to connect with them. Before Oliver could ruin the moment with an attack on Knox, Drew said, "Yeah, you're right, Knox. That's a good idea. I know other guys who said going to court helps."

"I'd think you'd want to serve the full punishment," Oliver said to Joe. "My dad got caught at one of those red light cameras and he felt like he ought to pay double, just to chastise himself."

"Oh, brother," Paul said.

"Being caught by cameras runs in the family," Joe said, looking directly at Oliver.

"Yeah, Oliver," Jon said. "What'd you decide to do about the pictures Joe got?"

"Shut up!" Oliver warned, looking dangerous to Ben.

"He's got 'til Friday to get up the courage to apologize to Morgan," Ben told Jon.

"Shut it," Oliver said, leaving his stretch to lunge at Ben.

Knox stepped between them, blocking Oliver with a shoulder to his chest. "Coach is here. Chill."

"Yeah," Drew said. "We told you. You don't *touch* your teammates."

"Coach won't like you guys picking on me."

"Coach'll like those pictures even less," Drew said, "so just shut up and be grateful we're letting you play on this team. All we have to do is hand him those pictures and you're history."

"Nuh-uh," Oliver said, "Coach hasn't cut a kid in ten years."

Joe rolled his eyes and shook his head, turning away. His team members did likewise, refusing to argue. The pressure they kept on Oliver was by mutual consent, fueled with their shared disgust. As Joe had put it, "It would be one thing if he were just hurting himself. But he's hurting Morgan, and it needs to stop." After their initial confrontation when they showed him the photographs, Oliver had claimed he needed time to pray and talk to his pastor. Joe had agreed to move the deadline, though to a man, they were sickened by Oliver's religious manipulation; now they waited, wary of his temper and his weird, offensive approach to life and faith, waited for him to—as Joe said to them yesterday—"man up."

Joe leaned over to him and said quietly, "We don't want you *cut*, Ollie. We want you to *change*."

"Stretched out?" Tom called as he limped toward them.

"Yeah," Joe said. "Are you?"

"Been stretching in my office while I was on the phone," Tom joked, coming up beside Joe and greeting him as he usually did during practice, with one arm around his shoulders while pretending to slap Joe's stomach with his clipboard.

"Oof," Joe said, laughing. "Mom said I'm not to let you practice with us unless you stretch out."

Tom tossed his clipboard to Brock and led the boys in their final stretches, watching them when they reached the last one, where, sitting on the floor, each player had to bend one knee back and touch his forehead to his extended knee. At this point Tom walked through the group, checking on each boy's flexibility.

When he was beside Ben, Tom said, "I didn't see your stretch," which meant he had to repeat it. Reaching for his toes, Ben touched his head to his knee easily.

"Good," Tom said. "Other leg."

Ben clasped his hands behind his back and bent again, touching his forehead all the way to the floor.

"Okay. I see what you're made of today," Tom said.

"Everybody see that?" Drew said. "Show 'em, Ben."

Ben repeated his feat, then, tucking his feet under, stood up quickly. "Let's play ball."

"First, prayer," Tom reminded him, one arm going around Ben's shoulder.

The team circled around Tom and he offered a short prayer. Ben had that same expectant feeling, but when he opened his eyes, Oliver was staring at him, eyes resentful and hurt.

Ben knew what it was about, Oliver's resentment of him. Jeff had told Ben that since last year, Oliver had been saying he'd start as point guard. At the end of the first week of practice, Tom had spoken to the best players, explaining how he saw things and why. Oliver's bragging and whining had increased with each scrimmage that Ben started as point guard. Ben supposed Oliver had hoped something would change before the first game, but Ben suspected, with a quiet and secret joy, that Tom was one of those rare coaches who knew that Oliver's attitude would poison the team.

Waiting for the start of the rebounding drill, Peter stood with the ball cage beside him, chucking ball after ball at the net. The boys lined up in their practice groups; the best players wore the gold side of their practice jerseys out and these grabbed balls from the cage and the floor, while the athletes wearing the blue side out trotted to the other end of the gym with Mr. Ridout and Al Brock, an alumnus who was the youth pastor at a local church. Doug Davidson, Flip's father, sprinted into the gym—just on time for his first day helping. Waving, he jogged up to Tom and shook his hand.

"Men, I want you to meet my brother-in-law, Doug Davidson," Tom said to the team, "Flip's dad. He played varsity ball in high school, club ball at Navy. He runs like a cheetah and he's fierce as death itself. So he's going to help us today." He motioned for Doug to join the gold shirts before saying, "Today you're going to use some of the skills we've been practicing as you work on keeping your cool. I don't want you waiting for the ref to call fouls on the other team and then get outraged when he doesn't. We had a problem with this last year. Remember? Refs don't call every foul and you've got to trust me and Coach Brock. We are going to be watching the game. Okay? If the ref is calling it slant, I promise you, I'll do what I can. But if you are waiting around for the ref to call fouls, you'll miss rebounds and all kinds of opportunities and you're going to fight about as effectively as a squashed bug does and that will *really* bother me. So, when you take a shot, these big guys will hack you. You don't let it get to you. Use the moves we've been practicing and work them out hard. If you get mad or you give up, you run. That will happen when we play, too. You show temper out there, I'm sitting you down. You get a technical for temper and you're out for the game. Understand? Play it cool and swift and hard."

"Coach?" Oliver said. "I don't think you should use running for punishment; some people love it."

Tom stared at Oliver for a full ten seconds. Quietly he said, "But you can count on me to do as I said," before speaking loudly to the entire team. "Score on those big guys, no matter what they do to you. Let's get started."

"Hey, Unca Doug," Joe said, tossing a ball to the muscular, dark-haired man whose eyes were precisely the same color as Bonnie Jean's. Ben recognized him from somewhere.

"How's it going, little Joe?" Doug punched Joe's shoulder.

"Can we call you Uncle Doug, too?" Jon said, shaking Doug's hand.

"Why not? I think I've met all you guys one time or the other. Except for this one," he said indicating Ben with a nod.

"This is Ben," Joe said. "He's new this year."

"Nice to meet you," Doug said, grabbing Ben's hand in a firm grip. He cocked his head a little when they shook hands, and his eyes opened wider.

"Unca Doug," Joe said, bumping into his uncle's shoulder affectionately, "Were you there when Dad saved that drowning kid?"

"No," Doug said, looking absently at Ben, his gaze sweeping once over Ben from head to toe. "I was zooming over the desert de*mol*ishing stuff for *Un*cle *Saaaam*." He motioned with both hands.

"Was the kid actually drowning?"

"Not according to Tom, and the newspaper didn't mention drowning. I don't know how deep it was."

"Newspaper?"

"Yeah, we'd better get practice goin' or your dad'll fire my sculpted Italian ass."

The boys lined up for the drill. Peter tossed the ball against the backboard and Knox, first in line, went after the rebound. Doug shoved up against him and Peter grabbed his wrist. Knox struggled, but Peter knocked the ball away. Knox went after it.

"Is he your mom's brother?" Ben asked Joe.

"My mom's *twin*, actually."

Paul could out-leap Doug, but he was equally matched in Peter. He got his hands on the ball and dribbled once. Peter slapped at it, shoving his hip into Paul's. Ben glanced to Tom to see him making notes on his clipboard. Paul, nearly squatting, attempted a shot that Doug and Peter shut down.

Doug stopped the play and told Paul he had to take advantage of his height. "Why bring the ball down to earth where the rest of us guys are? Don't squat. Shoot from up there. You bring the ball down here, we can all reach it."

"He's in pretty good shape," Ben said to Joe.

"Yeah, he runs. Fanatically."

"Oh. Right. That's where I've seen him before," Ben said, remembering Doug as the man who gave him water that day he ran so far. "Does he run with his dog?"

"Muffin. His black lab. She goes *everywhere* with him. She's probably in my dad's office right now."

It was Oliver's turn and Oliver could jump. He got the rebound glaring at Peter when he body-blocked him. He took the ball out, dribbling, and drove back for the basket, his form good. Peter stayed on him, reaching over his back, slapping at the ball, and finally catching it with the tips of his fingers, sending it flying. Oliver went after it, but so did Doug, and they ended up in a footrace for the sideline; they both dove for the ball and Doug crashed into Oliver, sending him sliding into the wall.

The boys yelled, "Jump ball!" and Tom came closer, his whistle blaring.

"Uncle Doug, he's crazy fun," Joe whispered to Ben. "He used to be a navy test pilot. Now he flies a Medivac helicopter."

"Good hustle, Ollie." Tom offered Oliver a hand up, but Oliver ignored Tom's hand and, rolling onto his knee, stood up, his jaw clenched. Tom said, "Notice how Ollie didn't wait for the ref to rescue him when Peter illegally got that ball loose. That's the way to do it."

"Good job, Ollie," Drew said as they passed when Drew approached the key.

Though Drew was not as tall as Peter he was quick, strong, athletic, and he was not particularly afraid of anyone. He had played ball with Peter since they were ten years old and when Peter went to chop at his arm with his fist, Drew twisted, shoving his shoulder into Peter's chin, getting the ball in his hand. Drew took his shot. It wobbled in the rim; Drew leapt up, and though Doug grabbed Drew's elbow, Drew tipped the ball in and came back to the line a triumphant man, while Tom called, "Great follow up, Drew."

Ben moved up close to Joe's shoulder while they were watching Scott. Ben whispered, "They expect everyone to go right, so once you come down with the rebound, keep the ball high and pump right. Then go up strong when they're on the way down."

"Just hope I can *get* that rebound," Joe grinned back at him. Peter bounced the ball off the backboard. When Joe went for it, Doug reached for Joe's face. Peter jumped too, reaching up over Joe's back for the ball. Joe flicked it back over his shoulder to Ben, who caught it, dribbled twice and passed it back to Joe who caught it, went high and pumped as if he were anxious to chuck it away. They followed, and Joe, jumping a bit as they were coming down, made a clean, two-handed shot that dropped in easily.

"Hey," Peter laughed, "no fair using the secret weapon."

"Nice fake, Joe," Tom called. "Good teamwork."

"It worked, didn't it?" Ben said, as he stepped forward for his turn. He watched Peter toss the ball and knew it would bounce left. Ben zipped around Doug to get it. Doug grabbed his elbow and yanked hard. Ben watched the ball's arc and twisted, and reaching hard with his free hand, scooped the ball out of the air and gave it a quick upward shove toward the basket. It banked off the backboard and swished through the net. Ben could hear Adam cheer as he fell, landing on Doug's foot and kind of bouncing onto the floor. "What just happened?" Doug muttered from where he lay on the floor. From the direction of Tom's office a dog barked, then barked again loudly enough to sound above the hollering of his teammates and Jon's squeaky whisper, "How'd he *do* that?"

Ben scrambled to his feet and offered Doug a hand. "You okay?"

Doug's black lab ran to him, barking her concern, bounding onto the court toward Doug. "Knew she'd open that door, just knew it," he muttered. He took Ben's hand and, once standing, said, "That was beautiful." He pounded Ben's shoulder and looked at him again, studying his face. "Why do I keep getting the idea we've met before?" Muffin got between them sniffing Ben's knees, tickling him, then licking his knee. "Stop it, Muffin."

"I think I've seen you out running with your dog, Mr.—uh—"

"You run?"

"Yes, sir."

"Maybe that's it," Doug said. "Muffin seems to know you. But call me Doug. Not Mr. Davidson." Doug looked at the line of boys before him. "Anybody see how he did that? I'm pullin' him to the floor, and I don't think he even knows who it is who's got him."

"You keep that up, Ben. Fight for the ball," Tom said, meeting his eyes. "You're doing great."

"How about I fight *you* for the ball, Coach," Ben said.

"You sure you're tough enough? I don't want you scared away from my gym."

"Yep. I'm sure."

"I'll give you exactly one minute." Drew tossed the ball up and Tom grabbed Ben's shoulder as he jumped. Tom pushed down, keeping Ben away, got the ball and laughed at Ben's protests.

Ben dashed after him, faced him. "Slow dribble, Coach, easy to steal. Want me to show you how I do it?"

"Is that your best taunt, Ben?"

"At least I'm not wearing a loser shirt like you."

"What's wrong with this shirt?" Tom said, swinging his hip into Ben, he switched the ball to his left hand. He drove toward the basket, switching hands again to weave around Drew, only to meet Ben face to face. Adam dogged Tom, moving his hands through Tom's peripheral vision.

"I hate to break it to you, Coach, but nobody listens to Kris Kross anymore."

"Pete wore this in seventh grade," Tom said.

"You're wearing your kids' hand-me-down T-shirts?" Ben laughed at him. "Pathetic."

Tom met Ben's eyes with a brief laughing glance, took the ball on the up-dribble, and lifted it toward the basket. Ben grabbed it, spun away, dribbling a rapid drum beat to the boys chanting, "Ball hawk, ball hawk." At center court, he turned, his right shoulder to Tom; he saw his shot, left the floor, and made a smooth, high shot. Too late, Tom grabbed Ben's arm and Ben crashed to the floor. Muffin barked the alarm and went to lick Ben's face. But Ben got up and stared at the floor. "Oh, man! I'm so sorry, Coach! I dented your floor."

Above their laughter, Tom said, "Okay, men, back to work. We've got a game tomorrow."

22

MUFFIN at his side and calmed down, Doug joined Tom at the sidelines to watch them run fast break drills. Muffin nosed Tom's palm, then licked his fingertips. Tom patted her head and she sat down between the two men.

"Kid Oliver's got an attitude."

"Flip's doin' well. He's gonna be a maniac on defense, just like his dad."

"Yeah. He's enjoyin' it, Tom. He's just afraid he made the team because he's your nephew."

Tom shook his head, "He's already proven himself."

"Flip tells me the kids are putting pressure on Oliver about something he did to a girl. Something on the bus back from band. He says Joe's given him a week to straighten up."

"Ah, I've been trying to find out what's been going on. I guess I'd better find out from Joe—"

"No." Doug folded his arms, watching the team. "Let Joe handle it. He's trying to help the kid."

"You think so? No harassing going on?"

"Just the good kind. But I think Oliver's also gotta be upset about the new kid. He's incredible. He's a hundred million miles beyond Oliver."

"Yeah," Tom said softly. Muffin stood up, eyes suddenly intent on the boys running.

"I keep thinking I've seen him before."

Tom opened his mouth to say it and stopped just in time. He looked at Doug and saw that Doug had not noticed Tom's near gaffe. Why had he agreed to Doug helping with the team? Why had he not foreseen this complication? Muffin sensed his turmoil and jumped up, her forepaws on his waist. She sniffed at his chest and chin.

"Down, girl. Mind your manners."

Tom knew that once Doug recognized Ben, once he put things together, Tom would have no more time for earning Ben's trust. And once Doug knew who Ben was there was no governing what Doug would say. He, Tom's closest friend, knew everything…pretty much everything.

"Maybe that or maybe he reminds me of somebody," Doug mused.

Feeling dishonest, Tom thought, *I'm running out of time.* If Doug's work schedule allowed him to come to practice regularly, it wouldn't be long before he saw Ben's name printed somewhere or—more likely—recognized the blue of Katie's eyes, the color of her skin, the set of Katie's mouth. In their Academy days, when they were running together along the sea wall in the predawn darkness, Doug had confided his torturing, devoted love for that compelling blond beauty who had dumped him for his own sister's boyfriend.

It had taken Doug years of trying to scare himself in navy jets to get over her. Tom thought, *Understandably so.* She had fascinated so many men in their small sphere. Impulsively, Tom put his arm around Doug's shoulder and hugged him with sympathy and compassion.

"Hey, Doug…"

"What?"

"We've been through a lot together and I love you. You know that?"

"Shit, Tom, don't say that kind of thing in *public*," Doug winced, despite his arm going around Tom's back. He patted Tom's waist with warm, hearty affection.

"I mean it, Doug. Thanks for coming out to help with the team. You're great with kids."

"You're the most sentimental son of a bitch I've ever met, Tom MacBride. I swear."

"Yeah, and I wish you wouldn't."

"And you're so tight-assed about language. I'd think you were a prude if—" he looked up at Tom grinning "—if we hadn't gotten into some pretty good scrapes together. Shit, every time I think about the stuff we did to Bulldog Charlie Johnson, I pee my pants laughing."

"Good times."

"Remember how mad your dad was that time on leave when we came home drunk?"

"Yeah. I'll never forget."

"Ruined you as my drinking buddy. If your dad wasn't such a great guy, I'd resent him for that."

Tom laughed. "So much for me trying to fix you up with *my* sister."

"Your sister was *not* my type, Tom MacBride. Scariest woman I ever met, next to your mother."

Tom laughed again. "Wish she were here to tell Ollie to sweeten up about not playing point."

Doug shook his head. "Kid's got enough problems without wishing *that* on him. But you got no choice, Tom. The new kid is *so much* better. And it's obvious Ollie can't lead with his attitude. You'd let the kids down if you pretended not to see just 'cuz ol' John Saunders gonna chew your skinny ass for it."

"I'm gonna tell him it was your decision. That way he can break his teeth on that bowling ball you call a butt."

After practice Peter lay on the bench between the lockers; his knees were bent, his head cradled in his hands. "What kind of noise was it making?" Paul said, rubbing his towel over his dark, cropped hair.

"Kind of a rough sound when you accelerate," Peter said, yawning widely, "Dad thinks it's missing. We took it over to Darden's this morning before school. Then I went and helped Mom at the store. Ate breakfast and lunch there. The food was *so good*. No joke. The food at college sucks so *bad*. You eat it and it doesn't do anything for you. No flavor, no nourished feeling. Nothing."

"You been spoiled by your mom's cooking," Jon said.

"Yeah," Joe said, joining them and snapping his towel at Peter's knees. "He's spoiled and he's soft and just a little girl. That's why Dad likes *me* more. I got testosterone pumping through my veins at a frightening percentage."

"Half bullshit, half testosterone," Drew said, shoving Joe playfully.

"If Dad likes you more, why are you always trying to get his attention?"

"Like when?"

"Like always," Paul said.

"I am not."

"Like smoking," Peter said. "Like getting a three-hundred-dollar speeding ticket."

"I was trying to *avoid* his attention, then, big brother. You haven't heard me volunteering information about our little trip to New Jersey or meeting distant relatives or getting speeding tickets or any of the fun stuff that happened up there."

"How do you think practice went?" Paul said.

Peter looked around to see if Ben were in earshot and when he saw him coming from the showers, he said, "I think we got ourselves an ace. A left-handed ace, boys." He smiled faintly at Ben, then lay back down. "Which helps make up for the lingering stench."

"Ollie left without taking a shower," whispered Jon.

"I think Joe's gonna cure him of showing his dick in public," Drew said.

"You think he'll submit to your terms?" Peter said, glancing around at his brother and friends.

"He has to. We know that stuff about talking to his pastor was a stalling technique."

"Meantime, he's working on the female population."

"What d'you mean?"

"Now it's like he's got *three* girlfriends. And Morgan doesn't seem to mind."

"Except she looks like she's crying all the time," Ben said.

"He's hanging around with Madison and Leeza now. And sometimes Tiffany. So, four."

"Leeza?" Peter said with a quick glance at Joe, who shrugged.

"She's okay," Joe said. "She doesn't take shit from anybody."

"Things completely over between you two?

Joe winced. "Nothing ever really got started with me and Leeza. We were just getting cozy when I locked her and the rest of the cheerleaders in the locker room, sooo—"

"Leeza's too feisty for you, Joe," Adam said, dropping a huge fist gently onto Joe's shoulder in an attempt to console.

"And too short," said Paul.

"And golden boy?" Peter said, glancing at Ben. "Is he in business yet?"

Ben shrugged and grinned. "Her dad won't let her date me."

"Won't let her date at all," Joe corrected.

"Bonnie Jean?" Peter said. "You know what you're getting into?" Ben shrugged again.

"What about you, Pete?" Adam said.

Peter shrugged. "I don't know. College girls."

"I can't believe it," Tom's voice surprised them from the door, invisible from their lockers. "I can probably count on one hand the times I've heard you admit you don't know something."

Adam rolled his eyes and whispered, "Will he *never* learn to knock?"

"I need you two," he pointed to Ben and Joe, "to hurry. We've got to stop at Grannie's on the way home."

"*We?*" Joe said. "What for?"

"I'm riding with you in the MG."

"What happened to *your* car?"

"They're both my cars, laddie," Tom said. "The one I usually drive is in the shop."

"That's what I was telling Paul," Peter said.

"Aw, man, it's *new*," Joe whined. "And I was gonna take Ben over to pick up his car. It's finally ready."

"We can do that afterwards," Tom said. "I'd like to see it anyway."

Ben nodded. "They're open late tonight."

Peter, Ben and Joe wrapped Grannie's air conditioner in a canvas tarp and carried it to the little shed at the back of her property while Tom worked in the basement to test a pipe he'd repaired the previous weekend. Rather than have them wait idly for Tom, Grannie directed the boys to carry her wood in from the backyard and bundle up the newspapers for recycling. When they were finished, they drifted into the kitchen in search of a snack.

Hers was a small house, tidy and quiet, with a faint scent coming from the gas stove. The counters stood in strict order, showing only a toaster, clean dishes and jars beside the sink, an electric coffee percolator, a small jar with lollipops in it, and one bowl of apples. Eyes sparkling, Joe took an apple, tossed it up and caught it.

"Maybe we shouldn't do this here," Peter said as he caught the apple Joe flung across the small kitchen. Peter tossed it over the little square table to Ben.

"Yeah," Ben agreed, giving the apple a gentle, high arch, easy for Joe to catch. "We don't want to break anything here."

"We've played this game for years and we've never broken anything except that one time with Ben." Joe winged it to his brother.

"Notice, Joe, I'm here again. If I'm the bad luck charm—" Ben warned, catching Peter's second toss and passing it swiftly to Joe.

"I don't believe in luck," Joe said. He tossed the apple straight up, caught it and tossed it again, this time ducking his shoulder so that he caught it behind his back. Peter and Ben murmured their approval. He tossed it a third time, dipped his shoulder again, but the apple hit his shoulder blade and bounced away into the canning jars, just washed and draining on the side of the sink. They leapt and crashed like bowling pins, smashing in the spotless white bowl of the sink.

"Uh-oh," said Joe.

Grannie appeared at the door with the urgency of a police car. "What's the meaning of this mischief, Joseph MacBride?" she shrilled, eyes ablaze with the certainty of swift judgment.

"What makes you think it was me?" Joe said.

"'Tis always you."

"Grannie," Joe pleaded, hands out to her. The old woman strode to the sink with a powerful determination that belied her age. When she saw the broken glasses, she let out a cry of one bereaved, lifting her apron to her mouth to muffle her wailing. "Those jars are ones my Eddie bought me."

Joe said. "I'll clean it up."

"I'll see to it that your father punishes you for this."

"Grannie," Peter said. "It was an accident."

Joe, beside her at the sink, bent to get the trash can. Grannie began pounding his shoulder with her small, bony fist. "Are you daft? The glass will cut open the plastic bag. You're a—"

"Stop hitting him," Tom's voice cut in. "Mother, I should not have to tell you—you're not to *hit* Joe."

"He deserved it, and more."

"There should be paper bags under the sink, Joe," Tom said. "Folded and standing up beside the trash can. Use one of those." He touched Joe's shoulder and said, "What happened?"

Joe swallowed audibly and without looking up from his task, said, "It was my fault. I started the apple game. Pete warned me not to."

"Y'see? Peter wasna at fault."

"I threw it as many times as Joe did, Grannie," Peter said. "I'm just as much to blame."

Grannie made a dismissive noise.

Tom said. "How did the jars break?"

"We tossed it around awhile and I started to feel guilty, like maybe Pete was right, and I was a little worried about Ben's arm in this small kitchen, so I started juggling it and I tried to catch it behind my back and I missed."

Tom looked to the other boys. "It hit his shoulder," Ben said, "and took a weird bounce."

"Dad—I—I may have been showing off," Joe said softly, bending closer to the sink so that he could pick up the tiny shards remaining.

"May have?"

"Yeah, I was."

"Be careful with that glass, son," Tom said.

"He deserves to be cut," Joe's grandmother said.

Tom turned to her, eyes bright and angry. "You don't mean that, Mother."

"I do mean it. You're to whip him. I demand it."

"I'll not paddle a kid for an innocent accident."

"I'll do it myself. *You* know I can."

"That is enough," Tom thundered. His mother gaped at him, then shut her mouth so hard that her teeth crashing together made sound. Tom grabbed a paper towel from the roll by the sink. "Are you finished?" he said to Joe.

"Almost," Joe said.

"Stand aside." Tom wet the paper towel and ran it over the sink surface, shoved it in the paper bag, took another towel so quickly that the roll hopped and clattered. He wiped the sink again, rinsed it, ran his hand over the surface, then snatched the paper bag, turned to Peter and Ben, and said, "Let's go." He put his arm around Joe and turned him toward the door. "Come on."

Tom held the door and waited for the boys to go through. He stepped over the threshold and looked back. "You'll have a new box of canning jars tomorrow."

"I dinna want new ones. I want the old ones and I want him punished."

"I'll see you tomorrow," Tom said and shut the door.

Outside, Tom strode past the boys to the trash cans at the curbside where he thrust the bag of broken glass into the can.

Joe whispered to Ben and Peter, "That'll show *you*, you sickening little bitch." They responded with silent, sympathetic nods.

But Tom heard Joe's whisper and when the boys reached the curb, he was waiting for Joe. "I heard what you just said."

"Sir?" Joe said, eyes gone wide, face stiff and serious.

"You behaved yourself *perfectly* inside Grannie's house. I was *so* proud of you." Joe gulped audibly. Tom said, "You were kind, you were honest, you were more humble than I could have been in that circumstance. You kept your temper when you had every right to lose it."

"Dad—"

"But you *know*," Tom said, pointing his finger at Joe, his voice clear and angry, "that I *do not* tolerate that kind of language, nor the hateful spirit behind it."

"Yes, sir, I know."

"I hear you speak that way about your grandmother again, Joe, and you won't sit for a week. Do you believe me?"

"I do, Dad."

"Let's go home." He rounded the car and opened the driver's door, took his playbook off the seat, and tossed it in the back. Lifting the seat lever for them, Tom commanded, "Get in." Peter and Ben squeezed into the cramped backseat. Joe took a deep breath, opened the door on the passenger side. Tom spoke to him over the car roof. "Or any woman, for that matter," Tom said severely. "If I hear you speak that way to—or about—any *person* who is of infinite worth to God, so help me, Joseph, you'll hear from me."

Ben's hand was shaking so that he fumbled the seat belt. "It's okay," Peter whispered, bumping his shoulder into Ben's.

"Was he exaggerating? Because—" Peter shook his head. "Does he mean it?"

"You heard him. You saw his face."

"He's really mad at your grandmother," Ben reasoned, "but I know he's mad at Joe, too."

"Yeah, because he wanted Joe to be respectful *in spite of* how Grannie treated him. He's said before he doesn't want us to strike back. Especially if the person is weak in whatever way." Peter motioned for silence and simultaneously, Joe and Tom ducked into the low car.

"Joe," Tom said over the roar of the engine start, "when you call names like that, you diminish yourself. You could have stood on your own admirable behavior. As it is, you stooped to her level."

"Ouch," Joe said, lips tight, squinting, breathing quickly.

"I won't allow that kind of abuse in your character."

"I know, Dad. I'm sorry." Tom glanced over at Joe, who turned to meet his eyes. "I mean it, Dad."

"I know you do. Don't forget this when you're angry." He reached over and tapped Joe on the chest. "You've got to form a resolve in here. Deep inside about how you're going to be."

Joe nodded, and Ben could see the bright tears in his eyes. "Thanks for—thanks for defending me, Dad."

"I'm ashamed that she behaved like that, Joe. You deserve so much better."

"What makes her so mean?"

Tom shook his head sadly. "Don't give in, son. Don't ever give in to the impulse to be cruel. It's *never* worth it."

"I won't, Dad," Joe whispered, snatching the wet from his eyes.

"I never should have taught you guys that apple game," Tom sighed.

"It's one of the things I like best about you MacBrides," Ben said to Peter.

"What was that, Ben?" Tom said.

"Hey, how is it you couldn't hear that, but you could hear me whisper when I was three yards away?" Joe protested.

"You're better off because I *did* hear you," Tom said. "All you guys are. You boys have to learn this."

"Yes, sir, Coach," Ben said. "But can I ask you something? Something purely theoretical?"

Joe turned a little in his seat and gave a half-smile to Peter, and Ben could see that with his teary eyes Joe told Peter he was grateful for Ben's ability to turn any crisis into an objective analysis.

"Ask away, Ben."

"What if Joe were using that term as a description? Not as an expression of anger."

"He can come up with a better description than that."

"Right, but what if he felt that was the *best* description."

"That word and others I object to you boys using angrily have such mean, derogatory connotations."

"But sometimes that's accurate, Coach."

Peter said, "You mean if you used that word in a very cold, calculated, thought-out way?"

"Yeah. What is your goal, Coach? Do you want us to be polite, or do you just want us to never describe someone that way, even if it fits? Is it the exact word or the *spirit* of the word?"

Peter and Joe exchanged grins, Joe rubbing his eyes.

"It is more the spirit behind the word," Tom admitted to Ben.

"You mean if Joe cruelly or angrily called a woman a rose or a beauty—but he meant the other thing—you'd be ticked. But what if he just calmly, objectively said something like, 'She's a witch, spell it any way you want.' How would that strike you?"

The boys knew this was one of Joe's favorite descriptions—a direct quote—and they waited for Tom's response. "Clever," Tom said, and laughed, first a little chuckle, then as if the spark caught, he laughed in a natural rush of amusement. The boys exchanged relieved glances, their tension lifting with laughter. Tom slowed the car as they approached their home. "I'm guessing that's something Joe says all the time," Tom said, still laughing.

"If either of you answer that," Joe said, "I'm jumping out this car door."

"You make sure you control yourselves, all of you. Be decent men, not cruel ones. Find a right way to express anger, but many times you're going to realize, there's no good, safe way to express anger. Then you just grit your teeth and do what's right," Tom said, pulling up the emergency brake and switching off the car.

"Hey, you were supposed to take Ben to get his car," Joe said.

"I'll do it later. Right now, he needs his dinner," Tom said. "Did you have dinner waiting for you on Porter Road?"

"No, sir. I'm happy to be here."

Tom put his arm around Joe as they went toward the kitchen door and Ben, walking with Peter a step behind them, heard Tom say, "If Grannie ever pounds you with her fist like she did today, I want you to very calmly put your arm out to hold her off. Without hurting her. And tell her to stop. If you're alone with her, leave the house and come home. Then I want to hear about it, if it happens."

Joe nodded. "It stinks."

"It is not your fault. Remember that. Her behavior is not your fault."

"It's probably *your* fault," Joe teased, slapping his father playfully on the stomach. "She probably still hasn't recovered from having you on that airplane in front of all those people." Joe looked back at his brother. "Can you imagine Grannie in that out-of-control situation?"

"Aye," Tom said absently and so seriously that the boys regretted Joe's gibe.

23

AFTER dinner, Tom asked the children to clean the kitchen so that Laurie could sit down for a while. When they were finished with the chores, Joe announced that he needed the computer to finish a paper, and Ben, Jeff and Bonnie Jean gathered around the kitchen table to study for their French quiz. Bonnie Jean took her seat in front of the fire and Jeff sat opposite to her. Ben took Tom's chair. Tom reminded them that they had to be finished by nine so that he could get Ben to the auto shop before it closed.

Ben took out his French notebook and turned to the chapter review. "Quiz yourself by doing this page," he said to Jeff and Bonnie Jean. "And mark the things you don't know well enough." They fell to silent work and in five minutes, Ben shut his book.

"Let me guess," Jeff said, turning Ben's notebook toward him. "You know it all."

"I told you before. The only way to learn a new language is to review every night. You have to learn the words."

"You have beautiful handwriting," Bonnie Jean said, her eyes mellow as she looked at Ben.

"For a lefty, maybe," Ben said. "Yours is beautiful, Jeannie. Artistic."

"You're making me gag," Jeff murmured.

"You make your ones funny," Bonnie Jean said, tracing the odd, looped numeral Ben used. "Where'd you learn that?"

Ben stared at it a minute. "Oh, that's the French way. I always do that on French papers. Don't you?"

"No."

"Ms. Bernadotte doesn't, either," Jeff said. "I don't think she knows any French."

"You don't, either," Jeannie said, "so study."

Coming into the kitchen, Tom said, "Does anybody know where I put my playbook when I came in?"

"You tossed it in the backseat of the MG when we were leaving your mom's house," Ben said.

Tom nodded, left the house, and in a minute came back holding his spiral-bound playbook.

"Are you nearly ready, Ben?"

"They need a little tutoring, Coach."

Thumping the book against his palm, Tom glanced at the clock. "I'm going to go and get some gas in the MG."

"Can I come with you?" Tommy yelled.

"Homework done?"

"Yep."

"I've got to stop at Giant and get diapers."

"I'm up for it," Tommy said, grabbing his jacket.

"You have to memorize the names of the verb tenses, Jeff. Then I'll quiz you on them."

"No," Jeff moaned.

"Yes," Ben said. "See, write them over and over like Jeannie's doing."

"I'll never get this stuff, Ben," Jeff complained. Shoving his French notebook away from him, he folded his arms and leaned his head down on the table.

"You can't quit," Bonnie Jean said. "It's hard for me, too." Bonnie Jean bent closer to her work then flipped her hair onto her back out of her way. It shimmered now in the winking firelight, wisps curling at the ends.

"What are you working on, Ben?" she asked.

"National Honor Society application." He shifted on the bench, biting his lip and drumming his pencil on his left shoulder.

"Yeah," Jeff said, "They begged me to try out, but I said no."

"Are you in it, Jeannie?"

"Not old enough. Have to be in eleventh grade to apply."

"It says I'm supposed to write my testimony," Ben confided. "But I'm not sure what that is."

"It's what everybody gives in chapel," Jeff said.

"Gives?" Ben said.

Bonnie Jean sat up straight to look at him. "It's the story of how you came to love God."

Ben squinted at her, thinking. "How is that part of NHS?"

"Your character, I guess," she said.

"It takes character to love God?" Ben said. "What if you have no character and you're just desperate for his goodness?"

She laughed, "I guess not—when you put it that way."

"I know what to say, just from what Jeff said about chapel and from Bible class. I can put down the expected answer, but I want to be genuine."

"You should be about this," she said.

"If you had to write it, what would you say about yourself?"

She sat back, put her foot on her chair, and hugged her knee. "I was

343

brought up to believe, you know, but I remember thinking my faith just didn't measure up to my mom's. She has this well of faith and love."

"Yeah. I'd never seen that before, either."

"But I got sick last summer—I had a fever for three weeks and my mom sat beside me, reading to me and praying for me, and one night my fever broke and when I got up the next morning to take my shower, I knew he was there in my thoughts and my heart. I believed. Really believed."

"I wasn't sure if God even existed before I came here—"

"And what happened?"

"Not until that first time you sang in chapel, and Joe was so calmed down next to me and I knew that…um…he and Scott and Paul and Adam and Jon all trusted each other. And it was weird but I felt something there— like living there inside me, and then things started getting better for me in a lot of ways."

"Start like that," Jeff urged. "Write that."

"And then one night on your porch, Jeannie, late one night, there was this reassurance, like something I could actually feel trying to soothe me."

"Were you upset?"

Ben said, "It's always when I'm around you MacBrides that I feel close to—"

"To God?"

"Not close to *him* so much as close to believing. But at home, it's harder."

"You could write that," Jeff said. "Tell them you're *trying* to believe, but you're not quite there yet."

"Is that your diagnosis?"

Jeff nodded. "You've sensed something real, but it's not yours yet." He smiled at Ben, his shy smile that rarely showed, and then, embarrassed, reached over and shoved Ben's shoulder. "Am I right, Joe?"

Joe came to the door between the rooms and, putting both hands on the doorframe, leaned in as if doing a pushup. "Yeah. I think you are, Jeff."

"Do I just write that, then?"

Joe shrugged. "It's a start, but you can't *try* to believe. Faith is a gift. Why not ask God for faith, see what happens, and then write about it? The thing's not due for a couple of weeks."

"Prayers take longer than that to be answered," Ben said.

"Not this kind," Joe argued.

"I take it you haven't started yours yet."

"My testimony or my application?"

Ben laughed. "Your application."

"Right," Joe said slowly. "I haven't started the application. I've got to think it through and besides," he added, "I'm putting all my energy into this English paper. I want it to be better than yours." Ben laughed again.

"You've got yours done?"

"Yeah."

"That makes me want to cuss," Joe said, turning, stretching and going back to the computer. "Don't anybody talk to me 'til I'm done."

Ben tapped his pencil on the paper where he had been writing, thinking about Joe's advice. He was comfortably warm, his stomach full; but the yearning inside him was keen and sharp as he considered some of the things that Tom and Laurie had said to him. He remembered that Laurie had known how much he weighed when he was born. Ben found this and the unlikely descriptions of Donna startling. Did a life exist beyond what he knew and lived—as if a life was waiting for him to discover it, holding out its arms?

Beside him, Jeff stared at his French book and Bonnie Jean hummed softly while she wrote. The firelight behind her flickered and leapt, stirring the air and sending her shampooed scent to him. She was so pretty, and if Tom and Laurie really had loved him for a long time…maybe in the end when he was a little older and was better inside they wouldn't object to his loving Bonnie Jean.

Jeff made a bored noise. Leaning back in Tom's chair, Ben studied Jeff with careful eyes. "Did you try writing the words over and over?"

"I did some."

"You've got to work at it, Jeff." Bonnie Jean nodded at Jeff, agreeing. Her hair slid down, falling onto her notebook with a whispering sound. Absently Ben looped it over his fingers and moved it up onto her back, away from her neck. Bonnie Jean glanced at him, surprised. Ben met Jeff's eyes, blinking slowly.

Jeff stood up. "I'm going to take a short break."

"You are not," Bonnie Jean said.

"I have to, Jeannie. My mind is blurry. Want to try to beat me in Mario Kart, man?"

Ben shook his head, eyes intense. Humming off tune, Jeff strolled away from them. When he was gone, Ben scooted his chair over, getting as close to her as he could. He tried to sit still, listening to Joe's thoughts race across the keyboard in the room beyond, feeling her scent and the intimate sound of her humming warm him further, somehow inflaming his restlessness.

"Is this the right tense, Ben?" she asked, pointing to her sentence where she had written, *Il avait déjà fini la leçon quand il a commencé à pleuvoir.*

"What are you trying to say?"

"I want to say, 'He had already finished the lesson when it started to rain,'" she said. "I'm writing about you, of course."

He answered her in French. Looking across her shoulder, she smiled at him. Again in French Ben asked the name of the verb tense she'd used.

"Hmm," she delayed.

"You know this, Jeannie," he whispered, as if English were forbidden. "You just memorized it."

"Oh. *C'est le plus que parfait.*"

"*Oui. Très bien.*"

"No," she said, tracing her finger along the next line of directions. "It's just that whenever you say, 'You know this, Jeannie,' in that certain tone of voice, it's *plus que parfait.* For *future anterior,* you always say, 'Think, Jeannie.'"

"You're memorizing my cues instead of the French."

"So?"

Once again her hair fell onto her book. Ben lifted it, wrapping it around his hand and laying it in a shining twist on her back. "That won't help you."

"It's not like you to touch my hair. You've been careful since that day."

"I think about you constantly," he said. Bending close he nuzzled her neck at the curve of her shoulder. "*Mais, je tremble de peur à ton pàpà.*"

"Tremble with fear," she laughed knowingly. "Today's different?"

She glanced at him, and meeting his eyes, he saw that she understood his intensity. "Kiss me."

"We promised we wouldn't yet." She pretended to read her homework sheet, her finger unsteady as it traced the printed question. "One of us has to be strong."

He moved in close, his lips beside her ear. "I'm not strong today," he said, his face close to hers. "I know you're a gift from God."

"That's the nicest thing anyone's ever said to me."

"It's what your name means," he said, "'Beautiful gift from God.' I looked it up."

"Ben, you are so sweet. Come with me," she said, standing up and taking his hand. She hurried him into the laundry room by the pantry shelves. She came close with a vibrant warmth that pounded his heart. Her arms went around him in that sturdy, eager way of hers, one arm around his neck with fingers gripping his shoulder, one arm tight around his back. Ben bent into her embrace, holding her close against him. At the thrilling, full-length feel of her, his strong heartbeat quickened and Ben went all hot inside, wanted to be closer, to hold her tighter. The sudden eruption shaking his stomach utterly astonished him.

"What's wrong?" she whispered, staying close.

"Um—I—"

"What?" She held him tight. "You're shaking." He tried to draw away, but she held him close, whispering, "No. What is it?"

"Something weird. Like I'm afraid of something…of God, I think."

She drew back only enough to see his eyes. "How do you mean?"

"I've doubted he was real most of my life. But with you so close it's like there's more at stake."

"Everyone doubts. He doesn't mind that."

"How do you know?"

"Doubting means you're seeking, Ben. When we seek him, he comes to us."

"I can't lose you now."

"Why would you?"

"What if you and Joe, your family—what if it's all a setup? A test or something. And what if God wanted me to trust," he drew back, a flush of embarrassment rushing up from his chest. "So he could slap me back down."

"Why would he do something so horrible?"

"Why shouldn't he? Horrible stuff happens all the time. If I could, I'd stop all the awful stuff. Just put an end to it."

"But that's his will. To stop the evil. He gave *everything* for that. It's people who won't cooperate."

"He should force people."

"He invites people to love him. That way it's true love."

Ben thought about this for a moment, and she came closer yet to him, her cheek touching his chin. He hid his face in the crook of her neck, in her hair, and breathed in her warm, live scent. Whispering, he confided things that made his voice shake. "What if I'm not one of the chosen like Mr. Bettinger talks about? Jeannie, obviously, I'm *not*. Look at my life. I've been lonely and hungry all my life. My whole life I prayed for relief. Do you ever wonder if you're chosen or what do they call it at school—elect?"

"You know that God is real now, but you suspect he's not good."

"Yeah," Ben said.

"What if he was with you in the dark years and you didn't know it?"

"No," Ben said, drawing back to meet her eyes again. "He wasn't there. He couldn't have been."

She touched his face. "How do you know that?"

"Mr. Bettinger says God can't stand the sight of sin. So, when sin was happening God turned away and left me there—"

"Ben, what happened to you?"

Ben shook his head, wary that the alarm in her voice would convince him to tell her those unutterable horrors he'd promised to hide. She rubbed her hand along his back. "Hey. Like the other night? At your house?"

"That and—" He shook his head.

She leaned back from him, moving one hand to his stomach, "Your stomach is shaking so much I can feel it. But listen. I've been reading this really difficult book in the Bible called Hosea and I read there that God is not like man. And that he won't come to you in terror. So, you see, it couldn't have been him who caused the terrible things that freaked you out like this."

"Oh, if that could be true, Jeannie."

"If I'm a gift from God, as you say, how can he be bad?"

They heard Tom's car on the gravel driveway, met each other's eyes, and by mutual consent stepped apart, lingering a moment, fingers touching. They were sitting at the table looking at their French books when Tom opened the back door. Tommy rushed in ahead of his father.

"We're back," Tom said.

"Where's Jeff?" Tommy demanded.

"Video games," Ben said.

"You two better not have been kissing," Tommy teased as he rushed by them, poking Ben in the ribs.

Ben looked at Bonnie Jean and her eyes answered his in deep understanding. How could they define the deep attraction and the powerful, almost supernatural response in Ben to their closeness? Could they explain how that blissful moment of touching had given life and healing to Ben? *I love you*, he vowed to her silently, beneath her father's watchful glance.

"How's the French coming?" Tom said.

"*Bien*," they answered in unison. Ben touched Bonnie Jean's book. "*Quel le nom pour cette tense?*" he began in French, conspiracy in his voice. "That means, 'What is this tense?'" he said with a glance at Tom.

"Future anterior," she said with even confidence.

"Good," Tom said innocently. "Does Jeff know this stuff?"

"Some of it," Ben said. "He's easily bored."

"I'll bore him," Tom said, and strode off toward the basement stairs where they heard him bellow Jeff's name. Up Jeff came, reluctantly, and took his place at the table.

Tom stood behind him, both hands on Jeff's shoulders. "You've got approximately ten minutes to get any help you might need from Ben. I'm going to vacuum out the MG and when I come back in, Ben's got to leave. Remember, you've got to pass this class."

"Aw, Coach."

Tom went into the pantry. He emerged with a garbage bag, a vacuum cleaner, and a loop of orange extension cord. "The MG's pretty messy, Joe. Lots of junk on the floor."

"Sorry about that, Dad," Joe called from the next room. "You want me to clean it?"

"Finish your homework. I've got time to spend while Jeff learns his French."

"Gonna need about a century," Jeff mumbled.

They rehearsed the French, including Jeff, cajoling him, forcing him to focus, and when Ben's eyes met Bonnie Jean's, when their fingers brushed accidentally, Ben murmured, "*Merci*," because during those beautiful, brief minutes, for the first time, faith flickered within.

24

WHEN Tom opened the kitchen door, his motion slow and quiet, Ben looked up. He watched Tom turn to shut the door, watched his coach moving deliberately, turning the big, brass doorknob and carefully, slowly, putting it to the latch. Tom slid a white envelope into the inside chest pocket of his jacket before shrugging it off and hanging it on the peg by the door. Ben saw that determined look in Tom's eyes and his stomach jumped.

"Where's Joe?" Tom asked, coming toward the table, solemn eyes meeting Ben's.

"Working on his paper," Bonnie Jean said without looking up. She pointed over her shoulder. "In there."

"Joe."

"Huh?"

"Come here." Tom strode past the table, past Ben, and stood just inside the family room. Ben leaned back to see Joe look up and ask, "What's the matter, Dad?" Bonnie Jean looked up, met Ben's eyes, questioning. They both looked to Jeff who made a face to say he didn't know.

"Come here. I want to talk to you."

"Yes, sir," Joe said. The room went so quiet that Ben heard Joe click the mouse twice. Ben stood up. Joe pushed his chair back and stood up. Ben pushed his chair in.

Joe crossed the room glancing through the wide opening of the fireplace at Bonnie Jean, then Ben. Coming close to his father, Joe's stance, his expression, even his readable eyes showed concern and curiosity, no alarm. But Ben knew better, and he felt terror quicken his blood.

"Is there something you've been meaning to tell me, Joe?" Ben's mind raced to the things he knew Joe was hiding—Oliver's picture, the ticket, the detention Joe had gotten in chemistry.

"No, I'm good," Joe said, but his eyebrows shot up in a glance at Ben.

"About your trip to New Jersey?"

"I, um—" Joe gulped.

"What do you know about this?" Tom said, opening his palm to show the rumpled ticket and the crushed stub of Joe's only smoke.

"Oh," Joe said, regret darkening his expression. "Where did you find that?"

"In the MG."

"Oh," Joe repeated, his voice dry. Ben felt it then, a whiff of danger, the dimension of Tom's relentless strength; he knew the measure of Tom's determination that his son meet his dearly held principles and Ben saw the beauty of Joe's wild, vibrant *joie de vivre* flicker and quail. He drew his breath; his body went tense, his mind cast for the right distraction.

"It's mine," Ben said, coming to them, soundlessly striding the few steps into the family room. "The cigarette's mine. I made Joe promise he wouldn't tell."

"Ben!" Bonnie Jean gave a hoarse whisper. But he could only glance at her, eyes pleading.

Tom looked at Ben, his knowing eyes sweeping over him. Then he squinted again at Joe. "I want to know why you didn't tell us about this ticket, Joe."

"It's *my* fault," Ben said, too loudly. "I was speeding. He had to keep up with me."

Eyes angry now, Tom turned to Ben, motioning for Ben to come closer. But Ben couldn't move. Tom gave Joe a look that commanded he stay put and went to face Ben, his hand extended toward Ben with the evidence there on his open palm. "You're telling me, Ben, that *you* were speeding? And because you were speeding, *Joe* got this ticket? And *you* convinced Joe to hide the ticket from me?"

"Yes, sir. That's what I'm telling you."

"Are you sure you don't want to rethink this, Ben?"

"The cop didn't even want to give Joe a ticket once I explained," Ben said, feeling his scalp burn as his mind raced to identify which of Joe's mistakes angered Tom most. "But he had to because he'd already called it in. Joe *wanted* to tell you, but I said—"

"Ben," Joe and Bonnie Jean whispered together.

Jeff said, "Come on, man."

"Ben, stop this." Tom pressed his lips together; it was Joe's emotional expression on Tom's face, angry and hurt. Ben clamped his jaw shut, and stared coldly at Tom, who returned his stare, peering hard. Ben shifted his weight to his left foot and glanced at the back door.

"Don't you even *think* about running out of here. You are in enough trouble."

Ben's eyes went wide. He glanced at Joe, to see Joe's lips pressed tight with emotion, his grayish eyes liquid bright in angry astonishment. He looked to Bonnie Jean, dismayed to see her disappointment, and Jeff behind her, shaking his head at Ben.

"Look me in the eye and tell me the truth," Tom said.

Ben tried. He tried to look his coach in the eye and repeat his quick and complicated lie, but his stomach was shaking so badly that his teeth crashed together, and his eyes had gone blurry staring at Joe's ticket and they refused to lift up. "I made Joe hide it from you," he said to the ticket.

"Get your stuff," Tom said, throwing the cigarette into the fire in a pitch so hard and sure that it skimmed past the narrow opening in the fire screen and hit the leaping flames with a thud. He slapped the ticket down on the kitchen table. "We'll discuss this in the car."

Tom started the car and waited for Ben to fasten his seat belt, but Ben could not get the clip into the latch. His hands shook and his eyes refused to focus.

"You need some help."

"I don't."

Tom waited fifteen seconds before putting his right hand over Ben's and, holding it steady, guided it. "You do," Tom said, giving Ben a hard look. He turned to look out the back, his hand going to the top of Ben's seat. Ben flinched. Tom waited, watching him. In silence, his jaw clenched, Tom backed out of the driveway and steered the car onto the road.

Ben managed only shallow breaths, fighting tears and the nausea they invariably evoked. "You're angry." Ben gulped, the internal pressure forcing him to speak.

"You have no idea how angry." Tom glanced at him.

"But you said we were going to talk in the car," Ben said.

"I'm considering what to say," The light ahead was yellow. Tom slowed the car to a stop, turned his gray, knowing eyes to Ben.

Whatever edge Ben imagined he had by taking the blame for Joe, Ben knew was now lost to Tom's strength, his strategies baffled. But Ben felt compelled to connect, careless of the cost. If only he could stop shaking so much inside. Words came out. "I—if Joe *had* smoked that cigarette—"

"Joe *did* smoke that cigarette," Tom said. "We both know that. And I would think you'd know I'm more concerned about his hiding things from me. About deception."

"But—but just theoretically."

"It's time we talked about you and the things you said back at the house."

"Please tell me what you're going to do to Joe. Please."

Staring at Ben, considering him, eyes sweeping over him as they often did in that seeking stare that was Tom's alone, his attention stopped at Ben's shaking hands. Then he seemed to see Ben's shivering and pity came into his eyes. Switching the heat on, training the vents on Ben, he said, "I have to talk to Joe and find out what he was thinking."

"Are you going to beat him?"

"I never have," he said, without looking away from Ben.

"Is that the truth?" Ben heard himself say, trapping his hands against his body to hide their convulsive shaking.

"You know me well enough to know the answer to that, Ben." Tom pressed his lips together in what Ben saw was clear, hot anger. Behind

351

them a car beeped to announce the light turning green.

Ben said, "But at your mother's house—"

"You don't have to protect Joe from me. Instead, let's talk about you. Let's talk about what's hurting you right now."

Ben gave a derisive laugh, tough and fake.

Tom glanced at him, waiting. The engine rumbled and sputtered and beyond the car windows, the sound of cars rushing by on the wet pavement underlined Ben's inability to reply. "Ben, I want you, as much as Joe, just *exactly* as much as Joe, to learn how to harness the willful thing inside that insists on telling lies."

"You've got me all wrong."

"Then explain yourself."

Bitterly Ben murmured, "Sometimes people have to lie."

"In the end, I don't think lying helps. It's wrong. It always hurts."

Ben said, "Now *you're* being theoretical. Face it, Coach, in real life, *every*body lies."

"Look, Ben. To my children, all their lives, I've always insisted that certain things were true: God loves us and gave his Son for our sins. I love their mother and promise to care for her and be faithful to her. I love them. These things sometimes are hard to believe, but I'm staking my life on the fact that they are true. If I lie about other things, it casts doubt on all the amazing, beautiful things I've insisted are true."

"Or else you told a dumb lie, probably for a good reason, like the rest of the world."

"No, when we trust someone, a lie is a betrayal and it rips something up inside us. I won't tolerate it in myself or my children."

Ben raised a shaking hand to his forehead and pressed his fingers into his flooding eyes. "So, you get the kid to admit he was lying and get him sorry for his lie—like you got Joe sorry for that prank the first day of school." Ben tapped his chest, remembering how Joe had done so, explaining that Tom was able to get to him in his deep places. "And once he was sorry, truly sorry—" Ben sniffed, breathing quickly, fighting tears and a nausea that rose in rapid power.

"Are you sorry?"

"People who lie are always sorry. They're always *immediately* sorry. So sorry it hurts inside. Like a sledgehammer smashing their insides."

"It hurts you because a man treasures his integrity. Without it, you can't be close to the people you love." Tom looked at Ben, eyes careful. "But Ben, you know me well enough now to stop this game. You want to know what I'm going to do about *your* behavior."

"You're not my father," Ben snapped. Tom went quiet, lips pressed together, nostrils flared, his deep breathing audible. Ben glanced at him, alarmed at his silence, sure he'd hurt Tom. "Coach, I wasn't brought up this way."

"How *were* you brought up, Ben?" Tom's voice was so sad that Ben's stomach lurched in panic. He shook his head, silently begging Tom to probe further, to ask the question that separated them. *Were you brought up to lie? What are you hiding? Say it, Tom, say it!* All he would have to do was nod his head and then the truth could come spilling out.

"I know you were lying," Tom said, taking the curve onto Spa Road slowly, with a glance at Ben that said he was waiting for Ben to speak. But Ben's words wouldn't come. Finally Tom tapped Ben's knee. "And now *you* know what I expect from you, just as if you *were* mine."

The confusion of disappointed relief washed over Ben. Tom—determined to think well of others, so sickeningly hopeful, so stubbornly decent—had not heard Ben's silent and forbidden cry, which now seemed to be moving up his aching throat.

"If you'd grown up with me, you wouldn't be *so torn up* at the thought of my correcting your behavior. And I can tell you that I'd never punish a child who is as frightened as you are now, Ben," Tom said quietly, looking at Ben. "Never."

"I'm not—I'm not—I—" Ben gulped, chest heaving. "It's just that—I'm gonna throw up."

"What?"

"Pull over," Ben choked. "Sick."

Tom swerved the car onto the shoulder and skidded to a stop. Ben reached for the door handle, forgetting that it stuck, and panicking, pounded on the door. Tom reached across, hit the door above the handle, punched the seat belt release button. Ben fell out of the car, crawled a few inches, and retched in the pebbled grass.

Tom squatted beside him, one hand on Ben's back, the other holding his shoulder. But Ben couldn't stop vomiting and it was several minutes before he rested his head on Tom's knee in the quiet of complete exhaustion. A few tears escaped his clenched eyes and they made a wet patch the size of an infant's fist on the worn knee of Tom's jeans. But Tom didn't speak, except to say, "Shhh," each time he patted Ben's damp, shuddering back.

When his breathing steadied, Tom said, "Can you stand up now?" Kneeling beside him, his hand on Ben's arm, his other arm across Ben's back, Tom got him into the car and shut the door. Once on the road, he drove very slowly, going only so far as the corner, where he pulled into a Wawa. "You stay here," he said to Ben, who nodded weakly.

Tom returned quickly with a bottle of water, a can of Coke and a cup of ice.

"Here you go. Rinse your mouth out," he commanded. When Ben obeyed, Tom said, "Now take a sip. Can you keep that down?"

"I think so."

"Good." Tom poured the Coke over the ice in the cup and put it in Ben's hands. "Sip it slowly."

Again, Tom drove slowly. Ben took several sips and seemed calmer by the time Tom turned onto West Street. "Feeling more steady?"

"Yes, sir. Sorry."

Tom pulled into the parking lot, bringing the MG to a stop before the shop's now darkened front door.

Staring at the cup he was crushing in his hand, Ben's chest heaved in a wobbling sigh. The tap on the window startled them both. Tom looked up to see a woman wearing a Franklin's Autobody polo shirt, hand on her hip. Tom rolled down his window.

"We're closed," she said, eyebrows raised. "He's about to lock the gates to the parking lot."

"We just came to pick up a car."

"Tell her it's paid for," Ben said to Tom. "I just need to know where it is."

"What make?" the woman said.

"Fiat Spider," Ben said to Tom. "It was supposed to be painted pink."

Tom's stared at Ben, eyes going wide. "*What?*"

"Oh, you're the pinkie," she said. "It's around back, but you shouldn't have left all that stuff in the back. Coulda got stolen. Keys are on the floor, driver's side."

"Thanks," Tom said. Tom puttered the MG around the back of the shop. Ben's car stood shining pale pink in the lamplight.

Tom brought the MG to an abrupt stop. "This is *it?*" Without waiting for an answer, he switched off the car and got out, slammed his door and went to Ben's car. Ben followed.

Tom opened the driver's side and slid in. He looked around the car, eyes wide, troubled. Leaning over to the glove compartment, he opened it, peered in, shut it abruptly and got out. "Where did you get this car?"

Ben steadied himself, one hand on the roof. "My grandmother's friend."

"You said that before, but I didn't think—"

"They've been fixing it up for me. Is it worth a lot of money? They didn't make me pay for it. I—"

"I have no idea how much it's worth," Tom said. He stood, arms clenched across his chest, gaping at the car. Ben stood beside him for a full minute, staring at Tom, then the car, baffled, exhausted, searching for what to say or do, searching and finding it impossible when he could not translate the signals of this new crisis.

Then he thought of a distraction. "Oh, I forgot," he murmured and opened the back door, moved the bag marked with his name aside, taking the one that had a card inscribed with the MacBrides' name attached. He held it out to Tom. "Mr. Bénet said to give this to you and I forgot until now."

But Tom's reaction worsened. He did not even reach to take the bag from Ben. His arms stayed slack at his sides and he gaped now at Ben. "Gregen Bénet? You *know* him—Gregen Bénet?"

"No, sir. I mean, yes, sir. That is, I *met* him when Joe and Pete and I went up to get the car. He's my grandmother's friend. The one who fixed this car up."

"You met him a few weeks ago for the first time?" Tom said, emerging from shock enough to reach out and take the bag from Ben.

"He remembered *me* from when I was small, but I didn't." Ben stopped, seeing a picture of Gregen arise in his mind…Gregen in the apple orchard, standing beneath a tree holding his arms out, telling Ben to come in for dinner that Marie had prepared. He remembered the defiance in his voice when he, Ben, told the venerable, generous Gregen, "No." It was a memory, wasn't it? Or was he imagining? How could he have been so rude to Gregen Bénet?

Now, Tom was touching his elbow, "Ben. You okay?"

Embarrassed, bewildered, Ben said, "I keep pissing you off, Coach, and this time I don't even know why."

Tom looked at the car again and shook his head. "Only *Gregen Bénet* would do this kind of a job."

"Yes, sir. I forgot you knew him."

"Laurie and I haven't seen him since…"

"That bag is from him. I was supposed to give it straight to you. Sorry."

Tom did not even look at the contents of the bag, but over its stuffed top, he peered at Ben incredulously and said, "Do you know the *history* of this car?"

They heard heavy boots on the pavement behind them. A booming voice called. "We're closed. Gotta lock up."

"Sorry," Tom called to the man. "We're just leaving."

"History? Mr. Bénet said he bought it from the owner—some real jackass—for a dollar and he and Gran have been taking their time fixing it up."

"I don't imagine *Gregen* called the owner a jackass."

"No," Ben said, ashamed, "I just filled that in from…I'm not sure where I got that idea, Coach. It wasn't you, was it? The owner."

"*No*, it wasn't *me*. And you honestly don't know who owned it before Gregen?"

"No. He didn't say."

Tom sighed and, shaking his head, squeezed his eyes shut.

Behind them a loud voice called, "Y'all got to quit jawin' or I'm gonna lock you in here."

"Is the word 'jackass' bothering you, Coach? Is that one of your forbidden words? Because I—"

"Hush, Ben. I don't want you puking again." Tom turned abruptly, carried the bag over to the MG, and swung it onto the passenger seat. Reaching into the back, he pulled Ben's backpack out and brought it to him. Again the angry call from the dark lot, "...lock you in or call the police."

"Sorry," Tom called to him. "We're going." To Ben he said, "I'm gonna follow you to Gate One, just to make sure you're steady enough to drive. If you start to feel sick, just put your blinker on and pull over. Okay?" Tom put the backpack in Ben's hands, patting it twice, as if he were giving it a fond good-bye.

"Yes, sir." Ben put the backpack in the backseat.

They stood there in the parking lot for a moment, staring at each other as the sound of swinging keys behind them forbid them linger. And Ben was sure that Tom, despite being extremely upset, wanted to hug him; Ben wished he knew how to reconcile.

"We have to go. We're being rude to this young man who I'm sure must want his dinner."

"Coach." Ben backed up to his car, holding his arms crossed over his chest as a shield against the shaking, but when he saw the deeply troubled look in Tom's eyes, he found he could barely speak. "Thanks for staying with me when I—when I got sick."

"Come and talk to me tomorrow at lunch. Come to my office. Okay?"

"But Coach, I just want to say—I didn't realize the old owner was a friend of yours. If I had I wouldn't have called him a jackass."

"*Ben.* This was originally your *mother's* car. Don't you *know* that? Didn't anyone *mention* that? Her father bought it for her when she was sixteen years old. The jackass you're referring to is your own father!" Tom turned away from Ben, one fist clenched around his keys, the other covering his mouth, which Ben saw was trembling with emotion. "I shouldn't have said that."

"What? Why?"

"I shouldn't have told you that."

"I'm calling the cops, fellas."

"No, Coach, look. That explains it. Don't be so upset. Mr. Bénet said it was wrecked when he bought it from the owner for a dollar. And this explains it. My dad wrecks cars all the time. So, it makes sense that Mr. Bénet—who's so careful and neat and all about order and growing things—would be offended by the way my dad wrecks things and throws them away. I must've picked up that opinion."

Tom stepped close to Ben and lay his hand on his shoulder. "You think very quickly under pressure," he said, the anger draining from his face.

Then, he touched Ben's face at the jawline in a brisk, affectionate gesture Ben had seen him use only with Joe. "You come and see me tomorrow. Don't let anything keep you away."

"Police on their way, fellas. Better skedaddle."

25

THOUGH every light burned at home, only Peter was to be seen. Tom shut the back door quietly and carried the bag from Gregen into the family room where Peter was stretched out on the sofa watching TV.

Tom came to the back of the sofa, which stood in the center of the room facing the fireplace. "What happened when I left?"

"Mom tried to talk to Joe and so did I, but he won't talk to anybody. Jeannie talked to Mom for an hour and cried a lot. I think she's in bed now. Jeff went home. Tommy wanted you to read to him when you get in. I offered, but he said no. He did fall asleep, last I checked."

Tom tapped Peter's knee in thanks and carried the bag from Gregen's house upstairs. He opened their bedroom door. Fighting sleep, Laurie said, "Joe needs you. I tried." He put the bag down, went to her, murmured some comfort, pulled the quilt up around her, and turned off the light.

Tom opened Joe's bedroom door quietly in case Joe had fallen asleep. When Tom sat down on the bed's edge, Joe lifted up from his pillow and turned to look at Tom. "Is he okay?" Joe asked miserably.

"No. Not yet."

"Sorry." Joe grabbed his pillow.

Tom touched Joe's shoulder. "Shh."

"So sorry," Joe cried.

Rubbing his hand across Joe's shoulders, Tom searched for the right words. "Joe, I—"

"Don't ask me, Dad," Joe burst out, lifting up to look at Tom. "Please don't ask me." Tears flooded out of his eyes. "I won't lie to you, Dad. Not again. Not after this. But I can't betray Ben. So don't ask me."

Tom nodded, tears coming to his own eyes. "Shhh." He patted Joe's back, rubbed his shoulders and neck with only gentle pressure.

"The worst part is," Joe said, "I've misrepresented you."

"How's that?"

"With all my pranks and half-truths and technicalities and giving him driving lessons when I knew you disapproved, and joking about your switch and trying to get around your expectations and complaining. Ben's been trying to get me to show you that ticket and I wouldn't. Like you were something to be afraid of in a foul kind of way. I made him think that by what I did. It's like I've painted this picture of you that's—not you."

"Oh, I see."

"He needed the truth. He needs you and I let him down."

"Shhh," Tom said. "Try to calm down."

"Dad, this is my fault. If you knew. If you knew how I really behaved and the stuff I've done and led my friends to do—the language alone." Joe moaned inarticulately into his pillow. Tom kept his hand on Joe's left shoulder, while he patted Joe's back in the center spot where his hand made a steady comforting thump, thump. Joe turned on his side, reached for his sheet, and wiped his nose.

"I am disappointed that you didn't come to me with that ticket, Joe."

"Every day I didn't, it got harder to bring it up," Joe's eyes welled quickly again.

But if this doesn't teach you, and there's a next time, I'll have your license and your keys. You know that."

Joe pointed at his night table where lay his wallet beside his keys. "You can have them now."

"No, I don't think so. I see something's happening inside you," Tom said and Joe nodded, quiet at last. "You need to pay attention to that, Joe. Give yourself to it. For my sake."

Tom wanted to speak to Gregen Bénet. But it was past eleven, too late for a polite call from an old friend who had been asked—*for Ben's sake*—never to call. Tom went downstairs, spread a quilt over Peter who'd fallen asleep on the sofa, went to his study at the back of the family room, and sank into his desk chair. A search in his top drawer found the old address book with Gregen's phone number. It had been that long since he had dialed this number. Though in Ben's earliest days, before Gregen also had been forbidden access to Ben, they had spoken nearly every day. Gregen had promised to call the minute that doing so would not jeopardize his relationship with Ben. That last visit with Gregen, when he had come to the grand opening of Laurie's shop in which he had so generously invested, he had explained the constraints Max had put on Ella, and the conditions under which Ella had reluctantly agreed to help Gregen see Ben. He had asked them to refrain from making contact, and though they were all three heartbroken, Tom and Laurie had seen that it was the only way. All his own efforts to be allowed even news of Ben had been utterly rebuffed.

But Ben did not remember Gregen, had obviously not spent time with him these last ten years, and so their restraint, their cutting Laurie off from Gregen, whom she loved so dearly, had not been the successful tactic they had so fervently hoped it would be. Oh, Gregen's lawyer had written to Tom every year providing a cash gift generous enough for Tom to "find ways to make Laurie's life easier." And so Tom had been able to afford to make this big, old house comfortable for his wife. He had been able to install the wood floors she admired, the air conditioning that allowed her to cook extravagantly even in the suffocating humidity of Annapolis summers; he had financed her grape arbor and her wildly prolific flower gardens.

And these were only the blessings that they could explain. Tom suspected that Gregen's vision and generosity were behind the miraculous financial breaks his family enjoyed—the anonymous yearly donation that paid his children's tuition, the fact that almost never in fifteen years had he paid more than one hundred dollars for a car repair, no matter how extensive it was. Yes, Gregen's presence had been with them but the contact—Gregen's loving words and wisdom, his intelligent, thoughtful perspective that they had so valued in the early years of marriage and raising children—had been suspended; Tom and Laurie had missed him so sorely.

Tom copied Gregen's phone number onto an index card and put it in his wallet beside the worn paper where he had written down the words he promised to say to Max when all this mess started. Now, he took this record of his promise out, and with it an old photograph he kept of Ben.

The photograph showed him bathing the newborn Ben who was sprawled and outraged, his tiny fists clenched; his face squinched and red, obviously squalling loudly though Tom held him securely against his body, a bright yellow towel draped beneath him. Remembering how Laurie had come to help with the bath and had soothed the baby by singing her favorite lullaby, Tom chuckled deep in his throat. His eyes burned with tears as he gazed into the past, *Sweetest little fellow, everybody knows, don't know what to call him, but he's mighty like a rose...*

Staring at the picture, Tom remembered how Ben had grown solemn and contemplative as they washed him, and remembered so clearly how Ben had watched them with wide infant eyes as if he were wondering about them. Once he was bathed, Laurie took Ben from Tom, and wrapping the towel around him to keep him warm, she held him, while Tom lapped the warm water over the baby's fragile, silky, round head with one hand, feeling a gentleness swell within him that he had never so much as dreamed a man in his circumstance could know.

Tom felt tears burn, sorrow for his own neglect of the matter, surprise at the enormity, the full-grown love he knew now for Ben, having nurtured it in silence over the years with daily prayers, many of them whispered late at night, with quick glimpses of this picture, and with painful and poignant memories only to water and feed it. He pressed his fists to his eyes, wanting to drive out the remembrance of things that never should have happened. He was to blame for so much, and now, finally, after all these years, for the fact that this same paper still rested with him, his promise yet unfulfilled.

Unfolding it, he forced himself to look. These were Katie's words, transcribed in his hand. He could not bear to read the first part—a confused, mumbled list of Max's betrayal that he wasn't even sure he'd heard correctly. How it would wound Max even today to hear these words, how it would tear at any man's heart. Tom's eyes rested on the last sentences, the ones that had, long ago, empowered him, or perhaps had flattered him and inflamed his pride so hotly that he had fought for five years with blatant confidence of winning custody of Ben, who by then no longer even remembered what he and Laurie looked like.

He looked at it now, dismayed that the folds in the paper had made some of the words vague, some unintelligible. As he read, he remembered Katie's pleading—*Do not let Max raise my son...not ever...please promise.* Tom kissed his finger and touched it to the photograph of Ben and he realized that in the silent house, he could hear voices upstairs.

26

HEARING the farewell salute of the old MG's horn as Tom turned toward home, Ben pulled up to the guard station at Gate One and showed his ID card to the marine standing duty.

"You can walk in, sir," the marine said. "But I can't let you drive in after dark without a DOD sticker."

"My car's new. I just got it and I haven't had a chance to get the sticker. I don't want to leave it on the street."

"Sorry, sir. Those are standing orders, sir. Just pull up there and turn the car around in the space beside the orange cone. Thank you, sir."

Ben went back up King George Street and found a space across from St. John's College. He took his backpack and the bag from Gregen, locked the car, and after standing beside it for several minutes, reluctant to leave it, he walked back down the street, surefooted on the bricks aslant in the sidewalks, and went around the corner to Gate Three. He was admitted on foot without protest

Ben paused at the chapel steps, shifted the bag in his arms, and stared at the high, blue windows above that made the space within the chapel dome look to him like the sheltered heaven of some secluded kingdom with a light all its own. At dawn when he ran, the realm beneath the dome looked as shaded as the dimming dusk. If the sun shone brilliantly on the Yard, the silent sanctuary within was midnight. Always it stood opposite to his world, Ben thought, noting now that the starry lights shining within the dome made a low, gold heaven sheltered from the chill night that held him alone.

The Yard looked deserted but for a few heedless mids hurrying back to Mother B many minutes past lights out. The moon hung low above, shrouded in sticky clouds. Ben could see down Porter Road to his father's quarters; the windows in his brothers' room were dark. He felt the night's cool dampness down to his bones.

Again the chapel called to him, its blue heaven called to him, promising a difference within. A cold gust from the Severn behind pushed him with damp, urgent breath, swirling past his ankles, urging him forward; he resisted for a moment, staring at that safe, covered heaven until his feet took him toward it, heart pulling him.

At the foot of the chapel steps Ben stared at the huge brass doors, knowing that they were locked. He saw a door a few steps up—a side entrance. Ben looked around before dashing up the steps. The door opened at his touch. He slid in and it sighed closed behind him.

In the quiet darkness the scent of the place seemed wide open and familiar, reminding him of the scent of the brook rushing over big rocks below his grandmother's home in Hillside. His eyes adjusting quickly, Ben saw the golden starlight from the dome illumine the first few pews and the altar steps opposite. The stony white moonlight outside this quiet sanctuary dropped through the circle of windows above and splashed gold on the pipes of the organ at the altar's right hand. In careful silence, Ben moved past the rows of wooden benches set perpendicular to the main bank of pews and he slid into the front row, which, set beneath the balcony's cover, remained just beyond the boundary of light. Ben stayed in the shadows, gazing up at that low heaven above.

Sitting on the edge of the seat, leaning forward slightly, Ben rested his arms on the rounded edge of the barrier that enclosed this box of pews, and saw that though he remained hidden in the balcony's shadows his hands extended beyond and they were bathed in the dome's light. For a long time Ben sat there, staring, thinking about the last day, about basketball practice and how Tom had been pleased with him then, about his blatant lie, his consuming terror, how he'd humiliated himself.

And then his mind coursed over all the baffling things that had happened since that day in August when the Hunter family had stopped their approach to Annapolis to watch the sailboats at the Eastport Bridge. He thought of his father's two car accidents and counted the times his father had hit or hurt him since they had crossed that bridge. He thought about Joe's insouciance, Bonnie Jean's honest beauty, the joy of school and of the MacBride's porch, the first time he felt something during chapel. He remembered the terrifying strength of Tom's anger in the car and felt again the moment when Tom turned the MG's heat vents toward Ben to warm him in a pity that ran concurrent with his scalding anger. "A different sort of anger," he murmured. And the blueness of the little expanse above him touched him somehow—the bright difference of it, the constancy, the shelter it provided—though he'd never thought to enter and hide here before.

He breathed deeply and felt himself calmer and terribly sad.

Aloud, Ben said, "How do I get back to Tom? How do I fix things?"

And the answer came swiftly to his mind the way it did when he took a test and somehow understood. *Tell him the truth.*

Ben knew just as surely that he could not. He rested his forehead on his arm and whispered a prayer. "Please, don't ask me to tell him the truth about me. You know I promised. And I'm too ashamed."

Lifting his head, Ben stared at his hands touched by the extraordinary light from above. They looked clean and smooth and gold. If he stepped out into that light and lifted up his face, would the rest of him be so changed? Would his eyes be washed of the sight of his father lying lifelessly on the stairs in a puddle of drunken vomit? Would the stain of his lies be wiped from his mouth, would his dark and deceitful heart be fresh and bright? Words flooded out of his mouth and he choked, whispering them, "Please help me. I know you're real. Please don't leave me here all alone, a liar whose father hates him. Don't let me stay this way without faith, drowning in lies. You've got to realize I've been alone all my life and I'm sick of it. Please don't leave me alone with my father. Please."

Getting up slowly, his lower back pounding, it seemed to Tom as if all his memories were stored there in the damaged tissue of his lower spine, heavy, pounding and unwieldy. He thrust his wallet back into his pocket, snapped the lights off, and labored up the stairs. When he was nearly at the top, he could tell that the talking came from Bonnie Jean's room. By the time he got to her door, moving as slowly as he was, there was only the sound of her bed covers rustling. Tom knocked softly.

"Joe?" his daughter whispered.

"No. It's your father." Tom opened the door to find her sitting up in bed, hugging her knees. He could see the shape of the phone beneath her covers. "Kind of late for a phone call. You won't want to get up in the morning."

"I know."

"Who was it?"

"Ben. Daddy, Ben's in trouble."

"What do you mean, Jeannie?" Tom said, coming into her room, sitting on the end of her bed.

"He needs you, Daddy. And he's really sorry about tonight."

Tom nodded. "Everything all right between you two now that you talked?"

"We had a good talk, but I'm worried about him. He's hiding in the chapel."

"I assume you convinced him to go home."

She shook her head. "I tried to get him to come over here."

"Is he coming back?" Tom said, in a burst of relief.

"He has to check on his brothers, and I think he still feels funny about tonight."

Slowly, steeling himself against the painful stiffness in his lower back, Tom scooted closer so that he could hold his daughter's hand. Their hearts and intentions in sympathy, they joined hands and bowed their heads. Together they prayed in silence and Tom sensed, as he always did when he prayed with his daughter, an openness above.

Ben pocketed his cell phone and sat still listening. He heard a whisper and then realized it was the murmur of the candle on the altar. He thought about holding his cold hands above its flame and finding his shivering soul warmed, too. He stood and hoisted his backpack to his shoulder. He left the pew and watching the candle flicker, he kept to the shadows with careful steps, feeling frightened of being caught but compelled to go.

He was so close to the candle that even in the discrete light of the sanctuary he could see the slight waft of carbon smoke drift up past its squat glass chimney. Ben had no thoughts, only wanting to touch it and own its bright warmth. Ben held his hand over it, feeling the heat, watching his palm gather the sooty traces of the spending of the candle's life. The liquid, yellow flame flickered like a live thing when Ben's close breath stirred the still chapel air. He stretched out both hands cupping them at the edge of the glass above the flame. The warmth from his hands quelled the shaking in his stomach.

Still standing in the candle's shadowed enclave, Ben turned to look up into the starlit dome. He wondered if he could decide to tell the truth and trust the God he sensed all around him to help him pick his way safely through the fallout. Ben sat down on the altar steps. His backpack slid off his shoulder with a thump and in an absent, automatic way, Ben took out his chemistry book. With just enough light falling slant on the homework page, he wrote, *Energy is the capacity for doing work or supplying heat, while heat is energy that transfers from one object to another because of a temperature difference between them.* Remembering the lab he and Joe completed, Ben answered the next question, *Heat capacity is the amount of heat needed to increase the temperature of an object 1°C. Specific heat...*

Ben worked through the problems quickly, heat calories, joules, and grams; the concept made perfect sense and its logic suggested to him that the universe was ordered by a clean, brilliant mind. He wrote the extra credit evaluations and, as was his regular discipline, forced himself to do the practice problems so that he felt certain, when he put his pencil away, that he understood how to measure the absorption of heat. Looking up, looking around, Ben thought, *Things are supposed to make sense. Things are supposed to be clean and beautiful and right. The messed up things are not God's idea.*

Ben lay back on the altar steps as if it were his home, arms spread wide in a gesture of helpless surrender. "I know Bonnie Jean is right," he said, staring up into the little blue heaven beyond him. "I'm living a lie. I'm a liar. And I'm so afraid."

He thought of something Bonnie Jean had said about what she'd read in the Bible. He looked in his backpack and, finding one, realized it was the French translation required for class and brought from his home bookshelf. He searched through the rest of his backpack and remembered that he had left his English translation in his locker. Heart thumping nervously, Ben hoped he could adequately translate the words, thinking, *If I ever need to be able to read something and understand, it's now.* He found the book she'd mentioned and skimmed through for the words. Drawing an eager breath when he found it, Ben read it aloud, heart mounting with excitement as he realized he knew each word, translating easily, "For I am God, the Holy One, in your midst; I am not like man. I will not come to you in terror." His whisper resounded in the low, sheltered sky above him, and Ben knew then to expect a difference, a separation between the ruined things that hurt him so much and the ideal realm that was meant to reflect this Holy One.

He stood up. He left the steps. He left the shadows and took two strides to stand beneath the dome of the little low heaven. There, with its golden light pouring over him, he murmured, "Yes, of course that's how it is." He took the book to his chest and looking up, hugged it's open pages tight with both arms.

Cross and Crown

27

The house was dark and noiseless. Ben made his silent way up the servants' stair. He showered, checked on Keith and Tim, and locked his bedroom door behind him. Wrapping Laurie's quilt around his bare shoulders he got into bed, moved the bag from Apple Tree Farm away from the door, and pulled his Bible from his backpack. He heard a noise and he sat forward to listen. He heard it again, a whispered sound like something moving across the hallway carpet. Minutes passed; he watched the clock. Then clearly and close by, he heard a woman say, "Come on, Max. It's late. Donna will be home soon."

Ben froze. A dim line of light showed now under his door. The woman spoke again. "I'll wake up the whole damn house if you don't get out here." Her voice was loud and scratchy. Guessing that they must have been in the guest room—the one Gran had fixed up for the midshipmen Max was supposed to host—Ben despised himself for not anticipating danger, for being so careless, trusting Max had gone to bed.

"Come on, Max—"

"Might be sick," Max said.

Ben leapt up and, throwing off the quilt, grabbed his trash can, scattering the few crumpled papers out on the floor on his way out the door. His father slumped against the doorway of the guest room. Ben thrust the trash can up against his father's chest.

Max dropped to his knees and vomited. The woman knelt beside Max, shaking her thin hands as if she were afraid to touch him.

"Run away," Ben told her; he folded his arms over his chest. "First he pukes, then he gets mean."

"But it's out of his system now."

"Suit yourself," Ben shrugged. "I've got a game tomorrow. I'm going back to bed."

"No, wait," she got up and, stepping over Max, extended her hand. Ben stepped back, did not take her hand. "I'm Patty Edwards," she said, "Sorry we had to meet this way. You must be Ben." His father was moving his head and would soon emerge confused and enraged. Ben felt a chill tighten his skin and knew he had to get away. "I've wanted to—meet you—for many years."

"Pardon?"

"I've known your father since—why can't I think? Since before you were born. Max and I were soul mates. We were…" She was blushing now, stammering.

"What? Married or something?" Ben asked, hoping she'd become irritated and he could get away. But surprisingly, her eyes filled with tears and she shook her head. "You're very beautiful," she whispered, the tears spilling out of her eyes. "I had no idea what I was doing, then."

"And now?" Ben asked, sounding disgusted and angry.

She looked at him, her expression a mixture of pleading and longing. He took a step back. "You should go," he said. "I'll take care of him."

"I might be too drunk to drive."

"Are you sober enough to call a cab?" She shook her head. "I don't want my mother to find you—"

"You shouldn't be here," Max said, thrusting the trash can aside.

Ben glanced at him and grabbed Patty's elbow. "Come on. Downstairs. Hurry."

"My purse—in there."

Ben saw that she meant the guest room, dimly lit beyond where his father lay in the doorway. Max pointed two fingers toward them. "Is that who I think it is standing there, because if—"

"I'm leaving as fast as I can, Max." Patty sounded hurt.

"Sounds like a woman…really does." But Max was staring at Ben, eyes intent, suspicious.

"That's Patty, Dad. I'm here, too."

"You. I wish you were dead," Max growled.

"What the hell does that mean?" Patty demanded, wrenching her arm free from Ben, taking a step toward Max.

"Don't. He's talking to me."

"How do you know?"

"He says it all the time," Ben said, working to keep his voice steady. "When he's like this."

"He says he wishes…?" she stared at Ben, her bleary eyes trying to comprehend. "But that's awful."

"Dead." Max fell out of the doorway onto his elbow. "Not me. Not her. You."

Ben tried to swallow, but his stomach was quaking again and his throat was closing. Ben knew that this was why his father hurt him. This was why he never hit Keith or Tim or Donna or anybody. That look came into his eyes, that look that accused Ben of some terrible betrayal, something worthy of a death sentence, and Max hit him. Ben had trained himself to respond to this atrocity with the chilling analysis he trusted would help him escape alive. But for the first time since he was thirteen, Ben was sure he was going to break down over hearing his father's most cherished wish for him. For the first time in years, Ben wanted to know why.

"*You* should be dead and I wish you were."

"Good God, shut *up* Max," Patty turned to Ben and reached out one hand in an attempt to comfort Ben, but unable to calculate the distance between them, she stumbled toward him, her hand striking vainly at the air.

Ben glanced at her. "Can you get your purse?" She looked at Max, then shook her head. Behind him, Ben heard Keith's timid voice through the door on the other side of the hall. "Is that you, Ben?"

Ben turned swiftly and leapt for the door as it creaked open. Blocking Keith's view of the hallway, he said as calmly as he could, "It's me. Go back to bed."

"What's wrong?"

"Dad's sick. I'm taking care of everything. Just lock the door and go back to bed."

"Are you gonna be okay, Ben?" Keith burst into tears.

"It's okay, Keith." He heard movement behind him, and panicking, he lowered his voice to a whisper. "Lock the door." He pried Keith's fingers from the door's edge. "I'll come say goodnight when I get him to bed." He shut the door and held it until he heard the lock click, but turned to find his father coming toward him. He saw Patty duck back into the guest room.

"You shouldn't be out here half-naked," Max said.

"Hurry up, Patty," Ben called, voice shaking.

His father said, "Do you *know* about Patty?"

"*Hurry*." But his father was getting close, stumbling closer. Ben touched the wall beside him, feeling for something steady. His shoulder scraped against the light switch.

Max reached for Ben, "I miss you so much."

Patty had her purse and was waving it happily as if this was an afternoon outing and Ben were not in the gravest danger.

"Your chest, I swear, babe," Max said, mouth full of saliva, reaching for Ben, empty, eager palms toward him. "Looks like a teenage boy."

Ben leaned against the light switch. Shuddering, he willed himself to trap it against his shoulder blade and trip it. He had to do it. He had to make his father awaken enough to understand that it was him—Ben—standing there. Blinking in the sudden, full light, recognition dawned on Max's face; he knew Ben now and that awful realization twisted his father's features with disgust and rage.

"No!" his father shouted. He reared up, torpid limbs made dangerous in some furious need to attack. Max's hand tensed like a claw; his fingers thrust into the hollow above Ben's collarbone. Ben faked left, biting down on his lip to keep himself from screaming in terror—sure Max wanted to rip the bone out—desperate to protect Keith from hearing him cry out in pain.

Max flailed for contact and he grunted, pinching the thick chest muscle. Ben lunged right and forward. Max hung on, twisting Ben's flesh hard, reaching with the other hand, dragging the savage, stabbing fingers across Ben's ribs. Patty screamed behind him. Watching his father, Ben grabbed Patty's wrist, dragged her toward him so that she broke the momentum of Max's attack as her hip and thigh and knee hit Max's body and knocked Max to his knees. Ben kept pulling on her and she stumbled over her fallen lover to the edge of the stairs. Holding onto her wrist, Ben moved down the stairs in terrifying speed, pulling Patty behind him.

Furious by the time he got her to the first floor landing, she had the surprising presence to rub her skinned knees and run a hand through her hair while Ben bent double, gasping for breath, fighting for composure. "This is absurd! Running down the stairs like—" But when she heard Max on the landing above, she ran out the front door and slammed it behind her.

Max made it to the edge of the stairs above before he fell. He reached out for Ben, his arms extended over the descending stairs. "I'm sick."

Ben fought for his breath, though his chest hurt like the flesh was torn. "Why do you hate me so much, Dad?" Ben whispered, the outrage in his voice echoing in the high, empty stairwell.

"Feeling mighty sick," Max whimpered. "Come help me to bed."

"No," Ben cried. "No." Ben ran up the back stairs, slowing only when he reached the top, though he knew his father would pass out where he now lay. The hallway stunk and Ben considered leaving the bucket of puke there. But he thought of his mother's heartbreak when she figured it out. She'd know Max had been drinking. She'd go into the room and…she would be crushed by this. Chest heaving with squelched fury, Ben made himself get the trash can. He cleaned it out and sprayed the bathroom with Lysol to mask the smell hovering now in the corners like so many sticky spider webs.

He took the trash can back to the guest room. The stench sickened him—a wrong combination of that sweating, fertile body smell, too much perfume, Kahlua and vomit. Holding his breath, he crossed the room and opened the window, but he could not make himself touch the bed to straighten it. He locked the door and shut it behind him.

Ben went to the bathroom, brushed his teeth savagely, washed his face, and scrubbed his hands and arms until they were red. Dabbing the raw places on his chest and ribs, Ben saw in the mirror that the bruises, showing so quickly, would be bad. Any numbing from shock had faded and now his chest throbbed so that Ben wondered if muscle could be broken.

He saw that the bruise on his collarbone would show when he wore his basketball uniform. He'd have to play with a T-shirt on underneath and be careful to dress alone before the game. After the game, all marks could be blamed on the physicality of play. Ben caught sight of his eyes in the mirror and saw the lie he intended to tell before he formed the words. But how could it be helped? And...Tom would know he was lying. His eyes flooded with tears and Ben could not stop them. He wiped his eyes, again and again, wishing for a glass of ice water. *I have to get a hold of myself,* he thought, dragging his hands over both eyes, *and check on Keith.*

Draping a towel over his neck to hide his bruises from Keith, Ben went across the hall to Keith's room. They kept the key on the floor behind the steam radiator. Once inside, Ben knew a moment of alarm when he saw Keith's bed empty, but Keith called to him from Tim's bed.

"I heard noises," his brother whispered. Ben went to him and found him curled up, knees to chest. He sat on the edge of the bed and patted Keith's shoulder. "Usually he's downstairs for this stuff," Keith said.

"I know. He shouldn't be up here. This is your floor."

"Ours," Keith said. Ben patted his brother's back, wondering what words could possibly help when Keith was forced to put up with this kind of insanity in the middle of the night. "Are you okay, Ben?"

"I'll be fine. I'm just a little cold and thirsty."

"Are you scared of Dad?"

"Yes," Ben whispered; the sad, terrible truth seemed indecent spoken aloud.

"It's not safe for you here, Ben."

"Shh, try to go to sleep," Ben whispered, fighting the pressure of tears again.

"But I heard what he said to you."

"He shouldn't have said that stuff. Fathers shouldn't say stuff like that. He should *love* me."

"When he gets drunk, it makes him crazy," Keith offered, looking up, eyes hopeful.

"Yes and no, Keith," Ben said firmly. "The booze brings out what's deep down in his heart. If he didn't hate me...there'd be nothing to say."

Keith puzzled over this, eyebrows drawn together. "You want to stay with us tonight?"

"For a while. I've got stuff to do."

"You have to write that down in your book. What happened."

"When you go to sleep, I will." Ben watched his brother's eyes falter and close.

"The book you write in is for the police to find. Right, Ben?" Keith murmured. "For when Dad kills you. It's...the missing evidence."

In his room, Ben's hands shook so violently that he could barely dress and he was ashamed that a groan of pain escaped him when he moved to stretch into his T-shirt. Wrapping the quilt around him, he sat on his bed and took his journal in hand. He pressed the quilt to his face and breathed in the scent of it. There were whiffs of Laurie's perfume and the scent of her kitchen, warm with vanilla and baking, but instead of strengthening him as this usually did, it twisted him with longing.

And writing—the motion of moving his pen—made the sore throbbing in his chest muscle worse so he recorded the night's terrors in a quick, bulleted list. *Keep writing,* he urged himself silently, but writing meant he relived his father's attack and Ben could not rid himself of the sensation of his father's ruthless fingers thrust into the hollow of his neck. Ben shuddered, fear rinsing through his gut, his mind reeling. He left his bed and paced. *I've got to get some sleep. I have a game tomorrow.* Unable to rest, he had no way to bring himself relief; his throat ached with holding back the tears he refused to cry.

Ben sank down beside his bed and saw that his Bible had fallen to the floor. He remembered the comfort of the chapel, the solemn stars above him in that calm blue dome, separate, gentle. What had he been reading? *I am not like man. I will not come to you in terror.* How could he then explain all that he endured unless it were somehow true that the terror he knew at home was against the very nature and will of God?

Ben looked up and caught sight of the bag from Apple Tree Farm. Ben reached for it, dragged it close, and peered in. Carefully wrapped in soft brown paper were three bottles. Ben took one out of its wrapping and, with the distracted interest of exhaustion, studied the curious wood block printing on the label, the words APPLE TREE FARM in an arc below the tree ready for harvest. Ben opened it and took a careful sip. It was cold and delicious with the fragrance of apples and the reddest berries; he drank the entire bottle and gave a funny, helpless hiccup.

Turning the bottle over in his hand, he noticed the style of the print on the label. The apple tree illustration seemed somehow familiar. Ben stared at it, and the remembrance of Gregen—his kindness, the order of his home, the amazing productivity of his creative spirit—made a quiet space inside Ben's sore and shaken chest. He took the Bible, got into bed, put it open with pages down against his stomach, pulled Laurie's quilt over him up to his ears, closed his eyes, and concentrated on the picture in his mind of Apple Tree Farm. He fell asleep.

When the sky began to lighten outside his window, Ben dreamed of Gregen's orchard. He was small—his hand not even the length of the slim, green leaves that cloaked the rosy apples—and he was climbing one of Gregen's trees at the edge of the orchard near a bench. Bees hovered around the fallen apples and the air hummed with their tart scent. Gregen reached for Ben and though Ben was upset about something, he went to Gregen, trusting him, reaching for him through the shiny green leaves that only moments before he had been certain could hide him. Reaching out of them, they brushed his hands and forearms with their stiff, vivid life.

As he emerged from his hiding place, he saw that Gregen looked younger—bigger, darker, his face and forearms very tan. There was a moment in the dream when Gregen's hands reached for him, just a moment when Ben leaned toward him, arms outstretched to Gregen as he pushed off with his feet, only one moment when he was airborne and unafraid. Gregen caught Ben in his arms. Ben pulled himself up close, knees hugging around the old man's tight stomach, and he put his face into Gregen's collar against the warm neck, smelling his clean, sunny scent, murmuring to him. Gregen's left arm held Ben close and his right hand went to the back of Ben's neck. Ben felt the rough ridge of calluses on Gregen's thumb and forefinger scratch familiarly against his hairline and behind his ear.

Ben woke to that sensation, so vivid it might have been real. He touched his neck, still it lingered. Ben got right up; his Bible fell to the floor. Rolling off his bed, he took his Bible and stared at the bookplate. It was inscribed with his name and the date of his birth. Ben saw that the writing was not his grandmother's and that the ones were made in that peculiar French way—each with the short upward stroke to the top. How could he have missed that detail all these years? Going to his bookcase, he took three books from different years, knowing what he would find. Each had a slightly different bookplate—one a sailboat in motion on a bright blue lake; one a mountain climber, rope in a coil on his shoulder; one a castle tower, flag unfurled—all three in the same wood block printing style, all three the same handwriting.

Heart pounding, Ben went to the bag from Apple Tree Farm, almost afraid to look. Beneath two other juice bottles and a box of cookies, he saw the stack of books, the yearly stack of books meant for his birthday, wrapped in a quiet blue-green paper, tied with a wood-brown ribbon, just as always.

"Oh." Lifting the stack out, Ben stared at it with reverence. "Gregen."

Beneath him, floors beneath him, he heard the sounds of his father's waking. Untying the ribbon, he took the top book into his careful, eager hands. He removed the paper with awareness, remembering its familiar pebbled, homemade texture. Inside he found an old book, just the size of his hand with a pale green leather cover, tooled in gold, entitled, *L'Histoire de Genève*. Below, Ben read the author's name, B. Guillaume Bénet, and the date, 1896. The cover showed an etching of a city beside a lake, surrounded by mountains. Ben ran his fingers over it and opened it. The bookplate, identical in style, showed the yellowing of age in a simple depiction of a boy reading beneath a tree. The name on the bookplate was B. Gregen

Bénet. Beneath the name in an old-fashioned curling hand was a signature Ben did not take the time to read because out of the book fell a folded cream-colored sheet of paper. Opening it, Ben drew a deep and expectant breath. He read:

My Dear Ben,

By now you understand that I have been the one giving you books as gifts and you are no doubt puzzled. The reason for the deception is simple: when you were small, I suggested that I supply you with books to feed your intellect and lift your soul. Your grandmother knew two opposing truths: first, that you required these books for your well-being, and second, that your father would object. She permitted me to purchase and wrap the books but insisted that they be given secretly—I was asked never to sign my name. Considering the good of your mind, I submitted to these disturbing demands with deep and abiding regret. Once, you trusted me. I do hope and pray that my choice will not inhibit the renewal of that now dormant kinship.

I have several copies of this book, but this one is signed by the author, my father. I present it to you in honor of your sixteenth birthday with the hope that now we can become better acquainted.

I am most sincerely yours,
Benedetto Gregen Bénet

Ben read it again and again, only slowly becoming aware of the sound of the shower running a floor beneath him; he had approximately fifteen minutes before his father emerged. "Once, you trusted me." *Just like my dream,* Ben thought. He remembered the joy and comfort the books had brought him. They had kept him company for as long as he could remember and now he knew the giver. Hiding the stack of books in his deep desk drawer under some old comics, Ben put the book he had opened, his Bible and one of the bottles of juice into his backpack with his journal and his school books. He dressed quickly and left the house in silence.

28

LAURIE put Cara down in the middle of the café floor and unzipped her little jacket, smoothing the hood off her head. Her dark, silken hair stood straight up, making Laurie laugh a little. Switching on the heat, Laurie read the note left by the cleaning service beneath the pieces of the *café au lait* bowl they had broken. Laurie tossed the shards into the trash and noted the loss before she switched the phone onto day mode and awakened the store's computer system.

Cara was calling, her coo musical. Laurie called back, narrating her whereabouts. "Mama has to turn all the lights on now, baby," she called. Laurie traced her finger over the schedule and saw that three employees were scheduled to work at the shop that day. Annette, whom Laurie was training to teach the machine quilting class, would be in before that morning's class at nine. When she read the other two names, Bethany and Chelsea, Laurie's concern over Chelsea's compatibility with the shop's philosophy resurfaced. On two separate occasions, Laurie had been forced to speak to Chelsea about her behavior around the customers.

The last time Chelsea had worked, another employee had phoned Laurie at home with a question from a customer whose sewing machine had broken again. In the background, Laurie could hear Chelsea's criticism about the shop's machine repairman; she could hear each loudly proclaimed word clearly. "Is the customer standing right there?" Laurie had whispered to her employee, horrified. And when she arrived at the store toward the end of Chelsea's shift, Laurie had been dismayed to hear her voicing her disagreement with Laurie's decision to repair the stubborn machine for free. Laurie hoped her direct discussion with Chelsea would be taken to heart; she dreaded negative employees any day—could not tolerate them—but today especially with Grannie planning to stop by to see Cara during the shop's busy midday hours.

Laurie took Cara to the back of the shop and, finding a sunny spot on the floor, spread out a thick pad for her blanket and toys. Laurie had designed this pad, constructed with built-up sides to block any draft that might sweep across the floor; it was made of six layers of thick wool felt covered with a removable quilted flannel cover. She took the contented, cooing Cara out of her infant seat and set her on her stomach on the blanket with toys scattered in front of her.

Right on time, she heard footsteps on the back stairs and several minutes later, when the door opened, Megan Chernosky's smiling face peeked in. "Mrs. MacBride?"

"Megan. I'm back here."

"I picked up the bread from Martina," she said, referring to her sister. "The baby was up a lot last night, so I thought I'd save her a trip. Am I late?"

"I've never known you to be late." Laurie went to meet her and took the sizable basket from Megan, who ducked back out the door to retrieve the containers of pastries, which were her own specialty. "Is Martina's baby sick?"

"I think he's teething," Megan said. She placed the three pastry containers on the counter and ran over to kiss Cara and coo to her. Laurie thought that Megan did not look much older than the high school athlete she had been when Tom first recommended she apply for an after-school job at Laurie's shop. Now married with three small children, Megan, her sister, and another friend did most of the baking for the shop. Their friend Amber had proven that of the trio of young bakers Laurie employed, she could best duplicate Laurie's specialized cookie recipes.

"Can you stay for a cup of coffee?"

"I wish I could, but I left everyone home with Jacob. He's waiting to leave for work 'til I get back."

"Thank you for all your extra effort, Megan. You are a dear." Laurie gave her a quick hug. "Do you have enough ingredients for tomorrow?"

"I'm good for another two days." Megan thrust her hand into her pocket and pulled out a piece of paper, apple green in color, folded in a square. "Do I put this in the box?" she said, indicating with a nod of the head toward the sleek wooden box by the cash register where notice of needs could be placed anonymously. "I'll take it," Laurie said.

"My mother's neighbor," Megan said, indicating the source of the information for the needy family.

Laurie took the paper from her, a form she had designed, through which knowing friends could refer candidates for Eight Hands Around's soup and bread service. Each day the employees processed the requests, added the names to their lists, and arranged for the leftover food from the shop to be taken to the address. Laurie read it quickly, noting the ages of the children and the problem—electricity had been shut off. "I'll take care of it. Thank you." Megan hurried out, waved, and shutting the door in her careful way, she ran down the stairs with the happy energy that had always been her gift.

Laurie read the request, touched by the described situation. She shook herself into action, giving a glance to check on Cara before going into the back room where she kept such supplies. Reaching for the warmest quilts, she took four in coordinating tones of yellow, rust and brown, shook them out to make sure they were not too worn, and arranged them in a large square basket like the one Megan had used to carry the day's bread. She tweaked the corners so they stood around the edge like starched napkins would in a bread basket. From another bin, she took a small cloth activity book for a toddler, two cloth dolls, distinctly different, and beside each she placed a paper envelope that contained everything the little girls would need to create miniature books for their dolls and little diaries for themselves. And oddly, with an aching sadness in her heart, she thought of Gregen and Sibilla as she packed the basket—Gregen and Sibilla in whose home she had learned to think about others. She pictured Gregen as she had last seen him, stalwart though his world had crumbled, Gregen who had asked so much of her and from whose generosity she had reaped untold benefits.

Would she speak to him again soon? Laurie thought about Gregen as her eyes absently perused the book stack. She took one Bible, which every package included, and two slim paperbacks. She went to the kit shelf and chose a beginning knitting kit, which had directions for five easy projects, needles and enough creamy ivory yarn to complete two of these. *I'll add the food at the last minute,* Laurie thought, satisfied with the contents. As she wrote the family's name on the apple green tag and tied it to the basket handle with trendy raffia strands, she wondered if the bag from Apple Tree Farm that Tom had brought home last night meant that her own estrangement from Gregen was soon to end.

The back door opened, jarring her from her reverie, and Joe called out, "We're here!" Laurie heard them talking to Cara and stepped into the café just as Bonnie Jean picked the baby up.

"Jeannie, she was happy playing on the floor. Now when you leave, she'll cry."

"She whimpered when she saw us. She reached out her arms."

"That's because she knows you'll pick her up."

Cara was cooing charmingly to Joe and Bonnie Jean, who laughed at her. Laurie took the groceries from Joe—large brown eggs, goat cheese, slow-roasted ham sliced thin for sandwiches and the beef she had ordered for roasting. There were fresh strawberries, raspberries, pears, spinach, asparagus, a stalk of basil, a bunch of dill and seven pungent tomatoes. "He had everything on the list," Joe said. "Can I take one of these croissants for Ben? He never eats breakfast at home."

"Of course, and could you put the groceries away for me? I'll hurry up and make you sandwiches for lunch. I'll make Ben a breakfast, too."

"Thanks, we've got to hurry. Dad wants me to play in chapel today. So I've got to practice up."

"Haven't you been all along?"

"No, I've been sitting with Ben."

Laurie looked at him seriously, patted his waist in her tender way, and turning to prepare their lunches, she glanced back at Joe and said, "I wish you'd told us about what happened on your trip to New Jersey, Joe."

Looking up at her from where he squatted in front of the refrigerator, Joe made a chagrinned face, eyebrows raised, jaw thrust out. "I'll tell you my thought process, but I realized last night I haven't really got an excuse. I was embarrassed and I didn't want to be more embarrassed by you two being disappointed in me for smoking...and speeding."

"Those are not the sort of things that are deeply disappointing," Laurie said, wincing at the private pang of conscience. She had been thinking of the boys meeting Gregen and Marie, not of Joe's mistakes. Aloud she said, "I trust you won't speed again. Bad driving causes accidents and accidents change people's lives forever. And not usually for the good." Memories long closeted pulled at her thoughts and she pictured the oddly angled intersection near her childhood home that she could not approach without holding back bitter tears.

"Take apples from the bowl," Laurie said too briskly as she wrapped the last sandwich. "And I have plenty of cookies, so take three each. Grab drinks from the pantry on the way out."

Joe stacked the lunch bags in one big plastic bag, while Laurie took Cara from Bonnie Jean. "Thanks, Mom," they called, running down the back steps.

A few minutes into the lunch period, Ben knocked at Tom's door. Tom saw him through the narrow window on his office door, frowning and somewhat drained of his usual tan color. The dark circles beneath Ben's eyes were unusual. Tom motioned for him to enter.

"Sorry I'm late," Ben said, stepping into the office, looking quickly around. He held a single paper in his hand.

Tom wheeled over to greet Ben, extending his hand, shaking Ben's hand, and clapping him briskly on the elbow. Ben's hands were cold and his eyes, up close, weary and confused. Tom shut the office door and motioned for Ben to sit down. Ben glanced at the cot beneath the window, but instead of sitting down, he held out the paper towards Tom. "Mrs. Bernadotte said I have to show this to you."

Tom took it from him. "What is it?" He turned back toward his desk to find his reading glasses and once they were settled on his nose, sat back to examine the paper.

"My French quiz," Ben said. "I failed it."

Tom looked over the top of his glasses at Ben. "But you knew this stuff last night." Ben shrugged, annoyed. "Didn't you know it?"

"Yes. I knew it."

"What happened?"

Ben glanced at Tom's face and looked away. "Mrs. Bernadotte wants you to sign it. Just to say you've seen it."

"Why is that?"

"I don't know. She's mad. She blew up at me."

"Why do you think she's angry?"

"I don't know. She's unbalanced. This isn't a big deal. I mean, even with this F I still have a hundred and twelve percent in the class."

"How do you know that?" Tom asked.

"I keep track."

"Really. In *all* your classes?"

"B—Of course."

Tom looked at him carefully for a moment, sure the fondness, the familiar recognition he felt, must show in his eyes, though as a father, as a disciplinarian, he wondered if this were the best moment for sentimentality.

"What?" Ben said, again vulnerable.

"You very nearly said, '*Bien sur*,' just then, didn't you?" Tom said quietly, thinking that in this same situation, surely Gregen or Guillaume or Katie would have automatically, unconsciously, said the same, showing that identical look in their eyes—bare, natural confidence.

Ben looked down, "Yes, sir. It fits the connotation I meant a little better. Not so arrogant as the translation sounds, as if to say, 'Anyone would.'"

"Hmm," Tom said. "So, what's your highest average right now?"

"French, but that's only because Spanish doesn't give extra credit and she will never curve a quiz. I only have a hundred percent in there."

"Impressive."

"Not really. It's easy for me."

"What does Joe have?"

"He's got a ninety-seven. He has trouble with the accents."

"Ah," Tom said. "And Bonnie Jean? What does she have in French?"

"She's doing pretty well. I think she has a ninety-two now."

"No doubt partially due to your coaching."

"No, she's smart all on her own."

"But this quiz helped her."

"She got the highest grade in the class today, so...yes."

"And Jeff?"

Ben hesitated, swallowed and murmured, "Sixty-five percent."

"Before or after this quiz?"

"After."

"So, he's nearly passing, or—with a curved grade—passing."

"He hates to study, but he also gets really stressed before tests."

"So, you threw this quiz on purpose."

"Why would I do that?" Ben managed to say, eyes narrowed to slits.

"You tell me." He met Ben's eyes, looking sternly into them.

Ben turned away. "Well, she wants you to sign it. She said under her breath to herself, in French, as if I wouldn't understand her, that she wants you to *fix* me. Whatever that means."

"Hmm," Tom said.

"It's insulting. And I don't see why she freaked out."

"She freaked out because it's *dishonest*."

"What?"

"Yes. You heard me."

"How?"

"Your teachers assume that you are trying your hardest and doing your honest best when you pass your test up front. To throw a quiz is dishonest."

"So anytime someone does less than his best it's dishonest?"

"No. Jeff won't study—that's not dishonest, that's lazy and stubborn. But you knew you could have absolutely aced the quiz and you acted as if you didn't know the stuff. That's dishonest."

"I was trying to *help* them."

"Perhaps, partially. But it is still dishonest. Especially because you knew mathematically exactly how many questions to throw to get Jeff and Bonnie Jean the grades they needed. Didn't you?"

Ben rolled his eyes.

"It is the same as a lie."

"You're overreacting!"

"No, Ben, I'm not. I told you last night that I want you to be truthful. This is lying and I don't want it to happen again."

"What do you mean? Not happen again?"

"Stop lying."

"It—it—I—"

"Is this something you do frequently?"

"You are impossible to please," Ben shouted and grabbing the quiz from Tom's fingers, rushed out of the office, banging shut the door.

29

INTO Dr. Deterding's math class Ben came slightly late, looking angry, his cold blue eyes bright and keen, his lips pressed together, jaw set.

"What's up?" Joe whispered as Ben took his seat between him and Bonnie Jean. She looked up, eyes questioning.

"Nothing," Ben said, then immediately burst out with, "I just yelled at your dad."

"What?"

"What's going on?" Adam whispered.

"Ben's in trouble again."

"About French?" Bonnie Jean asked.

Ben nodded.

"Why?" Joe said. "What happened?"

The teacher's voice interrupted their conversation. "Let's start class with a word of prayer," and she bowed her head and said a quiet prayer. After she said, "Amen," she pointed to the SAT practice question on the blackboard, their daily drill at the start of class. While Dr. Deterding wrote the day's problems on the board, students opened their notebooks to work on the SAT practice problem. Typically, Ben, Joe and Davy, still called "Baby," competed to finish first; Dr. Deterding had promised five extra credit points and a batch of her home-baked brownies to the student who solved the most problems quickly and correctly. But today, Ben opened his notebook slowly and flipped his French quiz onto Joe's blank paper. Joe read it and their eyes met.

"I wreck the curve in there and Jeff's failing."

"Oh," Joe said, squinting at Ben. "You failed on purpose."

"To help Jeff."

"Didn't hurt me, either," Bonnie Jean whispered so loudly that Baby glanced back at them.

"You knew almost everything."

"Ben," she said, eyes intense.

He met her gaze and realized that she was troubled by what he'd done. He tried to think of what to say to her and looked to Joe for help. But Joe shook his head, his eyes and expression serious, and said, "That's not honest."

"That's what Coach said," Ben said. He reached to take the quiz back, but Joe held it out of his reach.

"I understand why you did it," Bonnie Jean whispered, "but Joe's right."

"Yeah, well, Joe's one to talk," Ben grumbled, making another attempt to grab his quiz from Joe, but his bruised chest hurt when he reached out and Joe was able to hold it away.

"I know it," Joe said, meeting Ben's angry gaze, "I've been wrong. I've got to change, too. I realized that last night." Ben stared at his friend, not knowing what to say in the face of his stark humility. "And you know Dad's right," Joe said. "So, you yelled at him for telling you the truth."

Ben's face went burning hot. Baby leaned back to see the quiz Joe held and Dr. Deterding, having written all the day's lesson on the board, came close to them unobserved and snatched the quiz from Joe's hand.

"Oh, that's Ben's," Joe said, coming up out of his seat, hand outstretched to see if she would give it back.

"Now it's mine."

Joe looked at Ben and said, "Sorry." Ben shook his head in disgusted resignation.

Dr. Deterding looked up from the quiz and said, "But Ben, you're so good at French. Aren't you?"

"As you say, ma'am," Ben said.

"How do you explain this quiz, then?" she said, her expression stern.

Ben glanced around the room, noting that every single student was now included in his business and stared at him with expectant expressions.

"What happened?" Victoria asked.

"Ben failed his French quiz in a bad way," Baby drawled.

"Ben never fails anything," Michelle said.

"Ben never even gets an A *minus* on anything."

"He just had a bad day."

"This isn't just a bad day," Dr. Deterding said, shaking the quiz so that it rattled.

"I threw the quiz on purpose," Ben said aloud, face burning.

"What?"

"Why?"

Ben shrugged. "Someone in there is failing, and I honestly don't think he can learn it—well, not without *trying*—and he doesn't feel like trying."

Someone whispered, "Jeff."

Ben said, "And since I don't want him to fail and since I wreck every curve I decided to just put down the wrong answers—"

The class went silent. Ben heard not so much as the sound of one person breathing. He looked around at the friendly faces now all astonished and, in a weird sort of knowing and kind way, disappointed. Last of all, he met Joe's wise eyes and he heard himself say out loud, "Then, when Coach confronted me, I yelled at him and slammed the door."

With that admission, Ben hid his face in his arms on his desk while the entire class drew a collective gasp of astonishment so loud and pained that Ben's ears pounded with the roar of it. In the silence that followed, Ben fought back humiliated tears, shuddered with incredulity at his own public confession, and then simultaneously Bonnie Jean's and Joe's hands touched each of his shoulders.

Bonnie Jean said, "Everyone makes mistakes."

Joe said, "Yeah. We've all been there before. Especially me. Heck, every person in this class has seen me mess up so many times."

Then Ben felt Adam's mighty hand drop onto his back as the big man said, "We just never expected it from you, thinking you were perfect and all."

"I'm not perfect," Ben muttered from his hiding place. "And I know I was wrong."

"Well, then," Dr. Deterding said. "Let's just have a word of prayer for Ben. Then we'll get on with the lesson." Again there were murmurs and then sounds of nearby chairs scooting closer and friends walking quickly close. In a moment there were more hands touching his arms and back, his head and shoulders, and in the dizzying surprise of it all, he heard Dr. Deterding ask God's blessing on his health, his well-being, his school work, his basketball playing. "Father," she asked, "restore Ben to yourself and repair his relationship with Tom. Thank you. Amen."

Ben lifted up his head and looked around. "Thank you," he sniffed, and Dr. Deterding pressed a pad of tissues into his hand. Ben thanked her again and saw tears flooding out of Bonnie Jean's eyes and Victoria using her sleeve to blot her eyes. "Do you need to go to the lavatory and get yourself together?" Dr. D. asked him.

"No, thank you," Ben said. "I'm better now. Thank you. Thanks, everybody."

"We love you, Ben," Baby said frankly. And then suddenly, somehow,

Ben was pulled to his feet, being hugged by several of his classmates, then several more.

When she finally got everyone back in their seats, Dr. Deterding said, "Now, Ben, we'll have no more of that, will we?"

"Crying in public? Or cheating?"

"You can cry 'til the cows come home if it helps you, young man, and I'm glad to hear you call this what it was—cheating. No more of that. Not in any of your classes."

"No, ma'am," Ben said quietly. "That's what Coach said."

"I imagine you felt the pressure to fit in and not offend, as often as you've moved."

Ben murmured. "People get sick of me dropping into their world and wrecking the curve."

"We don't feel that way here," she said. "Do we?"

"No way," Baby said. "If I'm gonna beat you here in math, I want to really beat you, so don't cut me any slack. And," he said, "I'm sure I speak for everyone."

"Definitely for me," Joe said softly.

"And me," Bonnie Jean said.

"Can we get to work now?" Dr. D's voice held a hint of hope.

"I'm done with my problem," Baby said, grinning.

"You're done, but you're wrong," Ben said, pointing at Baby's paper.

"What!" Baby squawked.

"Look," Ben said, putting his finger below Baby's mistake.

"No!" Baby shrieked.

"Ben's back!" Adam shouted. "And he's better than ever."

"Good, that gives me another minute," Joe called out. They set to work, pencils scratching rapidly. The door squeaked open. Mrs. Poulard leaned in, met Ben's eyes, and beckoned him with her finger. "May I see Ben for a few minutes, please, Dr. Deterding?"

"Yes, as long as he gets the work from a classmate."

"Of course he'll do that," Mrs. Poulard said, her voice smooth as butter, as Ben gathered up his things. He put his finished problem on Joe's notebook and said, "It's right," then made his way to the door.

"Everything's going to work out," Dr. Deterding said, touching Ben's arm as he walked past her.

"Did she hear us praying over the intercom or something?" Ben whispered to her.

"No," Dr. D. laughed. "I'm sure Tom told her. He must be very upset."

When Ben left the room, the class giggled over Ben's comment about the intercom, but Joe met Bonnie Jean's eyes with their private concern.

After the second machine quilting class of the day, Laurie took a break to nurse Cara and phone Tom.

"How are you, Tom?"

"Everything okay, Laurie?"

"My class just ended and I'm feeding Cara."

"What's up, Laurie? You sound upset."

"I had to fire Chelsea."

"She couldn't get it together, huh?" Laurie recounted the conversation she had overheard between Chelsea and one of the customers. Tom said, "Imagine what she says when you're *not* in the store."

"It's nice of you to be sympathetic, Tom, when I know you would have kept trying with her."

Tom laughed. "No, you did the right thing. She's not a teenager."

"You keep hoping with Max."

"That's because I feel responsible for Max's problems in life," Tom admitted.

"He was like that before you met him."

"But I stole the most beautiful woman in the world away from him."

Laurie laughed. "You're sweet. But he didn't particularly want me..." her voice trailed off, her confidence faltering. "Or did you mean Katie?"

"What? Of course I meant *you*, Laurie."

"Oh," Laurie breathed deeply, "good. You scared me there for a minute."

There was an awkward silence. It lasted too long. Tom said, "Laurie, you're the one I love."

"But really, Tom," Laurie said with some difficulty, "you were attracted to Katie back then. She was much more beautiful than me with her long legs and her athletic—"

"No, Laurie." Another awkward pause held the space between them. Tom said, "Katie was attractive, there's no denying that. And I felt deeply concerned for her. She was needy and we were both—you and I—taking care of her. But you're the woman I'm in love with. Only you."

"Tom, I know you loved Katie. You may not have slept with her, but you *did* love her."

She heard Tom breathe, heard him swallow before he said, "That's what I meant about feeling responsible for Max's problems."

"I don't quite see the connection, Tom." Laurie caressed baby Cara's silky hair, surprised at the poignant stab of pain as she pondered again for the millionth time how both of the men Laurie had loved had turned, in startled fascination, to Katie. Even her own brother had been captivated. Maybe it was because Laurie had loved her; certainly she had introduced all three of them to her beguiling and needy best friend.

"Laurie," Tom said, his voice sorrowful and tender.

She knew he was embarrassed for having loved Katie at all, let alone so strongly; she knew he regretted the pain of doubt and jealousy it had caused. She said, "Max was used to everyone thinking Katie was gorgeous and interesting. Because she was. Totally."

"Laurie, I think one of the reasons I convinced Katie to go back to Max was because she was a temptation to me."

"You've said that before," Laurie murmured, thinking again, as she had so irreverently, so despicably, so many times before, that if Tom and Katie had slept together, things would have turned out better—for Katie. True, the affair would have shattered her own life—living with the knowledge that *both* men she had loved had turned from her to Katie's bed. It had been demoralizing enough to cope with Max's sudden and passionate preference for Katie, hard enough to understand Tom's interest. Inside she felt the torture of jealous fear just as vividly as she had that night at Rising Sun's New Year's Eve party when Tom had been so involved with comforting Katie. How could such a horrible emotion live through years of love and happiness and commitment? "You said that then." Laurie breathed deeply and hugged her baby—Tom's baby, warm and hungry and sweet smelling—close to her, knowing also that she, Laurie, would have labored to forgive them. How could she not? Tom had forgiven her so much; Tom had forgiven her Max. Aloud she said, "But no, Tom. Katie had to give Max another chance."

"Maybe she didn't tell us everything," Tom murmured. "And I sent her back into that lion's den partially to save my own soul. To protect you from my—"

"From your humanity? No, Tom. Stop this. Your motives may have been complex, but you were trying to do what was right. Part of doing right was wanting to stay faithful to me. Katie was tempting to every man alive. Even Charlie Johnson, for pity sake. And she had to go back. She was in love with Max, despite all their problems. You know that. She never could stay away from him." In the quiet of her office she held the phone, listening to Tom think and struggle.

Katie, in turmoil about her separation from Max, had come after Christmas to visit Tom and Laurie. Max wanted reconciliation, but Katie's family was vehemently against it. Laurie had been preparing for the New Year's Eve celebration at Rising Sun, sorting through donated blankets, coats and food, when Katie had returned from an errand to Graul's distraught and teary. Peter, eighteen months old, had tagged along with Katie because like every male, big and little, young and old, Peter was enchanted by her. Both of them returned in tears. Peter, crying in sympathy for Katie, came to Laurie's arms wailing and he clung to her neck, his chubby toddler legs balancing on her belly that had begun to bulge in pregnancy. Katie, sniffing back tears, held her head high, feeling foolish for her uncontrollable emotion.

All Laurie could get Katie to say was that she wanted a son just like Peter, and when people at the grocery store had assumed Peter was her child, she had been crushed by the thought that her prayer would remain unanswered. "Max and I had been trying for more than two years before we separated," she sobbed onto Laurie's shoulder, her emotion making Peter cry harder. Laurie's volunteers had arrived with armfuls of donated coats, and Katie had rushed into the back room where Peter usually napped—the back room that was today her office in which she sat nursing her new baby and remembering how her dearest friend had been unable to compose herself that cold winter afternoon.

Then Tom arrived with Charlie Johnson, in town for a few days. Twelve midshipmen followed, each carrying bags of donations. Tom took the whimpering Peter from where he clung to her shoulder, promising to distract him while she directed the volunteers' efforts. Midshipmen were great workers and Laurie quickly had the place humming with productive activity. Besides sorting the blankets and jackets, stuffing backpacks with toiletries and other donated necessities, there had been rising bread to put in the ovens, soup to stir and season, cookies to ice and tables to set.

So, it was hours later when she realized that Charlie and Tom, who yet held his sleeping son in his arms, sat in the back room talking with Katie. Still later, Tom emerged. Peter had awakened and was asking for Laurie. Then Laurie and Tom had their guests to greet, so it was close to midnight before she thought about Katie again and when she did, she went to the back room only to find Katie and Tom talking earnestly, Tom holding both of Katie's hands the way a man does when he wants to convince a woman of something that must happen. It was then that Tom must have advised Katie to return to the life she'd fled, to her estranged and waiting husband. It was then that Tom must have bargained with Katie's well-being for his own purity and Laurie's happiness.

"I was just remembering," Laurie said to Tom, her voice vague sounding in the phone.

"Me, too."

"Charlie remembers her fondly, doesn't he?"

"Yes."

"What was it about her, Tom?"

"I guess it was the tension in her and the honest way she tried to cope with it. She had so many philosophical questions about right and wrong. She thought about everything. Her spirit was yearning for faith, and her mind was demanding."

"Yes," Laurie said, knowing that just such complexity and the willingness to show that vulnerability defined Katie's attraction more than her stunning beauty did. "But she also had such strong physical and emotional needs. I think her wanting a baby so desperately drove her to ask those questions. And really, Tom, it was her wanting a baby that drove her back to Max. That's why she went. It wasn't your fault."

What Tom remembered of those hours in what now was Laurie's elegant and highly functional office, was how violently Katie had cried, how pitiful her eyes looked, the eyelids shiny and translucent, her eyes—without the disguising contact lenses—odd and compelling with their irises slit to look like twin keys. He remembered how Charlie had held her in his arms, had read from the Bible to her, and how Katie had wept over her faults and frustrations. Her desperation for cleansing, for new and vibrant life after the shattering experience of being married to Max Hunter, had been somehow tied to this longing for a child. And when faith became hers that night, both he and Charlie loved her. Her face shining with joy, her eyes bright with the light of hope, avowed that they—two idealistic men—had helped her or thought they had. They loved her for it. Later, when he had been alone with her, when they had talked, Katie confided questions and struggles that were so like his own had been—lofty and abstract and deliciously elusive compared to Laurie's rich, practical approach to life—that Tom had felt a kind of a kinship new and delightful to him. And somehow in those moments both he and Katie had known that she had to return to Max. The reasons for doing so were legion, and they were desperate ones.

30

MRS. Poulard's office was scented by the blousy bowl of gold and orange lilies centered on her conference table. She asked Ben to sit down while she poured him a glass of water from a decanter that stood on her bookshelf. She switched on an electric kettle before taking his file, a pad of paper and her phone to the table.

"I seem to be in here a lot," he said, "considering I was never in the principal's office before in my whole life."

She chuckled. "My teachers are required to report incidents—like your quiz—and Coach MacBride was concerned about you. Particularly about your slamming the door and shouting at him."

"Yeah."

"Help me understand what would provoke you to shout at your coach. I know you've been getting along so well."

Ben squinched up his face in frustration. "He has these standards for life that I'll never be able to live up to. I—I respect him, but I don't measure up."

"I see." Her kind eyes examined his face. "But you want to try or you wouldn't have felt so embarrassed and angry."

"Mrs. Poulard. I know I was wrong about that quiz. I see that now, but…I don't think I can be honest all the time." Ben looked down, not wanting her to see the angry despair he felt. Required to lie for the happiness and security of his parents, he could never give them what they wanted here at CCS.

"I tried to call your father to enlist his help, but it seems as if I have the wrong number." She turned his file toward him showing him the number he'd dictated to her during their last meeting. "Didn't you give me that number?"

"Yes, ma'am."

"Did you give me the wrong number intentionally?"

Ben hesitated, searching for what to say. The thought, *Start now, just start telling the truth,* came to his mind. "Yes, ma'am. I did. I know that wasn't honest, either."

"No, it wasn't. You're in the habit of lying."

"I am," Ben said.

"I need the correct number for your father. I could get it, but I want you to start setting things right."

"But I don't want you to call him."

"That's up to me to decide." Ben's shaky breathing could be heard above the wailing sound of water heating in the electric kettle. Mrs. Poulard held her pencil poised to write and Ben stared at his file, understanding in a deep, solid way that it was not really her, but God who was requiring him to tell the truth. The possible consequences of Mrs. Poulard telling his father flashed in Ben's mind like so many graphic and terrifying warnings and he swallowed, holding his jaw shut. He'd lied for years and how had it helped him? Mrs. Poulard said softly, "Tell the truth and leave what happens to God."

Ben thought that if God really was good, it might be better to do things his way. He forced the right numbers out. Fear pounded in his ears. Mrs. Poulard recorded the number in his file, and to Ben's horror, dialed it. He could hear his father's secretary, Mrs. Baird, say, "English and History Department, Office of Marine Affairs."

"Hello, may I speak to Colonel Hunter?"

"May I say who is calling?"

"This is Joan Poulard. I'm the principal at his son Ben's school."

There was a silence and then Mrs. Baird returned to the phone. "I'm sorry, Mrs. Poulard. Colonel Hunter is in a meeting and can't speak with you right now. Can he return your call?"

Ben was so visibly relieved when she hung up the phone that Joan Poulard patted his wrist. "Most boys are afraid of their fathers, yet when I call, they turn out to be reasonable men."

"No," Ben said. "It's different. Joe's not afraid of his father. He's afraid of his father's *principles*. Coach is committed to his principles and he's going to bring them to life in Joe, one way or the other. That's what Joe's afraid of, that process."

"What's different with you? Why are you afraid of your father finding out about this?"

Struggling to speak, Ben murmured, "The last time the principal called my father, it turned out awful."

"What happened?" Mrs. Poulard left the table and went to the hissing teapot.

"I had an ear infection and I threw up at school and they made him come get me. Things turned out bad."

"How do you mean 'bad?'" Ben watched her pour the hot water into two big mugs.

Ben tried to think of what he meant and how to say it. "I got the infection from swimming," he remembered aloud, tracing the events back. "I joined the swim team on base even though I wasn't allowed to swim anymore. But that didn't make sense to me because he *taught* me to swim and we used to love to swim together, so I signed up hoping to get him back into it. And didn't tell him."

"How old were you?" Mrs Poulard put a steaming cup of tea in front of him.

He put his shaking hands around the mug, breathed in the sweet scent. "Twelve." Remembering, Ben saw himself sitting on a bench at the Naval Hospital. He retreated into the privacy of his memory, grateful for Mrs. Poulard's silent patience. He saw himself resting his head back on the cold, concrete wall and he remembered the weakness that had weighed down his limbs. Both ears throbbed and his stomach, though emptied, had felt uncertain.

The doctor, a navy commander with dark hair put neatly back, smiled at Ben and looked at him with big, friendly brown eyes. When she lay her hand on his feverish brow, tears came to Ben's eyes. "You poor thing," she said. Ben remembered loving her with all of his heart. His father tried to flirt with her.

"You hardly look old enough to have been all the way through medical school," Max said.

"Isn't that something?" she said. "So young and yet I outrank you, Major."

"I like women who outrank me. Makes me feel kinda helpless."

"Both his ears are infected," she said, glancing at Max. "Looks like it started a couple weeks ago with swimmer's ear."

"My kid's not stupid enough to go swimming in February, *Doctor*."

"Not outside. On a swim team. Don't tell me he hasn't been complaining about his ears. This boy is in a lot of pain. I'm surprised he's conscious."

"He never complains. He's a stoic. I swear, I had no idea he was sick."

The doctor glanced at Ben. "It's true," Ben had said, "I didn't tell them." He never told his parents when he was sick. He understood that he was his own responsibility.

"This infection may be systemic. We'll have to do some blood tests to determine if it has spread to his bloodstream." She bent over Ben again. "I'm going to have to take some blood from your arm, Ben. It shouldn't hurt too much."

"No, ma'am." Ben watched her make the preparations.

"Make a fist, now," she said. Ben let his eyes drift over her kind face. "How long has your ear been hurting, Ben?" she asked.

"I don't know," Ben replied, glancing quickly at his father who shot him illegible warnings with his eyes. He remembered the doctor's smooth, dampish fingers probing his abdomen. "His heart sounds good and strong." She pulled a syringe from the drawer and took a vial from the locked cabinet. "For his pain," she said to Max. "He has a healthy body—a swimmer's body—look at the shoulders and the muscle development," she said, filling the syringe. "But he looks like he's been losing weight."

"He's not a swimmer, Dr. Chaney," Max said as the doctor injected the numbing liquid into Ben's bicep.

"I joined the base swim team, Dad," Ben's voice came trembling forth with the withdrawal of the needle.

"You *what*?"

Commander Chaney said gently, "When you get back in the water, you're going to have to use earplugs."

She turned to Max. "The corpsman will get a wheelchair for him. He shouldn't try to walk by himself and obviously shouldn't be left alone." Writing quickly, she ripped the prescriptions from the pad. "I'll see you in a week unless I call you about the blood tests later this afternoon." She smiled at Ben and stopped at the door. "Don't miss that appointment, Major Hunter," she said, "or I'll have a personal chat with your CO."

"Hey, no need for that. Have a personal chat with me. I'm a friendly guy. How about dinner?"

"I don't have dinner with married majors," she told him.

All the way home, Ben drifted on the sweet anticipation of his father taking care of him. He felt numb and happy. He had found the way to his father's attention; sickness demanded it. He forgot that Max had forbidden him to swim.

At home when he helped Ben to the bathroom, Max said, "You shouldn't have told her that lie about the swim team. That made me look like a jerk."

"I did join."

Ben remembered saying that. He remembered saying the words and hearing them echo off the bathroom walls, and then his memory went black. His next memory was pale walls, the sharp smell of Pine-Sol, and coarse white sheets all mixed with the delirium of codeine. He was in the hospital.

He heard Mrs. Poulard sip her tea and looked up to see the sympathy in her eyes. The systemic infection that Dr. Chaney had feared had been detected in his blood. She had called later that afternoon with the report and gave instructions to bring Ben immediately to the hospital. When Ben regained consciousness, Dr. Chaney told him that his eardrum had ruptured; his mother had discovered him unconscious on the bathroom floor. During his hospital stay, Dr. Chaney visited him daily and they became friends. She asked him, often, to try to remember how he ended up with bruises on his jaw and hip, but he could never remember. He still couldn't.

But he did remember what a dark time it had been when he got home from the hospital. "I guess Dad was in trouble for flirting with the doctor," Ben reflected to Mrs. Poulard after telling her as much of the story as he thought he could.

"No, I don't think so," she said so seriously that Ben stopped staring at his hands and looked at her to find her expression sad and worried.

Because of Donna's violent sadness, Ben had come to assume that Max's flirtation was the problem. He heard her yelling at Max, yet she seemed to blame Ben. Donna refused to look at Ben or speak to him until the day she told him he'd have to tell Dr. Chaney that he'd gotten the bruises because he got sick to his stomach and ran to the bathroom, slipped, and crashed into the tub. He was to tell the doctor that he had suddenly remembered everything. "I *don't* remember," he'd told Donna with the angry tears of honest protest. But his tears didn't matter to Donna, his outraged sense of justice was trivial compared to his father's need and in the end, to *please* her, to *soothe* her, he broke his friendship with Dr. Chaney and said what his mother required.

No, Dad must have been in trouble because of me. Finally grasping the implications, Ben met Mrs. Poulard's sad eyes. The tea had cooled in the cup he gripped in his hands and he pushed it away. Having endured the subsequent years of his father's escalating violence, Ben knew what he could not remember. Max had hit him, knocked him unconscious; the blow burst his swollen eardrum. And it was of this very crime that Dr. Chaney suspected Max. Now Ben was unsure how much he had revealed to Mrs. Poulard. Had he broken his promise of silence? Aware that his hands and voice shook he said, "My p-parents are not interested in the truth."

She nodded, biting her lower lip, and reached to grasp his shaking hand. "But Coach MacBride and I are."

"Yes, ma'am." He was unreasonably frightened, eyes burning again, stomach tossing.

She recognized this and withdrew her hand, turning her tone brisk. "Being honest is a discipline you must acquire. I have a good idea that this French quiz is not the only one you've given points away on."

"No, ma'am."

"You need someone to help you grow. That's why I had *planned* to call your dad—"

"Please don't, Mrs. Poulard. I know I've been a liar and you have no reason to trust me *at all*, but please don't get him involved. We will both be *really* sorry."

"What am I to do with you, then?"

Wincing, he said, "You could cut me from the team."

"Are you *serious*?"

"That would be better and it would punish me. I love basketball."

Her scrutiny of him grew sharp. "No, I won't cut you from the team. You need Coach MacBride."

Ben looked down, eyes stinging suddenly. "Apparently."

"And actually, I think that's the answer." She tapped her pencil on his folder; petals from her flowers drifted onto the table. "Tell me, Ben. Would you rather I turn you over to your coach—with all his stellar and impossible principles—than call your father?"

Struggling, Ben studied his clenched fists, noting the whiteness of his knuckles, the tight burn of the skin, fully aware of the traitorous and impossible choice before him. He opened his hands, the lines of those thin, childhood scars white on his reddened palms, and he knew in a flash of clarity that all he had to do was say what he knew was true. Ben said, "Yes, I would."

"Are you sure? He's going to be tough on you. You'll have to promise me you won't balk or give him any trouble."

Ben met her eyes. "If I have to pick between you calling my father or having to live up to Tom's impossible standards, I—I—still would prefer, even though it's not gonna work on me," Ben shook his head. "I still pick him—Tom MacBride."

31

STILL shaken from his discussion with Mrs. Poulard, Ben was drawn to the gym by the powerful sound of the piano, and only when he stepped through the doors did he see that his own friend, Joe MacBride, was making this strong music. He caught Joe's eye as he entered the gym. Joe looked up from the piano and nodded, giving Ben his serious, bracing smile, eyes squinted, not missing a note. Adam and Drew waved Ben over to where they were sitting in the bleachers and Ben took his seat in their midst, as they pounded his shoulders and back and teased him about Mrs. Poulard. He was greatly buoyed by their camaraderie.

Two other girls sang with Bonnie Jean that day, with Scott on the guitar and Michelle playing drums, but Joe made the music live with his particular touch. "He's really good," Drew said to Ben, who nodded agreement.

Their music seemed to build its meaning inside of Ben and he found himself thinking about the words in the final song. The tune had a Gaelic lilt, perfect for Joe's touch on the piano, beautiful in Bonnie Jean's heartfelt expression of it. And when the last note sounded, both Joe and Bonnie Jean looked to him smiling, their eyes bright with affection. Tom wheeled to the front of the podium and Joe left his piano, crossed the slightly raised platform, and jumped down. "Need help, Dad?"

"Thanks, Joe." Joe grasped his father's arm at the elbow and pulled him up. Tom took a moment to balance and Ben saw the look of intense concentration on his face. "I'm good," he said to Joe, patting his shoulder, and then impulsively Tom hugged him. He turned to the audience as though presenting his son to them and said, "Wasn't it great to have Joe back on the piano?" The school erupted in applause, his friends chanting Joe's name. Joe grinned at them, ducked his head down, and jogged off to the back of the gym with Tom's wheelchair, disappearing for a moment to put it in Tom's office.

When he came to where they were sitting, Joe squeezed between Ben and Adam shoving Ben so close to Bonnie Jean that Ben's thigh touched hers. He glanced at her; she smiled and took his arm at the elbow. "That was beautiful," he whispered to her.

"Things go okay with Mrs. P?" Joe asked in a whisper.

"She's turning me over to your dad."

"Good," Joe said. "That's what you need."

Tom read the announcements and when he finished, he looked straight at Ben, his expression directly conciliatory.

"It sometimes upsets students to see me use my wheelchair," Tom began. "But I'm not feeling too bad today, just bad enough that I figured I'd better rest my back so I can be on my feet for the first basketball game this afternoon." Here the students erupted into boisterous applause. "I hope you'll all be there. We've got a great team this year. They're going to be a joy to watch."

From a few rows behind them, Leeza whispered, "Too bad they can't play naked," setting off a brush fire of giggles.

"We ought to be allowed to," Joe grumbled, teasing. "Gymnasium actually *means* naked."

"You're such a nerd," Bonnie Jean whispered.

"That's what he told his dad after he mooned the school, you know," Ben said.

"You don't care about living, do you?" Adam scolded.

"Hey," Joe said. "He laughed."

Looking at their group, Tom put his finger to his lips, eyebrows raised, and they settled down to listen. "And anyway," Tom said. "Riding around in a wheelchair is not all that bad. When I push the wheels I keep building these impressive muscles in my arms and shoulders." Tom smiled at the boys' teasing response. "It helps me go where I need to go and much more quickly.

"Something about being human makes us want to go faster than our legs can carry us. Does anybody in this room remember getting your first bicycle?" Tom smiled at the crowd of waving hands.

"When I was eight years old, my parents gave me a bicycle for my birthday. My father was a plumber and though he was a successful businessman, always working, always doing excellent work, we did not have a lot of extra money. My mother did not work outside the home and my father had many expenses tied to establishing his business and obligations to relatives in Scotland. We lived a careful life and so, when he showed me that beautiful red Schwinn, I knew he had sacrificed to give it to me. He always knew what I was dreamin' about."

Bonnie Jean glanced at Joe and smiled. Joe whispered to Ben, "You would have loved Gramps. He was the greatest."

"As soon as I could ride, Dad let me go with it. I rode through our neighborhood and soon I was good enough to let go with one hand and wave to the kids who came out to admire it.

"I was feeling confident, so I decided to go to the main road because I wanted a nice long stretch to ride. Peddling hard up the hill, I rode past the corner grocery store, past the gas station. I had never been to this area by myself and I remember noticing the overflowing trash bins, doors left ajar, and a surprising number of people sitting on their steps. I waved and rode on finally reaching my goal—the long, sloping Cottman Avenue.

"I'll never forget the bliss of speeding along on that fine September day with the hot sun on my face and shoulders. The wind lifted me; it ruffled my crew cut; it filled up my jacket as if it were a sail. I was flying and free and nothing could catch me.

"I arrived home late and my legs were feeling like sticks of gum they were so tired, but I put the bicycle away in the shed, brushing off the dirt. I shut the door and I remember locking it. Dad kept his tools there and he had taught me to be careful.

"The next morning, I woke before my parents and went to take a quick ride before breakfast and church. The shed door stood ajar. The padlock and handle had been twisted off and left on the grass. I had to make myself look and when I burst into my parents' room, I was sobbing, 'It's gone! My bicycle's gone!'"

The gym went silent. Tom paused. "There was no question of replacing it. There was no way to justify such a luxurious expense—*twice*. It was gone forever. We all knew that.

"Four weeks went by with me waiting for the police to find the bicycle. Despite Dad's sympathy, I got angry. Along about the first week in October, the police called to say they'd found the bicycle. My mother and I considered it a miracle, but my father asked if he could talk to the suspected thief.

"I went with him. Now, you must understand, I knew my father. He was tough and principled, physically strong, and always interested in getting to the heart of the matter. I was convinced that Dad would talk to the thief, thrash him, turn him utterly subdued over to the police, and hand me back my bicycle in triumph.

"We met the policeman at the corner store on Cottman Avenue. He led us to an apartment that smelled of grease and boredom. My bicycle stood in the middle of a dim room beside knee-high stacks of newspapers and paper bags filled with empty glass bottles. Unwashed dishes rose from the sink. I counted five children standing very still, rubbing their eyes with the gritty concentration of the intensely itchy. I moved toward my bicycle, but my father's hand dropped on my shoulder.

"Dad introduced himself and then me to the only adult in the room— a thin woman who sat at the kitchen table before an open magazine and a full, steaming cup of coffee. Smoke curled from the ashtray beside her magazine in a slow, gray coil. He shook her hand and politely asked the names of the children.

"'Kevin's the culprit,' the mother said, pointing at the tallest. 'He's a handful and his dad can't see it.'

"'Where is his dad?' I asked.

"'He keeps his own schedule,' she said. 'Never know when he's gonna show up, do we, Kevin?' She said this without emotion, glanced longingly at her magazine, and then smiled at me.

"This gave me courage, so I asked her, 'But he lives here, right?' You see, I knew Dad wasn't going to thrash a woman and there wouldn't be proper justice until the father came home for it.

"'Course he lives here. You think I could take care of these children on my own?'

"My father said, 'When do you expect your husband, ma'am?'

"She looked at Kevin. 'When was he here last, Kev?'

"Without looking up, Kevin said, 'Yesterday morning.'

"'He'll be back anytime now get some clean clothes.'

"I looked around to see where these might possibly be kept. Kevin's mother said, 'What're you going to do to him, officer?'

"'That's up to Mr. MacBride.'

"My father said, 'May I have your permission to talk to Kevin, ma'am?' Dad always talked before he struck justice. He asked Kevin, just as politely, to wheel the bicycle outside.

"'How did it get all wrecked up?' I said when I saw it in the daylight.

"Kevin shrugged, rubbing his eyes and squinting.

"'I'm afraid that's not the answer I need,' my father said, getting down on one knee so he was eye level with the criminal. 'Tell me what you've been doing.'

"'You're not from here,' Kevin said rudely.

"'I was born in Scotland.'

"Kevin shrugged, then pointed to the bicycle. 'I been hiding it under that old truck," he said, pointing to his left where a lopsided pick-up truck with the grocer's faded logo stood. 'I can only ride it at night so I don't get caught and then I run into things.'

"'You run into things?' my father said.

"'It's dark,' Kevin shrugged again. My father glanced at me to see if I found the comment odd. A boy could always find his way in the dark, we both knew.

"'What kind of things?' I asked.

"'Stuff I don't see, like I'm riding along and *boom!* Last night I crashed right into the steps over around front the store. That's what bent the wheel up. That's when I got caught.'

"A glance at the policeman confirmed this. My father stared at the boy who was three years older than me and built solidly. But he was dirty, his hair the same color as his pale, grimy skin, his eyes looking weary, the eyelids puffed and cracked. In the awkward silence, we heard the boy's stomach thunder. My father stood up and indicated to the policeman that he wanted to speak to him.

"Kevin said to me, 'Your dad's nice,' and I began to tremble. I knew that things were not going according to my liking, something about the look on my father's face spoke mercy, not vengeance. I stared at my bicycle, barely recognizable with its bent wheel, scraped paint, broken basket, dented and scratched handlebars. The policeman went into the house—I hoped to talk to the mother about her son going to jail. My father returned to us and asked to speak to me privately. We walked over to the pick-up truck and stood on its far side. I kept my eye on the boy and my bicycle.

"My father went to one knee. 'Tommy,' he said in his solemn, quiet voice. 'There's somethin' we must do, you and I.'

"'No, Dad—'

"'To start, the child is ill. His eyes are infected and he needs food.'

"'He *stole* my *bicycle*.'

"'I'm thinking that maybe your bicycle was stolen so we would have an opportunity to love our neighbors as our Lord commands.'

"'But he didn't love me. Stealing isn't loving.'

"'But we're to love him first. That's what we're going to do. You and me.'

"My dad had a certain inspired look in his eyes that meant it was no use arguing, though I gave it my best try. The next week we began to fix the bicycle. Kevin and I worked for Dad on Saturdays, earning the money for the parts—one by one. And over my mother's protests, Dad invited the entire grubby family over for Sunday supper.

"In my opinion things had gone from bad to worse. I went with Dad when he took them a bag of groceries each Monday evening and though I knew they needed the food, I looked at the oatmeal I ate for breakfast with resentment, imagining the bags we took to them were full of bacon—or worse, Cocoa Puff cereal, deemed too expensive at my house. I read to the smaller children while my father visited with Kevin's parents. But inviting them to my house was too much for me. I was *so* resentful, I let it show. My father asked me to leave the supper table and when they went home for the evening, he came up to my room.

"I exploded. 'He *stole* something and you're mad at *me*?'

"'Here's your choice, Tommy. You can harden your heart and refuse to be kind. If that's what you choose, I'll leave you here to yourself. But if you want to be like Christ, you must turn away from your selfish behavior and forgive.'

"Now, the brilliant psychology of this bargain still impresses me. If I chose to keep being rude and hard-hearted, my father would not punish me, but leave me alone." Tom spread his hands wide in a gesture of surrender. "That's obviously gonna be less painful, less embarrassing. Very appealing, right?" He laughed and smiled at the crowd, his eyes ending up with a fond glance at Joe. Tom paused, looking around at the faces turned to him. "I bet you're saying to yourselves there's really no choice, right? Except when you love and adore your father as I did mine.

"I knew if I wanted peace between us, if I wanted him to be pleased with me again, then I had to change in here." Tom thumped on his chest with two fingers. "I started crying and asked him 'But why, Dad, why? He stole from us.'

"'We've been forgiven much, Tommy. It's a beautiful experience and one this lad needs.'

"'But you never just *forgive* me, Dad. You *always* punish me.'

"'And don't you think it is punishment to make the boy fix what he wrecked, all the time havin' to face you and me? Being forced to sit at dinner with the people he's wronged, just so he and his family can have the food they need? No, Tommy, God forgives first and then chastens us so that we can change.'

"It was nearly a year before the bicycle was fixed and Kevin looked as healthy as me. His eyes were better, he kept himself clean, and he had proven to be an excellent mechanic. The day came when we had no more work to do and the three of us stood staring at the gleaming bicycle. I'll confess I felt like crying, and by then Kevin looked like he was holding back tears.

"'I was wrong to take it,' he said. 'I'm so sorry.' He went to my father and he was hugged and kissed just as if he were me. They heard me crying behind them and took me into the hug. Finally, I said, 'I know. Let's sell it and buy two cheaper ones.'

"Both of them wiped their eyes and stared at me.

"'No,' Kevin said. 'It's yours. You don't owe me. I owe you.'

"'But I forgive you,' I heard myself say."

Tom glanced around the room, waiting for his audience to savor his words. His eyes met Ben's and he smiled his brisk, knowing half-smile. Touched, profoundly touched, Ben had to look away.

"What happened to Kevin? We sold the bicycle and bought two wrecked up ones. We fixed them up, same as we did the original, and I still have mine. If you're ever over, take a look at it in my garage to the left of the trampoline where I keep all the stuff with wheels. Well, you can't miss it. And Kevin worked for my father all through high school and on the weekends all through college. He took over my father's plumbing business when Dad retired and turned it into a tech school that is a halfway house for kids released from the juvenile system in Philadelphia. He calls it Water Runs Uphill.

"And so you see, my friends," Tom said, meeting Ben's eyes. "My father extended forgiveness way before the culprit had faith enough to benefit from it. Forgiveness was offered out of love, out of my father's understanding of God's love, and that forgiveness redeemed Kevin's life. This is what God has done for us, and this is what we must do for each other. Let's pray."

While Tom was praying, Ben thought about the lying his parents required, thought about the way he'd taken lying to his inner self as a way to live and he felt the tears again come up and when Joe and Bonnie Jean both put an arm around his back, he had to hold his breath and squeeze his eyes shut to try to keep them back.

32

HIS monthly meeting with the USNA and community volunteers of the Special Olympics committee was usually pretty enjoyable for Max Hunter, but today, his entire body hurt. Last night, at the sound of Donna's car behind the house, he had woken up lying facedown on the second floor landing. Eyes burning, stomach uneasy, and joints feeling wound with barbed wire, he made it to the bathroom before Donna got up the stairs. Two Excedrin Migraines had mitigated his morning headache; a double dose of Imodium and a glass of milk had settled his stomach, but he simply could not concentrate. Pain hovered like dark, building thunderclouds do at the edge of the parade field. When his wandering gaze looked out of his open office door, he saw Admiral Johnson standing before Mrs. Baird's desk with a big, white envelope beneath his arm. His headache returned in pounding waves; Max looked down quickly.

Mrs. Baird approached, her steps ominous whispers across the carpet, and when she informed him in her loud whisper that the admiral wanted to see him when his meeting was finished, the polite people on the committee shuffled up their papers and said their good-byes.

"Admiral Johnson, *sir*," Max said with strained enthusiasm, reaching to shake the admiral's hand.

"I need a few minutes of your time, Max," he said, stepping into the office and shutting the door. "Have a seat," Johnson said to Max, as if this were *his* office. He pulled out one of the chairs that faced Max's desk.

"Wouldn't you prefer to get a cup of coffee somewhere, Admiral Johnson?"

"No. Though you look like you could use a cup."

"I think I will," Max said. "Excuse me." He hurried out to Mrs. Baird and asked her to bring a cup of coffee. Max shut his office door behind him with care. Declining the seat beside Johnson, he took refuge in his big leather chair behind the desk. "What can I do for you, Admiral Johnson?"

"Max, after hearing how you've struggled to get Ben's birth certificate, I thought I'd use my influence and give you a hand."

"No, thank you. I'll handle it, sir. No worries." Mrs. Baird tapped on the door and Max leapt up to open it, stumbling over the flowers in the rug, which seemed to him at that moment as if they were ten inches high. He actually landed with a thump against the door, bringing Johnson to his feet.

"Are you *all right*, Colonel?"

"I tripped somehow."

"Maybe you should get your eyesight checked," the admiral said, watching Max take the green plastic mug from Mrs. Baird's outstretched hands. "What with two car accidents and this tripping."

"Twenty-twenty, sir," Max insisted, pointing to his eyes with two fingers as he crossed the room. He lowered himself into his chair and held the coffee under his nose.

The admiral said, "Here's my dilemma. I was asked to write a letter confirming Ben's age and identity. I wrote that letter in good faith based on the official documents in your file. Since then, I've been troubled because according to you, the information in your file is not correct."

"Like I tell my students," Max said, "history's a matter of perspective."

Johnson opened the clasp on the envelope, looked in, and took out a small, rectangular paper. "Regardless, I got you a copy."

"Pardon?"

"Of Ben's birth certificate." He flipped over his wrist, putting the document close to Max. "Here, take it."

Max hesitated; taking instead his coffee cup in both trembling hands, he raised it to his lips and tried to remember what he'd told Johnson when the admiral had mentioned Katie that Saturday in October. "Wait. There isn't a birth certificate."

"Indeed there is. Look. You'll see it's authentic." Again, Johnson offered the document. Max stared at it, hands clutching his mug tightly. "Take it, Max."

Max put down his coffee cup and took the birth certificate, remembering more of what he'd told Johnson. In the first years after Ben came to live with them, he had told the same tale to several colleagues who had known of Katie's pregnancy. He cleared his throat and murmured, "No disrespect intended sir, but this is the wrong baby. This is the one that died."

Johnson was silent. He stared at Max as Max grew itchy and a cold sweat came up under his collar. He sniffed the hot fragrance of the coffee rising from the desk.

"Let's stop this. I reviewed your file, confirmed the facts with the relevant official documents. There is no death certificate for this child." He patted the white envelope, suggesting it contained everything else.

"There should be."

"Do you have a death certificate in your possession? You are named as his father."

"This is none of your business."

"My officers *lying* to me is my business."

"Do you ask all your officers to prove their kids are their own?"

Johnson tilted his head and studied Max a moment. "As I said, I became involved when I was asked to write a letter for Ben—a letter I'm told is written by your CO at *every* duty station—based on information found in your personnel file. I've gone to the trouble to substantiate those facts." Johnson showed several documents from the big white envelope. "Sixteen years ago, Donna was stationed in Annapolis. Here is a copy of her marriage certificate, her divorce certificate, a copy of both birth and death certificates for a child who was born and died November 1982." Johnson said.

"How did you get this stuff?"

"You should ask yourself why I felt it was essential."

"You are a busy man, Admiral, with an entire military school to oversee. I can't figure out why you want to waste time proving what isn't true."

Max said coolly and sipped his steaming coffee.

"My documents prove that Ben was born to Katie Hunter October 1980, as I wrote in my letter based on your official file."

"Look, Admiral Johnson, if it will ease your mind, I ripped up that letter you wrote. No one has to know that you got stuff wrong."

"Max, I think you've concocted this lie, not to mention this absurd inconvenience asking your CO to write a letter, merely to avoid allowing Ben to see his birth certificate and discover that Katie Hunter is his mother."

"You want to talk about facts? Remember, Admiral, *Ben* asked you to write that letter, not me. I'm telling you. Drop it. Ben is not Katie's kid any more than he's *yours*."

"How can you even hope to convince anyone of that? He looks like his mother from head to toe."

"You knew her well?" Max said, voice thick with anger.

"I advise you to be very careful, Colonel Hunter. Don't cross the line your toe is on right now."

"Me? You are all over my business and you tell me to back off?" Max shouted. "I've got a crackerjack lawyer and I'll get her to pry you right off my ass!" Max stood up, meaning to look menacing but he fumbled his coffee cup and Admiral Johnson caught it neatly with two fingers gripping the rim.

With a cool glance at Max, Johnson set the cup on the table. "Not Major Kuhn?"

"Patty Edwards over on Franklin. She's retired Navy. She knows the ropes and she's *not your man*."

"I see," Johnson said. "Talk to your Ms. Edwards. She can phone me if she'd like, or Major Kuhn, and we'll reassure her that we have the documentation right here to support the information in your file. She can explain the ramifications to you." He patted the envelope now held under one arm. "By the day after Thanksgiving, I want you to have resolved the discrepancy between your story and your file. If you produce the missing death certificate, I will owe you a profound apology." The admiral paused by the door, opening it a crack. "If you don't, then you and I and both lawyers will outline a plan of how you are going to explain to Ben who he really is. I want it done before Christmas break."

Mrs. Baird tapped the door. Johnson pulled it open. She wrung her hands, "I hate to interrupt, Colonel Hunter, but this is the second time Ben's principal has called today, and I wanted to pass along her message. It seemed urgent."

"Absolutely," Johnson said, waiting for her to continue. Max saw that he had no intention of leaving.

"Mrs. Joan Poulard called," Mrs. Baird read from her note, "to invite you to attend the basketball game today at five-thirty. She said she would very much like to meet you. She asked that I phone her back to let her know if you plan to attend so she can watch for you and say hello."

Max cleared his throat. "Please tell her that as much as I'd like to see Ben's game today, I'm afraid that I won't be able to make it. As it turns out, I don't have transportation." Max looked pointedly at Johnson. "I've given up driving for the sake of the navy."

"Nonsense!" Admiral Johnson said. He turned to Mrs. Baird. "I would hate for Colonel Hunter to miss this opportunity to meet Ben's principal and watch his son play ball. Please let Joan know that he will be there this afternoon. I will drive him myself."

"Sir, no, thank you. I—"

"I insist," Johnson said firmly. "I'd love to see Ben play." He gave a nod to Mrs. Baird, who hurried away to make the call. Max stood with his jaw clenched, wordless.

"I'll be here at seventeen hundred to pick you up," Johnson said. "I'll give you a ride to the game and back."

"Sir, you're not going to show him the—"

"You have the birth certificate copy in your hand, Max," Johnson said. "You understand the deadlines I've set. You are the one who is going to tell him the truth. If you choose to do it tonight, I will applaud you."

Students left the chapel in a kind of satisfied hush. Ben hung back and his friends waited with him. When the crowd thinned, Joe said, "We'll tell Señora W. where you are," and the rest of them wore the same expectant look on their faces and stood there, waiting for him to gather up *their* courage for his own and go talk to Tom.

Alone now, Tom shuffled his papers and his Bible together and when Ben approached him, he looked up, smiled, and said, "Ah, there you are."

"You seem happy to see me."

"Always."

"Coach—"

"Joe still here?" Tom said, looking around.

"He went to class."

Tom reached out for Ben, his hand unsteady. "I hate to ask you this, son, but I'll need a little help back to my wheelchair. Standing here, my leg's gone absolutely numb. Do you mind?"

"No, of course not."

Tom rested his arm across Ben's shoulders and tentatively, Ben put his arm around Tom's waist to support him. They turned toward the back of the gym, slowly navigated the steps at the back of the raised platform. "This should be the other way around. Me helping you," Tom said. "I apologize."

"Come on, it's okay," Ben said, realizing, "you've done nothing but help me since I got here."

"It's still embarrassing for me to depend on one of my—young people."

It took only a moment for them to walk in step and Ben thought about the memory he'd visited in Mrs. Poulard's office, thought about when he had walked like this with his father when he had been so ill, thought of the countless times since then that he dragged the torpid, drunken body of his father to a safe and secret place.

"That was a great story, Tom. And the way you told it."

"Thanks, Ben."

"I wish I knew your father. He sounds great. Well, he sounds like you."

"It is my dearest wish to be like him."

At the water fountain near his office, Tom patted Ben's shoulder. "I think I can manage now."

"No," Ben said. "Let me get you to the chair. I've got you now."

"You talked to Mrs. Poulard?"

"Yes, sir. That's what I wanted to talk to you about."

"Go ahead."

"Mrs. Poulard wants to turn me over to you. She says I need someone to help me be honest about things. And I—I'm hoping that you—that you'd be willing to—kind of—take me on—tutor me or—"

"Yes, I will."

They had reached his office door and Ben twisted the doorknob, opening it. "I know I was wrong, Coach."

They stepped into his office, Tom edging through sideways, Ben still supporting him, and he patted Ben's shoulder as if to say he was ready for release, but Ben held on. The wheelchair was still out of reach and he did not want Tom to fall. He said, "Mrs. Poulard told me I'm supposed to agree, without arguing, to your conditions. She said you'll do *something* about the French quiz—and I guess about last night."

"I can do something," Tom said.

Ben bowed his head and drew a deep, resigned breath. Tom rubbed Ben's shoulder. "You know, Ben, my father had high standards for me, growing up, and I knew he would punish me when I did wrong. But I trusted my father. I knew he loved me. I knew he'd give his life for me."

"I guess you're saying I don't trust you, and I don't. I prefer you, though, I think."

"When you're honest, you're really honest," Tom laughed. Leaning on the file cabinet, he motioned for Ben to bring his wheelchair. "Lock it, please," Tom said, pointing to the lever at the wheel. With a determined grimace, Tom said, "Now turn your back, because this part's ugly."

"No. I'll help." Quickly Ben had his shoulder under Tom's arm, his arm holding Tom's waist. "Ready?" Ben said, and clipped the back of Tom's knees with his other hand. The knees bent and Ben eased Tom into the chair.

"Thank you," Tom said. "You were very kind, if disobedient."

Pulling the little cot away from the wall, closer to Tom's chair, Ben said, "Is there any way to make your back feel better?"

"Rest and peace and quiet," Tom laughed.

Ben sat on the cot and his hand went to the quilt folded at the end. He ran his palm back and forth over its softness. "Coach, I had been telling myself there was a greater good at stake. Bonnie Jean's and Jeff's happiness and, to be honest, their friendship."

"At the expense of your integrity? That's not an equitable bargain, son."

"Coach, this goes deep with me."

"I know it," Tom said gently. "But reason it out. If you commit yourself to the principle that it is *right* to tell the truth, then each time you do, you are deciding to leave the rest in God's hands."

"God," Ben murmured. "I'm just not so sure about him."

Tom shrugged. "Obedience can come from deep love or from blind trust. Either way, as you commit yourself to that principle, you begin to understand the deeper truths behind it. More than the reasons for the rule, rather how the rule reveals the bigger idea, including God's nature."

Ben grasped the idea. "Some rules are inevitable because of the way things are; math is that way, basketball is that way. You do the drill, hating it, and then you find yourself able to do stuff as if it came naturally, when really…it didn't before and then gradually you see how it all fits."

"It's something for you to think about, son."

Ben met Tom's eyes, wondering how it was possible that this man, who had known him just a few months, could understand how to motivate him. "But Coach, it's not so simple. For instance, this guy I really respect—well, you know him, Mr. Bénet—I just found out he's been giving me books to read all my life. I always thought they were from my grandmother, because he wasn't allowed to give a card or write in the books. And my grandmother let me think they were from her."

"Wait. What?"

"I get books to read every birthday and Christmas. A big stack and they've all been from Mr. Bénet. You know that bag that was in my car from Apple Tree Farm? There were books with a note from Mr. Bénet explaining. He said he was sorry for not telling me they were from him all these years, but he couldn't."

"Did he say why he never disclosed himself?"

Ben shrugged, "My father would disapprove."

"Confusing for you, I'm sure."

"Yes, sir. Mr. Bénet is a mystery to me, in a big way."

"He's a mysterious sort of man. But trustworthy. He must have felt that you needed the books and that your well-being was more important than your knowing who the gift was from."

"But they were *trying* to keep it from my dad. At least Gran was. I'm guessing that he hates Mr. Bénet."

Tom nodded seriously. "When we see Mr. Bénet in person, we'll have to ask him about it. He's a good man. I trust him."

"How much?"

"Well, if anything should happen to Laurie and I, our will is written that Gregen would raise our children."

"But you never *see* him. Joe didn't even *know* him."

"Yes. That's been difficult for us."

"Difficult, but why did it have to happen that way?"

Tom sighed. "Gregen told me the last time I saw him that if he wished to have any part in *your* life, he had to stay away from us. At the time your father was angry with me."

"Wow," Ben said, realizing how vast was the rift that stretched between his father and Tom. "But Gregen hasn't *been* in my life. So we both lost. And why does Dad want me away from you?" Ben considered the waste of the uneven trade— that Tom and Laurie had given up their friendship with Gregen for a biennial stack of books. But if he admitted what those books had meant to him, they'd traded for the feeding of Ben's soul. This stirred him to a pitying gratefulness that hurt without fear.

"Does he still? Want you to stay away from us?"

Ben glanced up, unable to hide a rush of tenderness he felt now for Tom and Laurie. Tom's face had that expectant look. Bracing himself, Ben said, "I think so, Coach, but I want you to tell me why. If you know why."

Tom hesitated, drumming his fingers on the wheel of his chair. "He was jealous of our—particularly *my*—relationship with your mother."

"What do you mean?"

"Your mother came to me for—I guess you could call it spiritual counseling. She believed there was more to life than she knew and she liked to hear about my faith. She loved theological discussions and we became very close friends. Your father objected to this friendship."

"Oh," Ben studied his palms again, considering the irony of his observation that people tended to judge others by their own weaknesses.

"How are things going with you and your dad?"

"Huh?" Ben looked up. "If they were going *well*, Coach, I wouldn't be sitting here with *you*, would I?"

"I'm sorry to hear that—"

"No, I need *you* to help me. You've got the kind of strengths I want in me."

Tom discussed the ways he wanted Ben to rethink his habits: come and talk to Tom—or Laurie or Joe or Bonnie Jean—the next time he felt compelled to lie, no studying with Jeff or Bonnie Jean for the next two weeks, and no more keeping track of other students' averages, but Ben felt unsettled still.

If I don't keep track of averages," Ben murmured, "I might beat Joe out on almost every test."

"Good." Tom had his game face on. "Competing with you is only going to help Joe. He needs the challenge. He relies far too much on his charm."

"Coach. Are you sure? Joe is—"

"The apple of my eye. Obviously. I adore the kid."

"Yeah."

"I'm capable of loving more than one. Try me."

What could he say to argue with *that*? Ben hesitated. *Tom said 'love,'* Ben thought, *but he means coach or discipline or…*He looked at Tom, just to see what else his expression would tell. Ben found he wanted to capture the sincerity, to memorize it, found that he had more to say. Ben touched the quilt again and traced the soft pattern with two fingers, considering the deep pull of Tom's invitation. Emotion swelled inside him and when he spoke, it sounded in his voice. "Can you fix the way I *feel*? Every time I think of how everyone who *cares* about doing things right will know by now that I've been lying and cheating—especially after how great everyone was in math today. I hate the way I've broken trust with them. I've done this so much."

"Apologize willingly and you'll do one of the most decent, brave things a man can do."

It took Ben a few moments to answer, during which his mind ran over all that Tom was requiring of him; inside his pounding heart and in the air around him he sought the courage he did not yet have. "Okay, Coach."

"You pick the time and place."

"How about before we're announced tonight? It will set things right before the game."

"That's just right," Tom said, putting his hands on the wheels of his chair. "I've got to cover Bettinger's class and I've got to get started over there before the bell rings. You stay here for a few minutes and think about your apology and jot down some notes. We'll talk again after school."

Ben stood up as Tom wheeled toward the door and he opened it for Tom, aware of a weird, gnawing discontent surfacing inside. "Coach, I— more than to the school, more than to *anybody*—I've got to tell you how sorry I am. Especially for disappointing you."

"I forgive you, Ben." Tom reached up from his wheelchair to pat Ben's elbow.

"For all of it, Coach?"

"If you mean for lying to me last night, yes. Let's put it behind us," Tom said, taking Ben's hand to shake it as if they were sealing a bargain. "And remember, there's nothing you can say to me that will chase me away. So, tell the truth."

Shaking Tom's hand, Ben felt the words—*My dad hits me and I have to lie about it*—pulsing in his throat. "Coach," Ben murmured, only managing a croaky, emotional, "Thanks," as he opened his hand and let Tom's drop.

Fighting his emotions, Ben shut the door after Tom, still feeling the grip of his hand and the weighty implications of his promise to Tom. If Tom knew all he was really hiding, if Tom knew the depth of the deception he practiced, so far beyond quizzes and tests, so much more important than grades…

He sank down on the cot, leaned against the cinder block wall, and remembered that there had been moments of peace. He put pen to paper and commanded his mind to concentrate, but the November chill moved through his tired body. He wrapped Laurie's quilt around his shoulders and drew his knees up to his chest and felt a new strength flickering inside. "Thank you," he whispered from his full, turbulent heart, took a deep breath, and closed his eyes to think. Before nine seconds passed, he went into a deep, dreamless sleep, clipboard clutched to his chest, pen in hand.

33

PUTTING the last quilt over her arm, Laurie went inside, shut the door of her shop behind her, and locked the door. The phone rang immediately and Laurie went to answer it

"Hello, my dear," she heard a familiar voice that trapped her breath.

"Uncle Gregen," she said, tears springing immediately to her eyes. "Oh, how I've missed you."

"I don't mean to alarm you, Laurie, my dear. But it is time we spoke."

"You know Ben is here in Annapolis, don't you, Gregen? He's at our house all the time."

"Yes, I know. I am so pleased. So very pleased."

"We're still so confused about how he came to be here and why you had to stay away."

"Laurie, I phoned Tom at school. He said you were here at the shop. Actually, I am right outside in my car. May I come in?"

Dropping the phone, Laurie ran to the front door, banged it open, and rushed down the steps, meeting Gregen when he had just stepped onto the sidewalk. She embraced him with the eager, heartbroken joy of a child.

"Hush, my dear girl," Gregen said, embracing her closely. "You mustn't cry so hard."

"You have no idea," she sobbed onto his shoulder, holding him tight, "I've missed you so much."

"I think of you every day, Laurie." He drew away, keeping one arm around her shoulders. "Shall we go inside?" Laurie nodded. Gregen took his handkerchief from his pocket and pressed it into her hand. "I've missed you and yours. There were times when your Christmas cards were all that kept me going."

"I know I wasn't supposed to, but I had to send them."

"They were more deeply appreciated than I can ever say."

Laurie stopped on the porch, gesturing toward the shop. "What do you think of your investment?"

"I am touched by it. To confess, I sat in my car and watched you take the things in. I just pulled up a moment before you waved good-bye to your daughters."

"You saw them? Bonnie Jean is walking Cara over to Tom's mother's house. It's about twenty minutes away. The baby needs the fresh air."

"What a beauty Bonnie Jean has become, Laurie. I've rarely seen a girl with such glowing radiance."

"I think Ben is in love with her, Gregen."

"How could he help it? He is to the manner born."

"Oh, dear."

"Does she return his affection?"

"As far as I can see."

"Well, let's arrange a marriage as quickly as we can and put an end to all this separation!" They laughed together, both of them fighting tears. Laurie opened the front door. "Come in," she said, "and see how your investment has prospered."

"I had no doubt that you would do great things with this business, Laurie."

"I can afford to repay—"

"Nonsense. I don't need or expect repayment. Anyway, it is *I* who owe *you* a measureless debt."

"No, Gregen."

"Yes. And Katie would have wanted the money invested this way. In you and your family."

Laurie looked at Gregen closely, thinking, scrutinizing, and he smiled his most charming smile at her. "You look very well, Gregen, fit as ever. Have you been well?"

"Well, but lonely. Striving with my soul. It has taken me years to forgive Max. I'm not sure I've done so, yet. But I've made progress and the Lord has rewarded me with this reunion and of course being allowed to see Ben right after his birthday."

"And Marie is well?"

"Oh, yes, and feisty as ever. She tires easily, but then she works much of the day."

Her hand on his arm, Laurie led Gregen into the store. He paused first in front of the *boutis* display, touched the scalloped edge of a wedding quilt, and sighed. "What a joy to know you are helping to keep this art alive."

"It has always been hard for me to understand why so many European shops would want to buy my *boutis* made in America."

"They are exquisitely done," Gregen said, his eyes sparkling. "And you've marketed them so cunningly. Cara makes a beautiful model for this little cap. I noted she was wearing one."

"Those have been so popular."

"There are only a very few, very old, women in France and Italy who have the expertise and interest to make these by hand. Your innovations with the machine make the design and look accessible to the modern woman who is really so much busier."

"We also teach how to make them by hand, you know, Gregen."

He smiled at her and pressed her hand, which he still held on his arm. "Yes, I do."

"Funny how I was able to get the secret family heirloom pattern for the bonnet, and funny, baffling really, how many inquiries for these I get completely unsolicited." Her eyes sparkled at him.

"Your eyes say that you are suspicious of me, and I will admit that I may have recommended your work to interested people. It is all quite innocent, Laurie."

"Thank you, dear Gregen. Knowing you were involved has certainly inspired me to keep my standards high. I know it was your way of saying you still loved me and—" Laurie stopped, tears coming quickly to her. Gregen squeezed her hand close to his side and then as if thinking that wasn't enough, embraced her again.

"Yes, of course. I was trying to let you know how much I loved you and how much I wanted to be part of your life. That seemed the only way. I can explain it to you, now, if you'd like."

"Come into the café." She led him past the cash register to the opening for the café and paused there, hand outstretched to show him. She had not finished cleaning up from the day's business and so the pastries, cookies, remaining bread, rolls and fruit salads still filled the display cases.

"CAFÉ SAN BENEDETTO," Gregen murmured, reading the small enamel sign above the entrance.

"In your honor."

"I am deeply honored."

"I had to incorporate the café separately," Laurie explained, "because it is non-profit."

"Brilliant idea, my dear. And have you accomplished all you hoped with this café?"

"Oh, much more," Laurie said. "I have several wonderful women who make food for the café and actually, one of them will be stopping by soon to get the leftovers for giving away."

"May the Lord bless you for your generosity, Laurie. You are the most generous woman I know."

"I learned from you and Sibilla."

"We merely encouraged what was in your heart."

"But come in. I want you to feel comfortable here. May I offer you *un petit café*, Gregen?"

"Do you serve coffee in the French style, Laurie?"

"You know I do," she confessed. "I have an entire line of French coffees, *café au lait* in the morning and espresso for later, of course. And cappuccino served all day just in case you ever came by, though I know only Americans drink it after noon."

He glanced down at her, his eyes bright with tears. "Then I would love a cappuccino, please."

Major Nels Lindquist knocked on Max's office door three times before opening it. Max, standing behind his desk at the big double windows, warming his shaking hands on the steam radiator, did not turn to greet him.

"Colonel," Lindquist said. When his commanding officer did not reply, he said, "Max."

"I heard you come in, Nels," Max said. "But I'm busy."

"Max, I heard you yelling at the admiral earlier and I—"

"He's a control freak. I called my lawyer and she's gonna meet me after Ben's game tonight."

"Nice lawyer," Nels commented and when Max's glance turned cold, added, "Ben's got a game tonight?"

"First one. Admiral Johnson's giving me a ride."

"I'll tag along, if you don't mind."

"Love to have you. The more the merrier," Max said blankly.

"Hey," Lindquist said. "Let's go to the 'O' Club. You need a boost."

"No, I—"

"Yeah, I insist. I'm buying."

Gregen chose to sit at a table close to the counter while Laurie set about making his drink. Laurie held the pitcher beneath the spout, and as it steamed, she glanced at Gregen.

"I owe you an explanation," Gregen said.

"I know your distance had to do somehow with Ben's welfare."

"I hope it has turned out to accomplish that."

"We all did the best we could," Laurie answered as she poured the hot, frothed milk into two cups half-filled with espresso.

"When my best is not good enough, I am deeply unhappy," Gregen confessed. "In so many relatively unimportant things in life have I been amazingly successful."

Laurie brought the steaming cups to the table and sat down. Gregen added sugar, stirred slowly, and sipped the cappuccino, murmuring his approval. "I was very close to Ben, you know, when he was a toddler. I saw him every day from the time you left until…you remember that Ella had asked me even then to avoid contact with you and Tom."

"We were involved in those lawsuits to try to get visitation rights."

"When he returned to his ship, Max had forbidden her to allow any contact with you and Tom. She was unnaturally frightened of him and would not hear reason."

"I did appreciate you telling me what you did in those days. It kept me going to know he was growing, was healthy and so smart."

"Of course. He's brilliant."

"He still is, Gregen."

"Yes, but essentially fatherless until Tom, I'm afraid."

"Yes."

"Max dropped in on Ella one day when Ben was three years old. Max made friends with Ben, which was very easy to do in those days, and announced to Ella that he was taking him to California. Evidently he'd remarried and his new wife wanted a child."

"Donna Boswell."

"I've never had the privilege. Do you know her?"

"Oddly enough. Tom and I do. She was a regular at Rising Sun."

"Ironic."

"Unless they were drawn together over hatred for us. Donna sued Tom and Rising Sun, you know."

"The logic of the American court system eludes me." Gregen shook his head. "What is she like? Ella claims she's cold."

"Defensive, nervous, doesn't trust anyone."

"I've seen pictures. That is all. But as I was saying, the next morning, as I was pulling up to the house to see Ben, they were hastily packing a rental car Max had driven from the airport."

"Oh, no."

"I don't think Ella would have had the courage to call and tell me. Why is she so afraid of him? She is his mother, yet she obeys him as though she were his slave. I do not understand."

"She's seen him at his worst," Laurie confided.

"Which was?" Laurie looked uncomfortable. "What actually happened between Tom and Max that last day, Laurie? The day he forced you to leave Ben."

"Max wanted to fight," Laurie said vaguely. "Tom wouldn't. Broke his back despite that."

"Naturally, I looked into it," he said, scrutinizing her carefully. "But the policemen—men I knew well and continue to see socially in town—would tell me nothing of use."

"They were Max's classmates from school." Laurie laughed at herself. "Well, they were my classmates, too, but—"

"But all their loyalty lay with Max. I believe they felt pity."

"And you read the police report?"

Gregen nodded. "Carefully written to say nothing."

"No. It was awful. Max showed no conscience."

"What did he do?"

Laurie concentrated on stirring her cappuccino, scraping the creamy foam from the side of the cup. She met Gregen's eyes. "Do you really want details now that you've come so far in forgiving Max?"

Gregen looked at her, looked deep in her eyes. "His behavior was that bad?"

"So bad that Tom will not speak of it."

He passed a tan, toughened hand over his eyes. "They were leaving, as I said, and I confronted Max, asking where they were going. Ben was, of course by that time, in my arms. He was happy to see me as he was every day, chattering to me in French about his daddy and their plans. Brimming full of the sweetest, happiest love. It broke the heart to see."

"I can imagine."

"Max said he was taking them on a little vacation to California to meet his new wife. I congratulated him, of course, and asked when I could expect them back, and Max said two weeks. I knew he was lying and so just to keep them there longer—just a bit longer—so I could think of something, I brought up Katie's car and asked Max what he wanted to do with it. Of course he wanted *nothing* to do with it, in the shape it was in—"

"So you bought the car from him."

"I had to have it. I had to have some reason to keep in touch with him and I thought this would at least require a title transfer and I knew I could drag that out. Off they went and I called regularly, but the phone calls were less and less communicative. They would not allow me to speak to Ben and finally, I could no longer get through. Oh, I obtained their unlisted number, but they didn't answer, or hung right up. Can you imagine such discourtesy?"

"Don't have to imagine, Gregen. That's how he is." Gregen shook his head in stern, brave disgust. Laurie patted his arm. "So, knowing you, you tried the legal system."

"But to virtually no success. In America I am not considered a direct relative, and I am not an American citizen, and when I could not give them what they called an 'emotionally satisfying' reason for why I could not become one, they refused to grant me so much as visitation rights."

"I'm so sorry."

He shook his head, dismissing her sympathy. "Similar to what you and Tom went through."

"But your rights are *legitimate*, Gregen."

"Yes, and so are my reasons for retaining my Swiss citizenship, but—"

"Your reasons being?"

"My responsibilities to my family, Laurie," he said a little sternly. "I am the eldest. That is not something understood here. And no doubt you know what I could not tell them—about my activities during the war."

"From Katie," Laurie said mischievously, "and Sibilla and Marie."

Gregen smiled. "None of you can keep secrets. Good thing no facts are known."

"We don't know any facts?" Laurie said in mock defensiveness.

"There are considerations that cannot come to light even now," Gregen said, smiling his strict smile, "and they would have to if I were to become a citizen here. I do not see what that has to do with my being allowed to see Ben."

"The laws are more favorable now, I think, Gregen, different family structures, maybe…"

"Maybe," he agreed. "I've begun to look into it in case my current plan does not come to fruition. But I still owe you an explanation for—disappearing."

"I always believed the best of you, you know that."

"I trusted that and it was a great comfort to me." He took her hand, lifted it to his lips and kissed her hand once tenderly. "My dear girl, I had to agree to refrain from speaking to you, avoiding any contact with you so that you could not obtain any details about Ben. Somehow while they were in California, Max convinced Ella that it would be better if Ben believed that *Donna* was his mother."

"That's what we feared."

"Ella only told me this when she returned from California—Max told her he was being sent to Okinawa and that the Marine Corps would not give them permission for her to accompany them, but in truth, he was sent to Hawaii." Gregen shook his head. "She was so brokenhearted that I was able to coax some information from her.

"Max had decided that Katie was to be kept a secret. That way Ben would forget her and learn to love his stepmother. Since I was connected to Ben through Katie, Max demanded that I also be cut out of all contact.

Ella had to give Max her word. He threatened that she would never see Ben again if Max discovered she had any contact with me, or with you and Tom. It took me two years to get this much information from her. And that only upon the promise that I would strictly avoid you and Tom."

"What else could you do?" Laurie said. "Getting to Ben was the most important thing."

"Yes. And once Ella began to trust me, we gradually devised the plan we are now executing."

"We?"

"Ella visits, you know, she has the privilege of the relationship and she knows more about their home life than I. And though she defends her son with an almost religious fervor, she has grown increasingly concerned about Max and Ben's relationship and, in that growing concern, has been more open to the idea that I try to re-enter his life. And recently, I helped convince her that it would probably be good for Ben to know you and Tom. She even admitted that she knew this was Katie's wish. For her to agree to this, I knew that she believed Ben was gravely unhappy at home."

"Ben has your cool composure, Gregen, but I do believe he's unhappy."

Gregen nodded seriously. "Once Ella confided that much, I knew I had to act. That is when Max was given orders to Annapolis." Gregen's brows creased together. "And Laurie, I have to ask your patience with this."

"How do you mean?"

Gregen held her hand tightly. "You know me and I'm sure you will believe that I've researched this subject. Children suffer terrible trauma from revelations such as Ben needs about his father and mother."

"I can understand that, but living a lie can't go on."

"No. It must *not* go on. But I think that short of Max confessing, the best way for Ben to accept this information would be for him to figure out as much of the truth as he can, little by little, as his memory comes back to him and he comes across the facts."

"But I don't want to be part of the deceit."

"Nor do I. But if we sit him down and tell him, he's likely not to believe us. He doesn't know us. As bad as his father is, Ben feels a loyalty to Max that is natural. Research shows that his emotions will be able to cope with the truth he discovers by reasoning and realization. You must be patient."

"And not tell him who you are?"

"Not yet."

Joan Poulard found Tom seated in his wheelchair at his desk, hands folded, head bowed, deep in thought.

"May I sit down?" she said from the doorway.

"Please, come in." He made an attempt to rise, but she prevented him and took his big desk chair from where he'd pushed it out of the way. She held up a brown paper bag. "I brought you a surprise," she said, "though I know you're well fed at home."

"That was nice of you. I smell coffee."

"Fresh coffee and the chocolatiest candy bar I could find." She took her gifts out and placed them before him on his desk, shooing away his thanks and settling into her chair with her own big cup of coffee. "Never drank coffee before I was a principal. Only wish I could put a big shot of brandy in it."

"Ha-ha," Tom said, lifting the plastic top off his and inhaling appreciatively. "This is just what I needed, Joan."

"I saw Ben sprinting late to class from this direction, so I assume you spoke to him."

"I did. I got back from covering Bettinger's class and he was sound asleep on the cot. Took me a few minutes to wake him up. I bet he was up all night."

"Listen, Tom," Joan said, and sipped her coffee. "Ben was absolutely terrified of me getting his father involved in his punishment."

"That is not good news."

"Ben seemed to be actually remembering a certain incident right there in our meeting. Either that or now that he's older he understands what it means." Joan's description of Ben's memory alarmed Tom and when she said, "During his stay at the hospital, the doctor discovered bruises that Ben could not explain," Tom's fists tightened.

"Bruises? Where?"

"I'm not sure. Ben said he simply couldn't remember passing out or anything. But because he couldn't explain where he *got* the bruises, I think his father was being investigated for child abuse."

"No. Oh, no."

"Hold on, Tom. And stop squeezing your cup that way. You're going to end up with scalding coffee in your lap."

Tom put the cup on the desk. "Go on."

"Ben told me—and I don't think he actually meant to let this out—that his mother convinced him to lie to get his father off the hook."

"Ben," Tom murmured, squeezing his eyes shut, clasping his hands.

"I know it, Tom."

"He was twelve? So, the information isn't current?"

"No, and his records say nothing about the incident. It must have been a suspicion only. But you can understand the doctor initiating the investigation."

"Absolutely. They should have done a wee bit more than *investigate*."

"As far as I can tell, Ben honestly doesn't remember anything happening. The lie was created to explain the bruises and get his father off the hook, not to cover up what he *did* remember."

"Lord have mercy."

"He gave no indication that his father had hit him. His purpose in telling me the story was that his parents do not value honesty. To show me that calling his father about his dishonesty would mean nothing to him."

"Uh-huh." Tom's mind whirled with regrets. "What's your plan?"

"I wanted to give you a heads up. I phoned and invited Max to the game this afternoon. I've yet to meet the man. I want make contact."

"Good move. I'm ready."

"I don't want you in any public confrontations."

"I thought you said you trusted me as a professional and as a Christian."

"I do, but I can see the violence in your eyes right now."

"Can you?" Tom said absently, his mind making wild plans—to call off the game, drive over to the Yard, and beat Max Hunter to a pulp. He could actually picture Max beaten unconscious.

"Yes."

But Tom wanted to fight him, now despising his own reserve the last time they'd met, worried that the man would again stoop to wield the only defense against which Tom would not strike. He clenched his jaw, clutched his hands together, regretting that he was far too angry to pray.

"Tom, if we don't do this properly, we'll lose Ben. And if our suspicions are right, think of the danger to him."

"That's what I *am* thinking about. The idea of asking your child to lie for your own sake. It's appalling."

"If that's the worst that's happened to him, then we're already working on fixing that."

"Joan—" Tom said, exasperated with her composure.

"Promise me, for Laurie's sake. No fighting."

"Have you ever known me to be anything but polite?"

"Well, you nearly slugged John Saunders last year when he said Peter would go to hell if he went to Penn."

"Nearly, but I didn't, did I?"

"You just stay in your wheelchair this afternoon and be polite. Anybody needs to be slugged, I'll do it." She heaved herself out of his chair, dropped her empty coffee cup in the trash by Tom's desk, and made a mock fist, trapping her thumb inside.

"Hit somebody that way, you'll break your thumb."

"Better my *thumb* than your *back*."

The front door opened. "Mama?"

"I'm caught," Gregen said, laughing ruefully. "Disgraceful for a man of my background."

"We lost track of time." Laurie squeezed his hand and whispered, "You'll have to come and surprise the boys at the basketball game."

"Good plan. Since we know your daughter is not likely to keep this meeting a secret. Does Max attend these games?"

"Mama?"

"I'm back here, Jeannie." To Gregen she said, "He hasn't been to any scrimmages."

Bonnie Jean maneuvered the stroller through the shop and stopped it at the edge of the café. At her approach, Gregen rose to his feet, his breath catching in his throat as he noted the high color in her cheeks, the brightness of her eyes, and the warm shine on her thick hair. "She is so like you, my dear," he said.

"This is Gregen Bénet," Laurie said. "My dear friend. You've heard me refer to him as Uncle Gregen."

"I've heard so much about you," Bonnie Jean said. She came to them, extending her hand. Gregen shook her hand and then embraced her in his way, taking both her shoulders in his brown, sturdy hands and kissing her cheeks in turn. "Bonnie Jean. I am so pleased to meet you. You are just as beautiful as your incomparable mother, my *dear* girl."

"Ben and Joe are crazy about you. Is it true you speak three languages?"

Gregen laughed, taking both her hands in his. "I speak eight fluently and read nineteen. After the first three, the others are easy." He squeezed her hands and smiled at her. "Your hands are cold, my dear. Don't you wear mittens?"

Bonnie Jean made a face. "They're in my pockets."

"Little good they'll do there," Gregen said, smiling and patting her hands as if to warm them, but clearly not willing to let go. "But I see you've kept your sister warm and happy. Sleeping so close to dinner time. You must have a special touch."

"She's a miracle with babies."

Gregen smiled at Laurie and when his eyes returned to Bonnie Jean's, they were bright with emotion. "Sit down and visit," Gregen invited her. She pulled a chair up to their table while Laurie took the stroller and wheeled it into the café. She bent down and loosened the ties on Cara's bonnet and opened her jacket. "Are you enjoying your sister?"

"So much. I've wanted a baby sister all my life. I prayed every night for her."

"Ah! And so you've discovered how faithful God is, how abundantly he answers."

"You're here to see Mama? Are you coming home to dinner?"

"I am in town on business, Bonnie Jean. I stopped by to see your mother and together we are going to surprise the boys at their game."

"Really? That's great! You know Ben is really good at basketball."

"Yes. I am looking forward to seeing him play tonight."

"Can I make you some hot chocolate, Jeannie?"

"Do you have any of the good kind left?"

"The good kind?" Gregen asked playfully.

Bonnie Jean said, her accent perfect, "*La cioccolata con panna.*"

"What is that like?" Gregen prompted.

"It's thick—more like chocolate syrup, or pudding, but without the sickly sweetness—it doesn't get you in the back of the throat like really sweet things do. And it's got a rich flavor, very dark. Then Mama puts a big mound of whipped cream on top and you stir that in as you drink it."

"Bonnie Jean," Laurie said, "Uncle Gregen's late wife, Sibilla, taught me to make that."

"Late wife? Oh, I'm so sorry!" She reached for his hand and held it.

"Thank you, my dear. You would have liked her very much. She is your far distant cousin, you know, through your mother's mother."

"Oh, so that's how you know Mama."

"When your mother was a high school student, she was a member of my wife's home economics club where they learned all the old and valued cooking and housekeeping techniques that your mother has turned into her successful business."

Laurie said, "Sibilla and I became great friends."

"Your mother traveled with my wife and my niece and I to Europe several times while she was in high school and college. Did she not tell you about that?"

"Just little bits."

"I was hoping she would fall in love with a distant Italian cousin of mine when your father captured her heart."

"Mama!"

"It's true. Giovanni. *Très charmant.*"

Bonnie Jean looked at her hands and realized that she still held Gregen's right hand in both of hers. But instead of apologizing or releasing him, she studied his face for a moment before looking at his hand. "Your thumb and finger," she said, looking up at him. "This ridge on them." She fingered the hard ridged scar that bisected Gregen's thumb, dividing his nail. "Ben dreamed about you last night. He dreamed about your fingers." Seeing bright tears come to Gregen's eyes, Bonnie Jean asked, "Are you upset?"

"Upset that Ben confides in you? Of course not. This is as it should have been always. Upset that Ben's memories are surfacing? No, definitely not. That is wonderful news."

34

DURING the initial warm-up when the teams split the court for stretches and a shoot around, Bonnie Jean tried to get Ben's attention, but he was focused and when he did meet her gaze, he gave a brief smile but he did not read in her eyes her desire to speak to him. Finally, she grabbed Drew's arm as he dribbled by her. "I've got to talk to Ben."

"Why?"

"Why should I tell you?"

"I'm team captain."

"Tell him it's important."

"I don't want you distracting him. Don't start a fight."

"Don't be stupid. Go."

Drew intercepted Ben beneath the basket and spoke to him, pointing to where Bonnie Jean stood. Ben sprinted across the gym to her. "What's up?"

"Gregen's here."

"What?"

She pointed out into the lobby where the graceful, straight-backed old man stood with Laurie, Cara and Tommy, talking to Ben's English teacher. "There. He's been at Mama's store. Visiting. Ben, I talked to him. He came to see you play."

Ben stood staring. He murmured to Bonnie Jean, "I'm supposed to apologize in front of the whole school. He'll be ashamed of me."

"No, Ben, he's wonderful."

"I can't—"

But Gregen looked up at that moment, saw Ben, and his expression brightened with delight. He excused himself and came to Ben. Despite his embarrassment Ben rushed to him, heart beating hard. He stuck out his hand. "Mr. Bénct, sir. It's great to see you. I'm sorry I'm so sweaty."

"Not at all," Gregen said, shaking Ben's offered hand, "you're an athlete." Too briefly to be certain, Ben thought he felt the ridge on Gregen's fingers scratch his hand and remembering his dream, stared into Gregen's eyes, searching for recognition. "My dear boy," Gregen said with strong emotion as he took Ben's shoulders and kissed both his cheeks. "I am happy to see you." Ben didn't know what to say. Gregen said, "Is the car running well?"

"Great. And I just got it back from the paint shop, so…"

"So it is safe from reckless drivers."

Ben nodded, frantically searching the man's face. "Sir, I—I—" The pep band played a flourish and Ben looked around quickly. "I have to go in a minute. But—can we talk after the game?"

"I hope so. I may have to leave early."

"Oh."

"If I do, I'll be in touch very soon."

"Because I realized when I found this year's books that it's been you—" Ben faltered.

Gregen made an expressive gesture. "I would have liked to give them to you in person, but I was not permitted to do so."

"Thank you for them, Gregen. For each one. They've been…so *important* to me."

"Thank you for each letter."

"I…"

Gregen chuckled. "We have so much to say that we can't find the right words."

"It's just that—"

Mrs. Poulard took the mic and called for everyone's attention. Ben looked around at her and back to Gregen, despair in his eyes. "What is it, Ben?"

"I failed a French quiz on purpose to help two of my friends," he said, finding that he could still meet Gregen's eyes.

"I can imagine Tom's response."

"Right. He was disappointed in me," Ben said softly.

"And did this crime provide your friends help?" Gregen asked, the expressive flip of his hand underlining the intent of his question.

"I don't know what the teacher's going to do. She may not curve the quiz now that she knows I tried to manipulate the outcome, but that doesn't really matter." Ben waited to see if Gregen might understand.

"True."

"I was dishonest and it's not the first time, Gregen. I've kind of had to…*face* myself."

Mrs. Poulard welcomed everyone and asked everyone to join her for the National Anthem. As the crowd rose to their feet in a noisy rustle, Ben leaned closer to tell Gregen, "Now I have to make things right. I'm going to apologize to the school."

"Are you? Good for you."

"Do you mean it?"

"I will never say what I do not mean." Gregen touched Ben's arm and nodded toward the flag. Joining the momentum of the crowd, Ben and Gregen turned to face the flag and stood together. At the last notes of the anthem, they turned back toward the front. Mrs. Poulard met Ben's eyes; he in turn glanced meaningfully at Gregen and trotted to where she stood with the mic in the middle of the gym. As he approached, he saw Tom limping slowly across the court from the team bench, his wheelchair abandoned.

Mrs. Poulard said, "Many of you know Tom MacBride as a neighbor or friend. Some of you may know him as a former Naval Academy classmate, some as the host at the coffeehouse Rising Sun back in the day. As the father of five, you may know him as carpool buddy, little league coach, or the man at whose house your son or daughter spends every Friday night jumping on the trampoline or sleeping on the porch." The crowd gave a collected chuckle. "He's our most popular chapel speaker here at CCS, teaches math and chemistry when we need him to, and he's coached almost every sport. He's been coaching our fabulous basketball team and he wants to say a few words."

Tom gave Ben a bracing glance and took the mic from Mrs. Poulard, thanking her and shaking her hand. "Welcome to the start of our basketball season. We've got a great team this year and we're excited to be playing our cross town rivals, the Key School Obezags. We want to start with a word of prayer, but first, one of our student athletes has asked to address the student body. As you know, here at CCS, we are concerned with cultivating and restoring all aspects of a person's life and this student has learned an important truth. Ben Hunter, a fine student, a superb athlete, and a young man of strong moral character—I would ask that you give him the full attention of your generous hearts."

Tom handed the mic to Ben, clapped his arm, and whispered, "Steady, now."

Ben turned to face the crowd. "As Coach said, my name is Ben Hunter and I'm new here. I asked to speak to…everybody…because I love being here and I'm grateful to be a part of this school." He looked around to the team, standing three yards behind him, legs apart, arms folded across their chests, "I love being on the team and in my classes and everybody's treated me like I grew up here the way all of the rest of them have. I'm grateful and I respect the great community you've got here. But I—um—I sometimes have been false to you and I wanted to apologize for that."

Ben felt waves of fire move across his skin, but he gulped and said, "For example, today, I—I failed a quiz on purpose to try to help other students because…" Thick quiet met him and he looked around anxiously, finding Bonnie Jean and Laurie and Tommy—three pairs of honest brown eyes full of love for him. "To tell the truth, most of my reasons were selfish. I did it and I've done it before and today a lot of you helped me admit that it's dishonest, so I wanted to tell you about it because I know you were trusting me to do my best and I didn't do it. I regret making that mistake." He gulped, struggling. "It's a weird way of cheating and I'm sorry. I hope to earn your trust back—especially now because I'm going to represent you on the basketball team. I'm asking you to please give me another chance and if you do, I promise I'll do my honest best." He wanted the floor to swallow him.

But what happened the instant he stopped speaking Ben remembered in a tumultuous clarity for the rest of his life. The auditorium erupted in applause; Tom MacBride hugged him saying, "Good boy," but Drew, Paul, Jason and Adam pulled Ben away from Tom, all of them around him at once, hugging him, pounding his body in unrestrained affection while the crowed chanted his name. "Ben…Ben…Ben." The rest of the team crowded in close and Adam picked Ben up, swung him around in an expression of delight. Up above the crowd in Adam's embrace, Ben saw Oliver standing a little way off, saw Laurie crying into a tissue, Tommy waving to him, and Bonnie Jean standing straight, fully composed but for the extraordinary brightness of her deep brown eyes. And as Adam swung him around he saw Gregen wiping his eyes and hurrying toward Tom MacBride, who hobbled across the gym toward the older man.

Mrs. Poulard tried to get everyone settled down and eventually, just as Gregen reached Tom, hand extended, she hushed them and asked Joe to pray. Ben was now held up above on a raft made of eight teammates' arms and shoulders and from that perch he watched Gregen embrace Tom, saw the concern on the old man's face as his tan, rough hand traced Tom's shoulder and down his back with a tender and kind of probing touch. Gregen's gestures told that he was inquiring about Tom's back and that Tom was dismissing the question's importance. Ben watched them embrace again, both showing deep emotion and both unashamed at plain and profuse tears. Adam set Ben down and the team lined up behind Joe who had made his way to the mic.

"Let's pray," Joe said. "Father, we thank you for providing a way for us to be forgiven through the sacrifice of your Son Jesus, and we remember him and all that he means to us today." Joe breathed deeply as if savoring the thought. "Please bless Ben and all of us who know we need your help to live as you want us to live. Give our team the grace and strength to honor you today. Let us delight our friends who came to see us play. Bless the Key School athletes and give them strength and conviction and focus. Amen."

The official warm-up music burst from the speakers and the cheerleaders leapt onto the court as the teams began the five minutes of choreographed half-court warm-ups before introductions, but Ben and Joe sprinted over to Tom and Gregen. After shaking Joe's hand, Gregen took his shoulders in hand and kissed both cheeks. "I can't believe you're here, Gregen," Joe said. "Thanks for coming." He pushed Ben to the forefront saying, "What do you think of our hero, here?"

"I am pleased with you," Gregen said patting Ben's shoulder. "You expressed your regret in a way that tells me you understand what is important now. And you are obviously well-loved here."

"Thank you, Gregen."

"Are you coming home for dinner, Gregen?" Joe asked. "The food's always great."

"If I can, I will. Thank you." Gregen held Ben's shoulder. He turned to speak to Ben. "If I cannot stay, I would like to know the outcome of the game."

"*Bien sur*," Ben said. They spoke in French, agreeing to write or call. Gregen reached into his jacket and took out business cards, which showed his numbers, address and e-mail. He gave one to Ben and one to Joe.

Again Gregen touched Ben's shoulder in a kind of patting caress. Ben heard the rough ridge on his finger catch on his uniform jersey, then scratch across his cotton T-shirt.

"We'd better go," Tom said, regretfully to Gregen, but before they hurried off to the bench, Ben grasped Gregen's hand to his shoulder, touching his forefinger, feeling to see if the hard ridge he remembered was really there.

Gregen allowed this, meeting Ben's eyes. "*Mon doigt*," he said, meaning *my finger.*

"I remember it," Ben said in French.

Gregen looked closely at Ben. "*Bien.*" He rubbed Ben's shoulder, his stance and expression saying that he wished to hold Ben there with him. Gruffly, he worried about Ben's flushed countenance. "You are too hot wearing two shirts."

Ben thought about his bruised chest, remembering his intent to deceive. His heart sank.

"Let's go now," Gregen said in French. "And do what is right."

Ben tucked Gregen's card into the side of his shoe before sprinting across court to his team. Mr. Ridout, the announcer, began to introduce the Key School starting line up.

Standing there, between Joe and Adam, standing across the gym from Gregen Bénet, standing where he could see Laurie and Bonnie Jean and Tommy watching him, waiting for him to shine, he knew he had to take off his T-shirt. Some strength within him compelled him to discard his mask. How he would avoid the inevitable concerned questions, he did not know, but if he had meant his apology, if this surge of desire to do right, to believe, was to survive in him, he knew that he had to do it. He ducked behind Adam and skinned off his uniform jersey.

"What are you doing? You gotta wear a shirt," Adam said.

"Taking off my T-shirt."

"Hurry up, man. The girls see you without your shirt and they'll be all the hell over this basketball court."

But Ben's hands were shaking and he was awash in nervous sweat. Mr. Ridout announced Oliver and Paul and Adam before he got his jersey back on. He called Drew's name and Ben looked down to notice that the jersey did cover the worst of the bruise and he was ashamed of the relief he felt. And as Mr. Ridout said, "Playing point guard, number fourteen, our very own Ben Hunter," he saw that Joe, beside him always, had seen the bruise and their eyes met. Joe thumped Ben's arm, "Go on, man. We're all behind you."

Adam tipped the jump ball to the right of Ben and he leapt to get it. Dribbling with his right hand, Ben circled around Key School's point guard, a heavy-footed, aggressive player with curling red hair. Ben led with his right hand to fake a shot and switching hands, dished the ball to Paul who dropped it in. He heard the approval in Tom's voice and when Key School inbounded and dribbled toward their basket, Ben looked uninterested, stayed a little behind the point guard's right shoe as if he couldn't quite keep up. When he figured the guy was sure he was winning the race to the basket, Ben quickened his stride, reached around him, and flicked the ball away on the up-dribble. Drew got it and seeing Ben's open path behind Key's guard tossed the ball out over Ben's head. Ben sprinted down the court following the ball, grabbed it, dribbled once, leapt and dunked it before Key's coach had time to holler. But the crowd did and again, Ben heard Tom's voice. "Teamwork!" he heard Tom shout and the surprise of Doug Davidson's voice call, "Nice shot, newbie," meant that he had arrived late. Ben dared glance at Gregen and saw the old man's intensely happy concentration and realized that Gregen understood the game.

In the defensive stance, shadowing the purposeful, slow dribble of Key School's point guard, Ben kept his glance moving from the ball to the kid's waist, watching for clues about where he'd go. Ben was getting bored and moved in closer. The guard murmured, "Hey, cheater, afraid to look me in the eye?"

"Terrified," Ben said. Ignoring the way he juked his head right, Ben saw his core stay centered and knew he wanted to play mean. Ben moved closer still, his chest above the ball now.

"Did you cheat on that quiz right handed or left?"

Ben made a rapid move straight toward him by thrusting his head and shoulders at the ball. The boy smirked and pulled the ball right with both hands. By the way Drew was moving, Ben knew that Key's forward was behind his own right shoulder; when the guard pushed the ball toward his forward, Ben didn't even have to look to grab it with his left hand. "Right or left, your choice," Ben said, dribbling around the sputtering guard. He put the ball into Drew's hands, who dribbled down court, Oliver right with him, while Ben and Adam set a pick beneath the basket. Ben took the pass from Drew, bounced it past the defender's hip into Adam's hands. Adam stood, both feet on the floor, and took his shot as he always did. Key School was furious and their center jumped after the ball, reaching for it as it touched the rim. Adam bent just a little so that Key landed on his shoulder; the shot went in, but the ref called the foul on Adam.

"He lands on my back and I'm called?" Adam said to the ref.

Tom called him to the sidelines. Joe came in to replace Adam, touching fists as they passed.

Ben heard Tom say, "I promised you. You argue with the ref, you sit out. Now sit down."

Key's power forward, a slim, friendly boy with long, straight black hair, got the inbound, took it out, dribbled and made a perfect three-point shot.

"Nice shot," Ben said to him.

"Thanks, man."

Ben inbounded to Joe, who dribbled crosscourt, passed it back to Ben just as Big Red came up behind him. Ben circled around him, keeping low, going fast. "Come on," he said, "keep up."

He went after Ben aggressively, taking big steps, spreading his arms, waving them, his big heavy legs shaking the floor with his steps. "Heard you're screwing the coach's daughter," he said to Ben

Ben slowed his dribble, turning slightly so his hip went toward the man, aware that Joe and Drew had heard the taunt. "That was rude, Big Red," Ben said. "You're going to regret that." Joe was a pretty good ball player, but he was best at sabotage, trash talking and other distractions; the guy guarding him was nervous. Ben saw that Paul's man was playing him tight and not watching the ball, Oliver was being chased by another, the fifth responsible for Drew. Staying two yards away, Drew kept his right shoulder toward Ben, Joe set a hard pick behind to Ben's right and Ben went left. Key's guard pivoted, following Ben's dribble around. Joe opened up, keeping his elbow tucked tight. Key followed Ben who rubbed off Joe's shoulder, bringing the point guard close enough that Joe, pivoting toward the basket, slammed his shoulder into the guard's solar plexus and pivoted back before Key's gasping could be heard. Ben burst right in a low sprint, the ball looking like a yo-yo strung from his hand. Alone under the basket, he leapt up, leading with his right hand, and moved the ball in a smooth lay-up that dropped through the net. Key's guard fell to the floor. The ref blew the whistle, motioning for Key's coach.

"You hurt, son?" the coach asked, helping him up.

"The—cheater—tripped—me," he gasped.

"No name calling. I like a clean game, got that, Coach?"

"Yes, sir," he said to the ref, before speaking to his athlete, as he took his arm and led him to the side, he hissed, "Don't say that again, Willie."

Before they were off the court, Oliver approached the ref and whispered, "In all honesty, sir, I saw Ben trip him."

"What?" The ref gawked. "You're speaking against your own team member?" The man glanced at Tom, who got the message that there was a controversy.

"What's the problem?" Tom called.

The ref dismissed Oliver. "Get yourself together, kiddo."

Key's shooting guard inbounded the ball to the power forward, who caught it and called a timeout.

"What happened?" Tom said, as they gathered around him.

"I was moving in to help Ben out," Joe said, "and set a hard pick. So when Ben broke for the basket, it messed him up."

"He told the ref Ben tripped their point guard," Paul said, jerking his thumb toward Oliver.

"You said *what*, Oliver?"

"Paul misheard me. I was being supportive, sir."

"You had better not be speaking against your teammate, Oliver," Tom said. "We'll talk about this later. You guys are doing great. Don't let the big guy's attitude infect you. Play a hard, clean game. Don't give them easy baskets—I want the offense picked up. Push the pace; let's get out and run. Oliver, that was a nice hustle for the rebound. And it looks like you're really communicating out there, Drew."

The whistle blew and Tom tapped the back of Ben's knee. Ben glanced down at him. "You're playing some beautiful basketball out there, son."

"It's fun, Coach. Really fun."

Toward the end of the second quarter, Ben dashed down the court, steps ahead. The other players were more tired than he was; his desperate physical training had given him endurance and a physical tenacity that made him able, even at the end of the second quarter, to drive hard, consistently hard, still concentrating intensely. And he felt both Tom and Gregen's concentration with him.

This time with the ball, he started down court dribbling slowly, moving in a zig-zag pattern, watching the brief expression of relief that passed over the faces of his exhausted defenders, knowing he had gotten them to relax just enough, then he stepped up his speed, circled around one defender so quickly that the man stumbled, only to find himself with two big, tired, irritated men on him beneath the basket. They blocked his jump, leaning in, and a third man joined them, their coach screaming at them from the sidelines. "Paul!" Ben yelled; he couldn't see him.

"Over here."

"Eleven and close," Drew said to help Ben see where the men had trapped him.

And Ben, twisting away from Key's big men, fell back; he was forty-five degrees to the floor and, hoping Paul or Drew would follow, took the shot. He hit the floor, his vision still blocked, knowing that it went in before the buzzer only by the intensity of the crowd's screaming. The score was thirty-one to eleven at the half. Ben had eighteen points.

35

ADMIRAL Johnson and Nels Lindquist waited half an hour for Max before Lindquist volunteered to hike to Max's quarters, suspecting that Max was still sleeping off the drinks he'd gulped at the "O" Club that afternoon. After rousing him, making him brush his teeth and dress, he led Max, with Keith and Tim in tow, to the admiral's car.

As they drove to the game, both Johnson and Lindquist talked to the boys, but when Lindquist rushed up the stairs to the gym with Keith and Tim racing behind him, Johnson drew Max aside. "A word of caution, Colonel. We are going to a public place. You will behave with all courtesy and military decorum. There will be citizens present at this game who witnessed one or more of your car accidents and who are convinced you are untrustworthy and reckless. I want you to change their minds."

"Yes, sir."

"Whatever comes up," Johnson said, "do not give me cause to reprimand you."

"I'll do my best, sir."

Admiral Johnson turned on his heel and went to the stairs. "I am quite certain I need to see a good deal more than your best, Colonel Hunter. Let's go."

They could hear the sounds of the game, the pep band and the tumult of happy voices. A buttery popcorn scent met them at the door, which Lindquist held open.

"Looking forward to meeting the coach," Max said in his most manly and amiable voice.

"You're in for a treat. He's the best," Johnson said coolly.

Max sputtered, "That's, uh, that's what I heard from Nels."

In a helpful tone, Nels said, "I heard he saved a drowning kid once. Local hero because of it."

Nodding his head in assent, Johnson stopped at the door, turned to face Max, his gaze frankly cold and intimidating. "You will do everything you can—everything—to please and support this coach. Tom's well-loved in this in town. And for good reason."

Gregen Bénet enjoyed meeting Joan Poulard when she came to sit with him, Laurie, and her children during the second quarter. Gregen could find common interests with nearly anyone, but Joan Poulard shared his chief interest—Ben's well-being. They were discussing the curriculum of books he'd sent Ben over the years when Gregen put his hand on her wrist. "If you turn around, you'll see Ben's father. He's late, but he's arrived. Look, there by the door with the admiral and another marine."

"Goodness. I forgot ol' Charlie Johnson was back in town. That'll make this easier." She sprung up and, proclaiming her farewells and pardons, made her way through the crowded bleachers to the floor.

"And now, my dear," Gregen said, taking Laurie's hand. "I must leave."

"No, Uncle Gregen," she said, her arm going around him.

"It would be ill advised to see Max today, Laurie."

"When will we see you again?" Bonnie Jean asked.

"As soon as I can manage it, my dear." He touched her cheek with great affection, then looked to Tommy. "Can you guide me out the back way, Tommy? I think it is best if I see Ben's father another day."

Max liked the clean look of the place, liked the way it was crowded with people, noticed the pretty girls selling concessions, was pleased with the roar of the crowd inside the gym; he felt his natural confidence return. He was sure he could turn the admiral's opinion of him back around.

They paid for their tickets and crowded into the open doorway where there was just room for them to stand. Tim tugged on Max's pants. "Me and Keith can't see."

Max dug in his pocket and produced a five-dollar bill. He put this in Keith's hand and told him to buy some snacks before Max turned his attention to the game. He could see Ben moving with the strength and agility that his performance promised at the last game Max had attended early last season. As point guard, Ben led the team; his fierce competitiveness cloaked in that sublime composure. Now, he moved down court dribbling in a pattern no human opponent could predict, dazzling the defenders, then slowing to signal to his big men. He did some crazy, circle dribble and pump faked, instead passing to the tallest forward. The pass was sure, and the big fellow made a two-handed set shot that went straight in. And when Ben leapt out of nowhere to grab the inbound from the other team's confident guard, the crowd erupted ecstatically, chanting his name.

Johnson looked at Max, his expression controlled, watchful. "Quite an athlete you've raised."

"Yes, sir."

"Are you kidding?" Nels shouted. "He's brilliant. He's coordinated, he's fast—Navy needs him *this* season. Does he have to finish high school?"

"Yes, he does," Johnson laughed.

It was a few minutes later when Ben went out for a rest and went on one knee beside a man in a wheelchair that Max remembered to look for the coach. *Can this guy be it?* he thought. *How can a guy coach from a wheelchair?*

A kid on the bench handed Ben a water bottle. Max identified him as the boy who was with Ben that day at the MVA. The coach said something to this boy and he went to the stat table, preparing to go in. A minute later, one of the big men came out and squatted beside Ben. Both boys listened to the coach with serious concentration, though both held their water bottles ready for the moment when they could take a drink. While they were drinking, the coach pointed to Ben's neck or chest—Max could not tell which—and Ben looked down, used his shirt to wipe his mouth, and shook his head. The ref blew the whistle and all three turned to note the progress of the game. Another team member leaned into the group to say something. Ben leaned up closer to the coach, talking intensely, using his hand to show something. The coach nodded and spoke again. The sound of the crowd said that the other team had scored. Ben stood up, tossed his water bottle to a teammate, tucked in his shirt, and at the coach's nod, substitutions were made and both players went back in.

"Is that the coach in the wheelchair?" Nels wondered aloud to his two comrades.

"Yes, it is," Johnson said.

"What's wrong with him?" Max said.

"Shh," Johnson counseled, leaning closer. "Nothing's wrong with him. He has a bad back."

"Must be tough coaching from that seat," Nels said.

"No tougher than leading a squad of men into battle with only one eye, Major. If you got what it takes, you got it," Johnson said with a slight smile at the major.

"Yeah," Nels said, smiling.

"Looks familiar," Max murmured.

"Does he?"

"Colonel Hunter?" The three men turned toward the right to see a vivacious woman standing to Max's right. "I'm Joan Poulard. Ben's principal. It's so nice to meet you. Thank you for coming." She offered to shake hands, which Max did. Her bright smile and no-nonsense style put him further at ease.

"Mrs. Poulard," Max said shaking her hand.

"Call me Joan," she said.

"May I introduce the superintendent of the Naval Academy, Admiral Charles Johnson."

"Goodness! I know Charlie. I taught his daughter in eighth grade!" And in an instant, she was in the admiral's embrace, the two of them laughing and talking in that rapid dialog of the once and always acquainted as Johnson filled her in on his family's news.

"You'll have to stop by some afternoon and bring me pictures," Joan said, before turning to Max.

"Mrs. Poulard, this is my good friend, Major Nels Lindquist."

"Lindquist," Joan said. "I think I may have met your wife at a class I'm taking in the evenings. Is her name Nancy?"

"Yes, ma'am. She's taking a quilting class at Eight Hands Around."

"It is very nice to meet you. Your wife and I got along like we were plotting a revolution!" she said, shaking his hand heartily. "When your boys get old enough, you've got to send them here, Major."

"That depends where the Marine Corps has me living, ma'am."

"You'll be back by then. Annapolis is like an elephant graveyard, isn't that right, Admiral Johnson? Everyone returns."

Everyone laughed at this and Joan took Max's arm with the comfortable warmth of an old friend and said, "I guess you've seen how your Ben is winning this game for us."

"He's doing well."

"It must take every ounce of self-control, Colonel, not to brag constantly about your son. He is absolutely a star."

"His mother and I are very proud of him."

"Did he tell you the news about his PSAT score?"

"Uh—"

"Well," she looked to Lindquist and the admiral for dramatic pause, "He got a two-thirty-four. The top score is two-forty. That means lots of scholarship money, Colonel. He's sure to be a National Merit Finalist."

"Really?" Max said.

"Congratulations, Max," Lindquist said.

"He doesn't need scholarship money," Admiral Johnson said. "He's coming my way. To USNA."

"We actually had two boys make that amazing score this year. We are so excited at the prospect of two National Merit Finalists. Ben and his best friend, Joe MacBride."

"Really?" Johnson beamed. "Identical scores? That's remarkable."

"And they're best friends?" Lindquist said. "I bet they compete constantly. That's good for them."

"What was that?" Max said slowly, blinking three times. "Who is this kid? What did you say his name was?"

"Joe. That fellow there—" Joan pointed at Joe, who Max recognized again as the kid with Ben that day at the MVA. "The one playing small forward. Number twelve."

"His last name is what?" Max croaked out the words. And then Max heard the coach shout about the rebound, and his eyes went reluctantly to the man in the wheelchair. The gray in the hair, the age in the man's tanned face had formed the disguise that now burned off like fog in the sun. Max saw him, knew him, and the air around him turned foul.

"MacBride. Joe MacBride, the coach's son. You know Tom. He said you were colleagues from Quantico."

Max did not reply. The room stretched out in a strange way so that everyone seemed inaccessible, faceless. And he stared at Ben, his son, who stood so far away at the sidelines waiting to toss the ball inbounds, so far that Max could not reach him. Ben's blond hair, wet from sweat, still gleamed like a halo; he was breathing hard, but breathing eagerly the poisoned air of Tom MacBride, and yet looked as clean and healthy and untouched as if MacBride's repulsive ideas did not bother him. Max's *own Ben* looked over his shoulder and listened—listened with concentration and comfortable obedience in his expression—to *Tom MacBride*.

"He's a former marine?" Lindquist said. "Well, that explains his heroism with the drowning kid. Was his back injured in Vietnam?"

"No," Mrs. Poulard said. "He did have an injury while in the Marine Corps, though, and had to get out because of it. That's what brought him to us…" Max knew she was talking, but instead he heard a loud whirring sound as if his head were too close to a ceiling fan and he couldn't seem to inhale. *Yeah,* Max thought, *I broke Tom's back so he was unfit to command marines and now he's coaching unsuspecting kids—my kid, the one I love.* He saw bursts of light pop around the edges of his vision. *I put Tom MacBride in this job,* Max told himself, and a wave of nausea flushed up his body in a wash of chilling sweat. "I—I better find my other boys," Max heard his own voice saying.

Johnson's eyes were on him and Johnson turned to let Max pass by into the lobby. Max rushed out there and found the air cooler and once again breathable.

"Hey, Coach," a brisk and friendly voice sounded from the locker room door. "Looks like you got yourself a winning team this year."

"Is that Smitty?" Joe said, as Paul and Adam simultaneously said, "Smitty," with knowing smiles.

"It's me." The stocky, grinning policeman poked his head around the corner and waved.

"Come on in, Smitty," Tom said, turning his chair to face him. "We're just finishing up." They shook hands.

Then Smitty shook Doug's hand. "Patrol car is waiting to give you a ride."

Doug ruffled Flip's hair. "Sorry I have to run. Accident up near the Magothy. Somebody needs a lift to Shock Trauma."

Smitty waved at Ben. "Remember me, ace? I gave you a ride the first day."

"Yeah, I remember," Ben said, getting up, leaving his socks and Band-Aids on the bench to shake Smitty's hand. "How are you?"

"I am *pumped* seeing you play. I was a little down when I got here, 'cuz my wife's on the night shift this week and I was feeling all sorry for myself. Then I see you jumping like you got springs in your shoes and I just cheered right up."

Oliver picked up one of Ben's shoes and looked at the sole. Adam grabbed it away from Oliver, his expression disgusted, exasperated.

"So they been treating you well here, like I told you they would, and you didn't believe me."

Again the door squeaked behind them and John Saunder's booming voice cut through the room. "I need to speak to ya, Tom."

"Can you wait outside, John, please? I don't allow parents in the locker room."

"Why not? Whatcha hiding in here?"

"John, please wait outside."

Smitty opened the door for him, sticking his chest out so that Saunders glanced once at the neat uniform, the gleaming police badge, and stepped out the door. "I'm waiting for you out here, Tom. Want to know why you took my boy out those five minutes during—" Smitty closed the door.

Tom said, "Those of you who have to, make sure you pee before you come out. There's not five minutes left."

Smitty held the door for Tom and spoke in a low tone. "Got news for you, Tom. Ben's dad is here, too. Miz Poulard sent me over to tell you."

"Thanks, Smitty. I'm ready for him."

"Yeah, you look ready," Smitty said, glancing at the wheels of Tom's chair.

"Help me up, Smitty. I don't want to face either one of these men in this chair."

"I dunno, Tom," Smitty said.

"Come on. Give me your arm." Smitty leaned over and grasped Tom's arm at the elbow. Tom pulled himself upright, wincing with pain. "I was up before. I walked across the gym and back."

"Try to stand on your own."

But it was no use. Not only did Tom have to cope with the pain of standing, but his legs were wooden, uncooperative, and he knew he would fall without his chair. Smitty helped him back down and gave him a sympathetic pat on the shoulder. "Tomorrow, you got to see the doctor and get a cortisone shot."

"The one time I need to be on my feet," Tom muttered.

"Be careful around Ben's dad. Y'hear, Tom? I don't want you gettin' in trouble."

"Just stay in here with the team and ride herd, will you, Smitty? They start playing around; they won't be ready. If I'm about to get in trouble, I'll holler for you. Keep me off the six o'clock news."

As he wheeled forward, Tom held up one hand to keep Saunders silent. "You signed the form agreeing to uphold the team rules, John," he said, looking up at the big, red-faced man. "First rule. No parents in the locker room at the half. None. For any reason. Second, Oliver argued with the ref.

Displays of temper, including arguing with the ref, means you sit out."

"So you can put your own son in."

"Joe is Ollie's sub."

"Shook his confidence. He thinks you don't like him. You saw how he played the rest of the half."

"I'm not having this conversation anymore, John. Open those doors for me. We're both going back into the gym."

Surprisingly, Saunders did as Tom asked, huffing and puffing about unfairness and his boy's sensitivity, as Tom scooted through to the gym braced to seek and find Max Hunter and face him down. And oddly Saunders stayed behind him. He did not have to look far. Admiral Johnson and another marine stood with Max by the stat table chatting with Mr. Ridout and the stat girls. Thinking that it was great of Charlie and so like him to come along with Max to ease this first meeting, Tom noticed first how *old* Max looked. Gone was the young marine with fiery eyes and the perfect, full-muscled physique. Oh, Tom could still see the impressive breadth of his shoulders, but Max had grown fat around the middle. He looked unwell, his color greenish, his shave, many hours old, showed bristles glinting of the silver that dominated his hair color. Deep circles under puffy eyes emphasized their weary—no, it was more *plagued*—expression. And for some reason, some reason he could not explain, some reason that was beyond his will to invent, Tom's heart betrayed him as his legs had moments before.

Though he could still call up Max's many crimes as though they were written in bold strokes, though he could actually see in his pained memory Max as he'd seen him that last moment sixteen years ago before he blacked out, Max's handsome grief-stricken face twisted with hate, fighting like the lowest coward, though Tom knew all this and feared even more was true, Tom's heart gave way to a powerful and gripping surge of compassion. The God he tried to serve had died for this man. And remembering the letter he had for Max folded in his wallet, Tom knew that Katie had loved him. *It would break her heart to see him like this.* Tom wheeled forward, determined to build whatever bridge he could to reach Max Hunter.

36

MAX Hunter kept his mouth smiling, but a frantic inner dialog demanded his attention. *Tom MacBride is Ben's coach? Ben's best friend is one of Tom's kids? I am standing in a gym waiting to say hello to a man I have vowed to pummel to death if I ever saw him again?* Max wished he could get the room to stop swaying. *I must be dreaming. I must be having a nightmare.*

When Charlie turned, Max felt an adrenaline rush that cleared his head for just a moment and set his hands tingling. Johnson pulled Max by the elbow toward the man himself, seated in a wheelchair, his facial expression the same supercilious, patronizing sneer it always wore. Max felt his fist tighten. He wanted to smash that face—that tan, smiling face. He wanted to hit him in the mouth and break all his white teeth.

Tom MacBride stuck his hand out toward him. "Max. It's good to see you again."

Max's eyes went over Tom, noting what looked to be good physical condition, except for the astounding wheelchair. Max felt Johnson bristle beside him.

"Don't tell me you don't remember Tom MacBride, Max. I know that can't be true after all he did for you and yours."

"Of course I know Tom," Max heard himself say, hoping with sudden, irrepressible glee that the wheelchair meant that Tom was paralyzed from the waist down. *Oh, that would be justice*, Max thought, *that would be justice!*

"Max," Johnson said, his voice gone low and tense. "Your son's coach, your fellow marine, wishes to shake your hand."

"Been a long, long time," Max said, stiffly offering Tom his hand but withdrawing it at a mere touch.

"Too long," Tom said with a smile that Max thought was so well practiced it didn't even look false.

Johnson made the introduction gesture toward Nels Lindquist. "Tom, let me introduce one of the outstanding marine officers stationed at the Naval Academy. This is Major Nels Lindquist. You may have heard of him. He is the officer who lost his eye in a knife fight at the battle for the ridge at Tan Phouc and managed to lead the troops back to safety."

"I read your story many years ago. Inspiring courage, Major," Tom said, extending his hand.

"You've got a fine team here, Coach. Ben played like a young god."

"He did. He's an amazing athlete."

"Last time I saw him play was ninth grade. And he hated the coach, didn't he, Max?" Max nodded woodenly and he listened to their polite inanities and his fury simmered within. Johnson *making* him act civil, or else his career was over, Lindquist making friends with the guy, no one able to see Tom's sinister magnetism lurking beneath that smiling face. Lindquist continued to gush at Tom MacBride like his ass was worth kissing. "Ben had talent, that was obvious, but you could tell he was holding back. You've brought him out, that's all. You've brought him out."

Max heard Tom speaking comfortably, and when Tom glanced at him with a friendly ol' smile, as if Tom had not put that blot on his permanent record, as if Tom had not snuck around behind his back with the only woman he had ever loved, as if they had not fought, as if Max had not crushed Tom's back last time when Ben was a baby and crying…just a crying baby…the pain of the memory swept back on him and he pushed it away because Tom was looking at him in a friendly way as if none of that had happened…as if none of it *mattered* any more.

Tom said, "I think it's because Ben feels part of the school and he's definitely an important part of the team. He's a terrific kid, Max. You must be so pleased with him."

Max glared at Tom, jealousy alive within him, wanting to shout out, *You don't tell me about my kid. I don't even want you to say his name. She wanted to give him your name—you snake. This whole mess is your fault!*

Tom said, "He was a hundred percent from the foul line and got eighteen points."

"That's nothing new for Ben," Max said, and at Johnson's bristle added, "but of course I'm proud of him. That goes without saying. He's a straight-A student, never any trouble at home, great with his brothers, and a superb athlete. So, there's nothing to worry about with Ben and everybody can relax about him."

"You have my congratulations, Max. Looks like you've done a fine job raising him."

"You almost sound surprised," Max challenged, the words out of his mouth before he could stop them.

"Pardon me, Colonel?" Johnson said.

"I was just asking Tom about his wheelchair," Max said to the admiral, whose face went to shock, then anger, in an instant. Max laughed amiably and bent to punch Tom's shoulder in a gesture that was meant to look playful. He was going to say it. He was going to taunt Tom—Johnson or no Johnson—he'd just make it sound like camaraderie. "Heh, heh. I know it probably isn't kosher to ask, but we *are* old friends and all these years, I've never imagined you—you know." Max pointed to the wheelchair.

Tom shrugged. "It helps me get around."

Voice in a grumbling conspiratorial whisper, Max said, "But like—are you paralyzed? Is that the problem? Because that can't be much fun for Laurie."

Johnson stepped toward Max. "Colonel—"

"Have you seen Laurie yet tonight, Max?" Tom interrupted the admiral, his face gone inscrutable. "She's over there in the bleachers with our children." Tom pointed and the men turned around. "Charlie, if you walk Max around that way—third quarter's about to start—you can steer Max to where Laurie's sitting and he can say hello." He stuck out his hand and said to Lindquist, "Nice to meet you, Major Lindquist. Charlie. Max, I hope to see you after the game."

Max realized, as they rounded the far corner of the court, that Tom had won that round. He knew it when he got close enough to see Laurie clearly.

If a man's wife said anything about his success, then Tom MacBride had it all. Her beauty—noticeable when they had been teenagers—was now arresting. Her perfect oval face, her dark hair with its shiny curls tossing insouciance, her chocolate-colored eyes alive as ever, her exquisite body with those truly astonishing breasts that made a man shiver with delight. In a memory that was both poignant and sensory he thought of the pleasures of her embrace, the embrace that had held for him the pleasures of initial sexual discovery.

Open-mouthed, Max stared at her as he approached, wondering how after so many years with Tom she could be more beautiful, glowing with happiness, looking rich. Beside her stood a smart-looking boy who held a baby. The boy's face was Tom's, but with Laurie's coloring; his expression was intense and lively—a singularly masculine boy. On her other side stood a teenage girl who was talking to several other friends. Max had noticed her before when they were standing in the doorway. She looked like Laurie with the same dreamy, enticing beauty, and though she was slimmer than Laurie had been at that age, her breasts looked just as delightfully round. Her hair was long, thick and straight; her mouth was fuller, her hands and eyes more expressive when she talked as she was now doing, and Max felt his heart sink with envy.

Johnson called to them. "Laurie."

"Hey, Charlie," Laurie called, then seeing him, met his eyes, blinked slowly and said, "Max." She touched her son's shoulder with some kind of gentle, private instruction.

"We'll come up there," Charlie promised, but there was no room and instead Laurie climbed down to speak to them. The boy gave the baby to the girl to carry and they followed their mother. Laurie hugged Charlie Johnson, who held her probably a little bit longer than was strictly polite before introducing her to a thoroughly charmed Nels Lindquist. She recognized the name and it turned out that Laurie *owned* the little shop in town where people like Nels' wife and that nice principal took sewing classes.

Laurie turned to Max and offered her hand. "Max. You spoke to Tom, I see."

"Laurie," Max said, taking her hand and holding it in both of his. "I— it—it's *terrific* to see you again. You look—wonderful."

"Thank you, Max. I haven't seen you since—" Max tried to interrupt her, making a dismissive it's-water-under-the-bridge gesture, remembering suddenly exactly how blunt Laurie could be; there were things he did not want the admiral to know. But she did not take the clue. "—since I drove away that day."

"Laurie, you don't—"

"You know, I still have the keys to the Fiat. I was holding them—and Ben's pacifier in my hand—and I didn't realize it until, I don't know, miles down the road."

"I don't guess Ben needs that pacifier anymore," Max said, sounding amiable and casual while wanting her to be quiet, just as much as he wanted to hold her and kiss her. Her perfume let him remember how fascinated he at sixteen had been with her body, he remembered how she felt in his arms, how many different ways he'd tried to get her naked, how every chance he got—Max thought about this, blinking slowly, staring at her. "You really look terrific. You look younger and more beautiful than you did when we were sixteen." Realizing he still held her hand, he lifted it to his lips and kissed it.

"I've missed you," she said, and further astonished him by grabbing him and hugging him, her arms sturdy and eager around his shoulders—those incomparable breasts barely brushing him. Max's hands went to her waist, just touching the slope of her hips, a caress that had always excited him and immediately his body tingled at the luscious feel of her in his arms. She kissed him quickly on the cheek, her lips just touching the corner of his mouth, actually making him salivate. She released him and stepped back, smiling, her eyes bright with emotion. He knew he must be blushing.

"I'm flattered," he said, afraid he sounded slurpy.

"It's natural that I should still care about you," she said, her voice blatantly meaningful in that crowded gym where his boss and best friend watched, where her children stood behind her, where her husband—was he impotent, or could he just not feel anything down there? How could he be incapable with a wife as obviously full up with this loving energy?

"I seem to remember breaking your heart," he said.

She laughed at him in that sexy, intense way of hers. "I forgave you that long ago. But I've still missed seeing you so much. And Ben. So terribly."

"Ben's fine."

"We were all meant to be friends." She gestured to include the entire room. "You just missed Doug. He lives here now, too. We've raised our children together. That's how it should have been."

"Really? Doug? I thought he was in the desert somewhere."

Laurie looked around. "He had to work, but you can see him at the next game." She put her arm around the boy beside her. "This is our son, Tommy. Tommy, Admiral Johnson, Major Lindquist, and my old friend from high school, Colonel Hunter. Ben's dad." The boy gave a hard handshake and spoke politely to each man.

"These are my daughters, Bonnie Jean," Laurie said, "and our baby, Cara."

"It is lovely to meet you," Johnson said to Bonnie Jean and Lindquist shook her hand muttering the same in the shy, brisk way he had with women.

Max took the opportunity to whisper to Laurie. "This is *your* baby,

Laurie?"

"Tom's and my baby. Obviously."

"So, he's not paralyzed?" He said close to her ear, drawing in the fresh fragrance in her hair.

"No, he's good, Max." Laurie moved to meet his eyes with a look that was sultry in its frank intention. "He's the best."

Max figured she was flirting, challenging him, and his flip dismissive expression said he could prove her wrong. And then some jealous memory dimmed the edges of the sensual high Laurie had evoked; life had been unfair to him, favoring Tom MacBride. He did not deserve all this.

"Any *more* kids, Laurie, or is this all you have?"

"Depends on how you count them, Max." And again, she touched him, her hand a brief, hot caress across the back of his hand.

37

LIKE a pit bull on a leash, Max went with Johnson down the length of the gym to stand again by the door. His two small sons had found seats on the first row of the bleachers in the middle of a row of teenage girls and they looked deliriously happy, eyes glazed from excess sugar consumption. Both of them tumbled their piles of candy into their laps to free a hand to wave to him.

Max lifted an arm that felt foreign, leaden. It was as if he were somehow detached from his body; he had not felt so numbly incapable of thought since Katie had gone. The blows of the day had been continuous and surprising and so absurd that Max startled in a panicky moment of horrible hope that he was actually dreaming. To wake up clear-headed and escape all this!

Out of the side of his mouth, Johnson mumbled to Max, "It was truly a gallant gesture of you to put your son in Tom MacBride's school. I tell you, Colonel, your good will toward Tom is a step in the right direction."

Max said, "Looks like I've finally done something right today." Johnson thought this was funny and, laughing, clapped Max on the arm.

Lindquist, looking concerned about the lingering tension, thought he'd help and said to Max, "Coach has got a great reputation, Max. It's super to think you started out together in Quantico and here he is helping your son reach his potential. I'm telling you, that last coach Ben had didn't know what the hell to do with him."

Max felt embarrassed that Nels knew more about Ben's last coach and how Ben played under him than Max did. He could not even remember what the guy looked like. He hadn't noticed anything about Ben's playing the one time he saw him last year, except that he was better than everyone around him.

Nels gushed, "This guy's great for him. Just look."

Max looked; he stood by Johnson, inanely obedient, as Tom MacBride coached Ben in a way that made their rapport palpable. The guy only had to call out a word or two and Ben's eyes would flick toward him, or he'd nod his head, seriously concentrating, looking as alive and vibrant as Max had ever seen him. No glimpse had Max now of the icy, controlled boy always distant and autonomous. No sense of some profound discontent, some hostile unhappiness in Ben that Max every day feared was not just his imagination, not just teenage shit.

The humiliating realization that he had put Ben under Tom MacBride's influence galled Max. How had that happened? How had he missed that? Wasn't his mother supposed to check out all the details? Max tried to retrace the steps of the decision. When he got his orders to USNA, he'd panicked about MacBride still being here. He begged to have his orders changed and when he couldn't make that happen, he had looked in the phone book. When he didn't find MacBride listed there—but he would *never* have guessed that Tom would be stuck working in a school. Max tried to watch the game but his mind refused to see it, though he was aware that Ben had slumped a little in the third quarter and Key had gained ten points. Thinking about their move in August, Max remembered telling his mother to *make sure* Tom MacBride no longer lived in Annapolis. He figured that Donna and the boys could live as far as Frederick if it meant keeping Ben away from so much as the *possibility* of breathing Tom's air. Now certain that he *had* asked her to check, he could not understand how she could have missed this.

Max's hands shook now and his tongue felt furry. He glanced at Keith and Tim to see that they were being fussed over by the girls. Tom and Laurie's daughter had joined the group and was bending over to whisper in Keith's ear. Keith laughed gleefully at something she said. *Good night, she's a beauty*, Max thought, and his chest flamed thinking about Laurie. Max looked up, looked across the gym to where she sat, his high school sweetheart. His mouth watered and his knees went weak. All these years he had never imagined her so happy, so vivid with life and energy. He had imagined Tom would have manipulated his way to the top of some sleazy church organization that made its money from giving people bad advice, but not this crowded and cheerful life. How had he managed to keep *that* woman happy?

Lindquist murmured, "Coach is gonna find out what's wrong," and he nodded toward Ben.

"Tom'll set him right," encouraged Johnson.

Max watched absently while Tom motioned for Ben to come out; the substitution was made, and Ben took his place beside Tom on the bench.

Max watched for three minutes while Ben leaned toward Tom, listening, his expression frustrated, troubled, and Max watched as Tom pumped Ben full of confidence. His blue eyes, now unguarded and noticeable across the gym, looked earnest, trusting.

Max shuddered. He had been so careful for years. He had destroyed every picture, every letter, everything that would lead Ben to Katie. He had even done his best—his very best—to destroy Tom MacBride.

From Tom's bench, Ben returned to the game like one inspired, dribbling like a maniac, making quick, sure passes to his teammates. The crowd roared their delight. No, Max couldn't bear to watch him giving Tom a victory but the only other place his mind would go was to memories of Katie's betrayal and when Ben dashed past him, inches away, instead of seeing just Ben, he saw Katie rushing through their home the night they had fought over her diary. He saw her crying frantically while she packed up her car, weeping brokenly while she stuffed the Fiat so tightly that he knew this time, she was never coming back. And this same blank rage paralyzed him so that he did nothing but stand there frantic with jealousy, unwilling to comfort her when she ran to the bathroom to throw up, unable to make her remember that she *loved* him, unable to make her even one bit sorry for cheating on him.

And here he was without Katie, her son having fallen under MacBride's spell, too. Max knew he had to shake his numbness and fight for Ben. He had fought before. For godsakes, that time when Ben was a baby Max had beaten Tom *unconscious* and still…*shit*. He had wrecked Tom's back so now all the interfering snake was fit to do was coach a bunch of marginally talented athletes.

When the buzzer sounded, Max applauded Ben's win with leaden enthusiasm. He found himself propelled through the moving, chattering crowd on the gym floor. He saw the MacBride girl sliding through the milling cliques of people, saw her hug Ben's neck, heedless of his glistening sweat, saw her whisper in his ear, watched them meet eyes before he whispered back to her, and saw her nod at him, hug him again, before he was pulled away from her by other students. She turned to congratulate her brother, then another player and another. Max stood awkwardly watching other people's happiness.

Johnson and Lindquist were ahead of him, shaking Tom's hand with ebullient warmth. Johnson turned back to him and nodded toward Tom. Coolly, Max shook Tom's hand, exaggerating his need to bend down to Tom in the wheelchair. "Good game, MacBride," he said.

"Thanks, Max."

Max looked around for an escape while enduring a fresh wash of nausea and a potent need to smash Tom's face bloody.

"Uh, Max. I'd appreciate it if we could *talk* sometime soon."

Other parents burst into the group to shake Tom's hand. He stood and watched them fawn over Tom, and he could feel Johnson's oppressive presence behind his right shoulder, threatening his career...his way of life...his family's happiness if he did not treat this snake with rankly undeserved courtesy.

Ben was propelled by the crowd toward them and bumped into Admiral Johnson's hip. Johnson shook Ben's hand and showered the kid with praise. Then Lindquist took Ben by the shoulders and presented him to Tom. "Aren't you gonna tell this kid how proud you are of him?" Lindquist laughed.

Tom reached forward and up to shake Ben's hand. "That was a terrific game, Ben."

"Thanks, Coach."

"Well coached," Lindquist said and bent toward Tom to explain some idea he had about zone defense. Johnson said to Ben, "Your dad is around here somewhere," and, turning right to Max, made a gesture toward him as if presenting Ben, as if introducing them. "I'm sure he has something to say to you."

"Good game, Ben," Max said, starting to reach for Ben's hand to shake, but in time, he saw Ben trap both hands under his armpits and he managed to drop his hand before the admiral recognized the hostility of Ben's rejection.

"It's a good team," Ben said, keeping his eyes from Max.

In the awkward silence, noted by the keenly observant, ever-smiling admiral, they were jostled yet closer to MacBride and Lindquist, Ben so close now to Tom that another push by the crowd and Ben would end up in Tom's lap. Max tugged at his collar; the place sweltered, the sweat stench of the athletes predominant and repulsive.

"Is the team celebrating after this?" Johnson asked as if he thought that was the most exciting and wonderful prospect on earth.

"I don't know, sir. To tell you the truth." Ben looked around, past Max, as if someone out there would provide the answer.

Max tried to think of something to say, something fatherly, but Johnson said, "You don't want to be out too late on a school night. You've got homework, I'm sure."

"Yes, sir. I've got lots of homework. And an away game tomorrow. So, you're right, we shouldn't stay out too late." Ben shifted, stared at his feet for a second, and then looked toward Max, but over Max's left shoulder as if he were searching for someone. The silence was making Max nauseous. In a habitual motion, Ben lifted the shoulder of his jersey to wipe his now-dried face.

Max saw Johnson's face go concerned, and following the admiral's glance Max noticed the bruises on Ben's chest and collarbone and blurted out, "What the hell happened to your chest, Ben?"

Finally meeting his eyes, Ben stared at Max, eyes squinted, but fiery with hostility. He stared so long that Max shifted from foot to foot and then said, sharply, as one accustomed to immediate, polite obedience, "I asked you a *question*, Ben."

"I *heard* you," Ben said, his opaque composure somehow worn thin; the deep undercurrent of his anger as palpable and alarming as the scent of leaking gas.

Max's expression went angry and expectant, not knowing what he'd do if Ben defied him in front of Johnson. "Give me an answer."

Staring at him, Ben said, "Some *jackass* grabbed my collarbone and tried to pull it out."

"Watch your mouth," a voice sounded behind Ben, *Tom's* voice, and Max saw Tom thump the back of Ben's knee with his fingers, the gesture so reflexive, such a comfortable punctuation to his correction that Tom did not even have to look.

"Sorry, Coach," Ben said immediately, turning to glance at Tom in a response that Max saw was not habit or convention, but genuine. Max's mouth went slack with shock and his eyes went quickly from Ben to Tom and back again to Ben.

Tom turned his wheelchair toward them, protruding knees nudging in a bit and he shrugged to show that he had made a mistake, his grin apologetic. "Sorry, Max. I didn't realize it was you talking to Ben. I would have left it up to you to correct his language if I had." And in the tense silence following, Tom's eyes went to Ben's, showing confidence and fondness, but Max realized that Tom could read Ben's expression, cloaked though it was now, in his beautiful, blond composure. In reading it, Tom's face changed to show deep concern.

Johnson said to Tom, "We were discussing this terrible bruise here under his shirt."

When Tom's eyes did not move from studying Ben's face, Max said, "I'm surprised that you, Tom—of all people—allow such rough play."

Tom tried to give Max his full attention but the man could not for long take his eyes from Ben, "You're right, Max, of course," he said, missing the mocking note in Max's voice because he kept glancing at Ben, watching as Ben turned away and squatted to speak to his brothers. The three men watched him in awkward collusion.

When Ben stood up, he offered to shake Admiral Johnson's hand. "Thanks for coming to my game, Admiral Johnson. I really appreciate it." He nodded his head in his father's direction, careful to avoid eye contact, and said to all present, "I'm gonna take a shower."

38

DONNA sat at the kitchen table before a tall glass filled with a fruit shake and some stiff, little book open on the table. When Max came in the door, she opened her mouth to speak.

"I'm warning you right now, Donna, don't give me any shit." Max said, putting Tim down and shaking him a little so that he woke enough to head toward the stairs. "About anything. Johnson's been on my ass all day."

"Now what for?"

"Get this, Donna. Guess who the *hell* is the coach of Ben's basketball team? Guess. Tom MacBride, that's who. I tell my mother to make sure he's *not* living in Annapolis and not only does she *miss* that choice little detail, but Ben ends up *at the school* where *he's* the *coach*. Ben, on his team and getting along with him like…And Johnson wants me to buddy up to Tom or he's gonna turn me in for a whole shitload of trumped up charges."

"What do you mean, charges? Like what?"

"He comes by the office this morning and I ended up putting him in his place. He thinks that was insubordination. Here he is—all up in my personal business and when I tell him to buzz off—I mean I've never had a CO who cared about the shit this guy does. Everything is PR to him. He wants to turn us into puling saints pursing up our lips to kiss his weird ring-knocking ass."

"Insubordination. What else?"

"He thinks I'm lying about everything! The accidents. Ben. Everything."

"You are lying."

"What *the hell* gives you the right to—"

"You might want to keep your voice down, Max. We have neighbors."

"Is that a *Bible*?" He flipped the Bible closed. "What *the hell* are you doing with that?"

"You know I wouldn't get this out unless it was an emergency."

Max stomped across the kitchen to the refrigerator. "Donna, I've had the worst day of my life. I don't need—"

"Your day may get worse, Max. Somebody named Patty Edwards called."

Taking a cold beer in hand, Max went quiet and calm. "She's my lawyer."

Donna's eyes filled up with tears. "That's what she said."

"Why *cry* about *that*?" Max asked, twisting the cap with thirsty determination only realizing he needed a bottle opener when he felt a warm gush of blood. "Shit, I cut my hand."

"Why do you need a lawyer?"

He grabbed a dish towel and stuck the beer into the opener mounted on the cabinet door. The sweet hiss of its opening made his heart pound.

And when he smelled the yeasty, homey fizz, his good nature reared up, ready to revive. Max gave Donna a careful glance trying to figure out what she knew, what she suspected, and why she was crying. "I need a lawyer because Johnson is stalking me."

"What do you mean?"

Max took a long drink, licked his lips, and sat down beside her. "Like I just told you. He's threatening to charge me. And it's because he's obsessed with Ben. He's demanding I give Ben his birth certificate and tell him everything."

"Maybe it's time Ben found out."

"No way. He's sullen enough without handing him ammunition. No. I'm not telling him *anything.* Not now, not *ever.*"

"Does Johnson know everything?"

Max raised the bottle to his lips. "I don't know. I think I threw him off the scent. I muddied up the story a little, so he can't know for sure, but he keeps bringing *Katie* up," Max made the quotation gesture with his free hand, "He 'was very fond' of her."

"Who wasn't?"

Max took a long drink. He couldn't argue with that and with even just that much of this delicious, soothing beer in him, he didn't want to.

"Don't drink too much, Max. Do you know where I found you when I got home last night?"

"Donna," his voice a warning growl, "I'm just starting to feel better."

"I found you on the floor in the bathroom. I had to clean up your vomit and—" Max held up his hand. "Disgusting," she said, her voice going emotional again, tears coming to her eyes. She ducked her head down.

"So you got out your Bible to try to fix me?"

"No." She gave a snort as if his comment were absurd. "I have to talk to Ben."

"About what?"

"Now, don't make like this is nothing, because it is very serious." From the seat next to her, she pulled up a Ziploc bag that held a bright purple thong. She held the bag between her perfectly manicured thumb and forefinger and dropped it on the table in front of Max.

"Ooh," Max said, his mind working quickly. It wasn't Donna's; she considered thongs unsanitary, never considering the fact that they didn't stay on long enough to contaminate anything…and then he remembered that this one had been the delight of his wild romp with Patty last night and suddenly he felt overheated. Max brought up a loud, unconcerned-sounding belch. "Where'd you find that?" he said, pushing the thing back toward his wife, and immediately taking another drink.

Donna watched him drink. He took his time. Still she was silent and when she spoke, her voice was quiet and small. "In the spare bedroom on the third floor."

"Ben," Max said.

"You don't really think it could be Ben."

"If he's my son, it is," Max chuckled trying to sound proud and not relieved. "That rascal. Sneaking girls in. Didn't know he had it in him."

"This is nothing to be proud of. I found condoms in the waste basket! Condoms! In the waste basket!"

"If he's doin' it, we want him to use condoms."

"There were three of them!" Max said nothing. He took another drink, draining the bottle. "Don't look so pleased with yourself. I know you are thinking disgusting things like you're proud of him for doing it three times, like he's some kind of a stud like you used to be, but this is all your fault."

"How?" Max asked, sounding as outraged as an innocent man.

She stared at him, angry, eyes filling. Feeling delightfully light-headed, Max went for a second beer.

"Don't drink too much, Max," Donna said.

"I'm not!" He remembered to go straight to the bottle opener and secretly congratulated himself, telling himself that this was proof that a little booze really did clear his muddled head. "Look, Donna, boys his age actually need sex."

"Oh, for God's sake," Donna groaned. "I don't want him doing it here. Right upstairs with his brothers down the hall. No! I want him to have some decency. So we'll sit right here and wait for him."

"Okay," Max said, with a glance at his watch. "But I have to meet my lawyer at ten."

Donna looked hurt. Max sat down again and took her hand. "Honey, you're going to have to get used to Ben being a horny teenage boy. Boys his age think about sex constantly. He's healthy, now we know he's normal, and let me tell you, he's got a hundred girls dying to screw his brains out. God, they were all over him after the game. He's probably doing it somewhere right this minute."

Right at that minute, Ben and Bonnie Jean ducked into a dark corner hidden by a dense blue spruce behind Johnny Rockets, where their friends sat inside awaiting the food they'd ordered. She put her arms around his neck as she always did and hugged him tight. "You were amazing."

"It was so fun, Jeannie."

"You are so fast! And the way you jump. Watching you in motion, I thought I must be in heaven."

Embracing her, his arms around her little waist, Ben pulled her close. "That's nice of you to say, considering how many inexcusable mistakes I made all day long."

"Not inexcusable. Forgivable."

Ben's face went serious and he studied her expression. "I hope you—especially *you*—can forgive me."

"Of course I do."

"I don't ever want to lie to you."

"It's simple," she laughed, moving her arms so that she tried to encompass his shoulders. She squeezed him tight. "If you know I will accept you, faults and all—"

Ben looked at her eyes, enjoying the sincere golden brown of them. Wrapping his arms tighter, Ben said, "You helped me so much last night. I'm starting to feel like things are changing."

"How?"

"Inside, despite all the bad stuff, the wish to thank God keeps coming up out of my heart."

"That's beautiful, Ben. You are so beautiful. Gregen thought so, too."

"Jeannie," he said, objecting.

"He said so."

"Like that? Like *you* do? I hope not."

"He mentioned your blind spot. He said he could see you compensating. The way you turn your head when the ball is up here." She pointed to the spot.

Ben nodded. "That's right, but how did he know that? I don't even know I'm doing it anymore."

"He seems to know you and love you."

"Yeah," Ben whispered. "But why?"

"Love has no explanation."

Ben smiled at her, then nuzzled her cheek with his nose, the euphoria of post-game exhaustion numbing his suspicions. "I guess you're right in a way. You know more about love than I do."

"I did find something out, though."

Ben waited, knowing she had to tell all she thought and knew. "Yeah?"

"Like I asked him was he a spy and all about the scars on his fingers."

"Isn't that weird?" Ben interrupted. "I dreamed it but his fingers are really like that."

"They happened during the war. He was in a *prison camp*, so I think it was part of the torture."

"No."

"Yes, and I was trying to get him to tell me why he gave you a car—"

"Jeannie, you are too bold."

"We have to know, and talking to him was so easy. He was the nicest, most—like right there with you kind of guy."

"Everything seems so whole in his life, do you know what I mean?"

She nodded. "I thanked him for the books, but I wanted to be able to ask him about it all. I wish he hadn't left but maybe it was better since my dad showed up."

She nodded. "Gregen said it would be better to see Max another day. Or something like that."

Jon jiggled the branches of the spruce and called. "Hey, Ben. Food's up. Got to come in."

Ben and Bonnie Jean joined the group, squeezing into the booth where their hot grilled burgers awaited them. "I am so hungry," Ben said, taking the plate of onion rings Adam passed to him. "I think I could eat this entire table."

"You eat up, boy," Mr. Ridout said from the booth behind them. He reached up over his head and ruffled Ben's hair. "You must of burned up seven thousand calories tonight. And don't you worry about payin' for it. This is my treat. My treat. You boys win a game for Coach MacBride, it's my treat."

Though Ben felt mellow and contentedly exhausted when he opened the kitchen door, the surprise of seeing his parents sitting in the dark, waiting for him, laying siege for him, rattled him to immediate nausea.

"Thought we weren't in here, didn'cha?" his father said, his voice friendly as he flipped on the light.

"Sit down, son," Donna said. "We want to talk to you."

Still partially blind from the sudden shock of light, Ben murmured, "Son?" She never called him that, he realized, or any term of endearment. "I have a lot of chemistry homework. And math."

"This can't wait," Donna said. "Sit down."

Ben saw then that she had a *Bible* open on the table, and he wondered if the school had called her about his cheating, or if his father had been there early enough to hear his apology. Inside he reached for the strength and resolve to bear their recriminations for his mistakes and sat down.

"Is that a Bible, Mom?"

His father had gone to the refrigerator and taken out a beer. Ben glanced at him, glanced around the room to see evidence of the toll. He noticed that the coffee pot held six cups and there were two used mugs on the counter. He caught a faint smell of beer but saw no empty bottles.

"It's my Bible. I wanted to tell you about how I became a Christian."

"You're a *Christian*?"

"Don't sound so shocked. You never hear me swear, do you? I've been faithful to my husband all these years. It's not so hard to believe."

"It's just that you never said anything about it."

"I'm saying something now."

"Go ahead," Ben said, genuinely interested. He heard Max pop open

445

his beer.

"When I was around your age, a little older, twenty, my parents caught me behaving inappropriately with my boyfriend." Ben's eyes went wide. "I was horribly ashamed. They said I had to start going to church and even when I went back to college after break, I kept going." Ben nodded, listening, hoping she would be all right, wondering if he might finally have some real conversation with his parents. "Some people at church told me that I could get rid of my shame by believing in Jesus." She pointed to the scripture. "See?" she said, tipping the Bible for him to see. "It says here that if we believe in him we can't be condemned for our sins." She looked up at him. "Sins are really bad mistakes, Ben."

She pointed again to the Bible and Ben read silently, "For God so loved the world that he gave his one and only Son, that whoever believes in him shall not perish but have everlasting life."

Donna said, "Perish means suffer and that includes suffering shame." She tapped the Bible again. Ben glanced at his father who was sipping his beer with the polite distance of a casual drinker at a Sunday picnic. Ben read aloud this time, "For God did not send his Son into the world to condemn the world, but to save the world through him. Whoever believes in him is not condemned."

"See?" she said.

"Yes," Ben said. "Do you know why it works that way?"

"They told me that a substitution was made. Jesus took our sins on the cross for us. Believing is like a check that gets what has been saved up for us."

Touched by her simple explanation, Ben nodded. He was afraid to smile lest he break the spell. He knew nothing of her past, nothing of her internal life. He added, quoting from the part in James that Mr. Bettinger had made his class memorize, "And without faith it is impossible to please God, because anyone who comes to him must believe that he exists and that he rewards those who earnestly seek him."

"Good. So you know that."

"From school this year." Ben waited.

"Do you have anything to say to me, Ben?"

"Um, I think it's really great that you believed." Ben glanced at his father, wondering if he should feel as comfortable and interested as he did or if he should try to escape. "Are you trying to tell me that time when your parents caught you was when I was conceived?"

"No," she snapped, emphatic, disgusted.

Ben did the mental addition, thinking that it must have been close to that date.

His father's eyes went sideways and Ben saw him looking at his fingers, counting. "Yes, Donna. Ben's right."

"No, Max. Stop. I want him to ask me about him making mistakes. Like the one I made." She raised her eyebrows at Ben.

Ben studied her earnest, almost desperate expression and the old worry for her, the desire to protect her and somehow try to get her to be comfortable if he couldn't make her smile, returned full and painful in his chest. "It must have been really rough on you."

"Yes, it was. Because—" she blushed scarlet and breathed quickly through flared nostrils. "I understand how it feels to make a mistake, Ben, so I'm not mad at you now. I'm telling you the way to deal with this."

"I appreciate that, Mom."

"So it would be easier on me if you'd confess now."

"Confess?"

"Confess."

"Um," Ben said. Though he knew it would not help, he glanced at his father to find Max's expression a baffling, patronizingly benign grin. "Like everything from when I was little?"

"No," Donna said, clearly at the end of her rope. She pulled her hand from beneath the table and revealed a Ziploc bag holding a bright purple, stretchy thing. This she dropped in front of Ben. "About this."

It took Ben a moment to figure out what it was. "A thong? What about it?"

"I found that," she said angrily, "In the guest room." Her voice went shrill. "On your floor! You've been having girls up there!"

"Not me."

"You have. I found this and—" she burst into tears. "And—you tell him, Max."

"She found three used condoms," Max said, looking at Ben meaningfully, eyes protruding, a slight, conspiratorial smile on his face.

"In the guest room upstairs," Donna sobbed. "Right down the hall from your *brothers*."

"I know. I know," Ben said, his voice rising with the injustice of it. "I *know* why you're upset but what makes you think they're mine?"

"They have to be yours." Donna snatched at her tears.

"I'm not the only one in this house with a penis," Ben said to his father.

"You're trying to blame it on me?" Max laughed, "I saw all those girls with the hots for you tonight at the game."

"Dad," Ben whispered.

"Mom knows about me and condoms. Can't function right with one," Max said proudly.

Donna nodded at Ben. "It's true."

"This is unbelievable!"

"*Please*, Ben," her eyes implored him.

"*It wasn't me—*"

"Ben, I thought about this all day…" Her voice drowned in the rising tears; she hid her face in her hands.

Taking the edges of the table in his hands, Ben glared at his father. *Tell her the truth, you worthless son of a bitch.*

Max put his beer bottle on the edge of the sink. "Just confess, Ben," he said and, walking toward Ben, patted his shoulder. "I'm goin' for a swim, darlin'," he said to his wife, bending to kiss the top of her head. "I'll be back right after my meeting."

"No, Dad," Ben said, rolling out of his chair and blocking Max's way to the back door. "You can't go and leave me with this."

Max took his cover from its hook by the door. He tried to muscle past Ben but Ben's feet were set and he stood. Max's voice went edgy. "Confess like your mother wants. You don't want to break her heart any *more*. Look at her crying there over you." And the moment Ben's eyes flicked toward Donna, Max muscled past him, his elbow in Ben's stomach, shoving Ben back against the wall. Max slammed the door, nearly trapping Ben's hand in chase.

Ben smashed the door with his fist.

"Pray with me," Donna said, holding out her hand for him to take.

"No, Mom. This isn't fair." He shook his hand savagely, then sucked on the skinned knuckles.

She reached for him, grasping at air. "Come back to the table." She pulled on his arm. He did as she asked and sat beside her. "Pray with me. Please."

"You first," Ben hissed.

"God in heaven, I want to pray that Ben will—believe what I said and be okay."

Ben sat in raging silence. He tried to recall the beauty of his prayers in the chapel, tried to recall the clean feeling of understanding he'd known today at school, but it was gone. His mother sobbed quietly beside him and in a gesture that was instinctual, Ben put an arm around her. As soon as he touched her, Ben understood the terror of her suspicions. It was as if he understood what to do, though he heard no words only a kind of sure direction inside telling him that he could be kind without lying. And then he knew a flood of some kind of clean strength not his own. "Mom," he whispered, "I'm sorry for everything you have to go through. It must have been really bad finding that stuff up there."

She nodded, groping for his hand.

"And you were all by yourself," Ben said. He wondered when in her attempt to get him to confess she had realized that Max was to blame, but somehow Ben understood that Donna knew.

She squeezed his hand, her tears dropping onto the table. "I failed you. I should have told you about God sooner. Then you would have had something to guide you to be...better than...I mean, to be good."

"It's okay, Mom," he said, but he wondered why her Christianity had left her so paralyzed and unhappy.

"It'll be okay if you pray."

Ben found he *could* pray. "God in heaven," he whispered, squeezing his mother's hand, "please forgive my faults and mistakes. You know them all. You know I'm a liar; you know how much I lie. You know all the other things I've done that you asked your Son to pay for on the cross. Forgive me." And while praying, Ben believed. He sat very still waiting for the peace that filled him to dissipate, but it stayed real and lovely like a round luminescent pearl within. He put both arms around his mother. "And Father, please comfort my mom and show her what she should do."

"My mom. You said, 'my mom.' And I've been so unkind to you."

"Come on, Mom. Please don't cry so hard."

"I took his side and you were just a child. I should have—"

"Hey," Ben said quietly. "What if I heat up some of that soup you like and bring it upstairs for you? You can get warm in bed and relax."

"I've got to go see Keith and Tim."

"I'll make it for you while you're with them, then, okay?"

"Thank you, Ben. All day I've been thinking about how good you've been to me. All day I kept trying to blame it all on you, but then I remembered how you are and what you are like."

"When did you know, Mom?"

"All day I worried and tried to think." She swallowed hard and shivered. "But when I showed him that *thing* and he asked where I *found* it, not *what* it was or where I *got* it, I got terrified." Her eyes met Ben's. "But it was your reaction. You wouldn't say you did it even when I begged you. I knew from experience that if you'd been guilty—I knew the shame wasn't there. I can spot shame. That's one thing I know."

39

ENTERING Lejeune Hall, the state-of-the-art natatorium, down the street from his quarters, Max went to his locker and greeted the few people still there. He needed to think and he could only really think in the pool. It stopped the shaking, it calmed him down; it was a tonic, an actual tonic. He folded his olive uniform trousers over a hanger, hung his shirt on the hook. He stepped into his faded Speedo racing suit and yanked it up, stretching the suit into place, settling it, comfortable finally, with the elastic below his hip bones.

Flipping his towel over his shoulder, Max pushed the locker room door open, and stepped into the blast of simmering air. He sniffed deeply for the clean smell of chlorine and pressed his lips together in a measured smile of approval feeling his mind clear, knowing he could here figure out what to do about Johnson.

The heavy door sighed shut behind him. He was alone.

Max scanned the big room. The pool stretched out on his right under small triangular blue and gold flags that had been strung above the swimming lanes. Blue and gold pep banners hung on the walls. To his left, three concrete towers loomed above the diving tank. As he walked toward the pool, his feet slapping against the wet concrete, Max was assaulted by memories of Katie that lingered like ghosts in swim centers. She had been home to him for *three weeks* and came up with a positive pregnancy test. Did she really think he'd believe she'd been faithful when they had been trying for a baby—really strenuously trying, screwing morning and night—for two years?

She was "mortally insulted," as she later told her uncle. That's the way she talked when she was upset—formally, drawing on her broad vocabulary, like she was mouthing the dialog from a book. Now he only had Ben to think of and he was losing Ben. That was clear enough from today. If he let Charlie Johnson push him into telling Ben everything, he'd lose Ben the next minute. He could not compete with Katie's appeal and all that being Katie's son would mean to the distant and dissatisfied Ben.

Warm air moved over his skin in a gentle caress. It was enough to urge Max into motion. He awakened to his surroundings, remembering that he was not back in the terrible past. He sucked in the clean air, the carefully engineered air that was constantly circulated by the superior ventilation system, which kept the room hot and ready and eliminated condensation on the windows and ceiling. A swimmer was never surprised here by a chill drip from a moldy, perspiring ceiling.

Max stepped onto the first starting block, pausing to drop his towel behind him. He noticed, when he stood ready to dive and begin his laps, that the water was the same clear blue as Ben's eyes. Max wondered what it would be like to dive into that widened black pupil of Ben's eye and swim, swim deep into his son's brain and find out what the boy was thinking. *Shit, the way he looked at MacBride all unsuspecting and…shit.* Max snapped his goggles into place. He sprang up and dived in, the cool pool waters parting willingly beneath him, rushing around him, yielding as easily now as if he were the same limber high school champion and his swim trunks were not cutting into his meaty buttocks.

Max set a fast pace. Bubbles gurgled in his ears and he focused on their waxing and waning rhythm, loud in one ear, distant in the other, as his arms pulled through the water. After ten laps, Max glided into the breaststroke. He could hear the filtering system whirr. It was too quiet to get his mind away from remembering those last days with Katie.

They had they lived together passionately, tenderly those few weeks until the day that she caught Max reading her diary. That day, when he got home from work, the place looked like a romantic restaurant. He went to take a shower, walked past the diary lying open on the bed.

His own name drew his eyes to it. There was something at the top of the page about him being sweet and him promising not to be violent. Max felt anger surge, wondering why she had to write something down about his "violence" as she called it.

So, he had to read further. And there it was, the very next thing. Something about having Tom to thank—*Tom MacBride* to thank—for the child she was carrying. He hadn't read anymore because she walked into the room. Of course he was shouting and whoever lived next door misinterpreted and called the MPs. So, Max was forced to stand outside in the garage with the MP beside him and watch her rush off in her little Fiat.

Hot now, the workout bringing his muscles that unique stretched feeling, Max gulped in air. When he thought about Ben in Tom MacBride's school, Max plunged his face and chest down in the water, switching to the grueling butterfly stroke. He lifted his arms, scooping the water, pushing himself up, gulping air, pushing himself to concentrate on the question he had to solve. Why was Johnson determined to ruin him and interfere with Ben? He couldn't care that much about the integrity of his personnel file. Hadn't Katie's journal mentioned Johnson, too? Wasn't he there, cheering Tom on when Tom and Katie "talked deeply into the night," as she had written? Clinging to the smooth tile at the side for a full minute before he tried to hoist himself out of the pool, Max's arms wobbled in protest. He needed to read Katie's journal again.

Patty waited for him at the little bistro on the ground floor of the colonial mansion that held her second-floor apartment. When she saw Max, she smiled her sultry smile; her kiss was as wet and sexy as always, so that the words she spoke honestly shocked him.

"You are probably the biggest jerk in the entire universe. I don't know why I'm crazy about you."

"I'm good in bed."

"Until you throw up."

"I threw up?" ·

"Don't you remember?"

"I remember how hot and sweet your little ass was last night." He licked his lips. "You know you left your thong in the bed upstairs?"

"I know! I walked all the way home without underpants! I was scandalized at myself."

"We got to be more careful."

She agreed, taking his hand across the table. "No drinking tonight.

Have you already started?"

"Just a beer at home. See, I'm not such a jerk."

"You are. You were absolutely cruel to Ben. I couldn't believe it."

"Ben was there?"

"He came out of his room while you were throwing up. He was being *so* nice and you were really horrible. What have you got against him to say those kinds of things to him?"

"Now you're the motherly type?"

"Don't get uppity with me, Max," Patty said. "How was I to know? How could I have known he would turn out to be such a gorgeous boy." Her face contorted into an uncharacteristic grimace—trembling pout, deep forehead wrinkles—and Max thought she was actually going to cry. "I was sick all night thinking that I'd given him up, when I could have—all these years—and you would have been all mine and I wouldn't be running through the streets of Annapolis half naked to avoid a woman you don't even like." And then, she *did* cry, big tears splashing out of her eyes so fast that she covered her eyes with one awkward hand and let her curls hide her face.

The waiter came to the table and asked what they wanted to order, Patty and her distress invisible to him.

"Two burgers. We'll split an order of fries. The lady would like a chocolate milkshake and we'll each have a Sam Adams Light." He put a napkin in her hand when the waiter turned.

"I can't drink beer and a milkshake," she sniffed.

"What the hell are you crying about?"

"I told you. Regrets."

"Patty, please. I've had a rough day. Did that ass-kissing Kuhn call you?"

Patty blew her nose into the napkin, took a deep breath, and flipped her hair back over her shoulder. "I didn't realize this was a professional meeting."

"Come on, Patty. I need you. All of you. Your brain, too."

She stared at him in silence while the waiter put the milkshake in front of her, the bottles of beer and mugs on the table. She watched Max sniff the beer before he tipped the bottle into the mug. Then slowly, as if all the muscles in her back hurt, Patty bent toward her briefcase, took out the folder and her glasses.

Setting the glasses on her nose, she said, "Did you read through this, Max?"

"Not yet."

"Johnson claims you're lying to him. And you are, according to these documents."

"What lie?"

"You claim Ben is Donna's and your son conceived when you were married to someone else. At a time when your legal wife was also pregnant with another of your children? A child who survived a well-documented car accident and died without any public record of his death? And Donna's child with you—Ben, according to your story—was conceived when Donna was single and attending Biola College in California while you were stationed in North Carolina, married to Katie. How did you come up with that one?"

"Patty," Max said patiently, "the point is that none of this is Johnson's business. No commanding officer asks his men to prove the kids living in their quarters are their own."

"Look, Max, Johnson got into this when Ben asked him to write that letter meant to substitute for his birth certificate. It was notarized. But you claim the info in the letter was false. So either he's guilty or you're lying. And he has the documents to prove his point." She reached into the envelope and took out a stack of documents. Flipping through them, she placed each on the table for Max to see. "Ben's birth certificate is really all he needs, and Johnson has a copy. Then he's got his early health records, his elementary school records…all consistent, all authentic, all in order. This child is the one who was born in New Jersey during that snowstorm and the same doctor who delivered him saw him until he was three for medical records. Dr. B. Gregen Bénet. Here are his credentials." She placed documents one by one on the pile. "He's a world-renowned physician, for pity's sake, Max."

"I know that, Patty."

"Then you should know that a man who teaches at Princeton and at the Lausanne School of Medicine and holds this kind of reputation…well, his word is not going to be discounted, Max. Bénet's records alone show he lived to age three. The doctor who delivered him would know if it was the same kid. Bénet's not going to make this stuff up. Then there are his school records. It's the same kid—eye defect, pictures look like the same kid. What the hell were you thinking?"

"I just told Johnson that shit because he was getting too personal about Katie and I wanted to throw him off. No one would have predicted he'd be so *obsessed* with Katie and Ben."

"Max." Patty held up a hefty stack of papers butterfly-clipped together. "All these details are a matter of public record. Were you sober when you talked to Johnson? Because that's the only excuse I can think of and it's one that won't help you at all."

"Now he wants me to admit I was lying like some kind of schoolboy. It's inappropriate for a colonel in the Marine Corps. I'm the head of the English and History Department! I'm the senior marine."

"Oh, he wants more than that."

"What do you mean?"

"Remember, he was burned by the last senior marine? The guy is living it up now at Fort Leavenworth for selling stolen cars to midshipmen. Johnson is under pressure to clean up the Academy's image. He wants your ass. And he wants you out of here. Not just a transfer. He told Kuhn that if you leave here, it's going to be without your eagles and without your retirement. That's off the record, which makes it scarier to me."

The waiter brought their food and placed the dishes ever so slowly down in front of them. Patty stared Max down, her eyes keen and penetrating behind her glasses, which fogged up slightly with the fragrant steam of her supper plate. "You've got to give him what he wants."

"I can't."

"You've got to go to him and admit you lied. Kuhn says Johnson will accept the words 'mistake' or 'error.' That's generous of him, in my opinion. Once that interchange takes place, he can't hold those idiotic lies over your head."

Staring at Patty's untouched beer, Max said. "If I do that, he'll blab to Ben."

She noted the path of his eyes and took a long sip from her milkshake, then picked up an onion ring. Max reached for her beer and poured it quickly into his glass, stirring with the sound of the bubbles, the scent of the yeasty froth. Patty said, "Why can't Ben know?"

"He can't. He doesn't even suspect. I got rid of everything—burned the pictures, kept the interfering relatives away. I made sure there was nothing of Katie's left around. Nothing."

"Nothing at all?"

"She needed to be forgotten."

"Max."

"What?"

Patty made an exasperated expression, took a spoonful of the milkshake and then murmured, "Then you can start from scratch and tell him."

"No."

"Ben will be fine with it. He's got a lot of heart."

"No."

"Max, you don't *know* this boy. He already accepts a lot of crap from you. He respects you and he takes care of you when you're really bad off—all this in spite of the *really shitty* way you treat him."

"You only met him that once, Patty, so *don't* tell me about him. You don't know how cold he's capable of being."

"*He's* cold? Look in the *mirror*, Max. You've lied to him his entire life about his mother. That shit about his birth certificate? Only someone with a really big heart would give his father the benefit of the doubt about that load of shit. And not only that, you destroyed all the traces of his mother's existence. Your first wife. That's cold, Max. That's arctic."

"I had some good teachers," Max said bitterly.

"Don't give me that crap, Max. There are families who adopt children and the birth mother is part of the family unit. People can deal with these irregularities. Just say, 'Look, Ben, I was wrong, but my heart was broken and I wasn't thinking clearly.'"

"No."

"I think you're still in love with her. This is your way of holding on."

"Shut up, Patty. Don't mess with stuff about Katie. Just give me legal advice. You're not my goddamned therapist."

Patty picked up her burger and took a huge, savage bite. She stared at him, chewing. Max was no longer hungry, but he drained his glass. He watched her eat, his breathing getting ragged with panic. Still chewing, a wad of food partially visible behind her small white teeth, she said, "Part of what Johnson wants is a plan of how you're going to tell Ben the truth. That's what he's demanding in the bargain."

"Why does he want this so bad, Patty? Have you thought about that? I'm telling you, he's got an agenda."

With her mouth full, she said, "Johnson has nothing to gain from this. It's about his job. What are you talking about, Max?"

He leaned toward her. "Look. Katie and I try for two, three years to get pregnant, and we were really trying. Night and day—all night some times." He made a descriptive gesture.

"Max, don't give me details. I'm your lover. I don't want to hear this."

"She couldn't get pregnant."

"So what?"

While we're separated she comes here to Annapolis for advice from her best friend and MacBride, the husband, who is this real asshole."

"Is this the man who was at the scene of the accident?" Patty asked, indicating the pile of documents.

"Yeah, so?"

Patty flipped through the stack of newspaper clippings and stopped to read, "Tom MacBride of Annapolis, Maryland...he's credited with—"

Max halted her, his hand up. "Yeah, so I've always wondered about MacBride, because Katie worshiped him. Even before this hot little encounter while we're separated. I mean, the man is married to her best friend and she's always going on about what a great guy he is."

"MacBride is still married? Still living here?"

"Yes, Patty. MacBride is—believe it or not—Ben's *basketball coach*. I learned that choice bit of news today."

"Oh, is that bad?"

"He's an interfering *asshole*, Patty. He turned my wife against me when she visited him. One night at this coffeehouse he ran, MacBride talked her into having some kind of emotional awakening. And guess who is there with her the whole time, holding her hand and God knows what else? Johnson, that's who. Wouldn'cha know it, he's buddies with MacBride. Academy grads." Max made a gesture, both palms upwards as if to say that his point was obvious. "She comes back to me, ready to *forgive me*—okay, she left me, right? She gets *real cozy* with this horny, self-righteous bastard, comes back to me *glowing* with love and benevolence like she's been to a fucking spa, and what do you know—three weeks later, she turns up pregnant. Fucking spa all right." Max raised his hand to call the waiter.

Patty wiped her mouth and sat back, staring at Max. "What are you saying, Max?"

"When you suspect your wife, it eats away at you," he whispered.

"Max," she reached across the table for his hand.

He held up his hand again to stop her words. "All I know is I can't see any of me in Ben. None. I may be a jerk, but I've raised Ben not knowing and I want to keep him. He's all I've really got."

"Of Katie."

"Yeah." Max pursed up his face to try to hide his emotion. "One more beer," he said to the waiter.

40

LATER when Laurie rested in his arms, Tom marveled aloud. "You absolutely have the magic touch, Laurie."

She laughed, patting his stomach, kissing his collarbone. "Love is stronger than magic. Feel better?"

"Like I'm twenty-five."

"Uh-oh. That's gonna get me into trouble."

Tom stroked her hip, "You were hot when I married you but now...I mean it."

"I wasn't so hot when you married me," Laurie reminded him. "You made that happen."

Tom thought about those early days, remembering. After Max's cruel and untimely desertion, Laurie had been jumpy about Tom's fascination with her body, associating certain caresses with heartbreak.

"How did you fix me, Tom?"

He laughed, having just enjoyed her healing touch, and remembered that he had coaxed back to life the creative love in Laurie that she now so freely bestowed. "Oh, it was easy. I'm in love with you," he said, kissing her head, enjoying the pleasure of the fresh scent, the shiny, smooth curls. He had known Laurie was thrilling when they were dating, when they fell in love. When they married, all their sex had been astonishing, volcanic and immediately satisfying. But real, expressive intimacy had terrified her.

Tom paid attention to the signs of her fear—a shudder, a tightening of her back that made her shrink away. His gift in bed was that he was both patient and passionate; he figured out how to evoke clean, hot desire in Laurie. Now lightly touching the curve of her neck, Tom remembered.

And sometimes, like now, when Laurie lay satisfied in his arms, Tom imagined that his desire for her, so intense and so infinitely hopeful that it had proven irresistible, had chased away the memory in her body and psyche of Max's touch. And now it was *his* hands and mouth, his entire aroused body, to which she responded in eager, heartfelt instinct. Now it was *his* eyes that gazed at her face and she had found that in their closest embrace, she could open her eyes and trust the face she loved.

"You were okay, seeing Max again." It was both statement and question.

Laurie came up on her elbow and moved her arm to hug him. "Tom, I almost burst into tears I was so happy to see him. I can't explain it."

"I saw you hug him."

"I hugged him *and* I kissed him on the cheek. I thought, 'This is stupid. With forgiveness we could have helped each other.'"

"Same thing happened to me. I was angry about whatever he's been doing to make Ben so uptight and I saw him and all I could think was, 'I am a Christian and the God I love died for this man. And for some reason, Katie loved him dearly.' And then, there it was—love. Though he did tick me off. Nothing like having to show kindness to the one and only enemy who's beaten you silly."

"You can't really say he's your enemy now, if you recognize God's love for him."

"I'm just afraid, Laurie, I'm just afraid I won't be able to live up to the standard I know I should reach. All my life I've been taught to love, to lay down my life for others, to see the best in others and see what I can do to help, but with Max, I may feel that urge, but it is so fleeting and a second later, I suspect him and then a second later, I want to rub his face in a roaring fire."

"Tom!"

"It would be so easy for me to fight him and if I'm honest with myself, I want to fight him. I want to fight him and I want to humiliate him and make him pay for what he did to Katie and really even more—for taking Ben away from us all these years."

"Shh," she stroked his shoulder, "we can't do it that way."

In the comfort of each other's arms they drifted toward deep sleep.

After putting the two paper cups brimming with steaming hot caffé latte on Ella Hunter's kitchen table, Gregen Bénet held the chair for her. When she was seated, he joined her and took from his briefcase a prettily wrapped package. "Is it Leonadis?" she said, eagerly unwrapping the box of milk chocolate pralines.

"Your favorite, no?"

"Now that you've spoiled me with these European things. I used to be happy with plain old coffee and Hershey's chocolate." She opened the packaged and offered him a piece. "How was your trip?"

"Successful and satisfying. The clinic I told you about in Milan has begun to thrive under its new director. I was fully pleased. Wonderful fellow, this doctor, typical Italian—meticulous about his work and full of passion."

"Glad to hear it."

"Thank you for looking in on Marie for me while I was away."

"She dislikes me, you know."

"No, my dear. It is your *son* she dislikes."

Ella drew a deep breath, then broke off another piece of chocolate. "Ben hasn't said anything about the books. He hasn't sent one thank-you note."

"I must tell you, Ella, I stopped by Annapolis yesterday on my way home."

"How is that on your way?"

"The flights through Baltimore are one hour faster. I always fly in and out of Baltimore."

"I didn't know that."

"Ben had left the books in the car while it was being painted. He just discovered them. He seemed quite pleased with them."

"So he knows? Did you see him?"

"Yes, I stopped by his basketball game for a few minutes."

"And spoke to him? How is he?"

"He has some wonderful friends at his school. He is doing well."

"He does seem to love it there. He has been a little bit vague on the phone lately. Used to be he told me everything."

"He is at that age when he talks to his friends. But he does look well, for the *most* part. He's gained a little weight and seems to be maturing."

"For the most part?"

"There was a bruise on his chest," Gregen touched his own chest to indicate where.

"He's always bumped up from sports."

"This did not look like a sports injury, and granted I did not see it up close. I was not able to ask Tom about it, either."

"But you saw Tom?"

"Yes, I did. He's well, but for his back, which is sometimes very bad. The poor man was in a wheelchair. He was making the best of it, but it was obvious that his pain was considerable."

"A wheelchair you say. That is too bad. Do you think it's from—?"

"He was too gracious to cast blame, but I think probably."

"Oh dear."

Gregen patted her hand. "We must look to the future. And how we can help so that all these people benefit and Ben has all that he needs."

"Max, too."

"You mentioned last year that you thought things were…I think you said 'getting worse' between Ben and his father, remember that?"

"I wouldn't have confided in you, otherwise. I told Ben to try to understand and to try to be cooperative. Teenage boys can be horrible to have in the house. And it's just that Max has had such a hard life. Now, don't be offended when I say this, Gregen, but Katie *did* break his heart and he's such a proud and sensitive man that he's had trouble getting over it."

Gregen smiled to cover his own struggle. "Ella, my dear," Gregen said, taking both her hands in his. "You know we are together in this for Ben's benefit; is that not so? Now think carefully. I hate to ask you this, but I think we must try to figure out what is best for Ben. When you said things were getting worse, did you have any indication that Max might use his fists on Ben?"

"Are you thinking about the bruise you mentioned? You can't blame that on Max. Ben has a wall up where Max is concerned. And Donna. Since that time he cut his hands when he was three. I saw the wall go up."

"I remember how hard that time was for you, Ella. But think back, even if it hurts to do so, think back and tell me if that's what Ben was hinting at last year when—"

Ella's cell phone bleeped. She whispered, "That's Max. I put that ring on for when he calls." Gregen made a gesture to indicate that he would not consider it impolite if she answered.

"Max, dear."

He spoke so loudly that Gregen could hear. "Mom. I tried to call last night."

"I saw that on the caller ID. I must have been asleep."

"Listen, Mom, I need something from you."

"Of course, darling. I'm happy to help in any—"

"What do you have left of Katie's?"

"Pardon?"

"Don't play dumb, Mom. I know that tone of voice. Do you have Katie's journal?"

"Her—?" She looked at Gregen, alarmed. Silently he sipped his caffé latte, watching her.

"You heard me."

"I'm just shocked is all. You told me to destroy everything."

"Yeah, but I remember you objecting to getting rid of her journals. I'm thinking you defied me and—"

"Now, why would I do that, dear?"

"Because you are all into that anecdotal history crap."

Her voice rising indignantly, "You know her journals provided an extensive record from when she was young detailing all her family history and travels and—"

"See? I knew you kept them. I just need you to send the one to me. Overnight it. Okay? Or if they can get it here in a couple of hours."

Gregen took out a pen and one of his business cards and wrote the word *Why?* on it. Obediently, Ella said to her son, "Why do you want it?"

"Is that any of your business, Mom? Isn't it bad enough that you kept the journal when I told you not to? I *told* you that you wouldn't see Ben again if—"

"No, of course not. I—I—" Caught as she was between two strong men with two opposing agendas, she faltered.

"Just send it. Get in your car now and hustle over to the post office."

Gregen wrote, *Tell him you don't have it. That's the truth.*

She shook her head at Gregen. "Max, darling. You told me to get rid of things and I did."

"But not the journals. I know you didn't. I can tell you're lying to me. So send them. Not all of them, just the last one."

"I can't, Max. I gave them to her people—"

"Her people?"

"Yes. I—"

"What people? Who do you mean? Not Gregen. It better not have been Gregen. That son of—"

"Darling, I thought if I got it out of the house and away, it would serve the same purpose as destroying it."

"Shit, shit, shit. You messed up again, Mom."

"But if you need it, you should be glad I didn't destroy it." Ella glanced at Gregen, distraught and humiliated. He bit his lips and tried to look sympathetic.

Max said loudly, "Where is that old geezer anyhow?"

"They moved back to Switzerland. You knew that. Katrina died not long ago."

"No, not him. The asshole. Gregen."

"Max, really." Ella glanced at Gregen and then turned her entire body away from him, shielding the phone with her other hand as if she could keep Gregen from hearing. Gregen stood up, and to give her the courtesy of not having to also watch his own disgusted expressions, he turned his back to her, clasped his hands behind him and stared out the back door.

"He is an asshole. Gregen Bénet is the biggest asshole I ever met. Next to Tom MacBride. Hey, Mom, by the way. Did you know Tom MacBride coaches at Ben's school? Didn't I tell you to make sure the guy didn't live in Annapolis? Didn't I say we could live in Frederick if we had to get away from him?"

"You are required to live on base in that house, Max."

"How did you miss that, Mom? I was depending on you."

"I'm sorry Max. What can I do to make it up to you?"

"Get the journal from Guillaume—get him to FedEx it from Switzerland and bring it to me when you come for Thanksgiving. Don't have Guillaume mail it here, Ben might find it."

"I'll see what I can do, Max."

"Make sure you get this done today."

"Wait, Max. How is Ben?"

"See for yourself when you bring me that journal. Don't bother coming without it."

"You don't mean that, Max."

"The hell I don't."

Gregen gave Ella a minute before he came back to the table, and when he sat down beside her she seemed to have composed herself. "He was unkind to you, Ella."

"When I think of how you are with Marie," she murmured.

"The disrespect he shows is inexcusable."

"Were you ever disrespectful like that, Gregen?"

"Only once."

"No, I mean as an adult." Gregen told her "no" in a voice that was gentle and belied the outrage he felt.

"I guess I'll need that journal back."

"But I don't have it, my dear."

"You gave it to Guillaume," she moaned.

"No. Of course not. He doesn't want it. I put it in the things we gave to Ben."

"In the bag with the books and everything?" she asked, looking horrified.

"No, I put it in Jim's toolbox." Gregen remembered how he had walked the tunnel from his house to hers for the purpose of putting the journal in there for Ben to find. He had considered putting it in the car's glove box until he learned that Ben meant to have it painted. As soon as Ella had called to say that the boys were driving up, he had brought it over. "When I had it carried out of the tunnel for you, Ella."

"Oh dear. Do you think it's wise for Ben to have it?"

"We agreed that he has to know and that the more he figures out for himself—"

"Max will be so upset." She wrung her hands. "I'll sneak it out of the toolbox when I go down there. I'll get it before Max gets home."

"If you do that, my dear, Ben might never know his mother."

She dismissed his comment as if shooing a fly. "There are the other volumes."

"This one is key. You know that."

"It does make his father look bad," Ella worried.

"Children love their parents, despite faults. The tragedy is if a child never knows and cannot love."

"That's easy for you to say, Gregen, since you have everything to gain from this."

Gregen stood up and reached inside his jacket pocket. "I took these pictures of Ben during his game. I thought you would enjoy them."

She took them up and stared at the top one. Gregen knew that he could not push her now. He bent to kiss her cheek and let himself out, determined to try once more to discover why Ella Hunter was unable to stand up to the tyrant who was her son.

Grandmother's Choice

41

Gregen Bénet caught the scent of the apple butter as soon as he opened the door of the taxi that had carried him home from the airport. He glanced at his watch and smiled. Thanks to an early arrival he would be in time to catch Marie once again disregarding his recommendations. These heavy kitchen tasks were not strictly safe for her, but she loved her seasonal routines and Emma Challant, a young relative of Marie's, felt bound to give the elderly woman her respect, not command her to behave. He hoped that one day he might be living in Annapolis and Laurie, always spunky enough to handle Marie, could help him protect the dear woman from herself.

He made noise going up the steps so that he would not startle her and as he expected, with her knitting in her hands, she sat in the rocking chair on the small rug by the kitchen hearth as if she'd been there all day.

"Bonjour, Gregen, mon cherie," with an innocence touched by the elegance of long practice. That she did not comment on his early arrival told him she wished to show she had no fear of being surprised. But her eyes sparkled and he knew how much she enjoyed her independence.

"Bonjour, Maman," he said, bending to kiss her cheeks. He greeted Emma and a few words whispered between them confirmed his suspicion.

He carried his suitcase up the stairs to his large, clean bedroom, pleased to note the fragrance of laundered sheets, the pungency of the chrysanthemums placed on his night table, and the scent of autumn air drifting from windows thrown open in anticipation of his homecoming. He glanced at the photographs of Ben and Sibilla that stood on his dresser and nodded, remembering the conversation he intended to have with Marie. Since he'd left Ella Hunter ten days ago, he had been increasingly troubled by Ella's behavior and wondered if Marie could give him wisdom about why a woman like Ella would tolerate the disrespect of her son.

Gregen took the gifts he'd brought his household and when he reached the landing, he saw Marie scurry to her chair as quickly as an old woman can. On the counter stood twenty-five jars of apple butter. Emma had brought out the little round table and placed it in front of the hearth.

"This looks cozy," he said. "It is good to be home."

Gregen listened to the news of Apple Tree Farm, pleased to note how well Marie looked. Her skin looked rosy, her eyes bright. Her hands did not shake as they sometimes did when she was overtired, and her fingernails looked pink with health. Emma described her first try at the SAT test, taking out the notebook she used to record her questions for when Gregen returned. "I'm sure you did well, Emma. And the results should be available soon."

"It costs extra to phone for them."

"You may spend the extra. It's only a little bit for peace of mind. And then you can get an early start studying for the next test."

She looked so tearfully grateful that Gregen hoped he wasn't indulging her, though he really could not help doing so with any of Marie's many cousins. And so with a shrug, he brought out the pink shopping bag he'd placed behind his armchair and held it out to her.

"Oh, you are ruining me," she said as she lifted up the trendy silk burnout scarf he'd found in Geneva.

"The idiom is 'spoiling,'" he said, "but I don't think so. You seem healthy and well-loved to me. There are things from your mother there, also, with a long letter for you." She kissed him, asked if he'd mind her opening them in her room, and she left them.

Marie merely shook her head at Gregen. Of all the many young people they had fostered over the years, Marie was particularly fond of Emma. Gregen held out a small package for Marie. "I drove down to Cogne to get you some cording and those replacement needles you've wanted."

"How very kind of you," she murmured.

He reached over and patted her hand. "You are important to me, Maman." Her smile was friendly and just guilty enough that Gregen knew he could press his advantage. "And how do you think I would feel if my mother hurt herself or exhausted herself making apple butter for my winter breakfast?"

"I am not officially your mother," she snapped. "I don't have to obey you. I am no Ella Hunter."

"Ah, that's not fair. You are and have, in every way, been my mother."

"Not every way."

"Whatever the technicalities, Marie, you are right in one sense. In an ideal world—a mother is not required to obey her son. But she would wish to do as he recommends. Especially when her son is a physician who knows what is best for her."

"I do not wish to spend my last years playing bingo. If I die making apple butter, that is better for me than to die sitting in this chair watching afternoon television where the people make love without the slightest art. Television and bingo! Never!"

"Yes, of course, Maman. But you must admit that the task you took on today strained you."

"I admit no such thing."

"If your heart had palpitations, you might faint. Think how that would scare Emma. If you are going to misbehave, please do it only when I am in the country and on the property!"

"My dear Gregen, stop speaking of what I may and may not do." She put her nose up in the air and gave him her most imperious glance.

Gregen refilled his teacup and took another slice of bread. Watching her, somewhat concerned to bring up the topic, he spread the apple butter over it. "It is delicious. Just as tart as I've always liked it."

"I am gratified to know you are pleased," she said to him, swiftly and softly in Italian, and Gregen remembered how often she had said those words to his father when they met—always so formally—over household matters.

In Italian as musical as hers, he gave his father's response. "With you, I am ever pleased."

Their eyes met, remembering.

"Maman," he said almost briskly. "I have a puzzle in my mind that I cannot solve."

"If I can help you, it would be my pleasure."

Gregen nodded. "Ella Hunter seems afraid of her son. Why is this?"

Marie snorted. "Her fear is no doubt the reason he grew to be such a man."

"Before they married, did Katie know or suspect that he was violent?"

"Even if not, she saw how he treated Laurie. Yet she took him to her bed and her heart. The girl was not strong."

"A wild girl, our Katie."

With a humble shrug Marie said, "We were wild, too. All of us. Your father was a most willful young man. And you, Gregen, made your *father's* youth seem proper. And me? When I was young, my blood felt like fire and I did as I pleased. This we have reaped and wept many tears."

Gregen nodded. Marie rarely said things that linked them thus and he feared that if he commented with too much interest she would say no more. "Thinking back to when they married, though, my brother's objections to Max were expressed in such a damaging way..." Gregen made a dismissive gesture.

"I am not blind to Guillaume's faults." Marie held one hand out, palm up. "If Katie had not married that man, her life would not have been marked by so much sadness."

"But we would not have Ben. So we cannot wish—"

"We still do not have Ben," Marie said, holding her hands out to show how empty they remained.

Gregen nodded humbly. "But Marie, her journal records two incidents of violence in their marriage. One of my questions is this: did he become violent in the marriage or was this his practice even before?"

"You think he may strike his mother," Marie said, her nose going in the air again, her eyebrows raised. "To understand Max Hunter and men like him is simple. He was indulged as a child so that when the wildness of sexual desire came upon him he had no deep strength upon which to return when forced to face his regrets. This makes a weak man and this is the difference. Your father and I were ashamed of our mistakes; we knew our parents wept over us. When we saw that God also wept—then we had to change our ways, didn't we? You did, too."

Gregen patted her hand, murmuring his assent. "I have never seen physical marks of abuse on Ella. But his commands are brutal. Forcing her to lie about Katie, forcing her to stay away from you and I, forbidding contact with the MacBrides. This is an unholy kind of domination. And did I tell you about the conversation I overheard when last I visited her house?"

"Several times," Marie said with a wry look at him. "She expects him to be a terror and so he gives it to her to the best of his ability."

"Yes, but also no. The look on her face when he is angry with her is one of fear and guilt, I think. There must be some reason why she feels she must obey him, never to cross or question him."

"You are worried that this tyrant treats Ben with violent contempt and his mother knows." Her hand tightened on the arm of her chair.

"I think if it were just that—and that is terrible enough—her love for Ben would compel her to say more. But why the sense of guilt? At times when she is distraught this is her emotion. Not fear."

"He is blackmailing her perhaps?"

"Yes. She is guilty about something and he uses this to force her obedience."

"How soon until Ben is back in my arms?"

"Very soon, now, I hope. I do apologize for letting him slip *out* of our arms."

42

BECAUSE the gym was reserved that evening for a fund-raiser, Tom scheduled practice for six in the morning. Ben was the first to arrive that dark morning and from where he parked at the side of the baseball field, he watched his friends' cars stutter and slide on the driveway, slick with black ice. Ben's car had skipped up the driveway with the ease of a mountain goat. And he sat in it, passing his hand over the pebbled leather cover of the steering wheel, filled again with gratefulness. Every day he discovered extras, a lifetime of presents to him from Gregen whose generosity was baffling and compelling. And everything he discovered, he wrote about *in French* to Gregen who replied quickly, with great warmth, lots of interesting information about all kinds of things and with careful corrections to Ben's grammar. Ben loved his car. It got him out and away so his frantic mind could soar briefly above the dark traps in his father's world.

He heard Joe's car and turned toward the sound to see the MG slide slightly on the crest of the hill. Joe handled it with his usual aplomb, steering into the swerve, then giving the old car a burst of gas that sent it skipping over the icy surface. When he emerged from the MG, giving the insouciant grin that always cheered Ben, Joe bragged that he'd had everything perfectly under control. On foot they slid across the icy parking lot together, catching up to Drew, Knox and Scott, and sliding past them. Laughing, Joe opened the gym, disarmed the alarm, and by the time they had turned the lights on, the heat up and had unlocked the ball cage, Tom joined them to begin their warm-up laps. As they were running, Oliver arrived, then Jon and the sophomores he drove. Paul and Adam came in last, grumbling about the ice on their steep driveway.

When they lined up for stretches, Doug, Flip and Muffin burst through the back door; Smitty in uniform followed them. "Ice is bad down our way," Doug said, coming up to them. Muffin sniffed Ben's hand, licked Joe's knee and tried to kiss Tom, getting so far as putting her paws on his chest. Tom and Doug shook hands, then embraced briskly as they always did. "Smitty and Flip and I were up before dawn checking out the bridges. School's got a two-hour delay," Doug said to his brother-in-law.

"I heard the announcement as I was leaving the house."

"What're we going to do with these maniacs for two extra hours?" Doug grinned.

"Laurie says come to the store for breakfast when we're done."

"Does she mean us, too?" Scott said.

"Yes, of course," Tom said. "As always."

Cheers broke out among the boys and practice resumed with Smitty helping Tom coach Ryan, Jon, Jason and Scott in a shooting drill, while Doug tried to carry out Tom's plan. He peered at the list Tom had written on an index card. "Drew, you and Paul work with Ollie and Adam to practice that inbound fast break we did yesterday. And uh..." he looked around to see who was left. "Ok, Joe, let's you and Flip, Knox and me guard Ben and see what moves he's come up with since yesterday."

"Four against one?" Ben protested.

"Are you *whining*, Ben?" Joe teased. "There's no whining in basketball."

"Especially when you're the star," Flip said.

Knox said, "How about if I'm with Ben."

"Yeah," Ben said, "Because no team will *ever* put *all* their men on me. And I bet it doesn't say that on Coach's little card."

"Heh, heh," Doug laughed. "Can't read his handwriting. I swear I never could."

Max walked through Gate Three and went carefully over the thin glaze of ice on the sidewalk to the place across the street to wait for Patty. From where he stood, blowing on his hands to warm them, Max watched the men setting up orange cones around the wrecked wrought iron fence where his Miata had incurred so many expensive damages. *Damned if I can remember that accident*, Max thought, squeezing the bridge of his nose as the recurring memory of a car he'd owned ten years ago—a big silver car—came to focus in his mind. The headlights glared against a window; that vision or memory—whatever it was—burst into his head every time he tried to remember that day he'd crashed the Miata.

Patty stopped close to the curb and unlocked the door of her champagne-colored Lexus. Once inside, Max leaned over and kissed her.

"Shouldn't we be more discreet?"

"That's a nice greeting," Max said. Patty drove to West Annapolis and parked at an old summer cottage that had been converted to a medical lab. She glanced at her watch. "They should be opening in a few minutes." Reaching into the back seat, Patty took her briefcase onto her lap. From it she took two slips of paper and put them in Max's hand.

"I hope this works," he said.

"I think Johnson will be impressed with this initiative on your part. You can clear your reputation with cold, hard medical statistics. We'll come here once a week. In six weeks, you'll have documentation that—"

Max shrugged. "And the paternity test? For that they have to take blood, right?"

"Just a little."

"I'm not *afraid*, Patty."

She stroked his arm. "This is the best way to set your mind at ease. The doubts have been eating you alive all these years. Get tested, get Ben tested, and you'll know for sure that he's yours."

"Or not."

"Well, that's why we're here," Patty said briskly.

"Yeah, but how do I get Ben in here? He was already gone when I went upstairs this morning. Keith said they had practice at six."

"I'd advise you to tell him the truth, Max. It's time he knew."

"I told you, *no*."

"He can handle it. He loves you. He's dedicated to you."

"You know this from having seen him for five minutes one night when you weren't exactly calm and analytical, to put it delicately."

"*I* was fine. You were so out of it you don't even remember how you treated him, so don't talk to me about who was aware of what that night.

I know Ben will listen to you if you explain what happened and why it's upset you all these years."

"No. I'm not telling him his mother was a—"

"Stop. I don't want to hear it," Patty commanded, opening her door. "I've given you my advice." She got out of the car and flicked her wrist as if to command him to follow.

He found himself complying. This further irritated him and he slammed the door shut. "I'm not telling him."

"You don't have much of a choice. Johnson's given you a deadline, so you have to tell him anyway," she growled, her voice like the grind of a gear, turning on her heel and leading the way to the now lighted medical lab.

"We giving you a hard enough time?" Doug grinned at Ben as he chased him in a low, defensive stance.

"Yeah, you're tough," Ben said with a slight grin at Joe and Flip. "If you were taller, you'd be trouble." He dribbled the ball out of reach of Doug's right hand, rotating his body slightly as he heard Flip scamper up behind him. He leapt up, gave it a neat bounce off the backboard. It dropped into the net.

Joe caught the rebound and dribbled out a couple of feet. "See if you can get it from me, Ben."

"We already know I can get it from you," Ben said, moving toward Joe, who lofted the ball over Ben's head to Doug. Ben whirled, following it and jumped to get it, but Flip grabbed Ben's elbow. Knox guarded Joe and Doug trapped the ball, slapping his palms against it and laughing gleefully.

"That's okay when we're fooling around," Ben said to Flip, "but you'll be called for that in a game."

"Yeah, yeah, yeah," Doug said. "Just guard his candy ass," he said to his son.

"Dad, remember your language at school," Flip whispered.

"Yeah, yeah," Doug said with a grin at Flip. "Anybody tell you how good looking you are, Ben?"

Ben laughed. "Nobody 'cept your son."

"Hey," Flip said from behind him. "Don't get personal."

"Yeah," Doug said, staring at Ben, his head held slightly to the side.

"I love how everybody gives *me* a hard time," Ben said, going to his ball-stealing stance close to Doug, arms open, knees slightly bent, butt down. "I can't even *say* anything. Why can't we play two on two?"

"There's five of us." Doug grinned, "And Coach said, 'Give Ben a hard time. Toughen up his candy ass.'"

"You made that up," Ben smirked.

Joe was beside Ben, ready for a hand off from Doug, but Ben stared down at Doug's shoe while Doug dribbled, inching closer beneath the hoop. The instant that Doug looked down to see, Ben tipped the ball up. Flip jumped for it. "Nice, Flip," Ben said as he glided up between Flip and the ball using one hand to scoop it out of the air; he twisted left with it, clearing Flip's stance. Swiftly he dribbled out to the top of the key, whirled right and shot. As soon as it left his hands, Ben knew it wasn't going in and he dashed for the basket in a footrace with Joe. The ball wobbled on the rim. Joe leapt up and got his hand on the ball, knocking it back to Doug. "That's goaltending," Ben acted angry.

"Yeah," Joe laughed at him. "I know."

Doug took the ball nearly to half court and Ben chased him. Dribbling, keeping his eyes on Ben's now, Doug said. "Hell, if this doesn't remind me of high school. Takes me right back."

"Shouldn't swear, Dad," Flip said. "I told you. Uncle Tom won't let us."

"That's not swearing. It's emphasizing, 'cause I mean it. I feel like I'm sixteen again." Doug said.

"You're playing like you're sixty." Ben said, jabbing his hand out toward the ball, but Doug thrust his shoulder at Ben.

"Heh, heh," Doug said. "That was pretty slick. Where'd you learn that? Where'd you play last year?"

"Quantico." He could see Knox on his right.

"Is your dad in the military? A grunt?" Doug handed off to Flip, then whirled around to follow as his son dribbled toward Joe who waited under the basket; Ben moved in, but Doug kept his hip and shoulder between Ben and Flip.

"You were friends with his dad in high school," Flip said.

"Where'd you hear that?" Joe demanded.

"Tommy."

"What?" Doug said, "Friends?" Ben got close to Flip, trying to un-nerve him and shut him up. Doug came up on Flip's other side, and Joe was suddenly at Ben's right. Flip dribbled off his shoe, the ball skidding into Doug's ankle. Doug grabbed it, traveled two steps before dribbling. Ben faced him again, hands out, quick on his feet.

"Wasn't there some guy you were lifeguards with," Flip said, "who joined the marines?"

"You're *Max Hunter's* boy?" Doug pounded furiously at the basketball but kept his eyes on Ben.

Ben looked for Knox and signaled him to come up behind Doug's left elbow. He did not want to answer the question, so when Knox closed in, Ben made a fake toward the ball with his right hand. Doug flinched left and, running into Knox with his hip, went low, dribbling the ball, his expression glazed with a distraction that seemed to be drawing him to intense inward concentration. "Wait." Doug caught the ball and held it to his stomach, his back going straight. "Wait. You." His face went stiff, frightened. "Oh, no. You—you're—How *old* are you?"

From the sidelines, Muffin stood up and whined.

Ben stood still and sensing a potent emotion rising in Doug, said nothing.

"He's sixteen," Joe said, "like me."

"You're—" He stared at Joe, but his fingers were thumping on the ball, counting. Over his shoulder, he shouted. "Hey, Tom!" He stared at Joe again, then timidly looked back at Ben for just an instant before looking around the gym. "Tom?" his darting glance made him seem disoriented. To Joe he said, "Does your dad know?" Muffin bounded across the court to Doug's side.

"Know *what*, Unca Doug? You okay?"

Doug took a step toward Ben. "Holy shit. I didn't realize," he said to Ben. "I didn't—" His hands shook so that he could barely hold the ball. "I *knew* you looked familiar."

"Dad?" Flip asked, and Muffin nudged Doug's elbow with her nose.

"Here you look *so much* like your mother and I didn't catch it," he said, voice breaking, his tanned face pale as dust. "I would have said something right away." Doug dropped the ball; his gold-brown eyes flooded with tears. "I never thought…" he murmured. Looking around at the other boys who stood watching silently, he said, "I'm sorry," before he spun away and ran, stumbling out of the gym and into the lobby, Muffin following.

Ben noticed, in his stunned blur, that Tom rushed by them to where Doug now leaned against the trophy case on the lobby's long wall. Doug stood with his back to the boys fighting powerful emotions, his sturdy, muscled body trembling with the effort. Tom touched his shoulder. Doug wrenched away from him. "Why didn't you tell me, Tom?"

The team of boys crowded at the open gym doors to watch.

"I'm sorry, Doug," Tom said, reaching toward Doug who held up both hands as a warning, "but I didn't want you going over to the Yard after Hunter."

"Okay. I'll kick *your* ass first. Then his. Do you remember what he did to my sister?"

"Hey, not in front of the boys."

"But you remember!" He jabbed his finger at Tom.

"I was trying to protect you."

"Yeah? And whose gonna protect *you*?"

"I don't need—"

"Oh yeah? The man broke your *back*, Tom! *You* want to keep me from kicking his ass? Half the time *you* can't even walk. I should have broken *his*

471

back after that *shit* in Quantico, then he wouldn't have been able to beat the hell out of you that time with *him*." He gestured toward Ben. "And what about his mother?"

"*Quiet.*"

"Yeah, you know all about quiet, don't you, Honest Tom MacBride? Why don't you *say* something? Talk to me. I'm your best fucking friend."

"Ben doesn't know about me and what happened—"

Again, Doug gestured toward Ben, his eyes wild with spilling tears. "The accident, Tom. Think of what he *took* from us." Joe, Adam and Jason moved closer to Ben so that their shoulders touched his. Jon and Paul took steps toward Tom; Drew came up close beside Flip, who cowered behind Joe's right shoulder. "What's my sister going to do if Hunter finishes the job? Huh? He swore to *kill you* and we know he's capable of it, don't we?"

"Doug. Stop." Tom moved toward Doug, his stance now showing something dangerous.

Doug squinted at him, breathing rapidly through flared nostrils. Hissing, his voice furious, Doug said, "You didn't know about that threat, did you, Tom MacBride? Because you were so fucking unconscious by then—"

Tom went for Doug, grabbing both the man's biceps. "Enough! Think of the boy," he commanded, speaking close to Doug's face. "Ben does *not know* anything about—".

But Doug was as fierce and intolerant as a wounded cat and when Tom touched him, he roared, "He doesn't know about his father?" Wrenching one arm away from Tom's grip, Doug stabbed a pointing finger at Ben. "I'll tell you about your father. He's a son of a bitch."

"Doug," Smitty barked, commanding Doug's silence. He stepped between Doug and Ben.

Above the voices meant to control him, Doug shouted, "He's the worst son of a bitch that ever lived."

Ben heard Joe's sharp inhale. He heard the tones of the fluorescent lights murmuring above the stunned silence of his teammates before he felt the violence of blood in his ears and face, before he felt shame pounding behind his eyes. He watched Tom release Doug, his hands going up and out as if he could catch his brother-in-law's words and keep them from Ben's ears. And when his eyes searched Ben's, Tom's expression was so grieved, so full of pain and anger, that the shameful thing inside Ben shuddered and broke. Ben stood very still waiting for his humiliation to rear up, but his heart stayed quiet. And no one moved. Ben saw that Tom was trying to speak, saw Smitty's hand on Doug's elbow, saw the agony in Doug's expression and felt behind him the heat of Flip's humiliation. With a glance at Tom, Ben stepped forward. "Yeah, you're right," he said. "I already knew that."

"He didn't mean it," Flip stammered behind him, and Ben turned toward Flip, whose face was so white, his freckles had disappeared.

Without smiling, Ben nodded. "He's just being honest, Flip. Your dad's a good guy. He's got a big heart. And he's right."

"No, Ben," he heard Doug stammer behind him. "I owe you an apology. I—"

"No—"

"Let him apologize, Ben," Tom spoke.

"No. Look, Coach," Ben said, bending to pick up the fallen ball. "You asked me to be honest. Wait. You *commanded* me to be honest. Are you gonna get after your brother-in-law for saying what's *true*? No. It's true and it stinks. Yeah, I've been completely humiliated by it all my life. And you know what? It's time somebody said it out loud."

In the silent tension a phone rang from beyond the closed office doors. Ben flipped the basketball from hand to hand. "So let's play ball. I didn't get up two freakin' hours early for nothing."

"Don't say *freakin'*," Oliver sniffed.

"Yeah," Adam chimed in. "Reminds Coach of the f-word and we all know he doesn't allow *that* in the gym."

"Which is why we're standing out here in the lobby," Joe said, his voice high and nervous. The boys looked at each other, eyes wide, bubbles of tension rising in their stifled laughter; it was Smitty who laughed first, a tentative kind of wry chuckle and Flip grabbed Ben to hug him, vowing, "You're the greatest!"

Paul took advantage of the moment to herd the team back to the gym.

Though closed in Flip's clumsy embrace, Ben heard Tom say, "Seeing him brought up all that hurt."

"No excuse," Doug vowed. "I behaved like an idiot." Flip eased his hold on Ben, both of them now listening.

"You would have taken care of me—of everyone—*Ben*, too," Tom said, "if you could have."

"Damn right I would have." Doug's voice wobbled. "Wanted to. Tried."

Tom said, "Think of Ben, now. He doesn't know anything about what happened."

"If she had just asked me," Doug said, allowing Tom to embrace him, tears wetting his tan cheeks. "*I* would've been his father." Doug sobbed brokenly on Tom's shoulder.

"She knew that too, Doug. But she was committed to Max."

Flip and Ben hesitated, watching them. "They're okay," Joe said. "They love each other."

"Dad says they been through hell and back together," Flip confided.

Ben felt Joe's arm go across his shoulders. "Want to go talk to them? It

473

might help Doug."

"Sure."

Doug saw them coming and opened his arms wide to Ben. He took Ben into his arms and held him as close as he could get him. He kissed Ben's cheek and pressed him tighter, kissing his head again and again, unashamed of the tears that wet Ben's cheeks and hair. "I never thought I'd get to see you. Never. And here you are, a wonderful, beautiful kid."

"Is there some logical explanation for all this emotion?" Joe said. "I mean because, Unca Doug, you're over the top even for you."

Doug loosened his grip on Ben and held Ben's shoulders, rubbing up and down his arms, then squeezing the muscles. "Yeah. I don't mind telling you. His mother and I—" Doug crossed his two fingers to show their closeness. "I loved her. Deep in love." Ben glanced protectively at Flip. Doug patted Ben's shoulders. "Don't worry about him. He knows I had a first love. And he knows I adore his mother. This isn't news to anybody."

"Just me."

"Yeah and *I'm* sorry about that," Doug said. "I was way out of line. When I realized who you were, I just lost it. No excuse. There was some bitter stuff between your dad and me." Doug motioned to include Tom. "But I'll never hold against you what I got against your dad. I should *not* have come after you like that."

"Thanks, Doug. I appreciate you saying that but—"

"No, listen to me. That was real quality of you just now. Real quality. And I want you to know, I'm here for you now. No matter what. You can't ask anything too big."

43

HIS friends were careful with Ben while he showered, the big men taking the spots on either side of him as if to guard him from heedless sophomores, but even they were wary-eyed and watchful. Their care for him, a shield upraised since the first day he'd stepped into their locker room, touched him and feeling as if his mind were somehow shocked numb, he showered in quiet thought, trying to sort through why Doug had gotten so upset and about something else he meant to ponder but couldn't quite reach in his mind.

Toweling off, he walked to his locker where Scott, Drew, Paul, Adam, Jon, Knox and Joe waited for him, looking purposefully casual. Joe shifted from foot to foot. Ben said, "Relax, MacBride."

"Ben, um, we—"

"Look, he *broke* your dad's *back*, Joe. That's proof enough of what Doug said. *If* I needed proof. Which I don't. Did you think I was so stupid that

I didn't *notice* my dad was the worst son of a bitch who ever lived? You met him for five seconds and you knew. I don't have to pretend anymore. That's all. Doug did me a favor." He looked around at his friends. "Now you guys know me."

But saying it aloud moved Ben and he turned away to open his locker. Joe grabbed him and hugged him and immediately, he was surrounded by his teammates, hugged by them all, his still damp shoulders and his back pounded with strong affection. Drew got him last and holding him tightly said in Ben's ear, "What you did for Flip. I swear I'll never forget it. That was big, man. That was gi*nor*mous."

"Doug just lost it because he loves so much. That's nothing for Flip to be ashamed of."

Drew released him. "So you ready for some breakfast, champ? Coach said he'd meet us at the store."

They decided to ride together in Drew's Suburban and were running and slipping across the wet, slick parking lot when the clean, high squeak of a car horn drew their attention to a new Lexus parked in front of the dumpster. Turning to look, Ben heard his name called as his father and Patty got out of the car and slammed the doors shut.

"Shit," Ben said.

"Is that *him*?" Jon whispered. Glancing at them, seeing their keen, tight-lipped expressions, Ben sensed their incredulity: this was the man who had broken their coach's back.

"Thought you guys would never come out!" Max said in a friendly way.

"What are you *doing* here?" Ben said, his eyes passing swiftly over his father, searching for clues to identify his condition and mood. Ben's eyes stopped on his father's right hand, struck by its ordinary size, it's benign and shameless shape. How did it happen? How had he been able to break a man's back and walk away?

"That's a helluva hello," Max said, laughing amiably as he nimbly crossed the icy distance between them and reached with that unfettered hand to clap Ben on the arm. But Ben dodged him in one of his quick, reflexive moves, making Max wobble off balance. The awkward silence endured while Max righted himself and scanned the boys' faces to see if they'd noticed Ben's cold snub. His teammates' singularly bland, wide-eyed expressions faked innocence so well that each might have been taking a charge for the team.

Except for Joe, who stepped forward, offering his hand. "Hello, Colonel Hunter. We've met before. I'm Joe MacBride."

"Right," Max said, shaking Joe's hand in icy acquiescence, but his lips tightened into a pursed expression as if he preferred not to touch Joe.

"How do you like having your dad coach? Puts you in an awkward situation, I bet."

"I only made the team because he's coach," Joe gave an amicable shrug and his disarming grin. "So—"

"Well, at least you admit that."

"He's *joking*, Dad. You saw him play." Ben said.

"I only had eyes for *you* that night, Ben," Max said and then swept the faces of the surrounding boys to survey their approval.

But Ben saw their façade wearing thin, saw that behind their composure, they were thinking about Tom and his back, that they were touched and concerned by Joe's bold courtesy; Ben stepped between them. "Dad, uh, these are all my friends from the team." Ben gestured to introduce and said their names in turn as each boy shook Max's hand and murmured politely to him.

"Hey," Max said to Ben. "Maybe all your friends want to sign up for the Polar Bear Plunge in the bay come January. Raise money for the Special Olympics." Max grinned at the boys. "I'm the Special Olympics coordinator for the Naval Academy." He jerked both thumbs at his chest.

"That must be quite an honor, sir," Jon said.

"We'll sign up if Ben wants us to," Adam said.

"That so?"

"Absolutely," Drew said. "We're behind Ben a hundred percent."

"Did you come all the way over here to recruit volunteers, Dad?"

Max made a funny genial gesture with his shoulders. "Nah, but I thought of ice when I saw you, Ben."

They waited in awkward tension. Patty cleared her throat. Without looking at her, Ben made the introduction gesture, his palm open to the sky. "And, uh guys, this is—

"My lawyer," Max said, taking Patty's elbow and bringing her into the group. "Patty Edwards."

"Your *lawyer*?" Ben said, meeting Patty's eyes, seeing that despite her drunkenness that night when he'd caught them *en flagrante*, she did remember their disturbing encounter. Max's arm went around Patty, his hand going to her waist, spread fingers pressing into the flesh of her hip with blatant intimacy. Moving away from Max, pushing his hand off her with a nervous laugh, she insisted it was great to meet everyone.

Ben stared at them, his jaw set sternly, anger glazing his icy blue eyes. "We're going to get some food now. See you later, Dad."

"No," Max commanded. "Patty and I need to talk to you, Ben."

Without speaking, Ben waited, lips pressed together.

"It's personal. No offense, guys."

"They know everything about me, Dad. We're teammates. We're tight."

"I want to speak to you—alone."

"Alone, but with Patty?"

"Remember your manners," his father stiffened.

"We'll wait right here, Ben," Drew said. "Right here. Two steps away, man."

Max stepped back by the car and Ben hesitated, then took one step closer, but turned so that he could see his friends, so they could still hear. Max looked to Patty, and though she whispered, her voice croaked loudly. "Just tell him."

Max shushed her, squared his shoulders, and said, "Did you—you didn't eat this morning, did you, Ben? Because of practice, right?"

"I never eat before practice."

"Good. Because I want you to go over to this—uh—medical lab on—uh—"

"Annapolis Street," Patty filled in, her smile strained.

"Right. You know where that is?"

"Yes," Ben said.

"I hate to bring your eye up in public, Ben." Max glanced meaningfully at Ben's friends.

Ben demanded, "Why?" just as Patty scolded saying, "Max—" Max glared at her and Patty shrugged, obviously annoyed.

"I'd rather not publicly embarrass you."

They stared at each other while Ben drew in a long, hostile breath, thinking. He held down his fury and said quietly, "I'm not ashamed of my eye, Dad. *You* are."

"Well, the point is that it's a serious deformity—"

"Max, really."

"Shut up, Patty."

Ben glanced at his friends to see if they had heard and they stood in a half-circle, arms folded over their chests, listening and ready. When he looked back to his father, he saw there only that ruthless sense of mission that his expression often showed. Discreetly, Ben sniffed, vowing silently that if he smelled alcohol, he was going to confront his father right there. He imagined it—his primed and wary friends backing him up, helping him exact justice.

"As I was saying. As the doctor explained to you before, there are health concerns that go with it."

"There *can* be. But I haven't got those. They already tested for those."

"I know," Max said, gesturing with both hands to indicate that Ben should stay calm. "But we have to retest."

"Why? I can't *grow* a kidney deformity, Dad."

"Don't be a smart ass. The doctor Mom works with wants to run some tests."

"Are you *kidding* me? Some random doctor just wants to run tests? Some doctor who's never met me?"

"We've been waiting for a good time and you're always so busy. We never see you." Max pouted a little. "So with this morning practice, I thought this would be the perfect time before you ate anything."

Ben shook his head in disgusted disbelief.

"It would mean a lot to your mother. You know how concerned she gets about things."

"She doesn't get concerned about *my* health."

Max leaned closer. "She is very worried about this. We're supposed to get these screening tests done every year."

"It's been six."

"Yes, Ben, I know," Max's voice dropped to a whisper. "And she's ashamed that she's neglected you. She feels terrible about it. Here she is a medical professional and she hasn't kept up with this. This doctor at work said he'd oversee it all for her. It would make her feel so much better."

"She has said *nothing* about this to me, Dad. *Nothing*."

"She doesn't confide in *you*. She confides in me."

"Are you *kidding* me?" Ben said, glancing at Patty in disbelief.

"Just take the envelope Patty's got there. It's got the referral in it. It should take you all of ten minutes. That's not a lot of time to do something that will give your mother peace of mind."

Ben knew his cold stare infuriated his father, knew he was in danger, but he did not care.

"Come on, Patty, jump in here. Tell him I'm right." Max took her arm at the elbow and caressed with one broad thumb.

She sighed, rolling her eyes. "Your father thought that since you had a two-hour delay this morning, you would have time for the test without too much inconvenience."

"I'm going to breakfast now with the guys."

"Good," Max said. "It has to be done before breakfast. So do it."

Patty pressed the envelope into Ben's hand. "They're expecting you."

On the sidewalk in front of Eight Hands Around, Adam plunked Ben's backpack down and they stood around it keeping Ben company as he wrestled with his irritation at Max's request. Muffin came to the edge of the porch and barked impatiently. Ben could smell the bacon and rich espresso from the shop. His mouth watering, he said that he wasn't going at all unless they went in and started eating. "Come on," Joe said. He took Patty's envelope from Jon and hefting Ben's backpack to his shoulder, pointed up the slight hill to the left of Laurie's store. "I'll go in with you. I love medical crap." Joe nudged Ben's elbow, steering him toward the lab, two doors away. They fell into step and Joe said, "I hate to have to say this to you, but there's something weird about this."

"No kidding."

"If you didn't have the kidney condition, did they say you could develop it?"

"No. It's like a parallel deformity with the eye thing, I think."

"Do you have to call it a deformity? They're pretty common. My cousin, Annie, Doug's little girl, she's got one—a coloboma—that's the actual name for it, right?"

"Right," Ben said.

"And um—and that old lady Marie had one."

"She did? I didn't notice that."

"Her eyes were so dark—black. It was hard to see, but it was there. Why hide it, though? It's cool."

"I know. It used to be my thing on the playground, like my superpower," Ben said, thinking about the puzzling frustration of not having a picture of himself as a baby or small child, not having the always-needed birth certificate. People who had a sense of personal history built from these homey artifacts never missed them. Ben looked for things to fill the void made by their absence. And this, his eye had long ago been. "Once, when I was bugging Gran to tell me about when I was little or when I was born or something, she got me some medical records. I think she said they were the doctor's notes on the birth. Like they describe my eye."

"Hmm," Joe said.

"It's cool to think it's written down somewhere, since it used to be my distinguishing feature and I hide it now and *instead* it looks like I'll be known as the guy whose father crippled the nicest coach in the world." He gave Joe a shy and reluctant half-grin.

"No, you're known as the guy who got caught with his hand up the skirt of the daughter of the nicest coach in the world."

"Be careful how you say that," Ben said, "since it wasn't *like* that." But he laughed a little in spite of himself and Joe, seeing that Ben's mind churned, bumped his shoulder with his own as he always did to cheer him.

Inside the office, Ben found a small sofa in a far corner by a window where he sat down, deep in thought. At the admission window, Joe wrote Ben's name on the chart.

"What do you carry in this thing?" Joe said, sitting down, standing Ben's backpack on his own knees.

"My entire life." Ben opened the outer zipper and looking into the backpack Ben reflected on his vagrant tendency to carry his important possessions with him. In the inside pocket, he kept his journal and the other things he treasured: his favorite pen, the bottom circle of the broken teapot from the first day at the MacBrides' house, the book about Geneva that

479

Gregen had given him for his birthday, notes from Bonnie Jean.

Joe reached for the fragment from the teapot, "Why keep this?"

"I don't know." Joe turned it over. "My mom wrote that," Ben said, explaining the words LAURIE MACBRIDE written in red indelible pencil.

"Could be *your* writing," Joe said, "with not as much slant."

"Stupid to keep it," Ben murmured, looking around for a trash can. "I should pitch it."

"You're not afraid of needles, are you?" Joe asked, plunking the pottery back into Ben's backpack.

"No. And it pisses me off that he tried to pass Patty off as his lawyer."

Joe's eyebrows shot up. "Oh, she—?" Ben nodded. "Her hair was down that night we saw her, so I wasn't sure, but I thought something was off with the way he touched her."

Ben made a disgusted gesture. "Somehow this blood test is for his benefit. It's got to be. It always is."

"Maybe they think you're using. And this is a trick way to get you screened."

"No, he probably had to get a drug test for work and he's making me take it for him." Joe just shook his head. "Stuff's all kind of spinning around in my mind."

"Understatement of the year."

Ben gave a tense laugh. "I know Doug said my dad broke Coach's back," Ben said slowly as if the words were foreign and incomprehensible to him. "But how can that be?"

"We've got to find out what happened."

"I believe my father *did* it," Ben said, reading Joe's thoughts, his mind warming. "I mean, how can Tom *not* hate him? And he doesn't. Tom really doesn't hate him."

"Uncle Doug does."

"Right, which proves it happened. Doug feels protective and I think, helpless, so he got mad. But your dad is over it."

"Dad believes in forgiving."

Ben turned to meet Joe's eyes. "Yeah. He really does."

Moved, Joe fiddled with the zipper on the outer pocket of Ben's backpack. "Maybe it was an accident. His back is his weak spot."

"Wait. Didn't you tell me before that he broke his back in Quantico?"

"Right. But that was in a training exercise."

"Joe, they were in training together. Your dad said so the first day of school. I bet my dad was involved in that, too."

"We could ask Doug. He'll tell us anything. Or Mom. We can ask Mom this morning."

The nurse called Ben's name, but instead of getting up, Ben shut his eyes in dread. Coming a few steps closer, she said, "Excuse me. Did you hear me? I called you." She seemed to be speaking directly to Joe.

"Me?" Joe said.

"It's your turn. I think I mentioned when you signed in that we try not to make patients wait more than fifteen minutes, but we're busy today."

Ben sat up and the boys met eyes. They stood up. Joe slung Ben's backpack over his left shoulder.

The nurse scrutinized them. "Oh, I get it," she said. "Twins, right?"

"What makes you think so?" Joe said, wincing. Beside him, shoulder touching Joe's, Ben understood Joe's temptation and thought, *He wants to play along but after that thing with the ticket he's determined to stop screwing around about serious stuff.*

"You look exactly alike."

"No," Joe said, his voice unsteady, his face reddening, the situation utterly irresistible to him. "Look at him. Hair's blonder, eyes bluer."

She turned and motioned for them to follow. They followed a few paces behind and Joe whispered to Ben. "If we do it, that'll be a good test. Whatever information they come up with about you from *my* blood will prove the whole thing was bogus."

"Any idiot *knows* it's bogus. All it will prove is you don't have a kidney defect either. *And* you're clean. We already know that."

"Right. Exactly. So if they say…look, the test proves you're using—or whatever—you can say, 'No. That wasn't even my blood. That was Joe's.'"

"But Joe, switching places is not strictly honest. It reminds me of passing that quiz forward and pretending I tried my best."

"I know it," Joe groaned. "I *know* it. But the opportunity."

"I realized on the way over here that it's not going to cost me very much to obey my father like Tom and Bettinger are always saying; I can do this even if it annoys me. He's only asking for blood."

"Heh." Joe shook his head.

In the little white curtained room, the nurse gave the technician the chart then told Joe to sit in a little student desk.

"Actually, he's the one you want," Joe said, his tone resigned.

She laughed and winked at her colleague. "Twins. And this one. The one who's supposed to get stuck is just a little bit afraid."

"No, really," Joe and Ben said simultaneously.

They laughed. "Even speak at once!" Then the nurse asked for the referral. From where he'd put it, folded in his pocket, Joe took the envelope and held it out, realizing as he did so that this further convinced the nurse that he was the boy to be tested. His throat flushed bright red as both boys insisted that Ben was Ben. And again the nurse and the technician laughed at them.

"You just think he's Ben because he signed in."

"Maybe you should wait in the lobby," she said to Ben, pushing lightly on his shoulder.

"You're making a mistake," Ben said.

"We're amused, boys, but we haven't got all day."

"Give me the backpack," Ben said, gesturing impatiently at Joe. "The front pocket." Joe swung it to his front and unzipping it, took out Ben's wallet. Ben grabbed it and flipped it open to his driver's license. "Look. That's me. Ben." Smiling, the nurse considered this. She asked to see Joe's and Joe, giving Ben the backpack to hold, patted his pockets and groaned aloud admitting he'd left his at school.

"Good try, guys," the technician said, but the nurse raised her eyebrows at Ben and put her hand on the phone. "You can stay with him if you promise to be good. Otherwise, out."

Ben gave up with a shrug and when they met eyes, both boys smirked helplessly. Joe slid into the chair. He offered his arm and when his dark blood filled one big syringe, he asked, "What's this for again?"

"Order says—" She squinted at it. "Hmm, that's funny."

"What's funny?" Ben asked, peering over her shoulder to read the order. The technician moved the order out of his field of vision and gave him a reproving look. "You stay still." To Joe, more gently, "Release your fist. I'll put this Band-Aid on."

44

"TOM," Laurie said, touching his shoulder. "I don't suppose you coaches have any objection to the boys having a cappuccino with their breakfast."

"Probably do them good," Tom said, "It's delicious." He took her hand and kissed her fingers. "But I don't want you serving them. Especially if I've been commanded to sit here like some sort of—"

"I'll show them how to use the machine and then I'll join you two."

Both men watched as Laurie coached the boys through making their hot drinks. "You've been good for my sister, Tom," Doug said, holding his fork where Cara, who sat in the crook of his left arm, could not grasp it. "Look how beautiful she looks."

"Mmm," Tom agreed, sipping his cappuccino. "She is gorgeous."

"You rescued her, you know."

"She's been a great blessing to me, Doug."

"I watched you heal her after Max, and I wanted to do that for Katie. Figured Max would move on and Katie would need me again."

"You came along just when *Beth* and *Flip* needed you." Cara cooed at Tom, seeking his attention. He made kissing noises to her and touched her cheek with his fingers.

"Much as I loved her, she didn't trust me. It hurts that she picked that asshole over me."

"You can't regret what you've done with your life. When you met them, Flip was afraid of dust settling. Now look at him."

Doug lifted Cara to his shoulder and both men watched Flip laughing with Austin, Drew, Bonnie Jean and Jon. "Yeah, he's a great kid."

"And he loves his dad," Tom said.

Doug's eyes filled up and he nuzzled Cara's head. "I think it's been ten years since he's had a nightmare."

"And Annie and Dougie, now, too? You've got a great family. Your wife adores you. Your career is fun."

"You're right, Tom."

"That's how God meant it to be. I actually think he's particularly fond of you."

"Stop trying to evangelize me, Tom," Doug laughed. "Anyway, I can't convert right now, I'm not done sinning. Got to kick Hunter's sorry ass before I repent."

"Promise me you won't do that."

"No. I'm *not* promising you. I'm gonna go over there, beat Hunter to a bloody pulp, grab Ben, throw him over my shoulder, and get him *the hell* out of there. Tom, if he knows Hunter is an SOB, it must be bad over there. Would your boys call you that?"

"I hope not."

"No. You're too damn humble. You *know* not. This is not the place for your freakin' humility."

Silence resounded in the café; Tom and Doug looked up. Doug lifted his free hand and made a calming motion. "Don't worry, fellas. I'm not gonna wig out anymore. Go on eating." Tentatively their chatter resumed, then burst to a roar. "Admit you want to beat Hunter up and get Ben away from him."

Tom tapped the back of Doug's hand with his cup. "I want Ben to find out about his mother. I want some explanation from Hunter about why he knows nothing about her. And if Ben is as unhappy as I sometimes see he is…" Tom said, his voice trailing off, he stared at his empty cup. He looked up at Doug, met his eyes. "At the first game, Doug you had to leave, but Max showed up." Doug leaned closer. "Something's wrong between them. You could taste the hostility between them, the stench of it was so rank."

"Okay, then, so what's your plan, Coach?"

"We answer any questions Ben asks us. That way we give him the truth as he's ready for it. In the meantime, we spend time with him and kind of set the stage for stuff to come up."

"Why not just tell him when he comes in here this morning?"

"Where are they anyway?"

"Drew said they had to do something."

"Gregen thinks we've got to help Ben figure it out. Or he won't believe us."

"Oh, Gregen," Doug sighed with a smile. "Once Max knows ol' Gregen's in town, I'll get my chance to fight."

"I can't understand what's taking them so long," Tom said impatiently and then called across the café. "Drew! Where did you say Ben and Joe went?"

From the little table by the window in Gisela's Delicatessen on Annapolis Street, Max and Patty watched Joe and Ben leave the medical lab, walk toward them, and turn up the sidewalk at a shop across the street.

"Good," Patty said, putting her coffee cup down with finality. "He got that done. Did what you asked with very little credible explanation."

Max looked displeased. "What is that place?" As Joe and Ben mounted the steps, Max squinted at the banner that hung from the porch, its yellows and blues vaguely familiar and disturbing.

"Some kind of crafty place for housewives with nothing to do."

"Why would two teenage boys go in there?"

They watched a car stop at the drive-through window and saw a girl open the window and hand out a big paper bag, then a tray with two cups, the rising steam visible even across the street. "They have food," Patty offered.

Max squinted, leaning forward so that he lifted from his chair. "I think that's one of the girls I met over at Ben's game."

"That's reason enough," Patty said. "Food and girls."

"I think that's MacBride's daughter. I think Ben's got the hots for her."

"Well, that's just more proof that Ben is yours. Surely Mr. MacBride wouldn't allow them to date if Ben were his child."

"Maybe."

"He'd at least be afraid of the possibility if he had slept with—"

"I *know* they slept together, Patty."

"How do you know that?"

Max shrugged. "You didn't know Katie. She was sexual."

"That doesn't prove anything. I'm sexual and I don't sleep with all my guy friends."

Max looked at her, nostrils flared, and gave a little shrug. She had tried to make him talk about this before. Patty wanted to find out if Max now considered *her* his sexiest lover. And because Max refused to discuss it with Patty, part of her strategy was to talk him out of his deep rooted hatred for Tom. He knew Patty's reasoning was this: if he no longer hated Tom, it would be a signal to her that Max thought she was a better lover than Katie, that the loss of Katie was surmountable. Why hate Tom for taking something that was not as valuable as what he now enjoyed? Patty lived to convince; her insistence was one reason he'd agreed to this paternity test, though he anticipated the outcome and had no intention of giving Ben up when it came back as he expected it would.

"What?" Patty said. "Go ahead and say it."

"She was different than you."

"You mean better, don't you?" She reached to get her handbag, looking for a cigarette, he knew.

Grabbing her wrist, Max prevented her. "She had ice in her veins, though, and you don't. You got so goddamn much fire, you could light that cigarette with one puff. So cheer up. And don't light one right now. Okay? You know I hate them."

Patty was tough and though he knew he'd hurt her, she shrugged, accepted the consolation he'd tossed her, lowered her glance, and growled at him. "You still haven't got proof that—"

"Yeah I do. Her journal. She said so in there. Where do you think I *got* the idea?"

Patty sat back stunned. "Max. Where is this journal?"

"My idiot mother gave it back to Katie's father. She's trying to get it back from him, but the old guy is a stubborn jerk. And he despises me. When we got married, that's the last time he spoke to Katie."

"What*ever* was the objection?"

"Hell if I know. I think they had it in for me because I'm a Republican."

"Huh. But I would think they'd have read it and if it *does* say—"

"*I've* read it and it *does* say," Max hissed at her, unwilling to explain the way Katie wrote things—so much stuff, a lot of it not even in *English*. But she'd made the mistake of teaching Max all the sex words in French and Italian. If Patty knew there was interpretation involved she'd never give him a minute of peace about it. And anyway, it was too damn personal to tell Patty how Katie recorded everything. Patty would never believe how Katie had described their first time together in raw, poetic detail. In her back-slanted, minuscule writing, she even wrote drafts of thank-you notes in her journal before copying them and mailing them. She wrote drafts of *post cards* in there.

Max drummed his fingers on the table, thinking of Gregen, his failed lawsuits, his relentless phone calls and letters. He decided not to tell Patty about Gregen. And like a bolt of lightening rinsing through his gut Max knew that Gregen must not have seen the journal, because he would have used it in court.

"Was Tom's paternity the subject of the petition he filed?"

"How do you know about that?"

"I'm good at my job. And now with the Internet, accessing public records is easy."

He wondered if Patty had been such a great idea. Everything would be all right if he could just grab all the loose ends himself and get Ben away from Tom MacBride. He told Patty, "He got nowhere with that because he would never admit to it publicly. Think of his goddamned image. He walks around Annapolis like a fucking saint."

"So he sued for custody. What was his argument? Did he use Katie's journal?"

"If he had, I wouldn't have Ben now. Claims he got attached to the kid when they were babysitting him. Claims Katie wanted him to keep an eye on Ben. He has some paper Katie gave him to read to me. But I already read it—or anyway the first draft of it because she always wrote stuff in her journal first."

"Max, I think it's unlikely that Tom's wife would put up with him visiting a woman he'd slept with, a woman who was bearing his child. From what you tell me about how she took care of Ben when Katie was ill, she could not have suspected."

"It's hard for me to believe Laurie didn't suspect."

"Because there was nothing *to* suspect," Patty needled.

"Shut up, Patty." Max gave Patty a withering look. "I get that you don't believe me, okay? But you weren't there. You didn't read what I read. So back off."

As waitresses always do, theirs came to the table at this tense moment of their discussion; she refilled their coffee cups while they glared at each other. Patty fumbled for her handbag, got a cigarette, and lit it.

"You can't smoke that in here," Max murmured.

"Try and stop me."

Tom watched Joe and Ben turn up the walk, heads bent together in conversation. He called above the noisy chatter in the café to Laurie, "They're here," and opened the door. "Food's ready, boys," Tom called to them as if he wanted to rush them up into the store.

"Good," Joe called back. "I'll eat a hunk of fabric if I don't get food, fast."

"Should have had some oatmeal before you left the house."

"Didn't want to throw it up during practice."

"I've never seen you throw up oatmeal."

"Just 'cuz *you* haven't seen it," Joe grinned, slapping his dad's stomach lightly, "doesn't mean it hasn't happened." Joe accepted his father's customary embrace with casual comfort before moving into the store to make room for Ben in the doorway.

"Where've you two been?"

"Running an errand for Ben's dad."

"Hey, Coach," Ben said.

Joe put Ben's backpack on the floor by the door and looking at Ben said, "Food, first."

The scent of fresh, rich coffee, roasting meat and cinnamon baking welcomed Ben into the room already warm with the first yellow glances of morning sun and the cheerful boisterous conversation of Tom's well-loved athletes. Ben ducked under Tom's arm to enter and the door bounced shut behind him ringing the shop's quaint, clear bell. Tom stopped him, his hand on Ben's shoulder. Ben waited as Tom's eyes swept over him with swift but fierce concern. "How's it going?"

"He's in shock. Be gentle with him," Joe called back over his shoulder.

"Is that true?" Tom said

"I'm a little confused."

"Laurie and I want to talk to you about all this."

"Coach, I just want to say that I—" Ben hesitated under swelling emotion. "I know you've forgiven my dad. I can see that. I can tell and I'm blown away by it."

Tom did not look away, but said, "If only he could forgive me."

"What exactly *happened* to make him so mad at you?"

"When your parents were separated before you were born—wait. Did you know about that?"

"*No.*"

"That's when I got to know your mother pretty well. She stayed with us for awhile and as I already mentioned to you, your father misinterpreted our connection and I think felt hurt by it."

"What did you—did you do anything wrong?"

Tom gave a short tense laugh, opened his mouth to speak. "No, he didn't," Doug said as he came up behind and grabbed Tom, trapping Tom's arms and jiggling Tom up and down. "Your mother and Tom—it wasn't like that. They *talked* about stuff. That's all. The only thing Tom ever did wrong to your parents was being a damn good friend. You have no idea."

"Doug," Tom pleaded.

Doug released Tom and grabbed Ben's shoulder. "Ben, you got to realize anything Tom tells you is gonna be against himself and is gonna make your dad look like the crap he did was worth him winning a Nobel prize."

"You *promised* me, Doug, not a half hour ago."

"Hey, I know, I know. I've caused enough trouble for today. I heard what you told me, Tom. I just want to hug my little man here."

Whatever emotion Tom restrained, whatever deep, loving enthusiasm was saddled in Gregen's austere commitment to decorum, Ben sensed that these fettered feelings were utterly free now in Doug and the man grabbed Ben in a warm, hard hug. Doug proclaimed in Ben's ear that he loved him and punctuated his sincerity by pounding Ben's back in hollow sounding thumps. Holding Ben by the shoulders he said, "I wish you were two years old and I hadn't missed a minute of you." Then, laughing at himself, he released Ben and elbowed Tom to elicit Tom's consensus.

To Ben's astonishment, Tom's eyes were wet as he nodded his head in agreement. And Ben could tell from Tom's face and stance that he, too, wanted to hug Ben. He imagined that he saw in Tom's eyes a brief and impassioned vow that said he'd trade all that he'd gained from a lifetime of discipline and courtesy to have had Doug's impetuous freedom for the last two minutes. But Tom did not even touch Ben, just trapped his hands under folded arms against his chest.

"I know we're embarrassing you."

"No," Ben said.

"You're embarrassing *me*," Joe said, approaching from the café, hands full with juice bottles and chunky golden scones. "Mom's making us omelets," Joe confided to Ben, putting a bottle of apple juice into his hands. "What's *with* you two? Are you having some kind of mid-life estrogen surge?" he said to his uncle and father. "When do you ever talk to *me* that way, or Pete or Flip? I mean *come on.*"

Doug ruffled Joe's hair, then patted his cheek. "I spent many an afternoon with you on my lap. All the hell you wanted to do was read."

"That was Pete."

"Right. Well, little man," Doug said to Joe, his arm encircling Joe's waist, pulling Joe close, his broad fingers digging into Joe's ribs so that Joe squirmed and giggled, working to balance the food he held. "You spent your first Christmas in my arms and the whole next month, too. Your grannie didn't like you much so *I* got you."

"Thanks, Unca Doug," Joe said with mock chagrin.

"And I walked you all night, every night, up and down the hallway while your dad was in the hospital, your mom pregnant again. She had to get some sleep. So don't whine. You got yours from ol' Unca Doug."

Doug did not notice the awkward tension his remark raised. Instead, he patted his cell phone and said, "Been ignoring my phone for the last twenty minutes. Gotta go." He grabbed Joe by the back of the neck and bringing him closer, kissed Joe's forehead, turned, punched Tom's shoulder hard, and banged out the screen door.

When his eyes met Joe's, Ben's thought was confirmed and Joe spoke for them both. "So, Dad," Joe said, casually, opening his juice bottle. "You were in the hospital when I was a baby?"

"Yes, I was." Joe glanced at Ben.

"You were in the hospital because that's when my dad broke your back."

"Yes," Tom said.

"Was it a fistfight?"

"On his part, yes."

"What does *that* mean?" Joe demanded.

"You didn't fight back? Right?" Ben guessed.

"Right."

"Why?" Both boys' voices joined in outrage.

"For good reason."

"You promised not to?"

"I can't explain why boys, so—"

"You didn't fight back *at all*?" Ben sputtered. "He hit you so hard he *broke* your *back*? And you—"

"You were protecting Ben's mother," Joe blurted out his guess. With keen, thirsty perception, Ben watched Tom's eyes and saw something like a sad glimmer of assent in them.

"I was trying to reason with Ben's father."

"But once he hit you, why didn't you hit him back?" Ben demanded.

"I can't tell you that."

"Why? You promised you'd answer any question I asked with the truth. Those were your exact words."

"It would be unkind to describe this situation. I'm telling you all I can without being unkind."

"I *told* you," Ben said, anger rising in him. "I already *know* he's a jerk."

"Hush. You must never refer to your father that way."

"Dad," Joe protested.

"*Never*," Tom insisted. "It's disrespectful."

Hands out in a gesture of supplication, Ben said, "Tom. Listen. You've taught me to be honest. You made that happen in me," Ben thumped his chest. "It's in here now. You'll never make me deny he's what he is. I mean, he *broke* your *back*. Didn't he?"

"He did. I don't think he specifically *went* to break my back, but he did mean to hurt me." Joe's pained breath drew Tom's glance and when he spoke again, his voice sounded definite and convinced. "But I know your father's anguish was genuine. So we do not need to stoop to name-calling. The issue is complex."

"Then explain it to me," Ben pleaded. "Did he have any reason to *fight* you? Any good reason to hate you? No! He—"

Tom held his hand up to halt Ben's words, saying "Hush," with a rock-ribbed strength that brought Ben to obedience. As he shut his mouth, Ben realized that, behind them, the café also had quieted. Both Ben and Tom glanced at the faces turned their way. Bonnie Jean, Jason and Tommy were crossing the store toward them. The phone rang at the counter. Joe turned toward the others, food-filled hands held up as if to keep the crowd away.

Tom turned his back to them, speaking quietly to Ben alone. "Your father hates me because—I don't know any other way to say this—in some ways, maybe the most basic of all, I'm responsible for you being here and that infuriates him."

Ben stared at Tom. "I'm not sure what you mean, Coach."

"When your parents were separated, I convinced your mother to reconcile with your father. That's when you were conceived."

"Why would he hate you for that? Wouldn't that make him happy?"

Wincing, Tom said, "*He* had been trying to convince her to reconcile and she refused. Wouldn't even open his letters. When *I* convinced her—"

"That can't be all of it," Ben burst out. "He doesn't *think* like that. I know him."

"Ben, listen. He believed that, deep down, her return to him was not because she loved *him* but because she—because she respected *me* more. That would hurt any man."

"She preferred you."

"Well...not..." Tom said, folding his arms tightly over his chest, wincing again. "Ben, it's..."

Coach and athlete stared at each other. Ben understood that in spite of Tom's excuses for his father's behavior, Tom knew Max. And he knew that Tom would throw himself—heart first—into the breach for Ben as he had done for Ben's mother.

"You know, Tom, if you *get* me to love my father, if you convince me to do it because of who *you* are and because of this faith you've brought alive in me—he'll hate you for that, too. You know that."

"Don't you love your father?" Tom sounded crushed.

"Me? Love my father? No," Ben said with a cynical shake of his head. "Oh no." Behind him, he heard Laurie call Tom's name. He heard the buzz of his friends clamor closer. His time was up. "Just like my mother," Ben said to his coach, "I prefer you."

45

LAURIE appeared by Tom's side with the phone in her hand. "Tom. It's Joan Poulard. She says it's urgent." Tom took the phone and walked toward Laurie's office in the back of the shop as Laurie ushered Joe and Ben into the café.

"Come and eat," Bonnie Jean said, taking his hand and pulling him to the table set for he and Joe. Big glasses of orange juice, a basket of steaming rolls, a plate of sticky buns with caramelized sugar glistening and a bowl of fruit salad awaited them. Joe sank into his chair, moaning with pleasure. Ben took his seat beside him.

"A line already at the drive-through," Tommy called. "Jeannie, help me."

"Thank you," Laurie called as she brought heated plates to the table and placed them down in front of Ben and Joe. She took a chair and joined them. Adam brought two foamy cappuccinos to the table, grabbed a chair, and squeezed in beside Laurie.

"Delicious," Joe said, his mouth full. "I love you, Mama. I swear to God."

"Mustn't swear, Joe," Laurie said, patting his arm.

Ben had been spreading butter on his roll, had not taken a bite. "Eat," Joe said, elbowing him.

"Take a bite of the omelet, Ben," Adam urged. "The one Mrs. Mac made for me was great."

It was hard to swallow. His stomach shook in the ruthless way it did; soon his hands would be shaking. Laurie pushed the cappuccino cup closer and he picked it up, hoping the warmth would quiet his body. Ben muttered to himself, "*C'est incompréhensible.*"

Ripping his roll open and tearing off a piece, Joe said, "No wonder he's freaked out, Mom. All this stuff with Uncle Doug." Ben put his fork down.

"Does your stomach hurt?"

Ben looked at her, so full of thoughts, he wanted to bolt out of there, but her familiar, searching eyes were careful and worried and he knew she loved him and wanted to make sure he was okay. "No, ma'am," he said. "I'm just weirded out by the news that my dad broke a man's back in a fistfight. Not just any man, but Tom. And then I find out about it and it looks like Tom is over it." Ben looked around the table. "And so far, his whole family doesn't seem to hate me either."

Pausing on her way to the drive-through window her hands full of merchandise, Bonnie Jean said, "I hate you?" and stopped to listen.

Adam said, "You gotta try to eat, man."

Ben nodded at him and looked helplessly at his food.

"Mama. Are you sure Uncle Doug wasn't exaggerating?" Bonnie Jean said. "How was Colonel Hunter able to break Daddy's back in a fight?"

"His back was weak anyway from a previous injury."

"Which my father probably also caused," Ben said miserably.

Laurie asked if his cappuccino needed sugar and Ben sipped it to please her, tasting first the sharp strength of the coffee, then the creaminess, the hint of sweet, and when he met her eyes to thank her, he saw, to his dismay, that his flip guess was right and that she would only say it aloud if he wished her to do so. He tried to swallow. He put down his cup. "What *happened*?"

Laurie hesitated. "Eat some of your breakfast and I'll tell you."

"The last thing I need right now," Tom prayed as he drove down Ridgely

Avenue toward school to meet with the insistent John Saunders, "is an-other fight, Lord. Please keep me from picking a fight with him. I'm likely to defend Doug; help me to honor you." He drove so slowly that drivers honked and passed him. This did not move Tom. He was safe from the phone for a few minutes and he had a question to ponder before he could face Saunders. His father had always advised him, knowing Tom's thirsty sense of justice, to pick his battles. Now Tom asked himself if he had chosen the wrong fights. Oh, he'd fought as tenaciously as a terrier over the resurrection of the wrecked coffeehouse—fought and lost ground in further spine damage. He'd fought to repair the building, fought to get the funding and time he needed to repair it after Max's car had smashed it. But that battle had been the distraction that had kept him from insisting the courts listen to him about Ben.

"I never should have let him go. Should have kept at it," Tom said aloud, remembering particularly one blunt lawyer who said that it would have been worth a fight *if* there had been proper documentation.

There was no police record of the fistfight when Max broke Tom's back, though Laurie had phoned the police, though she told Tom that they had come so quickly that they must have seen the way Max was hitting Tom; at the very least the police had already arrived by the time the ambulance came. The lawyer said Tom's suit looked like sour grapes—sour grapes that no court would understand because Tom looked the picture of happy success; he was married to a desirable woman with two healthy, thriving sons and a third child on the way. Why should another healthy child be given to this man already filled up with blessings? No court would rob Max Hunter of his only son.

Tom stopped at the gas station before the Ridgely Bridge. He set the gas pump on the slowest speed and began to clean his windshield, thinking that there would have been documentation if Katie's journals had not been destroyed and if he had pressed charges in Quantico, if he had been sure that Max's intent at the top of the Tower of Terror had been malicious.

That November at TBS, the platoon commander witnessed the mere end of their fight. The captain had not heard what Max had been saying nor had he seen Tom punch Max in the gut, but he had witnessed Max's fury, had seen the blow that split both Tom's lips. Tom had been angry and young and hot with pride. So, regrettably, Tom had not confessed, but let Max take the brunt of the screaming reprimand, thinking that Max deserved it for the things he'd been saying about Laurie. None in the platoon interfered; Max was disliked and everyone knew what kind of comments were off limits.

When he'd screamed himself hoarse, the platoon commander whispered that he'd foster camaraderie by making Max and Tom work the "O" Course together. Later in the hospital, the power of his legs and his future tentative as he waited and prayed for feeling to come back to his lower body, Tom had grown ashamed of himself for punching Max for so stupid a thing as an insult. His own father, come to sit by his bedside, read the New Testament verse to him: "So far as it depends upon you, live at peace with all men." When he learned that Max was facing a court martial upon the testimony of the witnesses in his platoon, Tom felt convinced that the platoon commander's partial knowledge had prejudiced him against Max. Back then, hoping for healing, he had decided that Max had not pushed him intentionally. No, Max had surrendered to the tower's mighty threat. Tom had seen raw fear in Max's muddy eyes that had gone wild with a glimpse of terrible, sudden and irrevocable death. His enemy had been frightened there at the top of the Tower of Terror. A man who is afraid thinks of himself. He does not purposely try to harm the man beside him even if...

The gas pump jumped in his hand, but Tom stood there gazing into the past, remembering the look on Max's face when he'd made the mistake of looking down, when his rope swirled wildly, when he realized that Tom had seen his fear. *He was angry, but did he intentionally knock into my shoulder when he was reaching for that crossbar?* At the time, Tom had insisted no. He had not been heroic, he had not been a good marine, but he had not intended murder.

Back in the car, driving slowly to school, he saw it again in his mind. The rope was damp and rough when he took it in his hands, making it both slick and abrasive as he pulled his body upwards. In his split lips, thumping with dull pain, Tom hauled Max's enmity with him up the rope. Upward, he climbed, forcing himself to concentrate, centering his gaze on the blazing coral lip of the sun rising above the low, gray clouds on the horizon. He swayed on the snaky thing, his insides still breathless from the fight, from the scathing rebuke of his own pounding conscience.

Nearly to the place on the rope where he had to lean and reach for the crossbar, he knew Max had caught up and squirmed just feet below him on the second rope. Max moved in spurts, jerking the rope with his weight and vigor. Tom's left forearm had begun to shake. His neck felt tight and hot. He reached for the crossbar, but was inches short. He struggled to inch higher on the rope. Max had nearly reached the top of his rope when he made the mistake of looking down.

Now, swinging his car up the icy driveway of his school, Tom countered the quick skid of his back wheels, remembering as his own stomach tossed again, the green, sickened pallor in Max's face, the way Max had groaned that he was going to be sick. Tom had looked down then, too, and it made his rope sway and swirl and the earth thirty feet below rolled beneath him as if it had melted. *Oh,* Tom thought, shuddering slightly despite the distance of twenty years, *it was rightly called the Tower of Terror.* He had hesitated, unsure of how to help Max, wavering as he was. Tom had called to him.

"Get going," Max grunted. "In my way."

Tom reached for the crossbar, missing it by a wisp. He pumped with his legs, swinging the rope toward the bar. It was now or never. He flexed his left arm, leaning away from the rope, reaching with his whole body, his right arm outstretched. He sensed Max's closeness, catching his movement in the corner of his eye. Their hips collided. In fleeting, dizzying glances as his body whirled with the rope, spinning so that he wasn't sure whether he was still holding on, Tom saw hostility in Max's expression. They collided again, Max's feet thudding into Tom's right calf. The impact drove Tom away from the crossbar, but on his return swing, Tom saw that he could reach it. As Tom's right palm skimmed the crossbar, he thought he saw Hunter reaching for the bar again. Or was it for him? But he swung past Tom, eyes frantic with a fear primal and raw. With his right hand, Tom gripped the bar hard. He felt his left hand burn as it slipped on the rope. Max's hand hit Tom's shoulder, the impact propelling Max backwards, whirling him around closer to the bar, and Tom's fingers slipped a bit—just a tiny bit—but then he heard the slap of Max's hand on the far side of the crossbar, felt the thud of Max's weight shudder through the bar into his slipping hand. The rope flickered through his fingers; he couldn't get it. Wind howled past his ears as he fell to the ground.

Tom yanked hard on his emergency brake as a cold sweat washed him. And once again, as he had so long ago in Quantico, Tom knew a breaking sense of compassion for Max. Something in Tom still refused to believe that it had been deliberate. If it had happened later…if it had happened after Ben had been born, Tom would have believed it, but then…at the beginning…Max had no reason to hate, only to fear, and as Tom told himself, climbing out of his car with a sense of gratefulness that he could walk, *I was scared out of my mind, too.*

After hearing Laurie tell the story about Tom's fall, Ben asked, "So, what was my dad mad at Tom about? Why does he hate him so much?"

Bringing Cara toward them, Drew called, "The child is hungry and I got nothin' to give her."

"I'll hold her off," Joe lifted up and reached for her.

"Got ten minutes 'til we leave," Drew said to Ben and Joe.

Ben turned his attention back to Laurie. "You were telling me what the problem was back then."

"True, Max disliked Tom, but it's possible that he started hating Tom *after* the accident at the Tower of Terror. Even though the charges were dropped and there was no court martial, your father was humiliated by the incident. It's to his credit that he recovered his…*poise,* I guess you could say, and standing in the Corps. He's done very well and with something like that on his record, that can't have been easy."

Ben met her eyes, saying no more, thinking how formidable a skill was the discipline of forgiveness. He saw the concern in her eyes, the searching look that was so compelling, so familiar to him. Deep inside his busy mind, he saw a flash of light and remembered a roaring crash.

But the searching look in her eyes intensified. *I remember you*, he wanted to say, not really understanding why the words pounded so strongly in his consciousness. *I know you, don't I?* His eyes left hers to quickly scan the café and the shop beyond. What was it about this place? "Have I been here before?" he said to her.

"What do you mean, Ben?"

"I know I was in Annapolis when I was six. My mom had something to do and Dad took me around. Did I see you then? Do you know what I'm talking about?"

"Yes," she said simply.

"Did you see me?"

"Yes, I did. Briefly, too briefly. Your father and Donna had legal business in town."

"That must be why I remember you."

"That's what I've been hoping," she murmured.

"That time in Annapolis, I imagined something about crashing off the bridge. I remember thinking I saw a mermaid. It's stupid, but her eyes remind me of yours."

"What did it look like when you thought you crashed off the bridge?"

"Murky and stuff floating. And a mermaid staring at me like you're doing."

"Come and see something." She stood up and taking him by the wrist, got him out of his chair. "The rest of you stay here," she said to the others.

Laurie led Ben to the front of the store and, switching off the lights, took him out the door, positioning him on the porch, so that he stood facing the bay window. Despite the cold weather, the sunny porch was summer hot and the scent of the ice-stung roses as nauseating as ever. "Look in through the window. Bend down a little and look."

She left him out there, but left the door open and when he did as she instructed, he saw her in the shop; she was squatting beside the bay window looking up at him and Ben gasped. The scent of the roses burned his nose and throat and for an instant he saw the crash again, saw his father's big silver car scramble up the steps. Ben whirled around to look. Max had crashed the car into this wall. He lay his hand on it and looking in, Ben realized that he had seen the debris, the dust of the broken house in the air, the change of light, and had imagined that they were underwater and Laurie, reaching for him with her capable hands outstretched, looking up at him with dark, knowing eyes, had somehow comforted him.

She hurried out to him.

"We crashed. I saw you."

"You were only six. And it was late at night."

"I only saw you for a few seconds but it was like—" he made a quick gesture with his hand as if to show an abrupt and final movement. "And I knew—I felt something strong from you. Then you reached for me. You wanted to get me out of the car. I knew that's what you wanted."

"My first instinct, I guess," she said with the saddest smile.

"I remembered that for all these years," Ben said, eyes wide in whispered confidence. "I held onto it."

"You held onto it?" Her eyes narrowed with concern.

Ben nodded. "Yeah." He bit his lip, determined to control his emotions. She moved her hands as if she would hug him but Ben straightened his back. If she touched him, he would cry. Their eyes met, his blurry and stinging, hers strong with understanding. "Were you hurt?"

"I was hurt."

"No! How did he get away with it? Didn't the police come?"

"I had a concussion. I guess that's what made me doubt what I saw. I couldn't believe he—"

Shaking his head, Ben squeezed his eyes shut. "Always," Ben spit it like a curse.

"Forgive me, Ben," Laurie said, stepping so close that her homey scent occluded the stench of the roses. She touched his elbow; he squeezed his eyes tighter. "I see now that God gave me that chance to reach you and I didn't take it."

"You don't know what you're saying," Ben murmured, trying to turn away. She held his elbow.

"Help me understand," she said quietly, glancing at the now restless crowd of teenagers milling just within earshot.

His mind spun imagining his life if his father had been punished—no, *imprisoned* for the crash—and away from Ben all those years. The sting of remembered blows lifted away to show his soul a smooth, green shoot ready for life, his mind quiet, free, concentrating. These images defied articulation, so poignant, so impossible were they. Instead he puzzled aloud, "He sped away. I remember the way the car swerved, so it must have been going so fast. I remember going over the bridge. It must have been the Ridgely Bridge—" he pointed. "I watched for you out the back window until it was too dark to see."

His eyes were dry again, his grief the ache of something torn inside, but Laurie's dark eyes spilled tears. With awkward tenderness, he reached one arm around her shoulders. "Don't cry. Please. You tried. I saw you. But you were hurt. You couldn't chase a speeding car. Please don't cry."

46

"TOOK your time, didn't you, Tom?" Joan Poulard greeted him, standing in the outer room of her office, holding the door for Tom.

"I'm here now," Tom said.

"Both Bettinger and I have tried to calm him down. I'm warning you, he's out for blood."

"Why? Doug was upset. He made a mistake. Why is Saunders even here?"

"He seems to be gnawing at things Doug disclosed about Ben's family. I think his agenda is to get rid of Ben. There's got to be jealousy there about Ben's success on the team."

"Okay," Tom said. "I'll handle him."

Tom held the door to the inner office open for Joan, walked in, going straight over to John Saunders to shake his hand. "Sorry to keep you waiting, John."

"I might have thought you'd know I'd be here soon as that practice was over."

"No. I'm astonished to see you," Tom said, finding a chair for himself and pulling it up close to the man. Joan retreated behind her desk and from where she sat, Tom could easily make eye contact. "Joan tells me your brother-in-law is not a Christian."

"No, he's not."

"And he brought up some pretty ugly stuff that proves the new kid's folks aren't church-going people."

"What's your point, John?"

"Oliver's thinking—and I agree—the new kid has brought a bad spirit to the team. Oliver tells me he showed no respect for his father this morning. Called him a filthy name. Now why are you giving a kid like that playing time when you have my Oliver sitting on the bench?"

Tom studied his hands for a moment. "I don't have my playbook with me, John, but I know Ollie's been getting in every game. He's still a starter, though to be honest with you, he's not hustling during practice and—"

"That's because—like I told Joan weeks ago—he thinks you don't like him. So he can't perform."

"For instance," Tom said. "Monday's practice, he was five minutes late. During laps, he complained of a cramp. He sat out until we got to the lay-up drills. He was good with those, but when it came time to practice boxing out and rebounds, he argued with Brock about it and Brock sent him to the showers. I can't reward that."

"Practices get to him. He just wants to play, Tom. Come on."

"If he wants to keep his starting spot, he's got to be on time and really pour it on in practice or I'm not starting him. It's that way for every team member."

"When you get the new kid out of here and Oliver's got a nice, pure atmosphere to play in, he'll be good again. Last year when he and Knox had the back court covered, he was happy."

"Last year he sat out every other game for getting technical fouls for arguing with the ref—"

"That was not his fault."

"Every *one* of them was *his* fault. That's what a technical foul *means*. It's a penalty for in*tent*ional misbehavior."

Joan Poulard said, "Remember, John, after Ollie threw the chair at the ref in the Grace Brethren game last January, many parents in the league complained. We suspended him for five games and then let him play again. Many of those parents thought he should be banned from the team, but Tom and I agreed we would work with him. Compare Oliver's behavior to Ben, who has shown no displays of temper. We're certainly not penalizing Ben because of what people may think about his father. His father is not a member of the team."

"He's a cheater and he disrespected his own father today!"

"That's enough," Tom said, pushing himself to the edge of his chair. "You're not to call any child a name in my presence."

"You don't know anything about this kid, Tom. Rumor has it he's after your daughter and you're too blind to see it. How'll you feel if he—"

"Really, John," the principal said. "Let's not talk like that."

"Ben belongs here. He's thriving. He's staying," Tom said. "I'll do what I can to reach out to Ollie, though. I give you my word on that."

"I think it would be smart," Joan Poulard said to Tom as they walked through the gym to Tom's office, "if Doug skipped a few practices between now and Christmas. Let this blow over a little."

"It's Ben that Saunders is really after. It's disgraceful," Tom sputtered. "A grown man targeting a child like that."

"Right. But if we can take down the general inflammation—that means Doug—we might be able to keep the heat off Ben."

"I bet Oliver's giving it to him every chance he gets."

"We're going to have to document any of that."

"Joan, I'm starting to believe that people shouldn't be given second chances."

"Don't say that, Tom! It's what I love best about you."

"Notice Ollie didn't make it to breakfast," Jason said to Joe as the crowd of boys ambled into school.

"Where did he go?"

"I saw him go into the john with his phone out. I bet he didn't even take a shower."

"He's probably bottling his sweat to sell to the girls."

Joe laughed at this, but grew immediately serious. "I guess we've given him long enough on those pictures. It's been almost two weeks. Probably he feels awkward around us 'cause this is hanging over his head."

"He feels awkward around us because he's a jerk."

"Yeah, but we've got to talk to him. Give him a chance to come around and apologize. We've got to make it easy on him."

"Holy shit! If you could hear yourself!" Adam said, "You know who you sound like."

"Coach," Jon said.

"Like Dad says, 'Somebody's got to be the generous one and God always wants it to be you.'"

"Ol' Tom MacBride rubbing off on you, Joe."

"So, what's the plan, chief?" Jon said, draping an arm around Joe's shoulder.

"We each try to talk to him today or tomorrow—like buddy to buddy—and encourage him to straighten things out with Morgan."

Drew said, "Then give him over Thanksgiving to think about it. If he still won't listen, we give Coach the pictures."

"Yeah," Joe said. "Hey, where's Ben?"

"He said he's meeting Bonnie Jean outside behind the gym," Jason said.

"You're supposed to cover for him if he's late."

"You know," Scott said thoughtfully, "we should really bottle *Ben's* sweat. I think it would sell a lot faster than Oliver's."

Holding hands, Ben and Bonnie Jean made it up the slippery hill behind the gym and hid in a little thicket of holly trees.

"Smells good in here," Bonnie Jean said. They sat down close together on a piece of PVC pipe. "Kind of earthy."

"The first time his back broke—at Quantico—was my dad's fault, too."

She squeezed his hand. "That's not what's important about you—to me or to them."

"Jeannie, it's not that I don't believe your dad or your uncle or anything, because I do. But something doesn't fit in what they're saying to me."

"I know what you mean. Something about what they're saying doesn't make sense. Like I'm glad I know your dad's reasons for resenting my dad, but is *that* why your mom hasn't called my parents or even *spoken* to them at all since you guys moved here, because it might make your dad jealous again? Especially when your dad is…not exactly faithful himself."

"That can be explained by a double standard. And he's absolutely capable of that. But it's hard for me to imagine my mom talking to your dad about the Bible and stuff. And if she hadn't just told me that she was a Christian, I would *never* have believed what Tom said about their relationship. Never. And even now, her...her way of being a Christian is kind of stilted and rigid and condemned, not like this sense of a powerful gush of life I've felt here." Embarrassed, he sought her eyes but she smiled and nodded, understanding him easily.

"Can you imagine how traumatized your mom must have been to have her parents catch her having sex with her boyfriend? If that forced her to come to faith—" Bonnie Jean shook her head. "It's not a natural awakening."

"True," Ben said, "but that's the other thing. If you count up the dates—if I understand it right—that must have been right around when I was conceived. But Mom says no. Like when my parents were telling me about when she became a Christian, you know when my dad was trying to blame that thong on me that night? He was just about to say to her, 'Yes, Donna, that *is* when he was conceived,' but it was like she didn't read his signals and said no. But the dates match up. And if the dates match up, other stuff doesn't. And today, I find out that she was in love with *your* uncle Doug. When was that? During high school? College? She's from California, so I always assumed that's where she went to high school."

"Where did she go to college?"

Ben said. "I don't know."

"You don't know?"

"They don't talk about the past," Ben said. "You don't understand. No one talks at my house. It's too confusing—all these connections, all these people who love my mom. I don't get it at all."

"And the only useful fact you got from Daddy was that your parents were separated, then he talked to your mom and she went back to your dad and that's when you happened."

"So, she left my dad and visited your parents during the January break from college, because that would have to have been it, right before I was conceived, nine months before October. Maybe she was having an affair with Doug and they convinced her to go back to my dad."

"This is making me nervous," Bonnie Jean said. "In fact I feel like puking."

"But then how did she *know* them to visit them? Tom said once she was stationed here. But that would have to be *after* college. Unless she was a mid."

"Wouldn't you *know* if she had been a mid? Midshipmen all have the trident and goat crap all over their houses and belts and rings and stuff," Bonnie Jean said.

"No. Obviously. Remember, my world is not like yours."

"Okay, let's think it out. If she *was* a mid, maybe that's when she and Doug were in love. Doug's a year behind my dad and when he was a senior it was the first year girls were allowed in. He talks about it all the time."

"Maybe...I hate to even *say* this, but...maybe Doug is my father."

"No. Then you'd be my cousin. Puke-a-rama."

"First cousins marry all the time in Europe. It's no big deal."

"Ben, *ick*. It *can't* be."

"But he *cried* today, Jeannie." Ben scrunched his shoulders together. "My dad never, I mean *never,* acts like that about me."

Bonnie Jean's class met in an upstairs classroom so she went into school by the art room, but hoping to put his coat in his gym locker before going to class, Ben jogged around to the gym door. Tom stood at his open office door, talking to Mrs. Poulard.

Tom made a gesture, fingers spread, palm up, asking for an explanation and said, "What's up?"

"I'm late."

"Late. Didn't you come back with the team?"

"Yes, but I skipped homeroom."

"That's an honest answer," Tom said, meeting his eyes. "Why?"

"I was trying to figure some stuff out from this morning."

"That's understandable, Ben. And I sympathize, but you know the team rules."

"Yes, sir. I knew them when I skipped."

"So you were expecting the penalty."

"I was hoping not to get caught." Ben managed a charming, cha-grinned smile.

Mrs. Poulard said, "I'm surprised you haven't learned from Joe that 'The Lord chastens those he loves.'"

"I just didn't realize I was in that group."

Joan Poulard laughed in a way that showed she thought Ben naive. She grabbed him in her exuberant way and hugged him. "You will get caught, and you're better off for it."

With a glance at Mrs. Poulard, Tom said, "Unless you feel it's your responsibility to handle this, Joan—"

"That's why I employ you principled coaches. But punish him, you must. Can't have our star pupil skipping class."

Tom glanced at his watch. "You're seven minutes late to class. You're going to sit out the first seven minutes of tomorrow's game."

"Coach! That's almost the entire first quarter!"

"Let's make it the *entire* first quarter then, since you're inclined to argue."

Ben opened his mouth to protest, caught himself, swallowed and said, "Yes, sir."

Behind Ben the doors opened. Mrs. Poulard said, "Oliver, Morgan. You're quite late."

"Really?" Oliver said, rushing in, leading with his shoulder, dragging Morgan by the hand.

"Whoa, there, Ollie," Tom said. "Mrs. Poulard and I want to talk to you." Oliver stopped, looking impatient, his eyes bright and angry. Behind him, Morgan's expression was smug and enigmatic, but Ben noticed that her uniform shirt was buttoned askew; if the adults saw it, they showed nothing.

"Where have you been?"

"Ask him!" Oliver said, nodding at Ben.

Tom and Mrs. Poulard looked at Ben, who shrugged to indicate that he didn't know.

Oliver said, "I've got a government test and I'm late."

"Come and see me before practice so we can discuss this. I don't want you to miss any more class. You too, Ben, go on."

Oliver hurried off; Ben and Morgan followed a few steps behind. Mrs. Poulard touched Morgan's arm. "Just a minute, Morgan. Mr. MacBride and I need to talk to you." Hearing this, Oliver glanced back without slowing his pace.

47

HIS brother's room was so hot that Ben opened their east window a crack and shut their door behind him. In his own room the steam radiators clanked and groaned, relentless in their generosity. Ben stripped off his sweats, straightened out Laurie's quilt, tossed his backpack on the floor by his bed, and stretched out to study. He was deep into reading *Last of the Mohicans* when he heard the tap of fingernails on his door. Before he could answer, Donna entered. Seeing her in his doorway, three ideas came to him: she had never been up to this room before, she might not like to see him in his boxers, and this is the woman who had left Doug Davidson heartbroken. But all he said was "Mom," as he tried to cover his boxers with his book.

"I had today off. A million errands to do so I ran out to the gym after I put the boys to bed."

Ben wondered if she wanted his approval for leaving them alone. Without smiling he said quietly, "Their room was hot, so I opened the window a little."

"We can't regulate the heat. The U.S. Navy doesn't think its dependents capable of regulating their own living space. They must spend thousands—millions probably—on wasted heat."

"How's it going?" Ben said. He thought about patting the bed and asking her to sit down, but the tone of their conversation had been so far from hostile, he was afraid of breaking the magic.

"Gran's coming tomorrow and I need you to pick her up at the airport."

"I have a game right after school."

Donna nodded. "She knew that and booked a later flight. I copied down the flight information and stuff from the e-mail she sent since our printer at work is on the blink." Coming into the room, Donna handed him the itinerary. "Dad is not happy about her coming, so we will have to be on our toes and run interference."

Ben tightened his lips and shrugged a little. Donna squinted at his neck and shoulder. "Are those *bruises* there?" She bent a little closer to look, then took the lamp on his desk and tipped it toward Ben. "About two weeks old? What happened?"

"Dad," Ben said.

She stared at his chest for a minute, avoiding his eyes. "I'm sorry about that."

"Yeah. Thanks."

"Did anyone see those when they were darker?"

"Yeah. Everyone did. They show in my basketball shirt."

"Oh, no! What did you say?"

"Nothing. But I should have."

"You promised, Ben. Remember."

"How can you *still* want me to keep that promise, Mom? He's not loyal to you."

"This affair will be over soon. I can tell."

"Mom, it's wrong."

"There's all kinds of wrong, Ben. Divorce is wrong, too, according to the Bible."

"You have scriptural grounds for divorce. He's cheating. You have proof."

"I pray with you once and now you're an expert on the Bible? Anyway, I have to think of your brothers. I can't raise them alone."

"Do you want to raise them with *him*?"

"He's never hurt *them*."

"Why does he hurt *me*?"

"He thinks you don't love him."

"I *don't* love him because he's been *beating me up*."

"It's deeper than that."

"I don't see how. I'm sick of it. It's wrong." It cost Ben a great deal to say that much; before he shut his mouth, his stomach seized up.

Folding her arms across her chest, Donna tapped one perfectly polished nail on her forearm. "Ben."

"You should *want* him to stop. Stop drinking, stop screwing around, and stop hitting me."

She raised her eyebrows at him as if he'd shouted the profanities he kept to his thoughts. "Please don't say things so graphically."

Ben swung his legs off the bed and scooted to the edge. She took a step back. Inwardly, Ben rolled his eyes. He could not help imagining how things would differ if Laurie had walked in to find him studying. Ben peeked up at Donna, surprised at himself for hoping to find even a glimmer of that love in her sternly vacant expression. In the disappointment he counted his birthright, he said softly, "But it's the truth, Mom."

"You intend to tell Tom and Laurie. I can see what's in your mind."

Ben lifted his head to meet her eyes. "*That's* what you see in my mind?"

"Promise you won't tell Tom MacBride."

"I think maybe…maybe *God* wants me to tell Tom."

"You're being influenced by Tom. But it's out of the question. God wants you to be loyal to your family."

Ben shook his head. "I've thought about it. I've been reading my Bible and it seems to demand telling the truth. We're consciously *lying*, Mom."

"Look. You *can't* do this to me. I don't want Tom to know anything bad about me."

"But why? Tom only says really nice things about you. He'll help."

"There are things you don't know. Things you don't understand."

"I know Dad beat Tom up. I know Dad made Tom fall thirty feet from the "O" Course in Quantico. I know Dad would have been court-martialed for it if Tom hadn't thought the best of Dad and got him off the hook."

Stunned, open-mouthed, Donna stared at Ben until a steely look came into her eyes. "Telling you that was manipulative."

"Tom didn't tell me *one word* of what I just told you."

She looked frightened, then shook herself. "If you tell them, Ben—" her voice went unsteady with panic. "I'm warning you, it would shame me so much, I—"

"Come on, Mom. Dad cheats on you and you don't seem even em*barr*assed."

"If Tom finds out about that or *anything*—" hand shaking, she made two fists, knuckles gone white. "I swear, I'll kill myself if he does."

Ben made a stunned noise as if struck. They stared at each other, Ben saw the quivering jaw, saw the cold, broken passion brightening her hopeless eyes and he remembered her depression after Keith and Tim were born. He remembered fearing he would say the wrong thing, the thing that would bring on the fits of weeping. "Mom, please. There must be a doctor or a pastor or somebody who can help you. Please don't say you'll do that."

"I could not face living if the MacBrides knew certain things about me. I couldn't face it," her voice guttural and sincere.

Ben could see how violently her chin trembled. Carefully, he said, "But if you patched things up with the MacBrides, they could help you get away from Dad."

"That is *one* thing I will *never* do, Ben."

"Why?"

"I took Tom's advice once, Ben. And I shouldn't have."

Her words hit him like the blow of a hammer and for an instant he saw stars in the edges of his vision.

"Listening to Tom MacBride was the biggest mistake of my life." Donna gestured to include the room, to suggest all she now lived with was part of the wreckage. Ben stared at her and seeing that she was sincere, his guts lurched, his heart pounded in frightened, uneven thumps. Tom's advice had brought him into the world and there was nothing she regretted more. She had finally said what he had always feared true. For just a moment the world stood still. Ben turned away, pulling the edge of his quilt up over his back and shoulder.

Then Donna's fingers moved rhythmically again, tapping their maddening rhythm on her arm. She peered at him suspiciously. Finally she said, "Where did you get that quilt?"

"Guess."

"Hadn't you better give it back?"

"No. Tom gave it to me. He put it around my shoulders when I was cold and hungry after sitting in the hospital for *six* hours waiting for *you* to get home from getting your nails done or something."

"You've always tried to make me feel like I wasn't enough for you, Ben, and maybe I don't measure up, but don't think for a minute that gives you the right to destroy our family by telling private things to people who will use it against us."

"You've got a lot of nerve telling me *I* make you feel unwanted, Mom. A lot of nerve."

"I just—I can't face it—I really can't. I need you to promise me that you won't go telling the MacBrides things about our private life. For once, try to think of somebody besides yourself."

In a single fluid motion, he rolled over and stood up, letting the quilt fall to the floor. She gasped and he remembered how little he wore. He watched for the unnatural reaction he anticipated and seeing her step back, her expression embarrassed with a dark blush rising up her throat, he lost his temper at her grimacing rejection. "You prayed with me. You took my hand in yours and you prayed with me. And now you still want me to take beatings and stay quiet about it?" he cried. "What is *wrong* with you?"

"The only thing that's keeping me going for Keith and Tim's sake is being able to depend on your silence. If I have to worry about you telling, I'll lose it!" She gestured with her hand, punching the sky.

"But telling would fix everything!" He held both empty hands out to her.

"I have no intention of being shamed *again* in front of the MacBrides. I'm warning you. Unless you want to be responsible for leaving those boys with only your father to raise them, don't tell."

"No," Ben said. "No, don't do this to me."

She whirled on her heel and slammed the door behind her.

48

"AND where is my son this evening that he couldn't be here to greet me?" Ella Hunter asked Ben. "Most people don't have to work the night before Thanksgiving. I can't imagine what a marine in his position has to do. Certainly all his charges here at Annapolis have gone home on leave."

Ben fit the key to the back door into the lock and glanced back at her. "I'm not sure where he is, Gran," he said, pushing the door open and holding it for her. He kept Keith and Tim back with his other hand. "Let Gran go first. You take her little bag, Keith."

Ben followed them, lugging both her enormous black suitcases. "I'll take these up to your room for you—"

"Before you do that, Ben," Ella said. "I need to ask you for something I put *accidentally* into that box I gave you from your grandfather James."

"Sure, Gran. First let me put these away for you."

"No, it's urgent, Ben."

"*Urgent?*"

"Want some chocolate milk, Gran? Ben showed us how to make it."

"Make it? Why not buy it and just pour it into the glass?" She waved them off in a way that reminded Ben of Donna. He put the suitcases down.

"I'll have some, Tim," Ben said in hopes of consolation.

His brothers stared at him, then burst into laughter, their disappointment fading. "That's a good one, Ben." To Ella, Keith explained, "He only drinks ice water and sometimes orange juice."

With a distracted nod at Keith, Ella said, "Did you put that box in a safe place, Ben?"

"What do you mean, 'a safe place?'" Ben said. He was annoyed now, and distressed at being annoyed with his grandmother upon whom he had always depended for his only family feelings of comfort and peace.

"Shh!" Ella glanced at the little boys who were busy at the counter. "Have you, um, how should I say this—looked—I mean—*used* any of the things in there? The tools or things?"

"No, ma'am," Ben said. He had not been near it since he and Joe and Bonnie Jean had carried it in that night when Patty and Max had surprised them.

"Can you take me to where you put it? I need to get something."

"It's down in the basement. I can get whatever you need out of it."

"Oh, I—" she wrung her hands. "I need a little brown book. Rumply looking, stuffed with papers and such. Not new. About yay big." She made a rectangle with her hands. "It should have leather ties and a couple of rubber bands around it."

"I'll see if I can find it." Ben ran down the back stairs to the basement and, flipping lights on, went through the rooms back into the little storage area where they had taken the box. Opening the latch, he saw the book right on top and as his hand closed on it, the familiar feel of the leather interested him. His grandmother called, "Ben?"

"I found it, Gran," he called, taking the book in both hands as he went up the stairs. He smelled its leather and ink scent; it was a great deal like the journal his grandmother had given him when he was twelve. Ben thumbed the corner above the rubber band, trying to remember if the journal had been in with the stack of books, if it had actually been a gift from Gregen.

Ben paused on the fourth step and turned the book over, noting the same stamp on the center back, a delicate fleur de lis, *Firenze* written below. Its scent, its familiar feel, its intriguing fullness of pages ruffled and heavy with clippings and souvenirs stuffed in, compelled him to open it. Carefully, he stretched one of the discolored, brittle rubber bands, lifting it up and off, sliding it onto his wrist.

Above him, to his left, Ben heard his father stumble on the wooden kitchen steps. Ben jumped, dropping the book, cursing himself silently for his lack of vigilance. With its usual creak, the back door opened announcing the end of peace. Ben grabbed the book, hearing some sort of commotion at the doorway. He saw that a scrap of a newspaper had slipped out of the book. He stooped to get it and in the dim light of the basement stairwell began to read the headline, *Three Dead in Two-Car Accident*—but his father's voice boomed into the kitchen above. "How *the hell* am I supposed to get in here with these suitcases blocking the door. Goddammit, Mom. You can't leave your stuff in the way."

Shoving the newspaper scrap in his pocket and tucking the book under his arm, Ben bounded up the steps. "I'll get 'em, Dad. Hold on a minute."

His brothers stood together in front of the sink, both clutching heavy tumblers of chocolate milk, feet together, eyes wide, lips parted slightly in careful anticipation. His grandmother's face reddened as Ben crossed the room. Her hand made a jerky kind of motion toward him. Her mouth opened, then she shut it with an audible snap. Ben smelled the liquor on his father when he stepped past him to grab the bigger suitcase with his free hand, the book still tucked under his other arm. "Drink your milk and go upstairs," he said to his stiff and frightened brothers. Hefting the suitcase quickly across the room, he took it through the front rooms to the stairs and came back for the other.

Max now stood too close to Ella, imperiously up on his toes so that he could glare down at her frightened, upturned face. "Did you bring it?"

"I—I—just have to unpack."

"Dad?" Ben said. He watched them as he went to get the other suitcase, watched his father's angry expression intensify, and adrenaline burned down Ben's arms. "What do you need? I'll get it for you. Gran just got here."

"This is between your grandmother and I." Max bellied up to her, bringing his left foot down on the toes of her right foot, his chest now brushing her upturned chin. Gran made a funny gurgling sound in her throat.

"*Dad*. Back *off*. You're scaring her."

Max looked at him, dulled eyes coming to focus slowly and as they did, he stepped back from his mother. "Upstairs, Keith and Tim," Ben commanded, keeping his voice quick and even. His brothers dumped their milk into the sink and bolted, scrambling under the table and out the other side to get through. Ben tried to pick the suitcase up to shield himself, then realized he was holding something there against his side. In his panic, he tried to think what. On his father's face dawned again the look that accused Ben of betrayal, the dark and unexplained forecast of the rising storm meant to bruise Ben. "*Dad*. I'll take it upstairs. Relax."

His strategy backfired. Max grabbed his mother's shoulders and shook her viciously. "He's got it. You see it? You gave it to *him*? To *him*? That was the whole idea! Stupid woman!"

"*Stop!*" Ben yelled. "You want the suitcase? I'm just carrying it up. You can have it. Let *go* of her."

Max shoved her and she landed heavily against the sink, stunned and silent, looking frail and broken, her gray hair a mop of chaos. "You're mine," he threatened Ben, coming for him. "Give me that book."

"What book?" Ben saw his grandmother stagger at the sink. "You okay, Gran?" Fear burned Ben's stomach making him move closer, reach for her.

Max slapped Ben's face, hitting his jaw below his ear so hard that

Ben arched back. Reaching out reflexively to break his fall, he dropped the book and the suitcase. Ben fell on the book; the suitcase thudded into his hip, flipped, and landed on him. "Give it to me." Max stood over him, "You're mine. Got that?" Max straddled Ben and, losing his balance, sat down hard on the suitcase. Gulping for air, Ben struggled to move, trying to get both hands under the suitcase to flip his father off. His father's open hand smashed his cheek hard, then again. He tasted blood.

"Give it," Max commanded, moving his feet, trapping Ben's face between them. "I've been so careful and my stupid mother," Max muttered, concentrating, his fury-blind eyes staring hard as if he were trying to read something in Ben's face. "How much did you read?" He trapped the edge of Ben's ear beneath the hard, gritty sole of his shoe.

Ben got his right hand free and pushed on Max's ankle, trying to free his ear, and when his father's face came closer, when his father commanded, "Give me the book," Ben spit his mouthful of blood.

Max screeched and fell back off the suitcase. Kicking and pushing, Ben fought to get to his hands and knees as he heard the hard soles of his father's shoes slap on the floor. Ben felt the point of Max's shoe touch his hip and then came a crushing, heavy pain and he heard his own voice cry out for Gran. Another kick hit lower and pushed Ben forward so that his head cut into the low corner of the cabinet; for a split-second, he saw black, he couldn't breathe.

Max flipped the suitcase, smashing it into the basement door, and he lunged for the brown leather book that had been trapped under Ben's hip. Ben scrambled to his feet. Max took the book in both hands and, breathing heavily, stared at it with the awed reverence of a fanatic. Ben looked to his grandmother who sat at the kitchen table holding the edge with both hands. Her eyes were wide and dry. "Gran," Ben said, "Are you hurt?"

"No. I'm perfectly fine." She had smoothed her hair. She did not look at Ben.

"Did you see what he did to me?"

"Try to understand," she said, voice wavering. Her eyes were brighter for an instant, then stared vacantly past him. "That certain things—"

"No," Ben said. "He's drunk. I told you. This is what he does to me."

She straightened her back as she did when she was ready to explain something. "Certain things upset your father and—"

"You're damn right," Max shouted. Holding the book in one hand, he shook it at his mother. A bit of blue and white plastic, flexible as a string, clattered to the floor then skittered under the counter. Two newspaper clippings and a scrap of ribbon fluttered out. Max watched as if stunned. Still clutching the book, Max went to his elbows and knees in a desperate scramble to recover them. "You both better do what I tell you."

"No," Ben cried. He spit another mouthful of blood on the floor.

Max said, "Hey," in protest as if Ben had spilled his milk.

"You did that to me—for that old book? You hurt me for *that*? And you let him," he said to Gran. The back door stood ajar. He ran out of it.

49

BEN saw Nancy Lindquist coming through the circle of lamplight at the edge of their yard, saw the frozen, appalled look on her face as he felt the warm gush of blood slip down his forehead, saw her fumble the big platter of cookies she held, and as he bolted across the grass and away, Ben heard her call him. He sprinted, speed coming to him now that it was too late, strength propelling him so quickly that he did not even remember breathing until he pressed his back against the darkest corner of the chapel's foundation. Ben wiped his forehead with his hand; there was enough blood to cover his palm. Disgusted, furious, sick to his stomach, Ben leaned over, wiped his hands on the concrete sidewalk. "Head wounds bleed," he repeated the wisdom he'd learned somewhere, finding it as comforting as the concrete had been. Ben unbuttoned his shirt, lay it over his knee, and skimmed off his undershirt. As if in a hurry, his blood made a quick, warm shiver down his cheek by his ear and dripped on his collarbone, ran down his chest. "Shit," Ben said and cursed his father in words vile and heartfelt.

Feeling the wound with two fingers, Ben tied the T-shirt around his head tight against it. Shrugging on his button-down shirt, he stood up and felt at once all the hurt places: pounding ear, throbbing skull, hips and butt and legs bruised and trembling and somehow worst of all the stinging soreness of his slapped face with the broken, pounding lips. He looked around. Now, where to go? He remembered the sweet sanctuary he'd found in the chapel and his heart leapt at the thought of the comfort that had strengthened him there. Tears burned in his eyes and his anger seemed now poisonous and vile. His senses returned with the metallic taste of his own blood as he saw the pools of golden light spilling from the chapel's windows, heard now the sound of the big organ tuned to praise and remembered that his family was supposed to have attended a Thanksgiving service, remembered overhearing Max's protests about Johnson ordering him to attend religious services, remembered Max's indignant ranting about how Johnson had no respect for a person's rights. Johnson was trying; there was life and comfort, but he couldn't go in there among clean, loved people looking like the bloody mess he was.

Ben staggered down the alley behind the chapel and out Gate Three at Maryland Avenue. Instinct turned him in the direction of the MacBrides' house. He limped past his own car down to the corner by Gate One before he remembered that it *was* his car. He stopped, stumbled back to it. In his left pocket, he found his keys. His stomach tossed, sick and unsteady. He could not fit the key in the lock. His hands were not working right. Frustrated, he leaned against the car and trapped his hands under his arms to steady them. Finding that the car was still warm, he moved to the front and put both hands on the hood over the engine. When they were warmer, he moved to try the key again and was horrified to see the bloody hand print that he'd left. Wiping it only smeared it and this upset Ben. If he drove to the MacBrides' he'd get blood all over the car.

The trunk was unlocked and opened with a pushed button. Ben lifted his backpack from it and hoisting it onto his shoulder, he set off on foot. He ran in spurts. He was tired; he'd played three hard quarters and won the game for the team with twenty-four points and more rebounds. His friends were lounging in their homes now, warm, satiated, not required to move. And he was empty, his stomach filled only with hate and fear and his own blood. He was cold and colder with each shivering drop of rain that wet his shirt and slid inside his collar. And something else. Something new had stunned him, making him unable to think. He ran, feet striking the concrete hard, ankles and pants wet with the splash from last night's ice melting in the rain and pooling on the roads and crooked sidewalks. He ran and tried to think about the dull and sickening outrage that filled his inner being.

As he came up the driveway, Ben could see the gold-lit windows through the thicket of trees that separated the MacBrides from their neighbors and relief flooded him so that he had to stop, had to stand still, had to bend double breathing and working to stop the rush of yearning. He heard sounds of a party and crept closer. Doug Davidson's Jeep was parked on the grass between the driveway and the towering hedge of cedar trees that swayed in the damp, salt wind that came up across the meadow from the river beyond. From the spilling window light he saw how dirty he was, saw the smear of blood and mud on his hands, the grimy stains, the splashes of dark blood on his school pants. Panic gripped him; he wanted to hide. A big silver van stood in the driveway, solid and dark; Ben limped cautiously toward it, hiding and crouching low along the scratchy wet fronds of the cedars, taking cover on the dark side of the van. *They're having company for Thanksgiving. That guy Kevin from Philadelphia*, Ben remembered as he slid into the shadow of the van that bore the logo of a plumbing business: MACBRIDE AND SONS.

He saw his face in the van's windows, saw the blood-soaked T-shirt, his oddly puffed ear, and looked for a place to hide himself. *Just go to the back door*, he heard Tom's voice inside his head as he took the bloody T-shirt from his head, knowing it would be easily seen. *Next time, come to the back door, son.* Then they would understand what kept him awake at night, what drove him during the day. Blood tickled as it oozed from his head. *Show them the blood running down your face.* The light moved in the kitchen with the hectic happiness of their party and the back door opened, spilling out yellow light and the golden fragrance of baking. Tom stepped out onto the little concrete landing. But there was a reason why he couldn't go in. Ben shivered with a conviction of shame and yearning that held him there in the drizzling shadows.

"Uncle Kevin and I have to put the clues out for the bonfire," Tom called back into the house.

"It's raining, Tom," Ben heard Laurie's voice call. "Can't you wait?"

"Rain's supposed to stop in a minute," Tom said as a big sandy-haired man joined him on the landing.

"Got a couple of flashlights, Tom? Laurie wasn't sure where they might be."

The two men ducked back into the kitchen but Ben stayed there, crouched behind the van, thinking of how his Gran—his dear Gran—had seen him beaten and averted her eyes. His back was soaked, his shoes sloshing puddles, when the kitchen door opened again. The man, Kevin, thrust a flashlight into the darkness and clicked it. "Doesn't work, Tom," and went back in. Ben grabbed the strap of his backpack and moved to stand but his head pounded so painfully that he could taste a kind of metallic tinge with every heartbeat. He could not fully straighten up, he was too cold and too weak and so he crept, bent that way, to the edge of the van where he stood gazing at the pool of yellow light on the landing. In shallow gulps of air, he drew in the late autumn scent of the fruited garden; the scent of baking and coffee spilled like light from the open door, drifted with the inviting smoke trail of the wood fire that he could see dancing deep in the well of the kitchen's warmth. Everyone he loved was in there. If they saw him beaten, would they, too, turn away? And if they figured it out, his mother had threatened to—

He understood what kept him in the shadows. He was alone. He had no one, not even Gran. He was alone in the world and had to stay that way, so he hobbled to the corner of the garage into the deep shadows along the basketball court and around back to the black, leafless apple tree.

He could hear Tom's voice, then the kitchen door squeaked open, banged shut. He climbed recklessly, propelled by panic, skinning his elbow, slipping on the wet boughs, nearly tumbling down when his backpack caught on a branch. The men were standing near the van, talking and laughing. At the window, he used the tips of his toes and wiggled the shutters apart, relieved to find that the windows inside were open. Ben heaved his backpack in and then swung his feet in, catching them on the windowsill, stood there, begging for balance, clinging to the tree with one hand, reaching for the roof with his left until he felt the shingles scrape against his fingertips. He let go and lunged forward. His feet went in and he sat so hard on the rough windowsill that he felt the entire structure shudder as he slid into the attic. His shirt tail caught on the wood and Ben tugged it free, thinking that Tom—who managed to hear the whispered fury of all his children—would have heard. Shaking and breathing hard, hoping Tom would come trotting up the steps or call to him from the ground under the apple tree, he slumped to the floor beneath the window and waited. And when he heard the men's voices—Doug's now among them—coming from the front of the house, he knew he had escaped salvation once again. He drew his knees to his chest, shuddering in bitterly confused disappointment.

Before his eyes adjusted to the darkness in the apple attic, he smelled the tart pungency of the apples stored below, smelled the tang of the onion and garlic ropes, the evergreen of rosemary and Laurie's fragrant, flowering herbs sheltered in the window beside Tom's workbench. He forced himself into action, shutting the windows, spreading out one of the spare sleeping bags, and building a makeshift barricade with whatever he could find—an old trunk, multi-roll packages of toilet paper, a box of books, two empty bushel baskets. Now he could lie down and be hidden in case the MacBrides and their guests came to jump on the trampoline.

He limped down the stairs and by the big square utility sink next to Laurie's potting bench, Ben stripped off his shirt and rinsed it. He ran cold water over his blood-soaked T shirt until the blood left only vague brown rings. It felt like hours standing there, his hands up to his elbows in cold water, peering at the dark murky liquid to try to see if he could get any more of the blood out. Then he wrung them out, trying to squeeze out every drop of liquid until his raw hands ached with numb cold. He took off his pants and rinsed the mud off the cuffs, wiping off the splatters with his hand, wondering about how to get his things from Porter Road. *I will never go back*, he vowed. Ben took his wet things back up to the apple attic and hung them on the back of the trunk by catching the fabric on the brass hinges, putting his shoes toe to toe behind Tom's file cabinet.

Shivering in his damp boxers, Ben crawled to the front part of the balcony hoping to be able to use the window there as a vague mirror so that he could figure out how to stop the bleeding. Squinting at his reflection, he saw movement at the corner of the porch and from outside came the sounds of many voices, then the screech of Joe's bagpipe. Grannie MacBride was seated in one of the porch chairs, brought to the edge of the garden and draped with quilts. Ben shivered in the chill draft that rolled off the little window, the sill open just a crack. "It is raining, this is insane!" she thundered. But Peter crouched beside her, adjusted a quilt around her shoulders, and pointed up. "No, look, Grannie, the stars are all out."

Ben looked too and then he noticed that along the edges of the meadow, candles and torches glowed and flickered like orange globes and the caught raindrops sparkled.

"Teams ready?" Tom called. It was then that he saw how everyone was paired, legs tied together as for a three-legged race. Peter was just adjusting the tie on his leg with Flip. Bonnie Jean was paired with a little red-haired boy, Tommy with another redhead. Laurie held Cara and beside her stood a red-haired woman who also held a baby. Ben saw Joe, his leg tied to a little dark-haired girl, hop over to Doug Davidson who stood with one arm encircling the waist of a spunky, athletic-looking woman three inches taller than Doug. With the other arm, he took Joe's bagpipe from him. "You win it for my little Annie, Joe."

"You bet," Joe grinned.

Tom's voice boomed above the commotion. "Just like last year, the flags hidden in the woods have clues to follow to get you to the candle with your name on it. You can only take the light with your name on it. Bring your clues and your lanterns back and stand them by the fire pit." Ben saw that they had made a pile of wood and bracken and that flags with names on them had been driven into the ground around it. "Be careful. Don't run with the fire." Ben almost smiled at the thought of Tom teaching his children to handle fire with care, and his heart lurched with painful longing. Together, Joe and Bonnie Jean looked up at the garage window, eyes searching, innocent, hopeful. But Tom captured their attention when he cupped his hands to his mouth and shouted, "Ready, Kevin?"

From the far edge of the woods, the answer boomed back. Grannie clapped her hands and the teams scattered, hopping and hobbling across the meadow. Ben crouched in the shadows of the window and watched the teams move in their hobbled gaits, fall, laughing as they made their way toward the flags beckoning white beyond the forest edge. His eyes followed their shouts, heard Joe cry out his, then saw him hoist Annie up with one arm so that her feet were off the ground. Holding her that way, he ran across the meadow, Annie shrieking with laughter.

Ben rested his head on his arm listening to the sounds of fun, enduring aching legs and a queasy stomach. He lifted his head after what he thought was a few seconds and saw that the fire was ringed with flickering lanterns made from little glass jars, and that the teams stood around the fire, each kid holding one. Joe and Annie, the winners, began the ceremony by reading from the paper tags tied to their lanterns. Annie read, "I'm thankful for my family and my dog, Muffin, and for God helping me win the spelling bee this year in Baltimore." The adults clapped and Grannie nodded at Joe. He read his little card and looked up to say, "I have so much I'm grateful for this year that I didn't have space to write it all down on this little card."

"I'll make them bigger next year, Joe," Laurie teased.

With a shy smile at her, he said, "But I'm really grateful for my family—everybody being here and Unca Doug helping out with basketball and Pete coming home for Thanksgiving, and especially for our new baby sister and for God bringing Mom through the pregnancy so well and all."

"You're t' read from your *card*, Joseph MacBride," his grandmother scolded.

"Let him speak," Tom said to his mother. "He won. He has the right to speak." Then to Joe, "Go ahead."

"And for my friends, especially Ben—" The color rising in his face, Joe said. "Ben's been a good friend and he's helped me not miss Pete so much and really made me think about a lot of things—"

"You've taken too much time. There's others waitin'—"

"Mother," Tom said sternly as Laurie bent to whisper to the old woman, who shut her mouth and pulled the quilts close around her neck.

Joe looked around and meeting his father's eyes said, "I wanted to say how grateful I am to God for working in my heart like he's been doing. It's hard to explain how that happens but," Joe tapped his chest over his heart, "it's important to me." Tom nodded appreciatively and Joe, visibly moved, pressed his lips together and glanced up at the apple attic with shining eyes.

So it went around the fire, every MacBride and every guest giving thanks. And when everyone had spoken, Joe and Annie tipped their candles into the wood and lit the bonfire. The others came forward in unison and toward the wood held their flickering lights. The fire caught in sections, the edges burning like flares on the rim of a dormant sun. Together they took breath, cupped hands, and whistled as if calling the fire up; it roared to life and the circled friends stepped back laughing, their faces glowing orange-gold, their wondering eyes bright.

After Major Nels Lindquist promised his wife he'd walk over to the Hunters' quarters, she began to calm down. He sat with her during the heaviest part of the rain, trying to come up with one acceptable explanation for what she'd seen. So it was late when he smoothed out his uniform, took his cover, and left his quarters to walk across the Yard. The rain had cleared and Nels looked up as he walked, wishing on all of the familiar, blinking stars.

Avoiding puddles, he took the alley to the back of Hunter's quarters and went up the sidewalk beside the garage just as Nancy said she had done. He found the house still but for a light that illumined the kitchen brightly enough that he could see the empty table and chairs in the middle of the room; one light also burned on the third floor. He tried to imagine what his wife had described for him, tried to imagine one of his own sons shouting at him and running from the house obviously hurt, and he, Nels, *not* running after him. He pictured it all as he stared with his one good eye at Hunter's back porch. If that had been his house, and his son, he'd rush out the door after him. If the kid kept running, he'd run after him. He'd tackle him and carry him back in—he'd do what ever he had to. It was too important.

Nels Lindquist had faced the enemy and rescued several of his men, he had faced disfiguring, frightening injury and had turned this into a party asset. When he'd gotten sick of people staring at his glass eye that just didn't quite match his live one, he had a party eye made for him with a bright red iris and the Marine Corps globe and anchor where the pupil should have been. The thing was so stunning he was often invited to parties just to show off his eye. Yes, Nels had faced loneliness and forced himself to talk to Nancy when he only knew her as the busy, kind-faced woman who had lived in the apartment three doors down from him and found out that she had so many interests that life became suddenly multicolored. He'd faced bureaucracy and prejudice in the closed-minded, if well-meaning, superior officers who thought a war hero like him couldn't do his job with only one eye. And now, if things kept going well, if exposing Hunter's problem didn't mess things up, he'd have his military retirement in a few years instead of disability pay. Nels took a deep breath and decided he'd expect good to come out of even something as unusual and risky as his confronting a superior officer. Just like always, he'd go with his gut and expect the best.

Though he saw no movement, Nels dared to step up the slick, wet stairs. Once on the landing, he saw that the kitchen stood empty. Stepping under the little metal awning that sheltered the back door, he put his hand over his brow and leaned close to the glass. Nels searched the darkened depths of the Hunters' quarters. Beyond the kitchen, past the dining room, he recognized Max sprawled on the living room sofa. But when he backed down, trying to descend the steps without making noise, he saw what looked like blood on the threshold.

He did not hurry the short distance to Johnson's quarters but lingered in the starlight thinking about Max whose story was not unlike Nels' own. Due to some misunderstanding having to do with his personal life, Max had gotten a bad fitness report for his duty on the USS Kennedy. He was assigned to Twentynine Palms to encourage him to resign his commission, but the accident there that broke both his legs had been the fault of the Marine Corps. Like Max, Nels had used the Corps' logic against them. They'd awarded him the Navy Star for bravery because he'd rescued those men *after* he'd been wounded—ignoring his own pain, finding his way with only one eye. After all that, he argued, how could they then say he was incapable of performing every day Marine Corps tasks with one eye? So they had paid for his education to sort of compensate him.

Once they did this, Nels applied for an officer's commission arguing that they must have believed him capable of serving if they paid for his education. Likewise Max used the Corps' own liability for his accident to finagle a great assignment recruiting in Hawaii. He did so well there that those who opposed his further promotion had the recruitment numbers waved in their faces and Max had the first of his scheduled promotions. But Max was his commanding officer and what Nels had to do now was not going to be fun.

Muttering to himself, "Can't be easy living with Max. Man drinks like a fish. You know that. You've seen it. You shoulda done more."

He wondered how loudly he had been scolding himself because the admiral opened the front door of his house before Nels had reached the top step.

"Admiral, sir."

"I saw you coming, Major Lindquist. You caught my eye, stomping along the sidewalk like some kind of madman."

"Yes, sir. I—" Nels saw the bustle of young adults and younger children in the big, bright house behind him. "May I see you very early tomorrow morning, sir? Before your company is awake? I don't want to take you away from your family."

"Nonsense," Johnson bellowed. "You'll come in right now. We'll talk in my office. These hooligans got to get to bed. The hour is late! And Grandpaw is tired!"

50

WHEN he woke up, Max was so uncomfortable that he thought his arm was still in the cast. Instead, he found himself sprawled on the sofa, his arm asleep under his body. He saw one light burning over the kitchen sink. Struggling to sit up, Max stared uncomprehending at the fat leather book he clutched in unfeeling fingers. He flung it onto the coffee table and sat up. Beneath his wrinkled uniform, his shorts and T-shirt were damp with sweat and shoved askew in lumpy wrinkles.

He found his legs unsteady as he mounted the steps to his bedroom and when a hot shower did not clear his mind, when the simple task of dressing made his temples pound, he made his way again to the kitchen, found a bag of pretzels and, disgusted with how bad he felt, just took the whole bottle of Jim Beam with him to the living room sofa. A handful of pretzels and two swigs later, he heard heavy footsteps on the stairs. *Who the hell could that be?*

His mother's voice broke the dark silence of the house. "Is Ben home?"

"The last thing I expected was to hear *you* clump down the stairs."

"But...earlier?" She stood three steps from the foyer now, bending over the banister, peering at him with a cautious, slightly disgusted expression. "You've started drinking again *already*?"

"Did you come all the way down from New Jersey to bitch at me?"

"I came down for Thanksgiving. Do you even know what *day* it is?"

"Yes, Mom. I know what day it is."

"Your boss called. He wanted to know if everything was okay since you missed some religious service. Max, really. I couldn't tell him you were passed out on the sofa. I'd think you'd make an effort on holidays, for the boys' sake."

"When did he call?"

"The boys refused to come down for dinner. And I can't blame them. Who wants to eat when their father is in a drunken stupor? What do they normally eat, Max? Keith said they like to have cereal for dinner."

Sitting up, forgetting his sullen cloak, Max said. "What did you tell him?"

"I told him they should have some meat for dinner."

"Not Keith. Admiral Johnson."

"Don't worry about it, Max."

"You covered for me, right, Mom?" Max looked at her, disgusted to see that she had a pack of cigarettes and a lighter in her hand. He grabbed his bottle and took one long pull. Making an unsuccessful effort to be quiet, she walked across the foyer and out on the front porch. Through the window that flanked the front door, Max watched her lighter flare, watched the red glow of her cigarette brighten as she puffed on it. She would come back in stinking of smoke, which he had never been able to stand without a lingering nausea.

He took another drink just to calm himself down. When he put the bottle on the table, he reached for the bag of pretzels and noticed Katie's journal just lying in plain sight on his very own coffee table. For a moment, he couldn't move. His heart pounded in his throat; his fingertips tingled with shocked desire. Then, he lunged for it, remembering that he had demanded his mother get it for him. A ripple of exhilaration warmed him from his scalp to his toes: he now had the last possible proof and could keep it from Ben. But when he touched it, when his fingers touched the smooth soft leather, he shuddered.

What would their lives be like today if Katie had not written everything in this damned book? He took it in hand, held it and thumbed the pages, breathing in deeply, and a thousand images rushed through his mind—Katie on that snowy night when he'd first convinced her to date him. Later, she had read her account of it to him. She had loved him so fiercely then.

Max held the leather to his lips. How could the book still carry the scent of her perfume powerfully enough after sixteen years to overcome the scent of the leather binding, the stink of the newspaper clippings she taped inside. He could even smell the graphite of her pencil tinged with that sweet provocative scent that would always mean love and betrayal to Max. Tears flooded his eyes. The front door opened behind him and after he startled, he held the book with feigned casual interest, again thumbing the pages.

"Don't come near me, Mom. You know I can't stand the smell of smoke."

Standing obediently in the foyer, she called, "Shouldn't Ben be home by now?"

"What time is it?"

"Quarter past one."

"He's fine. He's probably got some hot date."

"No, Max. You remember how he left here. He was upset."

"How'd you upset him, Mom?"

"For *pity's sake*, Max. Isn't there some way to check on where he might be?"

"He'll be fine."

"He may have been hurt. There was blood on the floor."

Max glanced at her and then stared at Katie's journal, holding it with both hands, remembering as if recalling a dream that he had kicked Ben. But that wouldn't make a kid bleed, Max thought, puzzling until he remembered slapping Ben's face. He remembered the blow in some odd, sensory memory that stung the palm of his right hand. "So, you think he's pissed at me and is driving around somewhere sulking? That doesn't bother me, Mom. If I slapped him, he won't be such a smart ass know-it-all next time."

"He wasn't smart with you." Ella gave a snort that annoyed Max. "How much do you remember?"

"Go to bed! The smoke is makin' me sick."

When she stepped heavily upon the second floor landing above, he took one of the rubber bands that held Katie's journal between thumb and forefinger. His hand trembled. He thought better of opening it and instead bent down the back cover, revealing the last pages written.

I'm expecting Max to arrive from the airport some time this morning. His CO ordered him home on emergency leave, which perfectly expresses the state of our relationship. Tom wants to be here, drives up every weekend to do what he can for the baby and me, but Max has to be ordered home.

But for the sake of my newfound faith, for the sake of my little son, I'm determined to forge a peace where we can at least speak. I can feel Max's anger as if it were a hot coal in my hand.

I asked Tom to bring the baby, already fed, to the hospital for when Max gets here. Max will be furious that Laurie and Tom have been so involved. But really, they have been so kind, especially considering Tom's impossibly awkward position in all this.

...This is poorly written, but remember, dear diary, I have been terribly ill.

That was how Katie wrote, that was how her diary read, just like that. He could see her and feel her and smell her and Max's eyes blurred with pulsing tears. *Nothing,* he thought, throwing the book down on the coffee table, *I've had nothing from Katie for sixteen years.* Tears streamed down his cheeks so fast that they dripped onto his chest. Max sobbed into the stiff pillow kept at the arm of the sofa. He cried so hard that he could hear his wailing echo off the high ceiling. Sniffing, chest heaving, he lifted his face from the wet pillow, then used it to wipe his nose. Upstairs he heard his mother's heavy tread come to the edge of the third floor stairs.

"Max, darling," she called to him. "Is everything all right down there? Is Ben home?"

"Go to bed, Mom," he shouted to her and muttered, "Things're so fucked up." He finally understood why people kept stuff even after the relationship was over. It brought the person back. You could remember how they sounded, how they phrased things, how they were. You thought you remembered, you thought you had them still in your mind, but with some of their stuff right in your hand, you realized. "Things been so messed up for so long." He noticed a piece of newspaper sticking out at the back of the diary. Carefully, as if it were hot, he took the book in hand again, peeked in at the piece of newspaper. Held in place by a bit of yellowed tape, the top third of the article had been torn off crookedly, leaving a fragment of the headline above three columns of print. He read:

> Captain Hunter, a Hillside native and a 1971 graduate of NHRHS, home on emergency leave from duty on the USS Kennedy, was driving the 1977 Volvo station wagon when the brakes failed to function on the wet street and he was unable to stop at the red light.

It told the story of the accident, he realized, and the words seemed sharply clear to Max. Who would have taped that in there? Probably his mother, he thought, knowing her obsession with newspapers. If Ella Hunter saw it in the newspaper, it was true and you couldn't argue with her about it. He stared at the bold print, the crisp authoritative columns. He had not been aware of this article's existence, back then, he had been aware of nothing but his confused fury.

His eyes scanned the article to see what it said about his guilt. Frantically, wanting assurance but forbidding the memory to form in his mind, unwilling to relive what he'd done that day, Max searched the facts listed in the article and shuddered in relief. Nothing about the moments before they crashed.

Physical relief washed across his senses, a grateful flush of heat to his chest and throat, a tingling all down his arms to his fingers that was so intense it almost itched. *Of course*, he told himself, *it couldn't be in there. No one knows about it or*—he stopped his mind, forcing himself to rehearse his defensive litany that gave justification for an act even his mother had said no one would ever forgive.

But if people knew what he'd been through. He had been crazy with jealousy after what he'd read in Katie's diary. His mother and Katie's aunt brought the baby to her hospital room not long after the taxi had dropped him off from the airport. While they were monopolizing Katie and going nuts over the baby, he had peeked into her diary. Any man would be furious at the way Tom MacBride had weaseled his way into his wife's heart. The way Katie told it there in the hospital room, she "owed everything" to Tom.

Max pressed his fingers to his eyeballs; he grabbed his bottle and drank deeply the scent and flavor. The smooth bite of the liquor distracted him. Max got up the courage to touch the torn edge of the headline with one trembling finger. Taping this here was his mother's way of verifying the story he'd contrived in the moments before the police arrived at the accident scene, in those furious, insane moments when Ella had chanted in broken sobs, "You're despicable! No one will forgive you. No one. Ever, ever, ever..." Ben's outrage sounded above the approaching sirens. Then the two of them saw Tom MacBride take the wet and squalling Ben to Katie.

From across the street Max and Ella watched Tom hold Ben close to Katie's cheek. Though Ella was grunting in a voice horrible in its knowledge and accusations, Max clung to her. Though her appalled evaluation of his actions frightened him, Max clutched at her flailing arms as if calming her hysterical gestures could wipe out what he had done. But neither of them stepped off the curb, both of them knowing that Max had thrown away any right either of them had to so much as approach Katie and Ben.

Max put Katie's diary on the glass coffee table and took his bottle in hand remembering with some satisfaction that the police had seen the events of the accident differently. The paramedics scolded Tom MacBride for picking the baby up saying that if he were paralyzed from the accident, it would be because Tom had moved him. The claim was absurd—Ben had been kicking with fury, his baby fists clenched, startled open, clenched again, as he bellowed his unfathomable testimony and showed a condition so far from paralysis that Max had taken hope in the blindness of the officials that controlled his fate.

It had cleared Max's mind. And when Tom's fervent and logical defense—that he'd picked the baby up because he was in danger of sinking under—met with the medics' scorn, Max exulted. Tom's defense, which was obviously true, was dismissed with the callous wave of the professional's hand and Max remembered thinking that the spin of the earth had changed in that horrible moment of the accident and *Tom*, whose fault all of this was anyway, would now suffer the judgment and derision of the powerful in Max's rightful place.

That was the last moment that Max had let the guilt hurt him. He had decided that he, the misunderstood and cuckolded Max Hunter, was being given another chance and so he took it. He grabbed his mother's arm and begged her to lie to the police. And Ella's reflexive ability to blow a thick, protective smoke screen up for Max had risen up like a filthy phoenix from her fiery vows to despise him forever.

Now Max tried to muster up the smug feeling he always enjoyed when his mother scrambled to make him happy and comfortable, but he felt oddly naked in front of Katie's diary, its truthful presence judging him. Max grabbed his bottle for a deep swill of whiskey and when his throat and stomach were still burning from its power, he spoke to Katie in his imagination. *You got no right to make me feel bad. I've supported him all these years. I didn't have to do that.*

But he knew it wasn't true. His mother paid for Ben's clothes, and really everything he needed. And now, she footed the bill for his tuition and she'd helped him buy a car. Max knew that this was because she never wanted Max to feel, even for a moment, that Ben was a burden.

But he did give Ben shelter—nice places to live—and food to eat. That was true and Max leaned back, wobbling the bottle back and forth in a moment of satisfaction that faded too quickly. He could still recall the stinging feeling in his palm. He had slapped Ben. Had he slapped him hard enough to draw blood? Tears sprang to his eyes as a fist-like grip twisted his stomach with the certain and inexorable knowledge that he had been a cruel father. Katie's scream echoed from the accident down the years and now it accused him: *You've hated Ben. Let him go. You have not loved him.* Because of one slap to the cheek? The memory of Katie's scream brought back those last moments in the car. They flashed in his mind like court's evidence.

"No!" he cried, reaching out as if to stop the memory from coming clear, his hands convulsing so that—he didn't mean to—the bottle slipped out of his hand and bounced so hard on the coffee table that it shattered the thick glass top, then it fell onto the plush carpet spilling the scant contents of its fire in fragrant, gold droplets.

51

GRIPPED by one of his recurring dreams in which muddy brown water rose around him, filling his ears, lapping up over his face, flooding up his nose, he was startled from the dream's grip by the sound of the wind. Ben gasped in air, tried to move, felt confused by the scents around him. His left leg was asleep under him. Had he been sleeping sitting up? His body was stiff and pulsing with pain. His ear and head throbbed, making him remember his beating, making him remember where he was. Frustrated with himself, Ben took his journal onto his knees; he had never slept after a beating until he had written about it. The last thing he remembered was growing warm and the words, "Find me in the river," sung in Bonnie Jean's clear voice. He had meant to close his eyes just for a minute.

Ben pulled the sleeping bag up around his shoulders and started to record his father's violence, his grandmother's betrayal. But writing about it made him sick, and his sore places hurt so badly that he wrote only this:

> Gran watched Dad beat me up. When I got away and he was standing there in a drunken stupor looking at that stupid book he wanted, she tried to defend him. After she saw it. How can this have happened? How am I going to explain that not only does my dad hit me and my mother want me to lie about it or she'll kill herself, but my grandmother—who I thought loved me—knows and doesn't care?

The lights from the house darkened. Ben crawled to the window and saw into the dim rooms where Tom banked the glowing bars of the kitchen fire. He watched Tom cross the family room, shut off the light and mount the stairs that now stood in the same shade of darkness that hid him in the apple attic. Ben looked up just as the light in Joe's room flicked off and then he saw Joe standing at his bedroom window squinting into the darkness. For an instant, Ben feared that their eyes met and he ducked down. Sitting at the top of the attic stairs, wrapped in the blood-spotted sleeping bag, Ben watched an hour pass on his watch.

He found the kitchen door unlocked. Entering silently, Ben went into the pantry and in the half-light he found a laundry basket with clean, folded clothes. Quickly he changed into dry boxers and thrust his into the hamper where he knew they'd be lost with the other boys' things. Feeling his way into the depths of the pantry, Ben found a plastic bag. Into it he thrust a couple of clean T-shirts, a pair of Joe's sweat pants and clean socks, shivering at the thought of such luxury. Ben tried to remember in what section of the vast and plentiful pantry Tom stored the Band-Aids and turned to one of the shelf coves beside the laundry area. Behind him something swooshed; he froze. Joe said, "Ben. It's me and Jeannie."

Ben exhaled a trembling half-sob. "I'm trying to find a towel so I can wash up. I'm not dressed."

They came to him in the darkness both reaching for him, touching his chest and stomach as if to make sure he was real before encircling his shoulders each with an outstretched hand. "What's wrong? Why were you hiding from us?"

"Your dad can't know I'm here."

"Why not?"

"Promise you won't tell him," Ben demanded angrily, "or I have to go."

Joe and Bonnie Jean stepped closer. "Why?" Joe said. Bonnie Jean whispered, "Why can't he know? He loves you." Ben shivered in their embrace; his forehead pounded.

"He won't believe me. He'll make me go back," he choked on the words. "And I can't. I hate it there."

"You're ice cold," Bonnie Jean said, her warm hand rubbing up and down his back.

"Are you bleeding?" Joe asked, sniffing as if he could smell the wound. Joe turned Ben a little toward the faint light that came from the pantry entrance and peered at his head. "I can't see."

"I hit my head. I need a Band-Aid."

"We've got to warm him up," Bonnie Jean said. "Feel his skin. It's like ice."

"You can use my shower," Joe said. "That will warm you up. Come on."

"No. Your parents might hear. I can't risk it," Ben said. "And if he catches us, you'll have to lie to him."

"Ben," Joe said, impatiently. "You're asking us to lie to him anyway."

"Just not to tell," Ben's voice went faint, his words muffled with the way his shaking rattled his teeth. "Please don't push me on this, Joe. Please."

Joe and Bonnie Jean met eyes.

"If Dad asks us," Bonnie Jean said, "we'll just tell him we can't answer the question."

"Yeah, that'll work," Joe drawled, taking Ben's elbow and pulling him toward the kitchen. "Let's try to get you warm. Then maybe you'll make more sense."

"I'll get towels from the dryer," Bonnie Jean said. "And a quilt."

The powder room off the kitchen was lit by a nightlight, and when Ben saw it he said he wanted to clean up by himself, but Joe and Bonnie Jean came into the room with him and commanded him to sit down on the toilet while they shut and locked the door. In the half-light Joe turned the hot water on at a soft trickle and Bonnie Jean took the first aid kit from the cabinet. When they turned to look at Ben, both MacBrides gasped aloud.

"Is that the light in here or are his lips really purple?"

"Blood everywhere," Joe murmured and flicked on the overhead light.

Bonnie Jean took a washcloth and dipped it in the hot water. "Are you cut anywhere else besides your head?"

"I don't think so."

"His mouth," Joe said.

"Yeah, maybe my mouth." They were silent, staring at him. Bonnie Jean snapped to action, wetting the cloth she held and began in a circular motion to wash the mud and blood from Ben's skin, instructing Joe to do the same. Ben sat stiffly, lips pressed together, squeezing his eyes shut.

"What happened to you?"

Ben startled at the question, his lips and hands shaking.

"Later, Joe," Bonnie Jean cautioned. "I think he might faint." As she whispered a gush of blood slid from Ben's head wound and splashed on his leg. Bonnie Jean grabbed a wad of toilet paper.

Joe moved the hair away to reveal the wound. "Look, Jeannie," he said, meeting her eyes again, mouth grim and tight. Bonnie Jean pressed the paper to the wound. "We've got to get his head to stop bleeding." Bonnie Jean took another clean washcloth and gently dabbed at the dried blood on Ben's face. Joe pushed blood-soaked clumps of hair apart. "All that blood…"

"Looks deep."

"I want to stick a Band-Aid on it," Ben murmured.

"You need stitches," Joe said. He stared at the cut, squinting, shaking his head. "I'd better wake Dad up."

"No."

"What do you mean? *Yes.*"

"If you wake him up, I'll run out of here. I mean it."

"Why? He loves you."

"There's stuff you don't know. If you try to tell him, I'm outta here."

"Then I'll take you to the ER myself," Joe said, angry now. "Come on, Jeannie, help me stand him up."

"No. I'm not going. My mom works there. I'm not going."

"She doesn't work in the ER."

"They'll *get* her. That's how it works."

"You can say you're me."

"Then they'll call *your* dad."

"When did this happen?" Bonnie Jean asked.

"I dunno. After the game."

"Six hours?" Joe growled. "We've got to go to the ER."

"*No!*"

"This is so stupid," Joe said. "Have you been in another car accident? Did he wreck your car?"

Ben thought about lying, thought of how the lie would work to his advantage, but Joe said, "No, that's not it. You wouldn't be so ashamed. And you need some real help. We should tell Dad." He went to put his hand on the doorknob but Ben's hand, trembling clumsily, reached for Joe's wrist and missed, knocking into Joe's elbow. Startled by his friend's weakness, Joe stopped, staring at him, heart pounding.

Bonnie Jean took Ben's hand between both of hers and rubbed. "Freezing and shaking," she took Joe's hand and made him feel the clammy chill of Ben's hand. A scant tear brightened Ben's left eye.

Seeing him weaken, Joe said sternly, "If you don't want to tell Dad, we should go get medical help *somewhere*."

"I want to. I can't."

"That doesn't make any sense, Ben. You're pissing me off."

"Can't you fix it, Joe?" Ben said. "Hold it shut with a Band-Aid."

"No! You're being an *idiot*."

"Joe, he's not thinking clearly."

"Right. So we're going to think for him. And I say we're going to the ER."

"Say that again and I'll leave," Ben whispered, furious.

"You can't even stand up," Joe said.

"You watch me."

"Shut up," Joe said. "Why are you being so stupid? You need a doctor. It's been bleeding for six *hours*, Ben."

"Things happened…it's worse…I can't talk about," Ben said, eyes a dull blaze of blue.

"It won't stop bleeding without stitches."

"You do it…you stitch me up, Joe," Ben said.

"No," Joe said, his anger now edged with fear. They stared at each other, the three of them, their breathing harsh, their heartbeats pounding in their ears. Bonnie Jean said, "I think you should do it, Joe. Stitch it closed."

"No! Bonnie Jean, no! He's just being stubborn and we ought to tell Dad."

"Awful reason for not telling," Ben hesitated, voice fading. "Sorry, but…" Ben's eyelids fluttered as he struggled to stay conscious. "I can't. Don't make me leave."

"Stupid!" Joe said. "You're stupid. You're a stupid—"

"Shh!" Bonnie Jean squeezed between them. "We'll get him to talk later. And do the right thing *later*. Now, we've got to stop him bleeding and get him to stop shaking."

"This is so wrong." Joe shook his head in anguish.

"Mama's got that water-soluble thread. I'll get it. I'll make some tea, so if they hear, I can say I'm making tea. We'll use the steam to sterilize it and the needle and you take just one little stitch to close the wound."

"Me?"

"Yes. You can sew. You used to do all that basting for Mama's store."

"You can sew and I don't see *you* volunteering."

"I don't know if I can stand to—you know—" she shuddered, "pierce the skin. You can do it."

"Shit, Jeannie. We *can't.*"

"Joe, we've *got* to. Look at him. Something awful's happened—"

"Shit. Shit. *Shit.* Get him to put his head between his knees if he looks faint again. I'll put the kettle on."

Joe returned with scissors, a curved needle, and three kinds of thread. Bonnie Jean pointed to the thread he should use, but questioned his choice of needle. "It said 'for leather' and skin is kind of like leather, so that's what I'm using." He took these out to the kitchen, threaded the needle, got the teapot ready, and sank down into his father's chair. Putting his head on his folded arms, Joe prayed in a whisper. "Please don't let me harm him. Please help me find a way to tell Dad without betraying Ben. Dear Lord Jesus, I'm so freakin' caught in the middle here. Give me wisdom. Please." Beside him on the stove, the kettle clamored with steam. Joe made the tea, set it aside, washed his hands while he let the kettle steam softly. "Jeannie," he called in a hoarse whisper. She emerged soundlessly. "Won't this thread disintegrate in the steam?"

"You have to soak it for an hour to dissolve it."

Joe nodded. "You turn everything off and follow me to the bathroom. I just washed my hands."

In the bathroom, Bonnie Jean gave Ben one of the towels then took the bottle of peroxide in hand. Joe said, "It's going to hurt and you can't move or say anything."

Ben met his eyes in silent assent.

"Hold the towel up over your eyes. Pour it on slowly, Jeannie." They watched it foam, then Joe told her to blot it. When it was clear, in the moment before the blood began to fill in the open edges, Joe saw that he could close the wound with three small, slanted stitches and this understanding quelled his anxiety enough. "Don't move. This will hurt like hell." Quickly, Joe slid the sharp needle through the edge of the wound. He felt Ben tense and he heard the pained changes in Ben's breathing as something distant and less important now. He caught the edge of the skin opposite and pressed the needle through the skin. He glanced at Bonnie Jean. "You go under to knot it, right?" Biting her lip, she nodded, and when Joe hesitated, she took the thread ends and knotted them as Joe had seen their mother do in her intricate handwork. "Hold the ends up so I can cut the thread," he told her.

The next stitch at the point of the wound made Ben's breathing go shallow and Joe felt Ben's shaking turn violent. "Hold on, Ben," Joe said.

Stooping to be next to him, Bonnie Jean slid her hand and arm under the quilt along his shoulders. "Just one more stitch after this one," she whispered to Ben, her warm cheek against his. "You can handle that. You've got to, okay? Let's breathe together. Ready? One, two, three." Together the three drew in breath deeply.

The wound had filled with blood. His nostrils flaring with the live, metallic scent, Joe wanted to spit. Instead he held the towel to Ben's forehead with his forearm and dripped on the peroxide to rinse the wound. Ben shuddered. Bonnie Jean tightened her arms around him. "Breathe with me," she whispered. She counted softly, and when Ben exhaled, Joe poked through the torn skin. Worried that he would pull too hard and shred the edge, Joe took both ends of the thread in hand now and carefully pressed on the wound with his thumb while he slowly, smoothly drew the edges close. The skin was surprisingly tough and reluctant to move and he knew that the pressure was hurting Ben. "Okay. Hold on now. Hold onto Jeannie," Joe said, and coaxed it closed.

He knotted it, and quickly made the third stitch and knot. With one finger, Joe patted the wound and found it tight; by just pushing a little he made it flat, though globs of blood spilled up over the edges. Putting his tools down, Joe grabbed the towel, held it to Ben's forehead and dripped peroxide on the stitched wound. He dabbed away the foam, tossed the towel into the sink and glanced at Ben's face, disturbed to note that he had gone gray again, his arms dropped slack at his sides. "If he faints, I'm getting Mom and Dad. I don't care what he says."

Nodding in agreement, Bonnie Jean got up.

Ben leaned his head back against the wall, watching them with half-open eyes.

She grabbed the ointment and a tissue. "How did he *not* faint while you were stitching him up, Joe? I mean he barely moved. He didn't jump or pull away."

"He's strong," Joe said peering at Ben through worried, squinted eyes while Bonnie Jean squeezed some ointment onto the tissue and dabbed it onto Ben's wound.

"You're a hero," she whispered to her brother.

"No, I'm stupid." Joe groaned and they began to dress him as if he were a child, fitting on sweatpants and a T-shirt.

"Got to hide now." Conscious again, Ben tried to stand up and Joe helped him.

"Let's go upstairs. The beds are soft. It's warm."

"No."

"Why?" Joe said, keeping his voice light, hoping Ben was too weak to reason and resist. Ben shook his head, then winced in pain. "You're right.

There's no reason why." Joe took Ben's arm over his shoulder. "Let's go."

"I promised my mother I wouldn't."

"You hate them and you're keeping your promises to them?"

"I can't tell."

Eyes meeting, Joe and Bonnie Jean noted the despair in his voice.

Shaking his head, Joe murmured, "I'm so far stepped into your mess now, you'd think I'd understand your freakin' logic." Joe told Bonnie Jean, "I'll take him out there. You be quiet while you get stuff. Try to get everything you need in one trip. Bring a flashlight, too. Okay?"

52

IN the garage, Joe helped the stumbling Ben to the stairs. "I saw you; when I was going to bed, you were at the window."

"I was afraid you saw me."

"Good thing I did."

Upstairs they found Ben's sleeping bag damp. Joe put it across the top edge of the barricade, made a tent that blocked the view from the window facing the house. "We don't want them seeing the flashlight," he explained. Quickly he found more sleeping bags, opened one and spread it out flat before unrolling the other three. He told Ben to lie down on the middle one. Ben struggled to lower his stiff body down and by the time he lay flat, Bonnie Jean called Joe from below.

"Be right back. Don't move."

Quilts slung over her shoulders, pillows under her arms, Bonnie Jean balanced a big tray with tea things, a flashlight and a bottle of water. "That was quick," Joe said with admiration.

When Bonnie Jean set the tray down, it wobbled. She slid it over until it sat steady on the floor revealing Ben's journal, which had been open beneath. "What's this?" she said, picking it up.

"I write in it. To remember and think," Ben said.

She turned it over, looking at it, biting her lip. When Joe asked her to help, so slowly did she put the journal into Ben's backpack that Joe said, "Jeannie, come on. He's cold." Together they helped Ben onto his side, put a pillow under his head and bundled the quilts over him. They coaxed Ben to drink sips of sweet, milky tea, their mother's remedy for every trouble, until he shut his lips and despite Joe's scolding and Bonnie Jean's imaginative encouragement, he would take no more.

Joe got into his sleeping bag and sat up by Ben's head. "Get in yours," he told his sister, "and get close to his back. You can get him warmed up. I'm going to watch this head wound and make sure it doesn't start bleeding."

"He must be exhausted," she said as she stepped into her sleeping bag and pulled it up around her.

"I'll take the first hour's watch," Joe said. "You get some sleep."

Bonnie Jean lay down behind Ben and put one arm over him. "It's cold in here."

Ben murmured. "Are you staying?"

"I'm trying to warm you up." Bonnie Jean snuggled closer, hugging her arm around his shoulders, nuzzling her face into the back of Ben's neck.

"Jeannie," Ben said sleepily. Joe pulled the quilts up close to their chins, then tucked them around their feet.

"You were awesome in there, Joe," she whispered, tightening her arm across Ben's chest.

"Yeah, and I'm gonna catch hell for it. So are you."

"You were so awesome," she repeated, her face serene, her eyes shutting. "Breathe with me, Ben," she whispered, and counted. In moments they both slept, leaving Joe with thoughts he wished to avoid. In a slow rhythm, tapping on his forearm, he counted to one hundred fifteen times, then switched on the flashlight and checked Ben's wound, wishing he could get his mother to look at it, wanting to go knock on their door. The blood flow had stopped; the wound looked neat and the edges seemed quiet, somehow. But Ben's ear showed puffy purple places and there was a discoloring on his jaw below. He wished Bonnie Jean would awaken and talk to him and he shined the flashlight on her hoping to wake her, but instead she shifted closer to Ben and burrowed her face into his shoulder. In a familiar and instinctual way, Ben sighed. Joe wondered how long it had been since his friend had slept well.

When dawn crept across the meadow frosting the low mown grass and touching the garage windows with a cold, white light, Joe awoke with a start. He shook Bonnie Jean. "Better go in. Dad'll be up soon."

She sat up and rubbed her face. "Didn't you sleep?"

"A little. The bleeding's stopped." He shone the light on Ben's head to show her.

Working to get her eyes open, she peered at Ben's wound. "Good work, big brother. It looks totally put back together."

"We have to watch for infection."

"Can you get arrested for stitching him up?" she said, wincing as she spoke.

"This is a *great* time to ask that question," Joe said, "after I've done it—after you *encouraged* me."

"Helped you, actually."

"Shit, shit, double *shit*."

"We had to."

"No, Jeannie, we should've found a way to tell Dad."

"We have to get *him* to tell Dad he's here," she said.

"I won't tell," Ben said, opening his eyes, fully awake.

"What makes you so crazy stubborn?" she said, exasperated.

"I just need a place to stay for a—"

"For the rest of your life," Joe said. "So tell them that and they'll take you in."

"I can't. I told you." He labored to sit up; succeeding only with Joe's help. He pulled his knees up to his chest, and groaning with pain and exasperation, rested his cheek on his knees.

"All you have to do is tell them he hit you and you won't *have* to explain."

Ben looked up. "What makes you think—that?"

"What?" Joe said, the challenge brightening his voice.

"What you said."

"Come *on*. You come over here to *hide*. You've got bruises on your legs, on your chest, your shoulder—"

"Basketball."

"Basketball, my ass. Don't give me that *shit*. The inside of your *mouth* is cut up. That didn't happen at basketball. You were *laughing* when we left the gym. Laughing. Then you come here totally broken. You drooled blood all night long, Ben." Joe gestured at the pillow Jeannie had brought him, now stained with watery red-brown rings. "Somebody beat you up and they beat you up bad."

Ben shook his head again. "I fell with my grandmother's suitcase. It landed on my legs. And I hit my head on the kitchen cabinet."

"Yeah, I know that's *part* of what happened. I know the code, now. But *you* don't just fall. You're the most coordinated person on earth. He hit you to *make* you fall. Or something like that." Ben met Joe's intense gray eyes. Joe said, "I know. Okay?" He jerked his thumb at Bonnie Jean. "She knows, too. We know."

Bonnie Jean nodded at him, tears standing in her eyes.

He needed them, but shame washed over him with its isolating feeling. Ben hid his face in the crook of his elbow. "I told you I was messed up."

"It's not you!" she vowed. "This shouldn't be happening. It's wrong."

"There has to be some reason why."

"That's bullshit," Bonnie Jean said. "Right, Joe?"

"Yeah. The way I see it, your dad is a freakin' bully."

"We don't want you to go through this any more," she touched his shoulder and he picked up his head to meet her eyes.

"Then let me hide here. No one has to tell anybody anything until I figure out what I'm supposed to do."

"We can't hide you forever," Bonnie Jean cried. "You're asking too much," She shoved her sleeping bag aside and stood up.

"No," Ben shot back, "*You're* asking too much!"

She looked back, furious. "If somebody was hurting *me,* you'd tell. You'd do anything to help me. Or Joe. Or any of us. "

"There's reasons. Reasons I can't talk about."

"Screw your reasons."

"Shh, Jeannie," Joe cautioned. He said to Ben. "She's right, man. She's totally right."

"Anyway, I've tried to tell. No one believes me."

"We do."

"Adults don't. They cover for each other. I told Gran and she didn't believe me."

Bonnie Jean's eyes went wide and sympathetic, she took a step toward him. "She tried to defend him," Ben said, his voice as taut as his frame. Bonnie Jean hesitated, then sank to her knees beside him and her hand touched his shoulder. "She tries to excuse him. His drinking, everything."

"Sick," Joe said. "Sounds like they're all a bunch of sick bastards."

"I'm so sorry," Bonnie Jean said.

"Can you imagine saying something like that out loud—finally getting the *balls* to say it out loud—and them not caring? Think about what it does to you inside." Ben gestured, moving his hand in a circle to indicate his turmoil. "That was last year. I've been dealing with that since last year. And then she's *there* last night, she *sees* it and—" he shook his head.

The MacBrides exchanged glances and Bonnie Jean said, her voice too bright, "But that's just one person, Ben. Other people will—"

"No. All I hear from your dad is—honor your father, respect your father, obey your freakin' father. If I tell him, he'll send me back there."

"But he's assuming your father is normal. He doesn't know—"

"He *knows* my father. Remember? My father *broke* his *back*—with violence, in a fight—and he *forgives*. You heard him say he doesn't even want me to say he's a jerk. And that doesn't begin to touch it. I can't go back. I can't talk and I can't forgive him. There's no way out for me."

"He's shaking again," Bonnie Jean said, meeting Joe's eyes. Together they pulled a quilt around Ben's shoulders and both knelt beside him.

"You don't understand," Ben murmured. "There's so much shit."

Joe thumped Ben's shoulder with a gentle fist. "Hey. We're listening." But he shook his head again and hid his face in his arm. Joe and Bonnie Jean inched closer, both of them hugging Ben with both arms. "We're not letting you go," Joe said.

"We're never letting go," Bonnie Jean echoed.

Ben shook his head in helpless frustration.

Joe gave an exhausted sigh and whispered to his sister, "Think of something."

She studied Ben, her eyes resting briefly on the bit of his face that he had not successfully hidden, on his red, puffy ear. "We could pray."

"Right," Joe said. "We've lied to our parents—basically—and we took Ben's health into our own hands *knowing* we shouldn't have and now we're just going to *pray* like we deserve God to hear us."

Bonnie Jean shrugged her shoulder. "We need help."

Joe sighed aloud. They inched closer to Ben, closed their eyes. "Lord, I know you're probably tired of me messing up and maybe even in a righteous way pretty pissed off at me right now. I got that feeling last night when it seemed like you were keeping me company when I was sitting there waiting to see if the stitches were good. I know you probably didn't want me to stitch Ben up, but I did it. I know you probably wanted me to run upstairs and tell my parents and I didn't. Jeannie, too. But...Lord, really, we *need you* to help Ben anyway. And us. He doesn't want to tell and he's been through too much and we don't know what to do..."

"Please God," Bonnie Jean prayed, "heal Ben inside and out. Help him to talk to us. Help him to trust us and you." And they continued to whisper their hearts' burdens until they noticed that it had grown lighter in the attic. Bonnie Jean lifted her head, stared out the window as she touched the hair at the back of Ben's neck lightly with her fingers. "It's morning now."

"You guys were here all night," Ben murmured, his gratitude showing in his eyes and the way he tensed his jaw.

"Yeah," Joe said. "We're in this together. Us three."

"'A threefold cord is not quickly broken,'" Bonnie Jean quoted.

"But Jeannie," Joe said, "you'd better get going. They'll never believe you were up this early." He stood up, and reluctantly she followed and turned to go but Ben had begun to shake and she stopped at the barricade with a despairing glance at her brother. "Go," Joe said. "I'll bundle him up."

She left quickly then, and before she had reached the ground floor, Joe had smoothed out both his and Bonnie Jean's sleeping bags. He told Ben to get in his and lie down on the others for extra comfort and warmth. Slowed by his quaking limbs, Ben crept into the makeshift bed. Joe layered on two quilts and tucked another around Ben's feet. Still Ben shook with an unnatural violence.

Joe squatted beside him. He touched Ben's forehead. "No fever. You're cold." He rubbed Ben's shoulders and the shaking slowed. "What hurts the most?"

"Inside."

"I didn't even *think about* internal bleeding," Joe worried aloud.

"Internal *meanings*." Ben's angry laugh initiated a big yawn.

"Okay, Emily Dickinson," Joe laughed, miserably. "When's the last time you ate anything?"

"Lunch."

"Shit, Ben. Nothing after the game?"

Ben shook his head.

Joe said, "I'll be back with some food as soon as I can, so don't run away, okay?"

"I have no place to go. You know that."

53

JOE MacBride went into the laundry room, silent as a cat. He put the bloody cloths and towels in the washer and bundled in Ben's soiled clothes, remembering as an afterthought to empty Ben's pockets. Pulling the trousers back out, he pulled out Ben's keys, a slip of paper with writing on it, a ten-dollar bill and a scrap of newspaper. Tossing the newspaper scrap into the little waste paper basket where his mother discarded clumps of dryer lint, he put the keys, the paper and money into the flimsy pocket of his shorts before setting the laundry to wash. Joe put on socks, found his running shoes underneath his gym bag and put them on. He took a bottle of water, drank half of it, and taking it in hand, slipped out the back door, ran down the driveway and along the street, Ben's keys jingling and thumping in his pocket like the rattle of a chain.

Joe ran and his stomach twisted as he thought of the way Ben ran to beat his anxiety and the reasons for Ben's anxiety that were now too vivid. When he breathed, the smell of Ben's bleeding wound seemed fresh and made him remember the dark ooze, the foaming peroxide, his certainty that he had to help Ben, tainted by the desire to call upstairs to his parents, the knowledge that he really should tell.

"Don't I have to keep his confidence?" Joe murmured aloud as he ran, the sound of his own voice startling him so much that he splashed into a cold, muddy puddle, the chill water splashing up his legs, all the way up his stomach. His mind's eye saw again how dirty Ben had been surely from his run in the dark rain last night. Joe ran and ran, going over the way he'd made the stitches, feeling again the pressure of the needle against Ben's wounded flesh, the tension as he pulled thread through his friend's bleeding skin, and his stomach soured at the thought that he might have infected Ben's wound with germs in the makeshift ER that the bathroom had become in the middle of the confused night. *Mom and Dad are gonna be so pissed*, he told himself.

He had run so far, he found himself standing in front of his Uncle Doug's house, still silent, curtains drawn. Joe bent one knee up to his chest, stretching. *Uncle Doug would be sympathetic; he'd be nice to me, but he can't keep a secret. Especially not from Dad.* Stretching his other leg, Joe considered if that might be the best strategy. Tell Uncle Doug knowing he'd tell Dad. That way Ben wouldn't have broken his promise to his corrupted parents and Ben could get away.

Joe wished his uncle Doug would sense his need and wake up. He waited, praying, until a neighbor opened his back door to let out the dog. He turned and sprinted for home. His heart cried out with a silent yearning, and he prayed distraught and penitent prayers all along the quiet streets now silver slick in the chill November dawn. He was walking by the time he got to his driveway and his stomach felt filled with salt water. Joe rushed past the garage, made his way down to the river and sat on the pebbled beach there, his head on his knees, his stomach gradually calming as the still and silver morning river lapped against his toes in a rhythm as gently familiar as the cadence of his father's voice when he read at bedtime.

As she measured the oatmeal into the big pot, Laurie MacBride thought she certainly did not know *everything* that was going on, but she knew that Joe and Bonnie Jean had spent the night in the apple attic. She had been thirsty when she had risen to feed the baby and checked on the children on her way to the kitchen. Their beds had been empty. Downstairs, the washing machine was running and her everyday teapot, the big tea tray, and all the commonly used tea things were missing, so she'd fixed her early morning tea right in the mug to her slight dissatisfaction.

Now, she covered the oats with fresh clear water, tossed in a pinch of sea salt, and set them to simmer, imagining that Joe had convinced everyone to sleep in the apple attic and that only he and Bonnie Jean had lasted the night. But lack of a good night's sleep was nothing to be upset about and did not explain Joe's intense emotion when she saw him earlier. He had been sick to his stomach and close to tears, but when she had asked him what was wrong, he had given his head a brief shake and rushed from the room.

Taping her morning's task list to the cabinet above her work area, Laurie considered these things as she mixed the bread dough and found her thoughts turning to prayer. As was her custom, she lifted each family member in prayer as she kneaded the day's bread, praying for health, for spiritual life, for guidance, for character. Today she prayed for Joe, considering his turmoil, lifting him up in her heart's attitude, covering his hurting places she imagined with her whispered words in a way that felt as if she were in some mysterious way bundling him up against the cold, strengthening him as she did when she fed him, building his manly character as she had once joined with God to compose his body and his fine mind in secret, in faith, in hope before she had even seen his face or the mischievous sparkle in his blue eyes. And Joseph Spenser MacBride was even more than she had imagined.

Always she included Ben and Gregen and Marie in these prayers and always she lingered over Ben, her heart pulsing with the same creative energy and hope that she had known in praying for her own children. Laurie set the bread dough to rise in her biggest bowl, draped a damp tea towel over it, and went to the refrigerator to get the coffee cake dough rising there all night.

Ben is not even my child, she reflected forming the morning's coffee cake, *and I've prayed for him more consistently, more passionately, and more imaginatively than all my own children put together.*

After Joe and Bonnie Jean left him at dawn, Ben shivered again until he remembered to breathe deeply as Bonnie Jean had coached him to do. He ducked down under all the covers so that is head was fully submerged and soon he felt warmer and calmer and the next thing he knew he heard footsteps and startled awake.

"It's me, Pete. Bonnie Jean sent me up here. I've got your breakfast." Peter put a box that had been covered with a thick towel down by Ben's sleeping bag. "First things first."

Peter made Ben get up, walk down the steps, and use the toothbrush and washcloth he'd brought. "Let's stretch a little," Peter encouraged Ben, pulling some mats out from under the trampoline. "That hurt?" he asked Ben as they tried a few of the team's easier warm-up stretches. Ben nodded. "Keep that up, then. You got to work all the stiff places today while you're hiding, okay? Or you'll get weak and depressed."

Ben gave an ironic chuckle, but told Peter, "Thanks."

Peter stayed with Ben and made him eat some of the oatmeal, pouring a pool of cream and a heaping spoon of brown sugar. "According to my father," Peter assured him, "this will heal whatever's wrong."

"They told you, I guess."

"Yeah. And Tommy knows some of the story because the little twerp was listening with the baby's intercom set. He'll be quiet unless Joe makes him mad, then he might tell just to get Joe in trouble."

Ben nodded, finding the taste of the oatmeal warming. His stomach rumbled gratefully. Peter said, "When you're done eating, I'm going to go for a short run and take a shower outside. When you hear the shower running, go to the toilet room at the back behind the trampoline. There's a low window you should be able to get out of back there."

"I'll try."

"You can shower. I brought a towel and stuff," Peter gestured toward the box.

"They'll see me."

"No. I put the shower curtain up on the ring where it's supposed to be. If Mom notices it's up, she'll be thrilled. She's always nagging us to put it up. Anyway, come around the back way and get in the ring. I'll watch for you.

"You're all gonna get in big trouble," Ben moaned.

"Yeah," Peter said, "but we're in it together now. So, it's okay."

"I'll leave as soon as..." Ben couldn't think of what he was waiting for or where he would go.

"No. You stay. Where are you going to go? We'll make it work. We'll figure something out."

"I don't want to be responsible for—"

"Hey, Ben," Peter said, "Listen. Do you remember how I knew stuff about your grandmother's house? Like we were supposed to park in back and stuff? The weird thing is, I remember Mr. Bénet, too. I remember him sitting at the table with me at your grandmother's house. Why would he have been there? Why would *I* have been there?"

"They were all old friends until my dad tried to kill your dad. For some crazy reason, that broke them up."

Laughing at Ben's sarcasm, Peter shrugged, "Okay, I figure you've got about twenty-four hours before Mama gets the truth out of one of us. Or before she figures it out and comes up here to get you. So think about what you're going to say."

"Like what?"

"You could say that you and your dad argued and you wanted to get away and think. That part's true."

"I thought you MacBrides believed in telling the whole truth."

Peter shrugged uncomfortably this time. "Yeah, I do. Of course I do, but it's just that if Dad finds out what your dad's been doing to you, I know he'll go over there and kick the colonel's ass. If he does that, Ben, he might never walk again. Or..."

"Or?"

Peter met Ben's eyes. "I overheard him and Doug one time when I was little. It was about somebody who'd promised to beat Dad to death the next time he saw him. That's got to be your dad."

"Yeah," Ben agreed. "Doug sort of brought that up yesterday when he was yelling at Tom."

"And even if your dad didn't go into the fight with that goal—we just don't know what another break could do. People die from..."

Ben held up his hand and murmured, "Sickening." He bowed his head.

"We've got to keep you safe *and* keep them apart."

"So many good reasons to keep on lying," Ben said, thinking of the way he'd kept Donna's awful threat from his loyal and trusting friends.

Ella Hunter stepped back into the kitchen and waited for Lindquist and his wife to round the corner where their view to the Hunters' backyard would be blocked by the small garages there. Under the sink, she found the cloth she'd used to wipe up the floor last night, wet it anew with water and vinegar, and scrubbed at the spot of blood on the threshold. Had Lindquist known what it was? Why had his wife stared at it with that stunned expression?

She lumbered up the stairs and knocked on the master bedroom door. At the muffled sounds of protests, she opened the door.

"Max. Wake up."

"I could be buck naked in here and you just barge in." He rolled onto his back and worked to open his eyes. "Some friend of yours—Lindquist—stopped by. Says he has to talk to you. He asked about Ben and—"

"What's going on?" Donna sat up and swung her feet off the bed.

"Max. I think he's going to come back and you two need to be up this time. He asked for Ben and Ben's not even home."

"Where's Ben?" Donna and Max asked simultaneously. Max rubbed his face with both hands. "Thought for sure he'd stay home with you here."

"And I'm sure this Lindquist fellow saw the blood on the doorstep."

"What the *hell* are you talking about, Mom?"

But Donna was up, wrapping her robe around her. She gave her mother-in-law a stern glance and stepped into the adjoining bathroom. Scrubbing her teeth vigorously, she commanded Max to get up, her fear and frustration distinct if her words were not.

As she came into the bedroom, again she spoke to Max. When he did not immediately rise, she yanked the covers off him and pointed to the bathroom. "Shower! And don't you dare take one drink—or a *sip* of a drink—in case Nels comes back." Turning to her mother-in-law, hands on her hips, Donna said, "The coffee table top was smashed when I got home. Did the Lindquists see that?"

"I cleaned it up first thing." Ella watched her son, disheveled and middle-aged, stumble into the bathroom.

"What happened?" Donna demanded.

"I don't know how Max broke the table but he went after Ben and Ben ran out the back door. I guess the blood dripped when he was—" her voice trailed off, panic seizing her.

Donna grabbed her elbow and shook her. "Are you sure they saw blood?"

Nodding, Ella watched Max at the sink. Quick as a cat, Donna shut the bathroom door and leaned against it, her hand behind her back, still clutching the doorknob. When they heard the shower run, Donna said. "*What* happened?"

"Max was upset about," she grimaced, shrugging her shoulders, "a *book* he wanted me to bring him and I asked Ben to get it for me and they fought over it."

"Over a book? What book is this?"

"Just an old—" Ella waved her hand in a gesture of dismissal.

"Are you going to stand there and lie to my face?" Donna hissed. "What the hell book is it?"

"Just something of Katie's." She said it so quietly, her head ducked down to her chest, that Donna hesitated.

"Of *Katie's*?"

"Don't worry about it, dear. I'm sure he's quite over her now and—"

Donna held up one hand to silence her mother-in-law. "You let Ben touch something of Katie's? No wonder Max lost it!"

"I know. I should have foreseen this, Donna. I feel terrible."

"Good," Donna huffed, folding her arms tightly across her chest. "It's ridiculous to think we've been so careful all these years and then you just—"

"That's why I couldn't believe it when Max wanted it. I should have tried to dissuade him, of course, but he was so adamant."

Standing still as a statue, Donna stared at Ella for a long moment "He *asked* you to bring it? I thought he told you to destroy everything."

"Yes, well, so he did, but this I had to get from her people."

"Is it that *diary* of hers he's always obsessing about?" Donna's mouth tightened.

"I suppose that *could* be it," Ella lied. "But really, Ben had no interest in it. He was merely carrying it to me so I could give it to Max, and now he's been out all night. All night!"

For several seconds Donna did not answer, but her chin trembled. "That's typical for Ben. He's rarely home."

"But he left so upset and injured—"

"Did you see an injury?"

"Blood. *On the floor*. I didn't really look at Ben. I—I couldn't."

"Next time, grab his arm and *make him* stay."

"*Next* time?" Ella gasped, her hand going to her mouth.

54

GREGEN checked his watch to see that he had yet fifty minutes before he had to leave for the clinic. This would be enough time to start Ella's car for her as he had promised to do daily while she was away. Sliding the documents into a folder, Gregen tucked it beneath his arm and left the house quietly. Taking his keys from his pocket, he lighted the small flashlight on the key ring as he descended the stairs at the back of his garage that led to the restored Underground Railroad tunnel. The motion-sensitive lights did not start until the first step taken in the tunnel. Inside, the cool, earthy dampness gave its familiar scent as Gregen began the short walk to Ella's house. Since that day when he had overheard Max's cruel rudeness to her on the phone, his friendship with Ella had been suffering one of its periodic strains. These happened, Gregen reflected, when he was approaching some important gain in restoring his relationship with Ben and from experience, from careful thought and yearning prayer, Gregen knew how to endure the wait, treating Ella always with deference, comforting her when she came to him with crushed feelings, all the while hoping she would tire of her son's tyranny.

Taking care of her car when it hardly needed it during her four-day absence was one of the ways Gregen could apply the gentle assurance of friendship. When he came to the place in the tunnel where Ella had been keeping James' trunk, he lay down the folder and opened it, glancing at his notes. For the past few days he had carried this file with him, reading, re-reading, studying the already memorized details. He was tempted to pause and read everthing again as he had countless times in the past, puzzling over the facts anew, searching to settle his mind about the details of the accident. He had not been there the moment it happened. He had not been able to resolve a peculiar unrest that gnawed at his gut whenever he thought about the details every account of the accident described.

His hand hovered over the file, he held the first page of notes up to the light and then shook himself, and took his hand away. He would leave the file there and get it on his way back through the tunnel. Gregen unlocked the door that led to Ella's basement. As he emerged from the tunnel into her kitchen, Gregen glanced around. Was there anything else he could attend to while here? Ella kept no pets nor plants, the house was neat and quiet. Gregen resigned himself to his unnecessary duty wishing he could do more for Ella, supposing that she had never recovered from her car not starting the day that Ben had been born. Too bad it had started that terrible day a month later when Max finally decided to come home to see his son.

In the garage, Gregen opened the door to Ella's car and as always when he drove her car after she had driven it, he tried to sit down but could not *get* in, could not even get his legs in, until he moved the seat way back. He scooted the driver's seat all the way back, then climbed in and sat down. He adjusted the mirror, put the keys in the ignition and abruptly—like a whiff of smoke—he sensed a new thought forming. Gregen sat perfectly still, his heartbeat quickening.

Think about the day of the accident, he told himself. He was driving, Tom beside him in the passenger seat, coming down Franklin Turnpike toward the intersection with East Crescent Avenue. They realized there had been an accident and slowed. He pulled over more than fifty feet from the intersection and before he had even stopped the car he had reached back behind Tom's seat to get his medical bag. They had opened their doors at the same moment, Tom made a noise, and as Gregen stood up he saw from the corner of his right eye Tom moving swiftly and then he saw Sibilla. He was running to where she lay in the middle of the street surrounded by witnesses. He heard the shriek of an ambulance. Beside her he knelt and she knew him though her eyes were vague. "It's just my arm," she said. But he knew that her pelvis was crushed and he was aware of the approach of two ambulances. One on Franklin Turnpike, one on Crescent Avenue. "Help is coming," he whispered to her. "Be brave." She stiffened as if pulling on her will and her eyes cleared, met his, frantic with fear. "But the baby!"

"I hear him crying," Gregen assured her, "he is alive."

Her eyes went vacant and fluttered shut. Her heart was beating; Gregen knew she was unconscious in pain, nearing shock. He shouted for the paramedics, seeing one team run toward Ella's car, which lay crumpled on the sidewalk in front of the Weiss' corner property. But Sibilla whispered. "Go. Comfort Katie."

"No, my darling," he had said.

"In his seat," her eyes opened. "His car seat. You must…He must…" Her consciousness wavered. The paramedics descended, ordering him away. He told them that her pelvis was broken, her arm, and he suspected several ribs. The internal bleeding was bringing shock. She was in grave danger. They worked quickly. He stood. He heard Ben crying, but could not locate him until he saw Tom run with the screaming child, who even from the distance Gregen could see was muddy and wet. His eyes followed Tom toward the crumpled car. It was only then that he saw Katie there on the sidewalk. The roaring in his ears made his mouth go dry. "The baby is unharmed," he said firmly to Sibilla, whose eyes met his for an instant in astonished relief. The look in her eyes—utter joy and thankfulness—he had never been so moved by anything else she had said or done. His hands shook, his chest on fire as he remembered. At the time he had told Sibilla, "Tom's got him and he's taking him to Katie."

"Our…poor…Katie."

"She is alive."

"Go," Sibilla had begged.

The next few minutes had remained as vague in his memory as when he had initially viewed them. The mental pictures he'd taken were misty from shock and fear—Katie's turmoil, her odd frantic words to Tom; he had heard some of them. "A father would want to hold him. You take him, Tom. Tell him the words. Don't *let* him have the baby. He doesn't want *to hold* him. I'm sorry, Uncle Gregen. I—I thought…" fretting though Ben's screaming quieted to whimpers at the touch of her cheek against his…drawing her attention for only a moment to the sweet presence of her child. He would never forget the beautiful rapture in her face when Ben murmured, "Ma," his wide, contemplative eyes knowing and clear and alert. It was then that Gregen had looked to find where Max was… he remembered hearing Katie's breathing change and he sought her wrist to measure a racing, then elusive pulse…giving the medics quick instructions…hovering over them as they stabilized her neck and back, as they lifted her into the ambulance…Ben screaming again when they strapped him to an infant backboard…finally locating Max across the street at the narrow pointed corner of Franklin Turnpike and East Crescent. In front of a chain link fence that held back two howling collies, Max clutched at his mother's arms while Ella, bent double with weeping, seemed to be pulling away from him…and in Gregen an uncomprehending anger was born that moment, despising Max for the distance he kept from his injured wife and frantic infant son.

An ambulance sped off with Katie and the baby. Gregen rushed back to Sibilla as she was being lifted onto a stretcher. Tom, embarrassed by a scalding reprimand from the paramedics for picking Ben up, stood again by his side. Sibilla, altered by pain, fretted about Katie and the car seat. Trying to help, trying to ease her anguish, Tom promised to get it from the smashed car. Watching Tom, Gregen held Sibilla's hand while the medic clapped an oxygen mask over her face. Unable to keep her eyes open, she moaned the words "In his car seat," again. To distract her, to ease her mind, Gregen had narrated Tom's progress in getting it from the smashed car. He kept his voice calm while his mind whirled with impatience to get her speeding to the surgery needed to save her life.

Both back doors were smashed. The left door had taken the impact of the oncoming car. The right door was folded to the hinges like a crushed can. Unable to get his arms into the back of the car, Tom tried to go in the driver's door to get the infant car seat out of the back. Gregen saw it play before his eyes like a film. Tom had tried to thrust in head and shoulders, had backed out, looked around. Gregen remembered saying to Sibilla, "The driver's seat doesn't look like it was hit. He should be able to get in and pull it out between the two front seats." Still she fretted—she couldn't see clearly. Could he tell her where the baby was? Was he back in the car seat now? Gregen gave the paramedics instructions. Her lips were edged in blue. She begged Gregen to strap Ben into the infant seat. He promised her he would and held the oxygen mask to her face. He glanced to see Tom squat beside the car and reach in, feeling around the glass-filled back seat for the lever to send the seat back. Gregen had known the moment when Tom sliced his hand on the glass, remembered seeing the man's arm jerk back, his body twitch in surprised pain. Then Tom had found the lever and forced the seat back just enough to get head, shoulders and arms in, reach between the front seats, release the seat belt, and wiggle the car seat out.

As the ambulance sped away with Sibilla, Gregen had taken his bag and stitched the gaping wound on the fleshy part of Tom's hand below his thumb. Gregen had insisted on ministering to Tom though Tom declared the wound inconsequential telling Gregen he wanted to wrap it up and hurry to the hospital. But it was a big wound, deep and bloody, and Gregen knew Tom would not be allowed near any of the patients if he himself required medical care. "I am fast," he assured Tom. *Quickly, they had to go quickly*, Tom had said, *to get the baby when they released him, Katie said so*, Tom demanded. *Didn't he hear Katie?* Gregen had heard her; he had not then understood her, had not understood until much later…and when he took the second stitch, Gregen looked up to see Max gesturing confidently to the policemen and a reporter who both recorded Max's words with dutiful attention while his mother, tears dried, stood by, nodding her head with a curious regularity. When he took the third quick stitch, Tom had murmured, "I don't think we can use that car seat, Gregen. When I moved the seat back, a hunk of glass fell into it from the back window." And Gregen had nodded in numb, shared grief as the two men stared at each other: the infant seat had become crucially important to both of them as if Sibilla asking for it meant something in an accident the dynamics of which neither man fully understood, the consequences of which both men dreaded facing.

Why Sibilla had wanted that car seat, he never understood. As Tom predicted, he and Marie never felt certain they'd cleaned out all the glass fragments and it sat useless in his garage for years while he had puzzled over Sibilla's frantic attention to it so many fruitless times that finally in despair he had taken it to the dump and had forbid himself return to even the thought of it. Because, really, despite her insistence and Tom's trouble, Sibilla had *not* wanted it. Thinking back, Gregen remembered that when Tom brought it over to her as they were lifting her into the ambulance bay, she shook her head in frustrated disgust and said into her oxygen mask, the words muffled, "Blame Max, not Ella." Gregen had always believed she blamed Max because Max was driving and had therefore caused the accident. Sibilla would not speak of it again.

Now as he sat remembering in Ella's newest car with the engine purring contentedly, Gregen realized that *Ella* had been driving that day of the accident, not Max. The position of the driver's seat proved it. Max, taller than he, as tall as Tom, could not have driven with the seat pulled so far forward. Why would Max say he was driving? Why would Ella corroborate this lie? Why had Sibilla wanted Ben to be in the car seat? Gregen saw again the picture of Ella and Max when he first located them after

543

the accident. Ella had been trying to get away from her son. Her posture told the story. Unharmed, she stood apart from the injured, not helping, weeping, and for the only time in the years he'd known her, looking as if she were saying no to Max.

Had she been unable to face the guilt of driving the car, of causing the accident by running the red light? Had Max agreed to take the blame and was she to pay for this favor by enduring his abuse for the rest of her life? Her posture did not support the theory. He looked the one to be begging, she the one resisting. For years, Gregen had assumed that Max was trying to get Ella to say she was driving and that she had refused. If he concluded that Ella had been driving, what could Max have been asking her to do? By saying Max was driving…where was the benefit? Gregen turned back to his house, the quiet sense of concentration deep inside him assuring him and for the first time in years, he thought he saw a new door to open.

Walking back through the tunnel, Gregen's concentration focused on the concept he had formed in his mind of the impact the other car had made on Ella's. He had never understood why it had hit in the back, behind Ella's seat. In most missed stoplight accidents, the car that failed to stop smashes into the car entering lawfully into the intersection. Usually the cars meet, crashing front bumpers, and the deadly accidents are the ones where the car with the right of way smashes into the transgressing driver's seat or the front passenger seat. The impact of the car had been so hard on the back seat that it had shoved Ella's car into the stone well on the Weiss' corner property. The skid marks from the oncoming car began well into the intersection. Police thought the man had not been paying attention. Gregen wished he knew the position of Ella's car at the moment it was hit. The only thing that made sense was that Ella was making a U-turn at high speed in the middle of the intersection where she had a red light. To protect Max, she was hiding something that she did not want Gregen to know…something he had to find out.

Nels Lindquist returned to Hunter's quarters without Nancy. She was far too upset. So, in the snug hours of Thanksgiving Day, while the turkey roasted and the family waited to eat it, he left her to be cheered by their own rambunctious sons and walked back across the Yard to his commanding officer's quarters. It was as if they were waiting for him. Donna greeted him with a smile as bright as a sun lamp. The kitchen was shiny clean, no drops of anything on the floor now. The room smelled properly of turkey. Donna invited him in to share a plate of crab dip with them, explaining that she understood from her mother-in-law that he needed Ben to babysit. Unfortunately, Donna explained, Ben had just stepped out for a pre-dinner run, but he couldn't babysit this weekend anyway. He had basketball practice. They thought all this practice was ridiculous, she assured Lindquist, her slickly polished fingernails tapping lightly on her folded arm, but Ben had made a commitment to the team and he had to keep it if he were to keep the honor of his word. Daunted by the performance, Lindquist gulped down three crackers loaded with crab dip out of sheer embarrassment before he could think of what to say. Even then, his statement had about as much fire as a wet match.

"I was hoping to say hello to Max."

"He's playing with the boys right now," Donna said, smiling at the crab dip.

"It's a work thing," Lindquist said. "That's why I'm here."

"Oh."

"It won't take long."

"Wait right here. Sit," she commanded and left the room with a hurried step. They came back together much more quickly than Lindquist expected. He stood up and reached to shake Max's hand.

"Your wife got you cooking dinner like the wussy I know you are or can you take a little walk with me?" Lindquist said quickly, his heart pounding. "Just a little thing, work related."

Max shrugged, "When's dinner?" he asked Donna.

Brightly she said, "Ten minutes."

Lindquist looked around at a neat and perfectly organized kitchen that showed no signs of a dinner nearly ready, then he made a little half-bow to Donna, smiled, and opened the back door. Max grabbed a jacket from the hook by the door and followed Lindquist down the steps. The afternoon sun had warmed the backyard and melted the frost they'd crunched across earlier.

"Something get tangled up in the Gaithersburg office again?"

"No. No, Max. I'm here—actually as both your XO and your friend."

"Hmm?" Max said, looking puzzled.

"Nancy—actually came by here last night to bring y'all some cookies she made and, she feels uncomfortable bringing this up, but if places were reversed, I'd want you to talk to me. You know? So that's what I'm doing."

"Relax, Nels. Tell Nancy no need to kiss up with cookies." He shrugged and made a face as if they understood each other.

"No, Max."

"Colonel Hunter," Max said coolly.

The reprimand so shocked Lindquist that he felt his ears burn. He chewed his lip, thinking. He had not expected this. "As I was saying, Colonel Hunter—"

"You felt embarrassed at your wife's insecurity and I don't blame you. Women like that make it look like there's something wrong with the officer so she's gotta buy his rep and his promotions by kissing up. That's why I like Donna. She's got a career and she trusts me to make mine a success. Donna would no more make cookies for Admiral Johnson than she would—"

Lindquist stopped walking. Max looked back at him and said, "Can't keep up?"

"I did not come over to apologize for Nancy. I'm speaking on her behalf because you are my superior officer and you have been my friend for years. Last night Nancy saw Ben leave your quarters looking real bad. She heard him shout at you. She thought she saw blood on his face."

Max made a dismissive noise. "Ben went straight to bed after his game. Slept 'til noon. He'll be running on back here soon. You can ask him then."

"Look, Max—Colonel Hunter—we've been friends for a long time now and lately you've been…unnerved or something. But if there's trouble between you and Ben, something you just can't handle—"

"The *only* thing that's unnerved me lately is the way officers—men I thought had the smarts *and* the balls to think about something other than women's *gossip*—poke their noses into *my* personal business. It's obvious you are so whipped by this little wife of yours you can't even remember how an officer behaves."

"Come on. Be real. We been through a lot together. Hell, I carried you home drunk from the 'O' Club not three weeks ago in the middle of the day. Don't talk to me like that. I know about you and I've stuck by you. If you had too much to drink last night and got into it with Ben, admit it like a man, Max, and get some help."

"*Colonel* Hunter," Max repeated, his voice even, his back straight. "If I have to remind you again, I'll put you on report, Major."

"Yes, sir, Colonel Hunter," Lindquist said, meeting Max's eyes with a steady, clear-eyed stare few men could achieve.

55

JOE opened the garage doors and slapped the coil of rope they'd used in their games back onto its peg on the wall before he clamored up the wooden steps. He peeked into the barricade, grinned at Ben, and then climbed in.

"Hey," Ben said, looking happy to see him.

"You look better and you sound like your old self," Joe said with a smile. "But I'll never forget how bad you looked last night."

"I needed a shower."

"You need a *new father*." Ben clenched his jaw. "Can I see your stitches?" Joe said. When Ben held his hair back, Joe shined the flashlight on the wound finding it clean, still flat, the edges neat.

"Joe, I know it's rough on you hiding all this stuff from your dad."

"How do you know that, oh brilliant one?"

Ben shrugged. "It's obvious."

Joe said, "Yeah, so?"

"So, I'm feeling better and I'm gonna go—"

"Your head looks good. It's healing like magic," Joe looked pleased and grinned again. "But don't even think of going anywhere."

"I don't want to split you from your dad."

"The idea is to bring you in, not take me away. If you could just trust him," Joe sat down, hugged his knees and nodded his head at Ben's journal. "Did you figure anything out?"

Ben shook his head. He shut his journal and then stared at it, turning it over in his hand, his finger tracing the design stamped on the back. "There was this book I was carrying. He wanted it. That's why he hit me and it looked just like this," he said, holding his journal out to Joe. "I keep wondering whose journal did my dad want so bad he'd fight for it."

"Wasn't exactly a *fight*," Joe said, anger springing to his eyes.

"You'd better go," Ben said. "They'll be looking for you."

"You're right," Joe said, meeting Ben's troubled glance. Joe clapped Ben's shoulder and stood up because he knew if he stayed he'd bust out crying. That or yell at Ben about his stubborn refusals to tell and his pointless questions. And what did it matter *whose* stupid journal it was? No real father would hit his son to get a book away from him. There had to be *some* way to make Ben see all this. "Don't go anywhere, okay? Jeannie and I are in this with you. We're gonna figure out a way to fix everything. I'll bring you some dinner when I can. Then we've got to bring you inside tonight."

Ben looked uncomfortable and Joe suspected he was going to try to run away, so on his way out of the barricade, he grabbed Ben's shoes and hid them in the garbage can beside Tom's workbench.

All during the early afternoon, when Laurie, the women and Uncle Doug were busy in the kitchen, Tom and Kevin lounged on the family room sofa, chatting, entertaining the babies and watching football. The kids and teenagers lay sprawled on the floor in front of the fire playing games and talking and laughing. As Joe lay there with them, thinking, he considered what he should do to best help Ben. He tried to understand what it must be like for Ben to fear his own father. The thought that Tom might possibly be malicious had terrified Joe all his life—that he could understand. It was what he was always trying to find out. He wanted to know if *really*, underneath, his father might wish him harm or might purposefully cause him harm or if his father would callously—even justifiably—reject him. These possibilities had all his life turned Joe's guts to water.

And when, a month ago, Joe had realized he'd misrepresented Tom to

Ben as if he'd made his fears come to life in Ben's imagination, he'd been more sorry about that than anything he'd ever done—secret drinking, leading his friends to misbehave, endangering their lives—because if there was one thing Tom's fathering, ever-present and demanding though it was, had given to Joe, it was this wild love for his father that was at times more vibrant and palpable than his own heartbeat. Though he would not speak of it, tested it all the way to the edge, and doubted Tom could answer his emotion in equal passion and devotion, Joe knew that he adored his father and that afternoon, he tried to figure out why. He had to explain it to Ben. This, Joe believed, would convince Ben to tell his secret.

He lay on the floor beside Bonnie Jean. Their cousin Annie sat on the small of Bonnie Jean's back, playing with her long hair. Tommy and Flip lay opposite them, the Scrabble board between. Peter was close by playing the first round of Risk with the littler cousins, paying only scant attention as he watched the football game. Using the letter "E" in the word *promise* that Joe had placed on the board, Bonnie Jean put down the word *bleak*. Joe glanced at her. Dark smudges beneath her eyes emphasized her turmoil and Joe worried about her; secrets made her uncomfortable to the point of physical illness, he knew, and she detested brutality and injustice. That with Peter's whispered reminder that they had to protect Dad from hurting his back again had bound her happy personality in pensive stares. It required every bit of her strength to stay quiet and wait. But they really did not know what to do. Joe looked up at his father sitting on the sofa with Kevin, Cara now on his shoulder, and knew that Tom was at his happiest with his family gathered. If his father never walked again…if Max Hunter hit Ben again…neither of these were bearable options. What could he do that would ensure everyone's safety and well-being? Bonnie Jean sighed beside him. And, Joe thought, his sister was falling in love with Ben.

"Are we changing into our kilts for dinner, Dad?" Joe asked.

"It would please Grannie."

"She asked us to bring ours," Kevin said, "for taking the picture."

"You know, Jeannie," Joe said, bumping into her shoulder, "I think I left my sporran out in the trunk in the apple attic."

"I'll get it for you," she said. Tumbling Annie off so that she fell onto Joe, Bonnie Jean was up and running through the kitchen and out the back door in a moment.

Tom said, "That was nice of her."

"Yeah," Joe agreed, studying his father's unsuspecting face, the knowing blue eyes that wrinkled merrily as he rubbed his tan cheek on Cara's soft hair, and Joe knew a whiff of comfort. One thing he had to make Ben see was that with Tom, a kid knew what he could expect. Tom was consistent in instruction and punishment. Tom based his instruction and punishment on Gramps' proverb that explained, "If you can't take telling, you gotta take feeling." Tom taught; he corrected when his child didn't follow his instruction. And he punished if the kid willfully defied him. Ben should have a sense of this because he'd already run into some of Tom's principles. And that was how Tom taught basketball.

Joe did not particularly like punishment, but for some stupid reason, it helped Joe figure out what his father meant in those instructing and correction sessions—or rather, it helped Joe believe that Tom meant what he said, and that what he said was important and true. And with that palpable belief, Joe tried to commit himself to live by those principles he admired and found so elusive.

When he was young, Joe was punished for the usual things—rudeness to his mother, disrupting class, going swimming in the river on murky and dangerous summer nights when the currents were swollen with thunderstorm waters and Tom thought he was safe in bed. This was how the punishment was typically given: When Joe was discovered, Tom made him meet his eyes and questioned him. "Did I hear you right, laddie? Did you really just tell your mother to go to *hell*?"

"Maybe," Joe said, already crying, trying to think of what funny thing Bonnie Jean would say in the circumstance and only coming up with a lamely ridiculous, "Maybe I said, 'Go ring the bell,'" and immediately realizing that Bonnie Jean would never tell their darling mother anything so mean and awful—though she *had* shouted it to Joe and his friends in well-justified rage.

"And you want to add lying to your crimes?"

"No, sir," he choked out, tears falling thickly.

"Good. Then go out to the apple attic and wait for me." Or if the weather was bad or there were guests jumping on the trampoline, he'd be sent up to his parents' room.

There he waited for a half hour or more during which time each of his siblings would have visited him at least once with advice, comic books to stuff in his shorts, or both.

When Tom opened the door, switch in hand, Joe tried to stand up straight and give a manly, dignified impression—which was actually a bit of advice Gramps had given him one rainy afternoon that time he'd been caught in a lie. And Joe could usually make this composure last while he told his father exactly what was wrong with what he did, but when his father said, "That's right. So you *do* understand," Joe always broke down in tears. He was guilty. He knew and he did it anyway and only his father's switch could fix that. So three, maybe four swats later, Joe found comfort in Tom's forgiving arms. It was always easy for him, after that, to re-enter family life. Being paddled didn't embarrass Joe, what embarrassed him was that he knew it helped him be the man he wanted to be and he considered this a damned weakness.

Thinking about these things, he lost three games of Scrabble to Tommy, Flip and then Peter. He lost a game of Risk, which was always his to win. When they all changed into their kilts to please Grannie, he felt a tingle of pride at his right to wear the MacBride plaid and Tom patted his shoulder when they gathered in the living room to pose for a photograph. This went quickly because Bonnie Jean was as quiet as he. She didn't so much as cross her eyes to wreck even one picture and Joe saw his parents exchange concerned glances. He tried to rouse himself from his reverie, but even when Tom asked him to play grace to begin the gorgeous, savory feast his mother had prepared, the entire time that he piped "Amazing Grace" so beautifully that even Grannie wiped her eyes, Joe considered how deftly and completely his father had won his heart.

At dinner, the conversation went on with only his scant attention. He was careful to be polite when Tom brought up the book he'd seen Joe reading on evolution, saying with enthusiasm that it was interesting but for the life of him, he couldn't remember why. He did remember to eat when Uncle Doug or Aunt Beth cajoled him to take bites. But now he had to figure out what to do with Ben, what to do to show Ben that he could trust Tom.

Bonnie Jean and Laurie rose from the table to clear the salad plates and reflexively Joe lifted up out of his seat to help, thinking that the kitchen was one step closer to the garage and he wanted to check on Ben. "This kilt is making me itchy," Tommy complained.

"Nonsense," Grannie snapped.

"Help your mother with the salad plates then, Tommy," Tom said. "Sitting's making you itchy." Tommy carried the plates with his usual careful intensity and when they were in the kitchen, Joe whispered to him. "You're naked under there. That's why you're itchy."

"It's tradition," Tommy hissed. "Real men—"

Laurie leaned her head close to them. "Tradition's always itchy."

Laughing, Joe said. "And Dad's gonna figure it out."

"You're awfully nice to help me, Joe," Laurie said.

"I figure the more I get away from the table the better chance I have of not pissing off Grannie."

Tommy said to his mother, "Can I see if there's a softer kilt out in the garage, Mama?"

"There isn't one, Tommy. But there are clean boxers in the laundry room."

Joe steered Tommy toward the laundry room and looking out the window said, "Oh, I left the hose out. I'll be right back."

Joe opened the kitchen door and the wind pushed him into the kitchen's fragrant warmth. The last three bowls of soup stood steaming on the counter while his mother drizzled apple essence in an "M" in the center. Laurie took two and meeting Joe's eyes said, "The last is for Grannie. She likes hers piping hot."

Placing the rimmed bowl down before his grandmother, Joe said absently, "There you go, Grannie, enjoy."

Glaring up at him, Grannie's eyes examined his hands and arms with squinted suspicion. "Y' ran outside. Did y' wash your hands before y' touched my food?"

Joe stared at his hands and said, "No, ma'am. I forgot."

Grannie made a disgusted noise and Laurie moved to get up. Tom said. "Trade with me," getting up out of his chair he took her bowl before she could protest and put his down before her.

"It's not hot as mine."

"Laurie just now brought it to me. It'll be delicious."

"Hurry back to the table, Joe," he called as Joe sprinted to the sink. Then, taking up his spoon Tom said, "Dig in everybody. Doesn't it smell great?"

When Joe slid back into his chair, he took up his spoon and set his mind back to the problem of convincing Ben. The hardest time between he and his father had been the spring of his sophomore year. He glanced at Tom, there at the head of the table, remembering. When Tom had discovered he and Adam and Scott trying the vodka lemonade they'd made with a half bottle of vodka Joe had stolen when he babysat at Uncle Doug's house, Tom's anger was nearly as palpable as his disappointment. Joe never wanted to see that expression on his father's face again and he knew that was what he feared today.

Joe had been told to wait in the kitchen while Tom drove his friends home and spoke to their parents. But Joe had hidden in the heat of the apple attic and when Tom found him there, Joe lashed out. Tom left him there and returned an hour later.

When Tom asked Joe to say what he understood he'd done wrong, Joe insisted that it was just a sip and it was not a problem. He would not even admit that stealing from his uncle—Uncle Doug who *loved* him, who trusted him with his *children*—was a problem. Tom didn't paddle him. He told Joe that they'd talk about it again the next day.

Joe held out for a week. At first, his family was furious with him, tense around him, pleading with him, but Tom was nearly the same old Tom. True, in public or at what had become a tense dinner table, Tom treated him with a careful courtesy, but he still read to Joe at night before bed, still had Joe's oatmeal ready when he emerged in the morning, head aching and eyes sore from crying himself to sleep, still patted Joe's shoulder affectionately in absent-minded moments. All that Tom did troubled Joe, weighed on Joe, and finally brought Joe to reconsider. And even though he knew it would convict him, Joe turned to his Bible for help. He had no idea the Bible said so much about pride and fathers and sons. The words were like a clean, sharp knife going into the infection that pounded in his knowing place. Into who he was. The cut was precise and it hurt.

So, on the eighth day when he answered Tom's question, he talked for an hour, explaining in detail every implication he had pondered.

Joe knew his father was telling him—as he had been for all those days—that Joe could not wear out his love. Joe had known that truth then as if he held it in both hands; he felt the steadiness of it, the enormity of it, the beautiful, bright, fear-banishing dimensions of it in the dozens of ways Tom told it.

Joe came back to the dinner conversation as if emerging from a dream. Peter, beside him, nudged him with his shoulder and held the mashed potatoes for Joe to take. Whispering, Peter said, "You'd better take something. You passed three things and your plate is empty."

"Oh," Joe said, looking down, fighting those insistent tears.

Kevin said, "Careful with that bowl, Tommy, you're gonna spill wiggling like that."

"Still itchy," Bonnie Jean murmured and Tommy forced himself to sit still but his posture was stiff and tense.

Pete and Joe smiled at each other. Grannie said, "You've been silent as the grave today, Joseph, but you can whisper to yer brother. Are you too good for the rest of us?"

"No, I—"

"What I want to know," Tommy interrupted, leaning forward so that he could sit on his leg. He flipped the kilt out back away from his bare skin and met Joe's eyes with a quick, conspiratorial glance. "Is when are you legal age to do what you want?"

"Never," Tom said.

"What do you mean, Tommy?" Laurie said. She held the turkey platter with both hands while her mother-in-law made her choice. In the living room beyond, Cara whimpered from where she had fallen asleep in her little cushioned seat. Laurie stretched her back and neck to catch a glimpse of her.

Peter murmured, "He wants to know when he's allowed to go naked."

Piling sweet potato casserole on his plate so that the sticky sauce made a pool in the middle, Tommy said, "No, Pete. Like when can I go and get *any* job I want and you know—be independent and have adventures?"

"What job do you want?" Beth asked.

"First I'm gonna fish for abalone off Cape Horn. They pay three hundred and fifty thousand dollars for three months of work. So you don't even have to work all year."

"That's the most ridiculous thing I ever heard," Grannie said.

"Now, now, Mrs. MacBride," Kevin patted her arm.

"That much money," Tom said. "I find that hard to believe, Tommy."

"That's because you make so much more as a coach, Dad," Peter teased.

"What's abalone?" Annie asked.

"Shellfish," Laurie said. "The shells are used for buttons and jewelry. Lovely, really."

Cara whimpered again in the room beyond.

"Why would they pay so much for some dumb fish?" Annie asked.

"The shells are *real* valuable," Tommy said. "And they can't get people to go get them. So I'll do it and I'll probably get real good at it and they'll want me back. So I can make tons of money."

"Plus you can swim naked," Joe teased.

Grannie glared at Tommy, who squirmed in his seat, reached back with his fork, and itched his upper thigh with the tines.

"Tommy," Laurie said, raising her eyebrows.

Reluctantly he brought his fork back to his plate.

"You're going t' let him eat w' that now?" Grannie shrilled.

Everyone looked at Laurie, who didn't know what to say. Tom opened his mouth and Joe stood up. "I'll get him a clean one," Joe said.

"He's mighty jumpy," Grannie said, leaning toward Tom.

"He's being helpful," Beth and Doug said at once.

Bonnie Jean said, "Maybe I'll go with you, Tommy. It'd be so cool to fish for a living."

"I'm surprised more people don't do this if it is so lucrative."

"They're scared of the sharks," Tommy said authoritatively. "Can I use this fork to scratch with since I can't use it to eat anymore?" He held it up for the table's inspection.

"*No*," his mother laughed.

"You'll be fishing for sharks, too?" Flip said.

"No," Tommy gestured with turkey on his fork. "There's tons of sharks in the water over the abalone beds. That's why nobody wants to go there." He jammed the fork in his mouth, clamped down, and scraped it with his teeth as he pulled it out.

"Good Lord," Grannie said. "He eats like a savage and his parents say nary a word."

Dougie giggled into his hand.

"Sharks in the water?" Tom said, "That's why you shouldn't go, laddie."

"I'm not afraid of sharks."

"You should be cautious. If they're paying people that much it must be dangerous."

"Verra dangerous," Bonnie Jean said in imitation brogue.

"I'll be careful, Dad, just for you, but sharks are not dangerous compared to hippos, for instance."

"Don't you remember all those shark attacks last summer?" Peter said. "Florida, New Jersey, South Carolina."

"No," Tommy said, gesturing with his fork. "Statistics say swimming with sharks is ninety-nine percent safe."

"Yeah," Joe said. "But fifty percent of statistics are made up."

Peter chuckled, but Tommy stared quizzically at Joe trying to sort out the logic of his statement. "No, see? Sharks bite people and then they don't like the taste so they swim away. It's not really a problem."

Cara, fully awake, cried for Laurie.

"We're talking about your *arms* and *legs* here."

"Would you trade your arms and legs for *money*?" Annie said passionately.

"For three hundred thousand dollars? Yes."

"Or your middle," Joe said, "or other valuable things that dangle in the water."

Above the stifled giggles, Tommy said, "I'm going. Soon as I'm seventeen."

"Eighteen," his father corrected, "and only if you're done college."

"No sense paying for his college, Dad, if he's going fishing with the sharks."

"One thing's clear," Laurie said. "No more public television for you, Tommy."

"Mama, are you sure I can't itch with this fork?"

"Come and sit here with me for a minute, Tommy," Tom said, his expression amused.

"Dad, I'm eleven."

"Still, if you mean to go harvest abalone, I'll miss you. Come and sit on my knee."

The attention at the table turned to the rosy-cheeked Cara who Laurie had brought to the table. But Joe watched Tommy and his father and he knew exactly what his father was doing. He would coax Tommy onto his knee and pat his flank to confirm that he'd left off his underwear in order to dress like a manly Scot. Joe could not see exactly where his father's hand was but he knew the moment when Tom surprised Tommy with a warm hand on his naked skin because Tommy sat up very straight and his eyebrows made arches. Beside Joe, Peter stifled a laugh as Tom whispered in Tommy's ear. But Joe caught the amused sparkle in Tom's eye as he spoke, with only a glance, first to Laurie, then to Doug about his findings. And when Tommy scooted away, Tom met Joe's eye and he smiled at Joe in camaraderie.

"Why is he leaving the table?" Grannie demanded.

"Never mind, Mother," Tom said.

"What's going on?" she demanded, "Is that child naked without his kilt?"

"Grannie," several people tried to shush her.

"Why do your sons always do this! And you, too, you were always tryin' to be naked, flaunting your manhood! Swimming naked in the town pool! Marching before your entire clan without your drawers! There was never such a son as you."

"Grannie," Bonnie Jean said. "It's a tradition for a Scot to go naked under his kilt. That's how the manliest of them dressed."

"It's a myth! You're perpetuating a myth. The Scots are a decent lot. It's the Italians got all those naked statues standin' everywhere. My father would have set all of you out the door in disgrace. It's disgusting. It is the core of decency for a man to cover his hind end. It should be covered and stay covered!"

Unless your ass is beautiful, Joe thought and he nearly said it. His mouth was open. But oddly, he saw, as if he had new eyes, that his father had come up with the same smart ass response. Tom met Joe's stare, his blue eyes twinkling with mischief and he winked. Yeah, Gramps, who Joe missed at that moment with a searing pain, Gramps had somehow gotten through to Tom and made him strong, though Tom had been born just as wild as Joe

56

HER arm in her husband's as they mounted the steps to Hunter's quarters, Claire Johnson said, "Shouldn't we go to the back door if that's where Nels saw the blood?"

Charlie said, "We'll leave by the back door. That way we'll get a good look around." Peering into the windows on the side of the door, he added, "I believe we were spotted comin' down the street." Donna was herding the two little boys into the living room.

He waited a moment, then knocked. Donna hesitated, but came to the door with a smile brightening her tense face and asked them in with studied gestures. The two little boys recognized his wife and ran toward her and threw themselves into her arms. "Mrs. Johnson! It's not even a school day!"

"We've brought you fellows something to play with," Charlie said taking a gift bag from behind his back and giving it to the little one. "Keep 'em busy," he said winking at Donna. The boys dumped the contents of the bag on the foyer floor and knelt down to see. Admiral Johnson and his wife smiled expectantly at Donna who stood with her back stiffly straight and smiled back. If he moved his head just a little to the right, Charlie could see Max's feet propped on the metal frame of a coffee table. Claire squatted down to speak to the boys and he heard her say quietly, "There's coloring books and a box of crayons for each of you. And those little cars are the same, only different colors. I think they wind up for racing."

"They're really cool," Tim said and gave her another exuberant hug.

"You should say thank you to Admiral Johnson," Claire said in a whisper that Charlie wondered if Donna heard.

Both boys leapt to their feet, squared their shoulders, and thanked him.

"Y'all are welcome," he said, ruffling Keith's sandy brown hair and the boys took their things to the living room.

Again, they smiled at Donna and waited. She glanced nervously at the living room, wrung her hands, smiled again and said, "Would you like to come in and meet my mother-in-law?"

"By all means," Johnson said. Donna scurried into the living room and they followed slowly but in time to see Donna bump Max's feet off their perch and shake his shoulder. "Wake up," she hissed. "I told you. Admiral Johnson's here." Max snorted and sat up.

"Happy Thanksgiving, Colonel," Johnson said cheerily just as an older, heavyset woman joined them from the dining room. Johnson bent over, clapped Max's shoulder in a patronizing way, saying, "We working you too hard here at USNA?" He stepped past the table, which he remembered as having a glass top, toward the older woman. Yes, it had. There had been a photograph on it of Max as a young man.

"You must be Max's dear mother," he said to her quickly scanning the room for the photograph, seeing it now on the bookshelf in the dining room. She offered her hand and so he took hers to give a handshake, pressing firmly, covering her hand with his left hand. Her discomfort was so palpable he could smell it. "I'm Charlie Johnson and this is my wife, Claire."

Claire gave a friendly handshake and a smile and Max's mother managed to say, "Ella Hunter. Yes, I'm Max's mother."

Max, on his feet, actually staggered over to them and gestured as if he had said something he wished to emphasize.

"Can I offer you something to drink?" Donna said.

"Oh, we're stuffed. But thank you so much."

Max said, "Can I get you something to drink, Admiral?"

"I'm not any more thirsty than when your wife offered me a drink, Max." Charlie clapped Max on the shoulder. "You are not awake yet, are you?"

Max rubbed his stomach. "After dinner, y'know?"

"We stopped by to say Happy Thanksgiving to you, and I wanted to remind you, Max, about that little deadline we set."

"Deadline?" Donna asked.

Johnson explained, "Max told you, I'm sure, Donna. He is going to have a discussion with Ben."

"What's a discussion, Mrs. Johnson?" Tim said, smiling at her from the floor where he was racing his new toy car.

"A discussion is where two people talk to each other," she said, bending down to pat his head.

"Admiral Johnson," Tim said in a tone that said he was scolding the admiral for joking. "Talking. Ben and Dad. That's funny."

Keith vroomed his car up over Tim's foot, then made a face at Tim, held his finger to his lips.

Johnson looked around. "Where is Ben?"

Everyone smiled. No one met eyes and Donna said, "He's napping. Teenagers. Sleep all the time."

Johnson watched Keith curl his knees up to his chest, hug them, and hide his face in his knees. Tim was busy making car noises and apparently had not heard. Johnson let the awkwardness stand, glancing from face to face.

"What happened to your coffee table?"

The Hunters stared at the empty metal frame. "Top broke," Max said. "Damnedest thing."

"How?"

Max, awakening quickly, shrugged, "Just put my book down...and pow."

"Defective glass," Donna said.

"Was anyone hurt?"

"No," Donna said, just as Ella said firmly, "Yes."

The women stared at each other.

"Ben," Ella said to Donna. "Remember?"

"Ben?" Claire said. "Oh, no."

"Right, Ben," Max said; he held his lips in a smile, but his eyes showed their dull hate in a brief glance at his mother. The admiral saw Max straighten his back, square his feet, flex his hands.

"He cut his hand cleaning up the glass," Ella said. "I think that nice lady who brought the cookies over saw him after he'd cut his hand."

"Yeah," Max said, his relief was audible, his smile practiced. "Ben. Can't stand the sight of his own blood. Practically freaked out. Must've scared Nancy," he glanced at Claire Johnson. "But it was nothing to worry about."

"How many stitches were needed to close the wound?" Johnson asked.

"Just a butterfly bandage."

"Hmm, because you see, Nels was so concerned from what Nancy saw when she was here that he came over here last night you know, and saw quite a bit of blood on the doorstep."

"I am a nurse," Donna finally spoke. "And I can assure you. Ben did not need stitches. It was raining last night. A little blood mixed with water looks like a lot of blood."

"Hmm," Johnson said. "I'm still confused."

Tim sat up and held his new toy car up, the wheels still whirring. "When Ben bleeds, he writes the story down in his book. So you just got to read that, Admiral Johnson."

Joe was nearly caught coming out of the apple attic when Grannie insisted that Kevin walk her around the house. He ducked back in and waited, but before he could get out, most of the family not involved in protecting Ben was out in the backyard calling for him. Annie had his bagpipes, holding them dangerously by the cording, while others milled around, juggling fussy babies and deciding who would carry what. Finally he just opened the door and stepped out, relieved when Laurie said, "Oh, there you are. We couldn't begin without you," because Joe always piped for the family while they walked to each of their closest neighbors' houses. It was a funny sight, the boys and men in their kilts, the women and girls wearing what they pleased but for a tartan scarf or sash or shawl and they didn't march to the music, they just went. After greeting their neighbors with a box of cookies and a song, they ambled down the meadow and around, walking and tossing a Frisbee, breathing the crisp November air as twilight fell and Joe played their favorites on the old bagpipes until Grannie demanded her dessert.

Tom and the others helped Laurie make the espresso and hot tea, whip the cream and carry the pies to the table. Cara was so fussy that she put her lower lip out and gave pitiful, neglected cries. This seemed to inspire Kevin's baby boy and so for several minutes before dessert was served, both babies fussed, Grannie complained and the telephone rang.

"Don't answer it," Laurie said. "It'll just delay dessert."

"What if it's Ben?" Tom said.

Joe glanced at his sister. The phone stopped ringing.

"Are you expecting a call from Ben?" Laurie asked.

Bonnie Jean shrugged. "Always hoping."

"Is this your new beau?" Kevin asked.

"He's Joe's best friend," Bonnie Jean explained with a disarming laugh. "I just happen to be completely in love with him." Kevin laughed as if she were a teenger prone to exaggeration.

"Have ye got your under drawers on noo, Tommy?" His grandmother asked him when he took his piece of apple pie and sat on the edge of his father's chair waiting for Tom to join him.

"Yes, Grannie."

The table was half-full, people helping Laurie with the hot drinks, walking with the fussy babies, helping little ones uninterested in more food to find a diversion. Tom put another log on the fire, then crossed the kitchen to wash his hands.

"Yer lucky yer father's such a soft man."

With a keen glance at her, Tommy stuffed a huge bite of pie into his mouth and Joe whispered, "Easy," to his brother.

"If I were yer dad," Grannie said, "I'd—"

"You're not his dad," Joe said to her quietly, his eyes meeting hers in a direct challenge.

"Oh, yer speakin' to me noo, are ye, Joe?"

Cara's fussy whimpers broke into an emotional wail. The other baby took a deep breath of surprise then howled much more loudly. The telephone rang.

"Yes, ma'am, Grannie," Joe said. "Tommy really didn't do anything wrong. And Dad—"

"Who are you t' judge this?"

The phone rang still and Tom, shaking his hands dry, crossed the room to answer it.

"Dad knows what he's doing, Grannie, and if you keep after Tommy you might upset him. So I—" He heard his father say, "Hello, Donna. Happy Thanksgiving. How are you?" and Joe shut his mouth.

Bonnie Jean stopped talking to Aunt Beth and straightened her back, staring at her father.

Peter stopped walking with Cara and the baby's tone shrilled an octave. Laurie crossed the room to take her from Peter. Tom listened intently, eyes focused somewhere in front of him.

Grannie said, "If this wild fellow's father was any good, he'd—"

"He *is* good, Grannie," Joe interrupted her, enmity rising in him in defense of his father and his brother. He whispered to Tommy, "Take your pie in the kitchen." But Tommy bowed his head and Joe saw his lip trembling.

Grannie's voice went shrill. "And who d' ye think ye are, interrupting me. Correcting me as if you had the good character to judge *me*. You—sneakin' around all day like a common thief."

Joe stood up, dragged Tommy to his feet with one hand on the boy's bicep. He nudged Tommy, trying to get him to leave the table. He heard his father's voice get loud. "I haven't seen Ben. No, Donna, I'm sorry."

"An' look at yer arm!" Grannie pointed to Joe's left elbow. "That bruise is the kind the addicts get." Joe glanced down and noticed the purple bruise inside his elbow where the nurse had stuck him Tuesday for that blood test. Remembering Ben's despair, his confusion, Joe felt a blush flood up his face. Two things became clear as his chest and throat flushed with fury at Grannie: for Ben's sake, he had to stand up for Tommy; for Ben's sake he had to show Ben what Tom was really like. Grannie, he saw from the midst of the furious, swirling currents that dragged around him, was making it easy.

Grannie pointed still, her voice angry. "Ye been sneakin' out to the garage to use yer drugs all day. And ye have the nerve to defend this immoral brat—"

Joe heard his father say, too loudly, "He sometimes runs over here but not today—"

Joe met his father's eyes briefly and knowing now what he had to do, quickly said, "Tommy's not an immoral *brat*."

"He is a brat. And you! Look at yer arm!"

He heard his mother's voice approaching, her words to Grannie muffled by Cara's crying. He heard his father say, "I'll have him call you, okay?"

As his father replaced the phone and turned to stop Grannie's assault, Joe said, "*You're* the *brat*, Grannie. You're an abusive, nasty *bitch*. So shut up."

The silence he expected fell hard, startling the babies to confused sputters. Joe glanced at his father to make sure he'd heard, turned and sprinted out the front door, down the steps and across the lawn to the apple attic.

57

JOE did not pull the door closed; his father would be there quickly he knew. He sprinted up the steps. Ben sat up, startled.

"I just swore at Grannie."

"What happened?"

"She was picking on Tommy and then she turned on me. I don't care. I had to do it.

"But Joe—"

"Dad's coming out here to deal with me."

"*Deal* with you?"

"I know. So I'm gonna get it. Don't try to protect me this time. You're gonna have to lay low and wait it out. I can take it. Okay?" Holding a hand up to silence him, Joe hurried down the stairs and Ben felt the structure shake when he sat down with a thump on the bottom step.

Tom pushed open the door and when he shut it, he saw Joe sitting on the bottom step, switch in hand. Joe stood up, took a step toward his father, and held the switch out to Tom.

"I know you're gonna whip me and I'm ready."

Tom stared at him, unable to clearly read his expression. The apple attic was dark as twilight deepened beyond its walls. Tom took the switch from Joe and stepped to his workbench to click on a light.

"What *happened* in there?"

Joe shrugged. "You heard what I said."

Tom nodded. "I'm not sure I heard everything Grannie said. I was on the phone with Donna Hunter."

Joe looked uncomfortable, shifting from foot to foot. "It doesn't really matter what Grannie said."

"Tell me what happened."

"Dad. Let's just get this over with."

"I want to hear what you have to say."

Joe shook his head—whether in impatience, repentance or disgust, Tom felt unsure—and when Joe spoke, his voice sounded determined and quiet. "Grannie was picking on Tommy. I tried to get her to stop." Joe's face flushed and he looked surprised at his own anger. "She called him an immoral brat. That's just mean."

"And from what I could hear, up to that point, I thought you were speaking to her very calmly and respectfully, Joe."

"I tried that."

"Then Grannie turned on *you*. Is that right?"

"Yeah."

"And you…?"

"I called her a bitch and told her to shut up."

"I thought that's what you said," Tom said softly. "But you were so calm and quiet about it. Usually there's a bit of venom in your voice when you have spoken so in the past."

Joe looked toward Tom, avoiding his eyes. "If you don't mind, I'd rather be whipped out here away from all the company."

Tom stayed quiet, waiting for Joe to meet his eyes, remembering Joe's typically passionate self-defense. At the very least he would demand the witnesses he knew loved him—his entire family—to be called to help prevent him suffering the earned consequence. Now he stood in stoic acceptance, jaw set, tired and shadowed eyes guarded, holding his arms to his chest as if to keep the wild boy inside him quiet and still. "Joe," Tom squinted at him. "I want you to apologize to Grannie."

"What? No."

"Yes. That's what you need to do."

"*No*, Dad."

"I appreciate you sticking up for Tommy—"

"No, wait. Wait. I was *perfectly* calm when I stuck up for Tommy. I got mad when she started picking on *me*."

"It doesn't seem as if you're angry, Joe."

"I am," Joe vowed.

"In any case, you shouldn't have called her an insulting name and you shouldn't have told her to shut up."

"No, I shouldn't have. But I *did*." Joe finally met Tom's eyes, his expression almost convincing. "I defied your principles. I disobeyed *you*. My language—you *hate* that. You warned me."

He squinted at Joe again, concerned about his stiff, controlled demeanor. Tom saw the deep, determined commitment in Joe's intelligent, gray eyes, his face, still tan from a long, fair autumn spent outside, was reddened with strong emotion, his lips looked swollen and he pressed them together in the way he did when he was upset, but Tom knew his son wasn't merely angry. In Joe, angry meant a profusion of poetic words proclaimed to convince followed by demonstrative action. When angry, Joe did some astonishing thing to express his disgust, to fix the situation, to initiate justice. Though Tom did not know what this was about, though he wondered about the bruise inside Joe's elbow, he knew that even this stance Joe was taking was somehow meant to communicate. The most impulsive of his children, Joe was also the most tenderhearted and the most difficult to understand. Was he so deeply hurt by his grandmother's cruelty that he had created this steely composure that would allow him to suffer painful punishment if it meant he could let the name-calling stand? Tom's heart had a heavy, thudding realization of his responsibility to Joe. "You must apologize to Grannie."

"Dad, come *on*."

"When you mistreat others, it damages you inside. Apologizing fixes inside you."

Joe gave an impatient laugh. "If I refuse—is that grounds for punishment?"

"You mean will I *whip* you until you relent and agree to apologize?"

"Yeah."

"Are you *kidding me*?" Tom said.

"No."

"Do you really not know me that well, Joe?"

Tears brightened Joe's eyes and he turned away from Tom. "You said if I used that language with Grannie ever again. And I did it. Now you've got to fulfill your promise."

"Something's wrong here," Tom said quietly, his voice toneless. He stood very still, thinking deeply, squinting at Joe. "What's going on with you?"

"Nothing," Joe said. "I just know I was wrong."

Tom lay the switch down. "Look at me," he commanded. Joe shook his head. Tom took his shoulders in hand and turned Joe to face him, but Joe stared at the switch lying useless on the workbench and tears pooled in his guarded eyes.

Joe whispered, "You said it wasn't a threat. Remember that day at Grannie's when Ben was with us?"

"I know, but I don't think—"

"You *said* if I spoke that way to Grannie or—I think you said it this way—to *anybody* for whom Christ died—I wouldn't sit for a week. Those were your exact words. So you have to."

"I did say that, and I meant it. And if the circumstances were the same…"

"The principle's the same, Dad."

"No, I don't think so. Something's different. And I think it's you. But I'm not sure—"

"Dad. You're a *man* of your *word*. Don't let me down."

"Let you *down*?"

"What will I say to the guys if you don't keep your word?"

"The guys?"

"The guys all depend on you doing what you say you will."

"It's just us here, Joe." Joe squeezed his eyes shut, shaking his head in what seemed to Tom either resignation or frustration. "This is between you and me. Father and son," Tom said. "And this time, I think I let you down. I won't punish you for what I should have stopped."

At the rims of his blue-gray eyes, tears pooled. Joe turned his shoulder to Tom. "I've always heard it hurts the parent more than the kid so you'll really be punishing yourself." Joe let out a frustrated puff of breath as if he realized how stupid he sounded.

Tom laughed. "Are trying to *convince* me to whip you? Against my better judgment?"

"Yes."

"*Why?*"

Joe shook his head, clearly disgusted with himself "I'm weak. It helps me behave."

"No. You're not weak anymore, Joe. I see courage and compassion." Biting his lip, Joe's eyes spilled their tears. Tom said, "But you were wrong to call her a name, to lose control, to speak so rudely."

"I know, Dad. That's what I've been *telling* you."

"I want you to say those things to her." Joe wiped his eyes, his cheeks on his forearm. "Can you do that, son? It will help you inside. It will show who you really are."

"Yes, Dad, I will," Joe said, tears spilling too fast now to wipe away. "You know I will."

Half an hour later, refusing Tom's arm, Grannie bustled out to the garage. Joe stood up when they entered and it was so quiet for a minute that Joe heard Ben swallow nervously above in the loft.

"I'd like you to both listen to me for a minute," Tom said, "then Grannie can speak." Tom squinted, folded his arms over his chest, and leaned back a little. "I owe you an apology, Joe. I knew your grannie was after you and I should have gotten off the phone more quickly. I apologize for not protecting you and Tommy. You shouldn't have been put in that position."

Grannie straightened her back, bristling. Tom raised his eyebrows at her, his gaze so stern it frightened Joe. Inside, he started to tremble. *This is not going to be easy*, he thought, *damn, damn, damn, shit, hell. Dad never makes it easy.* He thought he could engineer things so that Tommy'd be safe and Ben could learn. Now he was going to end up crying his eyeballs out, his heart putty as usual in his father's hands, because if he were honest with himself, Grannie's nastiness, Tommy's vulnerability, and Ben's need had given Joe the opportunity he'd secretly craved to get back at his grandmother, to strike out at her, to embarrass her in shameful cruelty and justify his actions. And none of it had worked. Tom had refused to paddle him so that Ben was not able to see what it was really like between Joe and Tom, or better yet, to rush down from his hiding place to rescue Joe and reveal his hurts to Tom. Instead, Joe's heart burned with the saltiest guilt.

"Dad, please," Joe said. "I could have walked away. I had it in me to do that. I could have ignored the comments. You gave me that strength and I chose to—"

"I know, but you shouldn't have had to do that. I put you in a terrible position. A boy should not be abused in his own home. He should feel safe. I could have stopped it but I was reluctant to take a hard line with my own mother. The fault lies at my feet."

With Tom standing there as he was, hands out to Joe, it felt to Joe as if his own half-truths, his scheming, his reckless choices were just a stinking pile of wasted effort big enough to fertilize his mother's garden for a decade or so. But as Tom stood there, quiet, solemn, eyes bright with tears, Joe felt Ben's interest in the loft above. It was as if they were again breathing together and he knew that Tom was winning Ben despite the failure of Joe's plan. "Joe," he said in solemn tenderness, "forgive me."

"I forgive you, Dad," he said.

"Thank you," Tom said to Joe, and when their eyes met, Joe despised all that he was hiding from Tom. Stepping into his mother's line of sight, forcing her to meet his eyes, Tom said, "You have something to say, Mother."

She shook her head.

"We discussed this inside."

"That was before you took the boy's crime on you. What have I to say now? Apparently yer son's appalling behavior was yer own fault. I canna whip you, now, I'm likely to be put out on the street wi' no one t' care for me if I speak against yer almighty opinion, Tom."

"No, that's not what this is about."

Joe felt a nudge inside him and he heard himself say, "Grannie, I want to apologize," his voice clogged and unsteady. "It's *not* Dad's fault. It's mine. I was mean and I am sorry. It won't happen again." He swallowed hard, and took a barely noticeable step toward his father.

"Mother?" Tom prompted.

Joe couldn't help it, he spit out the words, "I just don't understand why you don't like me. I'm funny! I'm smart! I—" Tom closed the distance between him, his arm going around Joe's shoulders. "Shh," he said. "She has no good reason."

"It would help me if I knew why you don't like me."

Grannie rolled her eyes and shook her head. "I'm not about to go all mushy and sentimental to ease your feelings, Joseph, but I offer you my—" she faltered and glared at Tom, "my apology since yer father demands it of me. Now, I'd like to go home."

"Thank you, Grannie."

"Smells like turkey in here." She squinted at Joe suspiciously.

"Okay," Tom said. "Let's end this here. Mother, don't say anything else to Joe."

"The remark about the turkey is addressed to you. It's your home!"

Tom offered his arm. "Peter will drive you home now. Remember what I said."

"I can walk by myself," she said and shoved open the garage door so hard that Tom and Joe looked at each other in surprise.

When Tom returned to the apple attic a few minutes later Joe sat on the landing of the steps, knees drawn up, head on his knees. Tom carried a quilt. "It's cold out here," Tom said sitting down next to Joe. He flipped the quilt out and wrapped it around Joe's shoulders. "And you've been crying." Tom's arm went around Joe's back; he rested his head on Tom's shoulder.

"She hates me," he said to his father, tears coming hard again. "She's always hated me."

Tom patted Joe's back. "It's not really about you, Joe. My father once told me she was inept at love. He didn't mean it unkindly, just as a matter of fact."

"Why would he say that to you?"

"It was on my thirteenth birthday. I'd tracked mud onto her new rug. She was hitting my head and shoulders and yelling about what a complete slob I was—ugly stuff. Dad blocked her blows and thrust me behind his back where she didn't dare reach for me. He said, 'He'll never be as neat and clean as you are, but he has a soft heart. If you keep this up, you're going to make him heartsick and bitter. I won't have that happen to him. I will punish him from now on. If you have a complaint about him, come to me.' Then, in front of her, he apologized to me for allowing her cruelty."

"So what happened? Did she punch Gramps out?"

"No, but the next twenty-four hours were tense, and sure enough I did something to aggravate her. I don't remember what I did, but I do remember thinking my dad was going to defend me and I could vent all I felt. And I'd stored up thirteen years of offenses. She said something to me, something mean, so I cursed at her. I called her every foul name I knew and when she raised her hand to slap me, I took a swing at her."

"No," Joe breathed.

"With my fist. Fortunately, I missed, but my father appeared out of nowhere and he hauled me up to his room so fast I don't think my feet touched more than two stairs. Then he whipped me harder than *you*'ve ever been whipped."

"Yeah, right."

"No scolding, no screaming, no blood drawn, but I still remember it. I said pretty much what you said just now to me. "I said, 'She hates me, Dad, she's hated me since the day I was born.'"

"So he told you she was incapable of love—as if that excuses it."

"He said *inept*, not incapable. He would never say anything that hopeless."

"I miss Gramps so much. He liked me."

"He was a loving man," Tom agreed. "He told me that he couldn't excuse her cruelty, but I should try to understand that she'd hardened her heart." Tom imitated his father's voice, slipping naturally into the accent that was his birthright. "'She was frightened when you came so fast on the airplane,' he said, 'imagine—a young girl all alone and you were so much later than expected. There were those in town who accused her of taking a lover once I had gone. You were so late, they thought you couldna' be mine.'

"Gramps agreed this was no reason for a mother to be cruel but I remember how broken he sounded when he said, 'I should never have left her behind—a young bride, her husband's half a world away and she turns up pregnant. Sick and scared she was, an' then t' be accused of infidelity when she was working so hard to earn money so we could be together again. It shamed her and it angered her—the injustice, the solitude, the fear.'

"I said something like you did to Grannie, wanting to know why she hated me. Everyone knows that mothers are not supposed to hate their children. And he said something interesting, Joe. Gramps, of course, would never say that she hated me. He explained it by saying that through my inconvenient birth, God had presented her with her life's trial and that the real issue was her unwillingness to submit to God's desire to change her. Gramps said, 'She never learned the lesson she was meant t' learn.'"

"Still hasn't," Joe said.

"I'd heard my birth story many times and I wondered about something, but never had the guts to voice it. I said to him, 'Dad, I don't mean it against Mother, but are you sure I *am* yours?'"

Joe said. "I can't believe you said that."

"I know," Tom nodded, patting Joe's shoulder. "He laughed and said, 'You're mine.'"

"'How can you know for sure?'"

"'How can you doubt, laddie?' he said, his warm hand on my back, 'When you love what I love, you smile at all that delights me, when we mist up at the same things? How can you doubt you're mine when our hearts echo the verra same beat?'"

"Yeah," Joe said, putting both arms around Tom, he hugged him.

"That's right."

"Good old Gramps."

"It was then I knew who I was. I saw that the important, good things in me came from him."

"Yeah."

"But when you struck out at her today, you turned away from what you know I love—honor, kindness, and self control. You became—just for a moment—just like Grannie."

"Ouch, Dad."

"That's not who you are. You are *my son* and you must guard against being like her. Never scold or swear. It diminishes you."

"It felt good to swear at her. It felt so good."

"Does it feel good now?" Tom said.

Joe shook his head, burrowing in closer to Tom, tightening his arms. "Dad, I—I've been thinking a lot and even though it doesn't seem like it, even when I do stupid things, I'm always thinking about you and—I love you."

When the garage door closed behind them, Tom and Joe walking in step, their arms around each other, Ben stood up from his hiding place and stared down at the landing. As if they'd left their images behind with him, he saw them there again, father and son in tense and real trust. Ben grabbed his backpack, shoved in his journal, and taking his cell phone, punched in his home number. Donna answered.

"It's me, Ben."

"Where are you? Gran is worried sick."

"You know Dad beat me up, right?"

"Gran said something…"

"Do you know what happened? She saw him beat me up."

"Stop. I need you to come home. Right away. The Lindquists were over asking for you. We had to pretend you were sleeping when the Johnsons stopped by! Your brothers—"

"Tell Keith and Tim I'm safe now. Nobody hits me or kicks me here."

"Where are you?"

"You know, I could be *anywhere* but your house. Anywhere else I'm safe from being beat up. Isn't that weirdly ironic? You're supposed to be safe at your parents' house. But not me."

"Have you been drinking?"

"No, I've been *bleeding*. The cut on my head bled for six hours. There's probably a blood trail from our house all the way here."

"Don't exaggerate."

"Could you please tell Dad and Gran I had to get stitches? I think they ought to know."

"No. I'm not bringing it up to them. I've just got them calmed down."

"Good for you, Mom."

"Are you trying to make me feel bad?"

"Yeah, I guess I am. Anyway, I'm at the MacBrides' house."

"Ben, you *promised*."

"I'm only calling because I know Tom will make me call when I go in there and I don't want them to hear us talk. They'd catch on right away to how you treat me."

"Oh, dear. Oh, no."

"I won't be home tonight. That's all I called to say."

He couldn't find his shoes and between bouts of searching for them with a distracted urgency, he stared out the window at the firelit scene inside the MacBride's home. From the apple attic, he could see in the living room window. The sounds of their music-making called him and the room looked safe with its dimmed light, golden glowing and candle flames flickering and the surprising Tom MacBride on the sofa beside his wife, his guitar on his knees, strumming and laughing. Ben could not wait longer to find his shoes, but left the garage and sprinted barefoot across the cold grass; he could hear Bonnie Jean's fiddle now, mellow and slow, and he hurried, wanting to get inside before he shivered again. He tapped lightly on the back door.

A few seconds later, Joe and Bonnie Jean rushed through the kitchen toward him; Peter and Tommy followed. Joe yanked open the door and a relieved smile broke across his handsome face. His intense grayish eyes, swollen and blotchy from shed tears, lit again with their lively joy.

"I had to come in after what you did for me. After seeing you with your dad. I couldn't stay out there, Joe."

Joe nodded. "I knew if you saw how he really is you'd be able to tell him and then—"

Ben heard Joe, Ben saw the hope in Joe's eyes, saw that Joe had expected to win Ben's safety and freedom but his mother's threat to end her life trapped the air in his throat. He didn't mean to do it, but he glanced over his shoulder at the dark driveway and shuddered at the urge to dash away.

Bonnie Jean grabbed his arms. "Come in and get warm."

Ben met Joe's eyes seeking his understanding yet again. "We'll deal with that tomorrow," Joe said, shrugging away his disappointment. "Just come in," Joe said as Bonnie Jean said, "Just stay." They pulled him inside, both of them hugging him at once, and Peter and Tommy stood behind them waiting their turn. Keeping Ben in the middle of their embrace, the four of them took Ben through the kitchen and dining room to the firelit retreat beyond. Standing before their parents, eyes bright, smiles beaming with tentative hope, they opened their arms to show Tom and Laurie their treasure.

Ben said, "You told me next time to come to the back door."

BOOK THREE

Shaded Trail
Eight Hands Around

Shaded Trail

1

Dreams visited Ben that night at the MacBrides' house. He felt cold; he was arching his back. Darkness lapped in, covering the edges of his vision. He could no longer hear Peter's ragged sleep breathing. Muddy water covered his unblinking eyes. He tried to call out, but he had no words, no English, no French, no words could break through the cold blanket that oppressed him. A shadow fell on his face and then he felt a hand touch his head, a hand pat his shoulder three times.

"Are you sick? Is it a fever?" Joe's voice. "Want me to get Mom or Dad?"

"I must have been dreaming."

Ben drifted to sleep again. He woke with a clear picture in his mind of the pantry at Porter Road. He could see the slim shelves on the walls of the back stairway leading to the kitchen. A case of water bottles stood on the landing, making it impossible to open the door wide. And wedged on the shelf behind the peanut butter jar was the book his father had fought him to get.

He saw it there, fringes of newspaper articles at the back edges. He could feel his hands closing over the book and shifted in restless anticipation.

At first light, Ben crept silently to the kitchen. After two glasses of ice water, he went into the laundry room to find shoes to borrow. As he reached into the crate of shoes by the dryer, a scrap of newspaper in the trash can caught his eye. It looked familiar and he remembered seeing it that night his father attacked him in the kitchen. Ben took the scrap in hand. He read:

> Three Dead in Two-Car Accident
> Infant Lands in Puddle, Survives
> ...though eyewitnesses did not report the baby's ejection from the vehicle, Mrs. Ella Hunter told police that her daughter-in-law was holding the baby when the accident occurred and the impact was so powerful, 'He was ripped right out of her hands,' Mrs. Hunter was quoted as saying...

"What are you doing?" Bonnie Jean stood right behind him, startling him so that he dropped the shoes.

"Look at this." He held it out to her.

"A baby—survives? What?" Bonnie Jean met his eyes.

"An accident where people *died*. But a baby lands in a puddle and *lives*? Weird," Ben said.

"Why are you up so early?" Joe's voice sounded behind him. They turned to see Joe in his gym clothes, rubbing his eyes.

Ben held out the article for Joe to see. "I found this," he said, "in the trash by the dryer."

"Oh, right. I found that in your pocket when I washed your clothes to get the blood out. I didn't even think to read it." Joe stared at Ben, shaking his head.

"That explains why it's here," Ben nodded. "I remember putting a piece of newspaper in my pocket right before my dad went postal."

"Mrs. Ella Hunter," Joe said. "That's freaky. Her daughter-in-law? This must be your mom, Ben. What do you know about this?"

"Nothing," Ben said. "Oh, wait. My mom mentioned an accident once when she was ranting about...something," Ben said, remembering her fear that Tom had told him something about Quantico and an accident. "Does it say where it happened?"

"The baby—that must have been you." Bonnie Jean pointed to the date at the top corner beneath the words *Bergen Record*.

"Me? No."

"The dates are right," Joe agreed. "The newspaper's from up where your grandmother lives, where you were born. We need to find out more about this."

Ben squinted at the print. "If my mother was holding me when the crash happened and I was thrown out...it's freaky that she never mentioned it."

"Right—because you were a miracle."

"That's right." Bonnie Jean touched Ben's wrist. "Unless she feels awful for holding you," Bonnie Jean shuddered. "If that happened when I was holding *my* baby, if I were responsible for holding onto him...and I couldn't...I'd never get over that. Never."

"But her baby *lived*," Ben said. He gestured, holding his hands out as if pleading his case. "You think your child is absolutely going to be dead. Then he's alive. Safe. Wouldn't you be happy about that?" Abruptly, he shoved his feet into the shoes.

"Where are you going?" Joe said.

"Running over to get that book. The one my dad fought me for." He squatted to tie his shoes. "This article fell *out* of the book."

"I'm coming with you." Bonnie Jean indicated that she was ready to go.

"You want to run with me, Jeannie? No offense, but I'm a real hard runner—"

"I had no idea you were so conceited."

"Or *stupid*." Joe blocked the door with one arm. "I put my ass on the line for you and I say you're not going over there."

"Look, if that's me in the article, if this incredible thing happened to me and nobody's talking about it, that's even more proof that I have to get the book my dad took from me. Maybe I can find the rest of the article," Ben said. "Anyway, I know where he hid it. I woke up with this picture in my mind."

"Fine," Joe said, "but I'm going with you." He looked at his sister for backup, adding, "You're never going there alone again."

"We'll go together," Bonnie Jean said.

Ben led them from Gate One to the alley behind Porter Road. They were walking now, dodging the slick spots and conversing in whispers. "Get whatever else you need," Joe said. "Like your uniform and books."

"Just let me get that book." Ben saw the worry in his friends' faces, then beyond them, through the window in the kitchen door, he saw his grandmother's silhouette. He heard his father's voice. Bonnie Jean was walking toward that door. Ben sprinted after her, Joe following. He heard his mother's Volvo sputter at the head of the alley and he rushed his friends into the basement.

"You stay down here," Bonnie Jean said. "I'll get your stuff."

"She's right," Joe said. "We've got to keep you safe."

"No, I don't want Jeannie upset or hurt or anything."

"They won't do anything to her," Joe said.

Reluctantly, Ben agreed. Together the three tiptoed to the bottom of the stairs. "The left side of the steps don't creak," Ben said. "Go slowly."

Bonnie Jean found the stairs as Ben had described when he told them his dream; looking up, she saw the water bottles on the landing above her, the edge of the book just visible behind the peanut butter. She started up, creeping silently, step by step. There were sixteen steps to the landing and as Bonnie Jean's toe touched the fifth step, she saw the kitchen door stood ajar; she could hear voices. She stopped moving; the boys below did not dare breathe.

Donna had not expected either her husband or her mother-in-law to be awake—much less standing in the kitchen with a strange woman—when she returned from work.

"I thought you were working late," Max said in a friendly way.

"I usually get home at four. I *am* late."

575

"Late to one man, early to another," Max said with a charming chuckle.

The woman stepped toward Donna, hand outstretched to shake. "It's early for anybody to have a visitor," she said. "I'm Patty Edwards, Max's lawyer. I'm sorry to intrude at this early hour. I can't believe it myself."

Donna did not take Patty's hand. "What lawyer comes to people's houses?" She looked to her mother-in-law for sympathy, but Ella fidgeted with her cigarette lighter, hands shaking. "And at this hour?"

"She's doing us a favor. So try being friendly, would you?"

"Max had some documents he wanted me to review before we meet with Admiral Johnson later this morning."

"Documents are not going to help Max at that meeting," Donna said, folding her arms.

Patty smiled. "Your mother-in-law was just trying to remember where y'all put a little book when you were straightening up yesterday before dinner."

"*She* doesn't know where it is, Patty," Max said. "My mother knows. Where is it, Mom?"

Ella glanced at Donna for permission but Donna said, "Don't look at me, Ella. My opinion doesn't count in things concerning Ben."

"Now, don't say that, dear," Ella said. "Ben loves you dearly."

"If I could just have what I came for," Patty said, smiling again, "I'll be on my way."

"It's just that I think Ben should have the diary," Ella murmured, head down.

"I can't believe you!" Max flared.

"Someday," Ella said. "Someday, of course I mean *some*day. It'll legally be his when he's eighteen, and as a historical document it is—"

"Yeah. I'll keep that in mind, Mom."

"Priceless. It's priceless. I'm sure Ben would prefer—"

Patty, laying a hand on Ella's arm, said, "You have my word. I'll protect it with my life." Ella glanced at the door to the stairway now open a few inches.

Max followed her gaze and banged open the door. "In here? On the shelves?" Groping for the diary, Max's hand closed on it. Then he saw Bonnie Jean on the steps, hand outstretched, and he yelped as if snake bitten. "Holy shit!" He stepped back, took the book in both hands, and held it front of his chest. "Wait. You're not—you're Laurie Davidson's girl, aren't you? What *the hell* are you doing here?"

Fear squirmed in Bonnie Jean's stomach, but she put on a confident face, grabbed a water bottle, and laughed at his shock, making her eyes dance, making her expression merry and teasing.

"I bet you *are* surprised," she said, stepping into the kitchen so that he had to back further away from the landing. "But you're right. I'm Bonnie

Jean. We met at Ben's game." She stuck out her hand to shake his, but he stared at her. "It's okay," she said, patting his elbow as if he were as safe as Uncle Doug. "Not every day you find a girl on your basement stairs." Smiling, she looked around the room. "Hi," she said to them. "You must be Ben's grandmother," again she offered to shake hands but the woman looked appalled to see her. Bonnie Jean looked at the two other women in the kitchen and said, "I'm trying to guess which one is Ben's mother, but—"

"Don't tell me you're Ben's girlfriend," Max said, coming to himself. He stuck out his chest and rubbed both hands up over his stomach, heedless that one hand held the thick leather book.

"Okay, I won't tell you," she laughed.

Max grinned and whispered, "He didn't have you sleeping down in that basement last night, did he?"

"Oh, *no* sir," Bonnie Jean said. "We were out running this morning, me and my brother and Ben, and Ben said there was water in here at the top of the landing." With the bottle of water in her hand, she gestured toward the door that stood open behind her. "And actually," she said. "I need a Band-Aid, and uh—do you have one I could borrow? I think I have a blister."

"Out running? In the cold?" Max laughed at her.

"They're in better shape than me," she said making her voice carry in the way she could, "so by now they must be halfway to the sea wall. They're gonna circle back and get me. Joe said we should meet in front of Admiral Johnson's house. I just need a Band-Aid. And this water, if it's not too much trouble. I hope I didn't interrupt your breakfast." She looked around the room smiling as hard as she could at the unfriendly faces.

"The Band-Aids are in the cabinet," Ella Hunter said.

"How old are you, honey?"

"Was fifteen in September."

"Really?" Max looked at the shorter blonde woman, his eyes bright with emotion, but she refused to meet his thoughts. Bonnie Jean guessed that this was Ben's mother, but the other woman in the room was tall and athletic—like Ben.

"Maybe you should introduce me, Colonel Hunter. I can't figure out who is Ben's mom."

Max patted Bonnie Jean's shoulder in a kind of caressing way. Bonnie Jean, uncomfortable with his touch, took a step away. "This is Laurie Davidson's girl," he said. "Mom, you remember Laurie."

"Of course I do, Max," Ella Hunter said, horrified at him.

"Doesn't she look just like her?" he said, smiling at Bonnie Jean as if there were too much saliva in his mouth.

"Thank you," Bonnie Jean smiled at him, glancing at the way he held the leather book in his left hand, close to his stomach; he held it so tightly that his fingertips had gone white. "But I have my father's chin."

"You *do not*." Max said. "Shit. Don't *say* that."

Patty stepped forward and offered her hand to Bonnie Jean. "I'm Patty Edwards. I'm Colonel Hunter's lawyer."

Bonnie Jean shook her hand and then said to Donna, "So you must be Ben's mom."

"Oh," Max said, stepping between them. "This is Donna. My wife. Yeah, and she's Ben's mom."

Bonnie Jean smiled in a hopeful way, expecting to hug her, but Donna looked uncomfortable, even irritated, and did not offer her hand, did not open her arms to embrace the daughter of a woman who had once been her dearest friend. Bonnie Jean pictured Laurie with Ben, and she squinted her eyes as if that forced distance of sight, that squinted perspective, would help her understand the woman. Donna's awkwardness gave Bonnie Jean a good excuse to stare, to soak in the details of this woman who was so important, so mysterious, and so awfully blank. Trying to connect with Donna, she said, "I bet you just got home from work and you're exhausted. Do you have breakfast when you work nights or just a cup of tea?"

When Donna fumbled for an answer, Bonnie Jean turned to Max and said, "I'm surprised you don't have a nice cup of tea waiting for your wife when she gets home from working all night."

"You think that's how Ben's going to treat you? Did he run in here and get you that water you wanted? You women have enough power over us men."

But Bonnie Jean knew he savored her taunt and when she heard a noise downstairs she said quickly, "What're you reading, Colonel Hunter? It looks like a *romance* novel or something else kinda girly."

Max chuckled at her, but his eyes went dull as he looked at the book. He quickly handed it off to Patty Edwards. "Where'd you get your trash-talking mouth, young lady?"

"I have three brothers."

"You say Ben's out running?" Ella asked clumsily. "How is he?"

"What kind of a question is *that*, Mom?" Max snapped.

"He has practice at ten," Bonnie Jean moved a little toward Donna, hoping to catch her eye, and said, "Mrs. Hunter. You should stop by my mom's shop and see her sometime. She would love to see you. She told me you two are old friends."

Donna forced a smile that came out looking grim. "I'm sure she has better things to do."

"No, *ma'am*." Donna dared to look up, and meeting her eyes, Bonnie Jean saw for an instant a stark and painful longing before she saw only shame. "She would really love it."

Donna went to the cabinet above the sink, took out a first aid kit and held it so Bonnie Jean could choose a Band-Aid. She squatted down to shove it onto her heel while the adults watched her in awkward silence. Finally Patty said, "I'll meet you at eleven o'clock at the admiral's house, Max." She took up her briefcase and Bonnie Jean watched her slide the book into it.

"Do you mind if I walk out with you?" Patty Edwards said to Bonnie Jean.

"Let's go out this door," Bonnie Jean suggested, pointing to the door that led directly outside. "It's pretty dark down in the basement."

She called her goodbyes and glanced back to wave; Colonel Hunter stood on the landing with the oddest, poignant smile.

As they walked, Bonnie Jean chatted to Patty in her friendly way. "I'm glad you came out with me because, to tell you the truth, I don't know exactly *where* Admiral Johnson's house is," she admitted, making Patty laugh, though as they approached the narrow street across from the mansion, Bonnie Jean felt the woman's tension lingering.

"There's Ben and that must be your brother."

Bonnie Jean took Patty's arm. "Come and say hi."

As they approached, Ben said, "You're up early, Ms. Edwards."

"Please. Call me Patty. I stopped by—that is—I had to get something from your father. Because I'm his lawyer."

"Right," Ben said, "his lawyer."

"You boys must be tired from having run all over the Yard."

Ben and Joe looked at each other and smirked. Joe said, "By this time in the season, we can pretty much run forever."

Bonnie Jean said, "Your dad gave Patty a really interesting brown leather *book* to read." She met Ben's eyes first and then Joe's. "When I was going up the stairs, Ben? I saw the water bottles, just like you described, and just as I was getting to the landing, your dad opened the door and grabbed this book from behind the peanut butter jar. Weird place to keep books, don't you think? Anyway, he saw me, so I met your mom and your grandmother, and of course Patty, who was there to—" Bonnie Jean turned to Patty. "Why *were* you there, Patty? Were you there to *get* the book?"

"Um...well...yes."

"Can we see it for a minute?" Joe asked.

Patty stiffened. "No, I'm afraid not."

"Come on," Joe grinned, his dimple showing. "Just for a minute?"

Bonnie Jean said, "Ben's grandmother—I heard her when I was going up the stairs—she said the book is a historical diary and it's *yours*, Ben." Bonnie Jean shook her head in mock bewilderment and looked to Patty for clarification. "Isn't that what she said, Patty?"

"Mine?" Ben said. "If it's mine, I'd like to have it." He held out his hand.

"Not until you're eighteen," Patty said. "Legally, that's when it's yours."

"That may be too late," Ben said. "I need it today."

"I can't give it to you."

"It won't cost you anything to let us look through it," Joe said, holding one hand out, eyes with his intense charm set to melt her will. She looked at each of them in turn, biting her lip and frowning.

"You could buy us all a cup of coffee and give Ben a chance to look at it," Bonnie Jean nudged her shoulder as if she were a buddy. "Come on, it'd be fun."

"I have a deadline." Patty's eyes went very bright and she shook her head. "I don't know the legalities but I'll look into it." She backed away. "Then I'll be in touch." She hurried along the sidewalk.

"I can*not* believe this," Ben said, turning to watch her escape, both fists clenched.

2

ANNAPOLIS Street, ice glazed and blinding in the sun, seemed busier than a normal weekday to Patty Edwards as she squeezed her car into a spot around the corner from Gisela's Delicatessen. Taking her briefcase, she turned up the sidewalk and was surprised to note the CLOSED sign on the deli. She decided to follow the crowd, which had formed a line at the little shop across the street. Patty stepped in line where she caught the fragrance of rich coffee and delicious baking. "What's going on here today?" she asked the woman who came up behind her.

"They're giving the first twenty-five customers a free yard of fabric and there's all sorts of free patterns and Christmas recipes. I come every year. It starts my Christmas season for me."

"But there's a café in there, right? That's the coffee I smell. Is it only drive through or can you sit down?"

"There's a café with chairs and tables and the absolute best chicken salad in the whole world. It's early for that, but there's everything for breakfast. And the macaroni and cheese is to die for. You should try the rolls. Out of this world!"

Patty smiled and nodded. "I will. Thanks."

The woman looked Patty over, noting her briefcase and black suit. "So, you're not here for the free fabric and stuff?"

"No, I don't even know how to thread a pin. I have some work to do and Gisela's is closed." She motioned across the street to the dark deli.

"While you're in there, look at some of the kits and see if you want to try quilting. Or other kinds of sewing. Helps with tension and mental clarity."

Patty wrinkled up her nose. "I work full time, so I don't really need stuff to do."

"I work full time, too," the woman laughed loudly. "How on *earth* do you think I can support my sewing habit?"

Another woman in line turned around, laughing and nodding her head. "The best thing about this shop," she said, "is that they have stuff going on after work in the evenings."

"What do *you* do?" Patty asked

"I cut hair," the second woman said. She stuck out her hand and introduced herself, pointing to her salon down the street. "Come see me; I could do wonders with your hair. Frizzy is my specialty."

With a grimace, Patty turned to the first woman and said, "What do you do?"

"I'm a pediatrician," she pointed in the opposite direction. "Our office is over there near Rowe Boulevard."

"So you all know each other, I suppose."

Shrugging, the doctor said, "Annapolis is a little world with all sorts of surprising connections. What do you do that keeps you so busy?"

"I'm in family law."

"What do you do for fun when you're not working?"

"I smoke," Patty admitted.

"*That's* gotta stop," the doctor said. "Try sewing. Costs far more than smoking and messes up your entire family room, but it's fun. All the color and texture!"

"Cheaper than therapy," the hairdresser said, making a questioning gesture. "Maybe not, but it works."

A cheer from the front of the line announced the open door. Patty did not go straight back to the café. She wandered around the store feeling a little drunk on color. Patty had the rare, imaginative sensation that she was looking at all the resources of sky and earth and ocean, captured and stacked on maple shelves. She shook herself, looked around for the café, and caught sight of the woman who must be the proprietor.

Patty tried to remember what Max had said about her that day at Gisela's when he'd been so obnoxious. She was part of the web that entangled and hurt him. Now, she stood at a counter cutting fabric and chatting with customers. Patty watched her. A skylight brightened the counter space and it seemed to Patty that this woman was the center of the entire cheerful buzz of activity. She could do three things at once. Measuring fabric, she answered questions called from across the table. When she bent to cut the yardage, her short, dark curling hair framed a knowing face with dark brown eyes that sparkled with life and interest as she recited today's café menu. Patty could already taste the pumpkin muffins.

Feeling as if she had a grasp of her surroundings, Patty hefted her briefcase and squeezed past the chattering women to the café at the back of the shop. While in line, she studied the menu, gaped at the glorious food in the curved glass display cases, especially the rows of cookie pretzels, chocolate dipped and seductive. Who ate like this? Yet, when she ordered her cappuccino and omelet, she asked for one of the cookies, a pumpkin muffin and a roll. Patty found a table for two in the back near the drive-through window. She sat with her back to the wall so that she could read and watch.

The drive-through was attended by a young boy. Patty was not good with ages, but she knew this one couldn't be in high school. Small, wiry and serious, with brown eyes as bright and quick as a hawk's, his competence brought a smile to her face. He typed the orders into his computer and called the total out the window. While the customer readied her payment, he ran quickly to fill the bag with items stacked near the little booth. Patty guessed that these were the most common items for the drive-through window. If he had to leave the booth, he dashed like lightening. Customers also ordered food from the window and the waitress brought this to him. Once the boy left his booth for the café counter to correct an order. "My mom wants all cookies ordered out to be in those little boxes," the boy said. "Sorry, but she's particular. I can do it, if you're busy." *So*, Patty thought, *he's her son*. She stared at him then, the quick athleticism of his motions, his handsome, boyish face, freckled nose wrinkling up with a grin that showed a brief dimple when the patron dropped a tip in his rapidly filling tip jar.

In a few minutes a teenage waitress brought Patty's order. She felt ravenous and cut a big bite with her fork. The waitress crossed the café to the window. "Want anything, Tommy?"

"No, thanks. I'm working. I'll wait for my break."

"Break? You may not get a break today. It's crazy."

"Not so crazy you can't come over here and talk to me."

"Your mother asked me to look out for you."

Patty devoured the omelet, watching the boy and listening to him. He did not look so much like his mother, but his way of working, his warmth to the customers, seemed her echo. She sipped her cappuccino, finding it so robust that she moaned aloud. Strong, not bitter, piping hot and creamy, she thought it the perfect complement to the sweets. *Funny*, she thought as she pushed her plates away, *to think of how much a boy gets from his mother*. Perhaps she would find what came to Ben from his mother. From her briefcase, she took a pad of writing paper and placed it on the table. Next she reached for the leather journal.

It's weight struck her until she thumbed its pages and realized how

many extra papers, photographs and fold-out sections had been inserted.
It began:

Dear Diary,

My oldest and dearest friend told me that my diary has
never been honest. Laurie said though the things I write shock
the reader to gulp for air, they hide the real me. There is a difference, she explained, in being candid and in honest self-disclo-
sure. I love this idea and I think it is clever of her to figure me
out! I write the most personal details—bright, distracting things
that hide what I think and feel. I've decided to use this new volume to provide the honest disclosure of my adulthood beginning today. My girlhood is past.

I was late for my own graduation yesterday. It's true. Those
children I've been tutoring from G.'s clinic called from a pay
phone to say that their mother's car had broken down *again*. I
drove right up to help. Of course they were hungry. And so I
was late, sneaked in the back way and into a seat with the zool-
ogy majors. I found my "party" sitting like hairs standing on
end—G. and S., Marie, faithful Doug, and Max, who seethed
with jealousy about Doug's presence. My parents were absent.

Despite the fact that I graduated *summa cum laude*, when
Father learned that I had gotten Max a ticket, he refused to come
and forbid Mother. Can you imagine? A Princeton professor refuses to see his only child graduate from his own university just
because she won't allow him to choose her mate? (Don't think
he'd prefer Doug, dear Diary, as he only tolerates Doug.) I kept
up a brave face through the beautiful luncheon G. arranged and
all afternoon as the unlikely group of us trudged around the beloved campus. I was composed until Max left, then I escaped
those who love me to my dear little car and sobbed for a broken
heart.

Doug found me there. He sat with me until I felt better, and I
let him buy me dinner because he is so dear and we have known
each other so long. There might have been an entire bottle of
Veuve Clicquot enjoyed between us! Then, of course, he came
back to my apartment and we made love to each other in the
most tender and comfortable way. This is one of those shocking
details behind which I am inclined to hide. How did I feel about
cheating on Max? I can make excuses—my broken heart, the
champagne, Doug's devotion, Max's early escape—but the truth
is—it's wrong. And if truth be told, in bed, Doug has always
been intent on my pleasure—our lovemaking is sweet, but...I
hate to say it...dull.

But Max has an emptiness inside that is eased by our love.
Max's jealousy, his desire for me, leads to captivating hours
of him confiding his hopes and disappointments, hours of me
soothing his inner fire with my cool body. I will tell you a terrible

secret—he trembles with what seems like relief or an infusion of
peace when we fall back on the pillows.

 Doug knows neither the compelling urges in my heart, nor
the volcanic nature of Max's passion for me. When I am with
Doug, my heart is quiet and comforted. But Max thrills my heart
to panic...

Patty put her open palm on the book and blew out her breath slowly.
Her hand shook as she lifted her cappuccino to her lips, feeling sympathy
for this writer in her coursing blood. Was that what attracted her to Max—
as Katie put it—his ability to "thrill the heart to panic?" Absolutely! On her
pad of paper, Patty wrote down the names mentioned. She thumbed the
pages, glanced at her watch, and eagerly, she read again.

...Of course, I phoned Laurie and told her what happened (even
about Doug). She was typically blunt with me. She is right; I
must give Doug up though Laurie would rather I gave Max up.
She has the right to say anything to me. She knows my faults—
has suffered because of my needs and actions and loves me yet.

 And so you see, everyone I love wishes I did not want Max,
nor do they love him as I do. He broke Laurie's heart and for
this, G. and S. distrust him, Doug despises him, and Laurie herself says she fears for me. But he hurt Laurie because he wanted
me. It is me who was at fault. There's something cold in me that
would allow myself to embrace Laurie's first love, don't you
agree, dear Diary? Some still, frozen thing within throbs with
life when Max grabs me to him careless of my plans, my loyalties, my duties.

 And this brings me to what happened today. I stomped into
my father's office, ripped up my diploma and tossed it on his
desk. He insists on an arranged marriage, insists he would have
preferred one for himself. That means he regrets Mother. And
me. With that knowledge in my heart, I could barely walk down
the stairs.

 G. was waiting for me. (How did he know I would need
him?) He gave me the greatest compliment: he would like to employ me at the Benedetto Foundation. I am to create an international branch designated to assist and rehabilitate any persons
without resources—those abandoned by their families, country,
neighbors—for whatever reason. That means I am to help anyone at all who is lost or hurt or alone! G. says my compassion is
my greatest gift. How kind G. is to notice me and to believe in
me.

"Whew!" Patty said aloud, thinking that this was not going to be an
easy read. She glanced at her watch knowing she would never make the
deadline and considering if she should skip to the end of the journal or try

to find where Tom MacBride was mentioned. She flipped across the edges of the book, noticing the vague breaths of a woman's perfume. Looking around the lively sewing store, Patty wondered about the secret lives of the women around her, wondered who here might sympathize with this story, or with her own story. Patty had the sudden inner direction to read the book, mind open, from cover to cover. She caught sight again of the store's proprietor and again glanced at the woman's son. Busy wrapping up a colorful stack of folded fabric, he looked up and grinned at her. "You want another cappuccino? I can order it from here and they'll bring it over."

"I'd love another," Patty said. "I'll be here awhile."

3

JOE and Ben found the locker room crowded, but silent. When they saw Oliver sitting on the bench between the row of lockers, they exchanged glances. Joe swung his gym bag to the floor. Adam and Knox opened their lockers and Knox whispered, "Morgan broke up with him."

"No way," Joe whispered. "What happened?"

"Her dad and her went to talk to Ollie together." Knox looked at the door that led to Tom's office. "Mr. Aldzimel is in there now with Coach and Miz Poulard."

Ben walked past Oliver to his locker and Oliver bristled, clenching his fist. Joe sat down beside him. "Morgan broke up with you?"

"Like *you* care," Oliver sneered. "This is your fault and you know it. You got exactly what you wanted."

"What did she say?" Joe said, bumping his shoulder against Oliver in the way he did.

Oliver moved away. "Nothing. Everybody's making a big deal about stuff that's none of their business."

"Did this happen because you apologized?"

"Yeah, right."

Adam said, "Victoria told me that Morgan told Miz Poulard everything." Joe glanced at Adam, one eyebrow raised. "Victoria said that if Morgan didn't tell her parents, Miz Poulard was going to."

"Look, Ollie," Joe said, his voice even, conciliatory. "If you had apologized, you would have seemed more of a man to them."

"That's your fault. We were great before you started laying down your law."

"It's not *my* law. It's common decency." Joe gestured to include all those in the locker room.

"*Morgan* wasn't happy," Knox said. "And you know it. You don't even love her."

"Shut up," Oliver shouted, getting to his feet.

Adam grabbed Oliver around the chest to keep him from lunging at Knox. "You've got to look at this as your chance to make things right," Adam said. At the squeak of the door, Adam released Oliver. The boys exchanged glances.

Tom came to the end of the locker row and said, "I want to see Joe and Ben and Adam, in my office immediately. Drew, you can start practice for me. And keep things on schedule, working hard. We've got a group of parents visiting to watch practice today."

Tom's office smelled of coffee and Mrs. Poulard's flowery perfume. Though he tried to turn his thoughts to practice and the team's problems, Ben could not free his mind of the image of that diary Patty had taken. He pictured it now in his father's broad hands, held open for Patty to read, and his frustration tingled down his arms to his fingertips with wanting to possess it. Tom shut the door behind Adam.

"Parents at practice? Why?" Adam said.

"Mr. Saunders asked some of the parents to watch practice after what happened last week," Tom sighed. "They're just checking up on me. That's their right."

"We'll work hard today, Coach."

"Before that," Tom said, folding his arms over his chest, "I understand you fellows have some photographs."

"Yeah, we do, Coach," Adam said.

"I don't have them with me, Dad."

"Who took these pictures?"

"I did."

"Joe," Tom said, frowning.

"We all were a part of it," Ben offered. "He did the right thing."

"Hmm," Tom said. "Morgan was traumatized."

"Right, I can see that," Joe said, a blush rising up his throat. "But—"

"They were goin' at it pretty hot and heavy on the bus, Coach," Adam said.

"So I understand."

"Dad, we had to let him know that we disagreed. Like Adam said, we could see—*everything*."

"You had to say something. I agree," Tom said. "But for Morgan's sake I did promise Mr. Aldzimel that I'd get those pictures from you and destroy them. Your motives were good, but *pictures*? It's—distasteful. Find another way."

Adam mused, "We all thought it was another stroke of Joe's genius."

"I wish you'd said something to me or your mom, Joe. Or Mrs. Poulard."

"I didn't think you adults would believe us."

"But you didn't *try me*, did you, Joe?"

"No, I didn't."

"Next time, come talk to me," Tom said. "I'll look into whatever concerns you."

"Not even MacBrides can stop bullies." Ben said, reddening, studying the floor. It came out all wrong, mixing somehow with his fury at his father, his frustration about the book he was so sure he was meant to have.

"Tell him why this bothers you so much, Ben," Joe challenged.

Ben gave a warning glance to Joe—whose expression ached with a hope Ben could not answer. *What's with Joe?* Ben fumed silently. *He knows I can't tell.* His anger, a foul and unnatural torrent, like dammed waters roiled. He found no words.

"Has Ollie been giving you a hard time, Ben?" Tom leaned on the edge of his desk.

"It's nothing I can't handle." *I hate my father*, Ben thought, *and when I recognize him in somebody else, no punishment is enough. None.* He started to sweat.

"Boys?" Tom said, glancing at Adam, then Joe. "You want to help Ben tell me why he's so angry?"

"Ben needs to tell you that all by himself," Joe said.

A few moments of awkward silence passed, during which Tom waited, watching them.

Adam shifted from foot to foot in restless confusion, and finally said, "Ben won't tell on a teammate, Coach, and neither will Joe or I. Ollie doesn't like Ben because he's fast and talented and strong, but Ollie hasn't *harmed* Ben."

"Is that right, Ben?"

Ben nodded, looking past Adam's shoulder to hide his embarrassment from Tom. *If I'm so fast and so strong, why does Dad win every time?* "Oliver doesn't like me, but it's nothing you should talk to him about. I just can't stand bullies."

Joe said, "*That's* what's important here, Dad."

Tom glanced at Joe and back to Ben. "Are we still talking about Ollie?" Joe stared at Ben, eyebrows up, willing Ben to speak. Ben clenched his jaw, mouth a tight line. Beyond their silence they could hear basketballs tapping on the gym floor, feet running, voices sounding. Ben studied his shoes. Tom touched Joe's shoulder. "I need those pictures, Joe. Right away."

"They're not even on school property, Dad." Joe winced. "Paul has one at home, Pete took one up to school with him, and I—I hid my copy in Grannie's shed."

"*What?*"

587

"Dad, before you get upset, remember, I did all of this before—"

"Imagine Grannie's *reaction* if she were to open that! Hoots!"

Joe squinched up his mouth to keep his grin from coming, but his eyes danced with mischief and his voice resounded with the echoes of his nature. "Okay, okay, I admit I *did* think of that."

Tom shook his head at Joe, lips tight. He grabbed his whistle, pointed toward the gym, swung open his door, and whispered, "Lord have mercy," as he stepped into the hall.

"Just another example," Adam quipped as they followed Tom out of his office to the gym, "of the genius of Joe MacBride."

Joe gave an uncomfortable shrug.

"I still think," Ben whispered, pressing down the edges of the Band-Aid that hid his stitches, "the pictures were necessary. They're proof. You should never give up the proof."

4

PATTY looked up to see if anyone noticed her scalding blush. Though key words in Katie's description of Max's lovemaking were written in French or Italian, from the context, Patty had harvested enough detail to understand what Max meant when he claimed that Katie was "sexual." This endeared her to Patty as her confessions moreover convinced that she was honest and that she truly loved Max, despite the different kinds of love and yearning she felt for other men.

She checked her list for people mentioned: G. and S., Marie, Guillaume—relatives; Ella and Jim—Max's parents. Her friend Laurie had married Tom MacBride with Katie as the maid of honor. Max did not attend. Katie seemed fond of Tom but referred to him as if speaking about a brother. No sexual activity or even attraction was recorded. The former lover, Doug, was Laurie's brother and Patty could feel Katie's tenderness for him. Patty wondered why Max had never expressed jealousy over *this* man. She turned the page to continue.

> October and terrible news! When he left Sunday night during an explosive argument, I thought he'd not call for weeks, but Max called today from what they call the brig (military jail). His commanding officer has accused him of pushing Tom MacBride off some training tower. He's to face a court martial and had no information on the state of Tom's health. I am driving down there but I've stopped at this awful HoJo on 301 for a cup of insipid coffee and to write for a minute…
>
> …I've seen Max—bars separating us—only able to touch hands. He insists they were just joking around when Tom got weird and hit him; then they fought. Seeing their strife, the CO

forced them to work as partners climbing this ridiculous, unsafe obstacle course. But Max says that Tom was still angry and pushed him at the top. Oh, dear Diary, do not think me a disloyal lover but I do not think Tom is likely to have done that. Tom is a strong, disciplined soul apt only to fight to defend someone. If he fought, who was he defending? The answer is obvious... his beloved Laurie. Defending against what? It does not require genius to imagine what Max might have said to...or about her. And Tom deliberately pushing someone to his probable death? No, it's not possible.

Thursday: G. has arrived and confided that Tom's injury is *écrasant*. By this G. means it is of the shattering quality—likely to defeat Tom. G. counseled alone with Max for hours and wore his sternest expression upon emerging from the brig. Laurie asks if I really want to marry Max.

Friday: Max insists his innocence. His lawyers have been with him all day. G. and I prayed together for the first time in a long time. Laurie and I cried together. Tom will never walk again. Tom's father came today.

Saturday: Doug is here. He talked to Tom. G. was attending. I stood, hidden, at the door. Here is how it went:

D: Why did you hit him?

T: He said something. I lost my temper.

D: About Laurie? Then he deserved it. Did he shove you?

T: It's hard to know for sure.

D: (coldly and without passion) If you don't walk out of this bed, Tom, I will kill him.

G: No, Doug. I implore you. That is not the way.

D: This from a man who killed more Nazis than I got hairs on my ass?

I left. This is too tangled. Max was angry at me last weekend because I didn't want to talk marriage. That's why this happened. I'm giving Doug up and I promise to marry Max and to be faithful.

Sunday: The way G. tells the story is that Tom was making his hospital bed when he, Edmund MacBride, and Laurie arrived to visit this morning. Tom's explanation? He forgave Max's insult, intends to apologize to Max for hitting him and for being so angry and starting the fight. This Tom said in prayer and God touched his back as if with a burning stick. He's well.

You would be proud of me, dear Diary. Last night I met Doug at a restaurant (not my hotel room) and told him never again. You know how I will miss Doug's sweet comfort. He begged me to see he's changed, but he doesn't understand I have moved on, that all this was my fault. That Max needs me to make a life with him. Today I intend to tell Max we can marry. But not until April. So much is happening with the dental clinic we've established for gypsies in Florence. I'll focus on that first.

Patty closed Katie's journal, pushed back her chair, and stood up. *Is this Tom MacBride for real?* Stiff from sitting, she hobbled over to the drive-through window and asked the boy if he would mind keeping an eye on her stuff. Busy but pleasant, he nodded. Patty took her cell phone, left the café area and went into the busy shop. She waited a minute near the proprietor and when she looked up, Patty got in her field of vision and gave a brisk, professional smile.

"Hi, I just wanted to say that I'm working over there and I hope I'm not taking up table space you need on this very busy day."

"I saw you over there," Laurie said. "It's funny, sometimes a noisy place is the perfect place to concentrate if the background noise isn't your responsibility or interest."

"Exactly. I've gotten so much done."

"I'm so glad."

"And the food is delicious."

"You're welcome to stay as long as you'd like."

"I just need to make a phone call." Patty held up her phone. "Do you mind cell phone use in the store?"

"I don't mind, but I wonder how well you'll be able to hear. Why not step into my office?" With a gesture to follow, Laurie excused herself to those around her and led Patty past the counter, past the rows of green fabrics to a closed door. "I am so happy to break away for a minute. I was wanting an excuse to run back in here and get my hand lotion anyway."

Laurie opened the door to her office, grabbed a little tube of lotion left on the edge of her elegant mahogany desk, and made a sweeping, gracious gesture to Patty. "Make yourself at home. If you hear a baby, don't worry. My daughter is just rocking my newborn to sleep in the next room."

Leaning against the desk edge, Patty called Admiral Johnson's office. The Admiral himself answered. "Oh, Admiral Johnson. I thought surely your secretary would answer."

"The day after Thanksgiving? No, I gave her the day off. Now, to whom do I have the pleasure of speaking?"

"This is Patty Edwards. I represent Colonel Hunter—he asked me to advise him on some legal matters."

"Yes. That's right. I do have you written down here for an appointment in a little bit. I am looking forward to meeting you."

Pacing in front of the desk, Patty was explaining that Max had given her some background material to read when her eye caught sight of family pictures on the desk. She told herself to concentrate on the phone call. But she could now hear quiet singing from beyond the door to her right and Patty's eyes focused on the photograph. The children she'd met today—the spunky Bonnie Jean, her handsome brother—*this* woman's children! Max had said, 'This is Laurie Davidson's little girl…' Laurie Davidson—

Doug Davidson's sister, who married Tom MacBride. Patty gasped. That was the connection that had eluded her this morning! And here she was. Small town indeed!

"Ms. Edwards? You were saying that you have reading to do?"

"Yes, sir," she croaked hoarsely, wishing for a cigarette. "I think it is vital that I understand the background of the situation and get a perspective that is not Colonel Hunter's."

"That may be, but more importantly, *Ben* deserves a perspective that is not Colonel Hunter's. I want all questions about the validity of the colonel's personnel file resolved before my Christmas break. And I take from this call that Max has not spoken to Ben and told him the truth about himself."

"Yes, sir. That was to be the subject of our meeting today. As Colonel Hunter understands things, you wish to force him to give Ben details about his first marriage. Admiral, any court in the country would side with Colonel Hunter on this issue. Legally, it is none of your business, though I don't mean to be disrespectful in saying that, sir."

"You can say it any way you want, Ms. Edwards, but I would argue that it most certainly *is* my business. Especially when you consider the stories with which Colonel Hunter is challenging the information in his personnel file. At USNA we do not take kindly to our senior officers lying. The mids themselves are held to a strict honor code. If I wink at Colonel Hunter—the senior marine—walking around weaving lies, what do I say to *them*?"

"Admiral Johnson, I respect your reputation and your instincts, sir, but documentation is vital. Which is why I *must* have time to examine the material Colonel Hunter gave me."

"Ms. Edwards, I like to fight fair. I should tell you that not only did I have the distinct pleasure of acquaintance with the *first* Mrs. Hunter, but I also have, right here"—she heard what sounded like a ream of paper slapped onto a desk—"a boatload of *documentation* I've dug up since my instinct kicked in and told me something was wrong."

What documentation? Aloud she said, "Admiral Johnson, sir, I would very much like to work with you to bring a good outcome to all parties involved—to Ben especially, to Colonel Hunter, and to the Naval Academy. I served in the navy for twelve years myself."

"Hmm," Johnson said, thinking.

"Working this out amicably would be best for everyone, sir."

"Have you known Colonel Hunter for long?"

"Twenty years, sir."

"Then you knew his first wife?"

"No. The first contact I've had with her is when I started reading her personal...*essays* this morning," Patty said. "Will you allow me some time to read this collection, Admiral? If I can understand her perspective, I will be able to help Max devise a way to begin the conversation with Ben that you've requested. If I know more about her, I can speak *for* her. From what I've read so far, I think she is more than worthy of my advocation."

Johnson was silent for a long moment. "Yes, I think you're right, Ms. Edwards. And I think I can work with you. Read it. Call my secretary on Monday to reschedule."

Patty's hands were shaking when she thrust them both into her pockets looking for a cigarette and lighter. She found two slightly bent cigarettes and honestly felt like smoking them both at once. Sticking the straighter one into her lips, she picked up a photograph and peered at it closely, marveling at the children's expressions, at the parents' joy. She took it with her over to the window, which she opened all the way. Sticking her head out, Patty lit the cigarette and pulled in a deep breath. She ducked back in to study the photograph, holding the cigarette out the window. The door opened behind her.

"Patty? What are *you* doing here? Smoking in my mother's office?"

She lifted her eyes to find Bonnie Jean looking at her with an appalled and amused expression.

Patty snuffed out the butt on the outside of the windowsill and dropped it down. "Oh, sorry! You caught me!"

"My mother's nose is her super power."

Patty hurried to put down the photograph. "I came in the café just to get a cup of coffee and read and I stayed so long I had to cancel an appointment. I saw your pictures and I got all distracted! To think I just met you and here I am! The only place open this morning," she explained. "What a gorgeous family." She glanced at her watch. "Oh, God! I still have to call Max!"

"He's not coming *here*, is he?"

"What's the connection between him and your mother?"

Bonnie Jean's expression told Patty that the teenager had noticed her hyper state, but she still answered. "From what I know, they dated in high school. He broke her heart, but she's totally over him now."

Patty nodded and tried to smile, reassuring herself that no woman would give up the sunny happiness she saw in the photograph for the turbulence that was Max.

"After you make your phone call," Bonnie Jean said, sitting on the desk, "I'll introduce you to my mom."

Patty punched in Max's office number and turned her back to Bonnie Jean. "Max. It's Patty."

"I know it's you, Patty. No one else croaks quite like you."

"Um. Here's the deal. I postponed your appointment with the admiral."

"Hey, I knew I loved you. What's the plan, now?"

"I call his secretary on Monday. This will give me time to finish my research."

"Research?"

"Yeah, you know."

"What? Reading her journal? Just look for that crap at the end! Don't overdo it. She literally wrote down everything."

"You know, Max, I'm in a public place, so I can't go into details about the case now, but I have research to do and I want to do it carefully and think about the implications."

"Can I see you for lunch, though?"

"I'll see how far I get."

"Prefer work over pleasure? Come on, Patty. I got the day off, pretty much."

"I'll call you when I feel like I have a grasp on things."

"You could have a grasp on—"

"I've gotta go, Max." She cut him off, pressing the red button on her phone.

Bonnie Jean's eyebrows were both in arches when Patty met her eyes, but the girl forced a smile. "Come and meet my mom," she said, taking Patty's elbow.

5

TOM'S sympathy for Morgan and her parents, his concern for Oliver, seemed heightened by the effects of a nearly sleepless night spent speculating about Ben's well-being after Ben showed up at their back door looking pale and skittish. When he saw that Peter had arrived and was visiting amicably with the group of parents gathered on the sidelines, Tom felt strengthened. He told himself to be careful not to let his irritation with Oliver and John Saunders color his responses to everyone else. Even Joe had annoyed him just now and the reality of the parents, inflamed by gossip, here to keep their children safe from his dear friend Doug Davidson—whose mouth might not be proper, but whose heart was big and generous—sickened Tom. So he greeted Peter first, hand on his shoulder. "Hey, Pete. Thanks for coming."

"I was just telling Mr. Cohen how my roommate found a used Band-Aid in his scrambled eggs."

Mr. Cohen chuckled, "I know Austin's mother will never stand for that when Austin gets ready to go."

"Yep," Tom said. "The least they could do is provide kids a new Band-Aid for breakfast."

The laughter helped. Tom and Peter greeted the visiting parents, shaking hands, passing a few friendly words, welcoming them with the disciplined MacBride courtesy—despite the unease dulling those parents' eyes.

Coach Brock and Drew had run the warm-up drills. A fifteen-minute scrimmage between upper and lower classmen seemed just the thing to awaken the boys and loosen them up after Thanksgiving. Tom hoped it would show the parents how much they learned in practice, how clean was the camaraderie, how organized was the instruction. By the time Tom blew the whistle, the energy of wholesome learning crackled in the gym. A couple of parents left, but John Saunders took his place at the center of those remaining. While Brock led the others in basic passing and shooting drills, Tom and Peter worked with the starters in one-on-one defense strategies. Tom glanced at his watch, wondering how Saunders could be so intent on this practice while waiting for an emergency appointment called by his son's principal.

After Drew had shown how to execute their moving, hand-in-the-face defense, Tom asked Oliver to demonstrate how he blocked shots under the basket.

Ollie hesitated, glancing at his father. "Just as review," Peter urged. "You're good at it." Oliver shrugged and as Paul jumped to do a lay-up, Oliver followed him, hand raised, and slapped at the ball. "Just go for it," Oliver said. "If the ref doesn't like you, he'll call it anyway."

"Well," Tom said, wishing that for once he could let this kind of false statement go. "It's not about who likes you, boys." He purposely did not direct the comment to Oliver. "It's about timing." He glanced at his clipboard. "We got eight goaltending fouls in the last five games. We're not anticipating the shot, we're just trying to stop it after we see the guy go for it."

"All those fouls weren't me."

"No, of course not, Ollie," Tom said. "We're all trying to improve."

Quickly, loudly, Drew said, "Hey, Ben. Let's review for everybody how you rattle the offense."

"Good idea," Tom said, handing off the ball to him. "Drew, drive to the basket, and Ben, you show how you do it." After their swift demonstration, Ben and Drew rejoined the group. "Well done, Ben," Tom said. He felt Saunders' hackles rise but said, "It's about composure and anticipation. Guarding is this fluid when it's working right. Let's pair up and everybody try that. Drive and then switch."

"Your Band-Aid's coming loose," Drew mentioned to Ben as they walked together to the half court line where the rest of the team was lining up. "Don't want that landing on the court."

"Oh." Ben flipped the ball to Drew and used both hands to press down the edges.

"I noticed that Band-Aid last night," Tom said from beside him. "What happened?"

"I got a cut," Ben said.

Drew peered at him. "Your chin looks—I don't know—swollen or something."

"I just need to shave."

Tom knew he had to keep the practice moving but he felt compelled to ask, "How did you cut yourself?"

"I...uh..." Ben looked to the sideline, past the parents lined up there, and glanced at the doors beyond that led to the locker room. "I hit my head on the corner of the cabinets. In the kitchen."

Joe made a coughing noise; Peter moved in closer.

"That hurts," Tom sympathized. Tom noticed Joe's odd expression, an intense stare, lips pressed together. Aware of the visiting parents, Tom felt he should not press it further, but Joe looked genuinely upset and Peter's laconic posture had gone tense.

"When did this happen?"

"Um..."

"I didn't notice the Band-Aid at the game."

"After the game. I hit it on the kitchen cabinet."

"That's not the whole story, though," Joe said.

"No?" Tom peered at Joe.

"Yes," Ben said, "it *is*."

"What's the rest of it, Ben?" Joe said.

"That's *it*, Joe."

"Right," Joe said, his voice rising in anger. "You *did* hit your head on the kitchen cabinet, but...*tell* him."

"You have something to tell me?" For some reason Tom's heart pounded in alarm. Maybe because he could sense the rumblings of discontent on the sidelines behind him, rumblings like the pawing of hooves ready to trample. This while Ben and Joe stared at each other, Joe's squinted blue eyes bright with anger, but Ben's expression was composed—no, it was cold—only his flared nostrils showed his steely and furious determination.

Saunders called Tom's name, his tone restless, eager.

Tom said to Ben, "Out with it."

Ben's eyes went swiftly to Joe's. "I had to get *stitches*," Ben said slowly, his voice a sharp blade.

"Stitches? Is that all? Let's get on with practice," Tom called to his athletes, backing away from the center court line. "Everybody in your pairs and go until the whistle blows. Then switch." Taking his whistle in hand, he turned toward the court and in his peripheral vision, he saw Joe lunge at Ben.

"Was that a threat?" Joe shouted, shoving Ben's shoulders with both hands. "Because I don't *care* if he knows about the stitches!"

Ben whirled around, went for Joe. Drew grabbed Ben, trapping his arms at his sides; Peter held Joe back.

"This is your *chance*," Joe shouted, twisting to get free of Peter's hold.

"Enough," Tom thundered, running back to them. He stepped between.

He took Ben's fist in one hand, Joe's wrist in the other. To Joe he said, "What did you do? Did you hit him?"

"I shoved him."

"Discourtesy is *always* a sign of weakness. You know that, Joseph!"

"This is *no place* for your principles, Dad. You have *no idea* what's at stake here."

Tom squinted at Joe. "Joe, you've run smack into my principles. You provoked Ben."

"I did." Joe squirmed, wrenching his angular shoulders to try to break free. "I'd do it again," Joe growled. "A million times."

"Not on my watch," Tom said.

"Stop," Peter hissed in Joe's ear. "Think of Dad's back."

With a warning glance that stopped Joe's writhing, Tom turned to Ben. He raised Ben's fist up to chin level so Ben had to look at it. Eyes squinted to a keen stare, he said, "You were going to hit your best friend?"

Tom saw the astonishment, the horror in Ben's eyes as he stared at his own clenched fist. "Just got a real ugly look at yourself, didn't you, son?" Ben's breath choked; he couldn't speak. "This is wrong," Tom said, his tone severe. Ben's fist in one hand, Joe's wrist in the other, Tom held them up, stared from one to the other. "You could not have done anything to displease me more." His eyes met Joe's. "Especially after what we went through yesterday." The look in Tom's eyes cut into Ben's conscience. "Boys," Tom said hoarsely, "you two are *brothers*."

From too close behind them, Saunders said loudly, "Looks like your kid's learning his manners from his uncle."

The gym went silent. Tom's back stiffened and he felt his anger rise. "Don't even look over there, Joe," Tom said in a tone meant to convince. "Don't make this worse. Remember Grannie. Remember yesterday," Tom coached quietly. "Ignore him. You're my son and I won't have you striking out in anger."

Joe slumped in Peter's grip, his throat and face going bright red. "I blew it, Ben. I lost my temper. But *say* it."

"You can't force this," Peter said in his brother's ear. "Remember what's at stake."

"Please." Joe said to Ben. "You've *got* to."

"I swear I'll cut off my hand before I make a fist again," Ben's hoarse voice sounded. "But *no*. I'm *sorry*."

"No need for drama," Tom snapped. "Your word will do." He made a gesture toward Drew and Peter. "Let them go." Taking each boy's shoulder in hand he held them away from each other and said to Peter. "Could you oversee this drill? I'll see to them." He nodded to Brock to continue as he walked Ben and Joe over to the bleachers away from the staring parents.

Standing between them still, his hands gripping the backs of their necks, he said, "I can tolerate your mischief, Joe, and all the testing you have to do to understand things, but I will not tolerate you fighting with Ben. I won't." He released Joe. Wishing Ben would look up, would look him in the eye, he spoke to the side of Ben's averted face, "You may not trust me. I understand that. But I will not tolerate you fighting with Joe. Do you believe me?" Ben nodded. Tom dropped his hand from Ben's shoulder.

"And you, son? Do you understand how important this is to me?"

"I do, Dad, but you haven't got the big picture."

"You're right. I don't know what's behind this, but you two will have to work it out." Thinking, searching for a way to make Ben and Joe see, Tom let his eyes wander around the gym. Practice was limping back into motion, but the remaining parents' attention had followed him over to the corner of the gym where he stood with the boys. Now, the parents were turned toward him and stared with mulish eyes at the backs of the two chastened boys. Did they not realize the sacred nature of the teachable moment?

Tom moved his hands to the boys' shoulders and drew them in a little closer. He was not angry now, but hoped for the sweet, fierce power to inspire. "Here's how you're going to do it. You're running for the rest of practice, which means neither of you starts against Baltimore Lutheran." In answer to their chagrined responses—the swift dropping of those defensive shoulders, both boys folding their arms, frustrated eyes meeting and giving identical, self-deprecating snorts—Tom said, "That's your penalty. You know better."

Tom raised his hand to forbid discussion. "First you will run this vinegar out of your systems. Then you will come to an agreement by each giving the other three concessions. The way you solve an argument is to see things from the other man's perspective and give him concrete evidence that you understand. Got it?"

"Yes, sir," Ben said.

"Dad, listen. I'm right about this."

"You're still fighting, Joe. No one is ever completely right. Not even you."

"It's *not* what you're thinking."

Tom willed Joe to cooperate, his heart yearning. "Trust me, son."

"You don't understand what you're *asking*," Joe warned him, his tone broken and angry.

"Oh, yes I do. You two are not going to fight. Things have to change."

"That's *why* I'm fighting," Joe murmured.

"You are going to work out a compromise like brothers. That's what Max and I should have done." He pointed to one, then the other. "That's the only solution I will accept. You're going to talk it out until you reach an agreement. Whatever it takes. You're both going to have to give. Now go."

"Tom!" John Saunders motioned for Tom to join the three parents still watching practice. Tom limped to them. "I've got to get back to practice, folks," he said politely. "But first, I'd like to say that I did *not* appreciate the comment about my brother-in-law, John."

Saunders shrugged. "It's true."

"It is neither true nor kind. I love and respect my brother-in-law. He did suffer a shock on Tuesday at practice. But he is a trustworthy man. Do not think you're welcome in this gym if you behave rudely to my family members…or anyone else I have set my heart to watch over."

Mr. Cohen broke the awkward silence by reaching to shake Tom's hand. "You have my full support, Tom. "I've got some errands to run. I'll be back at twelve-thirty to get Austin."

"Thanks, Basil," Tom said to him. Basil Cohen put an arm around John Saunders, and said, "Let's go get some coffee, John. Leave Tom to do his job."

"I just want to make sure that *his* kid is made to follow the rules."

"Why do you think I have those rules, John?"

Saunders shrugged. "Keeps the bad ones in line."

"No, it doesn't. Rules never keep *anyone* in line. The rules state the standard of behavior that I expect because I'm hoping—every day I'm hoping and praying—that my rules will show the boys some deep truths about life and themselves and about their maker. I help the boys live up to those rules—my boys, your boy, everybody's boy. What I suggest *you* do, is let Basil get you that cup of coffee and trust me with this practice."

6

AT nearly two o'clock, Laurie knew by the dry, quaking feeling in her limbs that she had to have a cup of tea. She ducked into the café and to her delight Beth had just made a fresh pot of tea. Laurie stirred in the cream and sugar, took a bite of the sandwich Beth had just been wrapping for her, and taking them with her, went the long way back to the counter.

As Laurie approached the woman Bonnie Jean had introduced earlier, she observed her. *She certainly is engaged in that book,* Laurie thought as she approached the little round table, noting that the woman's heavy, curling hair fell like a veil over her work station. Her long, slim legs crossed at the knee, she shook her right foot in a rhythm, the spiky-heeled shoe dangling from the toes. Though Bonnie Jean had introduced her as Max's lawyer, Laurie understood the eloquent shock glinting in her daughter's eyes. *Yes,* Laurie thought, *she is Max's type.* Tall, leggy, and probably a super athlete. Laurie felt sick, thinking of Donna's crushed feelings, Ben's disillusionment, but the demands of the store had given her time to regain her composure. Now she wanted to speak to this Patty Edwards, who flicked her hair back over her shoulder, then made a note on the pad of paper beside the book she read.

Laurie stared at the book. The extra papers throughout, the long ribbon marker, the gilt-edged pages wavy with age were so familiar that she recalled the smoothness of the leather binding as if she were holding it now in her hand. She stood still for an instant, the fragrance of the tea wafting up to her, reassuring her that she was not dreaming. Katie's journal, right there, and exactly what Ben needed.

Laurie put a smile on her face and walked right up to the table. "I'm sorry I couldn't visit with you when Bonnie Jean introduced you," she said.

Patty looked up, whipped her glasses off, a pleased smile lighting her face. Laurie was struck by the straightforward set of her mouth, was touched by the tears in her eyes. "Oh, don't be," Patty said. "I understand work."

"You—um—you're reading my friend Katie's diary."

"Yes."

"I recognized it, of course. I would know it anywhere. I'm the Laurie mentioned on the first page."

"I figured that out. Small world. I just met your kids this morning." Patty shook her head. "Have you read this?"

"Parts. Katie's the sister I never had."

"I hardly know what to say," Patty said. "It's so honest; she struggles, and I can identify with—well, you know, with her."

"Why are you reading it?"

Patty breathed in and out slowly. "Bonnie Jean told you that I'm Max's lawyer, right? He asked me to read it. Obviously, I can't say anymore, though I'd like to."

Laurie nodded. "It would be good for Ben if he could read it."

"Personally, I agree with you."

"But Max doesn't."

Patty shrugged.

Laurie said with a self-deprecating laugh, "You have me at a disadvantage, Patty, if you're reading Katie's diary. You know all about my wild youth."

"What was Max like when you dated him?"

"He was the new boy in town, brooding, lonely, gorgeous that summer at the pool," Laurie said. "He was so intent and demanding that foolishly, I felt more alive. I was the bookish type in high school." *And right now,* Laurie thought, *I'd give just about anything to get my hands on that book.*

"It's hard to explain his attractiveness unless you know him." Patty waved her hand over the journal. Laurie actually pictured grabbing it and running, but Patty said, "It sounds as if they had a rough marriage."

"Katie was a free spirit and Max was unreasonably jealous."

"But he had *reason* to be jealous."

"Once Katie made up her mind, she was faithful. This I'm sure of. Max has never been."

Patty looked hurt, upset. "That's because her behavior disillusioned him so much."

"Do you think so?" Laurie said. Against her will, her heart softened toward the loyal and deceived Patty and in a rush of compassion, her letdown reflex tingled deep in her breasts. She pressed her forearms tight to stop her milk. "Oh, gosh," she laughed at herself. "I'm nursing a baby and all this talk about Katie makes me emotional."

"I'm sorry…about Katie," Patty said, looking puzzled and hurt.

Laurie smiled. "Ben has Katie's dazzling blue eyes, you know—the kind you can notice all the way across the street—and the same kind of brilliance and the same contemplative composure."

"What does he get from Max, do you think?"

"Physical strength, math ability—Katie wasn't the best at math. Maybe the shape of his hands, those broad feet." To Laurie's surprise, Patty jotted this comment down on her pad. "So, you're Max's lawyer. Are you in the military?"

"I was," Patty said, blushing. "Actually, I met Max years ago; we were stationed in the Med."

"So you knew him when Ben was born. So you know everything that happened."

"I really don't know much, Laurie," Patty said, "I thought that if I read Katie's journal I might be able to help."

"Why does he need a lawyer?"

"I've said far too much already. I don't know what's wrong with me."

Laurie smiled again, meaning it. "If I can help you with your work…"

"Actually I do have a question or two. Um, do you know if Max has any other children…maybe fathered during one of their separations?"

"If he did, Katie didn't know about it."

"How about Katie? Did she have lovers during those times?"

"Why is this important?"

"I'm trying to reassure Max," Patty said in a confidential tone that

Laurie perceived to be only partially sincere, "so that his heart can be eased." Briskly she added, "So he can think objectively."

"Katie's life changed profoundly after she left Max. It is all recorded in there. I think you'll find it touching."

"For instance," Patty said, eyes narrowed. "Your brother?"

Laurie pointed at the book. "She gave Doug up before she and Max were married. She wrote about that, I know."

"Maybe you just didn't know about her affairs."

"Doug is my twin. We're very close. He wouldn't have kept something like that from me. And really," Laurie said, "Doug is not the cheating type. He loved Katie and wanted to rescue her from Max. That's why he hung on for so long."

"Rescue? That's a strong word. I hardly think—" Patty shook her head and gulped.

"I have to get back to work," Laurie said. "Patty, please come back and let me know if I can help you further. It's going to take you a while to finish that diary." She moved her hand in a gesture that included the shop. "You're welcome to the cappuccino—gratis, of course—if you want to come here and work and ask me questions."

"That's very kind of you."

Laurie offered her hand to shake. "I'm so glad we've met. I hope you'll come back, and in the meantime, take care of yourself."

Running, Ben kept his eyes staring, cold and unseeing in the way that he did when he needed to escape. He saw as he did in a dream—the only reality his thoughts and the steady footfall that propelled him forward to mete out Tom's punishment. His coach had been specific about how he and Joe were to run their laps. First they were to run in opposite directions three times around the gym. Ben approached Joe; they passed, shoulders nearly brushing. Ben stared through Joe's intent gaze. Tom said that the first man back to the starting point won the right to the first concession. Ben was sure Joe would demand that he tell, so he had to win, but his hip ached where his father had kicked him; it ached worse than it had when they jogged to Porter Road and back.

He looked up, Joe approaching, their eyes met again. Tom had said the second man gets the last word. They had one more lap this way and then they had to circle the gym fifteen times, the last five going backward. The sticking point here was that they had to stay together, help each other finish if necessary. If they refused, they'd sit out two games. Ben pushed himself, but his muscles ached; the deep bruises were calling out.

If Tom saw his bruises, the truth would come out and his mother's life would be lost. But part of the truth was that Joe had literally put him back together. He owed Joe his life.

I want to tell, Ben prayed silently, *but how can I? I risk my own life every time I'm near Dad, but I can't risk hers. If I take what I want — my freedom, the right to sleep at the MacBrides' house — it's at her expense. That's not noble. That's not right. Even if it were right, I couldn't do it. I've always looked out for her. Always, since I was little.* Ben remembered the heavy panic he associated with his mother's tentative happiness and he felt himself slow. A cramp jumped in his right calf. He met Joe's eyes in this last pass and Ben saw in them the same weight of fear. *He's trying to take care of me the way I have to protect her. Help me, Lord. I read that you look with compassion on the afflicted. If that's not me, who is it?*

Joe knew he'd win the first concession. He was far ahead of Ben and Ben's limping suggested pain and a bad cramp. Remembering how injured Ben had been, feeling in his own self Ben's need to heal, Joe also knew he would be loyal. It was his strength: Joseph Spenser MacBride was a loyal friend. He could not tell on Ben when he knew that Ben trusted him— knew that he and Bonnie Jean were the *only* people Ben trusted. Yet all the new growth, the clean yearning inside him, called him to live up to his father's baffling, stellar principles and say what he knew.

But Tom had taught him to be loyal; Tom loved and respected Joe's loyalty. Then there was Pete; Joe considered his older brother's impulses somehow purified from heaven. Pete didn't want Tom risking injury— maybe death—and Pete was right. That was the problem. Everyone he loved and respected had dearly held principles and these tugged against each other in this field of battle like determined and passionate opponents.

Joe could visualize, as clearly as if he held it in his hand, the strength and vibrancy that would be Ben's if Ben could speak about the horrors he hid. He desired it so fiercely, expected it so immediately, that his frustration boiled within him. It was right; it was necessary; it had to happen. His feet moving swiftly, racing down the sideline, Joe saw Drew give him a thumbs-up, saw Pete's sympathetic, encouraging nod, and he knew: even if Tom guessed the truth, Ben would deny it. No, Ben had to say the words, 'I hate and fear my father because he beats me up.' And Joe had to do everything he could to get Ben strong enough to say it.

Joe waited for Ben at the starting point, waited, breathing deeply. Joe greeted him by saying, "You'd be faster if you'd quit smoking," and grinned.

Ben smiled and nodded to show he wanted to keep running, though his panting denied this.

"Dad didn't say anything about speed," Joe said, as they started off in step. "Let's take it slow." Ben nodded again.

They did not speak as they pushed around the gym, but at points Joe thought he might have to support Ben's stride, and these times diminished his anger. Fifteen laps later, thigh muscles quaking, sides aching, they bent side by side to drink at the water fountains, and when Joe shut the door behind them in Tom's office, Ben said, "Sorry, Joe."

"It's just that I thought for sure you would have *told* by now," Joe said, guiding Ben toward the cot under the window with one hand on his friend's shoulder, making him sit down.

"I can't ever tell. Ever." Ben kept anxious eyes on Joe as Joe pulled Tom's desk chair around to the front of the desk. Ben leaned forward, elbows on his knees, head in his hands.

"But you can't keep getting beat up. You can't. He *hurt* you this time." Ben looked down. "Was this the worst time?"

"One of them," Ben said. "All the blood. There was so much blood. All for a stupid book."

Joe was quiet a minute. "This sucks so bad."

"Seeing Dad out of control, really out of his mind..." Ben shook his head. "It freaks me out, Joe." The quiet between them allowed them to hear their teammates' voices raucous in the locker room. "You won the first concession," Ben said. Joe saw Ben's hands shaking, watched him trap them under folded arms against his sides.

"This is it," Joe said. "You have to do whatever it takes to keep yourself safe. That's what I care most about."

"I thought you were going to say I had to tell. And I can't."

"So, that's your first concession? That *I* have to understand why you can't tell?"

"I didn't tell you why before—" the words choked in his throat.

Joe waited, thinking of Bonnie Jean's idea of the threefold cord. He wished she were there to help them. "You know I'm going to stand by you."

"If I tell, if Tom ever knows, my mom says she'll—"

"What? Hurt you? We won't let her."

"Herself. Not hurt, kill."

"Oh, no," Joe breathed. "No way."

"I can't risk my mother's life."

"She shouldn't threaten you," Joe shook his head, fighting for control of his emotions. "It's wrong."

"She's my mother." Ben gestured, both shoulders drawn together to illustrate the trap that held him. "She's depressed. I've always suspected she was this close to suicide," he said, squeezing the tips of his thumb and forefinger together. "At night, when I hear her in the bathroom, I lie there listening, so that if I hear her drop down, I can call nine-one-one."

"Okay," Joe winced, shuddering. "This is worse than I thought. But I'm going to help you. Whatever that means. We agree that you're going to keep yourself safe and away from danger. Next we agree that you can't tell my father because you have to protect your mother's life. I'll help you protect her."

"That means a lot," Ben said, meeting Joe's eyes.

"My next," Joe said, "is that we figure out how to get your mother some help. It can be confidential. Or let me and Jeannie ask someone besides Dad for help."

"Who could I ask?"

"How about your mother's parents?"

"I don't even know them. And Gran saw him beat me up; she just looked away."

"So your grandmother's out. But we need someone who can help your mom take care of herself," Joe watched Ben and spoke carefully, reluctant to rouse in Ben the inherent and implacable loyalties of sonship, "and help her see you need protection. Maybe a hotline or…"

Ben shifted uncomfortably, the cot squeaking and hitting the wall behind. His throat and face reddened. Joe hesitated to say what he was thinking—that Ben's mother had to be convinced to inform Admiral Johnson or the police or Tom himself. But Ben said, "I ought to be able to protect myself from him."

"No. It's because you hope," Joe said. "It's like me and Grannie. I fall for it every time because I'm hoping she'll be different—normal, then—whammo." Ben nodded, stared at the floor, lips tight. Joe said, "We could ask Gregen."

"Maybe."

"If we tell him she's suicidal, he's a doctor. He'll know what to do."

Ben shook his head. "What if he turns on me like Gran did?"

"I don't think he will. He's reaching out to you. He came to your game. He gave you a car."

"The car was from Gran, too, and when I really needed her…"

Joe said, "Or we could ask Smitty or Mrs. Poulard or anybody official like that. I know they'd say it was the right thing to do. We'll go together."

"I've got to think it through and make sure I'm protecting Mom. If I'm not careful, if things get out of control…I don't want to come home one day and find her when it's too late. Or worse—my *brothers* finding her."

Joe's stomach soured; he squeezed his eyes shut. "Ben. Shit. This is bad." Joe wanted to leap to his feet and scream his outrage, but something stilled him, cautioning him of Ben's fragility. "Okay," Joe said. "I promised I'd understand and if that means a little time, okay. I'll hang by you and help you think it through."

"We went out of order, so that's gotta be your final concession to me," Ben said.

"The last thing I want is this: you don't run away. No matter what. You don't shut me out, you don't take off running and hide away somewhere.

I've got to know where you are every night and I've got to know the truth. No half-truths, no tricks."

Joe stuck out his hand and Ben shook it and said he thought they should pray. And though Joe agreed, he experienced an initial burst of embarrassed discomfort. He was used to praying with his family, especially with Bonnie Jean, but he could not remember praying with the frolic of flip, faithful friends who daily had sat beside him in chapel, who followed him without question on his fearless schemes. When he and Ben bowed their heads, Joe knew that this was his to do. Silence held them for a few moments and in these, Joe admitted his fault, worried in whispers about deceiving his father and the entire adult world. To his astonishment a kind of wary quiet came to him. Reminded that he had obeyed his father to compromise with Ben, Joe marveled at Tom's method and the stuff it had brought out. The compromises they'd reached were workable and would begin to protect Ben. Now he had to hang on and gut this through to the end he hoped to see.

Joe determined to trust God to watch what he couldn't, to work the miracle that if it were up to Joe's own great love, his own adamant will, his own bright and hopeful vision, would already be as palpable as the sunlight that fell now from beyond the iced window and lay like a quilt on Ben's bowed shoulders. And in an instant, faith sprouted from his self-knowledge and regret: surely if he, the faulty genius Joe MacBride, could love so much and will such important, life-saving things, God himself—who was perfectly good and kind and who defended the poor and needy like Ben—had Joe's back. Clinging to that bolstering thought, he wished that God would also settle his cynical and uncomprehending stomach and found himself praying out loud and unashamed for Ben, who sat a foot away, still trembling, still broken.

7

TOM watched Doug pause to pat Joe's shoulder at the small table in the café where Peter, Bonnie Jean, Ben and Joe sat. "Somethin' must be real wrong when athletes like you two eatin' only soup for dinner. There's real food over there, boys."

"Thanks, Unca Doug. I like this soup and my stomach's not real good right now."

"What's a matter? Your dad burn your ass last night for cussin' Grannie MacBride out?"

"No," Joe said, "he was gracious to me."

"You're kidding me, right? He didn't whip you?"

"No, he didn't."

"He didn't," Ben confirmed.

"Tom MacBride!" Doug called as he approached the table where Beth, Laurie and Tom awaited him. "You are getting soft on me, old man! I was so worried about Joe when I left your house last night I actually said a prayer in the Jeep on the way home, didn't I, kids?"

"Yeah," Flip called from the table where he, Tommy and little Dougie were counting Tommy's mountain of tips. "If you call saying, 'Oh, Lord, Joe is gonna get it,' a hundred times over praying."

Doug laughed out loud, placing his mountain of food down on the table. When he was seated, Tom patted Doug's wrist, feeling grateful for Doug's company right now. His mind churned with confused concern for Ben; he was unsure about how much to say to his passionate wife and her doubly passionate twin brother. "I think you can come back to practice after exams," Tom said, hoping Doug had not been hurt by Joan Poulard's directive that he take a break. "Parents will be too busy with Christmas to build mountains."

Doug shrugged. "I'm gonna be busy. I got to get some action shots at three county wrestling tournaments and I'll be up at West Point the next few weeks off and on to shoot some pictures for the Army-Navy game stuff. I thought I'd drop in on ol' Gregen."

Laurie said, "I wish I could go with you."

"I'm sure he'd rather see you than me."

"Gregen liked you, but he didn't like you sneaking into the house through those tunnels, Doug."

"Yeah. I thought he was gonna cut off my—" Doug looked up to see his children, niece, nephews and Ben listening to him, staring wide-eyed. "But I'm a different man, now, aren't I, Tom ol' boy?"

"I hear the last thing to get redeemed is a man's mouth."

"I'm gonna become a Christian soon, Tom," Doug whispered. "Soon as I kick Hunter's ass. That'll show ol' Saunders," Doug whispered. "I'll even go to Saunders' tight-assed church. Doug Davidson, the ass-kicking, maniac Christian."

Annie, sitting on Beth's lap, craned her neck to see her mother's face. "Did you hear Daddy?" she said sleepily.

Beth whispered to Doug, "You don't have to give up ass-kicking to be a Christian, Doug. You just have to believe that through Christ, God has forgiven all your ass-kicking and so on. And then only kick the ass God commands you to kick."

Doug laughed merrily. "Hey, I'd have no problem with God if I thought he'd let me—" He glanced meaningfully at Ben.

"Shh," Tom said, the heaviness of heart falling hard again. "God is more interested in reaching Max than exacting revenge on him."

"I doubt that," Laurie and Doug said in unison.

Tom said, "Ask Gregen what he thinks about this subject when you see him."

"He's the one who turned me *off* to God. Said I had to forgive way back in Quantico. I thought, no way. This man does not deserve it." Doug's face fell into a deep, unhappy frown.

"Told me to forgive, too," Tom said. "If I hadn't, I honestly don't think I'd be walking today."

"You're *hardly* walking today," Doug said.

"Hush, you two," Laurie said. "Look who fell asleep." She pointed to Annie, asleep on her mother's lap. "Anyway, listen to this. Max's lawyer spent the day in here today. She had what she called 'research' to do."

Doug said. "What the *hell*'s he need a lawyer for now?"

"The one sitting at that table?" Beth pointed. "What kind of research? She hardly left her chair."

"Yes. It was the weirdest thing. The kids went over to Ben's house this morning to get some stuff and Bonnie Jean met this lawyer woman there. She usually goes to Gisela's in the morning and since they were closed, she ended up in here. I went over to say hello, and guess what I noticed?" Laurie touched Doug's wrist, then lay her hand on his. "She was reading Katie's last diary." Laurie met Tom's eyes.

"I thought Gregen had that," Tom said, his mind quickening, searching for implications.

"Evidently not."

"Whoa," Doug said.

"Thing is," Laurie said, "Bonnie Jean says that this woman is not *just* Max's lawyer."

"How does Bonnie Jean know a disturbing thing like that?" Tom said.

Laurie raised her eyebrows at Tom. "I know. Isn't it awful? Ben told her that Donna knows, too."

"I bet that's what those kids are all down about. That's rough for kids," Doug said. "Max, I swear your ass is calling me." Doug cupped his hand to his ear, "'Hey, Doug, I'm the world's worst jerk and I got a big fat ass. Come kick me all the way to hell.' You guys hear it?"

Tom said, "Oh, no. Poor Ben," imagining the bitter disillusionment, the struggle, admiring Ben's stalwart silence, understanding the dull pain in the boy's eyes.

Laurie touched each of them on the hand and said, "Ben didn't want us to know because he's afraid you'll think he's like his dad in that way."

"But of course Bonnie Jean couldn't keep that a secret," Beth said.

Tom shook his head. "I hate to see a kid disillusioned."

"Yeah, Tom," Doug said, a slight grin forming, "What's the Bible say? Something about a millstone around the neck if you rob a kid of his innocence. Right?"

"And Donna," Laurie said. "Don't forget her." The adults were quiet, thinking, shaking their heads, and Laurie continued, "So, here's the Hunter family—right here in Annapolis *finally*—and we find out that things are not at all good for them."

"I was hoping he'd changed," Tom said.

"Give it up, Tom," Doug said.

"Right," Laurie said, strangely energized after her busiest workday of the year. "We need a plan. The way I see it, both women are in trouble. I've already made friends with the lawyer—I invited her to come back to the café to finish her reading. Now, if I can just make contact with Donna…I don't want either of these women to end up like Katie."

"You're right," Tom said.

"God, I love you both," Doug said. "What can me and Beth do?"

They looked to Tom who sat forward, eyes staring as if he were seeing further than them. "Doug, try to discuss it with Gregen when you see him. This news about Max and the lawyer confirms what I've been suspecting. Ben is very unhappy at home. He hates his father, wants bullies punished."

"Hey, that's like me," Doug exulted. "Oh, wait, that's because *my dad* was a bully."

"I thought about that," Tom said, hesitating, measuring his words, "he's really hurting." Tom's lips went tight, he watched his dear ones' eyes go sad and solemn. In the hush, Cara's cooing from Laurie's office could be heard.

"What is your suspicion, Tom?"

"I think they fought on Thanksgiving. More than just a disagreement. I think Ben was upset enough by it that he ran over to our house to get away from them." Tom bit his lip asking himself silently if he should tell them his suspicions about Ben's stitches. He watched Laurie's expression, the clear flame of love lighting her eyes with that protective passion. And Doug—his passionate mouth frowning deeply, fingers drumming in that anxious pattern on the table edge waiting for something to do. "I can't imagine one of our boys being that upset."

"What do we do first?" Laurie said, glancing over at Ben.

Doug said, "We tell him what Max did to his mother and—"

"And what?" Tom interrupted, "Have him go after his father in a blind rage that could get him killed? No."

"So, we see what you *really* think of Hunter," Doug said. "You admit he's dangerous."

Tom gave a sardonic laugh. "That was never in question."

"Wouldn't it be better to tell him everything," Beth asked, "get him out of that house, and then try to repair whatever emotional damage he suffers from having to learn the truth in an abrupt way?"

"Right," Laurie said. "What's causing you to hesitate, Tom?"

"The past," Tom said. "I was so sure I was right...sending Katie back to Max, telling Donna to marry that coward she was in love with. It's all turned out so badly."

"Those incidents were advice, these are facts," Laurie said.

"I meddled, thinking I knew best."

Doug said, "Since Ben's not eighteen yet, we do have to be careful. With adoptions, for instance, kids can look for their birth parents at eighteen. While he's underage, if we force it on him and Ben freaks out, Max will have grounds to keep you two," he pointed to Tom and Laurie, "away from Ben. He's done that before."

"We have to get Gregen down here to help Ben realize the truth. We've got to push for it." Tom stood up abruptly, his concern for Ben coming into sharp focus. "What else? What else can we do to spark his thinking?" he heard himself murmur as his concentration whirled with another thought: *Ben is bruised too often; his lip has been smashed—I think three times since school started. That bruise on his collarbone...*Before he spoke his thoughts he left the table and called back over his shoulder, "I'll get Cara, she's starting to cry."

8

LEANING in, their heads together, Ben, Bonnie Jean, Joe and Peter kept their voices just above whispering. "My court date is right after exams. On the twenty-third," Joe said. "When are you done, Pete?"

"My last exam is on the twenty-second. Then I have a paper due by midnight in history."

"We can pick you up, Pete, early on the twenty-third, drive to the courthouse. Then, we'll go see Gregen."

"I can't go." Bonnie Jean said. "I've got a doctor's appointment for my stupid mole. And I've got rehearsals. We're singing at the chapel on Christmas Eve."

Ben said, "We'll call you on my cell phone. Will that help?"

"So, we only have a little time to keep Ben safe until we can get away. That's not so bad," Peter said.

"Yeah," Joe said, "I think with studying for exams, practice and games, he'll probably be at our house anyway. And I can stay at your house, Ben, when you have to go there."

"No. You don't want to do that."

"That part is not your decision."

"Right," Peter said.

A weird buzzing like an electric cricket sounded from deep within Ben's backpack.

"What is that?" Peter asked.

"His cell phone," Bonnie Jean said, reaching to open the zipper. "Should I answer it? It's your brothers."

"I'll call them back."

Laurie's office door squeaked open, drawing their attention to Tom. He held Cara against him but facing out, his arms around her stomach. She could see the store and her entire family. Tom limped toward them, his uneven gate amusing Cara so that she gave a delighted bubble of a laugh. "Somebody got a cell phone?" Tom asked.

"Just Ben," Peter called, staring with deep concentration at his father, as he walked to the counters to grab some napkins. Peter swallowed audibly. Ben, Joe and Bonnie Jean followed his gaze and wondered collectively at Peter's nearly trance-like stare.

"What's the matter with you?" Joe asked.

"I just remembered something else," he said. "In my mind—like a snapshot." Peter looked at Ben.

"What?"

"Tell us," Joe said.

Peter stood up and nodded at Ben, eyes sad. "I know why Dad wouldn't fight Colonel Hunter that day," he leaned in closer, lowering his voice. "I know why he wouldn't fight back. I remembered it. I remember seeing the fight."

"You were there?"

Meeting Ben's eyes, Peter nodded and said, "Colonel Hunter was using Ben as a shield. He was taunting Dad, daring Dad to hit him. Ben was screaming and Colonel Hunter was holding him, like draped over his arm—just like Dad had Cara there a minute ago. Except Colonel Hunter was trying to keep Dad from taking a swing at him. Ben's the shield. Ben's the hostage."

"No," Bonnie Jean said. "It can't be true."

"I'm sure it is," Ben said, eyes keen, cold and bright blue. "It doesn't surprise me."

"I believe it," Joe said.

Ben said, "It makes perfect sense. There could be other reasons he didn't fight back—like what if he'd promised your mom he wouldn't fight? But the fact that he won't ever *tell* anybody why—that means Pete is right. Tom doesn't ever want me to think badly of my dad. So he would never tell something like that. It must be true."

"Ben," Joe said, setting his jaw against a rush of emotion, clenching his fists. "If your dad would do that, he'd do anything."

Ben looked Joe straight in the eye. "Yeah. Pretty much."

The phone buzzed again and Ben's composure dissolved. He grabbed the phone and flipped it open. Joe began a frantic, angry drumming of his fingers on the table.

Keith screamed, "Dad's yelling at Gran in the kitchen. You gotta come home!"

Certain that everyone could hear his brother's frantic tone, Ben left the table, holding the phone close to his ear, and rushed to the porch. The door shut behind him.

"Where are you, Keith?"

"I'm on the stairs."

"Get back up in your room." Ben said, turning around on the porch to see his friends gathered behind him, eyes wide.

"Please come home, Ben. Me and Tim are so scared."

"By the time I get there, the fight will be over. Go in your room and lock the door."

"Tim's crying and we need you."

"Where's Mom?"

"Please," Keith cried, his voice a shriek. Ben met his friends' eyes, thinking of his father using him as a shield, realizing that without him there to absorb his father's anger, his brothers were in danger. His stomach lurched and Joe knew what he was thinking.

Joe said, "No. No way."

"Please!" Keith screamed.

Ben said, "Okay, Keith. Go hide in your room. Lock the door. I'll be there. I'll say the code word."

"You can't go," Joe said. "I won't let you."

"I have to. You heard Keith. We all know what he's capable of. I'm going."

"Let's call the police."

"I'm just going to sneak in and calm my brothers down. I'm not going anywhere near him."

"No. Pete, tell him *no*. Bonnie Jean, tell him *no*."

"You two go with him," Bonnie Jean said. "He has to go and you have to go with him."

"I'll get the coats and Ben's backpack," Peter said.

Inside, grabbing the things he needed with one arm, Peter gave a general wave to the adults with the other. "We're going to Ben's house for a bit," he said. "We won't be late. Ben's gonna stay the night with us, if that's okay."

"Stay with Ben," Tom said, with an obvious glance at the other adults at the table. "Don't be gone long."

"Don't worry, Dad," Peter called. "We'll be home in time for your 'this is your mom's busiest season' speech. In fact, I can give it, if you're too tired."

"Don't think I'm gonna pay for your education if it makes you even more of a smart mouth, Peter MacBride," Tom called, then, "Be safe, and call if there's a change of plans."

Outside, Bonnie Jean hugged Ben fiercely. "Be careful. I'll be praying every second."

Ben sprinted across the icy ground and around the corner into the dimly lit alley behind Porter Road, Peter and Joe following close behind. The graveled pavement glistened with patches of black ice and Ben ran nimbly over this, slowing to a jog when he saw his house. Keith and Tim's window blazed with light on the third floor. He could see his father in the kitchen, his posture antagonistic, and when he crept closer he saw that his grandmother sat at the kitchen table. He could hear their raised voices, though the words were indistinguishable.

Beside him, Joe said, "She looks terrified."

Peter said, "Where's your mom?"

"Mom works nights," Ben said, looking up the tree. "Sometimes I climb this tree and go in my window this way, but I don't know if it's open."

"And they might see you. They're right there."

Ben led his friends through the basement and up the dark, back stairs, whispering instructions to keep them from the creaky places. They crept step by step, rushing only when his father's voice boomed its threats. Ben wondered that the neighbors didn't hear, didn't object to the brooding violence in the Hunter house.

"Sit right there and listen to me. Don't you dare get up," Max shouted. "You're gonna keep your promise. It doesn't have anything to do with what I say or do."

Ben whispered to Pete and Joe. "Stay behind me." They mimicked his movements, stepping when he did, pausing, breathing only when he did.

Upstairs, Ben tapped with one finger on his brothers' door and when Keith said, "What do you want?" Ben replied, "Christmas morning."

Keith gave a relieved, hysterical note of laughter and they heard the door unlock. The boys flung themselves on Ben and burst into loud sobbing. Peter and Joe shooed them all into the room and Peter stood guard outside, Joe just inside the room.

"Why were you gone so long?" Tim asked.

"It's not safe here for me. You know that."

Keith nodded. "That's what I told Tim. But we're scared without you."

"He never hits you," Ben reminded them. "If you come upstairs and lock the door as soon as he takes his first drink, there's no way you'll get hurt."

"I was thinking, maybe we could get a frigerator up here," Keith said. "In case we're trapped."

"You're hungry now?"

"We had pizza with Gran before the shouting."

Ben nodded. "Good."

"Were you mad at us, too? Is that why you didn't answer the phone?"

"No, I'm sorry. I was really hurt this time."

"Is Gran gonna be alright?"

"I hope so," Ben said.

"Can you take care of Gran for us?" Keith asked.

"I'll try," Ben said sadly. He hugged them both and said, "Want to play a game before bed? We can play with you guys for awhile."

Two hours later, when he was sure that both his brothers were sleeping, Ben and Joe left the room and closed the door. Peter stood up from where he was sitting beside Ben's bedroom door, shut the book he'd taken to read, and lifted a stuffed pillowcase to his shoulder. "I took everything from your room I thought you'd need. You want to look and see what else we can take?"

Ben grabbed a couple of favorite books and Laurie's quilt. In the quiet his grandmother's heavy step sounded in the hallway. Ben opened the door an inch, saw her go to the guest room, and heard her dial her cell phone. "I need the number of an airport taxi," she said into the phone. Ben motioned for Peter and Joe to stay there and went down the hall.

"I'll drive you," he whispered, standing in her doorway and when she startled, he put a finger to his lips, and said; "Shhh. He'll hear you. He can't know I'm here."

"Where have you been?" she cried. "When did you get back?"

"Shh. Keith called me—hysterical—because you and Dad were fighting. What's he drinking right now?"

"Ben, really. Don't start. A man of his weight can handle a little liquor. Honestly."

"You've got about a half hour before he gets even meaner. So pack up fast. My friends are here with me. I'll take the heavy suitcase down the kitchen stairs and you go down the front stairs and distract him so he doesn't hear us. Walk out the front door and down to Gate One. You remember where I parked? I'll meet you there."

"A half hour? Why give into these dramatics? He's just having another sip, Ben."

"Okay, Gran. You're leaving *early* because he's been a jerk this whole holiday, including beating me up *in front* of you. Quit *pretending* he's okay. He's drunk all the time."

On the way to the airport, Peter and Joe squeezed their tall selves into the backseat of Ben's car with Gran's smaller suitcase between them. Ben was silent, angry, biting his lips, watching the scant traffic with unnecessary care. No one spoke. Ben's little car skimmed along the highway, its tires and gears the only voices.

Finally, Joe cleared his throat. "I guess this is pretty awkward for you, Mrs. Hunter. I mean, I know you're embarrassed because we heard you and your son fighting. Sorry about all this."

"I hate to have to discuss this with you children and I regret your involvement."

Ben's blinker filled the car with its musical urgency as Ben moved over to take the exit toward the airport. Joe began again, "Um, Mrs. Hunter, I feel I should say that Pete and Bonnie Jean and I, we know how badly beat up Ben was by his dad. Um, we saw him. He needed stitches. Did you know that?"

"We should talk about something else. Or nothing."

"Let's start with this, Gran," Ben said, the hostility raw in his voice. "Why didn't you say something to Dad when he came after me?"

"You have no idea about your father. If you understood—"

"I *understand*, Gran. He's made me understand exactly what he thinks of me."

"You don't realize why you're being so unfair."

"You know, Mrs. Hunter," Peter said in his friendly tone, "I think I remember the last day we stayed up there when Ben was a baby."

She gasped. "You were too young."

"I have that kind of a memory," Peter said. "And I remembered the fight. Ben's dad fought my dad. I remember how Colonel Hunter was holding Ben."

"You couldn't remember. And your mother didn't see—" She glanced at Ben. "I suppose Mr. MacBride told you that story to blame his—*giving up*—on Max."

"Dad didn't tell me," Peter said, his deep, honest voice a clear bell. "He won't ever talk about it. I remembered. I can see it play in my mind. I was in the car. Joe was in his car seat next to me."

"Ben was not hurt in that fight," Ella insisted.

Ben stared at her. "You saw that? He used his child—me—as a *shield*. You knew he hated me even then? And you left me with him?"

Gran stared out the window. "You have no idea what your father was going through. Absolutely no idea. After the accident…" she murmured, her voice trailing off.

No longer listening, Ben slowed his car and pulled up to the curb at the American Airlines area. He stopped, yanked on the emergency brake, and got out of the car. Peter folded down the driver's seat and climbed out, grabbing the suitcase.

While Ben opened the trunk, Ella heaved herself out of the low seat, opened her handbag, and despite trembling fingers, lit a cigarette and puffed desperately. Peter brought her suitcase around the front of the car.

"Mrs. Hunter, you said something about a car accident. Were you talking about the one when Ben was a baby?"

Looking up at Peter she blew gray smoke out to fill the space between them and in a clouded whisper that Ben could still hear she demanded, "What do you remember?" She took the suitcase from Peter's grasp. Her eyes were keen, almost cunning.

"About the accident?" Peter coughed. His eyes flicked toward Ben and Joe, who recognized that he was bluffing to make her think he knew more than what the fragment of a newspaper article had told them just that morning.

"You remember it? How could you? Were you back in the other car with your father?"

Peter frowned, biting his lip, and coughed again. Gran puffed the bluish smoke at him, "That was the diaper bag you saw. That's what that was. So put your mind at ease. Max was *driving*." She stared hard at Peter. "Max. Remember that, now."

Eight Hands Around

9

Past three o'clock, Patty looked up from Katie's journal briefly, watching Laurie move through the shop, baby in a neat, cloth carrier on her back, putting the green paper and the big basket she carried down to help customers. She had just finished Katie's description of two months that she and Laurie had spent in Europe. Both married to marines, both marines deployed, the two friends traveled through Italy and France gathering inspiration in a kind of a pilgrimage that Patty found herself envying. Looking around, Patty recognized items Katie had described. That 25-liter copper pot that steamed with the daily soup special, the red metal tray standing beneath the huge chalkboard with the menu—hadn't she just read Katie's description of bartering for them in a flea market? Patty turned back three pages. Yes, Saturday morning…Chartres. Here it was… the copper pot. Even more interesting was Katie's uncharacteristic spiritual experience. Well, Patty wasn't sure what to call it but she felt the reality of it in Katie's candor and description.

> …We walked to the cathedral and entered as a university tour was beginning. We followed along, staying within earshot never dreaming that in the professor's words about the Creation/ Good Samaritan window we'd find nourishment for both of our dreams.
>
> Here is the explanation of the window: The traveler leaves Jerusalem, or peace. He is harmed by life. Those who leave him to die stand for lifeless tradition and dogmatic scholarship. Who helps him? The Samaritan, the "everyman" with no learning or heritage to recommend him, takes responsibility for the broken man's restoration to well-being. Everyone knows the story! "Why does this window also show the Garden of Eden?" I asked, testing our young guide. To the first Adam is traced the world's sorrow and imperfection (as seen in any of my clinics). Why is Christ shown at the very top? Scholars refer to Jesus as the second Adam who restores those so harmed by giving his own frail human body. The patterns of Adam and everyman crisscross to show Christ.
>
> Both Laurie and I were moved to tears by the interwoven

truths, by the beauty of it, the miraculous concept illustrated. I remembered Donne's poem about illness expecting death:

> We think that Paradise and Calvary,
> Christ's Cross and Adam's tree, stood in one place;
> Look Lord, and find both Adams met in me;
> As the first Adam's sweat surrounds my face,
> May the last Adam's blood my soul embrace…

Frail because I'm human, I need the reality of Christ's life to transform mine; how do I get it?

Patty caught Laurie's eye as Laurie hurried to the drive-through window with a length of fabric. She moved her hand to call Laurie over to her. "Do you have a minute for a question?"

"Sure," Laurie said, coming to the little table and sitting down opposite Patty. "Where are you?"

"Chartres."

"Oh," Laurie sighed. "One of the most wonderful days in my life."

"Have you read Katie's description?"

"Yes," Laurie said. Annette called her to the drive-through. Laurie made an apologetic face and rushed off. Patty sighed and turned the page.

We wandered shoulder to shoulder, arms looped together as Laurie and I have done since third grade and when we reached the nave, we lit three candles each. You will think me daft, but this is what happened. I could feel something. I could feel the prayers of the centuries, dear Diary. Faithful ones have come here and bowed heads in the tinted light beneath the great, stone arches and their prayers still linger like the drifting scent of candles glowing and sputtering. We, too, knelt to pray. I told God things about Max and about me that I have not written. I whispered my fears and my regrets. If the second Adam was broken for me, it was to bring me life, not despair where I dwell now continually as Max's wounded wife.

What happened to me, dear Diary? I expected to be told by God that I deserved the hurt I felt, but it was as if I exchanged my regrets for his vibrant life. I lifted my head and—as if it were dropped into me like an apple into one's lap—I knew a fierce thirst for a child. I can see him. He is blond like Mother and I. He is like Uncle Gregen too, in that he can see into people, is brave, contemplative, steadfast. He is like Max in agility and competitiveness and runs as quickly as Max can swim. And so, I added my prayers to those whispered in Chartres by saints and sinners before me. I asked that God give me the child I saw in the clear new light of my soul. And what happened next, dear Diary? Laurie fainted.

She said it was because we'd skipped lunch and she had been so touched, so full of things to pray about, so intently pouring out her heart, but I know different. She is pregnant.

I helped her to the little café outside the cathedral. Slowly she revived and her color returned. At our hotel while she slept, I phoned Uncle Gregen and told him my suspicions. He will be here in the morning and then Laurie will know for sure and we can rejoice together. She has blamed her late period on traveling and says that she and Tom have not planned to have a child for another year—so it couldn't be. As if life is subject to a woman's will!

Dare I hope that it was God who awakened the desire in my heart for a child? If so, then he will hear and will transform my life to accomplish all that he has made me long for. Or did Laurie's and my prayers crisscross in the nave of holy Chartres, dear Diary? Did God give her the child I asked for?

When Laurie returned to the table and sat down, Patty said, "Have you read it all?"

"No. Once we were both married she never put the book in my hands, but read things out to me. So, I didn't have the same look into her thinking as I'd always had. If so, I might have been able to help her more."

"She didn't want you to know that she was always comparing Max unfavorably to your brother—and as she's starting to do—your husband."

Laurie regarded Patty seriously. "For a long time, Katie insisted that Doug was not right for her. Sometimes she said he was too nice for her. You see, Patty, this was Katie's inner fault. She hated herself and Max fit into that view of life."

"That's harsh. I have to remember that your opinion of Max is so biased."

"You can read for yourself. Maybe her perspective of Max and their marriage will prove my bias accurate."

"I doubt that. You really dislike him."

"I know him." Patty wiggled her shoulders and shifted position as if her chair were no longer comfortable. Laurie added, "Is he good to you?"

Patty stared at the pencil she tapped on the table. "I charge him a discounted fee for this legal work I'm doing for him, since I've known him so long." She glanced at Laurie, feeling her cheeks grow hot. "He pays by check. It's all above board. His wife knows he's hired me."

"Patty, come on. You've read so many intimate things about me. We're friends."

Patty made a frustrated noise. "I don't know what's wrong with me. I don't do shame. I just don't. I guess I just don't want it all over Annapolis. Max's boss is absolutely maniacal about Max's personal life."

Laurie touched Patty's hand. "I think Katie's diary is getting to you."

"She was so accomplished, Laurie," Patty whispered, her eyes bright. "So outgoing and compassionate…so amazingly brilliant. I can see why Max loved her. He's not over her. Not at all."

"No one ever gets over Katie."

"You said before she was faithful to Max. Are you sure? Because I bet *everyone* wanted her."

Laurie considered this. "That's Max's way of thinking about her charisma." Patty's grin flickered uncomfortably. "What?" Laurie said, "What are you thinking?"

"Don't you know how tortured Max is by the idea that she was never faithful?"

"I can believe that, Patty, and I'm sorry for him. I know he's suffered a lot." Patty felt hopeful that Laurie would share some passionately withheld secret. "You should know, Patty," Laurie said, seriously as she reached across the table and touched Patty's hand. "Max became hostile and threatening to Katie. And after that first separation—during which Max *did* see a counselor—Tom advised Katie to reconcile and except for Ben being conceived, it turned out so badly. We feel responsible, Tom and I, for sending Katie back to Max—it's what keeps Tom up at night."

For the past few days after practice, Tom had found himself standing at the window of his office as he was now, his right leg gone too numb to stand on, all the panes of glass in the window clouded from his breath. And each day, Tom's blood thundered with the premonition of battle. He could smell conflict mounting as if it had a scent as familiar and rank as the boysweat smell of his locker room. Knowing it was coming never helped; he could never manage to avoid the battle especially when it meant fighting Max for Ben's sake.

He turned from the window and shoved the letters scattered on his desk into a neat, brown file folder. Tommy, who had been tossing a football outside with some friends, was coming toward his office and he did not want the boy to see that he'd written letters to each of his children, letters to tell them everything he had not had time to say or to show them, just in case he didn't win this time with Max. Eyes blurred, Tom fumbled with the folder's clasp and felt a friendly punch on his elbow. "Ready, Dad?" He caught Tommy's small fist. "Gotcha," Tom laughed. Tommy laughed too, twisting free. Tom glanced at his watch, then ruffled Tommy's hair.

"Let's go."

"Can I wear your jacket?" Tommy said, reaching for Tom's old favorite, the football jacket from Navy.

"You've got a coat," Tom said, pointing to the one Tommy wore as he shrugged into his own and felt the padded crinkle of the envelope with Ben's name on it that he'd tucked in the deep, inner pocket that night when he'd found Joe's ticket. How many times had he reminded himself to hand it to Ben and forgotten once the jacket was off his shoulders, once he did not hear it against his chest?

"You call this a coat?" Tommy looked critically at his black nylon jacket lined in blue fleece. "It's a three-time hand-me-down. And it still smells like that stinkin' grape junk Bonnie Jean used to squirt all over her head. Besides, it's practically a rag. Look at it."

"It's newer than mine."

"Man."

Taking the back roads across the bridge at Weems Creek, Tom let Tommy select the radio station and the volume level as he drove to Eight Hands Around. Tom found that he enjoyed Tommy's pick—a wacky arrangement of Christmas tunes turned up so loud that the coins in the ashtray danced.

"How come you have to work at the store today?" Tommy shouted as Tom swung the car around in a U-turn heading for a parking spot he wanted.

"Your mom needs to go visit a friend."

"Dad, you should say 'yo mama,' not 'your,' if you want to be cool."

"But I didn't mean it as an insult."

Tommy laughed, pleased. "You could be so much cooler if you'd just let on that you get it."

Tom eased his car expertly into the tight parking place on the side street perpendicular to the storefront. "More than anything I want to appear cool," Tom sighed.

"Can I just hear the end of this song before we go in?"

Tom gave him a thumbs-up. He left the car, shut the door, and leaned back against it waiting for Tommy. In the lamplight that brightened the area around the drive-through window, Tom could see that the shingles near the gutter had torn loose. He reached into his jacket pocket for his little note pad. Ben's envelope came out with it and Tom glanced at it, then studied it: on the front Ben's name had been typed. Beneath the clear tape that fastened the back he saw Charlie Johnson's signature, fractured when the envelope had been opened. Tom decided that it must be some sort of a recommendation. *This has been in my pocket for weeks. I have to remember to give this to Ben.* He opened the door and grabbed a pencil from the console. "Hurry up, Tommy," he said before shutting the door. Opening his pad, he scribbled down: *right front roof—shingles loose* then, *give envelope to Ben.* Tom glanced again at the storefront, doubting he'd notice any other needed repairs in the dark and twinkle of the December evening, and unexpectedly, the sight of the place stirred Tom.

The store's hallmark banner, flapping noisily from a small flagpole, caught his attention though it was small and pastel beneath the bright

Christmas flag. Tom let his eyes rest on it a moment and his memories sank upon him like a fog. Once he'd lettered an old sheet with poster paint and hung it from that same flagpole announcing FREE SOUP AND BREAD 4-7. But that was when their coffeehouse, Rising Sun, had flourished there beneath that same roof.

The coffeehouse had been a dream since he and Laurie had met during college. By the time his back problems forced Tom to resign his commission and take a job at CCS, Rising Sun was a rousing success. Several local churches supported the ministry with donations and volunteers. Tom spent every spare moment there; Laurie made soup and bread daily for the soup kitchen.

"Whatcha staring at, Dad? Something broken?" Tommy's voice jolted him into the present. The boy had joined him, unnoticed, and stood at his side.

"Just thinking," Tom said, and slid his notepad back into his pocket. Tom dropped his hand on Tommy's neck and guided the boy across the street.

Patty Edwards felt the pleasure of new friendship when young Tommy MacBride said hello to her as he burst into the café, but she could not stop the hot rush of emotion that flooded her when she looked up and saw the man who must be his father kiss Laurie MacBride so tenderly on the lips. *Oh, I've finally seen him, Tom MacBride.* Katie had included first drafts of her letters to Tom and Laurie so Patty felt Katie's fondness, her respect for him, and quivered with anticipation of his real presence in the room.

Funny, she thought as she stared at him, *Katie never once described his looks.* He was a tall man, with a casual, athletic stance and wide shoulders. He walked with a slight limp. His full head of dark hair was shot with gray, his nose looked as if it had once been broken, his eyes the off-blue of the bay on a windy afternoon. He was happy, his eyes showed it, but he was a thinker, worried, his eyes showed that, too, as did the lines that framed his mouth. His stance beside his wife was adorable: the expression on his face, the way he leaned toward her, arm around her just touching her elbow in an awed way that said he was thrilled, unable to resist. But he caught Patty staring and she ducked her head down and blushed at the irony of reading about the man himself in a private, very candid diary.

> July…en route to Firenze…
> The woman in the seat beside me has kindly fallen asleep and so, dear Diary, I have a moment to write. Max will be on maneuvers from now until Thanksgiving and so I am flying away! I booked my flight out of Baltimore so that I could see Tom and Laurie and their darling new son and have just left their arms three hours ago. The baby is sweet-natured and Tom adores

him. Laurie, of course, has buckets of milk and he is thriving. He looks at her with adoring eyes. Who can blame him? I love her, too. She is so kind and giving, not jealous of me needing to talk to Tom about so much.

And that is how I am getting to know Tom so much better. He is even more than the dear brother I have always wanted. Though I wish Max would get over his problem with Tom, I enjoy the freedom of being able to stay up late talking with Tom, which would never happen if Max were here, too. Laurie falls asleep on the sofa beside him, her head on his shoulder.

One of my questions for Tom is this: Max and I have been trying (and how!) to conceive the baby I so desperately want. I wonder if God is reluctant to give us a child because…one only needs to flip though the pages of this journal to list a million moral misjudgments, flaws in character that cannot be denied. I am still ruthless in satisfying what I need: my husband does not know that I am visiting the man he hates. I had to be near Tom; something in me craves these conversations with Tom more than I ever wanted Max in my arms, more than I ever craved physical joy.

I asked Tom, "Is God punishing Max and I because I have always known better and did what I pleased anyway?"

But you see, Tom has the idea that God is strong and outgoing in his love for us. He is the perfect father and according to Tom, he will correct, but is not vindictive. I have met Tom's own father, the jolly Edmund MacBride, so it is easy for me to see from where his inspiration arises. He has never been disillusioned; it is easy for him to believe. For me, not so. Tom says that when he goes to bed at night, he thinks, "God loves me and speaks to my heart. He forgave me. I've had a good day." What do I think before and if I fall to sleep? I think this, dear Diary…"I have failed to make my father love me and be proud of me. I have failed my mother's hopes for my character and choice of husband. I have hurt my good and faithful friends. I have failed to help Max improve and grow. I have failed to conceive the child I so desperately want, a child so real to me, I could count the freckles on his nose and tell you that his breath is scented with salt and cinnamon." It is no wonder I cannot sleep.

Patty looked up to see Tommy busy straightening up the drive-through window, chatting to the woman running it. Father and son were alike in their slender build, in the way they walked, one shoulder slightly higher than the other, in something about the intent, but amused look in the eyes. Tom MacBride was handsome, a well-built and attractive man, but to Patty, he did not seem worthy of Max's hate.

According to the diary, Katie had been faithful to Max. Patty trusted the narrative because of the stark discussion of her faults, her fears, her disappointments. Katie was not prudish and talked freely about her sexual desires and thrills. If she had indulged outside of marriage, Patty believed that Katie would have recorded it as she recorded her temptations, her arguments with Max, and the sometimes cruel things she said to him. Max's responses to her, though, Patty noted on her yellow pad, Katie never recorded. The thought stopped her a moment—long enough for a fierce desire to rise in her: if she could just free Max of the hate that tortured him so, of the fear that Ben was Tom's! Could she see any resemblance to Ben in Tom? She leaned forward. If anything it was his elegance. Yes, this man before her was in some way, elegant, and Ben had that, too. Maybe it was a superiority of some sort.

"You ever met my dad?" Tommy said, standing over her.

She slapped her hand over the diary; he looked startled and stepped back. "No, no, I haven't," while thinking she'd drawn attention to the diary as now the boy stared at the open pages. Could he read upside down? This child probably could.

"When you're done reading I'll introduce you," the boy said. "You've been reading that for a long time. You might want to talk to an actual adult human."

Tom always said that he was bad for business. When he minded the store, the customers liked to *talk* to him, but their suspicious expressions told him that they didn't believe he could cut fabric straight. And he couldn't. But then, no one could. Laurie had taught him to measure, make a snip, and then tear the fabric. The quilting fabric tore straighter than anyone could cut it. When Laurie tore fabric, he watched customers sigh with awe. When *he* tore fabric, they gave him grief. "Does your *wife* know you're *ripping* everybody's fabric?" *Ah*, Tom thought as the sixth talkative and empty-handed customer shut the door behind her, *the prejudices a loving husband must endure.*

Tommy, however, had been busy. He made a list of every task he'd finished. This he would show to Laurie and be paid for his work. He'd cleaned the café, put away all the fabric bolts stacked by the cutting table, and was now at work alphabetizing the books, a job he knew his mother hated. *That alone will earn him a good bit*, Tom thought, grateful again for the immense success of the shop.

One lone customer wandered past the counter—a man. "Can I help you?" Tom asked.

He placed a hand-written list on the counter before tumbling down the contents he held in his arms.

"I think I've got almost everything," the man said straightening his tie in a reflexive kind of motion. "You ever heard of a…magnetic seam guide?"

"Sure," Tom said, reaching for one. "They're a big help for a beginning quilter."

"Yeah? Okay," the customer said, looking at the device suspiciously and questioning the use of each item that Tom rung up. "Last year was easier. All she wanted was a flannel nightgown."

"Have a merry Christmas," Tom said, chuckling as the man left still shaking his head and staring into the bulging shopping bag. Tom thought, *Enough quilts on the bed and your wife won't need to wear a flannel nightgown.* Though if he were to be honest, if Laurie did wear flannel, despite *all* the quilts—seventeen years of quilts—he found flannel just as provocative as lace. And when the flannel nightgown came off...those quilts—with their magnetically guided seams—made a snug tent for them.

From where he stood, Tom could see the front display window crowded with handmade things. The tiny white Christmas lights outlining the window gave the blurred look of perspective to that part of the room. In his memory he could still see the room as it once had been, before the store had been shattered and rebuilt.

One hand on Cara's wiggling foot to keep him grounded in the present, he let his mind drift. He could see the room alive with people talking seriously about significant subjects. Ordinary people from diverse backgrounds grouped together, searching for the truth as they shared a loaf of bread and were warmed by Laurie's soup. It was here that he had helped Katie piece her life back together, here that Donna and hundreds of others had sought friendship. The coffeehouse was at its busiest, its most vibrant, when Max had shut it down with that lawsuit he'd forced Donna to file and the violent crash. It was awful to think that Ben had been so close, that Ben had literally been on the front porch.

After the crash, Tom had worked to restore the damage, but his wrecked back gave out. The brittle, twice-mended vertebrae cracked, pinching already damaged nerve tissue.

Laurie had been a steady, sympathetic listener during the long weeks when he was hospitalized. She drew Tom's grief and questions up out of him, and from it, she had patterned a business that would reflect what they loved, as well as assuage her fears. After all, neither of them knew if he would ever walk again.

Tom remembered one day, exhausted and sweaty from a therapy workout, he lay spent on that stiff, chilly hospital bed. Laurie explained, "The trouble with the coffeehouse was," she said, laying her needle down, "that thinking has to be...worked out."

I could use some work, myself, just this minute, Tom thought with another quick glance around the shop. Gently, he extracted the quilt corner from Cara's mouth and offered her pacifier. He pulled open the top drawer, thinking he'd add up the time sheets. Tommy strode past him toward the back of the shop. "What now?" Tom asked the boy.

"I'll do the bathrooms. Then I'll close up the café and wash all the coffee stuff. You had enough, Dad?"

"Yes, I have, laddie," Tom told him, watching the boy's confident athletic bearing with a gratefulness that made him flush, his chest going hot again with memories.

When Rising Sun was wrecked, Tommy had plenty of life. Determined to walk at eight months, he fell so much that Laurie was frantic over his bruises and his constant need for activity. He could climb out of his crib or scale the side of his playpen in fifteen seconds. Peter and Joe had timed him, cheering him on. If left alone for a moment he zoomed on hands and knees to the stairs where he liked best to climb up the outside narrow ledge extending beyond the banister spokes. Laurie wanted to keep him strapped in his highchair, or buckled in his stroller. There was no other safe place.

Tom protested, knowing the child's passion for mobility. "Let him go," Tom said from his new wheelchair, "I'll watch him." So, Tom watched his tiny, bright-eyed son work himself to his feet and struggle to master the meaning of balance and coordinated movement. Tommy's problem, he realized, was that his legs weren't strong enough to support his desire. He pitied and admired Tommy, and he knew he could help him.

After all, he had walked once, he'd walked for thirty-three years, and he knew the rage of uncooperative legs. So, he coached Tommy along, tottering and stumbling behind him, falling beside him, surging with frustration, dripping with sweat. He coached Tommy, coaching himself. He practiced with his son, knowing that Tommy would walk, doubting himself daily, until he finally understood the purpose of those agonizing hours of therapy, something Laurie had already seen. An idea must be coached and sweated into reality if it is ever to happen at all. He and Tommy learned to walk together.

10

AWARE that the bustle of the shop had quieted around her, Patty looked up to see Tom MacBride sitting against the edge of the counter where they cut the fabric. His arms were folded across his chest, emphasizing the broad angularity of his shoulders, and he gazed into the shop's colorful space. Patty had the feeling that he would not rush her and felt grateful; Katie's story compelled her attention.

> ...Just last week at a party, Max and his buddies were so drunk they crawled on the floor looking up skirts of wives too drunk to stop them. When I confronted him later, Max shrugged it off.

It does not seem normal to me; I was hurt and disgusted. I am growing sick of this crude stuff.

It may be because of what happened at the clinic in *Firenze*—which is doing well. We serve thousands of gypsy or homeless children, giving them urgent care, immunizations and basic dental care. I think continually of one family the clinic treated. I was enjoying my morning cappuccino at the little café across from the *Duomo*, which is right around the corner from the clinic. I think some of the shops are a bit unhappy with us. They do not want tourists to see the reality of the children's poverty; without us, many would not own toothbrushes let alone be able to fill the huge cavities one can see if the child finds something to smile about. Anyway, there I was and a child came up to my table to beg. She was ten years old. And when she smiled at me, it was the same awful story—a huge black spot had eaten half her front tooth; her breath reeked of decay. I told her I would take her to the clinic, but she said she needed money; her mother was sick.

I gave the child caffé latte and a soft pastry, which we had to break up and soak in the coffee or she could not bear the pain chewing caused. The waiter had to move us to a table inside near the bar where no one sat in the morning; his other patrons would object to a gypsy child and a rich, blond woman getting to know each other.

The mother is really an "older" sister—a girl of 14. They are new to the begging community in the city; she had only been there one month from the country outside Sienna. Her illness? A kidney infection, strep throat, syphilis, her body torn up, her heart broken from a brutal rape. I will never forget the dull look in her eyes as if having seen the ugliness of the world had forever eclipsed the sun. I want a cleaner life.

Max does not object to my work with the foundation, but he does not care. He does not share my passion for a family. He said he will never adopt, "I'm not taking care of somebody else's mistake." How could we be so different? He is no Tom MacBride.

I am the one who wants a child with a desperation that dwarfs any mountain and I am the one who is dissatisfied with my husband and wary of the God I need.

The shopping bags that Laurie carried bulged with colorful quilts, soft stuffed animals and packages of warm, hand-made baby clothes. She met several people she knew on the way to the hospital nursery and so was later than she had hoped. When she explained the nature of the donation to the charge-nurse, the woman agreed to break Donna's "do not disturb" rule and escorted Laurie back to her office.

At the sound of her knock, without turning around, Donna commanded, "I'm not officially on duty until seven. I'm catching up on some paperwork."

Laurie opened the door a crack and said, "Can I come in, Donna? It's me, Laurie."

Donna gasped, whirled around in her silent desk chair. Laurie opened the door enough to squeeze in, hefted the stuffed bags in with her, and plopped them down at Donna's knees. "I didn't want to leave these things out front. I wanted to make sure they got into the right hands. Tom said you were the supervisor here."

"I'm so surprised to see you," she mumbled, standing as if her legs were numb.

Laurie opened her arms and hugged Donna; her cheek, warm with nervous excitement, met Donna's thin cool skin. "Here you've been in town and I haven't made the effort to get in here to see you. It's just not right."

Donna stepped back, folded her arms over her chest. "I wouldn't have expected any contact from you or Tom."

"But Donna—"

"When you were here for the birth of your child I stayed away on purpose. I didn't want to upset you at such a time."

"I would have been happy to see you," Laurie said, measuring Donna's discomfort, her whole soul open in sympathy and hope. She decided that Donna felt horribly embarrassed. "I brought you some things from my shop. I read about the hospital's Get Ready, Get Set program for new mothers. It's a wonderful idea, Donna. I love it and would love to help. You can include these things in the packets you give out." She pulled out a tiny pink cap and thrust it into Donna's hands hoping its soft beauty would ease the awkward tension between them. Donna's fingers moved over the petite quilted rows of the cap and along the satin ribbon.

"I love that color," Laurie said.

"This pink is my favorite."

"Mine, too. By far."

"Is this what you do at your shop?"

"That and other sewing projects. There's a café in the back, now."

Donna stiffened. "This is too expensive for this program." She held it out to Laurie.

But Laurie gently pushed Donna's hands back. "I'd very much like to donate these things, Donna. My store is doing well. I have plenty to spare and I wanted to see you again." Her tone was a bit plaintive. Donna's frown deepened. Laurie said, "Tom told me you have two sons of your own, now. How wonderful!"

"Don't pretend to be happy for me, Laurie. I ruined your coffeehouse to make you and Tom pay for my not being able to have children again. Now I have children and Rising Sun is gone."

Laurie reached for a stiff little metal chair and pulled it up to the center of the room beside the bags. She sank into it. "Why would I be angry that God blessed you with children?" she said, looking up to Donna. "In a way, they redeem all the differences we had back then. You blamed Tom and his advice—given at Rising Sun—for all you had lost. God saw fit—through difficult circumstances for sure—to close the coffeehouse. Then God kindly gave you children to replace that loss and he helped us change Rising Sun into the quilt shop, which is doing all Rising Sun did and much more. How could that do anything but make me grateful?"

"Because I meant it to *hurt you*." Donna shook her head and Laurie knew that if Donna could, if she did not consider herself so unworthy, she would apologize.

"It's noble of you to admit that to me, Donna. At the time it was all so confusing. You were never mean or vindictive. It was so unlike you."

"No, it's Max who's obsessed with the law and lawyers."

Laurie took out a fleece bunny. "Your child would have been about fourteen now, right? What happened that the doctors said you'd never be able to carry another?"

"Miscarriage. Twenty-two weeks. I hemorrhaged. There was a tear in the uterus. It was weird."

"How awful. I'm so sorry."

Donna sank down into her chair and stared at the bunny Laurie held on her knees.

Laurie held it out to her and she took it, touching the silky ears. "Do you know if the baby was a boy or girl?"

Donna said, "A girl. I didn't even get to see her. I passed out. Max saw her."

"It's impossible to ever fully get over something like that," Laurie murmured. She wanted to take Donna's hands, to hug her, but she didn't dare move.

"How would you know with your perfect life?" Donna snapped at Laurie. "You have so many children and the husband you wanted—" She broke off, her anger palpable; she tossed the little bunny into Laurie's lap as if she feared its influence.

"I am happy and loved, it's true," Laurie said, gently. "But I've lost people, too." Donna straightened her back and sniffed, wrinkling her nose, but her eyes were filling again so quickly. "And I do understand how you must have felt—especially since she was your first—and then to be told that you couldn't have any more! I wish we could have talked," Laurie said. "Losing friends as I have is almost as painful as losing people to death. I have lost some very dear friends. And until this afternoon you were one of those."

"How are you not furious about that lawsuit?" Donna cried.

Laurie shrugged. "I saw it as your way of trying to express how hurt you were. In a strange way, I understood. I was upset by…" Laurie gathered her courage and said, "I only wish Max had stopped when he—when he crashed into the side of the building."

Donna gasped. "How do you—did you see?"

"Yes. When it happened, I was confused, because I thought I was imagining you and Max together."

"No. It's reality," Donna said.

"Lawsuits and car wrecks," Laurie said. "When we really needed to talk. That was hurtful to us and I think to you, too. If you knew I understood and sympathized, if you knew how sad I was about your baby, how concerned about you…"

"I felt completely alone. I didn't believe anyone cared."

"So you met Max during that really painful time."

"He broke both his legs in a training accident. I was his nurse. I was pregnant and he loved me anyway."

"That is dear," Laurie said.

"I thought he was so great and special because he got behind my anger. I didn't realize his connection to you, Laurie. And it turns out he was really angry about—Katie. He used me to get back at Tom."

Knowing it was healthy for Donna to admit the truth aloud, Laurie nodded while she straightened the blue satin bow tied around the soft bunny's neck. "The boys are how old now?"

"Keith is eight and Tim is only six."

"They must be a joy to you. Do you have pictures?" Laurie looked around the sterile office.

"No, I—"

Donna looked miserable and Laurie regretted embarrassing her, thinking, *No pictures, all that storehouse full of anger, so miserable, the poor woman is so depressed*…Laurie said, "It must have been wonderful for both you and Ben to form a family together."

"I can't decide," Donna interrupted, her voice trembling, "if you are really *so nice* or if you are fishing for information." She stood up, angry and stiff, arms clamped over her chest. "Did Ben put you up to coming here?"

"No, Donna. Ben did not send me. Ben is entirely loyal to you." Laurie put the bunny on the top of one of the bags.

"Why did you come? Why?"

"I had to. I couldn't stay away." Laurie stood up. "I wanted to come sooner, but I had Cara. And well, something's happened recently that made me know I had to come to see you. Listen, Donna. There's been a customer in my shop, in my café, she's there nearly every day now. She is Max's lawyer." Laurie stepped closer and met Donna's eyes. Her hand went to Donna's arm. She touched her, then held on. "Donna, I know Max. I know what's going on with this woman and I just can't bear the thought of you being alone in Annapolis and going through that all by yourself when I'm right here just wanting to be friends again with all my heart."

Donna's mouth dropped in surprise. "How dare you!"

"Oh, please don't," Laurie said, tears coming to her eyes, her let-down reflex prickling deep inside her so that she had to quickly fold her arms and hold them tight. "Remember, I was the first woman Max ever cheated on. *I know* how it feels. You know my story."

Eyes filling, Donna stared at her. "We'd been married for years before I found out *Max* was the one who hurt you." Donna collapsed into her chair; she pulled one knee up to her chest and dropped down her head so that she could cover her face and head with her arms and hands. "Laurie, then I thought—" She was sobbing, gasping for air. Laurie knelt before her and coaxed her into her arms.

"You thought maybe his cheating wasn't your fault."

"Sometimes when I just know he's—this rage comes on me so heavy. Not towards Max, but me. I'm a useless failure."

"You don't understand how he can turn from you because you've given him everything, haven't you?" Laurie said, her hand on Donna's convulsing shoulder. "And he still won't stay with you."

"You have no idea what I've given him. What I've *compromised* for him." Donna nodded against Laurie's shoulder. "One time, I—I had the pills right in my hand, and I imagined you standing there in the bathroom with me."

"You did?" Laurie's eyes showed tender concern.

"You said, 'Don't give up, Donna. You can still do worthy things,' or something like that."

"Hmm."

"That's when I decided to take extra training so I could work here in the neonatal ward and become the supervisor."

"As you've done. I am sure so many mothers have been comforted by your expertise. I know I was."

Donna looked up. "I met her, you know. In my own kitchen. She said she was there on 'legal business.' Can you imagine? In my own house? I stood there and I was civil to her even though I knew. She must be a horrible person to come to my house like that."

"Donna, you don't deserve this from your husband."

"He had her up on our third floor. Ben knows about it."

"Oh, no."

Donna started to weep again, "I've been so awful to Ben. I depend on Ben when Max is…like this. And now for him to know about it."

"That wasn't your fault, Donna. That was Max's responsibility."

"But there's more that *is* my fault. You don't know." She sat up alarmed. "Do you?"

"I know that Ben is very unhappy, but that he loves you and always speaks very respectfully of you."

"Have you told him about Katie?" Donna was trembling, hands gesturing as if in supplication.

Laurie shook her head. "I've tried, but he does not even suspect. I don't know how to begin."

"He knows nothing about her," Donna confided. "Max burned everything of hers and forbid his mother to mention her. Do you know Ben has been completely cut off from his grandparents? That was because of me. Ben was cold to me at first and Max thought if we blocked out any connection to Katie, he'd have to forget her and accept me. Max actually threatened his own mother."

"To be honest with you, Donna," Laurie said, controlling herself with difficulty, "that doesn't seem right to me."

"I would suspect you of being a liar if you hadn't responded that way," Donna laughed bitterly.

"Ben is loyal to you. That is why he is so unhappy. He knows something is wrong and I think—emotionally—he can't make himself suspect."

"He has good reason to be unhappy at our house," Donna said, then shut her mouth tightly. "I tried to make up for it about a month ago. I shared the gospel with him and Laurie, he was so dear about it. I mean here I am a wreck of a Christian. Nothing to offer that boy but apologies."

"I think you have a great deal more to offer him, Donna."

"Ha! Like *what*?"

"You're his mother now."

"I'm a terrible mother. I've been awful. Worse, much worse than my own miserable mother."

"You could change that now," Laurie said, her voice irresistibly soft and true. "You could be, to your three boys, the mother you always wanted."

"That would mean..." Donna looked at Laurie. Her eyes went over Laurie once, then back over her again, peering with careful scrutiny. "Your children love you, don't they?"

"Yes, they do. And yours *need* you. You have to take action. Doing right for them will make you stronger. It will comfort them and it will *save* you."

"But that would be..."

"Difficult because you'd have to stand up to Max."

"I can't do it."

"I think you can.

"I can't even *talk* to Max."

"You can find a way, Donna. You can start with the way he's treating you. Have you ever confronted him about his affairs?"

"What good would it do?"

"Probably won't change him, but you'll be speaking up for yourself. You'll recapture some of that integrity and self-respect you laid down for him."

Donna pressed her lips together. "That's putting it bluntly."

"Old friends," Laurie said, "should tell each other the truth."

11

GLANCING up now to see young Tommy MacBride sweeping the café floor, Patty knew she had to hurry to finish this section.

> Camp Lejeune, December 1
>
> Home again and my pen compels me write what I have thus far refrained from declaring on paper. What keeps me now from writing the truth about Max? My parents will not read this. I have written down all my intimate feelings, the record of my cheating on Max in the early days before we were engaged, my continued longing for Doug. Max has no doubt read portions. He confronts me about what I write. What keeps me from writing the whole truth about him?
>
> Dear Diary, since I was tiny, I have loved and believed the written word. When I saw my family tree drawn so beautifully, written in Isabella's lovely hand, then I believed that I really belonged to my parents. I did not believe my intelligence until I read the test scores, the grades, the comments of those who wrote down their measure of my mind. If I write the truth, if I describe what it is really like to live with Max, why the panic that once thrilled my heart now chills me so deeply, then I will have to face the enormity of my mistake. So, I will not write down why, I will hide the proof from my reading eyes. But if tomorrow is like today, if when I try to discuss "the problem" with him and he shows me that he is truly all that I despise, I will leave him.

Patty turned the page in both dread and avidity. Katie had stapled in a newspaper clipping about her clinic in Florence and after that a copy of legal separation papers. *So, without writing why,* Patty thought, *she left him.* Six pages after that were clogged with clippings, notes pasted in, pictures. Patty shut the diary and slid it into her briefcase with a glance at her watch. Max would be waiting for her at their corner in just an hour. She needed a cigarette and wanted to stretch her legs. But how to get out of the store without actually speaking to Tom MacBride, who for some reason, brought out in her the most tender and vulnerable sensations. *If Max knew the effect the man was having on me, it would absolutely finish him,* she thought. Taking out her cell phone, Patty saw that she had three messages from

Max. She gathered her things, looked around for Tommy and not seeing him, decided to hold her head up confidently and stride through the store looking as if no one dare stop her.

She was past the cutting counter when she heard his voice behind her. "You can't leave without us meeting," Tom said in his friendly way. He was close, maybe two feet away, and she could feel his power like the pull of the sun. She turned around.

He had taken the wide-awake baby from her seat and held her perched on his left elbow. Up close he was kissably handsome—those lively blue eyes, those broad, lean shoulders looked even more appealing. Patty's mouth watered. "I'm Tom MacBride. Laurie's husband."

Saying her name, Patty shook hands, her palm moist. "Yes, I know, I figured." She wished she could smother the fire she felt in her skin, along her scalp, in her deepest core, at the electricity of Tom's handshake. *He's just your everyday man*, she scolded herself.

"I happen to know, from my wife's description of you, that you are my marine colleague Max Hunter's lawyer."

She gave a brief nod, pushing her hair out of her face. "Laurie's been kind enough to let me camp out in the café. I'm entirely addicted to the food and the cappuccino."

"What's your favorite so far?"

The question, so light-hearted and full of life, startled her. "Oh, I could never pick! The chocolate Scottie dog cookies with the little bows! My mother would flip. And the gingerbread!"

"I like the jam filled cookies," Tom confessed, patting his middle. "They're my weakness."

"I only wish she'd let me smoke. I was just headed out for a cigarette." Patty gestured toward the door.

"It is nice to meet you, Patty. Naturally, I've heard that you're reading our friend Katie's diary."

Patty laughed, thinking that the MacBrides certainly did believe in saying what was on their minds. How would he react if she told him what she was thinking now about him? But Tom said, "How's your reading going?"

"It's…slow reading. Such small handwriting, so much detail."

"What do you think of our Katie?"

Patty's eyes opened wide and a different, deeper emotion flashed through her being. "I think she's the most—lovable, vulnerable, interesting person."

"She was an astonishing woman. Every man in the room—young and old—was fascinated by her."

"Really?" Patty said, she narrowed her eyes, hoping for an important confession. Tom peered at her, his expression quizzical. Patty reached into her pocket frantically, while Tom stared at her as if he wondered what she could be searching for, as if he were ready to help. "Was your wife okay with your...*fascination* with Katie?"

"None of us who knew Katie at that time is *okay* with anything that happened back then. We've come to terms with a lot of it."

"How close were you to Katie?"

Tom motioned toward Patty's briefcase. "It's in her journal."

"I see."

"Say, Patty," Tom said. "I know we've just met, and I know you've been friends with Max for a long time and you might object to what I'm about to ask you—" Tom stopped, his expression showing alarm as Patty wished she could stop the embarrassed, scalding flush that rose up her throat. Tom said, "Are you *okay*?"

"Quite. Go ahead." She now had a pack of cigarettes in hand and was squishing it. This she brandished at Tom as if to explain the reason for her red face.

"Um, I need a lawyer to update some of my personal papers. Maybe you could help me."

She gave a loud guffaw, tried to recover herself, but giggled. Tom smiled cautiously, watching her. "I've heard about you, Tom MacBride. You know practically every person in town. You've *got* to have a lawyer you went to school with or something like that. You don't need me."

"I do have a lawyer, but I don't want to alarm him...or my wife."

"Oh, so this," Patty choked, gesturing between them, "is to be kept a secret."

Tom shrugged. "I just want to create a legal document to attach to my will—in order to clarify a few things—and if I do, my lawyer will tell my brother-in-law because they play racquetball together and then Doug will tell Laurie and she'll be worried," Tom confessed. "It shouldn't present a conflict of interest with Max. But if you think it does, I'll think of something else."

"Call my secretary," she said, scrounging again in her pocket and coming up with a business card dusted with crumbled tobacco leaves. She shook these off and handed it to Tom. "I could actually use the business. I've been so caught up with—" She waved her hand as if to indicate the confusion of her current life. Tom's eyes were steady and she found herself asking, "What changes do you want to make?" She lifted her briefcase to the counter, unlatched it quickly to pull out her legal pad. Flipping to the back, to the clean pages beyond the notes recording the history of Max's heartbreak, her fingertips tingled with the possibility of new information she could use to ease Max's mind.

Tom smiled slightly, waiting for Patty to get ready to make notes. Patting Cara's back, he told Patty that first he wanted officially to include the baby in his will. "I think the current will says something about subsequent children born, but still…"

Patty scribbled the baby's name as Tom spelled it. "And my mother's house belongs to me. My father left it to me I think because he felt a little awkward about leaving his business to his foster son." Hesitating he added, "I don't want to drag you through the pile of my ancient laundry, Patty, but—"

"No, please, *go ahead*," Patty said,

"My mother resented my father's will. She disagreed with his leaving the business to Kevin and she was very resentful that he left the house to me. And if I die before her, she will be frightened about her future. She doesn't trust easily and though I know my family will take care of her, I'd like it spelled out."

"Give me the details, I'll write it up," Patty said.

"My mother is entitled to live there—rent free—as long as she wishes and the family should continue to rent out the dock space on her property. The revenue from that goes into a savings account that I keep for her so that she can afford things like visiting my sister and you know…whatever. They should keep that up."

"When you phone my secretary, give her the specifics about the property."

"I'll do that," Tom said.

"Do you want to include anything—um—anything about *Ben* in this document?"

Tom sighed deeply. "That is also what's on my mind. How insightful of you to see that." His eyes were sad, but amused. "If…if this paper is needed soon, I will need someone to tell Ben how sorry I am that I failed him."

"Failed him? How? You're of no relation, how could any failure of yours matter?"

"Can that be written in somehow?"

"It's not a legal or financial matter, Tom."

"Maybe *you* could *tell* him. If it comes to that. You've got the official legal stature."

"How have you failed him in the official legal sense?"

"No, it's moral failure," Tom said sadly.

"That's not my thing, Tom."

"I could write him a letter like I did for the other kids," Tom said, frowning. "But I wanted something—I don't know—something more official."

"Your *other* kids?" Patty urged, hoping her fishing for a confession wasn't as obvious to Tom as it seemed to her. But Tom just gazed into the distance, patting Cara's back. Patty said, "And anyway, what makes you think you're going to die? Have you had bad news from the doctor? Because you *look* great—um, I mean *really* healthy."

"Just a premonition. I've had them before."

Patty laughed. "But they must have been wrong!" She opened her arms to gesture, emphasizing his life-size, breathing stature there in the shop.

Tom laughed too, a full, amused chuckle at himself. Still smiling, he said, "It would mean a lot to me to have this buttoned up." Tom waited, still patting Cara's back, looking at Patty with hopeful intent.

"Okay, sure, Tom. I think this is unnecessary and sort of melodramatic, but your wife has been extremely kind to me and I see you're a nice guy, so if it will make you feel better, I'm happy to do it."

"Okay, thanks," Tom said, offering to shake her hand again.

He seems so genuine, Patty thought, *his handshake so warm, his manner so straightforward.*

"Why are you so attached to Ben?"

"You haven't gotten to the end of the diary, have you?"

Patty shook her head. "I'm at where Katie has just left Max. Poor guy."

"Mm," Tom said, pressing his lips together, eyes solemn and full of regret. "Ben came about right after that separation."

"What convinced her to go back to him?"

"I asked her to."

"Please explain your reasoning," Patty said with sudden boldness that made her heart thump.

"In part, my motivation was self-preservation." Tom looked unspeakably sad.

"You mean covering your own ass?"

"Max had been a problem to me. But he seemed to deserve another chance."

"I need facts, not vague confessions," Patty said, briskly. It usually worked with male clients; they would confide almost anything if brought to believe they were merely recounting facts. But Tom just shrugged as if he'd given all and offered to shake hands again. "I'll see you soon," she said, shaking his hand.

12

OPENING his car door Joe said, "We have to go to Ben's house to get some of his math homework."

"I thought you finished it at our house last night," Bonnie Jean said as she got into the car.

"I'm missing part of chapter seven. Dr. D. looked through my notebook today and told me if I get that section in her mailbox by the time she's done tonight, she won't count it late," Ben said.

Bonnie Jean put her head back against the seat. "My math notebook was a mess, but I turned it in and I don't care." She shut her eyes.

"How are you, Jeannie?" Ben touched her arm. "Rough rehearsal?"

"Yes. And my head is throbbing. I had nightmares all night. I can't live with all this lying we're doing. I feel like I'm going to burst." Joe made a sympathetic noise and glanced at Ben, who leaned toward Bonnie Jean from the backseat.

"I'm sorry," Ben said.

"I'm so frustrated and I hate being dishonest. During lunch today, I looked up the suicide hotline," she said, pulling a paper from the backpack between her feet. "Here." Ben took it from her. She said, "I called them from Mrs. Poulard's office. Don't worry, she wasn't there. And it's strictly anonymous."

"What did they say?"

"The guy on the hotline said we should tell your dad. Of course that won't work because what are we going to say? You're hurting Ben and we can't tell because your wife will kill herself? No."

"We could try it," Joe said. "It might wake him up to find out we know."

Ben hesitated, pressing his lips together. "I don't know if I'm right about this or not, but all day today, I *have* wanted to try and talk to my dad."

"Are you serious?" Joe said.

"If you two are willing to come with me, I think he's less likely to hurt me if anyone is there. I'm not sure, but I think I have something to say to him. With you guys there, I could stay calm and…just say it."

"Yes! Hurray!" Bonnie Jean shouted.

"I know he doesn't love me and I don't think he loves her in the way we think of love," he said softly, "but I think they're *attached* and he should know what his behavior is doing to her."

"Let's try his office, then," Joe said.

"Yeah, if he's still there. An official, crowded place would be safest. But he may be home by now."

Joe said, "What will you say, Ben?"

"Um…I'd say…okay, just like this, 'Dad, I don't know how much you remember because of being drunk so much but you've been hitting me—hurting me, really, and um…'"

"That's good, Ben," Bonnie Jean said. "Say that."

"And then I can say how its affecting Mom and how she's threatened suicide. What's the worst that could happen if you two are there? I mean, we won't try it if he's drunk, but if he's sober he's not gonna hit me in front of you. And maybe, just maybe we can reach him and he'll see."

"That would be a great and needed miracle," Joe said.

Bonnie Jean sat up, eyes bright. "Okay. Let's go for it."

They walked into the Yard, showing picture ID cards, and circled around the alley behind Porter Road. "Mom's not home," Ben said, pointing to the empty garage. "My brothers should be at the Lindquists'. Let's get my math notebook stuff and check to see if he's here."

Joe and Bonnie Jean followed Ben to the basement, amazed at the stealth he practiced so smoothly. Without a sound he opened the basement door, ushered them in, and shut it. There was a rustling noise above them, they froze, listening. Finally, Ben whispered, "Okay, that's him. He's here. I'll get my math papers so I have them in case things get ugly. You stay here."

"No," Joe said. "We're following you. It's not up for debate."

They tread in his footsteps all the way up the back stairs. Once Ben had the missing notebook pages in hand, they stood on the landing of the kitchen stairs, confused by the noises they heard beyond the door. "Is he watching TV?" Bonnie Jean asked.

Ben frowned, leaning his ear to the door, trying to discern his father's mood. He whispered. "I don't want to go in there if he's drunk."

"Let's go out and come back in by the front door," Bonnie Jean said. "We can see in and back away if he looks out of it."

"Shh," Joe said. "Listen. Is he alone? Is he hurting someone?"

"Sounds like someone's sick," Bonnie Jean whispered.

They listened at the kitchen door, holding their breath. The boys frowned, concentrating. "Let's go," said Joe.

"No. It might be your brothers," Bonnie Jean said. "What if they came home because they were sick and no one was here?" The moaning came in a different pitch, deeper. "Gosh," Bonnie Jean said, her voice a bit too loud. "It's both of them and they sound miserable." She put her hand on the door, the volume mounting. Ben covered her hand.

"No," he said, his voice flat and quiet. "It's them. Forget it. Let's get out of here."

"What do you mean, *them*?"

Ben met Joe's eyes. "Patty and Dad doing it. They're in the living room, probably drinking, too."

"Sick," Bonnie Jean said. Joe's eyes went wide, then narrow.

"Hurry," Ben whispered and turned to creep down the stairs.

Once in the basement, Bonnie Jean kept her hand over her mouth. "This is awful. This is unbelievable."

"I'm so sorry," Ben said, shaking his head, his color gone ashen. "Let's go."

"No," Joe said, with a hand on Ben's arm. "Wait." He met Ben's eyes, then Bonnie Jean's. "I just had the most genius idea." He motioned them closer, their three heads together. "We thought someone was sick or getting beat up. What if we call nine-one-one and report it that way?" He watched their reaction. "Report it as if we *don't* know what's *really* going on. The police come and..." Joe shrugged, "serves him right."

"Let's do it," Ben said.

"I'll use my little kid voice," Bonnie Jean whispered as Ben motioned for them to follow him into the laundry room where a phone hung on the wall above the light switch. He dialed and put the phone to Bonnie Jean's ear.

"Huh-woh," she said in a baby voice. "I camed to my friend's house to see if he can play and I think somethin's bad."

"Is your mother there?" the operator asked.

"My mommy at home. I at my fwiend's house and camed in the basement like aways and he won't come down. I think there's a bad man upstairs hurting him. He's crying. I'm scared a go up thewe."

"Where are you, honey?"

Bonnie Jean gave the address but when the operator asked for her own name and address, she started to cry. "Hurry! Do you promise to hurry?"

Ben sprinted down the alley toward Gate One, his math papers crumpled in his left hand. Joe and Bonnie Jean ran after him. Two yards down he cut left and led them down the sidewalk, past the tennis courts and into Dahlgren Hall. Pee Wee Ice Hockey teams practiced on the ice. Mothers stood by the boards watching. In the large open area near the doors, teams of older boys dressed for the next round of practice.

Trying to look casual as they strolled the length of the ice rink toward the steerage and the stairs to the upper deck, they heard the police siren outside. Joe led, running up the steps three at a time. Once on the spacious upper deck, they rushed past mids lounging in the plush chairs set up around the balcony rail. They found a coffee table and dragged it to a high arched window opposite Ben's house. The three climbed up and clung to the lower edge of the window, watching.

A white car bearing the insignia of the police assigned to the Naval Academy was parked, lights still flashing, in front of the Hunters' quarters. One officer rounded the back of the house, one mounted the front steps. They saw him pounding on the door. Inside, someone turned on a light that for the three friends' vantage point, lit the entire first floor of the Hunters' quarters. The officer shouted. "Open the door, sir. Police, here. Open the door!"

The door opened, and Patty's curly head peeked around it. She was shaking her head, gesturing with one bare arm. Ben, Joe and Bonnie Jean stared openmouthed. The second officer appeared inside the house, leading Max to the front of the house. Naked, he held a sofa pillow in front of his groin, his open mouth showing his astonishment. Ben pointed to his right. Down the street, walking briskly, head up, gleam in his eye noticeable even at their vantage point, came Admiral Johnson. "You're a genius, Joe," Ben said, backing away and off the table, he sank down on the floor. Bonnie Jean joined him.

"Oops! There Patty goes up the steps. I guess she's looking for something to put on."

"Shh," Ben said. "Whisper." He glanced at Bonnie Jean, took her clenched hand in both of his. "This is awful," she groaned.

"Awful justice," Ben said.

It took Ben, Bonnie Jean and Joe some time to find a few of the math papers that Ben dropped during their rush through Dahlgren Hall. "I'm just going to have to take a B," Ben groaned as he glanced at his watch, then at Bonnie Jean smoothing the muddy, trampled papers.

"Just sit down here and re-do them," Joe said.

After borrowing paper and pencil from a friendly mid, Ben began again. Joe and Bonnie Jean waited; Joe studied, Bonnie Jean rested her head back and closed her eyes. When he finally finished, Joe looked over Ben's papers only to discover one still missing. "I'll get my backpack from your car," Ben said, "do that last page, and drop them off at school." He glanced at his watch. "The girls' game is probably just finishing up. You guys should go home. Your parents will be waiting."

"Then come over," Joe said. "We'll save dinner for you.

This agreed upon, the three left Dahlgren Hall. As they stepped out into damp cold evening, Bonnie Jean asked, "Why don't you ever fight back, Ben?"

"If you were around him when he's drunk, you'd understand. He's bigger than the room and he's got this weird power about him...It's overwhelming."

"I believe that," Bonnie Jean said. "He's overbearing normally. Too much personality or something in him."

"I can't get away from the fact that I'm so ashamed for every time he's hit me."

Joe said, "But he's a big guy, and athletic, so that fueled by his anger and with alcohol wiping out his inhibitions—and the fact that he's your father. It must handicap you."

"Lots of times, I do get away—those are the good days. But when he actually hits me, when his fist or whatever—actually makes contact," Ben said. "It's because I'm surprised. And after I'm hit, I—I don't know. I freeze."

"Gosh!" Bonnie Jean said. "That is *awful*."

"It's like…you know, on some hopeful level deep inside, you don't expect to be in danger around your own father. And then when I realize he wants to hurt me, or like he says sometimes, he wants me dead, I'm astonished. It's like realizing the nightmare you're having isn't a dream… it's reality."

Joe put an arm around his sister, another around Ben, their habitual way of walking.

"Puke," Bonnie Jean said. "I have now felt like puking for the last two hours."

"Do you think it would be wrong for him to hit his dad, Bonnie Jean?"

"No. I say deck him."

"No," Ben said. "It's wrong. I won't do it. It's like the one thing I have to hang onto. It's the one thing I don't have to feel bad about. I've never hit him. I may be a crappy son or have disappointed him in some way or I don't know, I piss him off so bad he wants me dead, but at least I can say I never hit him. Everyone knows that's wrong. Hitting your father. It proves I'm not like him."

They stopped on the street, huddled together, their heads together, the wind whirling around their knees.

13

AFTER he said good-bye to Joe and Bonnie Jean, Ben walked up King George Street to his car, backpack on his shoulder. He mourned the lost opportunity to confront his father. The will, the courage to do so, had submerged in his anger at finding him there with Patty. And he knew that the time he could impose on Bonnie Jean's honesty was fast closing. He had to do something to relieve the pressure she suffered. Joe was only holding up because his dedication to protect Ben fed and inspired him.

Ben unlocked his car door and swung his backpack into the backseat. His desire to talk to his father returned and with it the flickering hope that he would survive what was in his heart to do. He ducked his head into his car to slide his math papers into his math notebook when he heard his father's roar behind him.

"How did *this car* get pink?"

He felt his father's hand grab his waistband and pull. "That better not be Ben!" His father yanked him back, pulling him out of the car; Ben's head hit hard on the door rim. He stumbled trying to right himself and Max smacked Ben's ass with an open hand. "You stay away from that car," Max growled. Though his knee hit the brick sidewalk, Ben got away, stood, watched his father go to the back of his car to stare at the bumper. Behind Max, the lamp-lit street was a long, quiet stretch of twinkling white

Christmas lights; no footsteps sounded, everyone inside. Ben turned to look for Patty behind him finding only a family of three walking away toward Gate One. The place where Joe had been parked stood empty, the MG and his friends now gone. "Dad," Ben said, recapturing only a glimmer of the strength and purpose he'd felt moments before.

"What are you doing in that car?"

"Are you okay, Dad?"

"Where did you get this? Let me see," Max said, pushing past Ben to the door, crawling in, punching the button on the glove compartment so that it bounced open. Ben squatted behind him to follow his father's investigation and saw the old-fashioned wallpaper lining the glove-compartment, the one area that Gregen had not restored. Max scooped out the maps, sending them to the floor and then he saw the same small photograph of Max that had been framed on the coffee table. It was stuck to the wall of the compartment, not visible when maps filled the space. Ben remembered that on the night they picked the car up from the paint shop, Tom had also looked in the glove compartment, remembered Tom's rush of emotion at the sight of the car. *Maybe this is the car in that accident—where I was thrown out,* Ben wondered.

"What's wrong, Dad? Why is your picture in my car?" Ben asked as his father rolled to right himself and stand.

"*Your* car?" Max growled, his hands coming up fast, he lunged for Ben, who dodged him. "Where'd you get this car?" He stepped toward Ben, hands out as if he wanted to grab him. Ben, wary and alive, went on his toes, ready to move. "I thought your grandmother got you a car."

"She did. A friend of hers restored this."

"Goddammit! Goddammit! This was a worthless piece of trash when I got done with it."

"Is this the car from the crash when I was a baby?"

"What the hell do you know about that?" Max shouted, reaching for Ben's arm. Ben let him grab it then whirled around swinging his father away from the car so that Max's back brushed the Academy's brick wall, giving Ben access to his car's open front door. He could get in, shut the door, get away, but something compelled him.

"I'm sorry you're upset about the car, but I need to talk to you, Dad."

"The hell you do. Sneaking around behind my back with your grandmother. I'm taking you out of that school. This stops here."

"What? No. Wait," Ben said, planting his feet. "This has nothing to do with school. Mom is in trouble. She's depressed. You've got to—"

"What do you know about your mother, you little shit? I'll tell you about your mother!"

Max went for Ben, hand out to shove him, but Ben juked right. "Dad. Stop. You have no right—"

Max laughed. "No right? After I raised you? All I went through for you?" The angry hysteria in Max's voice mounted. "I'm the *only one* with rights." He swung hard at Ben, his eyes bright, clear and angry. Ben dodged the punch and when Max stumbled, he grabbed his father, both of his strong, young arms trapping Max. Nostrils flaring, Ben measured his father's sobriety in the whiffs of beef and garlic that hung on his breath. Ben held him tight and close; they struggled face to face, their bodies touching, chest against chest, stomach on stomach, thighs hard and straining.

"Stop hitting me," Ben whispered. "Stop treating me like shit."

Max cried out in a wrenching, guttural shriek. He twisted right and thrust his arms up hard, loosening Ben's hold enough to get one hand between them and he shoved Ben away, shouting, "You're the one who messed your mother's life up! You!" Ben stumbled, hands back, reaching for his car. Head down, Max tackled Ben. Max's head smashed into Ben's stomach, shoving Ben up against the car. Max staggered back off Ben. Ben's vision skipped and flashed and then he saw Patty running up the sidewalk.

Ben found his feet, pushed off the car, and stood. In the same instant he saw Max's fist form, saw it coming and jumped left, so that Max hit air, stumbled, lost his footing and grabbed for Ben, getting his hands on Ben's jacket and pulling Ben down with him. Ben's shoulders hit the edge of the door. Max crashed on Ben's legs; Ben's chin hit the curb. Ben fought to get out from under, his churning legs giving Max some leverage to get to all fours. Patty pulled Max up, getting his chest up, getting Max's legs under him. Ben rolled left, his hand reaching in for his steering wheel. Max shoved Patty away and he kicked Ben back down so hard that Ben's head hit the corner of his front bumper.

Ben cried out, saw his own arms and legs shoot out in terrified spasm, saw bright images in the night black sky that mirrored the pain like glass slicing deep, like a sledge hammer crushing ice—a penetrating and permanent accusation. He felt the blow in his legs, in his spine, in his right jaw. He saw his father raising his foot again with vicious intent. Ben pulled his knees up, but they would not bend. He rolled, clawing the brick sidewalk, grabbing for his car, getting his hand on the running board, pulling, trying to get in.

"Are you all right?" Patty screamed as she slapped at Max's bent knee with savage fear. "Are you hurt?"

Ben made himself look at them, saw Patty trying to hold Max back, saw the intentional fury in Max's eyes, saw that he was not drunk, and a quiet came to Ben that blanketed his pain. He reached for the steering wheel and pulled himself into the driver's seat of his car, his right leg regaining a feeling that mimicked life. He looked again to see Patty pound Max's arms and finally rear back with her brutally pointed shoe and kick

Max's knee. With both hands, he lifted his left leg into the car, slammed the door, locked it with his shoulder while he fumbled for his keys with hands not yet again his own. When the car purred beneath him, he rolled the window open a crack. "You saw him hurt me, Patty. I know you saw and I know you're not drunk."

"Get out of here!" she screamed. Breaking away from her, Ben's father lunged for the car, his fingers screaking against the window as Ben bucked the car into gear and lurched it out into the wet, empty street.

By the time Ben turned into the school parking lot, he felt queasy and he drove quickly and carelessly past the crowds of athletes and fans leaving the girls' game. He let his car roll to a stop behind the dumpster at the back of the auxiliary parking on the hill above the gym. He rushed out, stumbled to the edge of the woods where his stomach heaved in empty effort. Now his strength was shattered, but his body did not hurt—numbness and calm, the disciplines of his sonship. When he could move, he crawled back to his car and crouched beside it, the silent, waiting engine radiating the only warmth available to him. Ben felt the cold descend through the darkness, the scent wet, metallic and familiar. It touched his head, closed his eyelids; he imagined snow falling, sat still without thinking and clung to an odd, threadbare feeling of quiet.

Hours passed.

Hot and pounding, his aching ribs woke him. It hurt to breathe. He heard the cleaning crew open the gym back door and heard the plump of the trash bags as they were set on the concrete there.

"I've got to get into the school," Ben thought irrationally, "or I'll get a B in math." Staggering he stood, and the wind fought him all the way to the gym door, taking his breath and hitting his tingling and unsteady knees in strong and steady gusts. The door had not yet been locked and Ben opened it, stepped in, and went swiftly to his right up the few steps to the stage. He hid behind the black scrim curtains, awaiting the crew's exit. When he heard their truck on the gravel of the driveway, Ben went back to the door, left his shoe in it to prop it open, and hobbled back outside to his car.

Above him, the stars faded in the blue-black night beside the moon's full light. Sensing his father's fury, unsatisfied and alive, he felt it approaching; Ben decided to hide his car. He drove it around to the dirt driveway that led into the woods. He drove until the road curved then pulled the car off the gravel onto a grassy place invisible from the parking lot. Taking his backpack, Ben made his way slowly back to the school.

In the dark school, he shivered, alone and cold. In the locker room he stood in the dark under a shower of steaming water. But he couldn't get warm. Thankful that he wouldn't need stitches, he blotted the oozing skin on the back of his head and measured the damage by looking at the bloody towels through the dim light of the locker room windows. Wondering how to hide them, he finally took them with him to Coach's office.

Using the first aid kit kept under the cot, Ben made a clumsy patch for his head wound. It hurt too much to sit. To finish his overdue work, he stood up at the window, the sill serving as his desk where the cold, night air shivered through the glass.

At two-thirty in the morning, Tom tucked the covers around Laurie's feet and walked quietly down the hall to check on Bonnie Jean. Though she had been unusually quiet and subdued the past several days, she hadn't complained of feeling ill until tonight. Tom felt her forehead, thinking that her fever had lessened, but he could see from the hallway light that bright red patches still burned on her cheeks. He replaced the damp cloth Laurie had placed on her forehead earlier and went out into the hall. Joe's room was empty. Tom went back to his room, pulled on his jeans and a sweatshirt, and hurried down the stairs. Joe stood, clad only in boxers, staring out the back door window.

"What's going on? You should be in bed." Tom touched Joe mid-back.

"Can't sleep." Joe glanced up slightly to meet his father's eyes.

"Do you feel all right?" Tom brushed Joe's forehead with the back of his hand. "No fever."

"Just worried about Ben."

"Anything unusual happen today after practice?"

Joe gave a deep sigh. "Okay. I'll tell you, but I don't want you to go crazy. Okay?"

"I'll try my best, son."

"We went over to Ben's house today on the way here—we being me, Ben and Jeannie after we picked her up from rehearsal. You're not going to like this, Dad. You're not going to like what I'm going to tell you at all, but I don't want you to hold it against Ben. He doesn't want you to think he's like his dad."

"I don't think that. Good Lord! If I thought that it would mean I'd given up all hope! Go ahead. You went over there and…"

"And we got the stuff he needed, math papers, and we're on the way out. See, we always use this back staircase, and we heard this stuff on the main floor and Jeannie thought someone was sick, but at first it sounded like *maybe* someone was being beat up because there was all this groaning and this thumping sound. Try to see it from our perspective, Dad, okay? Something was wrong or unusual so we listened."

"What was it?"

"Ben's dad having sex. With a woman. Not Mrs. Hunter."

"Oh, no. And you walked in on them?"

"No." Joe put a hand on his father's arm. "No. We were going to just get out of there, but then I got this idea."

"Oh, no."

"We called nine-one-one and Jeannie used her baby voice to report someone being beaten up. Then we ran away."

"A nine-one-one call on false pretenses?" Tom said, his voice strained. "It's illegal, Joe."

"I didn't think of that."

"I don't know, honestly, Joe, what I'm going to do with you!"

"Dad, it just kind of happened."

"With you, Joe, it always 'just happens!' You have to look ahead and imagine the consequences before you act." Tom rubbed his forehead. "I am going to have to think of a way to make that real to you. I cannot believe—"

"Dad," Joe said, his voice sober. "I'm thinking of the consequences now. It's torturing me. If that helps you any."

"You're thinking that Ben is in trouble for this."

"I don't see how the call could have been traced to him unless someone saw us leaving the house."

"Max may have suspected it was Ben, though, and confronted him."

"But I didn't think he was going *back there*," Joe protested, upset. "He was going to go to school, finish his math stuff, and come over."

"He's not in the apple attic, is he? It's too cold tonight."

Joe met Tom's eyes, relief rushing up in him, sympathy palpable between them. "No. I checked."

"And he said he'd be here?"

"We agreed," Joe said. "But...maybe his brothers needed him. I don't know..."

"Or what?" Tom said.

"He said something about wanting to talk to his parents. I wish you could talk to his mother, Dad."

"I'll go see if I can find him," Tom said. He shoved one foot then the other into the shoes he'd left by the door.

"You're not supposed to go near Colonel Hunter."

"Says who?"

"Everybody. Mama, Unca Doug."

"Don't worry about me." Tom shrugged into his jacket and felt, as had become habit, for the envelope. "I'm looking for Ben, not Max."

"I'm coming."

Tom dropped a firm hand on Joe's shoulder. "No. You're not. You're going to bed. Go to bed and go to sleep. Trust me and sleep soundly." Tom kissed Joe's forehead. "Go on now."

14

BEN tried to sleep on the cot beneath the window in Tom's office, but when he lay down, cold air rolled off the glass and drifted over his face. The shivering he could not stop aggravated the aching in his ribs and even the weight of the quilt rubbed the sore skin. The act of sitting up hurt so much he feared he would not be able to think, to test, to play ball, to hide the truth. And once sitting, his butt sinking down into the low, sagging cot, his knees high, his stomach bent almost double, he could neither tolerate the pain nor take a full breath.

He rolled on his good side and plunked off to his knees. Pushing himself up with his arms, he stood; he paced. Though he had survived, things felt worse for the pressure in his heart. He had to end things somehow. He had to stop torturing Bonnie Jean. He respected and loved her honesty, yet he was forcing her to discard it. Today's prank was the first time he'd seen Joe laugh since Thanksgiving, but his laugh had lost its free insouciance and was edged with pain and disillusionment. And Joe's relationship with Tom was tainted now due to Ben's required deceptions.

He had done what he wanted. He'd confronted his father and it hadn't helped. Max's hatred now needed no alcohol to fuel it. So weary he couldn't keep walking, Ben went to Tom's chair. In too much pain to sit, he knelt in front of the chair, resting his head on the seat, arms at his sides, and for the first time realized that he was hurt badly enough this time that people might actually realize the truth. His father would be arrested, his mother, alone and in despair, would take her life or at least attempt to do so. Keith would find her and never be a child again. He had to spare his brothers that terror. He had to go away before anyone saw him; he had a car and three thousand dollars in the bank; he could drive to Quebec. They spoke French there. He looked eighteen. He'd hide and work for a couple of years until everyone was safe.

He heard footsteps on the concrete stairs that led up to the gym. He lifted his head. Was it Tom? Joe?

The pounding on the gym door was palm-flat and arrhythmic. It was his father. Drunk. He knew it. Then the voice came, angry words slurred. "I know yer in there."

The pounding stopped. Despite shrieking pain, Ben lowered himself to sit on the floor, the cold reached up all around him, pulled on the aching in his ribs.

"Come out here, Ben," The voice was closer, then he heard his father's hand slap the window above the cot and Ben jumped. Terror shot through Ben. "You messed up my life. Come out here and pay for it."

The ranting sounded insane—threats, name-calling, Max's lethal wishes for Ben, who inched deeper into the knee well of Tom's desk. He pulled the chair in close and held onto it. The glass smashed. Ben stifled a scream. Max shouted, "Ow, shit, hurt my hand." Then came the moaning and the drunken sobbing that always came when pain broke his father's anger. Ben pressed his eyes to his knees and cried out to God for help.

He heard Tom's voice. He heard him calling, "Max? Don't move. I'll help you." He approached, the call steady, calm, closer every second. Ben held his breath. His father cried and pleaded. Tom said. "Here. I'll get your arm out. Hold still. Every time you move it you cut it again. We've got to lift it up."

Ben heard his father's relieved crying, heard the sound shift, move away, heard his father say, "If it isn't Tom MacBride."

"What are you doing here, Max?"

"I gotta get Ben outta here. I'm gonna put him in St. Mary's."

Tom's voice came through the window. "Are you in there, Ben?"

Ben kept still. Tom said, "He's not there."

"He is. Can't you smell him? I can. Same stink as his mother."

"Hush, Max. Show some respect."

"I'm getting him out. I'm getting him away from you."

Tom said. "I'll go in and get the first aid kit. You stay here."

Ben listened to the keys work, the footsteps approach. He reasoned this way: if he revealed himself, Max would attack him. Max's injuries didn't matter, alcohol ruled Max's brain again and would release him to act out his passionate wish for Ben's death. Tom would fight to defend Ben at any cost and get hurt. Tears stung Ben's eyes. He fought them, asking for strength.

Inside, Tom switched on the light. Ben heard him grab the first aid kit, his big hand making a hollow pop on the metal box. He heard the whirr of the tape dispenser and realized that Tom was patching the hole in the window. But Ben could still hear Tom when he was outside. "He left some stuff, but he's not there, now. He's probably home in bed."

"I'm getting him away from you."

"First I'm gonna patch up those gashes. Then I think we'd better go to the ER."

Max's mumbled cursing continued without any words from Tom until Ben heard Tom tell Max to get up. He heard the sounds of struggle and feared for Tom's safety. "How did you get here?" Tom said.

"Walked. Patty's mad at me and wouldn't drive me. Nervy bitch. I want Ben away from you. Away from you or dead."

"Stop that," Tom said. "That's ridiculous and cruel. You should be ashamed of yourself."

Their voices grew distant and when he dared, Ben crawled out from his hiding place and crept up to the splintered window. He watched Tom help his father into the car, watched them drive away.

At the ER, Max was admitted, Donna was called. She came to the waiting area to thank Tom, looking grieved, tense and angry. Tom stood up when she approached. "How is he?"

"Drunk on his ass," she whispered. "I guess you noticed."

"I tried not to," Tom said. "The gashes?"

"They hope stitches will be all that's needed. But, thank you, Tom. For bringing him here."

"He was looking for Ben," Tom said, expectantly. "At school."

"Drunken fool. It's humiliating."

"Would you like me to wait and take him home for you?"

"They'll keep him until I get off," she said. "You seem no worse for the wear?" It was a question. Tom saw genuine concern touch her jaded eyes.

"I am just concerned for you and Ben."

She seemed to be struggling, then whispered, "I suppose your school will do something official about the window."

Tom shrugged. "We like to keep good relationships with our parents, Donna, but you know, it depends on how Max handles it."

"It would be bad for the boys and I if the school pressed charges."

"Maybe not," Tom said. She reminded him of Ben just then, too terrified to submit to correction that would save, would strengthen the character.

"Things might come out about you and your past. About why Max hates you."

"I don't care about that. I care about you and Ben having to live like this."

"Tom, give me a little time, I beg you."

"This can't go on, Donna. It's not good." Tom squinted at her, searching her eyes to confirm an earnest determination he felt quickening in her. "If Ben is home when you get there, would you mind giving me a quick call? It doesn't matter how late."

Ben thought of his brothers sleeping unattended while his parents struggled at the ER. Frustrated with his lame and foiled attempts to solve his own problems, broken, weary and unable to get warm, he went home. Shaking Keith gently, Ben woke his brother enough to let the boy know he was there. He kissed Tim's head, then took a pillow and leaned his folded arms on the top of their bookshelf and dozed, standing there, for two hours.

He had been dreaming of Bonnie Jean. She walked in his dream as when they first met, summer tanned, quick-witted, honest, happy. And when he woke, he had two thoughts: *The strain of keeping secrets is damaging Bonnie Jean,* and *This must have been what happened to change my mother. Keeping my father's violence and drinking a secret has warped the amazing, vibrant woman that everyone remembers.* He envisioned that framed photograph of his young father he'd seen, unable to reconcile the difference in him either.

He woke the boys early enough so that he could oversee their showers, made them breakfast, and while they were eating, he stood by, holding onto the back of a chair to ease his pained breathing.

Tim asked Ben if the nice lady had interviewed him at school, too, and the question revived him.

"No. What nice lady?"

"We had a conference," Keith said. "And Mrs. Johnson was there. The lady asked us about Dad and you and we told her how nice you were and how you take care of us all the time."

"Not recently," Ben said sadly.

"Mrs. Johnson said it was okay that Tim told the lady that Dad is after you and that you wrote it all down for the police to find after you're actually dead."

"That's good that you said that, Tim," Ben said, feeling sick.

"But Mom and Dad say never tell. Never," Keith reminded them of the family code.

Tim said, "But the lady said it won't get anybody in trouble. And she smiled and I liked her."

"What did you say, Keith?"

"Dad *can* be good," Keith said with a glance at Ben. "He never hurts me or Mom or Tim. Only you." The shame was more than his embarrassed flush showed; it's alienating depth felt so unnatural. "But we've never seen that. 'Cause you make us go out of the room," Keith added.

"Look," Ben lifted up his shirt to show the bruises on his torso. Though it hurt to lower his chin, Ben looked, too. The sight of the puffed skin, of the wine-dark stain that pooled at his waist then dripped in triple currents down below his waistband, turned his guts to water. He swayed, gripping the chair with one hand, holding Tim's impulsive, compassionate hug off with the other. Tim started to cry. Keith, stricken, said, "Is that gonna happen to me?"

"No, Keith." Ben ruffled Keith's hair in a gesture of reassurance "There's something basically wrong between me and Dad," he said to himself, thinking about Tom's statement, "I'm responsible for you being here," and Tom's reproof to him and Joe, "You two are *brothers*." It wasn't so much that his father hated Tom. Max hated Ben enough to want him dead. The hostility spilled over onto Tom for his conspicuous liaison— so special and strong, so unusual and undefined. Max should have been grateful that Tom convinced his wife to reconcile, that Tom coached a reconciliation just in time for Ben to be conceived; instead Max blamed Tom for Ben's presence in the world. Suspicions vague and horrible, leering in his mind like nightmares, came to life.

15

BECAUSE fewer steps led up to the gym, Ben parked in that lot. Tom was there at the top of the concrete steps, sawhorses set up, toolbox open, patching his office window in the chill winter dawn. When Ben started up the steps, Tom glanced up and said, "Hey," his slight smile strained but sincere. He turned back to his work.

If Tom noticed how long it took Ben to climb the eight steps to the landing, he gave no indication. But when Ben steadied himself by gripping the iron handrail, his breath, pained and shallow, making quick frosty puffs, Tom looked up at Ben and said, "Joe and I were worried about you last night."

"I'm sorry, Coach."

"Were you in my office last night?"

"Coach, I can tell you're pissed at me."

"I've got a lot on my mind, Ben. You being the chief concern."

"I *was* here, in your office. I had to finish my math notebook."

"I don't like the idea of you being here, *alone*, at *night*," Tom said, stern eyes meeting Ben's briefly. "I can only imagine the reasons." Tom lay a metal yardstick on a sheet of glass, took an odd bulb-ended tool from his pocket and drew it along the ruler's edge making a scraping noise.

"I went home, after being here." The truth, spoken so plainly, deceived completely.

"Are you okay?" Tom said, his voice gruff as he retraced the line that the diamond tip of his glass cutter had etched.

"I need to tell you something, Coach." Tom stopped his work, turned around, faced Ben. His eyes went over Ben with their coach's scrutiny, growing gravely concerned. Ben likewise gathered his strength, squinted his instincts to observe, memorize and analyze Tom's reaction to what he knew he had to say. "I know you said not to, but..."

Tom put the glass-cutter into his pocket and folded his arms over his chest, squinting at Ben. "Go ahead," he murmured, the words making clouds in the air between them.

"Jeannie and I. No, wait, your *daughter* and I"—that was how it had to be phrased—"we're not allowed to date and I want to know the real reason why. Because we—we're in love with each other."

Tom's sigh was a burst of steam in the winter air. "Bonnie Jean has a fever and when she was suffering chills last night, she did tell me all about that. I wasn't sure if she was delirious or not." Tom raised his eyebrows at Ben, pressed his lips together, then bent over his sheet of glass and moved his left hand, bare and reddened with the cold, underneath.

"She's sick? I didn't know that."

"Fever of one-oh-two. A little better this morning." Tom made a fist and tapped the glass. It broke cleanly and he moved deftly to catch it.

"I'm so sorry."

"I doubt it's your fault."

"I think the stress of keeping things secret from you…got to her."

Another sigh fogged the cold space between them. "That may be part of it," Tom said as he shifted the pane of glass to hold it in both hands. "And that's another reason why you should—" Tom's hand jerked back. He shook it, quick blood droplets scattering on the concrete, then he took the glass in hand again and lifted it.

"Coach," Ben said.

"Step back a bit, will you, Ben?" he said as he turned toward the window. "This is sharp."

"Can I help you with that? You cut yourself."

"I've got it."

"But your hand's bleeding."

"It's just a scratch; it always happens when I fix stuff. Clumsy, I guess." This time when Tom glanced at him, Ben saw Tom notice his shivering, saw the worried compassion in his coach's stern eyes, but Tom turned quickly away to fit the glass in the empty window frame. Ben's heart thumped, needing to connect, to ask and understand despite a gnawing and unnamed terror.

"Coach, I want to apologize for putting Bonnie Jean in the position of being dishonest with you and for disobeying you."

"Thank you for that, Ben. I'm glad you brought it up this morning," Tom said with a backward glance. He ran his fingers around the perimeter of the glass, then stepped back, hands out to catch the glass if it fell. In the awkward silence, Ben listened to Tom's hard, purposed breathing, watched the breath clouds form, puff against the window, and fade. "Have you…um—" Tom turned toward Ben, gave him one hard look, stepped toward the sawhorse, took up his caulking gun, and strode back to the window. Over his shoulder he said, "*How* have you expressed this love to each other?"

Ben moved a little. He could see the vague reflection of Tom's disquieted eyes in the new glass. "Do you mean have we made love?"

"Yes. That's what I'm asking."

"We've kissed. Lots of times. I love her, Coach."

"That's what Bonnie Jean told me," Tom sighed, his breath obscuring his reflection now in the glass, but Ben saw his hand trembling. He balanced the caulking gun on the narrow windowsill and shaking the gathering blood from his hand, he turned toward Ben. "This complicates things, Ben, I'm—"

"Is there a reason I shouldn't love her, Coach? Is she really my cousin or—" He couldn't say more.

"No, she's not your cousin."

"Not my *cousin*?"

"No," Tom said, looking as if that wasn't the point. He shook his hand again, the spatter of his blood a constellation on the concrete around his feet.

"Then why are you pissed about this?"

"I asked you both to treat each other like brother and sister. You should have done as I asked."

"But—no. I *should* have and I'm sorry for that part of it, Coach. Even though I don't always act like it, I respect you and…I think…I thought…I wanted to live like you do, be like you, but—" The frustration pushed on his chest like he'd swallowed a basketball and the throbbing of his ribs mounted. "But why ask that of me? Why should I stay away from this gorgeous, loyal, fun girl who loves me and understands me and challenges me to grow as a human being and a *Christian*? I'd think you'd want that."

"She can be all those things to you as a sister."

"But that's a weird request. Why should I treat her like she's my sister if she isn't and I'm attracted to her?"

"It's my way of saying 'be friends,' that's all."

"Why? Falling in love is a *good* thing. It's natural. You did. What if someone had said that to you about Mrs. MacBride or"—he had to say it—"or even my mother?"

Tom's eyebrows went up, his mouth shut. He turned back to the window, grabbed his caulking gun and guided its point along the window edge. Blood pounding behind his eyes, Ben watched Tom's reflected face, watched the distant concentration as those solemn, blue eyes stared at the caulk flowing now in a line as straight and severe as the set of Tom's mouth. Again, blood gathered along the line of Tom's gashed hand. With a breath that fogged his reflection, Tom said, "I did, in the end, love your mother as a dear sister. So I know it can be done."

"You treated my mother like she was your sister? That's it? No sex?"

Though he looked surprised by the bluntness of the question, Tom said, "I will admit to you that I was attracted to her. We were very close friends and she was an extraordinarily beautiful, lovable woman. And once, when she was terribly upset and weeping, she was in my arms in a way that she shouldn't have been."

Ben tried to focus, eyes pounding with an odd pressure, blurring as he searched Tom's posture, the side of his averted face, hoping to discern the gold in the confession. Was it like his own dissembling—meant to disguise, never to reveal? "What does *that* mean, Coach?"

"There is no excuse for my behavior." Tom faced Ben.

"But what—*exactly what*—did you do?"

"She said that her journal characterized the moment as a tender, meaningful kiss in which our souls touched."

Ben shut his mouth; his stomach began its shaking, raising swells of pain against the broken cage that held him.

"She saw it as that, but I know in my heart that it was—well—a betrayal. So there you have it, Ben." Tom moved his hands, one bleeding, the other holding the spent caulking gun, out to Ben in a brief suppliant's gesture that seemed to ask for understanding.

"If it was just a kiss then I don't think that's as bad as—"

"It wasn't *just a kiss*," Tom insisted. "My wife was hurt, my father ashamed of me, my integrity compromised. However briefly, I took advantage of a woman in despair."

"Took advantage," Ben repeated in dumb confusion. The concrete with its red stars receded and Ben watched the nebulae of his own breath. A thought, like a vague shadow, gathered shape in his mind. Was his mother hiding herself from him as he hid from everyone? He had never known her to speak descriptively or was it—was it meta*phor*ically?—as Tom described. A journal? She kept a journal that Tom had read? Breathing hurt in sharp stabs now. If he passed out, Tom would know he was hurt, then his mother would end her life. He wanted her to live, wanted her healthy and happy so he could know her that way. He had to stay upright; that part was clear. Why couldn't he get his mind around Tom's bedimmed answer?

"Ben, what's wrong?"

"*What?*"

"I wonder if Joe is here yet," Tom said with a glance at the parking lot. "Joe's bringing some breakfast for you. I suspect you need some food."

"No. Please, Coach. Questions, still." He saw Tom's expression soften and heard his own voice, tight and distant, ask, "Has my father read those words?"

"Yes."

"Is—*Coach*—is this incident…because of me?" Ben said it clumsily; the question was not precise. Tom's painful regret, his palpable sense of guilt, reminded Ben of his own deep currents. If Ben didn't ask the right question, he'd be left wading these dark waters. "This is when I was—conceived, isn't that what you said before?"

"Yes. Remember? I told you before your *mother* wrote *everything* down." Tom stepped closer. "Max read your mother's diary—uninvited—and took offense. You see, because of what happened between your mother and me, she—well, I guess I might as well tell you—she wrote that she wanted me to take a significant role in raising you. Laurie and I had already been taking care of you when your mother was sick—"

"You mean right after I was born? You knew me when I was a baby?"

"Yes," Tom said slowly. "We didn't lose touch with your family until you were a little bit older than that, Ben. Your mother became very ill just a few days after you were born and had to be hospitalized. Laurie and I stayed to help."

Ben remembered how weak and listless Donna had been after Keith and Tim's births. Did it all start with him? Was it *because* of him? "So, you were there because my dad was in the Med and my mom was too sick to take care of me."

"Well, yes and no, Ben..." Tom hesitated.

Ben felt as if he would crumble. What did Tom mean? His mouth went dry, the floor of his stomach suddenly gone. *I'm missing something,* Ben thought frantically. *He's not saying something. He wants me to understand something he's not saying. I feel it. I know it.*

Tom stepped closer, his hand open, and Ben flinched reflexively. Tom hesitated, hands up as if guarding Ben. "I want you to come and stay with us now. Officially. Let's just get it out in the open."

"What?"

"That's what your mother wanted. No more doing homework in my office late at night. Being attached to Bonnie Jean in this way is going to make things awkward and uncomfortable—for a while anyway until we sort through all your questions. But I think it needs to happen. We'll just have to work through all this stuff."

Ben's quaking became visible. "Wait. *What*?" His mind slammed shut.

"Are you *okay*?" Tom said, reaching for him with instinctual speed.

"Don't touch me," Ben warned.

"What?" Tom's arms froze, open, empty.

Ben put both hands up to stop Tom's touch on his bruised shoulders, to ward off Tom's one-time coveted hug. His own response sickened him. Why fear Tom when there was this deep, undeniable truth: he loved Tom, he nearly trusted him.

But should he?

His thoughts were double sided: love compelling trust, suspicions revolting, body so sore and Tom's touch tainted now with a possible father's power. Ben made himself lift his arm and touch the brick wall to steady himself. Tom said, "You look like you're going to fall over. What's wrong? Are you *sick* or *injured*?"

"No!" Ben said, his shallow breaths making him lightheaded. Inside him, something tapped, begging he open his mind. *I can't think. I can't figure this out. There's something wrong. Something awful.* "You said my mother was sick but...What won't you tell me?"

Tom squinted at him, frowning. "Come live with us, Ben. No more nights alone in my office—for whatever reason. When you're safely in my house—"

"Wait," he said. "She didn't want me, is that what you're afraid to tell me? That's nothing new. She can barely stand the sight of me." He wanted Tom to say it, to identify from all the whirling suspicions the one explanation for his misery. "Just tell me if that's what you're afraid to say."

"That's not it at all. She wanted you—as she wrote once—'with all the golden power' she had inside her."

What? No! It doesn't fit! Think! But he couldn't and it made him so sick that he had to turn his head and spit. The sidewalk came toward him and he felt for the brick wall though his hand lay flat against it. "I don't know what you're smokin', Coach." He patted the wall to make sure he knew right where it was. "But you've got my mom confused with somebody else." Slowly, Ben leaned his weight against the gym wall, forgetting the bruise on the back of his skull until his head went back and touched painfully against the brick. He thought he might have said, "Ouch" out loud. And then he imagined Tom could hear the broken rib bones squeaking with each breath.

"Ben, you know I don't appreciate that kind of comment."

This was the coach Ben knew. "Okay. Everything's back to normal now."

"It's too cold out here for you."

"Ohhh." It was a groan he'd meant to keep inside.

"Let me help you inside, Ben."

Tears came to Ben's eyes. He squeezed them shut. His head cleared a little. He wanted to say yes, his mouth was opening with the word, but Tom said, "Tell me how you were hurt so badly," and the fear confused him again. *Should I answer that? Why can't I think?* Tom's voice sounded so familiar. "Tell me what happened to you, son." *It was a foul word; one Tom should not use. Should he?* His mind, fearful and sluggish, suggested that something had spoiled Tom. So Ben shook his head, knowing that for some terrible reason, he could not answer Tom's question, thinking he ought to say, 'Don't call me son,' but finding himself incapable of hurting Tom, his love for his coach so clear, so potently felt, brimming up and squeezing out the corners of his shut eyes in tears hot and quick as sprinters.

Sunlight looked orange beneath his closed eyelids; squinting he opened his eyes and looked around. The parking lot, bright sun reflecting on the wet pavement, swarmed with chattering students. Joe's car pulled into its spot. Adam, holding Victoria's hand, walked up behind it. Students hurried up the steps. Beside him Tom's tools lay scattered, their job finished. Ben remembered the glass smashing last night; he stared at Tom, remembering the comfort Tom's voice brought him when he hid from his father, cowering beneath the desk.

Quietly Tom said, "Let's go in now, Ben. You left your backpack in my office."

"I did? I meant to take it to the math classroom." Looking to his left, Ben saw Joe mounting the other steps in a group of friends. Joe lifted up a big paper bag to him, the sign that he had food. The new window glass glinted in the sun, catching Ben's attention. "You sure…fixed that…window…neatly," his words rocking out in little puffs of breath.

Tom took a step backward, watching Ben, his eyes never leaving Ben, and without looking at the gym doors, he opened the left one, held it open. "Yeah, I did," Tom said. Ben stole a glance at Tom's face and their eyes met; the sympathy in Tom's expression more real than the dull thump of Ben's pain. "Repair is my specialty."

He stepped past Tom into the little hallway between the locker rooms. Quickly Tom opened his office door, grabbed Ben's backpack and the quilt and towels now bundled into an untidy ball.

"Oh, it is in here."

"I'll carry it for you," Tom said as he swung Ben's backpack onto his shoulder.

"I know my dad broke the window," Ben blurted it out.

"I'm good at fixing what he breaks."

"Not always. My mom's not fixed." It was both challenge and plea. Tom nodded seriously. "Is that your fault, Coach? That she's so different than what you tell me?"

"You don't know who your mother is, Ben."

I don't know who my father is either. Ben thought as Tom limped through the gym beside him.

16

JOAN Poulard saw Tom pacing outside her door. She glanced at her watch, then at John Saunders and his sullen son Oliver. "I don't understand, Joan, why you won't take action. Oliver here heard Tom say it out of his own mouth that this kid is his bastard son."

"John, you can sit here all day but you are not going to convince me to do *anything*—much less fire an excellent teacher and student mentor like Tom—"

"I want this man to be brought to justice. He claims the boy as his own bastard."

"Tom would never even say that word," she mumbled, rising, pushing herself up with both hands flat on her desktop. "Excuse me a minute." Poulard walked to her office door and blocking the Saunders' view with her body, stuck her head out. "Tom," she hissed. "What's wrong?"

"We need to talk," he said, holding up a pink form that she recognized as the one used to initiate action by the school's crisis action protocol.

"Ben showed up?" Tom had phoned her before dawn with the report of the broken window.

"He says he went home last night." From where he grasped the quilt under his arm, Tom pulled out from its folds two crumpled, bloody towels. Whispering, he confided, "I found these under his backpack in my office. And I'm afraid he was beat up last night."

"Did you see any bruises or cuts to tie him to those?"

"No."

"Did he admit it?"

"No. But we only have to *suspect* to call. He's traumatized. I've seen him like this before, not to this degree, though. I'm gravely concerned."

"Okay. Make copies of the observations you've documented since Thanksgiving, fill out the form, and I'll call as soon as I can end this with Saunders."

"What's his problem now?"

"You don't want to know."

Two hours later, Dr. Deterding tiptoed back to Ben's desk. "Are you finished?"

"Yes, ma'am."

"Did you check your work?"

"Yes, ma'am, I did. I think I got them all right."

"Do you, now?"

"Well, maybe not all of number seven. But I did the extra credit just in case."

"You can work on something else now, Ben, or read. But you have to stay here."

"Okay."

Ben looked around the room. Joe was nearly finished, Davy still la boring. He imagined Bonnie Jean at home; his heart lurched. He took his pencil in hand again. Brushing the eraser crumbs from the unused piece of scratch paper, Ben sent his mind back to his morning's encounter with Tom and confusion tumbled down around him like the scatter of snow flurries he watched beyond the window of his classroom.

He began to write:

> Tom's trying to tell me something…Do I want to know it?
>
> What was Tom's exact association with my mother? What did he mean when he said he "took advantage" of her? He's old fashioned. Back in the day that meant…
>
> Why did Tom tell me, "I'm responsible for you being here?" He says because he told her to go back to Dad, but everyone's so mad at each other and Dad hates the man who tried to save his marriage…
>
> I know why she changed so much—Dad ruined her—but… well, here's my question…why would a man feel that way about his own son? He's so…sick.
>
> Dad used me as a shield or hostage to win the fight with

Tom. That's why Tom wouldn't fight back. This shows that Tom loves me and Dad doesn't. That's obvious anyway. What else do I need to know, then?

Ben's head pounded; he had to lift his eyebrows to keep his eyes open. He leaned on his right fist, staring at the page in front of him, trying to make sense of his broken sentences, his disconnected thoughts. Finally, he wrote, *I need to know WHY Tom loves me*, before he put down his pencil and closed his eyes.

Patty Edwards stood behind her desk staring out her office window, which allowed her to see past the hospital across the street and down to the fingers of Spa Creek that touched the graveled end of Charles Street. Behind her back in clasped hands, she held her notes from the lab's call reporting the results of Max's paternity test. Chewing her lip, she glanced back at Katie's diary, lying open to the description of her seemingly endless visits with a family reunification psychologist.

"What haven't you told me, Katie?" she said aloud, took a deep breath, and went to her phone.

She recognized her cowardice, but she dialed anyway, wanting Max to get the news in a place where he would absolutely be forced to control himself—where his reaction would be witnessed by tough marines who could do something about it. Her hand shook. She couldn't hold the phone. Again, the vision of Max's foot raised over Ben's body flashed in her mind's eye. Patty sat down; she popped a piece of chewing gum in her mouth and chomping savagely, tried again.

"Mrs. Baird? Hi, how are you? It's Ms. Edwards, Max's civilian lawyer. Could I speak to Colonel Hunter?"

She heard Max's voice in the background, booming, laughing. This was good. He was in the central lobby of the offices and not alone. In a minute, he spoke into his phone, the other voices distant.

"Max, it's me, Patty."

"Hey, babe," he whispered.

"Is your door open? Can anyone hear you?"

"Why do you think I'm whispering? If the door was shut we could make as much noise as we wanted like always."

She swallowed, wanting to get it over with and get off the phone. "Max, I have the DNA test results. I spoke to the doctor after I got the results in the mail and he explained them to me." Max was silent. Patty said, "Of course, since they don't have the mother's blood, you have to take that into consideration, but basically there's almost no chance that you and Ben are related."

Silence.

"I'm sorry, Max."

Still silence. For some reason, Patty left her desk, grateful that her phone was cordless, and she walked to her office door to lock it and bolt it. "The doctor said you should have been able to tell just by his blood type. AB negative just isn't possible when the father is O positive and—well, the journal says she was a universal blood donor and that's O negative."

"So," Max finally said.

"And the DNA matching confirms that. I know you're disappointed, and in my opinion, things being as bad as they are between you and Ben, I think the thing for you to do would be to find a more agreeable living situation for Ben."

"Stop me if I'm wrong," Max hissed into the phone, "but I don't remember *asking* for your opinion."

"You hired me to help you wade through this. That's the same as asking." And then, like a stick of dynamite lit and forgotten, rage burst in Patty and she slammed the phone down.

Checking the locked door, Patty went back to her desk, crammed a new stick of gum into her mouth, and took Katie's diary in hand, believing that the confession had to emerge soon. Max had said it was in here, she hadn't believed him. She read another three pages, tears stinging her eyes; she didn't want to believe it, but if it meant getting Ben away from Max, she was determined to find it.

Hair done perfectly, nails gleaming Christmas red, wearing a white blouse, tight black pants and a chic leather jacket, Donna walked briskly to Sampson Hall where she hoped to find Max sober in his office. The events of the past few days had jolted her and she clung to the vision that she might still be to her sons and Ben the mother she would have liked. One thing was clear: she was not living through another day like the last one had been, beginning with that humiliating visit from Child Protective Services. The woman had been so kind when Donna had sobbed after reading the transcript of the nine-one-one call she had included in the file. She was so broken and embarrassed then that when Tom MacBride—from whom she wished most to hide her failings—brought Max to the ER, drunk and crying, she had decided: no more. No day for the rest of her life would be as bad. So Donna hurried up the circular staircase, grateful that the time she'd spent in the last fifteen years hiding from her family had at least put her in great *physical* shape. She screwed her slim bit of courage up as if she were setting an arrow taut in a bow ready to pierce the target's eye.

Mrs. Baird went into titters at her unexpected presence. Max made a big show, for Mrs. Baird's sake, of being glad to see her. Donna smiled, thinking over and over again what she would say, how she would start. She coaxed Max back into his plush office where she shut the door behind her, its whisper on the thick wool carpet assuring their privacy. Max was smirking at her with lusty amusement. "Hell if you don't look like a new woman! Aren't you usually asleep this time of day?"

"I took a nap during my pedicure."

"What's that sparkle in your eye, babe? You ready for some hot Christmas love?" He came for her, arms open.

"Oh, that's not a sparkle, Max."

"Coulda fooled me," he slurped.

"A woman from social services came to see me at work." Max blinked. His arms went slack to his sides. Then he bent to smooth the creases out of his trousers. He came up, eyes keen and cunning. Shuddering, Donna stood straight, holding her keys in her fingers as taught in scores of self-defense courses, suddenly aware of the power of the truth.

"Let's talk when I get home, babe."

"You're drunk at home. We're talking here."

Without meeting her eyes, Max rounded the corner of his desk and stood behind it. A preening smile glazed his expression. "This isn't a good idea."

"Did you hear what I said, Max? Someone from social services."

"I heard." His voice made a low, angry growl. "And I don't want anyone in the office to hear." Calmly, evenly, he said, "Someone already came to the house, asking all kinds of questions about what happened at Thanksgiving. Ben gets a little cut on his head, somebody calls social services. It's bullshit. But I took care of it. Told her it was an accident. Ben bumped his head on a cabinet, so I took him to the ER. He was running to the car, that's all."

"Don't you realize they check all that stuff? They checked the *ER records*, Max."

"He could've gotten stitches anywhere. I told you, I took care of it. I answered all her questions. She's not going to bother us anymore unless you told her stuff you shouldn't have."

"Don't try to blame this on me. She knows. You're so out of control. People know. Do you remember what happened last night?"

"Don't take that tone with me. I am the head marine for godsakes."

"And how did the head marine get to the hospital last night?"

Max touched his forearm, his sleeve making a crinkling sound against the bandage beneath. "I probably didn't even need stitches. If you weren't a nurse and blew the whole thing out of proportion."

"Do you remember where you cut your arm? What happened?"

"Enough!" Max roared. "I'm not a child."

"You don't remember. Great. Do you know how many people saw you drunk there?"

Max's intercom buzzed. He took the phone in hand. "Tell her I'll call her back," he said, angry eyes on Donna. "I don't care if she says I'll want to be interrupted for this. I don't want to talk to her."

"Patty?" Donna asked coolly.

"Donna, let's not fight about this, because we've got some real shit to talk about. Patty called earlier with some—"

"Speaking of Patty," Donna interrupted, crossing her arms over her chest. "The social worker mentioned a nine-one-one call to our house." Now her voice was shaking. She clamped her teeth together. She had been doing so well. "These calls go in the emergency network computers. I looked it up. I checked it out, Max. I read the report."

"Donna, babe, do they know who that brat was who was in our house? Because that kid needs—"

"Don't bring Patty to my house again."

"No, listen. Patty has been helpful."

"I'm sure. But not at my house *ever again*."

"No, see, it's all real important. There's actual evidence that Tom is his father."

"Max, you are out of your mind. Tom is not Ben's father."

"Patty's been helping me gather the evidence. You've got to see that."

"I know what Patty's helping you with and I want it to stop."

"Tom's gonna try to take him away! I need a lawyer."

"There are male lawyers."

"Every male lawyer in this town belongs to Tom MacBride. He either went to school with them or he coached their kid or their cousin or their uncle or their cat. Hell, Donna, I need someone on my side. I got to figure out what to do with Ben."

"I know what to do with Ben. We have to tell Ben the truth."

"We talk to Ben—like you say—just in case he finds out about Tom being his father. We say that you and Tom had a thing and then—you know. That explains everything."

"I'm not confessing to an affair with Tom. You must have dreamed this up in one of your drunken stupors with Patty."

"Okay. Forget it, Donna. You have no rights in this. You're not even his mother. I'll do what I want."

"No. You can't anymore! You *hit* the child. You kick him. You hurt him."

"I do not."

"You've beat him up for *years*. You scream at him that you want him dead."

"Maybe I've got reason to be upset." Max's eyes narrowed. "I've got hard evidence that Ben is not my kid. Patty got these blood tests done. That's what she called about." He gestured at the phone. "Once Tom finds out, I'll lose Ben. *We'll* lose Ben."

"We deserve to lose Ben. Your mother is coming down tomorrow.

We're going to ask Ben to come home. You're going to be sober and we're going to tell him everything."

"That's inadvisable, legally. You know Tom and you know Katie's family."

"We have got to try to save our lives, Max. We are messed up. I'm going to ask Ben to forgive me. And if you don't tell him the truth, I will."

"You're just mad about Patty, which is really hypocritical of you." Max's chest heaved with frantic breathing, his face red, eyes darting. "When we started, you were still married. Remember? You were so desperate for sex it made you lose that baby girl."

Donna stared at him, her mouth open. She felt herself crumbling, the cleaned places throbbing with guilt. "That was cruel," she croaked. Just saying it gave her mind back some clarity. "Things have to change."

"You are so uptight, you sound like a Puritan preacher, Donna. No wonder I have to look for a little human kindness other places."

"I'll tell you what, Max. I'll ask Admiral Johnson if he has a room where Patty can give you all the human kindness you need. Or wait, maybe he won't mind if you use his nice big living room during his Christmas party. You can lap up all the human kindness your lawyer has to give right there on *his* sofa instead of mine with all your buddies watching instead of *my* children. Then we'll find out who else around here is uptight."

Donna meant to bang the door shut behind her, but the carpet stopped the door mid-slam so that when Max threw Ben's picture into the mirror on his clothes press, everyone in the silent and wary office of the English and History Division heard the glass shatter and fall.

17

IF Patty Edwards felt embarrassed to have to unlock her office doors to let Tom MacBride in for his appointment, she was mortified when he asked if she had been crying.

"That's quite a question!" she roared at him.

"It's just that your mascara…" Tom said, pulling out a cloth handkerchief. "What's wrong? Are you trying to quit smoking?"

"Smoking and drinking!" Patty thundered, the tears rushing into her eyes. She grabbed Tom's handkerchief and hid her face in it.

"Can I buy you a cup of tea?" Tom said. "There's a nice little café in the hospital."

"If I want tea, coffee, or anything else, I will have to go to your wife's place."

Tom smiled. "Ah, you are a changed woman, aren't you?"

"Maybe it's just a new addiction."

"Want to sit down?" He took her elbow and guided her back to her desk where she dropped into her chair and wept furiously into his handkerchief.

"Katie's diary is getting to you," Tom said. "Where are you?"

"I wish someone would just tell me the truth and not make me read anymore!"

"What do you want to know?"

"Why didn't you tell me before that you slept with her?"

"What?"

"I've been defending you to Max! And then I find out you did! How could you have left Ben with such a monster? He's as much yours as Joe or that adorable Tommy or—"

"Hey, slow down a minute. You say you found out that I *slept with* Katie?" Tom asked.

She almost thought he was suppressing a grin. "I suppose that was the quintessential joke on the man who almost paralyzed you. It's *almost* poetic, but really, Tom, it's pathetic." Patty dropped the handkerchief and searched frantically for the test results finding them tucked in the back of the diary. "I've been accusing Max of being paranoid and I've worked so hard to prove Katie loved him. I thought that would get him free of her."

"So he'd love you," Tom put in.

"So what?"

"I'm just saying," Tom said.

"I made him and Ben submit blood samples for DNA testing. So he could rest at ease."

"About?"

"Whether he's Ben's father!"

"Max is questioning that?"

"Duh," Patty said rolling her eyes as if she were an eleven year old. "He has been ever since!"

"When was this test done?"

"Back before Thanksgiving."

"Oh."

"Oh, what?"

"Exactly when was this, Patty? What day?"

"Um," Patty skittered her fingernails on her desk, thinking. "That day we had ice on the roads and Ben had an early practice. That is weird, by the way. Practice at six in the morning? Give me a break."

"Right, I remember. The day before Thanksgiving. And it came out that Ben and Max don't match?"

"Yes."

"There's a logical reason for that, Patty."

"No kidding, *Daddy*."

"Ben didn't give a blood sample. My son Joe did."

Patty sniffed, staring at Tom, uncomprehending. "Say again."

Tom made a gesture with his hand as if to say that he faced this kind of situation every day; his eyes showed muffled amusement. "My son Joe is prone to pranks. Joe was the one with the Band-Aid on his elbow and the bruise. Joe gave his blood. No doubt about it. Did Max tell Ben it was for DNA matching?"

"What? No! Are you crazy? Max lies to him about everything!"

"They thought Max was testing to see if Ben was using so when the nurse mixed them up, Joe gave his blood."

"They do look alike…" Patty squinched up her face, trying to think.

"I spotted the bruise inside his elbow and Joe came clean about it. I meant to have him call Max and straighten that out, but honestly, with everything else that's been going on with Ben, I forgot."

"You *forgot*? That's a lame excuse."

"Well, in my defense, Patty, I didn't know it was DNA testing. Still, you're right. We should have called."

Patty's mind whirled. If she'd called Max with the wrong information…if she called him back and gave him Tom's excuse…

"Do you have those documents you drew up for me? I'd like to sign them." Tom reached into his pocket and took out a check he'd written. "I have another couple of errands before the game this afternoon." He glanced at the check then placed it on her desk while she fumbled for his folder, which she flopped open. In silence, Tom signed the papers, waited for her to witness, then notarize.

"Patty," Tom said, when his hand was on the doorknob. "How angry was Max when you called him with that misinformation?"

"*Mis*information? Not so fast," Patty said, coming around the other side of her desk. "I still say you could be lying. Who would dream up taking somebody *else's* blood test? It's utterly outlandish and ridiculous!"

Tom held up his hand. "Okay. For instance. It was Joe's idea to call the police yesterday." He winced, his expression part sympathy.

"What?"

"Sorry."

"You—he—oh, no!" She sank into her chair, hid her face in her arms folded on her desk and burst into violent weeping. After a minute Tom walked carefully around to the back of her desk and touched her shoulder. "Can I drive you to Laurie's shop?"

From beneath her mountain of frantic curls, Patty said, "I don't ever want you to see my face again."

"Come on, now. I just feel bad for you and embarrassed by my son's escapades."

"Yeah, right."

"If you go to the shop, Laurie'll fix you up with some soup. And cookies. She's got all your favorites there today. And free gingerbread hot chocolate until Christmas."

"Okay, you win." Flinging her hair back, she sat up, hands flicking out frantically in search of Tom's handkerchief. "But I'll drive myself." She mopped up her face, grabbed Katie's diary, shoved it into her briefcase and took a deep breath. "Tom, you don't think Max will think to look for me at Laurie's shop, do you?"

"It's probably the safest place in town," Tom said, "if you're avoiding Max." He took a single step, reached her coat on the hook by the door and held it for her. "Here. You'll need this. It's cold outside."

Driving behind Patty across town, Tom thought about his morning conversation with Ben. He feared that he had said too much, explained too little. He was impatient now, trying to honor Gregen's request to allow Ben to figure out as much as he could, feeling sure in his heart that he must always honor Gregen's wisdom, though it no longer seemed like the right course to Tom.

Giving Laurie a meaningful look, Tom escorted Patty to her usual table, got some soup and bread for her, and left instructions for a teapot and cookies to be brought. He glanced at the drive-through window and waved to Annette who was handing out Christmas cookies packaged in big white boxes tied with red string. Ordered earlier in the season, customers flocked to get them the last few days before Christmas.

He and Laurie stole a minute in her office. "Joe called from school this morning to tell me Ben was there. How is he?"

"I'm not sure," Tom said, meeting her eyes, trying to decide how much to tell her. "I asked Ben to come and live with us. Officially. I let on that I knew he was hiding places and said I didn't want him doing that any more. I don't know. I may have said too much. I told him it was what his mother wanted. I told him he didn't know who is mother is, but…"

An employee called Laurie's name. Laurie said, "I'm glad you did. We've been far too circumspect."

"Doug is talking to Gregen today," Tom said, looking at his watch. "I think it's time for him to come down and we—all of us—talk to Ben together."

"Finally!"

Tom touched Laurie's shoulder, then lay his hand on her back. "I stopped by the house earlier and checked on Bonnie Jean. She was doing a little bit better."

"Mother is coming to keep Cara for me so I can run home in a few minutes. Then I'll go home again before the game."

"Don't come to the game today, Laurie." With the tips of his fingers,

Tom touched Laurie's cheek, wanting to protect her, his premonition looming. "Jeannie could use the company; you could use the rest. Think of going home and having three hours of quiet with your girls."

"I have so much to do at home I can't really rest."

"Then if Jeannie's well enough, she can keep you company while you wrap or finish decorating. If I didn't have the game, I'd certainly like to do that. Keep you company." He kissed her, his fingertips on her chin, treasuring the intimacy of her soft skin. "I love you."

Impulsively, Laurie threw her arms around his neck and hugged him tightly. "You'll tell the boys why I'm not there?"

"They'll understand. They like having you home when they're sick, too."

On his way to find Max, Tom stopped at Charlie Johnson's office only to find that he had flown to South Carolina to help his daughter and her children drive to Annapolis for Christmas. He wrote Charlie a note, then reconsidered and tore it up. He found Max's office by following the signs, passing office after office down the hall where doors stood open in the ample USNA heat and dedicated civil servants worked in silent concentration. Max's name and titles, COLONEL MAXIMILIAN J. HUNTER, MARINE CORPS REPRESENTATIVE, DIRECTOR OF THE ENGLISH AND HISTORY DIVISION, topped the listed names on a black sign that hung by the door to a large circular office suite. Tom squeezed by a cart from Public Works, which had been parked in front of the main door. Beneath a wall-sized painting of the battle off Tripoli with its burning ships, an elderly secretary sat at a neat desk drumming her pencil on her silent phone. Her powdered demeanor looked strained, her red jacket a bit too big and somehow off center. Tom read her nameplate. "Mrs. Baird? I wonder if I can see Colonel Hunter. I'm Tom MacBride, his son's basketball coach."

"Colonel Hunter is not in right now." She glanced nervously toward the primary office of several that were attached like spokes to the central office's axle. This Tom took to be Max's and his eyes followed there to see the Public Works chaps busy with something inside the door. "Is something wrong?" she asked.

"It is urgent," Tom said in a low voice. "I do need to see Colonel Hunter right away. Can he be reached by phone?"

"If you give me your name and the nature of your message," she said, doubtfully.

Tom wrote his name for her on one of those little pink message pads. "Can I call him? Is he at home?"

"If you'd care to take a seat, Mr. MacBride, I'll try his home."

Tom sat opposite Max's office so he could watch the work. He took out his little pad with his own tasks listed on it and flipped to a clean page.

He wrote: *Max, please disregard the DNA test results. My son Joe's blood was submitted for analysis not Ben's. Please phone me so I can ask your pardon.* He signed his name and wrote his phone numbers. He copied the note word for word, folded the copy, and put it in his chest pocket.

Tom made his way over to Mrs. Baird. "When do you expect him back?"

"I don't know if he'll be back," she sounded frantic. "And he hasn't answered his home phone."

"Mrs. Baird, I have an urgent situation concerning his son. There must be procedures for locating your top marine."

"Have you tried calling the child's mother, Mr. MacBride?"

"I need to speak to Ben's *father*."

"I can't help you."

"Are you telling me there is no way to find him? Is he AWOL?"

"Actually, I think so." Her eyes got very bright, then she looked down biting her lip.

Tom was silent a moment. "May I borrow a couple of pieces of tape?"

"Of course."

"I'll just tape this note to his office door." Tom put the note at eye level and as he was turning to go, saw a torn photograph of Ben in a broken frame that had been set on the windowsill. He watched the new mirror being lifted into place, bowed his head, and whispered a heartsick prayer.

18

AFTER his math exam, Ben awoke to find the classroom emptied of students, Dr. D. grading at her desk, and Mrs. Poulard knocking lightly at the classroom door. She came to stand beside him. "Ben, dear, there's a woman here who would like to talk to you about a few things. And Dr. D. has agreed to let us use her room since my office is just crawling with people for some reason."

Ben's pulse quickened. He stood up slowly, painfully aware that Mrs. Poulard and Dr. D. watched him struggle to move. "A woman? What about?"

Joan Poulard motioned to someone in the hall and as an elderly woman stepped into the room, said, "She spoke to your brothers at school recently. Did they tell you about that?"

"Yes, ma'am, they did."

"Would you like me to stay here with you, Ben? Tom thought you'd prefer he not be here, but I can phone him if you want him here."

"No, thanks. I'll be fine by myself."

"Are you sure?"

"Yes, ma'am." Ben felt a familiar dead calm enter his being, felt his own back straighten though the room had grown uncomfortably hot.

As his teacher shut the door, the older woman, Mrs. Spraig, introduced herself to Ben with an offer to shake his hand. "Your brothers spoke so highly of you, my dear boy. I have been very much looking forward to seeing you." She covered his hand with hers and patted three times. "Would you like to sit down so we can talk?"

"I'd prefer to stand," he said adding, "I sat for two hours for my math exam so…"

"I'll sit if you don't mind." She did so and smiled up at him. "My, you're tall and good-looking."

Ben tried to perceive her. She was around his grandmother's age, he supposed, maybe older, tiny, wrinkled. Her crisply ironed blouse, showing neatly above her bright red sweater, her straight nubby gray skirt and those clunky lace-up black shoes all suggested old-fashioned propriety. She opened a folder and clicked a pen to ready it. "You've guessed by now that I'm from Child Protective Services. And what I like to do first in these cases is reassure everyone that I am not here to break your family up or take you away from your parents. We want to offer families support when they need it. That's all. The family lets us know what kind of support they'd like." She smiled at Ben.

Ben tried to smile. He concentrated on breathing in as deeply as he could and out slowly through his mouth but the air in the room had gone uncomfortably dense. If he could just keep his insides from quaking and the pain from building again.

"We had a phone call from someone who thought you might be in a situation at home that you couldn't handle. There was an incident where you were seen with blood on your face." Ben said nothing. "That's what I know," she added with the tone of one having placed their best, if mediocre, word down in Scrabble. "Can you tell me how it happened?"

"Have you met my dad yet?" Ben asked.

"Why yes, Ben."

"How did that go?"

"He's a most charming man." Ben studied her expression, trying to see if she had been swayed by Max or was suspicious. "Your mother seems conscientious and professional. Did she stitch up that head wound for you?"

"Since she's a nurse, you mean?"

"Yes."

"Did you have a good talk with her? What did she say?"

"She said that now that she's adjusted to the move and her new job she should be more available for you and your brothers. We understand that sometimes families go through adjustments. Did you know, Ben, that moving is one of the biggest stressors for people? And you have moved so frequently."

"Is she feeling less stressed now?" Ben asked, hoping wildly that she might have confided in the prim and modest Mrs. Spraig.

"Does your mother also hit you?"

Ben flinched at the question. He felt his throat burn, sweat forming along his back. "I'm a lot bigger than her." He always allowed the artlessness of such questions to prod him into an angry defense of his guilty parents. The internal writhing began with his inner man urging him to tell the truth.

"Ben, abuse is not deserved."

"I guess you're right," he said, not really knowing how to say more, simply unable to put into words the hell he endured at home, utterly unable to put Donna's life at risk. "Were you able to help my mom at all?"

"I think she understands the support system available to her."

"Such as?" Ben asked, his heart leaping up to hope.

"Well, our office of course."

"What happens after my interview? Do you come back? Do we all go see a shrink or a regular doctor or a minister or what?" There had been reports made before at other duty stations, but the interviews always stopped with his slick and convincing father and there was hell to pay when he locked the door behind the social worker. Mrs. Spraig had gotten farther than any.

"I piece together my report."

"Like what we said or...nuances and things you might observe?"

"Um, Ben, is there anything you'd like to add to what I already know about your home life, your parents?"

"That's a big question, Mrs. Spraig." He wiped his forehead on the cuff of his shirt. "I really can't say."

"Some people are concerned that your father, particularly, is abusive, violent."

"The people who called?"

"Is he?"

"What did *he* say when you asked him?"

"He said you hit your head on the kitchen cabinet."

"I did."

"Ben, what else would you like me to know about you?"

"I wish we'd met under different circumstances." Ben glanced at his watch. "And I have a game in a few minutes."

She raised her eyebrows. "Ben, is there anything you would like me to know *about your father*? I'd like to know what *you* think. How you're doing at home. You have something to say about your father, don't you?"

Ben gave a tense laugh, random quotes from English class running through his fiery brain…*look like the innocent flower, but be the serpent under it…false face must hide what false heart doth know*…on and on. Ben knew a sharp pang of conscience; he had to say something or continue to be like him—the fiend who lies like the truth. He opened his mouth and heard himself say, "You know, my brain is probably fried from that math exam, but I just keep thinking of how much my mother needs a friend. If you could, um, think about that. If you could do something about that. If you could find her a friend. That would really help me."

Before she left the shop, Laurie made Patty lie down on the sofa in her office and close her eyes. "Don't you dare light a cigarette in here while I'm gone," she warned and the weary Patty laughed, though tears puddled out of her squeezed-shut eyes. Grannie had Cara in her arms, Beth had taken over the drive-through window, and the café stood unmanned, unusually quiet, patrons probably scared away by Patty's weeping at her table. After racing home to check on Bonnie Jean, Laurie returned to a buzzing hive, counting fifteen customers browsing the hand sewn treasures.

Her mother-in-law grabbed Laurie's elbow. "Cara is sleeping and Tom said you were t' go home early today. I mean t' see that happen."

"You could come with me, Mother, and help."

"I've got to finish baking the little shortbread dogs and dip 'em in chocolate."

"Those are Joe's favorites!"

"He can have some, I suppose. You'll not have time to bake as busy as it is here."

Laurie noticed Donna then, standing stiffly hunched by the pink fabrics, and blinked in surprise. Her mother-in-law squinted at Donna and elbowed Laurie. "You need to go to her. Crying in a store. What next?"

Laurie put a hand on Donna's shoulder, "Come and let me make you a cup of tea."

Donna cried, "Oh, Laurie," and dissolved into her arms.

Behind her Grannie commanded, "Go to that table in the far back. I'll make the tea."

Laurie coaxed Donna into a chair at Patty's usual table, her back to the café. She sat opposite her, facing her store and held Donna's hand as she wept in unintelligible murmurs. Grannie brought a steaming pot of tea, a cream pitcher filled to the brim and a little flowered bowl piled with sugar cubes. "I think we may need three cups, Mother," Laurie whispered.

"Aye," Grannie nodded. "If that will keep the quiet."

"You talked to him," Laurie said, pouring the tea. She glanced up to see Annette at the window, Beth circling the shop to help customers, a few of whom glanced her way to give her an encouraging smile. The café had cleared out and Laurie was touched to notice her dear customers' support.

"I said things," Donna gasped. "He's furious. There was a scene."

"Of course." Laurie plunked two sugar cubes into Donna's milky tea and slid it in front of her. "Take a sip, Donna. It will strengthen you."

"I told him no more with this woman."

"You did the right thing."

"He's such a bad husband. He's such a horrible father."

"Now, now. Things will improve."

Grannie brought another cup and a plate stacked with cookies. Loudly she whispered to Laurie. "Since the baby's asleep, I'm going t' clean out under yer sink. It's a disgrace." To Donna, she said, "She can thank God I'm not the health department!" She turned on her heel and stomped around the back of the counter and for some reason, Donna smiled.

"Is that Tom's mother?"

"Yes."

"That explains a lot about Tom."

"Doesn't it? I wonder if she'd like to have a word with Max," Laurie said and Donna's smile brightened into tense giggles. Laurie laughed with her, squeezing her hand. "Grannie MacBride's boot camp!"

"Why has it taken me so long to do this, Laurie?"

Shrugging, Laurie pushed the plate of cookies close to Donna's hand. "What was decided? Anything? Or was it just a kind of clearing the air?"

"I told him about her and that we have to talk to Ben."

"Donna. That took so much courage."

"Social services came to see me. Did you call them?"

"No, I did not."

"Do you know who called them?"

"I don't, Donna."

"Wounds from a friend are better than kisses from an enemy."

Laurie looked up to see Patty standing at the edge of the café, shoes off, purse slung over her shoulder, eyes puffed and face bare of make-up, hair in a panic of frizz. Staring at them, she rubbed her face with both hands.

"She's here, Donna. Max's lawyer. She came here crying today."

"Here now?"

"About twenty feet behind you." Laurie looked around and noticed Patty's briefcase standing against the wall behind the table's empty chair. "She usually sits here at this table and I guess that's her briefcase left behind. Oh! Here she comes. Courage, now."

Moving quickly, voice brisk, Patty said, "Laurie, I'll just get my stuff out of your way. Gosh, it got crowded in here." Patty bent to grab her briefcase and saw Donna's face. She gasped, stopped moving and stared.

"Patty," Donna said.

"You've been crying!" Patty burst into tears again. "That's my fault!"

On her feet, an arm around Patty, Laurie whispered, "Sit with us, Patty. Let's talk." Patty slumped into the chair, hiding her face in her hands, her weeping immediate and profuse. "Come now, Patty, take this napkin and mop up. Grannie's made you a cup of tea."

Instead she pulled Tom's rumpled handkerchief from her purse and rubbed it over her eyes. Laurie and Donna exchanged glances. "I've had a tanker full of tea and I'm still crying," Patty sobbed, dropping her hands and grabbing the cup as soon as Laurie filled it. She gulped down the scalding cup and held it out for a refill. "You can say anything you want to me, Donna. I know I deserve it. I know how I hurt you."

Donna was quiet, battling for self-control, but tears again filled her eyes. Finally she said, "Thank you."

"Sitting here with you I feel really shitty for ignoring you. I acted as if he wasn't even married."

Donna shook her head slightly, overcome with emotion. "Things have to change for me."

"No kidding."

"Have you spoken to Max this afternoon?"

"No. Just this morning. To tie up business," Patty said, "I've had it with Max. I didn't realize how bad he was. He used to be able to hold his liquor. I think I made him worse." Her sentence ended in a wail. Laurie looked up to see her customers turn their backs, trying to maintain the bubble of privacy they'd created for her. But Grannie signaled her to look toward the drive-through window and when she did, she saw that Beth had one arm and shoulder out trying to clean the convex mirror. Snow swirled thickly around her, catching in her hair. "Did y'all know it was snowing?" Laurie said as she stood up. "Excuse me just a second."

Donna said to Patty, "Max has been…this way for years…and I should have…I have some hard regrets."

From her purse, Patty drew out the worn leather book she had been reading. "This is his problem," Patty vowed.

"Katie's diary?" Donna asked.

"I finished it in there," she gestured toward Laurie's office. "You need to read this."

"Me?" Donna raised both hands to protest. "No thanks. I've been competing with Katie for years. I don't ever want to hear her name again."

"Look, I know you have every reason to hate me. And I don't blame you. I was wrong. But I think if you read this, you'll feel better. Free." Patty put it in Donna's hands, folding Donna's fingers around it. "Just don't let Max get his hands on it."

"The one thing of Katie's he didn't destroy," Donna murmured, staring at it.

Patty swallowed audibly. Her breathing quickened. She stood up, grabbed her coat and briefcase, shoved her feet into the shoes she'd left under her chair. "How is Ben?"

"What do you mean?"

Looking around, Patty whispered, "Max was horrible to him last night. Violent." Donna flinched, her eyes went wide. Patty shifted her weight, adjusted her briefcase. "Um, he needs to read that, too."

"Are you talking about Ben?" Laurie said as she approached their table, brushing the snow off her sweater. She saw the journal in Donna's hand. "Oh, good. You can give that to him, now."

"It's the least I can do," Donna said, clutching it so tightly her fingers went white.

19

GREGEN Bénet picked up fallen pine cones from his snow-dusted front lawn while he waited for Doug Davidson. When he saw the bright red Mustang convertible round the corner, Gregen walked to the end of the driveway. Doug swung the car in and pulled to a quick stop. The two men shook hands and Gregen walked beside the car as Doug drove slowly down the driveway to the parking area in the back. "A bit cold for a convertible, isn't it?"

"I had to drive a car that would impress you, Uncle Gregen."

"It is a beauty. Is it a rental?"

"Borrowed it from the whoop general. He thinks if he loans me his antique car I'll throw out all the shots that show what a shabby place Army is." He laughed.

"General Morrison? You are being used, Doug. He's been trying to sell me this car for three years now."

"What?" Doug bellowed, leaving the car, slamming the door for emphasis. "I forgot you know everybody in the whole d—darn world!"

Gregen offered his hand again saying, "I am so very glad to see you, Doug."

"Same here," Doug said, taking his hand and pulling him into an embrace. "Been too damn long. Pardon my French."

"Yes, it has been too long, my boy." Gregen patted Doug's cheek. "You look very well. You're healthy."

"Yep. How's Marie?"

"She is well and visiting my brother and his wife right now in Switzerland. I've just returned from taking her there. She is too old to fly alone. Your family is well?"

"They're terrific. Thanks for asking. Well, Annie, my little daughter, you know, has that coloboma thing like Marie and Katie. Proves Marie and me are distant cousins, I guess. She gets UTIs, too, like Katie."

"You should bring her to see me. My clinic in Baltimore specializes in kidney problems."

"Clinic in Baltimore? Who knew! Will it take me three years to get an appointment? You're a hard man to get in touch with. Been trying for two weeks."

Gregen gave a charming shrug of his shoulders and reached into his jacket to get a pale blue business card. "These are my private numbers. I'm surprised you didn't get these from Tom or Laurie. Tommy also has my numbers."

Doug took the card and slid it into his chest pocket. "Didn't think to ask. I'm not the smart one in the family, remember?" He elbowed Gregen, who put an arm around Doug to steer him toward the house.

"The universal rivalry of twins is speaking from your mouth. My brother and I are also still competing. Though I try not to, it seems it cannot be helped." Doug laughed.

The moment he stepped inside the house, Doug's breath caught. The candlelight-colored walls, the warm, old wood floors, the elegant, clean furnishings, the unusual, old Christmas things—red and white, pine and gold, hand carved wood and burnished silver—the scent of a clean house warmed by apple wood burning in the fireplace. It was too familiar, too much the same: lovely but lonely.

"It looks as beautiful as ever," Doug said, as Gregen led him to the library where a table had been set by the fire. "Remember how Sibilla used to say, 'Beauty makes people feel at home.' It's not the same here without her."

Gregen touched Doug's arm. "Thank you for saying her name. Hardly anyone will mention her. I grieved so violently, I suppose they're afraid of me."

"You had a right to grieve," Doug said. "She was a great lady. One of the greatest I've ever known. She and my sister..." He reached his hand up as far as he could.

"Yes. They are alike. Love makes people become like each other, don't you think?"

Gregen motioned for Doug to sit down. He uncovered the thickly stacked sandwiches, took the lids off the little soup bowls, and poured the Bordeaux. "I hope so, Uncle Gregen. I love Tom, but I don't think I'm much like him."

Doug found as they ate and discussed their beloved MacBrides that the awkward tension he'd always known in Gregen's presence had crumbled to dust in the years apart. "Talk about great kids, your Ben—there's a prize."

"My Ben," Gregen said, ruefully. "How *is* he?"

"You know, Uncle Gregen," Doug said, draining his wine glass, staring at the leaping fire in the big stone fireplace. "Neither of us wants Tom to have to confront Max. His back couldn't take it."

"I agree," Gregen said, pouring another half glass of wine for Doug, refilling his own glass.

"Tom thinks Ben's in danger over there."

"What do you know? Tell me. Don't spare me."

"We don't *know* anything. We have no facts. Ben hasn't said anything, but Tom says he's too emotional to be happy at home. Rage toward bullies, way too upset over mistakes. And he's bruised up a lot."

"This confirms my suspicions." Gregen said, his voice, the voice Doug had once so feared, sounding thinned with wear. "Since his grandmother came home from Thanksgiving there, she has shut me out. Won't return phone calls. When I drop in on her, which I have been in the habit of doing daily when I am in town, she will not look me in the eye and sits at the table, hands folded, not speaking. Even if I ask her a direct question, such as, 'What happened to upset you so much?' she gives no answer."

"That woman never was a match for Max."

"No. And great tragedy has come of that lack."

"You blame her."

"I don't mean to blame her. I have forgiven."

"Oh, come on! You can't mean it. After what you've been through, you can *not* tell me you still believe in God and forgiveness and all that shit. When you gave that speech at school about the war and forgiving your enemies, I couldn't accept it then, but after Max—*forget it.*"

Gregen considered Doug's statement, staring at the fire. He put his wine glass down, moved the table a bit and left his seat. He took the used plates and bowls and Doug began to sweat, sure he'd offended and was being ushered out. But Gregen brought a small silver tray that was stacked with the French pastries Doug had gobbled up as a teenager waiting for Katie to dress for a date. Gregen rang a little silver bell and sat down.

"These are your favorites, are they not? Little eclairs and the citrus tarts with raspberries. Here is a clean plate for you. The espresso will be here in a moment. Oh, there is Mrs. Bonaparte now."

Mrs. Bonaparte remembered Doug and greeted him warmly, placed the tray down and left. Gregen gave Doug a small white espresso cup and took one for himself. "You don't smoke, do you, Doug?"

"No, sir," Doug said, feeling uncomfortable with this gracious response to his outburst.

"Doug," Gregen said. "When I was asked to come to your high school to speak, my commitments had me extraordinarily busy. Like all our decisions, Sibilla and I considered the request and prayed together. The strangest thing happened to us. A vision formed in both our minds of a boy.

He was the most darling child and we both described him to each other. Spunky, athletic, full of life, with the brightest brown eyes. And we both knew, with a surety, that he hated his father. Why did he hate his father? We didn't know, but it didn't matter. Sibilla said to me, 'For this boy, you must tell your story.' Of course, Doug, we both know now, that child was you."

"Gregen—"

"You got away from home as you determined, but you have always reacted violently to the suggestion that anyone forgive the tyrant. But forgiveness is the way out of prison."

Doug held his hand up. "I've heard your story. Don't tell it to me again. How can God let these beautiful people suffer? I want it to stop! I want it to stop now."

"I want it to stop, too. But striking out in rage is what caused me to lose Ben to Max."

"Tom does not deserve that bad back any more than Katie deserved missing out on raising a kid like Ben. She would have blissed out over him. People are innocent. They're full of faith and God lets disgusting people hurt them. Did Sibilla deserve—" Doug stopped, appalled at his own insensitivity, he hung his head, shoulders bowed. "I'm sorry, Gregen. I should not have said that."

Gregen put his espresso cup down. "The truth is that everyone makes mistakes, Doug. Everyone. You just did and you'd like me to reassure you about that mistake. You've made others."

"None to deserve—" he broke off, emotion choking him.

"Of course not," Gregen said, astonishing Doug so that he looked up to see again, the bright tears in Gregen's eyes. "Yet, I must ask, isn't there any mistake in your life you feel was worth at least *some* response from God?" Gregen asked, gently. "Perhaps a word of correction as you've seen Tom speak or as you've no doubt had to speak to your own children? I know you are a kind and gentle father, but surely you've occasionally seen a mistake of theirs and had to respond. No?"

Doug wrung his hands. "I wish I'd killed Hunter in Quantico."

"That's a regret for something you didn't do. I'm glad you didn't."

Doug stared at the fire, embarrassment mixing with an irresistible urge to tell the truth. He finally said, "Katie thought she was pregnant, you know. She freaked on me and said we had to get married. I told her no. I was going to the Academy and I couldn't be married."

"Hmm," Gregen said quietly.

"We hadn't even had a pregnancy test, but she was convinced it was there and she already loved it."

"Compassion was her strongest motivation," Gregen said. "You are like her in that way, Doug, always wishing to protect the vulnerable."

"I learned it from her. From this. But too late. I did *not* want to give up the Academy. It was my ticket out of my house and I wanted to fly and I wanted her to go with *my* plans. Here's the worst thing, Uncle Gregen, I told her I couldn't see her as a mother. I told her she wasn't the type. I saw her as this hot, sexy woman meant to be worshiped in bed and I thought motherhood would wreck that. That hurt her."

"Yes, she wrote about that in her diary."

"I was an idiot to say it. But you could tell that she believed me. She shouldn't have. She changed some inside picture of herself because of my stupidity and I think—I think that made her able to settle for a jerk like Max."

"I think you're right," Gregen said with keen precision.

Doug gulped. "If I had tried to understand her. Because you know in a week she got her period. She knew I was relieved. But I stayed up all night with her cramping and crying. I wonder if maybe she miscarried. I wonder all the time if we've got a kid in heaven, Katie and me."

Gregen nodded, eyes solemn and quiet.

"After that, she didn't trust me. She loved me, but I'd damaged her." He looked up at Gregen, eyes brimful of tears. "It was our moment, our chance, and I blew it. I was into my dick and my ego and I didn't have any idea who she really was. And she knew that."

"That's a significant regret, Doug. And in it you must recognize that neither you, nor Katie, were innocent."

Doug shook his head. "Uncle Gregen, I feel responsible for *everything* bad that happened to her after that."

"You are responsible and you are not responsible."

"You sound like Tom."

"Think about the complex operations involved in helicopter flight. At any one moment three or four things must happen in concert for flight to occur. Aren't the workings of life more complicated than a man-made machine? The answers are not simple, and one truth pulls against another. God is more than us, that is why our minds struggle to understand."

"I *loved* her."

"No man on earth loved her more than you did, Doug. May the Lord comfort your grief."

"Can he?"

"You dare to ask me that?"

Doug shook his head. "No. I shouldn't have said that. I'm still a smart ass. I'll always be one."

Gregen took Doug Davidson's hand as if he were a child. "Are you ready to pray with me?" Doug nodded, squeezed the old man's hand and thumped to his knees. Finally he whispered in prayer, "You're God and I'm not. But please protect my brother-in-law and Ben. Don't let them suffer for how Katie and Max and I messed up."

After some time, Gregen made Doug get up off his knees and stretch out in the chair. Thrusting a clean handkerchief into his fist, Gregen patted Doug's shoulder and left the room briefly. He returned, refreshed the fire, and poured Doug a brandy. He sat down, sat on the edge of the armchair, hands clasped between his knees, and said, "May I speak frankly to you now, son?"

"Yes, sir," Doug sniffed.

"Drink your brandy. Mrs. Bonaparte is bringing you some tea and she will not approve of the brandy before dinner. I don't want her scolding me in front of you."

Doug laughed, a funny, boyish giggle rising in him like a bubble. "No, but I'd sure enjoy seeing you scolded." He took a big slug of brandy and sighed, his breath wobbly and weak.

"Doug. The little boy that Sibilla and I saw—" Gregen pressed his lips together as if he had to give Doug a terminal diagnosis. He exhaled slowly and said, "The picture we saw illustrates more than you. We all hate those who cause us pain. If that pain is unjust—especially when our fathers hurt us. We attribute their cruelty to God's character and the anger imprisons us so that we hate God, when really he wishes and wills it not to be so."

"If he wills it," Doug said, sleepily swirling the brandy in his glass, "it happens, right? So he's responsible."

"You know, now, don't you, that we humans don't always do what his will is for us to do. If you could make a mistake, anyone could."

Doug stared at Gregen, eyes coming clear. He nodded, biting his lip, tears swelling again. "I see."

"Yes. And you know now, son, that the little boy who Sibilla and I envisioned was you, but not *only* you. It was many other children. It was also Max."

"I'll have to spend the night, Uncle Gregen," Doug sniffed. "If I have to forgive Max, I'm gonna drink the rest of your freakin' bottle of brandy."

20

TOM returned to school so late that he missed the pre-game meeting. His search for Max had been unsuccessful. Before he left Max's office, Major Lindquist had stopped him and together they scoured the Yard, finally standing in the falling snow on Hunter's front sidewalk waiting for him there.

Lindquist, who had confided his own fears about Ben's safety at home, finally convinced Tom to go by saying, "Look Tom, if I stand right here at the corner, I'm not going to miss him if he comes home. I can see all the way to the front door of Sampson Hall. I can see almost to Lejeune Hall. I can see the 'O' Club in between. The man doesn't have a car. He's got to walk. I'm staying right here until I find him, so you go ahead."

Entering the noisy locker room, he scanned the players' faces, looking for Ben. He walked toward the back, where Paul, Knox, Ben, Joe and Adam stood; Tom was relieved to see Ben standing upright.

"Tom!" Brock called from the front of the locker room, his tone urgent. Tom signaled to Brock that he'd be there in a minute.

Raised voices and someone called, "Can you see him? Are you sure?"

"Uncle Tom," Flip said, touching his elbow. "My mom's out there. She needs to talk to you."

"Tell her I'll be right with her."

"You'd better come now, Coach." Brock took his elbow, pulled him away.

Beth had worked her way through the crowd into the locker room and when she saw Tom, thrust a crumpled piece of paper into his hand. "John Saunders is giving these letters to all the parents. I hope Tommy hasn't seen one."

Tom took it and scanned, catching Ben's name and the word *bastard*.

"Where is he?" Tom said, pushing past Brock and the crowd of parents arguing in the little hallway between the locker rooms. He saw Saunders now in the gym, talking to Key School's coach who, red-faced and flustered, when he saw Tom pushing through the crowd toward him, literally jumped and lunged for Tom, offering his hand. "Tom, am I glad to see you. This parent—" He broke off, rolled his eyes.

Without a word, Tom got his hand on Saunders' shirt, grabbed the collar opening, feeling his hand snatch the curling hairs beneath. He hauled the big man, pulling him after him as if he were a mattress, big, bulky, stiff and ready for the junk pile. The crowd parted for Tom, falling silent. When he got to the doors, Beth was there and opened one. Tom whirled Saunders to face him. "Don't you ever insult one of my students again." He shoved him, forcing him to step out into twilight's dark cold. Saunders bobbled like a bowling pin and sputtered his protest. "Get out and stay out."

Tom pulled the door shut, found his keys in his pocket and despite shaking hands, locked the gym doors. With a glance at Beth, he said, "Call the police. Then call Joan. See if Jim Ridout will guard the front."

Tom turned toward the gym ignoring Saunders who pounded now on the glass doors with the desperation of a drowning man. Hoping the police would arrive before Saunders figured out he could walk to the front of the school and re-enter, Tom made a gesture toward the crowd of staring parents, both hands out as if to ask what the problem was. "Game's ready to start. Better get your seats." He walked into the crowd then, grabbing

Saunders' slander sheets from the parents' surprised, clutching fists with a look on his face that dared them to provoke him. They dispersed.

Tom was never so grateful for cheerleaders as he was during that warm-up session. Their forced cheerfulness distracted neatly. The team, trying to warm up, was wary of Oliver whose aggressive antics mounted by the minute. Ben lasted two minutes before Adam brought him to the bench and sat him down where he struggled to control his roiling emotions. Finally he turned around, back to the gym, straddled his chair, hid his face on his arms against its back. This brought a hush of guilty concern to the parents who had allowed Saunders to inflame them, a prayerful concern to the others. The gym was as quiet and tense as an August twilight.

Tom caught his sister-in-law's eye and nodded. He walked over to Ben and touched his shoulder. "Aunt Beth wants to bring you a little cup of Gatorade. Is that okay?"

Ben nodded. Without lifting his head, he said. "Unca Doug here?"

"Not yet."

"Is Mrs. MacBride here?"

"Not tonight, Ben. She's home with Jeannie."

Tom watched Oliver, thinking about Ben, glancing back, wanting to give him a little space. None of the other players would pass to Oliver who was actually hip-checking his teammates who got close enough and calling out taunts. Tom caught Brock's eye. They met at the half-court line. He whispered to Brock, "If he's upset about his dad and has the guts to admit that, we can either work it out with him or he can choose to leave." Brock agreed and when Oliver approached, Brock called his name. Without stopping, Oliver snapped, "What?"

"Come here," Tom said, reaching out his hand to block his progress. Oliver stumbled to a halt. "What's going on?" Tom said.

"You ought to know."

"You are hip-checking your teammates." Tom motioned with his head toward the bench. "Go sit at the far end of the bench away from Ben. Don't go anywhere near him. And when you're ready to change your attitude, come find me." But Brock had to escort him over there and in the end plunked himself down next to Oliver who had folded his arms over his chest and glared at the court.

Until the police arrived, Ridout and Bettinger stood beside the gym doors that led into the school. Then Bettinger kept John Saunders company in the lobby where his ranting could be heard when the cheerleaders drew breath. The refs warned Tom that any disrespect shown by CCS fans would force a forfeit. In the prayer before play began, Paul asked God for a miracle. And, the game went badly.

Ben could not start. He'd calmed down enough to face the court, but could not control the trembling that shook his body. Tom refused his request to play. Biting his lip, Ben sat stiffly upright in the chair beside Tom. Five minutes later, they were down by fifteen points. Tom gave into Ben's begging when Ben showed Tom that he could hold his hand out steady.

In the next twenty seconds Ben scored. Paul grabbed a missed bank shot off Key's goal and flipped it to Ben who dribbled at half his normal speed, right handed, to the basket. Key's guard got close and when Ben juked away, the sound of his breath catching was an audible gasp, but he recovered and made a stiff set shot that went in.

Ben was scoring on reputation, Tom thought. The shots he'd taken were simple to block but because Key was expecting his fancy footwork, they hung back. Next Key went to the hole and Ben could not keep up. He tried to cover this, but as soon as Key scored, Joe got the rebound and called a time out. Ben limped to the sideline and just made it to the bench before he threw up into the spit bucket. Tom put Flip in, and that was when Oliver got up, walked the length of the bench followed by Brock and said he was ready to cooperate. Tom sat beside Ben and coaxed sips of Gatorade into him.

"Can I try again, Coach?"

"Ben, something's wrong. We both know it."

"I've had a rough day, but I can play. Please, Coach."

"You throw up again and it's over for you."

"Okay. Agreed. I just don't want to go into the second half down."

Tom put Ben back in; put Oliver in for Joe and when Joe sat down beside him, Tom asked, "What's going on?" They talked facing forward as if watching the entire game, seeing only Ben's tarnished play, his stilted, one-handed dribbling.

"I don't know. I think he's hurt, Dad."

"He hasn't had an injury since Thanksgiving," Tom said, "not that I've seen."

"No. He's been safe. But this is so much worse than Thanksgiving."

"What do you know about that time, Joe?"

Joe met Tom's eyes. "That cut? In his hairline? I stitched myself because he has to hide what's going on."

"Oh, no. No."

Joe hung his head. "Dad, I think he's really hurt this time."

"But he wasn't *with* his father last night," Tom said, thinking aloud. "He was with *you*, he was here for a while, then his father was *looking* for him, then *I* took his father to the ER."

"There were hours, though, after we left Ben and before you found his dad here."

"You're right," Tom said. "I didn't realize that."

"Yeah," Joe said.

"Joe, is there anything else? Any other possibility? Ollie? Could Oliver have beat him up?"

"Dad," Joe pleaded.

"Okay. I've got it now, son, I've got it."

Feeling danger like a draft around his ankles, Tom looked toward the doors. He saw that Ridout and Bettinger had abandoned their post in the lobby and stood now at the corner of the bleachers squinting at the scoreboard with disappointed frowns. The gym doors opened and Lindquist entered with his two small children and his wife. Behind him came Max with Ben's brothers. John Saunders slid through the doors behind Max and stood belly out, mouth oddly shut. Tom gave Brock the "it's your watch," signal and started walking down the length of the bench.

From the top of the key, Ben passed to Knox who drove to the basket, handling the ball low and fast. Saunders cried out, "Sin in the camp! Sin in the camp!"

How the refs didn't hear that, Tom never knew, but when Tom got there, Ridout was trying to reason with Saunders, who now screamed his taunts. The crowd of CCS fans booed him. "Get yourself under control, Saunders," Tom told him, the police taking Saunders' flailing arms.

The refs stopped play. Tom explained to the refs, "I called the police on him earlier. He's taunting my students. I'm going to ask the police to escort him out."

With a whistle, play began again.

"It's a misunderstanding," he heard Saunders promising the police. "I just want to see my kid play."

They looked to Tom for instructions. "You can watch from out in the lobby. Open the doors, and if you men are willing to stand with him, he can stay."

"Who died and made you king?" Max's voice. Tom turned slowly, feeling his own fists tighten. Max sneered, "You afraid he'll spoil your little kingdom? What will happen if all your fans find out the truth?" Max brandished a copy of Saunders' flyer.

"Daddy," a little boy begged.

"Hold on, Max," Lindquist cautioned.

"I have stuff to say to you, Max. So stick around. After the game. You and me." Tom pointed to Max, then himself.

"This time I'll make sure you're useless below the waist."

Tom got in Max's face, his finger pointing, "You can beat me senseless for all I care but don't you *ever again* lay one finger on Ben. Do you understand me?"

Lindquist pulled him away, Ridout wrapped his arms around Max and held him away. Tom heard a crash behind him, heard the ref's whistle shrill long and loud, heard the fans cry out, "No!...Ref, did you see that!... Oh, God!" and then the gym was silent. Lindquist released Tom and turning he saw one ref making a T with his hands. Tom scanned the court. Oliver stood defiantly, hands on hips. The rest of the team crowded around Key's bench, which had been demolished to a pile of upturned chairs. Tom sprinted across the gym. Paul made way for him and at the center of the huddle Ben lay on his right side, his knees drawn up, skin white and damp, his lips two gray lines.

Tom knelt beside him. "Ben." His eyelids fluttered. "He's conscious."

"I don't know how," Joe said. "Did you see what happened, Dad?"

"No."

"How bad hurt are you, Ben?" Joe said.

"What happened?" Tom demanded.

"Didn't you *see*, Coach?" Drew said. "Oliver *shoved* him. Shoved his own *team*mate. Where is he? Where is that snake?"

Tom grabbed Drew's wrist. "Hold on. Don't make it worse."

"Can you get up, Ben?" Joe asked.

"Don't let Tom fight..."

"I'm right here. You quit worrying about me. Can you get up?"

"Saw you...and Dad...didn't see Ollie."

"Let me pick him up," Adam said. "Me and Paul can."

Behind them Saunders cried, "You see this justification? My son is the only one left standing! There it is!" To this the Key School fans hissed and booed. The CCS fans groaned and stood up and jeered as one man, their chanting like a heartbeat. Adam got his arm under Ben's shoulders. Paul and Drew took his hips and legs and stood him up. Key School's coach elbowed his way into the huddle of boys.

"Must be a full moon or something, Tom."

"I apologize. This is ridiculous."

"What say we call this?"

"Yeah," Tom said. "Absolutely. I need to forfeit."

"We'll reschedule," he stuck out his hand.

"No. You won. Fair and square." Tom shook his hand. Behind them the refs' shrill bleat ended the game. Both sides of the bleachers resounded with booing fans. Tom watched Adam, Paul and Drew carry Ben into the locker room. He turned to join the refs who were speaking to Oliver. Four crying cheerleaders made an arc of palpable sympathy behind Oliver.

One ref said, "Shoved his teammate, then kicked him. Saw it with my own eyes. Kid, you're not only out of the game, you're never playing in this league again." Oliver opened his mouth to speak and the ref held one hand up. "Your coach and your principal will figure out what else to do with you. Go on home now."

The other ref said, "More like a hip check. Sent the kid flying and then went after him. Didn't you see it, Tom?"

"I did not." Tom shook his head, turned to Oliver. "Do you understand what you did, Ollie? It would have been *inexcusable* to treat your opponent with such violent disrespect, but your teammate?"

Oliver shrugged. "You're a really bad judge of character, Coach."

"You're right, Ollie," Tom said. "I thought for sure you were better than this.

21

"YOU going to shower, Ben?" Jon asked. "It's emptying out."

"In a minute," said Ben. He leaned against his locker, eyes shut, head bowed.

"Do you need anything?"

"I just need a minute."

"You're shirt's all wet, man," Paul said.

"Look, just take a shower," Drew said. "Just to clean the stink off."

Ben looked up. Four friends stood around him, faces scared, pleading for a sign that he was okay. He thought of the times he'd found his father lying motionless on the floor and knew they needed a sign of life even if there was just so little in him right now. As long as Joe wasn't there. He couldn't let Joe see. "All right," Ben said, with difficulty, not wanting to show how hard it was for him to breathe and speak. "No fooling around in the showers."

"Anything you say, man."

He kept his T-shirt on, waiting until the shower was so steamy he was less likely to be seen. He hobbled, holding with one hand to the lockers all the way to the far end and chose a shower head well away from the group, hoping they would not be able to see through the steam, and only then undressed. Keeping his back to them, he soaped up his neck but wanted to touch no skin below that. He couldn't bend over without pain. Realizing the futility of trying to shower, Ben stuck his head under to rinse off, jumped away when the hot water ran down his side across his bruised skin, and mumbled, "Shit." He heard Austin's shriek approaching through the steam and he knew the sophomore was skidding on his backside toward Ben's end of the shower. Ben jumped out of the way, landed on his feet and slid backwards, hitting against the far shower stall. He yelled at the underclassmen, his irritability so sharp and uncharacteristic that his friends drew near. At their approach, the steam clearing, Ben realized he was without a towel. And there was Joe rubbing a towel on his wet hair. Joe saw his bruises, stared at them, then looked at Ben, stern sympathy turning to bald fear. "Ben, no."

"I just need my towel."

"No."

Drew pointed.

Adam reached for a towel and brought it to him. "Bad bruise, man."

"How'd that…get like that so fast?" Paul said.

"It's okay." Ben watched Joe's grieved expression.

Scott said, "I'm gonna beat the crap out of Oliver."

"We've gotta tell Dad," Joe said. "Where is he?"

"No. Why?" Ben clutched the towel to his chest, hiding the purple.

"You know why!" Joe shouted.

"Look, man," Paul said evenly. "It happened on his watch. He's gotta take care of it."

"I'm fine."

"You're not fine, man."

"Plus he needs to know how hard Oliver actually shoved you," Jason said.

"That ought to figure into what happens to the jerk," Jon said.

"No." Ben said. "I'm not going to be the cause of Ollie getting it."

"He's gonna get it, Ben," Adam said. "We all saw it. Parents saw it. My mama saw the whole thing and she's hoppin' mad. She's not gonna let it drop."

"He's in enough trouble. Why bring me into it?" Ben snapped.

"Stop this," Joe whispered to Ben, coming closer. He reached to move Ben's towel, but Ben held him off with one hand out. "Tell them you came here like this. This happened last night."

Ben turned away.

"Forget it," Joe muttered, eyes flashing. "Don't reason with him," he said to Drew, grabbing his boxers and stepping into them, "and don't let him out of your sight. I'm getting Dad."

Joe grabbed his jeans as he ran out of the locker room and assuming his father was in his office, ducked in there. Finding it empty, he pulled on his pants and ran out into the gym. Colonel Hunter was across the room, talking heatedly to John Saunders while a powerful looking marine that Joe had met before stood by, listening. Two little boys hung around this marine. Crowds of parents talking animatedly, hands in gesture, were scattered around the gym. He did not see Tom. Aunt Beth was talking to a group of cheerleaders. The refs were bustling out into the lobby. Wanting to avoid a confrontation with Colonel Hunter, Joe decided to go the long way. He strode toward the back door that led to the band hallway beside the stage.

His team stayed with Ben, trying to say something, glancing at each other, listening to Ben's uneven breathing, staring as Ben groped for the shower wall, then leaned against it. Drew took a cautious step toward Ben. "We agree with Joe," Drew said. "This has gone too far."

"No." Ben said. "We're not telling Coach. You don't understand."

"Not telling me what?" Tom said, stepping onto the slick tile.

"Careful, Coach," Adam said. "It's pretty slick in here."

"Not telling me what, Ben?"

"Nothing." Ben turned toward the wall and tried to wrap the towel around himself so that it covered everything and was still high enough to hide the bruises, but his hands were shaking.

"I'm sorry, Coach," Austin offered. "I accidentally crashed into him in the shower."

"We told you guys no fooling around," Jon snapped. "He's hurt, man."

"Ben," Tom said.

Feeling their eyes on him, Ben couldn't control his back muscles flinching. Bands of pain tightened around his chest, and his shoulders heaved in rapid breaths.

"Can you cover up or do you need help?"

It took Ben more than a minute to get the towel wrapped around his waist. Tom dropped another clean towel on his shoulders. "Unusual place for a bruise," he commented. "Come on, turn around and show me your ribs."

"No, sir."

"Ben. I got a glimpse of it. I know it's bad." Behind him, Adam tapped Tom's elbow. "Offer him this," he whispered. Nodding, Tom said. "Okay, at least take this cup of water from me. It's nice and cold."

Ben reached back for it, but Tom put it just to his left side. Hand trembling, Ben turned toward it, with his right hand got it, but couldn't hold it steady. His teammates surged and crowded around him, behind him, enclosing he and Tom in a protective circle. Tom took the cup and held it up to Ben's lips. He shook his head after a sip.

"Let me see your chest." Tom turned him around.

Ben bit his lip hard. "Don't make me puke again," Ben warned.

"I won't."

Watching Tom's eyes, Ben saw Tom's expression go hard and angry. He met Tom's eyes, tears threatening with the tremor erupting within. His team was behind him, around him and Tom. "Did Oliver kick you right there where it's bruised?"

"I can't say."

"That means yes," Adam said.

"I know."

"That is where Ollie kicked him," Flip vowed.

"You're overreacting," Ben whispered.

"Shh," Tom said again. "Your teammates saw it."

"Yes, sir, but—"

"Does it hurt to breathe?"

"Coach. I'm okay." Ben glanced at his friends for support, but they stood with arms folded over their chests and their eyes were hard and bright with determination.

"Unusual for a bruise to develop that quickly," Tom said giving Ben a challenging glance.

Growing agitated, Ben groaned, "Look, I'm okay!"

"I'm gonna take you over for x-rays and get you fixed up."

"No! Ollie didn't do this. I know he's a jerk, but this isn't his fault."

"Whose then?"

"Mine. It's my fault. I just tripped."

"You never trip, Ben."

His friends exchanged looks and too late, he realized his mistake. His eyes stung sharply; all of his life he'd used the excuse *I tripped* or *I fell*, silently begging someone to see through the flimsy lie, further hurt and then embittered when no one did. Tom was right. He never tripped; only Joe had noticed before, but this was the wrong moment for Tom to figure it out. He couldn't allow Oliver to take the fall for his father.

"You're the most coordinated person on earth," Tom said, softly, his eyes going over Ben, thinking. "In fact, I've never seen you stumble. No. That's enough. No more of this." Tom guided him away from the showers toward the locker room. "You're getting dressed and then I'm taking you to the ER." Tom looked back. "Adam, run and see if your dad's got his truck ready. And Scott, get the first aid kit out of my office. Does anyone know where Joe is?"

Tiffany, Leeza and Johanna stood in a cluster by the back door and they turned when they heard Joe walking toward them. "Do you know where my dad is? He's not in the gym. I've got to find him."

"Don't show him," Leeza said, grabbing the flyers from Johanna's hand.

"Don't show me what?"

Tiffany shoved one of the flyers at Joe despite Leeza's cry of protest. Joe read it, crushed it in his fist and pushed past the girls to open the back door. Barefoot, he sprinted up the hill that was slick with a frost of snow and dashed around the back of the school, the wind flicking his bare skin with a scatter of icy flakes. But Tom was not in the main office. Mrs. Poulard had arrived and said she hadn't seen Tom yet; she scolded Joe for walking around school without his shirt.

He checked in the faculty room and made a quick sweep of the upstairs, exited by the art room, and slid down the hill on his backside. Hoping the guys had not been naive enough to let Ben slip away, he jogged across the back parking lot toward the gym entrance.

"Hold him up," Tom said to Drew who took Ben's right arm and held it out so that Tom could fit on the sleeve of a T-shirt and stretch it over Ben's head. Ben winced at the touch of the cotton on his skin. Ben heard Adam and Mr. Ridout approaching, their step duplicated and heavy. He turned away to hide his ribs.

Tom said, "Hey, Jim. We need to take Ben to the ER."

"Please listen to me, Coach."

"Don't bother begging, Ben," Jim Ridout said. "School policy. I got the truck running outside; it'll be nice and warm in a minute."

"I can't go right now. Where's Joe?"

"Show Mr. Ridout your chest, Ben."

"Coach—" Ben shook his head.

Moving quickly, Tom yanked Ben's shirt up. "Look."

Ridout moved to see, his face showing his alarm. "No doubt those ribs're broken."

"No. You don't understand."

"Everyone saw Ollie kick you," Flip said.

Tom peered into Ben's eyes and waited. "What happened to you, Ben?" He took a stretchy bandage from the first aid kit Scott had brought him and flipped open the end. "Let's give those ribs a little support." He took Ben's left arm and laid it against his chest, wrist tipped up toward his right shoulder. "If I tape your arm here, it will hold the ribs steady and it won't hurt so much." He pried open Ben's clenched fingers and got his palm flat. "Like that," Tom said, peering at Ben. Their eyes met and Ben knew that Tom could measure the immediate relief in pain. Tom nodded. "That's better. Now breathe as deeply as you can without hurting yourself, okay? And try to hold it." Tom lifted Ben's right arm, glanced at Drew who took Ben's arm and supported it for him, and Tom wound the bandage around Ben's arm and torso wrapping the last third up over Ben's shoulder to keep his left hand bound in place. "You guys stay right beside him, in case he sways. He'll be a bit unsteady."

Tom knelt by Ben's feet. "Drew, pick this leg up so I can put his sock on. Don't want him to pull with his stomach muscles. That's right."

"I feel much better now, Coach, so let's just call it a night."

"School policy," Ridout repeated. "Your coach has to get you medical help."

"Coach, please. This isn't Oliver's fault."

From where he knelt, Tom looked up at Ben. "Okay, it's not Oliver's fault. Whose fault is it?" Ben stared at Tom, eyes pained and filling. "Tell me," Tom said, glancing down to tie Ben's shoe. "Just say it."

"God. It's God's fault."

The silent locker room waited. "This is not God's will."

"Not in *your* world. Not for *your* kids, but it is for me. He's all-powerful. It must be."

"No, son. This should not be happening to you. No way."

"If you're not my father, you have no right to say that."

"I'll tell you what," Tom said, pushing on the bench to help him get to his feet. He got close to Ben, pointing one finger in his face. "God is mad as hell about this. And as far as you're concerned, from now on, I *am* your father. You got that, Ben? No more of this."

"Are you confessing?" The voice crackled out from behind Jim Ridout. "Down on your knees, too."

"Max. I want to talk to you." Tom gave Ben one silencing glance. He strode toward Jim Ridout, touched his arm and said, "Find Ben's jacket or use mine and get him in the truck. I need to talk to his father." Facing Max, Tom said, "Out here. Right now." He shoved Max's shoulder, forcing him to turn slightly, then keeping his hand there, forced the man out the side door into the men's bathroom.

"You want to be alone when I crush your back again? Fine with me."

Max went for Tom, swinging for his chin. But Tom dodged him easily and when Max stumbled, he grabbed Max by his uniform jacket and shoved him so hard up against the bathroom wall that the door stuttered on its hinges. "I know you've been hurting Ben and I'm telling you right now, I am taking him. Katie wanted me to raise him and you know that."

Tom heard the door swish open behind him and in the mirror saw Adam, Drew, Paul and Scott enter.

"Coach."

"Stay back, boys. I've got it." Max thrashed in his grip. Tom shifted his weight, getting closer, forcing his arm across Hunter's chest. "You had your chance. You have failed that boy. I'm not giving you another minute."

"Yeah, Tom. Top athlete, first in his class, Ben sure looks like I failed him."

"Ben sent us in here to help you, Coach."

"See? He knows you can't stand up to me. Want to see me crush your coach's back, boys?"

"Drew," Tom said. "Get my wallet out of my back pocket."

"Got it, Coach."

"There's a piece of paper folded up beneath the dollar bills," Tom said. "Pink paper. Get that out."

"I tried to fix him so he'd stay away from other men's wives. This time I'll—"

Tom shoved his arm against Hunter's throat. "That's enough." He glanced at Drew. "Listen while Drew reads it." Paul, Adam and Scott closed in. "We got your back, Coach."

Max's throat gurgled.

"Read it. The whole thing. He's listening."

"Coach?"

"Go ahead. *Now.*"

Drew began:

> To my husband, Max,
>
> I am close to death. After our son was born I succumbed to a kidney infection. Your violent disdain and stubborn disinterest toward our baby from the moment I announced my pregnancy to you until now, convinces me that you should not be permitted to raise him should I die.
>
> I've written you every day for the last nine months in hopes that you will come to believe that I left for my safety, not because there is any truth to your accusations.
>
> I am afraid that if anything happens to me, this little boy will have no parent to look after him. Uncle Gregen is willing, but old. Your mother has been kind, but she's not good with children. Laurie is closer to me than a sister could be and she will continue to love our little son as if he were her own. If you had been here you would have seen that in all the most important ways, Tom has been a father to this little boy. So, I am choosing Tom and Laurie MacBride to raise my son. I am dictating this to Tom MacBride in Hillside Hospital, on October 27, 1980.

Drew looked up.

"I promised her I'd read that to you. Now you've heard it."

"You tried to use that in court," Max croaked. "You couldn't get custody then. You won't now. It's worth shit."

Tom stared at him a minute, remembering when he had it in his hand sixteen years ago, when he'd tried to read it to Max, how Max grabbed Ben from his grandmother's arms. "Give me that paper," Max had screamed, "I'll break his neck." The memory shuddered Tom, the weight of the years' consequences falling on his back like a terrible stroke of a lash. Now in his own gym, Tom commanded, "Stay away from Ben."

"Don't threaten me," Max wriggled and reared up, raising his knee to smash Tom, but Adam blocked the blow, one huge hand gripping Max's knee. Paul shoved an arm between the men, pushing Max's torso up against the wall. "We got him, Coach."

"Hit him," Scott said. "Show him you mean it."

"He knows I mean it," Tom said. "He knows he's wrong; he just doesn't care." Tom opened the door to the hallway. "Put him outside with the trash."

22

OUTSIDE in the dark parking lot, Joe saw Oliver and his father putting a big box into the trunk of their Honda. "Have you seen my dad?" Joe asked jogging up to them.

"Why would I want to see *him*?" Oliver mocked.

Joe said. "Ben's really hurt. I need to find Dad."

John Saunders grabbed Joe's arm, held tight. "You must be mighty disappointed in your dad."

"Let go of me," Joe said, wrenching away, but Saunders held hard, trapping Joe with his other arm around Joe's chest. Joe fought, twisting and jabbing with his elbows.

"Here's your chance, Oliver," Saunders said, grunting to control Joe, "Tell this troublemaker something that will change his life."

Joe hollered for help and stomped his foot onto Saunders' just as Oliver said, "Give this to your dad," but when Oliver spit at him, Joe stopped in astonishment and he heard the back door creak, heard the girls' voices and feet on the gravel.

Tiffany grabbed Tom's elbow just as he stepped onto the driveway in front of the gym. "Mr. MacBride," she gasped, "they're beating Joe up." She pulled on his arm, pulling him toward the back parking lot.

Jim Ridout opened the door of his truck and looked back at Tom.

"Take Ben to the ER," Tom told Ridout. "Don't leave him alone for a second until I get there," he shouted as he jogged away.

Max Hunter stepped out in front of Jim Ridout's truck as it rolled toward the stop sign at the entrance to the school. Ridout rolled down his window. "You get things straightened out with Tom?" Ridout asked.

"Sure," Max said, shading his eyes and peering into the truck. "He's just nervous about me suing the school," Max lied. "You know Tom."

"Why would you sue the school?" Ridout asked. "Taking Ben to the ER means we're taking care of him."

"I've gotta go with you to authorize medical treatment," Max said. "Good thing I'm here."

"No," Ben said from the backseat where Ridout had buckled him in, the latch below his bound left arm.

Ridout glanced back at Ben. "You okay back there?"

"He doesn't need to come with us," Ben said as Max hefted himself into the front seat. "That's what the insurance forms are for at the beginning of the season. He signed them."

"Don't worry, Ben," Max said, glancing back and patting Ben's knee. "Ben's a big worrier."

"Your boy's bad off," Ridout muttered to Max putting the truck in gear and rolling it forward. "I had to plum carry him out here to make him leave. Tom insisted I step in when he had to go off and help his son Joe out. Ben's ribs look bad."

"If you want to loan me your truck, I'll drive Ben wherever he wants to go."

This made Ridout laugh. "No, sir, Colonel Hunter. Nobody drives Big Red but me and my boys. No offense intended."

By the time they pulled up to the curb outside the ER, Max had regaled Jim Ridout with stories of his amazing career, about his rapid promotions, his awards and medals, his great job at USNA, about his responsibilities as the USNA military liaison for the Special Olympics in Annapolis, and even in the dark truck cab, Ben could see Mr. Ridout's jaw working in silent thought. Finally Ridout said, "So you were just a bit too young for Vietnam? Did you see action at Granada or Somalia?"

"Been in recruiting most of my career. Are you military?"

"Retired army," Ridout said. He shut off the truck and hopped out with swift agility for a man his size. He opened the door for Ben, reached across him to unlatch his belt, thrust his arm behind Ben and lifted him out of the seat as if he were as big as an undersized first grader. "I'll get you inside and signed up. I know Tom wants you seen soon as possible. My neighbor works here. Might be on tonight. Didn't see her at the game."

In they went with Ben under Ridout's formidable wing, Max following behind. The waiting room, which formed a corner around the triage window smelled of latex and bleach. Ridout left Ben to lean against the wall beneath the TV. Max stood three feet from Ben watching Ridout who got in the line formed for the triage window. Jim Ridout glanced back, looked satisfied, faced front, folded his arms over his chest to wait.

Max stepped closer to Ben.

"Stay away."

"Don't make a fool of yourself, Ben." Max turned his back to the room, his shoulder to Ridout, and faced Ben. "Everyone in this room can see that I am a uniformed member of the armed forces, respectable in every way. You're the one who looks like a junkie right now. God, you look like shit."

"Don't come any closer."

"Look, let's get out of here. We both know this visit is bogus."

"It's not bogus. My ribs are broken. You broke them last night."

Max reached for Ben's arm. "Shut up and come with me."

Ben flinched away, the movement hurting him. "No. I'm not going home with you." He whispered, "never again."

Max stepped closer, trapped the toes of Ben's right foot under his shoe and leaned down hard. "Where you going to go? You gonna live with Tom?" Ben hesitated. Max said, "You think Tom'll treat you better than I do? You think that?"

"I know he will. Are you kidding? He's nothing like you. He doesn't drink, for one thing. He doesn't punch his sons."

"No, but he abandons them."

"You don't know what you're talking about. Leave me alone. I swear I'm gonna puke if you don't get away from me."

"I'm gonna tell you a little secret, Ben."

"I don't want to hear it. Go away."

"Remember when your mom got all weepy about how sinful she is and all? She got her Bible out? That's because she was trying to tell you something really bad she did. Only she was too scared you'd hate her."

"Leave her out of this. You're the one who messed everything up at home."

"See, you're wrong about that. You've never felt comfortable, you've never felt like you fit in because you don't. You're not my kid. You're Tom's kid." Max laughed and pointed at Ben's face. "Don't stare at me like that. I've known it all your life and I took on the responsibility anyway."

"You're a liar."

"Your mother, you're so concerned about her. You think *I* ruined her life? I stuck by her after she cheated on me. I raised you, just to cover her ass. Of course I'm gonna drink, she's gonna feel guilty. It's because of you. You are someone who never, ever should have been born."

Ben couldn't breathe. His gorge rose. "Not true," he croaked.

"Yeah, she described it in detail in these sick diaries she used to keep. I didn't want you to know, so I kept it from you. That's why I took that diary away from you at Thanksgiving. Your mom and Tom. Broke my heart."

"No."

"Right. You remember how upset I was? I'm trying to protect you because I knew how much it would hurt you to learn that your mother is a slut and your father—this coach you love so damn much—was willing to pass you off as another man's kid just to save himself the embarrassment."

Ben retched. Max leapt back. Ben's vomit splashed on his trouser leg and his shoes. Ben stumbled over to Mr. Ridout, who caught him in his arms. Behind him, Max squealed so loudly and pitifully that the busy nursing staff called security to tend to him while the waiting patients backed off in confused disgust.

"Can we get this puppy in a room?" Ridout called.

23

BEN had been put on a slender hospital bed with a pink plastic tray beside him in case he was sick again. The nurse opened the curtains and announced, "Your dad is here!"

"He's not my dad," Ben said.

The nurse looked at Max. "Does he have a concussion? That explains the vomiting." Max gave her a broad, supercilious smile. She patted Max's arm and left.

"Where'd Mr. Ridout go?"

"I sent him home." Max said, coming close to the bed. "He didn't want to leave, but I told him we were fine. It's none of his damn business anyway." Max came around behind Ben to speak in his ear. "Just don't puke on me again."

"Give me a chance and I will."

"Listen. You're upset. I'm upset. Let's get out of here. No need to stay, right? You understand what I was upset about and how I took you in. Let's just go home now. We'll start over."

"My ribs are broken and I have a concussion."

"You'll be fine."

Ben nodded. A dead calm lay on him as if cold rain could fall from a clear sky. Tom wanted him to be seen, Max didn't care. Now he knew why. Now everything made sense. He wondered if he would feel better soon, if he would discover that truth was better than fear. For the last couple of days the suspicion, the fear that Tom was his father had tortured him. Terrible truth now sickened him and he had not gained the sense of peace he expected the truth, however bald and ugly, would bring. "Okay," he said. "Go talk to that nurse. She seemed to like you. See if you can sign me out before anyone sees how bad my ribs are."

"Okay. Great. Great to work with you on this, Ben." Max punched Ben's sore shoulder in light-hearted camaraderie.

Tom's right leg was going numb by the time he reached the back parking lot; Tiffany clinging to his elbow, talking as they ran. There in the center of the lot stood Saunders' car. He leaned against it, Oliver next to him, both of them leaning on their hands, both of them open mouthed, staring at Joe who was flanked by Johanna and Leeza. More students hurried toward them from the back door.

As Joe talked, he glanced over at Tom walking across the lot. "…So, that's how it kind of happened inside me on Thanksgiving. I know who I am now. I have a lot of regrets about how proud and flip I can be; if I hadn't been, things might have been different between us, Oliver." Joe held both hands out to them in a conciliatory gesture. "But man, you've been wrong, too. What you did to Ben tonight, that was the worst possible thing. First those bogus flyers and then hurting him on purpose. That's criminal, Ollie. You've got to take a good look at yourself."

Tom stood beside Joe, his hand went to Joe's shoulder. "Son? You all right?"

"Yeah, Dad. I'm fine. I was just explaining how I know who you are. How's Ben?"

Ben used the handrail to pull himself up enough so that he could roll to his feet. He peeked out of the curtains, found the hallway empty, slipped between the curtain panels and walked away. He hurried past the bathrooms and the nurse's lounge and through the double doors marked NO ENTRY. When the alarm sounded, Ben ducked into a dark room and hid behind the door. After several minutes, the alarm subsided.

He found his mother's empty office; he stood in the corner, in the deep shadows listening to the newborn cries and the padded feet of the nurses rolling the carts in and out. As soon as she opened her door a crack, he said, "Mom, it's Ben," so she wouldn't scream.

She flipped on her light. "What's wrong?" but when she saw him, her hand went to her mouth. "Your ribs are broken."

She stretched out a hand but Ben snapped, "Don't touch me."

"Did this happen at the game?"

"Dad did it last night."

"Oh, no, Ben."

"Mom, he told me everything."

"Really? Good. I can hardly believe it. You need to know."

"Why didn't you tell me?"

"He wouldn't let me. I've been begging him."

"I wouldn't have blamed you. It's worse now thinking of what I would have had if Tom had gotten custody of me."

"Why would Tom get custody of you?"

"As my father, my real father, that's normal, Mom."

"What?"

"Even part time. Even if Tom had visiting rights like other dads. That would be some compensation for having to put up with *his* abuse."

"Wait. He told you *Tom* is your dad? Ben, don't believe him."

"Don't believe him? Okay, then who do I believe? You? After all that shit about you killing yourself if Tom knew you had a shitty life? What was that? When you said that to me, Mom, you chained me just in reach of Dad's fists. Do you realize that? I believed you. I *cried* for you. I stayed, I took *hits* to keep you alive. I could have been sleeping at the MacBrides— safe at night, safe in the morning. You—you cheated me out of the life I should have had."

"Please try to calm down. You're right. I shouldn't have manipulated you, but—"

"Just think!" Ben was frantic. "Just imagine it! I would have had food and somebody to talk to. Do you know he *reads* to his kids at night. Still? He reads to Joe stuff Joe's *interested* in. That's how Joe falls asleep instead of like me trying to decide which way to lie down based on which bruise is the oldest, lying there all alone trying to figure out why my father hates me. You took all that from me."

"Ben, you're right about one thing. I have greatly wronged you."

"Did you think I'd judge you for being with Tom? I prefer him, too. I don't blame you. You were probably desperate. Like me. Did you forget how great Tom is? Do you know, like the stuff he understands and how he's full of hope and like even when he's mad—*really mad*—he controls himself. I mean, Mom, Tom is so much better than Dad—than him—" Ben's breath caught painfully, his broken body wrestled with sobs. "Except for," Ben couldn't say the words he was thinking—*except for cheating on his wife*. He stared at Donna, trying to perceive the connection, to imagine the passion. Tom had said she had come to him hungry for discussion about God. Had he taken advantage of that? Is that what he had been trying to say this morning? How was that any better than what he despised in Max? Wasn't it the same preference for his own will and pleasure? This was so wrong. *He abandoned me to a violent, bitter father. Isn't that a worse crime than hitting someone?*

"Do you really think Tom is the kind of man to cheat on his wife and abandon his son?" Donna said.

"No!" Ben shouted. "But it explains everything. It explains why Dad's hated me all this time. You have no idea how I've tried to understand why he's so *unnatural*."

"Shh, Ben, calm down."

"I won't be quiet. I can't calm down. My insides are a spewing volcano. I mean, just now, just downstairs. He knows my ribs are broken and he wants me to sneak out of the hospital without being seen so no one will find out about him hurting me. He *can't* be my dad. It explains everything." Quaking with rage, Ben balled up his right fist, turned and slammed it into the wall.

"He's not here so you'll harm yourself *for* him?" Ben pulled his hand back to hit again, but Donna grabbed his elbow. "Don't be like that." Her grip was astonishingly strong. She turned him away from the wall. "You'll break your hand." She held his wrist, covered his fist with her other hand. He heard her tears and looked to see them bright in her eyes, which were for the first time unguarded. "I'm sorry, I'm so sorry. What can I do to start making it up to you?"

"I need help," he whimpered. "And you owe me. You owe me a lifetime of good stuff, Mom."

"Let me get someone to look at your injury."

"First call Tom and tell him I'm with you at the hospital and they're keeping me overnight." She picked up the phone, but hesitated. "Call him. Otherwise he'll be over here as soon as he can and I don't want to see him."

She dialed. "You know their number?"

"Why would it have changed?"

Ben paced Donna's office while she called. Tom was not yet home, but Donna asked that Laurie pass on the message that Ben was just about to be x-rayed and would be kept in the hospital for observation. When Laurie asked, Donna said it would be better to wait until the morning to visit. She phoned the school with the same message. Listening, Ben's aching eyes passed over three photographs of him and his brothers in what looked like shiny new frames. He'd never seen the one of him before. Very small, he stood under a palm tree holding a colorful quilt in one arm and a ball nearly as big as himself in the other. He looked worried. Donna squatted next to him, her brightly manicured hand helping him hold up the ball; the expression on her face was pure rapture. She hung up the phone, dialed again and spoke quickly using medical lingo.

"You left the boys alone tonight," Ben accused her.

"Gran is here. For Christmas." She looked up at Ben. "We wanted to talk to you. Maybe you'll be up to it tomorrow."

"No. I'm going now." Ben looked around, unable to focus, frantic with pain and exhaustion. "But I told Laurie you'd be x-rayed and watched over. We can't lie to her. I don't want to do that."

"You've been lying to the entire world for years," Ben said. "Remember? You let him—" he gestured at the floor, "yell at me and punch me and kick me all these years and said shut up about it. That's lying."

"I know I failed you. But trust me this once, Ben." She took out her keys and unlocked an adjoining room. "They're bringing an x-ray machine up here."

"I don't want it. I know my ribs are broken. I need a support but I need my arm free."

"Don't you want to make sure your lung isn't in danger?"

"It's better breathing since Tom put this bandage on."

"He did a good job on that. Now come with me, please."

"No," Ben cried. "Dad will find me here. You don't understand. He's still obsessed with me."

"Oh, I do understand. He won't find you here. I know you have no—" she gestured between them, "no experience as to why you should trust me, but did you hear me say 'code pink,' on the phone? That's our way of saying we have a victim of a violent crime. There will be someone from security, too. You'll be safe. And they can give you something for the pain."

The little room had a sink, standard medical emergency equipment and two beds, a recliner chair, a television and a refrigerator. "We use this for all kinds of things," Donna said as she maneuvered the height and slant of the bed so that Ben did not have to exert himself to get on it. In the ten minutes that they waited, Donna created a chart for him, entered his information into her computer, took his vital signs, gingerly cut his bandage off, and coaxed him into taking three sips of ice water while Ben watched her in a thoughtless stupor, rocking on waves of pain-edged rage. At a knock, Donna moved the blinds on the glass door and unlocked the door to a burly-looking guard, a nurse practitioner and a radiology techni-cian. The bedside x-ray machine meant he did not have to move and he lay there, clutching Donna's hand tightly.

When pain medication was mentioned, Ben snapped, "No!"

"Can you give us a minute?" Donna asked the nurse practitioner. She nodded and they moved a few steps away.

"I need to go," Ben pleaded. "I can't drive on medication."

"Is your car here?"

"No. I'm gonna walk back to school to get it."

"Sleep for a couple of hours, Ben."

"You're not going to give me back to him, are you? Trick me into going to sleep and next thing I wake up in his quarters? I won't go back there."

"No. I agree. You must live somewhere else. For your own safety."

Ben swallowed, meeting her eyes, searching them. For the first time in his life, she seemed solid, calm. She took his hand and whispered, "Let me start making things right between us by giving you a couple of hours of care to show you I understand how things should have been."

"You can't let him near me," Ben whispered, tears filling his eyes. "I can't pay that price to make you feel better. I'm bad off this time. I can't protect you right now."

Donna nodded to the nurse practitioner who came quickly to Ben's bedside and swabbed his arm. "Things are going to be different now. I know I should have gotten help. I should have protected you. And see? These people are helping us. They know you're my child. I told them your father hurt you. That's the first step. Can you rest in that?" The hypoder-mic injection pierced his bicep and he felt the liquid burn into his muscle, pulling with it a warm, numb cloak that tugged his eyes shut.

"If I'm asleep, I can't protect myself."

"I won't let your father near you."

"Neither one of them," Ben murmured. "I don't want to see either one."

Ben woke and looked around the little hospital room. The clock read three o'clock in the morning. A new bandage covered his ribs and with his freed left hand he felt the velcro straps that held it.

After removing the IV needle from the back of his hand, Ben grabbed his shoes and shirt from the plastic bag beneath the gurney. On the door, his mother's note in her loopy, childish handwriting read, I'M ON ROUNDS. I'LL BE BACK AT FOUR.

The latch on the door clicked open with two and a half turns to the right. Down the hall, the security guard chatted with a nurse. Swift and silent, Ben found his way in the dark hallways to the stairs, through the sleeping hospital, and went the opposite way of the signs to the ER. He emerged at the grand front doors and stepped out into the dark blue night, his nostrils flaring with the icy damp of the cold. Wisps of fine snow lay in lines along the base of the curbs and on the forks of dark, trembling branches. Ben thought he could run as long as his side was numb and stepped off the curb with that intention, heart and body positioned to go, but a car beeped and pulled up behind him.

"Ben."

Ben dashed off, a car door slammed behind him and he heard his name again, then, "It's me, Nels Lindquist."

He stopped, clutching his side. *No, I probably can't run all the way*, he thought as Major Lindquist took his arm. "Hey. I'm a friend, remember?"

Ben stared into the car, looking for Max. Lindquist said, "Your mother called. She said you'd take off as soon as you woke up and she was right, I guess, huh?"

"I've got to go, Major Lindquist. Nothing against you."

"I'm to drive you to the MacBrides." Lindquist steered him toward the car. "Tom spoke to your Mom but he's still very worried." Lindquist opened the passenger door for him and waited while Ben lowered himself into the seat with pained deliberation. "I've been waiting here all night."

"What happened to Joe?" Ben asked as Lindquist pulled away from the hospital.

"He handled Saunders and his kid like some kind of Ghandi. Not a punch thrown. Great kid, that Joe."

"Can you drive me to school, Major? I've got to get my car."

"You can get that tomorrow, can't you?" Lindquist said as he guided Ben to his car and helped lower him into the seat. "Joe took your backpack to his house. They're expecting you."

"I'd really like to get my car."

"Ben," Lindquist said. "You've got a runaway look in your eye and I can't help you run. You need to go to your coach's house, they've got a bed waiting for you. No one will hurt you there."

Ben teared up, looked down, studied the bloody patch on his hand. "How long have you known my mom and—and the colonel?"

"I first met y'all in Hawaii. You were a little tyke."

"Yeah, I remember Hawaii. No shoes. It was nice."

"Your dad's been a friend for lots of years, Ben."

"Yeah, I know," Ben snapped. "Everyone likes him. He's fun at a party."

Lindquist pulled into the MacBrides' driveway. "I was going to say that being his friend, even *I* know he's in trouble. He drinks too much. You stay with Tom until your dad gets himself straightened out."

"How long have you known Tom?"

"Just this year. That's all."

"Are you sure he's any better than my—than the colonel?"

"Yeah," Lindquist said. "I'm sure."

Ben stared at Lindquist, his uneven gaze only half-convincing. "Thanks for the ride," Ben said.

Lindquist offered his hand. "Give me your word that you'll go in and stay here." Ben hesitated, staring at the offered hand. "I'll take you in myself if I have to."

"No, sir," Ben shook Lindquist's hand and with the touch remembered the man's years of kindness. "I'll do as you ask. You and Mrs. Lindquist have been great to me. I'm grateful."

Ben walked slowly across the gravel driveway to the back door. He pulled the door open and stepped inside, watching as Lindquist backed his car out of the driveway. When Lindquist's headlights disappeared, Ben crossed the yard in the darkness, jarred the garage door, and slipped in.

In the morning, Ben hid in Tom's pantry until Tom left the house to warm up the car for Bonnie Jean. He stepped into the kitchen just as she shrugged on her coat.

"Jeannie," he whispered.

She gasped, opening her arms to him, and cried out his name. "Shh!" He held her off. "I'm sore," he explained, unable to meet her eyes.

"I thought they were keeping you in the hospital? Are your ribs okay? Not broken?"

"Are *you* feeling better?"

"Yes. But I have to take the make-up exam this morning."

"Jeannie, I have something to tell you."

"Dad suspects your dad's been hitting you so you can just tell him now."

Ben looked at her earnest face, the lovely brown eyes, bright with passion and life, the dash of her dark, straight-across brows, the high curve of her cheekbones pink-flushed, the sunny scent of her open lips. "Stuff's happening and I'm scared, Jeannie."

"We're here. We love you."

"No matter how it turns out, I just want you to know that I love you. I love you and nothing will ever change how I feel about you."

"We usually kiss when you say that."

"I can't do that right now, Jeannie. I'm so sorry."

"It's okay, Ben. I think Dad is just worried about it being awkward when you live here, but that's no big deal to me."

"It might be," Ben said. "You don't know everything about me—" He couldn't say it, he couldn't tell her Max's foul news and spoil her shining innocence. "I think your dad's ready to go. He's almost got the frost off the windshield." Ben bit his lip to keep from breaking down.

"Will it hurt if I hug you?"

"Very much," Ben said.

Every time Tom started to drum his fingers on the table where eight students worked on various make-up exams, one of them looked up to reprove with silent eyes. It was true, he wanted out of the silent, windowless room, but told himself that it was just as well that he was so confined. It gave him time to think about what he intended to do.

Tom reflected on what he knew of his father's thought process in the great crises of his life. He had loved Tom's mother though her negativity and abuse, speaking the truth, always kind. He had seen, somehow, what to do to reach Kevin, to turn the boy who had stolen from them into a genuine family member, worthy to be given the MacBride plumbing business. Tom had tried to follow his father's loving, creative example in each of his failed and violent encounters with Max. Last night, Tom had promised Max punishment for hurting Ben and Tom had every intention of fulfilling that promise, but he wondered, sitting there in the chill room watching Bonnie Jean's concentration wander, hearing the phones outside the door buzz, hearing the muffled sounds of urgent voices beyond the walls, Tom wondered if there were something he could do to turn things.

He imagined what his father's response would have been if Kevin had scorned Edmund's generous open-handed training. What if Kevin had stolen, again and again, from Edmund MacBride and Sons? What would his father have done? *He left my mother's house to me so that she would have to try to get along with me whom she despised...And to me he gave always the most careful, clear and honest responses.* "Do not think yourself stronger than you really are," he had counseled Tom when he observed Tom's fascination with Katie Hunter's spiritual awakening.

Tom leaned his chin on folded hands, his elbows firm on the table. He closed his eyes and prayed, "Lord, bring justice to Ben. Let me be your servant and his servant as you rescue him as I know you want to do. I can't think of any way to reach Max. I can't change his heart, but I do ask that you would." Tom let his eyes wander to the students around the table wishing he had been able to see Ben this morning, but Bonnie Jean had only mentioned him being there in the kitchen when they arrived at school. He remembered that today was Joe's court date in New Jersey and felt sure that Joe would take Ben with him to get Peter first. At least Ben would be out of Max's reach for the day.

24

BEN woke in the passenger seat of his own car when Joe slowed it to curve onto the exit ramp that would dump them out three blocks from Penn. Joe glanced over at him, gave a brief smile. "You were already asleep when I stopped at the store for breakfast, but there's food there, by your foot."

Ben shook his head. Joe touched the lid of a paper cup in the console. "It's not hot anymore, but it's still good." Taking the warm cup of chocolate in hand, Ben shifted in his seat. He unbuckled the seat belt, which pressed too tightly on his ribs. Joe glanced at him with worried, hopeful eyes. For Joe's sake, Ben put the cup to his lips and Ben watched Joe drive, wondering if he were strong enough to bear Ben's terrible burden. "You've been a great friend, more like a brother," Ben suggested.

"Brothers fight. We don't."

"We fought that once. And remember? Tom said we *shouldn't* fight because we *were* brothers."

"No, he said we should work it out because we were brothers. Even he and Unca Doug have words sometimes," Joe said. Ben sipped the chocolate, remembering the immediate, almost telepathic connection between he and Joe and a crowd of memories of Joe's daily kindnesses, the protective stance he had immediately adopted with Ben, who was five months younger and crippled by his bruised confidence. Ben realized the implications, now, of his missing birth certificate. He glanced again at Joe, saw the bay-blue eyes in their serious aspect, moving to watch the road. What Ben had to say to Joe today would darken their spark forever.

From the back seat, Tommy's deep sleep breathing caught, the boy muttered something and pulled his jacket up over his face. A buzzing, muffled and distant, sounded in the small car. "What's that?" Joe said.

"Probably some weird contraption Gregen put in the car for tracking it during blizzards in the Alps."

"You sound bitter."

"*This* is why I'm bitter." Reaching for the glove compartment, Ben opened it, took out the maps, and tapped on the picture in there. "Remember when I went back to my car the other night? After I got my backpack out of yours?"

"Yeah. Your backpack's at my house, by the way. What happened?"

The colonel came up behind me when I was putting my backpack in the car and he freaked out—right there on the street—because of this car. Can you see?" Ben pointed at Max's picture taped there. "This is him. When he was young. His picture in my car."

Joe glanced quickly, then back to the road.

"He recognized the car. Even painting it pink didn't help. He totally pulled me out of the car and got in here and went for the glove compartment expecting to find something."

"And then he hit you?"

"You know how I wanted to talk to him? I didn't get much out because he was so angry. I don't know why that picture's in my car, but I feel like ol' Gregen set me up. I mean, the way the colonel acted about this stupid car—Gregen with the way he thinks of everything—he *must* have suspected the colonel would freak. The colonel used to own this. Gregen absolutely knew that because he bought it from him. Remember?" Tommy made a stretching groan in the back seat. That electronic buzz sounded again. "That sounds like a cell phone. But mine is in my backpack, isn't it?"

"Are you calling him *the colonel*?" Joe asked. He glanced in the rearview mirror, set the blinker going, and merged neatly right.

Ben looked at Joe. "Yeah."

"Why?"

"Joe, don't you think it's unnatural the way he hurts me? I mean you know a little of it."

"Yeah, it's unnatural. It's also criminal and sick."

"You saw how bad off I was at Thanksgiving, and then this time, I wasn't doing anything. That's like always. And he wasn't even drunk." Ben pointed to his ribs. "He stomped on me. I think he was actually trying to kill me."

"Anything I say," Joe murmured, "can't really show how outraged I am at him. This is so wrong."

"Why do you think that is, Joe? Why does he hate me and want me dead? Mr. Ridout doesn't want to kill his sons. He would never act like that to Adam and Paul. Even Oliver's father defends Ollie to a fault. You see what I mean? Mr. Saunders is wrong—he's completely ruined Ollie but not because he *hates* Ollie and wants Ollie *dead* but because he's convinced that Ollie is faultless and unappreciated. He's blind and wrong, and his brand of love is deformed, but he's totally dedicated to Ollie."

"Yeah," Joe pulled the car into an empty parking lot behind a tall dorm. "Absolutely. It's bizarre. I agree. Confusing." In his heavy coat, a nubby wool cap Grannie had knitted, gloves on his hands, Peter stood by the back doorway, a backpack on his shoulder, a duffle bag by his feet. Joe waved to Peter, his grin dimpling. He coasted the car to a stop, letting it bump softly into Peter's knees. Pete came to the window as Joe was lowering it. "Hey, Ben. How you feeling?"

"I'm alive," Ben said.

"Gimme the keys, I'll open the trunk." Tommy said. "You're letting all the cold air in."

Joe switched off the car and let Tommy out. The car rocked as they slung his stuff into the small trunk. "I'm taking him in to the bathroom," Peter called as he tossed the keys back to Joe, who caught them, got back in, and started the car. He switched the fan on, trained the vents on Ben.

"I'd let you drive your own car, but I think you're still too drugged." Joe backed up, turned the car, and let it coast parallel to the sidewalk.

"It's wearing off."

"Are you in pain again?" Wincing, Ben tried to find the words. With one last glance at Joe's bright eyes, he whispered, "The colonel says he's not my father."

"Ha. That's no excuse," Joe sneered.

"He says Tom is."

"What?" Joe stomped on the brakes. Ben fell forward, his hand on the dashboard stopping him from hitting his head on the windshield. "No."

"I know it's hard. I know it's awful, but it makes sense."

"No. It doesn't. It can't be. He's lying to you."

"Think about it." Ben gestured to illustrate the deep connection they both felt. "The way your parents take care of me." He added, quietly, "The way they love me."

"But what about my mom?" Joe argued. "She'd be hurt and mad if…"

"We're not talking about normal people here. Tom and Laurie MacBride forgive the most hurtful stuff. Your mom would totally embrace a mistake like me. They both loved my mom, now no one speaks. I'm why."

"No, Ben. Think about it. Your mom is the one who doesn't want to be friends. If he was—if they did—wouldn't it be *my mom* who demanded they cut things off?"

"You don't understand shame. If you're ashamed you hide and keep away from people."

"No. No. It can't be. It's not like him. I won't believe it."

"You're loyal. That's who you are, but it all fits together…" Ben hesitated. "It makes sense." Peter and Tommy hurried toward the car, breath clouds puffing around their faces.

"What. Except what? You were going to say except something," Joe demanded, searching Ben's face for information.

"The way Tom describes my mom. It doesn't fit. That's the only thing."

"It's not the *only* thing!" Joe looked away, stared out the window at his brothers approaching, shifted the car into neutral, and yanked up the emergency brake. "There's him. Who he is. His integrity and all he's taught me."

"Maybe he learned all that from messing up with me. Maybe he's determined to make you different—better."

"No. It can't be." The buzzing sounded again from the back seat. They ignored it, staring straight ahead.

Peter hesitated on the sidewalk, reading the expressions on their faces. Ben opened his door. "Sit in here, Pete, I'll move."

"No," Peter prevented him. "Stay there." He glanced from Ben to Joe, back to Ben. "I'll get in the back."

"You can't fit."

"But I can *bend*, you can't," Peter said and when Joe held his seat up, proved it by doubling over and crawling into the back. Tommy followed.

Joe drove slowly, lips pressed together. Angled into the back seat, sitting with his hips in the corner, Peter studied Joe's face, then what he could see of Ben's. The tires whirred against the concrete, the blinker sounded its stiff dinging. "Smells like snow," Tommy said, cheerfully. "And it's way colder since this morning. Did anyone listen to the weather?"

"Yeah," Peter said. "Both systems are gonna miss Baltimore."

"Like those storms that roll up from the south?" Tommy asked, but his brothers didn't answer and Joe's fingers drummed on the steering wheel in a frantic pace until that buzzing erupted again.

"What is that?" Joe snapped. "Is that one of your gadgets, Tommy?"

"Hey. What's wrong? You were nice just a minute ago. It's just Ben's cell phone. I took it out of his backpack in case he needed it." Tommy stretched one hand under the front seat, finally pulling the phone out as the buzzing stopped. He handed it to Ben, who flipped it open to read the display. He said nothing. Tommy asked, "Did Dad call?"

Ben glanced at Joe. "My brothers and my grandmother." The phone vibrated in Ben's hand. He flipped it open, put it to his ear. "Keith?"

Everyone in the car heard Max's commanding voice. "I've been calling every ten minutes for the past two hours. Where the hell are you?"

"Don't call me again. We have nothing to say to each other." He snapped the phone shut.

The phone buzzed three more times as they drove in thick silence. The busy road, too, attended that insistent phone, cars speeding with them, their urgent noises distant, irrelevant and muted by speed and the urgent buzzing. Rising in a dense, whitish sky, the muffled sun strained to shine in Ben's window, to warm Peter's shoulders, which were pressed against the small pane of drafty back-seat glass. The cold air silenced the world beyond the silent car.

Ben watched the guardrail flicking past. A flurry of snowflakes, big and lacy, swirled around the side mirror, sploshed on the window. Twists of the road brought them closer to the swelling green river below. When his phone jumped again in his hand, Ben hit the window lever. In vicious jerks he pushed and pulled to make the window glide down, catching cold air like gulps. Ben aimed for the river, snapped his wrist and released. The phone flew straight out, then fell in an arc, making a small, white splash that Tommy pointed to as Peter turned and Joe glanced in the rearview mirror. Ben slumped in his seat, the captured snowflakes softening to blots of white on his eyebrow, his sleeve, the worn knee of his sweat pants.

In the light of the mirror, Peter met eyes with Joe. Ben watched this from his angle, lips pressed together. In the mirror, he saw Tommy glance from face to face, make a knowing grimace and bend out of sight. He emerged with a Walkman and earphones. He put these on and with a resigned grimace at Peter, turned the volume up.

Peter said, "I know he hurt you again. Joe called me last night. I'm sorry." Ben was silent, though he looked up to meet Peter's eyes in the mirror. "You know, there's something really off with your dad. Because after Joe called last night, I remembered something else. I remembered why Dad didn't fight back that time Colonel Hunter broke his back when Ben was a baby."

"Yeah. We got that figured out," Ben said.

"No. I remembered something about the fight. I remember being put in the MG. Mom strapped me in. It was parked in front of your grandmother's house, Ben. Mom ran in the house and I remember being scared because I was all alone in the car. Joe wasn't there and Dad was like right in front of the car with Colonel Hunter shouting and gesturing. Not like Dad at all—really angry and freaked out."

"The fight," Ben said. "That must be what you remember."

"Yeah. Dad was saying something like, "Give me the baby. Give me the baby. Don't hurt him." The weird thing is, Ben, I remember seeing you. Really close, right outside the car, like you were hovering there or floating there. You were screaming and I remember I tried to give you the pacifier that was in Joe's car seat next to me."

"That's weird," Joe said.

"Then I remember Dad—like flipping backward and hitting against the car door."

Ben glanced at Joe. Peter said, "They fought over you."

To Joe, Ben said, "Notice who was trying to rescue me. Notice who got himself hurt over me."

"No," Joe said. "He's just like that."

"I mean, this proves it. Why did Tom demand I be given to him? You gotta see the implications."

Joe made a frustrated noise and glanced in the rearview mirror at Tommy who bopped to the music and who met Joe's eyes with an intensity and concentration that showed his understanding. Glancing at his older brother, Joe said quietly, "Pete, here's the problem. Last night Colonel Hunter told Ben that—" Joe shook his head. "You say it."

"He told me last night, I'm not his kid. I'm Tom's."

"No."

"He said it."

"Oh, I believe he said it," Peter explained.

"It makes sense," Ben said. "There are too many clues."

"Then why do you live with him?" Peter said.

"Different mothers."

"But," Peter shook his head. "It doesn't fit."

Joe said, "I won't believe it."

"Look, I know it's hard for you," Ben said, "I know it means Tom is not who you thought he was. That makes this hard for the whole world. Me, too. I got what I wanted, I'm his, I'm Tom's, and now that ruins everything."

"Yeah," Peter said, the implications seeming to scroll down his expression.

"Plus, the worst is, Tom let me stay there with *him*—that *jerk*—while I could have been here and then I wouldn't be so messed up and I wouldn't be so confused."

"Bonnie Jean," Joe said, realizing.

"Yeah," Ben said, angrily. "Yeah. What do you think I've been getting at?"

"You didn't know," Joe murmured, his voice weighted with compassion and horror. "Not your fault."

"Yeah, but she's the one I want. I'll never love anyone else."

"He's still our dad," Peter said. "And if it's true, he's sorry now. Especially that he let Ben out of his hands. I mean, don't you think that explains the grief on his face when he looks at Ben sometimes?"

"No," Joe said. "That's because he knows Ben's a liar and his father's a violent creep."

"Maybe. But either way he's still the same honest, compassionate man we respect so much."

"I don't believe it. I *won't* believe it."

25

HER exam finished, binomial irregularities or whatever the heck they were explained, Bonnie Jean was dropped off at home and told by her father to rest. But she had been at home, and alone, for too many days and didn't want to rest. And there was nothing to do. Last night, waiting for Tom and Joe and Tommy to get home, between frantic phone calls, waiting again for word of Ben's diagnosis, she and her mother had worked off their anxieties in a whirlwind of Christmas preparations. Now the MacBride home looked like an imagined snow-touched world with the funny little Father Christmases her mother had made over the years from outgrown undershirts dyed in tea, clothing them in capes made from her children's torn woolly jackets. Remnants of clean, odd socks covered the Santas' little feet. Despite their scrappy origin, the Santas sold swiftly at the store, remaining in constant demand. But their home housed the originals now displayed whimsically and attended by cunning elves, soft-eyed deer and laughing lambs. She and her mother had put the Christmas tree up and it waited now to be decorated if ever the entire family was together again in the living room.

No one had slept much. All night, the house had that considerate feeling of everyone lying still and awake waiting for news that the loved one feels better. Bonnie Jean waited to hear Ben's footstep on the stairs knowing he would not submit to a hospital bed for an entire night. Calls to his cell phone buzzed endlessly. This morning—what had he been trying to tell her? With Ben, deep waters churned above that perfect composure; every gesture a subtle clue.

And now, she was alone and ineffective again. Bonnie Jean found herself in Joe's room and then went into the closet and opened the hidden door that led to attic stairs. She looked for photograph albums that might show the time when her parents still claimed Ben's parents as friends.

Her mother, creative, always making something, did not like organizing pictures. Aunt Beth did an album a year for Laurie but the other pictures stood in shoeboxes. Not knowing what she was looking for, she was flipping through two boxes of memories of her parents' early years when a picture caught her eye. It was taken on Tom's birthday. Tom was bending over a birthday cake helping Peter cut a slice. Beside Grannie and Gramps stood her mother with a tiny Joe swaddled in a blue blanket in her arms. Bonnie Jean put the picture aside and flipped through the box for more.

Back further in the stack a wedding picture stopped her. The picture was taken inside, the wedding party standing before an altar under arches of stone the color of butter. Light streamed in the tall arched windows and touched the bride's blond head. Bonnie Jean recognized her mother first, standing to the right of the slim, elegant bride. Beside her were two middle-aged women, but only one smiled. The groom looked familiar. Squinting in the dim attic light, Bonnie Jean brought the photograph up close to her eyes and then gasped. Yes, the groom was Colonel Hunter. But he was young and slim and tan with a smoldering beauty she saw had been polished to a bright shine in Ben. She flipped it over. *Katie's wedding, Beaune, France*, had been written in her mother's handwriting. The photograph had been printed in 1975.

In the next hour, Bonnie Jean found a packet of letters, all written by Katie—Katie of the broken teapot, she surmised. She also found a stack of pictures of Ben as a baby. These were clipped to the front of a thick, shabby manila envelope that held pages and pages of letters and documents written in obtuse legal language. As a baby, Ben was adorable; she saw in the pictures the yearning already present in his blue eyes, the strong arch of those eyebrows, the mouth waiting to speak.

Shivering, legs stiff, she gathered up her finds and stood. This is when she saw on the floor an envelope with what looked like Ben's handwriting the word *Laurie*. Bonnie Jean picked it up. She hesitated, then opened it. Two pictures and a folded piece of paper fell out. A note written on a small card decorated with a branch of gold apples read:

Dearest Laurie,

I can never thank you enough for your kindnesses great and small. How does one thank a friend—a sister really—for saying yes to my request that you mother my little son while I'm hospitalized. I will never know how you had the time to finish that gorgeous quilt for my little one. And to take the time to sit with me here in the hospital when you are looking after two infants and caring for that precocious toddler!

I do so enjoy hearing you tell all the funny and endearing things each of the boys are doing. But hearing about your dreams and goals helps me to look up, to dream of the future myself. Thank you for that gift especially. In my mind's eye, I can see your little quilt store. Uncle Gregen and I have talked about it and we would like to help you bring this to life, as you and Tom joined hands with us to bring my son safely to birth. Uncle Gregen has purchased for you Rising Sun's building. Now you can make it your own as you have time—a quilt store that is a refuge for the poor and poor in spirit. You are and always will be my hero, dearest Laurie.

Love,
Katie

One photograph showed Katie sitting on an elegant sofa with Joe, a smiling, sparkly-eyed infant sitting beside her, and Peter, a huge-eyed toddler, on her other side patting Katie's round, pregnant tummy.

The other photograph showed Katie holding her newborn baby. Along the white margin of the photograph, Bonnie Jean's mother had written, *Katie counting baby's toes*. Bonnie Jean saw the coloboma in Katie's eyes. Thin slices divided her pool-blue irises, but one of the baby's eyes was whole, the other eye was notched with a keyhole shaped pupil. Bonnie Jean's breath caught. "Oh, this is the problem," she said aloud.

Downstairs, the house felt chilled. Cold air rolled off the windowpanes and Bonnie Jean wondered when the house had been so empty. She got Ben's backpack and carefully slid the folder, stuffed now with all the pictures of interest, behind his chemistry book. She sat the backpack on the table, its zipper open, its contents visible to her. She circled the table once. She heard the urge, felt the desire to read his journal somewhere between her heart and her fingertips, which tingled now with an itch only the journal's leather would ease.

Turning abruptly, she put the kettle on—this her mother's solution to any trouble. The water heating, she tried to distract herself by sweeping out the fireplace that flowed with wispy gray ashes. Then she built a fire, stalling, but when the tea had steeped to that gorgeous chestnut brown and the fire crackled in the hearth beside the lonely kitchen table, she wrapped up in one of her mother's quilts, took her tea and opened Ben's journal to read.

26

SNOW fell in fast batches from rushing gray clouds as Joe sped away from the courthouse. Despite Tommy's muffled music, Ben dozed, waking whenever Joe braked and the slowing momentum of the car thrust him forward, putting pressure on his side. When Joe turned left onto Lake Street, the car slid a bit on the wet road. Waiting in the courtroom had given Joe a sense of peace. Though he would have liked to call his father, he felt certain he was doing the right thing, going to Gregen's house seeking answers. At least Ben was safe. Joe glanced at Ben's face restless in sleep, understanding his need to believe what Joe felt sure was Max Hunter's lie. And if Joe were honest, Tom's unique love for Ben suggested this. It was true that his parents welcomed all sorts of kids, fed them, helped them with homework, but not even Jeff had come close to provoking that certain look of tender care from his parents, none had so deftly suggested family membership as Ben had.

"We should probably find a weather report." Peter said from the backseat.

"Tommy probably knows the weather," Joe said to the boy, meeting his eyes in the mirror. Tommy lifted one side of the earphones and whispered to Joe, "Last night they said two systems. One passing south of Baltimore with snow. This one up here they called it 'arctic cold with some snow squalls.'"

"Hmm," Joe said thinking, *So you can hear with those things on.* "Maybe it will pass. I guess we'll have to hurry."

Ben opened his eyes. "See the X pattern the snow is making?" Ben said. Joe looked and nodded. The flakes were smaller and seemed to be falling in alternating streams making an X. "That means it's cold and it's going to snow for awhile."

"How do you know that?" Joe laughed at him fondly, eyes scanning to see if anyone else in the car shared his relief in this bit of normalcy—Ben reciting some odd fact he'd read.

"I read a book on snow once." Ben's eyes went far away, Joe knew, remembering the book.

"What else did you learn?" Tommy asked.

Ben scanned the sky as if he could read it. "If that southern storm you mentioned stalls out over the ocean it could generate a lot of snow. How big was it on the radar?"

"Big. It looked like a big swirling puddle of spilled milk."

Sitting up and stretching, Peter said, "You turn right up here, Joe."

"I remember, Pete. Thanks."

Snow lay in an even blanket over the rolling lawn, made puffed coverings of white on the manicured bushes, sat atop the lanterns burning now in the dimmed light of day. Oddly, the sidewalks and steps were wet but clear of snow, suggesting Gregen's efficient, hard-working presence. The boys hurried out of Ben's car, Peter and Joe pulling Ben out by his arms so he didn't have to crunch his abdominal muscles. Joe ran to knock on the front door while Peter helped Ben up the steps. While they waited, knocking every few minutes, Tommy walked down the driveway, backpack on his shoulder. Peter was peering into the windows, Joe knocking again, when Tommy walked back.

"Since nobody's home, let's look for the entrance to the Underground Railroad tunnels. Uncle Gregen says he's got a few entrances on his property."

"*Uncle* Gregen *says*?" Joe came down the steps.

"Yeah," Tommy pulled a new digital camera out of his backpack. "I called him yesterday to tell him thanks for sending this. He's not home. He's going to our house for Christmas."

"Wait," Joe said. "Back up."

"He sent you a digital camera?" Peter said. "And he's going to our house for Christmas? Why didn't you tell us when we decided to drive up here?" Peter gestured around them at the snow falling in sheets.

"You didn't ask."

"Tell us everything you know," Joe threatened.

"Mom hit it off with Uncle Gregen's wife, Aunt Sibilla, and she taught Mom how to cook and sew and all the stuff Mom likes so much. And when Mom was afraid because things were bad at home, she stayed here. They took her to Europe bunches of times and Uncle Gregen paid for her college and invested in Eight Hands Around after his wife died in some accident. In her memory. And if you want or need anything, you just have to ask Uncle Gregen and he ships it to you. I told him Dad's too careful to buy the new stuff we want."

"If he's not here," Joe said, "let's go."

"I need the bathroom," Tommy said.

"You pee more than anyone I know. Just go over there."

"Not at Uncle Gregen's house," Tommy scowled at Joe.

They were standing in the driveway together now, and Ben looked around. "Wait. Tommy said 'tunnels.' I remember what Gran said about the tunnels under the house and at the Hermitage where she works. They were used for the Underground Railroad, but built for bringing water into the houses. This house is around the same age, so…" He started walking down the driveway and the MacBrides followed him. The garage was locked; Ben tried all the doors. They stood in front of the garage, looking down at the apple orchard covered now in a thickening blanket of snow. "Water would flow this way," Ben said, pointing and they went down the thick stone steps together into the apple orchard.

The orchard's lines looked neat in the snow, and they walked down the hill beneath branches frosted in white against the darkening sky. They left deep footprints now in the grass; the furrows between the row pointed toward a place where three fir trees grew from the hillside into which the stone steps had been cut. Snow covered the roots of these trees, and now lay in straight lines along the top of what looked like a line of rectangular stones cut three by four feet and placed end to end. The front face of the stones were just touched with snow and beneath them was a dark doorway. They hurried toward it.

The tunnel was dry and smelled of earth and tree roots that ran like veins in the walls. Tommy ran ahead. Lights anticipated their steps and Ben saw neatly painted wooden signs on the timbered walls. The first, GARAGE, was underscored by an arrow. The door was locked as was the next labeled PANTRY. They saw that the tunnel forked. "Let's explore," Tommy said. "We might find a bathroom…or anything." In the warm darkness, they forgot the snow and walked down and south following the tunnel's signs, past a door labeled CAREY~RING BELL, and SCHARFF~OPEN MAY TO SEPTEMBER. CALL TO ARRANGE TOUR. After this another passage intersected with stone steps that lit up as they approached. The scent was different and a gasp of cold air fell on them, drawing their attention up. The steps led to a cylinder made of stone. The sign read HEISS' WELL and was marked with a gold cross.

In another thirty yards, they came to a door that stood slightly ajar.

"No way," Joe said.

Beyond the door Gran's hermetically controlled, perfectly organized storage shelves waited. There, placed carelessly on the edge of a shelf lay a folder with Ben's name scrawled bright red in Gregen's curled hand. Ben put his hand on it, hesitated.

Peter picked it up. "It's yours, man. Read it while I take Tommy up to find that bathroom."

Ben opened it and peered at it in the half-light of the tunnel. Gregen had written:

> What I know about the accident—
> 1. While Tom and I saw to the bill, everyone else left Valley Hospital in Ella's car.
> 2. Max went through the red light at the intersection of Franklin Turnpike and E. Crescent Avenue.

3. Ella's car was hit by a van driven by Terry Pandora who did not survive the accident.
4. Eyewitnesses say that Ella's car appeared to be making a U-turn when it was hit.
5. This turned the vehicle so that Sibilla, sitting behind the driver, bore the force of the impact, breaking her pelvis and causing her death.
6. The impact was such that the car was pushed within inches of Heiss' Well.
7. Some eyewitnesses thought they saw an adult leaping from the car moments before impact.
8. No eyewitnesses saw the baby's exit from the car.
9. The puddle, at the northwest leg of Franklin Turnpike, was where Ben was found.

Note: Because he was unharmed, I've *assumed* that upon impact Ben was thrown through the sunroof, which was found open.

What I need to know—
1. Why did Max remain on the north corner of Franklin Turnpike and E. Crescent Avenue, not investigating the health of his wife or his infant son?
2. What were Max and Ella arguing about right after the accident?
3. Why did Sibilla insist I take Ben's car seat from the car?

Ben and Joe stared at the paper. They met eyes. "Whoa," Joe said. "That *was* me in the accident." Ben whispered. "My dad was driving and it killed Gregen's wife."

"Your dad didn't even go check to see if you were okay?"

"Right. Unnatural. See? And this has got to have been what messed my mom up."

Peter and Tommy rushed from the house toward them. "We'd better get going. It looks like a blizzard out there."

27

WHEN the boys passed the lettered sign HEISS' WELL, Ben and Joe explained why they had to go up and see the intersection. Looking up the steps to the patch of sky visible through the well's round opening, they saw the snow swirling in from the sky above, coating the round wall of stones on the well's west side on a wind that wailed across the open stone rim. Joe took the steps two at a time. Tommy followed, then Ben with Peter helping.

The steps ended at a plank ladder, which hurt Ben to climb; he went slowly, Peter behind him encouraging him in a voice Ben could hear beneath the rushing sound of snow splashing on them like buckets full. Peter pointed to his right. There, just to the right of the ladder in the wood rim upon which the stones of the well stood, were carved initials. The snow fell with glints of light, brightening the well, falling in the grooves carved by pairs of lovers. Following Peter's finger, Ben read, "Doug loves Katie," in bold block letters above a heart decorated with an infinity sign. "There are lots of names," Ben told him, "and probably lots of Dougs." But with a glance of his damaged blue eyes, swift in the darkness, perceptive in the half-light, he quickly read them all and did not see letters carved in hope and passion that claimed any Doug loved anyone else but an unknown Katie.

Ben had to grasp Joe's arm to get up and over the rim of the well and when they stood there, the four of them, snow falling thickly on a vocal wind, they blinked away snowflakes to stare at the intersection that had divided Ben's life from the ordinary. The roads crossed like scissors, Heiss' well at the open point of the blades. The northern fork of Franklin Turnpike ran west of East Crescent down which came the descant of the wind. "Our car was coming that way," Ben said, pointing up Franklin Turnpike. "It ran a red light so I guess the two cars hit somewhere in the middle, but our car was pushed right here, right up to this well."

"The article you showed us said you were taken from a puddle."

"It must have been over there," Tommy said, pointin behind them toward the Celery Farm beyond.

Joe said, "No, Gregen's note said the northwest corner."

"But the physics of that don't make sense," Ben said. He moved his hands as if they were the cars and fine snowflakes gathered on them.

"Good thing I asked Gregen for this, too," Tommy said, pulling a compass watch from his backpack to identify the spot.

Following the direction Ben noticed the corner anew, though he had seen it, had walked or driven by it hundreds of times. A concrete half-wall curved around the corner and was topped by a mounded, terraced garden that lay fallow now, covered in snow. A small house sat on the hill above. An elderly woman stood at the curb, leaning on a snow shovel and tossing handfuls of sand at a sidewalk quickly filling again with snow. She called to them. "Only one place you guys could've gotten into that tunnel and that's Dr. Bénet's orchard." They looked at each other, unsure of what to do. "Don't think I'll scold you. If he's visiting his uncle, I'll note the date!"

They crossed the street, footsteps showing snow to the tops of their shoes.

"May I help you with that sand?" Ben asked politely.

"You've got to be the Hunter boy…Ella's grandson."

"Yes, ma'am. Did you say 'his uncle?'"

She nodded. "I've known your great-uncle since he moved here in the sixties. I've seen you grow up. I bet you don't remember meeting me here around town, though."

"You do look familiar," Ben said, "but I don't know your name. I'm sorry." She put the bag of sand into Ben's outstretched hands. Peter took it from him.

"We drove all the way from Annapolis," Tommy said. "Have you lived here long?"

"Fifty-three years. I'm Lou Van Dyke."

"Do you remember an accident that happened here?" Joe asked.

"*The* accident?" The woman glanced at Ben. "Sure."

"We can't figure out where the puddle was," Peter said. "Dr. Bénet says it's somewhere over here. Somewhere back on this side of Franklin Turnpike." He pointed to the sidewalk, humped and cracked by the knuckle of an ancient tree root now caped in snow. Beneath this, the gutter dipped to make a deep, wet hollow. It was canoe-shaped, about four feet long and a stream of dark water pooled in its deepest part and trickled over the brim at its point into the metal grate of a storm drain. "Has that drain always been there?"

The woman glanced cautiously at Ben and, blinking the snow from her eyes, nodded. "The water gets to where you see the snow collecting there on the sides and it pools during storms or thaws or such and when its high enough it drains down the gutter. Always been that way. They tried several times to fix it, but it's the natural way of the water draining here. Maybe from this tree, the sidewalk, who knows? Water will run downhill, though, no matter what you do!" Tears sprang to her eyes and she lifted her hands reaching for Ben's face. "So you see—!"

Despite his ribs, Ben bent to her, his face showing the great compassionate tenderness that watching him, Joe thought was the one thing that might convince *anyone* that Ben belonged to Tom. She kissed his face, her hands tender flames against his cold cheeks. "I am so sorry for your loss. I've always wanted to tell you. Could never say it in front of Ella. So sorry."

"Thank you," Ben said with the restrained poise of a prince. "Do you mean Sibilla?"

"Good God, as if that wasn't enough to break your uncle's heart. You poor, poor thing."

"Did you *see* the accident?" Tommy asked. "Because I don't understand how Ben ended up here," he pointed to the spot. "If the accident was there."

"I was at my daughter's. I never saw it. But I blame Max. Sorry to speak ill of your father but there it is. He drove way too fast since he was a kid. Used to shout at him racing past when I was out here working on my garden."

"Are you sure the baby—I mean Ben," Joe said, "landed there? In *that* puddle and not somewhere else?"

"Like I said. I never saw it, but when I got home and the police cars were all over the intersection, I see the blanket, caught right there, on that corner of the grate with the melting snow water pouring down over it. I don't know how it was still there." She pointed to the storm drain. "Every time I think of that baby," she grabbed Ben's forearm, "*you* so close to danger—so I asked the police if I could take it and wash it—which I did—and then I give it to your mother," she pointed to Peter and Joe, "to fix the tear because she's the one who made it in the first place."

"How do you know who *we* are?"

"I got eyes, don't I? Laurie Davidson grew up right down the street." She pointed to the house's shadow in the swirling snow, northeast. "Didn't I see her all my life?"

"Yes, ma'am. I'm Peter. This is Joe and Tommy."

"The yellow and blue blanket?" Ben asked.

She nodded. "You kids better get going. They say this is just a squall but we know better, don't we?" She winked at Ben. Peter said, "You're right. We've got to get going, but we'll scatter this for you and I'll set the bag on the front step." Joe took her arm to walk her up her stone steps.

28

SHE had been expecting her brothers to be back long before they were supposed to give her a ride to her rehearsal. All day alone in her house, Bonnie Jean watched the snow squalls coat the ground with more than an inch of heavy white snow while she read Ben's palpable and poetic descriptions of his heartbreak. The abuse had confused and tortured his mind as much as his body, making him unable to speak about it. She had not cried; she was far too angry. She finished; the afternoon looked dark. The sky beyond the kitchen door looked like a thick, gray blanket on the tops of the tall trees that edged their meadow now white with snow. Bonnie Jean decided to try to get an early ride to her concert before it was canceled due to the weather and she lost her excuse to be on USNA grounds.

Bonnie Jean had called her mother, but the frantic sound of the shop forbid her from confiding what she'd read. Instead, she called the school; her father was in a meeting. She called again later; her father was out on an errand. She called her Aunt Beth's cell phone and in five minutes Aunt Beth was in the driveway.

Grabbing the garment bag, she thrust in Ben's diary with the pictures and notes she'd found.

Aunt Beth was talkative. She had purchased a new pool table for Uncle

Doug and it had just been "installed." She'd put a big bow on the door to the game room and forbid anyone from entering lest they snoop before Doug could get home. He was stuck at West Point in a snowstorm that was supposed to last all night and wrap back around maybe, Aunt Beth hoped so, giving them a white Christmas, which she always felt was so *romantic*.

"Does it ever bother you about Uncle Doug and his first love?"

"That's a funny question."

"Sorry. But I'm in the first love stage."

"There's something sweet about first love and even better if it lasts, I say."

"You had a first love. Do you wish it had lasted?"

"I used to. For Flip's sake and my sake. But Doug is so wonderful and I can't imagine life with anyone else, now."

"But do you begrudge him his first love?"

"Of course not. She helped make him the person he is."

"What happened to her?"

Beth looked at Bonnie Jean now, all the frantic Christmas excitement gone. "Katie? You want me to tell you Katie's story?" Bonnie Jean's breath caught. "I don't know if I should, sweetie. You should ask your mom."

"That's okay, Aunt Beth," she said. "I'll do that. I'll ask Mom." She picked at her thumbnail. The name confirmed what she already knew.

When Joe came down the steps, the others stood in the snow staring at the intersection. Ben glanced at Joe and said, "If I landed here, I would have had to come out of the car way back there." He pointed north on Franklin Turnpike, his hand shaking, "If the car was hit back here, head on, I would have been thrown forward, making it possible for me to land in this puddle. But we know the car was hit in the middle of the intersection. And we know I did land here. So there must have been some other sort of force that thrust me back here. Another car, hitting again when the car spun toward the well? Nothing like that in the notes. And I don't think the wind is strong enough to send a baby back over there."

"Unless it's like today," Peter said, shielding his eyes from the stinging onslaught of driven snow.

Joe put a protective arm around Ben's shoulders. "We have to get going. Ben's shivering too much. I bet that hurts, too."

"I don't think he can make it back down that well," Peter said. "It was tough going getting up."

"I can do it."

"No. You and I will walk up toward Gregen's. It's not far. Pete, you and Tommy run through the tunnel, get the car and pick us up." Joe turned Ben to the north and glancing down the street, guided him to cross it.

"Keys, Joe," Peter called. As he rushed Ben across the intersection, Joe tossed the keys back over his shoulder. He heard them plunk to the ground and glanced back to see Peter fish them out of the hollow beside the storm drain.

"Another inch and you would have tossed my keys right down that drain," Ben said, then stopped walking. From where he stood in the middle of Franklin Turnpike, two yards from the center of the crossed roads marked by the traffic light above rocking on its wires in the wind, Ben turned to look back.

"Don't see Peter's perfect hands fail often, huh?" Joe said with an aching tenderness, following Ben's concentrated glances.

Ben said, "If the car was here where we are now when I—" Ben explained, vaguely, eyes traveling again and again the distance to the hollow by the storm drain. Beside him, Joe felt Ben stiffen. "Then it went two yards or so forward, started making a u-turn before it was hit."

"What?" Joe said.

"I can imagine it, like careening to the intersection, hurtling out of control. He ran the red light, the other guy probably couldn't stop." Nudging Joe forward into the center of the intersection, Ben gestured as if Joe could also see what seemed so clear in Ben's mind. "Here. See? It had to have been hit smack in the center of the intersection to have ended up by the well." Ben stood still, staring through the descending snow as if he could see his history written in its pattern.

"Come on," Joe said, once again putting an arm around Ben's shoulders and leading him forward up the hill.

When Aunt Beth stopped in front of the chapel, Bonnie Jean told her she'd walk over to her mother's store when rehearsal was done. She hurried up the snow-coated steps and pushed open the towering bronze doors. Hiding just inside, she watched until the car drove away. She draped her garment bag over the back pew, unzipping it to take out Ben's journal, yanking it back up until it caught on her dress. "Shoot," she whispered into the echoing light of the mellow building. "Aw, who cares about a stupid dress," she told herself and left it there to hurry out the side door toward the alley that ran along the King George Street wall.

Ben and Joe turned, hearing Ben's pink Fiat Spider crunching through the snow behind them. Peter tried to halt, but the car slipped past them, finally sliding to a stop as Peter pumped the brakes and coaxed it into the mouth of a driveway only a few feet from the intersection. Tommy and Joe had to push the car back out into the street before they squeezed into the back, Tommy taking the smaller space behind Peter. Despite Ben's protests, Joe squeezed his arm between the door and the front seat, to work the lever lowering the seat until Ben was lying as flat as possible. They could hear the wind now, crying at the edges of the window to be let in, and the snow's icy pings were as rapid as the spray of a hose.

"Come on. This is rough going," Peter said as if coaching the car. The tires crunched along the snow. He glanced at Ben whose brow showed the pallor of pain and then at Joe in the mirror.

"Do you have Tylenol in your stuff, Pete?"

"No. What am I, a girl with a pack of Tylenol in my purse?"

Joe shrugged out of his jacket and put it across Ben's chest. "I'm not taking your jacket from you," Ben said as Joe motioned for Tommy to hand him Peter's. "Shut up," Joe said, squeezing his torso between the two front seats to lay Peter's coat across Ben's knees. "You'll feel better if you stop shivering. Think about it. Every time you shiver it irritates those breaks."

"I think the motion of the car hurts him a little, too," Peter said.

"Do we have any food?" Tommy asked.

Peter reached into the space beside Ben's feet, grabbed the bakery bags there, and swung them back to Tommy. "Three bottles of apple juice, a ton of Christmas cookies. Two croissant sandwiches and four apples. That and half of Ben's hot chocolate. We're set for a while."

"Go easy, Tommy," Joe said. "We've got a long trip and I don't want to risk stopping and getting stuck."

Stamping her feet to keep them from numbing, Bonnie Jean went over the things she knew about Colonel Hunter. She hadn't been able to find him at the Officer's Club or in his office. The Hunters' quarters were dark; no one was home. Swimming—Ben had said his dad liked to swim. She took off running again, the cold air seemed to stop part way into her lungs so that when she got to the natatorium near the entrance at Gate One, she was coughing and her nose was streaming.

Bonnie Jean found a restroom and got herself together. She hid in the stalls and prayed. Now she felt the sweltering indoor heat, but reasoned she ought to take her coat with her. She held Ben's journal in the crook of her arm and draped the coat over it to hide it.

She found the pool by following the scent of chlorine, opened the door and stepped into a room that was warm as a bath, the moist air stinging with chemicals. Two elderly men swam laps in the Olympic-sized pool. And there was Colonel Hunter, lying on the wet tiles like a beached whale. A lifeguard stood over him. "It's been a half hour since you threw up, Colonel. You can go in, but I wouldn't advise it. We can't have you throwing up in the pool."

Max sat up, rubbed his face. "I made it to the head, didn't I?" Bonnie Jean noted in dismay how well his now absent uniform hid all that bulged out over the tight little Speedo he wore. She squared her shoulders and marched forward. "Colonel Hunter?" she called.

He saw her and for an instant, his face brightened, then he looked flustered. He plopped into the pool, ducking down up to his neck. She edged toward the pool.

"Missy," the lifeguard said, "you got your shoes on, what are you doing here?"

"I'll just be a minute."

"Do you know this young woman, Colonel Hunter?"

Max sputtered, but Bonnie Jean said, "I'm his son's girlfriend." She stood at the end of the pool, ten feet from where Max squatted in the water. "I need to talk to you, Colonel Hunter, sir." She faked a disarming smile.

Max, flushing red, flicked his hand to dismiss the lifeguard who turned in a huff and took his chemical vials over to the diving tank. "You kinda caught me in the middle of something, sweetie."

"Um, Colonel Hunter, I don't know how to say this to you but I have to say it." She straightened her shoulders and when she spoke again, her voice carried its full volume. "I've been reading Ben's journal."

"Ben's what?"

"Ben's written down every single time you kicked him or punched him."

"Hey!" Max hissed, looking around. The lifeguard, his shoulders hunched over the blue waters of the diving tank, did not look around. "You don't say things like that!"

She tossed her head. "I read it and I want you to know that Ben was a gift to you. He's great. He's thoughtful and he's kind and loyal and beautiful and you had the chance to love him and help him and you betrayed him."

"I thought more of you than to let your father put you up to a low trick like this." He put one hand on the edge of the pool and slid his hand toward her. "Your dad wants to make me look bad."

"No. This is about how you hurt Ben."

"Ben. Right. Your half brother," he was whispering, moving closer and she found herself wanting to lean in to hear. "Did your father tell you that? Is that written in your little book? A nice little description of how he screwed my wife and sent her back to me with his little brat growing like a tumor inside her? No. No one knows about that."

Immediately, the air seemed poisonous, her mind stunned, but Bonnie Jean felt something peculiar in the way Colonel Hunter was watching her. She knew he was watching for the moment that his words entered her heart, piercing her clean, strong love and befouling it. She saw the vicious intent in his eyes, the flare of his nostrils, the sucked-in set of his lips determined to wound. The expression looked familiar; it had leapt to her mind again and again all day as she read and now Ben's words echoed in her mind and with their haunting poetry defined Max's expression. This man was ruthless; he had already told Ben this lie and it had robbed Ben of all clean light and peace. Her mind cleared. She feigned a look of utter disillusionment to test him. Max's eyes narrowed, a smug smile formed. He despised her with eyes that moved in slow, leering scrutiny. He turned away, began a deliberate breaststroke away from her.

She followed him. She stayed a body's length behind him, reasoning that if he came after her, she'd have time to turn and run. Screwing up her courage, Bonnie Jean opened the book and called after him. "Listen to this. Ben wrote this:

> We had my birthday party anyway even though I had a black
> eye and my lip was so sore I couldn't smile. Mom stayed right
> next to me during the whole party so I couldn't tell anyone what
> really happened..."

Max swam faster, splashing. Bonnie Jean breathed in and projected, her big voice resounding in the heavy, damp air. "Listen:

> And then Dad punched me right in the stomach. I didn't see it
> coming. I threw up...I told Gran about all three times Dad hit me
> this month and she said not to say anything and to try to under-
> stand what he's been through..."

Bonnie Jean read another entry, then another. Max stopped, rose up in the water. He stood, his hand groping for the side. She stopped walking, terrified, furious. She flipped the pages to the end and when he turned around, moving toward her through the water, his big, bare self menacing with shoulders drawn up, elbows out as if to grab her and silence her, she backed away one step, then showed the page where Ben had made a bloody lip print. "This happened this year," she said. "You hit him and he lies about it because your wife said she'd kill herself if he tells. That's sick." She was bellowing now, her voice as big and full as if she'd swallowed the sun. "And I'm gonna stop you, you coward, you...you criminal."

He leapt out of the pool, his speed and agility startling her. She stepped back. He tottered on the edge of the slick tile, speaking with a raspy, out-of-breath fury, "You want the whole world to know about your father? You threaten me, I'll ruin him."

She wrinkled up her nose but could not stop the nervous laughter that was her first response to fear. "You're afraid of me and I'm fifteen. You know you're wrong, that's why!" She backed away, her steps quick and frantic. "You can only hurt Ben because he loves you and every time he hopes you'll change. You can't hurt anybody else." She saw his fist form, she saw his body tense to lunge for her and she yelled, "You're just a fat, drunk wuss."

She twirled on her toes, leapt away and ran. As she ran, Bonnie Jean was aware that the two elderly men had abandoned their workouts and stood in their lanes, shaking the water out of their ears and looking confused. As she pelted out of there, she saw the lifeguard moving and heard the splat of Colonel Hunter falling, felt the earthquake of his big body shudder the floor behind her.

She banged the door open and leapt out into the cold fresh air. Sprinting through a fine, hard snowfall, she ran, sure-footed, leaping over the ice slicks nearly hidden in that short time with drifts of cold snow, the air too cold, unfriendly. She pressed the book to her side, her coat flapping from one arm. She didn't look back, she ran for the sanctuary of the chapel. Would he dare step foot there?

29

TRAFFIC on Route 17 inched south as the snow gathered on the road and covered the strip malls beside it, whirling in white fury from a dark gray sky. Ben's eyes were closed, but Joe knew he was not sleeping. He was thinking and still shivering. Joe touched his forehead finding him too cool to even suspect a fever. He reached forward from the backseat and trained the heating vents on Ben. To their right, Joe saw a lighted traffic sign that posted the news of an accident on the Turnpike. "Look," he whispered to Peter.

"Oh, no."

Radio reports of the snowfall conflicted, but after they heard two stations claim that the storm had stalled off the coast they reasoned that driving inland would mean less snow. "We can use Tommy's compass, go west, then south," Peter said. "It was supposed to go south of Baltimore. It probably did that and now it's hanging around off the coast up here."

"We're so used to seeing it on the TV radar," Joe mourned shaking his head. "Sure wish we still had that cell phone."

"So sorry," Ben whispered.

"Try to sleep."

The first five miles of Route 80 were okay. It was snowing, but not so much; fewer cars, no visible accidents. Peter got off at the first exit to get gas. Joe climbed between the seats and out Peter's door. Between them, the boys had fifteen dollars. Peter took ten for gas and Joe went into the shabby convenience market. There he bought Tylenol, a travel toothbrush, and toothpaste and begged the girl for a free cup of ice water. At the payphone, he dialed home with a glance at his watch. It was four o'clock. Even if the roads had been clear, they wouldn't make it home for Jeannie's concert as his parents expected. Joe left a message on their answering machine. "Um, hi. It's Joe. Instead of coming straight home from the courthouse, we...

uh…we went up to see Gregen for some good reasons which I'll explain later, and…uh…it's snowing here." He looked up then, up to the northeast from where they'd come and he saw the nearly black clouds rolling with the power of the incoming tide, the snow line visible as a descending veil. "We're taking 80 West and then going south. We probably won't make it in time for the concert, but we didn't want you to worry. Okay. Gotta go. Love ya."

He sprinted to the car calling Peter's name and pointing. "That's what they meant by wrapping around!" For seven minutes they outran the front and then felt the icy rattle of the wind wooshing past them, clearing the air in the car like a vacuum would and the snow hit the back window, then rushed over them and they were in it again.

Bonnie Jean slipped on the chapel steps and fell hard. For an instant she couldn't draw breath and when she did she sucked it in too quickly and the cold hurt all the way down her throat. The clouds above dumped snow and the wind swirled around her ankles and up the steps. She scrambled to her feet finding that she still clutched Ben's journal close to her chest. She thrust her arms into her coat and shoved the book into the inner pocket where it settled against her side. Buttoning her coat, she went carefully now up the slick, snowy steps hand outstretched to push open those sturdy bronze doors that had always meant staid ceremony to her. But the chapel door was locked. She panicked, looked back and saw Colonel Hunter chugging toward the far corner of Porter Road. Then she noticed the sign taped on the chapel door; the letters running like black tears in the wet of the snow: CONCERT CANCELED.

Bonnie Jean knew that if she cut diagonally across the space beyond the chapel, she would end up at Gate Three. Once she was outside the Academy's gates, she thought she'd be safe from Colonel Hunter and it was not an overly long walk to her mother's store.

As she jogged in approach, Bonnie Jean could make out the snow-swirled shapes of two marines closing the big iron gates at Maryland Avenue. She sprinted toward them, calling "Wait!" They seemed to hear and switched positions to push the gates open again. Bonnie Jean sped up and slipped, hitting the ground hard and sliding into the street, unable to stop. The approaching Volvo lurched, swerved and skidded, coming to a stop with the front left tire just inches from Bonnie Jean's hand. The marines helped her up. "Are you okay, miss?"

"I'm fine. I slipped, I'm sorry, but I'm in a hurry."

A door slammed and Bonnie Jean saw Donna Hunter hurry from the car to her side. "I thought I recognized you! Are you all right, Bonnie Jean?"

"I am. I'm so sorry. I slipped." She glanced back over her shoulder but could only see the vague gray outline of the chapel in the distance.

"What are you doing out in this? Let me give you a ride." She took Bonnie Jean's arm. "Are you sure you're not injured?"

"Ma'am, we can call the ambulance. It'll be here in a jiffy," the marine said.

"Thank you," Bonnie Jean smiled at him. Would he protect her from his boss? She tried to listen for the sound of heavy sloshing feet, but heard only the muffle of snow and the skirl of the wind. "I just need to get to my mother's store. My concert was canceled and if she hears it on the radio, she'll be worried."

"I'll drive you, Bonnie Jean."

"Oh," Bonnie Jean said, hesitating.

Donna met her eyes. "You don't trust me."

Again, her nervous laugh bubbled up. "You're pointing in the other direction."

"Ben's told you."

"No! He would never! He'd protect you no matter what. It's just that Joe and I guessed."

"Did you see Ben this morning? He left the hospital last night and we've had no word."

"He's with Joe."

"Ma'am, I'm going to have to ask you to move your car."

"Let me give you a lift, Bonnie Jean, please."

"No, that's okay. You're almost home anyway." Bonnie Jean gestured, pointing.

Donna nodded, circled her car and got in. She pulled away into the snow curtain. The marine held back the impatient trio of cars so that Bonnie Jean could step carefully across the street, and when she was half-way down the block, she heard a car purr to a stop beside her. It was Donna Hunter. She leaned across Ben's grandmother to speak out the passenger window. "I'm pointed in the right direction now, can I give you a lift to Eight Hands Around?"

Bonnie Jean saw the hopeful smile in her eyes and when the little boy opened the back window, she saw that only Keith and Tim were in the backseat. "Thank you," she said and got in with the little boys.

"You remember my mother-in-law."

"Yes, I do. How are you, Mrs. Hunter?"

"I think it's foolhardy driving out again in this weather. We just made it home. Really, Donna!"

"She is the daughter of an old friend."

"I know who she is," Ella whispered loudly. "That's the point."

Donna drove slowly and skillfully. "Are you feeling any bumps or pain now that it's been a few minutes?"

With a laugh Bonnie Jean said, "Really, I'm fine and it is so nice of you to drive me."

"We saw you before," Keith said.

"You're Ben's girlfriend, right?" Tim asked.

"Yes, I am. We love each other and we want to get married some day."

Donna looked back at Bonnie Jean using the rearview mirror. "Ben will make a wonderful husband some day."

Gran snorted. Donna said, "I suppose Ben will come home to your house tonight and when he does, could someone please call us? I've been so worried."

"Of course."

"He ought to answer that cell phone I got him."

"He's a little...I guess he's feeling a little betrayed right now, Mrs. Hunter," Bonnie Jean said. "You know, since Thanksgiving."

"I don't know what you mean."

"Oh, um...try to put yourself in his shoes for a minute. He always told himself you'd stick up for him if you saw his father hit him and when you didn't...well, you can imagine how bad he felt."

In the shocked silence, Bonnie Jean studied both women's faces. Donna met her eyes briefly in the reflection of the mirror and said, quietly, her voice trembling, "Ben has every right to feel betrayed."

Tim tugged on Bonnie Jean's coat. "We're not allowed to talk about this."

"Shh!" Keith said and poked Tim.

"Actually, boys," Donna said, "Remember, I told you? Gran and Dad and I are going to talk to Ben. For Christmas, we're going to make our house different."

"I just hope there's more cookies," Tim said.

"Donna, hush. She is not family."

"I won't hush, Ella. She knows anyway. Don't you, Bonnie Jean?"

"Yes, Mrs. Hunter. I do know. Not because Ben says much. He's too loyal. But Joe and I have seen his bruises. We knew something was wrong. And then today, I read his diary—he left it at my house. It's all in there. All written down."

"Ben has a diary?" Donna asked.

"Those stupid journals. I never should have let Gregen give him one. They cause only grief!"

"He only writes what's true in there," Keith said. "Mom said we're going to start telling the truth."

"Not while I'm here!" Ella shouted. "Not after all I've done to protect my son."

The tires crunched on the street thick with snow. Ella snapped open her handbag. "I don't care what you say. I'm having a smoke."

"Not in here, Ella."

"Yes in here." She drew out a cigarette and flicked at the lighter.

"Gran," Keith whined. "Mom said no."

She opened the sunroof a crack, inviting a spray of tiny white flakes, opened her window a bit, too. Donna warned her, "Be courteous to us, Ella."

"And who is courteous to me? You pick this girl up and drag me back out in the snow. You bad-mouth my only child and I'm supposed to sit here and take it?"

"You're only feeling bad because you know you're wrong," Bonnie Jean said. "Look how much happier your daughter-in-law is now that she's come to terms with what has to change. That takes courage but it's also really good for you."

Donna said quietly, "Do you have his book with you? Can you read me some of it?"

"Oh, for God's sake," Ella snarled.

Bonnie Jean took the book from her inner pocket, opened it. "This will hurt to hear it."

"I need to hear it."

She kept her voice firm and even and read the three passages she'd read to Max earlier. Tim sneaked his hand to hold the edge of Bonnie Jean's coat; Ella filled the car with smoke. Keith begged for air. Ella opened the sunroof another two inches. Cold air dropped in and pushed the smoke down into their eyes.

"Thank you," Donna said. "You can stop now. We're nearly to your mother's store."

"I would let you have it to read," Bonnie Jean said, "but I can't."

"No. It's Ben's," her voice broke; a sob rose painfully in her throat.

"Watch the damn road," Ella snapped.

"Please, Gran, the smoke," Keith whined.

Ella slammed the sunroof fully open. "That make you happy?"

"Please be nice;" Donna said. "This is so hard."

"See what you've done?" Ella said, turning toward Bonnie Jean. "She's a mess and she's driving us. We'll all get killed. Now give me that book before you make it worse."

"No."

Ella stabbed at Bonnie Jean with her cigarette, aiming for her knee.

"Stop!" Donna screamed. Bonnie Jean thrust out her hand to block the fiery blows but Ella stabbed rapidly, hitting her sleeve, singeing the wool. Donna stomped on the brakes. Ella stabbed again at Bonnie Jean's knee. Donna slapped at her mother-in-law's hand. The car swerved, horns sounded and Bonnie Jean swung Ben's diary up at the cigarette, batting it out the sunroof. But Ella grabbed the diary, yanked it out of Bonnie Jean's hand and flung it out into the snowstorm. The car careened sideways down Annapolis Street, coming to a stop beneath the blinking, yellow light across from Eight Hands Around. Behind them two cars hit.

Twilight fell on the boys in that eerie way it does when the air is boiling with white snow. The wind roared above, around them, and Peter, exhausted, said he was reluctant to stop. Ben's eyes moved beneath closed lids and Tommy stretched, awakening.

Joe stared at Gregen's list in the folder Ben had taken from the tunnel. Tommy sat up and leaned toward the folder. He pointed to the last item on the list. "They didn't always make kids sit in car seats, back in the day. We saw a video on it when we had a sub. But they found out a kid loose in a car is like a torpedo or a bullet—because of the momentum. A loose kid keeps going when the crash happens and if somebody's in the way, too bad."

"Tommy," Peter said. "Think of Ben's feelings."

"Three people died," Joe said, with a glance at Tommy. "Let's remember that as we discuss this."

"I'm just saying, he couldn't have been in the car seat," Tommy said. "Ben must have left the car before they got to the intersection."

"Babies don't just *leave* cars," Peter said with uncharacteristic sharpness. Joe looked up. Snow fell so thickly that Peter's visibility diminished each foot they traveled.

"No," Ben said, opening his eyes. "Of course not."

The car fell silent, the boys watched whiteness fall on the white car and the white road. Tommy said, "I have a couple of theories about how Ben was ejected."

"I know how it happened, Tommy," Ben said, pushing with his elbow so he could sit up as Joe flipped the lever to raise Ben's seat. "I've known since we stood out there in the middle of the intersection." Ben glanced at Peter. "Remember when you were pumping my grandmother for information about this and she tried to convince you that—somehow the diaper bag flew out of the car before the accident?"

"Sure. Something was really wrong."

"It was like she had to cover something up. She assumed you saw something and she wanted to define that as the diaper bag. It was a warm day. We know that because the snow was melting. The sunroof would have been open because my father hates the smoke smell in my grandmother's car. Something flew out the sunroof. Not the diaper bag. Of course not. A lost bag is nothing to be upset about, to lie about. That something was me. And the only way I could have gotten out *before* the accident is completely obvious—" his voice broke. "He threw me out." Ben lifted his arm and flicked his wrist. "Like that. No one could stop him because no one would expect it."

Ben heard the air trap in the MacBrides' hopeful chests. Ben hid his face under his open palm. From there he said, "Gran must have been driving because she made such a big deal about the fact that *he* was driving. You have to be able to translate the language of lying. That's supposed to give him an alibi in case anyone figures out that I was thrown out of the car *before* the accident—on purpose. Gran probably freaked out, ran the red light, and the other people died. I lived." Ben took a shaky breath. "I lived, so he's spent the next sixteen years trying to kill me."

Gripping the wheel his knuckles frozen white, Peter's eyes blurred and reflexively he stepped on the brake. The back wheels skipped and swerved. He tried to turn into the spin, not realizing his foot was pressing hard on the brake until Joe yelled, "You're braking!" But the car spun, careened off the road between huge cedar trees, up over a berm, across a stretch of snow and slid nose first into a steep, snow-filled ditch.

30

BONNIE Jean saw immediately that Donna was alert, unharmed and angry. The boys, though crying, seemed okay. She climbed over Tim, pushing open his door and stumbled into the snow. The crashed cars blocked the road and their passengers were getting out, slamming doors as they bent to inspect the damage, eyes squinting in the wind-whipped snow.

"Everyone all right?" she called, running toward the cars, but she was looking for the mark of a splash in the snow, for Ben's book. She heard the whine of a police siren approaching from the station on Taylor Avenue, one block down.

One angry lady held her hand over her cell phone and said, "Did something fly out of that car?"

"Yes! Did you see where it went?"

"Do you know you caused this accident?"

"Are you hurt?" Bonnie Jean asked.

"No. My car is wrecked." She gestured. "And my dog peed on the back seat."

"Oh, gosh," Bonnie Jean said with a hasty glance at the frustrated, freezing people around her.

Behind her, she heard Donna's raised voice. Bonnie Jean tried to imagine where the book would have fallen and she looked left. There it was, near the curb, its pages bleating in the wind. On the down-facing pages, the ink ran into the gathering snow. Carefully, she blotted it on her coat sleeve, then slipped it back inside her pocket.

Bonnie Jean ran back to Donna's car. "Do you want me to take the boys to my mother's store?"

"Are you okay?" Donna said, her makeup running in inky streams down her face.

"Yes, I'm okay."

"Boys. Go with Bonnie Jean. You can warm up in her mother's store." She told Ella, who sat arms clamped down over her chest, staring straight ahead, to get out of the car.

Crossing the street, a policeman stopped Bonnie Jean, one hand on her elbow. "Were you in the accident, ma'am?"

"I was a passenger in that car. I'm just taking these kids over to my mother's store." She pointed across the street. Laurie was coming down the steps, hurrying toward her.

"That's your mother's store? You're Tom MacBride's daughter?"

"I am."

He waved to another policeman. "Help these kids across the street." To Bonnie Jean, he said, "Do you know what happened?"

She nodded and when the second policeman came to them, she put Keith and Tim's hands in his and waited until they were walking away before she confided, "The older woman tried to burn me with her cigarette and the driver tried to stop her. She swerved and couldn't stop."

"Tried to burn you?" He squinted at her. Bonnie Jean lifted up her arm, pointed at the ring of burnt wool, lifted it to his nose, which he wrinkled and drew back, nodding. "All right, then. Let me take you to your mother. Don't want you to slip and fall."

Though they were only a hundred yards from the road, the berm and the trees blocked the sound of the cars creeping along the highway. Joe and Ben, without seatbelts, were tumbled in the crash so that Ben fell forward and Joe landed between the seats. Peter got them out of the car. Joe's lip bled profusely and Ben crouched in the snow unable to stand up.

"He can't walk anywhere," Joe said. "And we're not splitting up."

Tommy remembered the flashlight in his backpack and by the time they got it, Ben had pulled himself to his feet and insisted he was okay. They trained the flashlight on him to see and the falling snow scattered its electric light around him. He managed a grim smile. "Is everybody okay?"

Tommy said, "Do you think we can dig out?"

This they tried. They dug in the dark and when the wheels were free, the MacBrides pushed. Their feet slipped and they couldn't get a foothold, so they tried to dig the snow away. Snow filled each handful they scooped. When they finally gave up, slipping and exhausted, they struggled to the top of the berm. In the distance they heard a siren, the highway now scant of traffic. Peter waved to the first car they saw. The tenth car stopped.

"Need a ride?"

"No. Our car's back there. Can you call the police or a tow truck or something when you get to a phone?"

He agreed, but to the boys it seemed doubtful. "Next person, give them our home number."

Now the cars were scarce and people waved back, but the boys reasoned that since their car was not visible, drivers thought they were playing. Finally, a car stopped. Into the window Peter thrust a gum wrapper on which he'd scribbled their home number. "Can you call our parents when you get to a phone? Tell them our car slid off the road."

"Sure you don't want a ride? I can fit two of you." The cab was stuffed with bags of laundry, the truck bed covered with a bulky tarp.

"No, we'll stay together. We'll wait in the car."

"Supposed to snow all night. Like this."

Peter hesitated. "If you could call."

In the snow-lit darkness of Ben's car, they scraped the clumps of snow off their clothes and forced the snow into the empty juice bottles, plunked it into Ben's half-drunk, cold cup of chocolate.

"We're not that far from civilization," Peter said. "We should be okay tonight. The storm can't last too long."

"It just seems so much more hilly and rural than what we normally see of New Jersey," Joe said.

"We could try to walk to see if there's an exit or a house or a restaurant or something," Ben suggested.

Peter and Joe exchanged glances, knowing that for Ben, they had stayed out in the cold flagging down cars too long. Even in the anemic flashlight, Joe had seen the blue trembling lips and had called a halt to their effort.

"I'm cold," Tommy said, his voice a little shaky.

"Make sure you've got all the snow scraped off yourself." Joe said, leaning close to peer at him.

Once in the car Peter gathered up all the food and piled it into Tommy's lap. "You're in charge of the food. Better divide it up, some for now, some for later. Okay?" Tommy nodded, counted and made four little groups of food. He set these up on the back shelf. Ben looked in the glove compartment, took out the maps, the owner's manual and found a compact first aid kit.

"I bet there was Tylenol in there the whole time!" Joe said, leaning up to see.

"Yeah," Ben nodded, finding the kit complete. He held up three packs of waterproof, strike-anywhere matches and said, "But no cell phone. I sure wish I hadn't thrown that away."

"Yeah," Peter agreed. "We'll be okay, though. We can run the car for ten minutes every hour."

In the dim night of the storm, Tom and Laurie stood shin deep in shifting snow drifts on the front porch of Eight Hands Around talking with Donna Hunter, Smitty and two other policemen. Tom was turned so that he could watch the female officer who was guarding Ella Hunter.

Smitty said, "I know she's an older woman, but the people whose cars are wrecked are not going to let this pass."

"Nor should they," Laurie said.

"With respect to her age, I can send her home with you for Christmas, Mrs. Hunter. She won't get jail time, probably just a fine, some community service and you know, ma'am, with all due respect, she's gonna need to see somebody. Talk about this."

"Yes, of course," Donna said. "I'm just so grateful that no one was hurt. Especially Bonnie Jean."

The MacBrides stayed on the porch while Smitty herded the Hunters into his big Suburban. Tim rolled down his window and swung the white box of cookies Laurie had packed for him. "Thanks for the cookies," he sang out.

"Poor, poor child," Laurie said. Tom's arm went around her and he urged her into the store where a few of the accident victims lingered still in the café waiting for their rides to make their way through the deepening snow. "Not a word from the boys."

"No doubt they're stuck in the snow somewhere."

"No doubt," Laurie said, "Doug's stuck at West Point, Gregen called to say he can't get out of Brooklyn. It's the entire East Coast."

"We have a lot to be grateful for," Tom said, drawing Laurie's attention to Bonnie Jean cheerfully serving a gingerbread latte to one of the accident victims, who was chatting with Grannie as Cara slept soundly on Grannie's lap. "Let's look up." But the thing that worried him most, the thing he'd only whispered to Smitty, had not said aloud to Laurie, was that Max had also been gone all day. Neither Johnson nor Donna had seen him despite looking and calling. When Tom had called Patty around dinner-time, she also had not seen him. What Max would or could do to subdue three smart, strong teenagers and Tommy, the most innovative kid in the world, Tom could not imagine, but Max was dangerous and unstable and his boys were missing. And unfortunately, when he confessed his fears, Smitty admitted to the same worried thoughts.

31

MAX Hunter walked coatless in the snow all the way to Patty's townhouse and pounded on her door. When she heard her neighbors yelling at him, she shrugged on her coat, put her wallet and phone in her pocket, grabbed her keys, and opened the front door.

"I'll drive you someplace, but you're not coming in."

"Aw, Patty," he groaned. "I've had an awful day."

"No. Let's go." She took his arm and pulled him down the steps. He followed her over to her car. Patty opened the door for him and shut it behind him.

She started her car, trained the vents on the windshield, and let it warm up. Max rested his head back and closed his eyes.

"Do you want to go get a bite to eat somewhere?" She shook her head. "You still love me, don't you?"

"We're never getting back together, Max. Not after what I saw you do to Ben. No way."

"Tom," he whined.

"Even if that were true, it doesn't excuse you. And it's not. The blood tests were switched, messed up."

"How do you know that?"

"Tom told me."

"What do you expect him to say?"

Patty glared at Max, commanded him to put his seat belt on, and switched on her wipers, which quivered, made a bumping sound, then pushed the heavy snow away. Patty scooted up close to the steering wheel and peered out the little fans of clear windshield.

"Police gonna pull you over for driving like that."

She pulled out into the street slowly, not slipping, kept going. "Where do you want me to take you?"

Max dug in his pocket and pulled out a scrap of paper. "You know where Admiral Heights is?"

"Yeah, I went to a party over there."

Max stared out the window, rubbing his hands up and down over his arms. Patty drove through the snow to Rowe Boulevard, which was slick, the bridges over College Creek and Back Creek treacherous. Patty crept along knowing it was stupid to be out, wanting to be rid of Max. The going was slow, the wind strong enough to drive the snow hard against the windshield.

"The guy says turn up here," Max said.

"Who is this guy?"

"Some guy Saunders. His kid goes to Ben's school."

"Why are you going there?"

"I called him. Told him the fix I'm in; he invited me."

"What fix are you in? No booze at home?"

"Ha-ha, Patty. Like I can't do without the stuff. I haven't had a drink since sometime after lunch. No, this guy and I are trying to show the world the truth about Tom. Since my lawyer deserted me."

Patty's front tires spun halfway up the hill. There was no one behind her so she slowly let the car roll back down. She inched forward, but slid again. She put the brake on and told Max to get out and push.

"No. I just got warm. Try going backward again."

She did this, letting the car slide backwards to the base of the hill. Now another car crawled toward her from behind. Max said, "I'd like you to reconsider, Patty. If you're mad at me, I can wait for you to get desperate again. But it's unprofessional of you to quit on a client."

"You haven't got a case. You've got a drunken imagination. Now shut up. I'm in a pickle here." She rocked the car back, went forward a few inches, and turning the wheel, gave it a little gas so that she steered the car onto the side road where the grade was more gradual.

"This isn't the way."

"We'll have to go this way. I can't get up that hill."

She went slowly, keeping the car going; when the slope increased her wheels spun again.

"Let me drive," Max demanded.

"Never. You get out and push."

"You're the one who got it stuck, *you* get out and push. I'll drive."

Patty looked at Max. She saw the cunning in his eyes. She moved her hand into her coat pocket past the bulk of her wallet seeking with her fingers to feel the antenna of her cell phone. "Okay," she said. "Let's switch."

He opened his door and when he swung around to get out, she switched off the ignition and hopped out. She shut her door, saw that he was picking his way through the mounded snow around the back of the car and went quickly around the front. She pressed the automatic lock, dropped her keys into her pocket, and shut his door.

"Oops!" she said as he reached for the handle. "I think I locked my keys in there."

"What?" Max demanded. "Why did you shut it off anyway?" He yanked at the handle. Patty played along, bending to peer into the dark interior. "Yeah, there they are, right on the floor. That was stupid of me."

Max glared at her. She stood up very straight. "Well, you've got your directions. You're close enough to walk now."

"Hey, wait a minute."

"I'll just walk on over to Graul's and call a cab."

"No cab's going to come out in the *snow*, Patty." She turned to walk away. "Better hurry, Max. You don't want to freeze your ass off."

He startled her, his hand on her elbow, grabbing her, pulling her back. "I need something from you."

"No!" She wrenched her arm away.

"I need that diary back. Katie's diary."

"Obviously, I don't have it with me." She held both hands out, showing that she was empty handed.

"You didn't give it to Ben, did you?"

"No, I didn't." She backed away. He stood still, eyes bearing down on her.

"You know Ben has a book like that. They say he's got all kinds of bad stuff in there about me."

"I don't know anything about that."

"If the wrong people get that, Patty, they could use it for evidence. You got to help me."

Patty had not noticed his utterly disheveled state before. Uniform shirt wrinkled, shoved unevenly in a beltless waist of trousers that looked as if he'd slept in them. And he wore no socks. She took another small step backwards widening the curtain of white snow between them. "Honestly Max, that won't mean anything to the police."

"You don't think so?"

It bought her another step. "Are you kidding? Like you always say, who would believe a teenager, like Ben, when they have *your* own testimony?" She gestured her gloved hand sweeping to invite the entire blizzarded world to regard him. "I mean, just look at you."

He glanced down at himself, eyes lingering, seeing the disheveled uniform, the snow caked on the trouser cuffs, on the tops of his good leather shoes, and when he looked up, she was gone.

The snow flew so thickly that it took Tom nearly two hours to drive his family home from the shop. But he knew God was with him—Grannie and Cara slept the entire way. Smitty had assured him that no car fitting the description of Ben's Fiat had been reported in an accident.

Finally Laurie said, "They're not near a phone, that's obvious."

"Looks like every light is on at our house as usual."

"Oh, maybe they're home! We've been on the road so long."

Their driveway had been shoveled. Walls of snow four feet high lined the sides of the driveway now coated again with six inches. Three snow-blanketed cars were parked on the basketball court. Beth Davidson and Flip waved to him from the just-cleaned walkway.

"Oh, my word," Laurie said, waving to Drew, Paul and Adam, Tiffany with her entire family, Morgan, Michelle, Victoria, Jeff, Scott, Jim Ridout and five of their neighbors. "Half the school is here. What will I feed them?"

"Any word from the boys?" Tom said stepping out of the van.

Beth shook her head.

Inside the kitchen, their friends had been at work. The room sparkled, the weeks of holiday cooking and frantic shop-keeping swept and polished away by anxious friends that crowded now around them offering words of assurance, pats on the back, promises of prayer. A bright fire roared in the fireplace beyond the table abounding with lovely offerings of food. Laurie was crying and laughing, hugging one, then the next.

"We heard on WNAV about the boys being missing," Victoria said. "My mom thought you could use the help. Most of us came with Mr. Ridout in Big Red."

"Hey," Bonnie Jean called. "There's a message here from Joe." The room went silent, then resounded with the muffled, open-air sound of Joe's message. It was hard to hear, garbled at points, but it was Joe's voice, serious, with its undertone of enjoyment and irony. "They must have gotten stuck or lost sometime after four."

They crowded around the table, examining maps. Adam carried the television into the kitchen and set it on the counter. The radar pictures of the storm's track showed that the road Joe had named was in the thick of the storm. We know they're somewhere in there," Tom said, his finger on the map. He dialed Gregen's number while Beth called Doug.

Long past midnight, Ben convinced Joe to give in to his yawning and sleep. He knew he would not sleep again and assured Joe that despite sore ribs, he could keep watch. When he heard Joe snoring, Ben left the car. Using his forearm, he cleaned the foot of snow that had gathered again on the roof, on the trunk, and as much as he could away from the wheels. He trudged up the berm and gazed through the fine snow falling at the empty highway. It looked as if plows had been through, but the snow lay in thick rows beside packed trenches dusted anew. The wind whimpered now over him, the temperature bitter. The thing to do, he decided, would be to try to get the attention of those weather helicopters that would be flying as soon as it cleared. They might see his pink car, but he thought it might be too far off the road or too deep in snow to catch their attention. Then he thought of it: a snowman.

His cold hands and feet made him forget his sore side; he rolled and packed the snow until the base was chest high. He rolled a huge middle ball up onto the base and it made the snowman at least eight feet tall. Ben packed the back of the snowman, making a shelf so that when he clothed it with his varsity jacket, the back was flat to the sky, the school insignia and his name easier to see from passing traffic helicopters. Using his little pocketknife, Ben cut branches from the cypress trees they'd skidded by. He used these to make the arm of the jacket point to the car's location. By now his hands were numb, his lips stinging and the trembling within again painful, but he needed a head to secure the jacket. Clumping snow together, he wished for a bright red hat. *Maybe Pete's got a hat with him*, he thought, and then remembered that he was wearing Joe's orange boxers with the little Santas on them. He stripped down to get them off, tugged his snow clogged sweats back on, piled a mound of snow for steps, and climbing on, put the head with the bright boxers on the top, rotating it to make it stick. Shivering so much that his bones ached, Ben trudged back to the car.

32

FAR in the left corner of his peripheral vision, Doug Davidson saw a flash of bright orange. He swung left and pointed so that Smitty, riding shotgun, located it too. Smitty radioed the police following some distance behind on the treacherous highway while Doug called, "Tom, come see this."

Circling down closer, Doug saw the shape of the snowman towering above the drifts.

"It's pointing," Tom said leaning between the seats.

Doug hovered his aircraft, making low circles over the highway while the New Jersey State Troopers stopped the scant traffic. "Look there," Tom said, "I bet that's Ben's car." Doug circled above it, powering down. Peter emerged from what looked liked a pink-edged cloud and shielding his eyes, tilted his head and waved.

Tom waited, hoping, and saw Peter dig at the snow bank, a yawn of darkness out of which Tommy tumbled, looking up, waving and yelling. Joe crawled out next, shaded his eyes to squint up at them, then ducked back in.

"Where's Ben?"

"We're about to find out," Doug said. "Have a seat, strap yourselves back in."

Inside the car Joe MacBride heard the whine of the chopper recede and glanced up to see Tommy and Peter trudging and leaping through the drifted snow toward the berm. He lay his hand flat on Ben's forehead, sickened by the chill pallor of his skin. Ben's eyelids fluttered.

"We're going to be okay," Joe said to his friend. "Dad and Unca Doug are here."

Joe shook Ben's shoulder. Ben opened his eyes a slit, blinked, lay still, mouth shut. "Come on, Ben." Joe felt the dampness of his sweatshirt and reached to brush clumps of snow off Ben's sweatpants, alarmed to feel only cold; the damp fabric felt frigid and Ben's knee beneath no warmer. "What did you do, get out and play in the snow?" He patted Ben's cheek with frantic force, glancing up to see his father and uncle mount the top of the berm, and together tumble Peter and Tommy into their arms. He heard the tumult of shouting, voices raised in grateful questioning.

Using the driver's door, Joe crawled out of the car, tromped in the places Peter had trampled down and then dug frantically to the other side. His strength aroused, he shoveled the snow away from Ben's door with both arms. He had just gotten the door open when his father's hand touched his shoulder.

"Ben's alive, but he's chilled."

Tom yanked the door open, scraping its edge along the snow. Doug tousled Joe's head, elbowed past him, then reared up and shouted. "Stretcher. He's hypothermic. Hurry."

"Let me see him," Tom said, crowding in beside Doug. He ripped off his glove and lay his hand against Ben's face. "Ben. Son. Wake up. Come on now." Joe squeezed in between his father and uncle.

"Any injuries from the crash?" Tom said. "You split your lip I see. What about Ben?"

"He was thrown forward. But he was already injured."

"Did he complain of headache, back pain, neck ache after you crashed?"

"He never complains, Uncle Doug. But I think he went out in the snow." Joe gestured to the clumps of snow that clung still to Ben's ankles and knees.

"Ben," Tom said, "Can you wake up? Does anything hurt?"

"You hurt every one of us." Ben tried to sit up, fire brief as a match lit his eyes. But he stopped and a mist seemed to pass across his vision; his shoulders slumped back and his eyes shut.

"Hurry them up," Tom said to Doug.

Joe kept shaking Ben's shoulder. "Come on. He's here. Wake up and tell him how mad you are."

"Step back, son."

Doug helped with the stretcher; once the paramedics reached Ben, they commanded Tom to back off. "Careful. He's got broken ribs," Joe called as they lifted Ben, who had gone blue-lipped and very still, onto the stretcher.

They strapped him in and lifted him over the snow. Tom followed, touched Ben's foot. Ben's eyes opened and he tried to focus. "Hey, Ben. It's me, Tom." Ben frowned, squinted, looked at Joe as if he were trying to remember something. Tom said to the paramedic. "His sock is wet." He touched Ben's knee. "His clothes are soaked."

"I guess we found out which one made the snowman," Doug said.

"Snowman?" Peter asked.

Pointing, Doug said, "Saw it from the air. If it weren't for that snowman—" He shook his head. "Hurry everybody. Must be twenty degrees out here."

The New Jersey police and paramedics herded Joe, Peter and Tommy on board the big police helicopter Doug flew and told them to strip off any wet clothes and find dry stuff from the laundry bag Tom had brought from home. Tommy and Peter acquiesced but Joe stood in the center of the aircraft every sense alive, watching and praying.

Joe could just stand upright in the cabin though his hair brushed the top. Peter and Tommy were shepherded to a three-seat bench attached to the wall across from the door. Joe sidestepped the brisk New Jersey medics and moving further into the cabin he bumped into a stack of green, woolen blankets. Two slim, paper-covered pillows toppled off the stack onto the floor below another small jump seat that was now upright. He stood in front of the jump seat with his back against the chopper wall, shoulders bent with the curve of the cabin there.

Smitty emerged from the narrow opening that led to the cockpit, helping Tom and a stout female paramedic, whose name badge read HODGES, guide Ben's stretcher into the long, empty space in the cabin's center. Ben lay still, eyes shut, lips blue; his chest moved slowly in breathing. Hodges snatched one of the pillows from Joe's hands and thrust it under Ben's head. *Wake up, Ben,* Joe begged him silently. *Wake up.*

The MacBrides made a half circle around Ben while Hodges and another medic made a quick evaluation. Someone snapped a monitor onto Ben's finger, it's weird clip reddening the tip. Behind them, on a screen, graphs of green lines burst to life, clicking with the slow, cold rhythms of Ben's torpid body. Hodges said, "We'll warm him up, get an IV started and fly him home. Only forty minutes by air. Better n' being stuck in traffic down there. If he declines, I'll call Wilmington, Chestertown, lots a places to stop on the way."

This agreed upon, the paramedics talked to Tom. "You're satisfied that the other boys are okay?"

"They say they're fine. They'd tell me if they weren't," Tom's eyes swept over his sons as he squatted down next to Ben and took his icy hand in his. "Ben, can you wake up and tell me where you are?"

Cold air gusting into the cabin from the open door made a puffing sound and rattled the plastic wrapping on the sterile equipment and muffled Hodges words, "Got to get the wet clothes off him."

"It's too cold in here," Tom looked at the open door. "Doug, can you shut that door?"

"Yeah." Doug offered to shake hands with each of the local paramedics and emergency personnel. "I'm gonna rev this bird up and get going. You guys've been the best." Doug shut the doors as soon as the men stepped into the snow. He told everyone to get belted in and grabbing Tommy by the back of the neck, said, "Come on up front and help me out. Got a little jump seat for you there."

Hodges ripped the sterile seal from a pair of scissors. "You keep him calm. Watch his arms."

Patting Ben's hand, Tom said, "Your wet clothes are robbing you of all your body heat."

Hodges lifted Ben's ankle to cut off his sock but Ben flinched and kicked. "Don't touch me."

"Don't usually see 'em violent."

"It probably hurts his stomach to lift up his foot like that," Joe said to Hodges. "His ribs are broken on the left side." Joe moved in close, stood beside Ben's foot, captured Ben's torpid gaze, and held eye contact.

Hodges spoke sternly to Joe, "Your instructions were to get wet clothes off and put one of those blankets round your shoulders. We don't need two with hypothermia."

"Thanks, I'm fine," Joe said, squatting, laying his hand on Ben's ankle. "And he trusts me." Joe smiled into Ben's dull questioning eyes. "We'll need a blanket. He was wearing those boxers he put on the snowman's head. Which was a great touch by the way, Ben."

"I've never been so glad to see my son's boxers," Tom joked, he too, smiling to encourage Ben. At the sound of Tom's voice, Ben broke eye contact with Joe and squinted at Tom, trying to pull thought up. Joe helped Hodges cut off Ben's sweat pants, wet and chunky with clumps of snow, and Tom dried him, rubbing the towel briskly over his icy skin.

"Mr. MacBride, if you want to help," Hodges said, "I need someone to transfer body heat." He pointed at Joe who was carefully making a slit in Ben's bandage. "I'd rather this one got out of his wet stuff."

"You said on the way up here you had warmed air and a way to warm the IV fluids," Tom hesitated.

"Right. I'll start that soon as you're transferring body heat. Just take off your gear and get on the cot with him."

Doug called from the front. "We can take off as soon as you tell me Ben is stable."

"Okay," Tom said. He dropped Ben's hand, shrugged off his jacket, bent to tug off his boots. As soon as Tom lay down, Hodges told Joe, "On the count of three, we roll him toward your dad."

Doug came toward them, checking seat belts. Hodges counted; he and Joe moved Ben so that his face rested on Tom's scratchy wool shirt. Hodges placed Ben's arm across Tom's stomach and bent Ben's knee across Tom's legs. "Rarely see a bruise that bad, Mr. MacBride."

Tom said, "Get this bird going." He put both arms around Ben and Joe saw Tom hold Ben carefully. "You've got to warm up and wake up, Ben," he whispered. "We want you back, full strength."

Holding the corners, Joe flicked two blankets open and glided both over them while Hodges wheeled a small oxygen tank set in a padded capsule next to the stretcher. She bent down next to Ben's face and fitted the clear plastic mask over Ben's nose and mouth. Turning the dial, she said to Tom, "Warm, moist air to help raise his core temp." She checked the monitoring clip on Ben's finger, then tucked his hand back under the blankets. Joe watched the graphs again and he opened his mouth to ask about them when Hodges snapped her fingers in front of his nose and said, "Get over there and let Smitty look at you."

Smitty put a hand on Joe's shoulder and took him to the little jump seats on the other side of the chopper where Peter sat, pushed him so that he had to sit down, and clapped the seat belt on Joe.

"Everyone's stable and buckled in," Hodges called.

"Let's go!" Doug called and the helicopter's whine built to optimum. It lifted up and forward. Peter moved with the chopper, holding his cup of hot chocolate so that it wouldn't spill, but he met Joe's eyes as they lifted off, his expression serious, emotional. "Mom sent dry clothes."

"And the hot chocolate," Joe said.

"How did we not wake up when he left the car?" Peter mourned.

Joe said, "Silence is his super power."

"Okay," Smitty said, "Look straight ahead, Joe."

"You're not even a doctor, Smitty."

"Got emergency first aid training, smart ass."

Doug called from the front, "About forty minutes to Tom's backyard. Another five to the hospital."

33

FROM where he lay on his back on the stretcher, Tom could not really watch Ben as he would have liked to do because Ben's face lay against Tom's chest, tipped away and partly covered by the oxygen mask. He could not hear Ben breathing, only the whirr of the warmed air flowing through the tube into his mouth. But he could feel Ben's chest move with breath and he felt the boy's chill seeping into his own body like an ice cube numbs a scalded hand. Tom concentrated on absorbing Ben's isolating pall as if with his will, as if with his heart he could draw all that cold away and dissolve it in his great and angry love.

Hodges had brought Peter to sit against Ben's back at his waist, and Joe sat at his bent knees. Joe reached for Tom with the gaze of his intense blue eyes. "Ben feels he's been lied to," Joe said.

"He has been."

Both boys sighed, eyes meeting. "We thought we might find answers in Hillside," Peter said.

"Did you?"

"We saw the place—the puddle. Where the accident was. You were there, Dad?" Joe said.

Tom shuddered. "It was horrible." Hodges approached with IV equipment and another nylon contraption on a steel stand. She took Ben's right hand out of the blankets, placed it on a sterile pad and looked at Tom. "You might have to hold his arm. Remember how he kicked before?"

"I'll do it," Joe said. "He won't fight me."

Beneath the blankets, Ben tensed. Peter startled. Ben ripped off the oxygen mask and threw it. "What's going on?" Ben said.

"You're hypothermic," Hodges said. "We're warming you up."

"Who the hell are you?" he demanded, pushing away from Tom, thumping Peter off the narrow cot. Joe stood up. Eyes wild and unfocused, Ben crawled backwards, rolled off the stretcher. Standing now at its foot, he pointed at Tom. "You—you have to explain."

Tom heard Ben's demand but he was staring at Ben's body, marked with bruises, huge and purple. Tom squinted to remember. In the locker room Tom had seen the bruised shoulder and chest above Ben's towel before he'd given Ben clothes. He had been thinking of the child's dignity and safety, not of gathering evidence for the police. *Hadn't Ben been examined that night when he was x-rayed? Did he run away before they saw him?* Slowly Tom got to his feet, staring with eyes dry though tears swelled in his throat.

Hodges said, "We use body heat to restore a patient's core body temperature. Monitor says you got to lie back down, boy."

Tom counted the bruises, estimated the age of each, searching for something to say, aware in the periphery of his vision that Ben looked angry, too.

"Screw the monitor," Ben said. He glanced at Hodges. "I'm not going near him. Except to kick his ass."

Eyes on Ben, Tom reached for a blanket, couldn't quite touch it. Ben took his defensive stance standing on the balls of his feet, knees slightly bent, hands poised to follow Tom's movements. "I've never seen anyone with bruises that bad," Tom said.

Ben's derisive laugh made Tom squint. "This is nothing compared to what you've done."

"Tell me what I've done."

"You're guilty about me and you won't come out and say why. You want me and Joe to tell the truth all the time but you hid the truth about me." Ben was pointing to his chest.

"Ben, I've wanted to tell you about your mother. But I—"

"But what? You're afraid? No. Not you. Not Tom MacBride who takes a broken back from my father and forgives him."

Hodges stood by them, one hand·outstretched to each. "Look, you gotta get back down on that cot. No activity or excitement. You're temp is gonna go back down." She pointed to the monitor.

Ben kept Hodges off with his right hand extended, finger pointed, the monitor glowing red. "You didn't fight him back, Tom, did you? Because you were guilty. You took that broken back instead of facing up." Ben ripped the monitor off with his left hand and dashed it down. It hit the oxygen tank and skittered away.

"Hey, we're in a helicopter, kid. You can't act rough here."

"Ben," Tom said, "You were found hypothermic. You've got to cover up."

Hodges looked to Tom, then to Joe and Peter. "See him going gray so fast in his skin? See it?"

"At least put the blanket on, man," Joe said, picking one up.

"What's going on back there?" Doug called from the front. Smitty stuck his head out of the cockpit. "Uh-oh." They heard his buckle open, heard Smitty's feet take the cabin floor.

Ben held them off, one hand toward Joe, one toward Hodges. Peter said, "There's more of us, we'd better take him down."

"His bruises," Joe warned.

Doug called. "People got to sit down back there."

Tom glanced at Smitty and said, "I don't want him harmed or traumatized." He stepped toward Ben.

"You come any closer and I'll beat the crap out of you," Ben shouted at Tom. "I'm gonna get you back for all you've done to me."

"Son, your bruises are terrible. You poor kid," Tom said, lifting his eyes from Ben's bruises to his face. "Good Lord, I had no idea it was this bad."

"What do *you* care?" Ben taunted, swaying slightly, panting for breath, his hands and limbs shaking, his teeth rattling together. "You whine about how you're responsible for me being here and then you let me *live with him* all these years. You *left me there* to protect yourself while you're living this great life!"

Hodges said, "Mr. MacBride. Quickly."

Tom nodded at her, then made deliberate eye contact with Ben. "Ben— tell me all this while you're getting warm."

"First you're gonna tell me the truth." Ben juked, fists up. "You've always got an excuse to keep you from telling me the truth. Every time. No more."

Joe moved behind Ben, creeping silently toward him. Peter moved closer to his father, put one arm out between Tom and Ben. "Don't be on his side, Pete. He did this to you, too."

"He's going downhill," said the paramedic, moving toward Ben, hands open, but Ben lunged for Tom, shoving Peter's arm away, taunting him to fight, making a fist. Peter grabbed his arm from behind. Ben twisted away and leapt back, hitting the back of the cabin and crying out.

"Tom!" Doug called. "He's shaking me up!"

"Yeah, Doug," Tom replied. "I'm working on it."

"You—" Ben winced, squinting, wavering slightly on his feet. He used his fists to rub his tears away. Then blinked, disoriented. Tom saw the bright blue cup of his contact lens sticking to the back of his left hand.

"Whoa, son," Tom cautioned, reaching for his hand to rescue the contact from loss.

"Stay away," Ben snapped, rubbing at his eye again. The lens drifted off his wrist and fell beside his bare, bluish foot. Frowning, breathing rapidly in confusion, Ben squinted at the sudden brightness, feeling the air in front of him as if to see with his hands.

"I'm right here," Joe said. "I'm in your blind spot. I can help." Joe touched Ben's shoulder. Hands out defending himself, Ben moved, looking for Joe, his expression exasperated, confused. Joe said, "You've got to get warm, Ben. Then I'll help you kick his ass, okay?"

This upset Ben, his confusion building as rapidly as his color grayed.

"Put this undershirt on, Ben," Tom said, tossing it to him, "I don't want to fight a naked man." He said to Peter. "Find some boxers in the bag."

Doug called, "Get him to sit down. He's rocking this thing."

"Hypothermia's nothin' to fool around with, kid," Hodges said. "It's why you're feeling so confused."

Ben squinted at the T shirt. "And I had something else to say."

Tommy called from the front, "Put some clothes on. Get warm, then fight."

Ben seemed to hear this and concentrating, put the shirt on. Tom stepped closer and held out the boxers. "Get dressed, then you can fight me."

"Don't come near me."

Tom tossed the boxers up in an arc. "Put them on, Ben."

Ben snatched them from the air and when he bent to step into them, moving slowly, one hand going instinctively to his bruised side, Tom grabbed wool blankets from the floor and thrust one at Smitty. Both men moved just a step closer.

"You come near me, I'll fight you."

"Okay," Tom said. "I'm ready. As soon as you're dressed." Tom's meaningful glance at Peter and Joe as he tossed Peter a wool blanket told them to get ready. He signaled Ben with both hands, saying, "Come on, then."

Tom stepped close and Ben swung at him. As Ben's shoulder dipped to punch, Tom reached over Ben's shoulder, grabbed the back of Ben's

T-shirt. He yanked it up over Ben's head, trapping his arms and confusing him just long enough for Peter and Joe to wrap the blanket around Ben from behind, trapping his arms to his sides. Smitty held his blanket out, Tom grabbed one corner and they wrapped this one around him too, making a tight bundle of Ben's writhing, weakly bucking body.

Hodges fretted, "I'd tranquilize him but I can't slow anything down in him right now."

"Get him down. Sit on him if you have to," Doug called from the front.

"It's okay. I've got him." Tom held Ben in front of him, both arms holding him. Smitty encircled him from the side. "That wasn't fair," Ben growled.

"Get his feet wrapped up."

Ben tried to twist away. Tom held on. "Stop it, now. Don't you dare kick the paramedic, Ben. You going to behave indecently because you're ticked about something? I thought you hated that."

Peter and Joe caught his feet in the blanket and Peter held the blanket on with both arms wrapped around Ben's flailing legs. "We got him, Uncle Doug," Peter called.

"Damn good thing," Doug hollered.

Peter, Joe, Smitty and Tom, holding Ben, lifted his stiff and wiggling body up and laid him flat on the stretcher. Eight gripping hands fingered a bruise old or new. Ben tried to get away. He could not focus his eyes, all that extra light pouring in without the blue plastic barrier of the contact. And the fury inside his mind, the jolting of his bucking body, made the inside of the dazzling bright helicopter dip and blur.

He heard Hodges fret as she gathered up the equipment he'd trashed. "You got to get good and warm. This ain't nothin' to fool around about kid, so settle down." She taped new, flat white sensors to his cheekbone and neck; Tom watched the monitor, eyes concerned.

Immobile, Ben waited until Tom's eyes came to him and he whispered, "I hate you."

"Just so you get warm," Tom murmured.

"You should have told me why you didn't want me to date Bonnie Jean. You took advantage of Mom when she came to you for help. No wonder he hates me."

"Who hates you, your father?" Smitty asked, leaning in he took out a small note pad and pen.

Ben opened his mouth, then shut it. His eyes were injured, wide and tearless. Ben's chin shook, his lip crumpled like a broken, frustrated child's.

"Dehydrated, too. See? No tears. I was going to start an IV when he got wild," the paramedic said.

"He'll be good so you can start one," Tom said. "Ben, I want you to stay quiet and cooperate with the doc here." Ben shook his head. "You haven't even got any tears."

"I'm not—crying—not—one—more tear—for you. I cried—all my life for you."

"Give me that oxygen mask, please," Tom said to Hodges. He took it in hand and held it up where Ben could see it. "I'm going to put this over your nose and mouth. Don't fight me. This is giving you heated air to warm up your insides."

"There's no hope for my insides. I even *tried* praying. Doesn't work."

"Try again," Tom ordered, his voice inexorable as he fitted the mask on Ben's face. "Breathe and pray," Tom's voice so terrible that Ben knew, albeit unwillingly, the misery of Tom's deep concern. "It has worked. It will work for you."

Ben tried to bite his quivering lips, but couldn't. He tried to close his eyes but they moved restlessly, sore and dry. "Hush, shh," Tom soothed him, stroking his forehead, ignoring the way Ben shuddered and feebly tried again to pull away. "If Hodges has to put the IV in your ankle or your groin, it is going to hurt a lot more. So I want you to let her put it in your arm, now. Okay? She's getting it ready. In your arm, it will hurt so much less."

"Please, Ben," Joe said, leaning over Ben's body to try to make eye contact with him. "Don't fight anymore. We'll get everything straightened out. You've got me and Pete to help now. We promise. We'll take up your cause with Dad." Ben turned his face away and squinted with dry, angry eyes at the glaring green monitor that said he was alive.

"Whatever you're doing back there, keep it up!" Joe heard his uncle's voice with its casual authority and he watched Ben's silent, impassioned face for any sign of kinship. He breathed with Ben, giving out shallow puffs while Ben's chest pulled up to inhale the warmed air given to him through the oxygen pump. Peter and Smitty helped hold Ben down while Tom sat at the top of the stretcher, took Ben's head onto his knee. Ben opened his eyes briefly, but uttered no protest. Every time Tom's hand passed over Ben's head in his absent caress, Ben winced and shivered.

The paramedic squeezed between Joe and Tom and coaxed a vein to accept the needle. Ben's eyelids fluttered and he drifted beneath consciousness.

Tom said, "His face is green, skin way too cold." Tom unbuttoned his woolen shirt, pulled it off and rubbed it on Ben's hair to dry it. Ben lay still, eyes shut. When Ben's hair stood up in straight, static wisps, Tom tucked his shirttail into the edge of the blanket at Ben's neck, making a kind of tent. "Keep the warm air in," he explained, mumbling.

Peter got up, changed places with Smitty, who seeing Ben's closed eyes, reminded them that they couldn't let Ben sleep.

"Wake up, Ben," Tom said. "Tell me why you want to fight me."

"Hate you," Ben murmured with a dry sob.

"Blood pressure's not so bad's I expected. Should come to."

"Do you know why he's so angry at me?" Tom asked Joe.

Joe looked at Peter, then met Tom's eyes. "He thinks you're his father."

Tom shook his head. "God knows the boy has reason to be angry at Max. I've never seen bruises like that."

"No, Dad," Joe said, watching his father carefully, "He knows it's you. He knows you're Tom MacBride. He thinks you, *Tom*, are his father."

Tom laughed sadly. "I wish I were his father," he said. "Oh, how I wish it." In Tom's brief, direct glance at them, Joe saw the same steady expression, uncloaked and approachable, that distinguished those blue eyes he had been born to love and trust. He watched Tom's eyes brighten as they went from Peter's patient gaze to Joe's own searching eyes, he saw his father's eyes brighten with yearning. Then Tom turned his face toward Ben and rubbed Ben's arm and shoulder, trying to generate warmth.

Joe met Peter's eyes and the recognition of their father's innocence passed between them. "No, Dad," Joe said, softly. "He really thinks that."

"He thinks what?"

"You said you were responsible for him being here," Peter prompted, his voice gentle. "So…"

"I am. I'm responsible for him being here. I convinced his mother to reconcile with his father."

"Yeah. But Ben thinks you did that *after* getting her pregnant."

Tom gave the same rueful laugh. "How much lighter my burden would be if Ben *were really mine* and my only fault sexual immorality. I could have kept him all these years. Kept him and taken care of him like I wanted to."

"But—"

"No, I knew what kind of a man Max was." Tom choked up, swallowed hard, his body shuddering with grief. Joe saw Ben open his eyes, saw lucidity dawn in them as if the tremors of Tom's emotion had awakened him. Tom said, "Deep down, I knew Max was dangerous, but I wanted her where she would never be a temptation to me. I know that I sent her back to Max with that thought polluting my motives. My reckoning is going to be severe at Judgment Day. When I have to account for every one of those bruises he's suffered." Tom's voice choked; tears rushed to flood his eyes. "When I think of what he's gone through—"

Tom pressed his fingers to his eyes, but the swift tears coursed to his chin and one splashed onto Ben's cheek. Ben looked up, his reluctant eyes meeting Tom's, squinting in the light that was now too bright for him. Quickly, without breaking eye contact, Tom wiped away the tear's blotch from Ben's face. "You boys see to it that you don't follow my example."

"Dad," Joe said, moving to get up, "No."

"Stay there," Tom commanded hoarsely. "Warm him that way, and hold him in case he tries to get up. You too, Peter," he added, as Peter reached for his father, one long arm circling around Tom's back.

"Be at the hospital in fifteen," Doug called.

When Doug puttered the helicopter down to a stop on the landing pad atop the hospital on Franklin Street, Tom came to the cockpit.

"Smitty wants me to go with him to start the police report. Can you stay with Ben?"

"Sure thing. Soon as he feels better we'll take him home to Laurie and all talk some sense into him." Tom touched Doug's shoulder in thanks. "We got a lot to be grateful for, Tom."

"Don't I know it. Don't leave him alone."

"I'm not that stupid." Doug said as he followed Tom back into the cabin, watched his nephews run out into the snow-deep landing pad to the open door across the roof. He saw Ben stirring, saw how much his color had improved, quickly scanned and read the monitor. They watched Hodges unhook the IV drip, tape the needle down on Ben's hand. "Be right back," Hodges promised, rushing out.

Ben moved, trying to sit up. Doug went to him and loosened the blankets. "You look pinker, now, little one," he said helping Ben sit up.

"From the way everything looks," Ben said as Doug helped him to his feet. "I must have lost my contact."

"Just as well," Doug said. He draped one of the blankets around Ben's shoulders. Ben held it close with both arms, clutching another blanket around his waist. "I need some clothes."

"Tom took all the dry clothes with him so you wouldn't run off."

"Forget it. I don't need clothes." Though he was barefoot, wearing only boxers and a T-shirt beneath his blankets, he stumbled toward the door.

Doug blocked his way. "You sure were ugly to your coach, Ben. Said some rough stuff."

Ben tried to push past Doug, but his attempt was feeble and Doug stopped him one hand across the door opening. "I don't know what's gotten into your drawers, young man, but don't you speak to Tom that way. You owe him. You have no idea how much."

"He owes *me*," Ben spit the words out. "He's my father."

"Your father?" Doug said, his face close and angry. "You think if you were Tom's he'd a let you out of his sight for one minute? You see how he dotes on his kids."

"They didn't come from a fucking *affair*." Ben said it coldly, eyes hard, he tried to duck under Doug's arm.

"Show some respect." Doug smacked Ben's ass, his open palm popping harmlessly on the blanket. Open mouthed, Ben turned to stare at Doug, who took Ben's shoulders in both hands. "Your mother was not *like* that. She was beautiful and idealistic and elegant. And if she were here, she'd be ashamed of you right now. A-*shamed*."

"Tom left me with him when he knew," Ben said. "Because he was ashamed of what he did with my mother."

"No," Doug said. "Tom tried everything. Courts, everything, 'til you were six years old. He had a written statement, too. But Max fights dirty, you know that, right? When he broke Tom's back, he was threatening to break *you*. That's dirty." Ben's legs buckled. Doug scooped Ben up in his arms with a swift and decisive power. "Come on, I'm not waiting until these bozos get their act together. I'm taking you inside."

Doug held him up close, forcing Ben's face to his shoulder so that the air Ben pulled in was warmed and smelled of Doug's flight jacket. "Come on, Uncle Doug's got you now."

"That proves it, Doug," Ben whispered. "All he did to me proves I'm not Max's. What father would do that to his own kid?"

"Yours. He hit your mother. He was violent."

"How do you know?"

"She wrote me." Doug made way for the ER. "Your mom found out she was pregnant and instead of dropping to his knees and thanking God, Max slapped her. Slapped her." Doug punched the elevator button, and when it opened, maneuvered in with Ben, talking loudly, heedless. "Accusing her of—you know—being with Tom. She wrote me. I told her I'd take care of her and you. I begged her to let me. I loved her with all my heart, but she was too confused to make that decision. At least she was safe during the pregnancy, staying with her aunt and uncle."

The elevator beeped open. Doug rushed out.

"Are you sure I'm not *your* kid?"

Doug stopped walking a minute. He lifted his knee to help hold Ben's weight and shifted Ben in his arms. "Oh, so that's what this is about. Any port in a storm?"

"I'm desperate," Ben whispered.

"No. There's no way."

"Are you sure?"

"So you think I would have let that—piece of work—raise you if I even *hoped* there was a possibility you belonged to me? Or Tom? I woulda committed murder to get you away from Max if I thought you belonged to Tom. I woulda spent my life in jail and been happy to do it, too."

"Doug," Ben murmured, astonished.

"Yeah, *Uncle* Doug to you from now on. Learn some respect, like I said, or I'll teach you some."

34

BEN could not move. They had discarded the helicopter's wool blankets and wrapped him in some soft white ones that had been heated. His head and feet were wrapped, his left arm bundled in, only his face and his right hand, with the IV catheter, were exposed. He closed his eyes and breathed in the warm moist air from the oxygen mask; the heat from the blankets seeped into him in a way that felt like health and sunshine were being infused into his cells. He felt warm, quiet and hungry.

Some time later, he heard Donna's voice approaching and opened his eyes a peep. Light flooded into his widened pupil and it startled Ben. He had not been without his contact lens for years in daylight. Waiting for focus, he realized that Doug stood beside him. Ben found Donna's voice was coming from a gap in the curtains surrounding his bed. He could see that she carried stuff in her arms and was listening intently to someone in a white coat standing beside her. Her eyes grew animated when she spoke her medical language with the doctor who seemed to regard her with respect.

Doug's hand patted his shoulder and he left Ben's bedside.

"Mrs. Hunter?" Doug said, opening the curtain wide to invite Donna in. "Hi." Doug offered to shake hands. "I'm Doug Davidson."

Ben's mind jinked.

He squinted at Doug in the room's stark brightness and saw him standing in perfect calm, hands as if waiting to be of service, his eyes bright, the passion dormant. When Doug saw Ben looking at him, his grin flashed—happy-go-lucky like he'd landed his chopper or found a penny. Not, Ben thought, like he was in the same room with the woman he loved with all his heart and from whom he'd lived unwillingly apart.

Donna said to Doug, "It's nice to meet you. Over the years, I've heard so much about you."

Ben's heart pounded. Things Tom and Laurie had said came back to him, descriptions that had startled him, quoted poetic phrases that invited kinship. What was it Tom had said? "You don't know who your mother is, Ben." Comprehension dropped into Ben's soul, creating a great open space.

Donna glanced at Ben. "You're awake."

"Yes," he said. "I'm awake now."

She came to his bedside. "How are you?" Her eyes swept over his face, went quickly to the monitors.

"Better," he said into the mask.

Doug stepped forward and tweaked Ben's blanketed toe. "I'm gonna take the chopper back to the airport and let you two get caught up." He touched Donna's elbow. "Nice to meet you, Mrs. Hunter."

"Thanks again, Mr. Davidson. I'm grateful for you rescuing Ben and the others."

Donna pulled a stool up to his bedside and removed the oxygen mask. Ben saw her notice his naked eye but she did not reprove him. Instead, she used the foot pedal to raise the head of the bed. "Your vital signs are perfect."

Ben stared at her. He didn't know what to say. Held still in a bath of light as he was, this lie seemed their darkest and most terrible, but he could not conjure due fury against her. He could never again be stunned or wounded by the awful knowledge that she did not love him as mothers love their sons. True, she could have fostered that sweet, late-planted love that the generous ones give to children not born to them; but Ben knew that her lies had robbed her of the nobility to give it.

"Somewhere on the flight home I started to get better," he said, looking into her hazel eyes. Gone was the cold fury, the fear. The flickering changes he saw within satisfied the protective burden he'd always felt for her.

"I stopped on the way here and got you some new clothes," she offered, patting the bag beside her.

"Oh. You did? Thank you."

She breathed out a little sigh. "I figured if you were hypothermic, yours were wet and they'd cut them off."

"Some of them anyway. I used my boxers—well, I'd borrowed them from Joe—I used them on the snowman."

"That's what I heard."

He thought she wanted to say more and there were so many questions Ben wanted to ask. *What do you know about my mother? What is she like? Why don't I know her? Why did you keep her a secret from me?*

"Ben, I—I know you won't stay here in the hospital."

"No. I want to run."

"You shouldn't run just yet. After all you've been through, it wouldn't be wise." In her quick efficiency, Donna disconnected him from the IV and the probes that monitored his well-being. She loosened the tuck that held his blankets in place. "There." She took a step back and tried to smile at him.

"I still have so much to figure out…so many questions."

Nodding, she said, "I have something for you." She opened her purse and took out the book Max had fought to take from him. Bigger than his own journal, it was worn and stuffed with papers. "After you get dressed, go to one of your safe places. I know you have them. And read this." Tears brightened her eyes. "This diary explains…everything. About Tom, too. Read it from start to finish so you won't misunderstand."

She stood up. "I'll put it here. With your jacket."

Ben pulled his blankets away so he could sit up and see what she meant. "I don't think that's mine."

"It's the only jacket here, so it must be meant for you. It's awfully cold outside and now that you're warm..."

"Okay," Ben said. "I'll wear it."

"Thanks. And leave the bandage on your ribs. I'll go sign you out and when you're ready," she opened the opposite corner of the curtain, "see out there to the ambulance bay?" She waved. "That EMT is a friend. She just got off duty and her vehicle's warmed up and ready to take you wherever you want to go."

"Thanks."

"I'd like you to go to the MacBrides—"

He shook his head, looked down.

"But I know you have to read this first." She put the book on top of the jacket and turned to leave.

Heart longing, Ben took the diary she'd left for him into his eager, careful hands.

The side door to the U.S. Naval Academy Chapel had opened to Ben's touch. He stepped into the dark east arm of the cross-shaped building where the soft blue carpet muffled his presence and the scent of pine and candles urged solemn reflection. Taking a seat in the rows called Sleepy Hollow that stood cross-wise to the main rows of seats, he found it a perfect place to read in secret. The breath of the wind against the high windows on the west side reminded him that he sat sheltered and hidden. Though the rim of the balcony curved above him, he could see up into the perfect, arched dome that rose above the place where the arms of the transept crossed the main aisle of the nave. Tiny lights hovered there amidst a cupped bluish ceiling that seemed, once again to Ben, a little low heaven.

Above him, the dome's star-like lights shone dimly; as the afternoon passed, they glowed brighter and brighter in answer to the quick, cold sinking of the sun. The great arch behind the altar was lit only by the flickering of a commemorative, perpetual flame that cast its solitary light on the magnificent stained glass, which proclaimed the navy's hope: ETERNAL FATHER STRONG TO SAVE. Christmas trees had been grouped on the altar; their subtle fragrance, their gold, symbolic decorations suggested a world beyond even this snug one in which he had been kept apart all afternoon. With a hunger that encompassed his quest to know her and to discover, in her candor, the truth about Tom's role, he hid, reading her diary, though evening had come.

Ben took the pages he had not yet read between his thumb and forefinger to measure an inch. He suspected that his solitary hour had passed. To the heights of his indoor heaven he whispered, "He was a violent jerk to her. That's why she left him. That's what drove her away." The handwriting was his own with its peculiar slant. Ben pictured Donna's note to him the other night stuck on the hospital door, the writing dark and loopy. The diary's dates were right, but it was the affinity he felt with this woman's voice—this woman who wrote everything down, this woman with heart and compassion whose poetic descriptions and beautifully expressed inner struggles made sense to Ben.

His fingers touched the description of Katie's visit to Rising Sun, the coffeehouse where Laurie's store now stood. She wrote:

> New Year's Eve, 1979
>
> I was in his arms—the moment holding all the passion and tenderness of two souls touching in a kiss. I moved away from him and asked him if it were true and he blushed to admit it. "I doubt my motives are pure when I advise you to return to your husband," said my dear humble friend Tom MacBride.
>
> Dear Diary, I have made love to men when I felt so much less than I felt for Tom at that moment and to the *old* me, to my *natural* self, love-making at that gorgeous, intimate moment with Tom MacBride was inevitable.

Ben looked up, his gut echoing the panic Max must have felt when reading this confession. Despite Doug's assertions, despite Tom's off-base regrets, Ben unwillingly suspected Max was right. Doug's loyalty to Tom might blind him, and on the helicopter, Tom had admitted he'd done wrong in protecting himself; he'd sent her back to save his soul and his marriage. Sent her to Max he did, but these words implied—too late.

True, Max had said those things to crush and manipulate Ben. But Ben could imagine this Katie with Tom. Try as he might, he had not been able to picture Donna and Tom joining together to create life in brilliant though mistaken passion. But this woman's desire to know Tom was palpable and her penned words thronged with the lively color that had conjured Max's accusation that Tom had fathered Ben.

At the front of the chapel, doors opened, admitting busy voices on gusts of cold air. Choir members, directors, chaplains, ushers, musicians, military men and their wives who bore the responsibility for the pending Christmas Eve service streamed in, ripping the silence from Ben's grasp and loosing it to hover above among the domed lights of that indoor heaven. Ben crouched down behind the pew to hide. He heard the Lindquists—all four of them—but what Nels said chilled him.

"You and your mother sit right here in the front row, Max. Admiral Johnson wants us all to run through the readings. It won't take that long. Your mom can watch and see how you do. Is that clear, Mrs. Hunter?"

Ben had only the diary with him; he could run. But torn by dread and longing, Ben wanted to read; he had to hide. He moved it into the inside pocket of the jacket he wore and froze when he heard it crunch against paper already there. He knelt in still silence and when he calmed, he realized that even the dome was filled now with sound—enough sound to hide him.

He crept along the pew and hurried to the staircase that emptied out at the back of Sleepy Hollow. Up in the balcony he watched the sanctuary below. Now someone had thrown a switch and modern torchlight streamed like uplifted arms from big iron goblets along the rail of the balcony. Though the decorations looked pristine, women buzzed around them; someone vacuumed the immaculate carpet, another tweaked perfectly placed ornaments, straightened bows that stood at attention, fussing to ensure the readiness of a building for its most solemn purpose. In the warmth of candles bursting to flame, the stone walls took on the translucent gold of summer twilight and all the colors in the stained glass windows blinked to life.

Ben watched Gran fidget in her seat, fingers drumming on her purse, unbuttoning, then buttoning her coat. Max was pressed and clean in his dress uniform, but his face was ashen, lips bitten ragged, dark circles visible even from where Ben crouched above. Max's hands shook as he took the podium to practice the reading assigned to him as the senior marine on campus and he botched the verses badly. Ben shook his head wondering what they possibly were thinking to allow Max Hunter to read poetry in public.

Another marine major had taken Lindquist's place beside his grandmother whose posture had gone stiff. He heard her ask for a bathroom and the man pointed to the stairway. He heard Gran on the stairs coming up toward him and impulsively went to meet her.

She gasped when she saw him. "Where is your contact lens?" Anger blazed in her eyes.

"I don't see why you're angry at me," Ben said. "He's been lying to me all my life. You have, too." Somehow, the atmosphere around him, the steady lights in the dome above, made the words come out gently. And anyway, he loved her. Wasn't that part of the problem?

"I sent you those books, didn't I? I let Gregen buy all your clothes and made sure you got opportunities. Do you think that didn't take some sneaking around? I lied to you, but I also lied *for* you."

"Gran," Ben said. "Your own son shouldn't have asked that of you."

"Oh, make no mistake," she said. "He did not *ask*."

"I have a right to know the truth. Even if it cost you saying no to him for once."

"You try opposing him and let me know how it goes for you." Ben stepped down so that they were standing on the same level. This close he smelled the lingering cigarette smoke in her clothes and hair; heard the clicking of her nails in nervous repetition. Her eyes were too bright when she said, "So, you are going to turn your back on us, aren't you? Well, just be *quiet* about it. Live with Gregen for a year. But don't let that snotty little girlfriend of yours give your journal to the police. Don't do this to us."

"Wait. Bonnie Jean has my journal?"

"I should have torn it to pieces."

"Did you read it?"

"That brazen girl read it out loud to Donna and me. What were you thinking, Ben, to write like that? One page alone will destroy your father. Please."

"We've got to stop lying, Gran. I don't want to be beat up again. I want to know who I am, who my parents are."

Gran rolled her eyes. "Biological parenthood is so overrated. Think of how random it is."

"Please just say it. Please just tell me the truth."

Lindquist's voice sounded from below, his hard shoe on the first stone step. "Mrs. Hunter?"

She grabbed his wrist. "Your father is not a strong man. Your diary will destroy him. Please, think of how his misery will hurt me."

"Mrs. Hunter? Is that you up there?" Ben raised his eyebrows at her and backed away. She turned and hurried down the steps. He heard Lindquist say, "Major Hernandez said you went to the ladies' room. That's downstairs."

"Ben is up there," she said, her voice tense, superior.

"So? He's a free man. He can be where he wants. You, on the other hand, have to be escorted until day after Christmas. Remember what the judge said this morning?"

"Who died and made you boss?"

"You could try to enjoy having a handsome marine escort like me, ma'am. I'll show you were the bathroom is."

35

BEN knew that as soon as Max finished murdering the reading from Isaiah, Gran would tell, so bending over, he crept along the balcony rail all the way around to the back of the chapel. The stairs led to the basement, with a landing on the main floor beside the nave entrance. Ben saw a place underneath the stairs where he could remain unseen.

Without his contact lens, his widened pupil gathered faint strands of light; he could see in the dark. He stepped back as far as he could beneath the stairs, leaned against the stone, and feeling cold, he shrugged into the jacket he carried. He drew the journal out of the pocket, taking the papers there with it. He recognized the opened envelope by Admiral Johnson's writing; it was the letter meant to replace his birth certificate. He flipped open the jacket, saw *Tom MacBride* embroidered on the inside pocket, and remembered the jacket put over him in the helicopter. *Tom had this letter all along?* He shoved it back into the pocket and flipped pages to find where he'd left off. Was this it? The start of a new page said:

> February 14
>
> Meadowlark Inn somewhere north of Richmond. I meant today to be the happiest of my marriage so far. After a visit to the doctor, I prepared a marvelous dinner, roses on the table, a fragrant fire in the fireplace. Somehow, I had forgotten to buy more beer and also needed one more lemon for the fish and so I ran back out. When I returned, Max's car was there. I heard the shower running and went in to surprise him. There he was, naked, ready to shower, my diary open in his hand. "What are you doing?" I asked for I have not let him read it since we were married.
>
> He put it down. He seemed embarrassed and so I said, "Well, never mind. I have wonderful news!" The doctor confirmed what the pregnancy test indicated; the baby is due in October. I expected his joy to match mine.
>
> I was so wrong.
>
> I did not think he would hit me. I thought that his accusations would be the only abuse. Max believes that Tom is the baby's father. He asked me to deny it! I could not even speak; I said, only, "Max," in a pleading voice and his blow was so fast and so hard that I did not react quickly enough. He knocked me down. My head had snapped back and I felt very strange and stunned with pain and a numb shock. He threw my diary at me and it hit my shoulder. This roused me enough from my shock so that when I saw his foot go up I know that he meant to stomp on my stomach. With both hands, I held the diary up and when his foot hit it, I pushed with all my strength and flipped him so that he lost his balance. I got away, grabbing my purse as I fled. I do not even have a coat. In loyalty, I guess, I have never described our "fights"—his violence. Now I carry his child, have written the worst report that can be written about a man because his child must know, must beware. I've left him before; this is why I will never again live with him.

Despite the building noise of worshipers gathering in the nave of the chapel beyond his hiding place, their excitement bidding Ben join them, Ben read the passage again, realizing that if she had fled, Max would not have read this part. He stared at the words, soaking in the tone, strong compassion rising in him for her. She had made the spiritual journey Ben had tried to begin. As recorded in the pages of her journal, she was honest about her mistakes, open about her struggles, comfortable talking about her questions; he understood her shock, felt the dizzying betrayal in Max's blow. Ben looked up. Now he heard people speaking in their familiar Maryland accent the cadences of Christmas greetings. He heard a familiar voice say, "Ben?" He slipped the journal back into the jacket.

From his hiding place, Ben could see Bonnie Jean peer into the darkness where he hid. She'd fastened her hair up so that in the incandescent light of the chapel her creamy neck and chin and bare arms looked luminous as she craned to see around the curve of the stairwell. Against the plush of her long black dress, she clutched *his* journal looking like she held onto a piece of the brown earth.

"Bonnie Jean." He stepped out of the shadows.

She ran toward him, one bare knee revealing a ragged tear in her dress.

"Your eye," she said, one hand reaching out for him. She touched his arm.

"Lost my contact."

"It's very cool that way." Her eyes went over him, brightening with tears and longing. "Just a little naked-looking." She smiled her impish smile, eyes hopeful.

"I can see better," he said, stiffly, but the entire fabric of his being stretched toward her.

"I read your journal." She patted it, still clutching it close. She glanced behind her. "I'm sorry I read it. I shouldn't have. I couldn't resist."

She held his journal out to him. Ben made no movement to take it. "You couldn't help it. People are utterly irresistible when you…love them." This terrible truth hurt him. What he was finding out was tearing him from every person he loved—even if he loved them painfully or in outraged chains of duty.

"What you've been through, Ben," she said, her voice soft and unsteady. "I couldn't have *really* understood—if I hadn't read it, but, I *didn't* read it to Mom or Dad or tell them what it said. I didn't want to steal *that* from you, too. But maybe tonight you can tell them. They want to talk to you."

"I was wrong to ask you to keep stuff a secret," Ben said.

"Yes," she nodded. "I think you were."

He said, "Did you read what I wrote in there about you?"

"Every word."

"So you see what trouble I'm in with you."

"He's lying about my dad."

"Maybe not."

He heard footsteps approach. Then Joe's face appeared just below the curve of the stairs that hid them. He saw them, came to them and extended his hand to shake Ben's. "Why are you hiding?" Joe said.

"I'm hiding from my best friend who is wearing a *skirt* in public," Ben smiled; he couldn't help it though Joe looked comfortable with his blue-green plaid kilt and those nerdy, nubby knee socks.

"Tradition. All the MacBride men are wearing kilts tonight." Joe said and grabbed Ben, hugging him. "It is so good to see you smile," and immediately, too, Bonnie Jean's arms were around Ben's neck in that sturdy, tight embrace of hers that he loved so much.

"Come with us," Joe said, encircling Ben's shoulders with his arm. Bonnie Jean took his arm and held it close to her side. They moved in the crowd down the center aisle. An elderly usher gave them slim white candles fitted with a paper holder. "We light these at 'Silent Night,'" Bonnie Jean explained. "The whole place goes dark. I'm so glad you're here."

Ben spotted Max, his grandmother, Donna, Tim and Keith on the right side of the chapel in the space under the balcony. "I might not stay," Ben said, hesitating.

"You have to," Joe said. "We have a good surprise for you."

Just as they turned toward the east side of the transept where Ben had hid all afternoon, Ben saw Gregen's white head. Dressed in a suit and tie, overcoat over his arm, he was talking to Tom, Peter, Tommy and a group of elderly people Ben did not know. "Gregen?" he whispered.

"He got here around two."

As if by instinct, Gregen turned toward them. He left his conversation and met them when they were still some distance from the MacBrides. He held his hands out and Ben went to him. Gregen took his shoulders in both hands and kissed each cheek. "*Joyeux Noël*, Ben," he said, quietly.

"*Joyeux Noël, monsieur*," Ben returned, adding, "It is so good to see you."

Gregen embraced him, held him close, Ben felt him draw his breath in. "Does the rib brace you're wearing help with the pain?"

"It really does."

Gregen peered at his face. "You know that Tom was utterly traumatized by the sight of your injury. Joe, too, of course." With his left hand, Gregen smoothed Ben's hair up away from the scar at the hairline, glanced at Joe with eyebrows raised and nodded his head. Then he smiled at Ben patting both cheeks. "Ah, to have you here, in my arms after so many years."

"Does Gran know you're here?"

"She knew I was considering it. Have you spoken with her yet tonight?"

"Yes, sir. Briefly. She's sitting across the chapel," Ben said, pointing directly opposite across the centre aisle with the forward facing pews to the other arm of Sleepy Hollow. The gesture brought him to face Tom, who approached in his kilt, his kilted sons following. Tom smiled at Ben, eyes bright and eager, but he crossed his arms over his chest showing his restraint.

The strife of Ben's unanswered questions held Ben those three steps away from Tom whose concern for Ben showed plainly in his stance and in his face and eyes. And seeing him, Ben remembered the way Tom had humbled himself to warm Ben up on the helicopter. He recognized that, somehow, a clean, grateful respect for Tom had been woven inside him. He recalled Tom's stalwart love, his concentration on Ben's well-being in the quaking fury of Ben's rage, remembered how Tom had used his own shirt to dry Ben's hair.

He took a step toward Tom, but stopped as quickly as if his shirt were caught on a nail; Ben remembered Tom's humble admission of fault. Exactly what had Tom said when Ben was sinking into icy unconscious?

Ben's dilemma was a rope around his neck: *If you are my father, I don't ever have to go back to Max.* Now in Tom's presence, the possibility burned like a temptation he should shun. He couldn't—*shouldn't* want to be a MacBride because his sonship would convict Tom; he couldn't *want* Tom's fatherhood because his rescue would prohibit his fiery, inalterably sensual love for Bonnie Jean. *The truth will stand regardless of what I want,* Ben reasoned with cool detachment, asking himself as he stared into Tom's still solemn, still approachable eyes, *Do I have the courage to find out?*

Tom said, "You are looking much better than the last time I saw you."

"I feel a little better." He had to say it. "Thanks to you."

Everyone looked at each other, the awkwardness thick and itchy. Ben said, "Did Mrs. MacBride stay home?"

"She's downstairs feeding the baby so Cara can make it through the service."

"Do you think she's done, Dad? I've got to get her to mend my dress." Bonnie Jean poked her knee out. "I got it caught in the garment bag zipper."

Peter and Tommy laughed at her, a little too loudly, and still the tension did not flee. "You'd better hurry, Jeannie."

"How can she sew it here?" Ben asked.

The MacBrides gave him a collective, knowing laugh. "Far be it from Laurie to be anywhere without needle and thread…and if she is, she'll think of something." Tom said.

"She duct taped Scott's basketball shorts on me once when mine got blood on them," Peter said. He demonstrated her spinning him, rolling the tape around his slim waist. They applied more strained laughter to the tension, the result like ice sent to melt a snowdrift.

Gregen said, "I'm afraid Tom and Laurie were displeased with the risks you boys took. And I must agree with them, Ben."

"Did you—" he glanced at Joe and then at Tom. "Did you get in trouble?"

"We all," Peter included Ben in the circle he drew in the air, "have to pay to repair your car."

"I'm included in this?"

"Duh," Tommy said. "You're one of us, now."

"And to make up for the anxiety we caused Mom," Joe said, "we have to give her as many hours of peace and quiet—clean the kitchen, keep the fire going, chop wood. All over Christmas break."

Again Ben glanced at Tom who seemed to read his question.

"Pete and Joe were mistaken, not defiant."

Though thoughts flew thickly, justifying him, Ben felt embarrassed for the way he had shouted at Tom. "I was defiant, Coach."

"Yes, I know, Ben." They met eyes. "I think you were objecting to your bruises," Tom said quietly, as the organist leaned on the keys as if with his entire forearm, "as any man would." The music was a thunderclap above them, around them.

Bonnie Jean said, "I have to go. We're singing part of the prelude since our concert was canceled last night." As she passed behind Ben, she slipped Ben's journal into his hand and whispered, "Do what you think best with this."

He took it and held it behind his back. Katie's diary, heavy against his bruised side, had to stay hidden.

What to do with this one? Ben considered. Ben rubbed his thumb across the soft leather of his own testament. *If I put this in Tom's hand now, or in Uncle Gregen's...*He thought of his grandmother's plea. *Would I be cruel to ignore her?*

"Um, Coach," he said nervously, glancing at Tom, tugging at the collar of the jacket he wore. "I think this is yours. Do you mind if I keep it until the end of the service? I need it."

"No, I don't mind at all. I'm glad to see you're dressed warmly."

"Thank you," Ben said, with a glance at Gregen. He slipped his own journal into the right hand pocket of his jacket. It was smaller than Katie's, not packed with papers as hers was, and it fit there, though it made a lump.

"Will you sit here with us tonight, Ben?" Gregen said.

"I don't know," Ben said, his voice thick as he glanced at Tom and touched the diary just to remind himself that the truth was within reach. "I'm not sure."

Gregen nodded. "I will walk with you, then, and greet your grandmother and parents."

"You don't need to do that, sir."

"Of course I do." He turned to Tom and touched his arm. Gregen gestured toward the other side of the church. "It has been a very long time since I spoke to Max. Would you accompany me, Tom?"

"I will," Tom said.

Ben sputtered a protest, but Gregen shook his head and whispered in French to Ben, "There will be no argument." Aloud in English he added, "May I take your arm, Ben? I wish your father's initial impression to be that I am old and harmless."

They fell into step, Gregen holding Ben's arm at the elbow, Tom with Joe, Peter and Tommy behind them. "Tom and I are grieved about Max's cruelty to you. There is no excuse for what Tom and I suspect he has done."

Somehow, walking along with Gregen, Ben knew the depth of his conviction. "How long has it been since you've seen him?"

"I saw him in court until you were past six, but he would never speak with me."

"In court…" Ben shook his head.

"The last time I spoke to your father face to face was when he brought you that ball at your grandmother's house."

"I remember that day, but I don't remember you."

"I came to see you the next morning. You told me all about it, *en français*. You were bilingual. Officially you lived at your grandmother's house, but you had a room at Apple Tree Farm and saw me daily until your father took you to California where he was then stationed. That is when we lost touch despite my efforts."

Slowly they rounded the corner to approach the pew where his family stood. Ben said, "But we won't lose touch again."

"No, never again."

"The books you sent were so important to me. Thank you. And to hear you went to court…"

"Tom and I both tried desperately to win you."

"I have to tell you, there's a ripping inside me now." Ben's eyes went to his family standing by the front pew on the right side.

"I know it has been difficult for you to know how to honor your father, and I know your giving, generous heart still seeks to do that and to understand him. But you must not put yourself in danger. And I must talk to you seriously after this service."

"He told me," Ben whispered, nodding his head toward Max, "about Tom being my father."

Gregen studied Ben's eyes, acknowledging the deep hurt. "No doubt you have suffered enough without this *nonsense* from Max," Gregen said, with infinite sadness.

Ben gestured to include Gregen and Tom. "To believe you and Tom means to have the most beautiful things, except I won't be free of the colonel." He sensed that the MacBrides were no longer right behind him and glanced around to see that they'd been stopped and somebody was hugging Joe. Tom met Ben's glance, looking impatient, torn. Ben turned back to Gregen. "And besides. His story about Tom makes sense. I don't fit with the colonel. It explains his hate."

"You don't fit with Max because he discarded his true rights to father you by his behavior to your mother. Her journal explains this. And, from what Tom suspects, he has continued to forfeit that privilege. And in you I see that you understand things that set you apart from Max and you've made choices with your heart and spirit that have set you at enmity with him."

Ben was quiet, touched by Gregen's insight. He nodded solemnly but said, "You have to understand, sir, I grew up feeling the colonel's hurt about all this. When I was asleep, it was the dark shape lurking at the end of my bed. It was the gas that I could smell permeating every family meal, exploding when I blinked the wrong way. I know how real a reason it is and I know how bad it hurts him."

"I know you must analyze and understand, but why believe your father when he has so mistreated you?"

"But he couldn't *be* my father," Ben said, his cool analytical stance crumbling; his voice broke. "He threw me out of the car the day of the accident. He tossed me out the sunroof like a piece of gum. Fathers don't—"

Gregen stopped walking. For an instant his fingers gripped Ben's arm too tightly. Ben felt a tremor move through the old man. He turned to meet Ben's eyes, his own blazing with grief too awful for tears. With his other hand, Gregen reached up and touched Ben's cheek in a gesture of deep compassion, the ridged scar on his thumb scratching the edge of Ben's jaw. *"Mon Dieu,"* Gregen whispered. Ben covered Gregen's hand with his own, holding it there against his face, meeting the old man's pained, brown eyes to search them. *Ah,* Ben thought, *he didn't know. He couldn't have known because he and Tom got to the accident afterwards.*

"Bien sur," Gregen said as Ben felt the man rein himself in. "That explains what I could not," Gregen said, but Ben felt also Gregen's inner anger. "That's what Sibilla tried so hard to tell me. I did not deduce it because how could I have imagined such behavior from a father? Never!" He dropped his hand to Ben's shoulder. "But you figured it out."

"It fits," Ben nodded. "I'm convinced it's true."

"How that realization must have hurt you."

"Yes," Ben said. "But it explains things. So that helps."

"This lie has tortured your grandmother all these years," Gregen said. "She is in the gravest danger. Let us go to her." They turned again, side by side, to walk.

"I'm so sorry about your wife, Uncle Gregen."

"She was also your great-aunt and loved you dearly."

"How are you not out for revenge?"

"Do not think it has been easy for me to forgive your father. It has been the greatest challenge of my life. When I think of what you've suffered, I know I will have to fight through the most intense feelings of outrage again to forgive."

"Don't take this the wrong way, sir, but you seem calm about it."

"I am composed. Any man can learn self-control. I have done so through much intense work and prayer."

Ben squeezed Gregen's hand close to his side as they walked in step. They were now a few feet from his family. "Max," Gregen said, his voice stern and formal. "It has been a long time."

Max turned and his mouth went slack, his eyes flicked quickly to Ben. Lindquist moved closer to Max's side. Keith and Tim, seeing Ben, shrieked and tried to run to him, but Ella prevented them, her whisper hissing low. She made the boys stand behind her, but they looked around her bulk to return Ben's wave.

"Dad," Ben said, taking Gregen's arm again, "You remember Dr. Bénet, don't you?" Max stood more immovable than stone. Ben glanced at his grandmother, eyes urging her cooperation. "It turns out that Dr. Bénet is a relative. But you guys all knew that, right?"

No one moved or spoke.

Gregen extended his hand to Donna. "I am pleased to meet you after so many years, Mrs. Hunter." With a disgusted glance at Max, who stood glaring at them, Lindquist moved forward and offered Gregen his hand. They exchanged pleasant words, Lindquist introduced his wife and sons. Gregen greeted Ella Hunter; she mumbled the requisite response.

Stepping away from Ben, whispering to him in French to stay behind, Gregen stretched forth his hand to Max. "Will you shake hands with me tonight, Max?"

Max pointed at Gregen. "You should not have given him that car behind my back."

"This is not the place to list who should not have done certain things." Gregen looked around, gestured at the crowd, smiled at Donna and Gran. "It is Christmas and I have forgiven you for the past heartbreak you caused me. Let us shake over that, and I promise you we will discuss your latest deeds in a place where doing so will not upset Ben and your young sons."

Hands clasped in front of his body, Max glared, jaw wagging as if searching for words he'd lost. Ella moved to his side, put a hand on his shoulder. Tom and his boys joined the group, inadvertently making a circle of friendly handshaking with those who crowded close. Still, Gregen and Max stood in perpetual opposition.

"Ah, the kilt," Lindquist said, shaking Tom's hand with obvious warmth, his teasing eyes seemed grateful for the distraction.

"It's like your fancy eye, Major," Tom said, smiling at the special occasion prosthesis made to look like the Marine Corps symbol—red iris with the gold globe and anchor blazoned across it. "An honor for a man to wear." Tom checked to see that his boys stood beside Ben, and alongside Gregen, he offered his hand to Max. "I'm glad to see you here tonight, Max."

But Ella Hunter's hand shot out to block Tom's way. "He's nervous about his reading," she snapped. "Let him be."

Several voices speaking Gregen's name turned them from the redoubling tension as Admiral Johnson and several other men joined the group. "Dr. Bénet?" Johnson said, "May I introduce my son, Dr. Arthur Johnson?"

The admiral's son, his wife and several doctors crowded close to meet Gregen, clasping his hand in both of theirs, mentioning mutual friends, studies Gregen had written, clinics whose locations Ben recognized from the diary. Several military men and their wives joined the group all greeting Gregen with enthusiastic warmth. The crowd distracted Gran enough so that Ben's brothers sneaked to him, clung to his legs, begging him to take them home. Ben urged them to be patient; he wanted to stay as close as he could to Gregen, hungry to learn the details of the adults' admiration.

Now the coach from Key School was shaking Gregen's hand, and waiting to speak to him was Smitty's twin, his double in a suit and tie, and Mrs. Miller from school with her family. Ben noticed Ella's fiercely protective stance with Max. She kept her right shoulder and hip just in front of his body, her expression threatening to deck anyone who came too close. Ben slipped his hand into his pocket, feeling the incriminating journal there.

When the organ music swelled, the crowd around Gregen dissipated. Joe touched Ben's arm. "Looks like mom's having to fight off the crowds to save our seats." Ben saw her standing in the pew opposite them, Cara on her shoulder, Grannie frowning beside her. Laurie waved to Ben, her eyes beckoning him. "Tell her I said hi."

"Come tell her yourself," Peter said. "We're saving you a spot."

Ben glanced at Tom, who, though he was talking with Donna, kept his eyes moving around the group. Joe said, "If it's true—which it's *not*—you won't be telling her anything she hasn't already forgiven."

Ben glanced at his brothers who clutched the fabric of his jeans in their fists, then at Max. He saw Bonnie Jean's choir filing onto the altar. Once in her place, Bonnie Jean lifted her knee to show the mended place in her dress. Her eyes, full of hope and courage, called to him. Admiral Johnson thrust himself into Ben's field of vision. He stuck out his hand. "Merry Christmas, Ben. Glad to see you're safe and warm."

"Merry Christmas to you, too." Ben said. He reached inside his jacket and took out the envelope from behind the journal. "Remember that day the Miata crashed, Admiral Johnson?" he said. "Thanks for writing this letter for me that day."

Max reached for it, "You haven't looked in there? Just give it here, now."

"I wanted to say," Ben said, putting the letter back into his jacket pocket. "I wasn't thrown clear of the accident that day. I wasn't in the car." Ben met Max's eyes. "Just like the very first accident. I was out of the car *before* the crash, wasn't I, Dad?"

Ben saw the boil burst in his father's soul, saw his grandmother flinch and shudder. She covered her face with both hands.

Ben's breath caught. So it was true. A terrible sad peace settled in him.

The music changed. With a look at Admiral Johnson, Lindquist spoke in a conciliatory tone. "Admiral, sir, we're certain to attract the attention of the entire city if we stay right here." He winked at Ben. "And I hear the choir from CCS is not to be missed."

"Max," Johnson gestured toward the altar. "You'll sit up in the front row with me and go over that passage so you don't disgrace me further." His fingers prodded Max's shoulders to turn him toward the altar. Lindquist tried to reason with Ella Hunter, but her weeping grew violent and loud. Gregen spoke to her, but she shoved his hand away, fell to her knees with a thud, and threw her arms around Ben's legs. "Please, Ben, please don't do this to me."

"Gran!" Ben said, pulling on her arms, urging her to stand up. "Get up!"

"Ella," Gregen said.

"Ella, stop it!" Donna snapped.

"It's okay, Uncle Gregen," Ben said into the murmuring, stunned chapel. "I'll stay with her until she calms down a little." With Donna's help, he pulled his grandmother to her feet and she stumbled into Ben's arms, hiding her face on his shoulder. Gregen nodded his assent. Turning her away, Ben met Tom's eyes, sure that the longing he couldn't quench showed again in them.

Pete and Joe walked with him. "We'll stick with you."

"She wouldn't want it," Ben shook his head. "It'll make her worse."

"We're right over there," again, Joe pointed the way, directly across from where Donna had gone to sit in the perpendicular rows on the west side of the chapel's crossed arms.

36

DONNA'S face was bright red and she sat stiffly on the pew's edge. Ben sat beside Gran, his arm around her, trying to muffle her weeping on his shoulder. Keith and Tim bickered over who would sit near him. Donna pulled them past Ben to her other side. Both boys whimpered and pouted. Ben and Donna exchanged glances.

"Shh," Ben whispered, patting his grandmother's back. The first notes of the choir's song erupted from the organ in a solemn prelude. "Gran, try to calm down," Ben said.

"How could you humiliate us? How could you?"

"Dad's an alcoholic. He's in bad shape. The admiral's seen him mess up so many times. You have to face the truth."

"I don't know what's gotten into you," Gran sobbed. "You never were so damn interested in the truth."

"Of course I was," Ben whispered. "It's just that I believed you. Or I kept trying to."

Three girls stepped out in front of the choir close to the microphones set there for them. Victoria, Michelle and Bonnie Jean opened their mouths and the tense quiet around him evaporated in a hush.

"In the bleak midwinter…" The choir resounded behind them; the organ swelled softly beneath and Ben breathed in. The song took him, Bonnie Jean's shining eyes seeking his. He sat up. Gran noticed and pulled away, sniffed and followed his gaze. He heard her grunt beside him and glanced at her. With a disgusted glare at him, she moved away from him, took Kleenex out of her purse and mopped her face. When she settled back against the pew, it shook. Donna sighed.

The choir's song flowed into a processional carol sung by the USNA choir who stood at the far back of the nave in a balcony choir loft. The ministers walked down the aisle holding flickering candles before them. Aged ushers followed, shuffling proudly. As her choir filed off the altar, Ben saw Bonnie Jean take her place with her family in the front row they filled there. By moving his head just a little, he had a clear line of vision past the people in the pew perpendicular to where Tom sat directly opposite him.

The music spilled from the gold-colored pipes clustered between the three arches of the main part of the sanctuary, it spilled with the eager power of the congregation's unity and joy and purpose. The music called to the deep wells of Ben's torn heart.

The congregation rose to their feet in a solemn, corporate movement. It was the sound of ceremonies to Ben, the prelude to worship and the giving of honor. The sound of countless soles met the floor in firm, synchronized salute, and hundreds of coats and trousers and dresses swished as people rose to their feet. Around him the scent of perfume, of a thousand melting candles made solemn their offering. He, also, rose to his feet.

> O come all ye faithful,
> Joyful and triumphant!
> O come ye, O come ye to Bethlehem.

In the sound of all those voices lifted, he felt someone's eyes on him,

Tom's watchful glance reaching all the way down the row perpendicular to his own. From that safe distance, Ben kept his eyes on Tom. Ben was trying, as he had since the day Tom wheeled into Mrs. Poulard's office, to measure the quality of him. Now Ben tried to find the truth in his stance, in his expression of comfort reaching through the tension that held them apart. Tom put his arm around Laurie, whose tears Ben could see even at his distance. Gregen leaned across Laurie to speak to Tom; Joe pointed across the rows and waved. Ben brooded over the distance that separated them, rows going different ways, clogged with people, but he had chosen his spot, compassion and loyalty once again keeping him in uncertainty and dread. He touched her diary, hidden in the pocket close to his heart, wanting to read and know.

The congregation sat for the reading given by one of the chaplains. Donna forced Ella to switch places with her and when she was next to Ben, she placed her huge purse on her knees. "You haven't finished reading, have you?"

"No."

"My purse will hide it."

He glanced at his grandmother. She held a tissue to her nose and stared blankly in front of her. Sighing with a mingled compassion and disgust, he drew out the journal and looked for his place.

He had missed a page, the end of the part in the coffeehouse right after Tom's incriminating quote and Katie's assertion that...*to the old me, to my natural self, love-making at that gorgeous, intimate moment with Tom MacBride was inevitable*...There the page ended and Ben had stopped reading, but on the top of the next page, Katie had written a little bit. This he had missed. He saw why. The corner of the page, itself stained and buckled, was crimped to the next. Ben smoothed out the wrinkle, felt the stickiness old, but virulent, in the corner.

> January 1 later...Oh, my narrative was interrupted! You see I am here alone and I was writing and I thought I heard something and jumped like a nervous cat! I spilled my cup of chocolate all over the table!
>
> You may be surprised to know that I am alone when earlier tonight I was not. While Tom and I were talking, Peter awakened crying and had a fever. Tom insisted we all go home and be comfortable. They went and I stayed. Laurie deserves her own husband to herself; she has been so kind to lend him to me for all my desperate questions.
>
> Ah! Dear Diary, I sense your laughter. Is it joy or mockery? Of course we did not make love. Oh, no! You see, though I may remember how I would have behaved, I do not have to do so any longer. As Tom said about himself, he "might have certain thoughts and physical sensations, but he loves Laurie and Laurie

alone and he wishes always to be gracious to her." This is how he actually talks, dear Diary!

He left me saying he was not sure I should return to Max, not sure I should trust his advice, but I have decided that I must return to Max as a way of demonstrating my forgiveness to the man I chose for my husband. I did have a choice, as you remember, dear Diary. I'm going. Tomorrow. I know I'm right to do it.

He looked at Donna who was reading over his shoulder. She nodded at him. "Keep going," she whispered. Ben read hungrily, reviewing in this new light the description of Max's violence that had driven her to flee her husband. The congregation sang again. Gran declined, sitting arms crossed, tearing her program into little shreds. But Ben rose, keeping the diary hidden in the pages of his own folded program, he rose and read, he sat and read, and only when he felt the room go still and hold its breath did he look up.

He felt a hand on his shoulder and turned. Lindquist leaned forward. "I'm right behind you, Ben. Right here." Ben saw Nancy beside her husband and she smiled at him; their sons waved. He smiled. He looked up searching for the reason that the room seemed changed. In the pews that separated him from Tom, he recognized so many people: the Ridouts standing in the last row of the section, Tiffany and her family, the lady who owned Middleton's tavern, one of the nurses who stitched up his arm that day in the fall. Knox and his parents, and with them Mrs. Poulard and her family. Davy gave him a tense wave. In front of them stood a man Ben recognized as Smitty's partner from when he'd climbed out of the Volvo's sunroof. He had been one of the men who reached up to catch him if he fell.

The organist sounded the notes to the familiar carol "Away in a Manger." The congregation bustled to their feet, looking around. Ben moved the diary and saw Max's reading was scheduled next. He touched the pew railing in front of him. The swell of the organ's power vibrated against his palm and the congregation joined him, singing in full voices. Ben gripped the railing, his hand, his arm quickening with the mounting vibration of the song.

When it ended, the congregation sat expectantly. Ben perched on the edge of the seat, waiting. Johnson stood up, hand on Max's elbow, pulled him to his feet. Ben's nerves piqued in the quiet, still room. He glanced at the MacBrides, whose eyes were cast in identical apprehensive expressions at Max. Uncle Gregen, eyes bright with compassion, met Ben's agonized gaze.

Max got to the podium, clearly undone. His shaking was visible from where Ben sat. His attempts to smooth out his papers sounded as if he were ripping them in half. The microphone, bent toward him, broadcast his dry-mouth swallowing across the big room.

Beneath that sublime dome, Annapolis waited, eyes front. Max coughed, and the licking of his lips crackled in amplification before he murmured, "Um, I…um…I'm going to have to ask my son to help me tonight." He looked up, peering into the crowd. "Ben? Can you help me read this?"

Ben stood up before he thought. He saw the faces turned to him, all those familiar faces. Now, too, he saw Patty crying in the pew behind the MacBrides where Beth Davidson and Doug sat on either side patting her back. Dr. Deterding nodded at him from the balcony, her face smoothed by the softened light of that heaven-come-down above them. Tucking the journal back into the jacket pocket, Ben went quickly to the altar. When Ben stood beside him, Max said to the congregation, "Guess I need glasses or something."

A tense, hopeful laugh rippled down the center aisles and into the wide open arms of Sleepy Hollow.

Max pointed to the text lying on the podium. Ben stepped closer, his father's scent threatening to overpower him. He took a deep breath and spoke clearly into the microphone:

> "The Spirit of the Lord God is upon Me,
> Because the Lord has anointed Me
> To preach good tidings to the poor;
> He has sent Me to heal the brokenhearted,
> To proclaim liberty to the captives,
> And the opening of the prison to those who are bound;
> To proclaim the acceptable year of the Lord,
> And the day of vengeance of our God;
> To comfort all who mourn,"

Ben looked up, saw the relief, the joy in the faces upturned to hear him.

> "To console those who mourn in Zion,
> To give them beauty for ashes,
> The oil of joy for mourning,
> The garment of praise for the spirit of heaviness;
> That they may be called trees of righteousness,
> The planting of the Lord, that He may be glorified.
> …For I, the Lord, love justice…"

Ben saw the pride glittering in Tom's eyes, saw Laurie snatching her tears away. And when he glanced at Gregen, expecting to see reproof for his impulsive decision to stand so close to his dangerous enemy, he saw instead the look of brightest love that he had ever seen in his life. Ben knew that in their years apart, Gregen had paid a costly price to forgive the cruel man now standing broken beside Ben. He breathed in and said, "Isaiah sixty-one, verses one through eight." He saw that Smitty stood by the corner of the altar, his partner at the other side.

Max grabbed Ben's elbow. He covered the microphone with his other hand. "We're gonna walk right out the side door. You and me. Right now. Let's go."

"No," Ben shook his head. He pulled his elbow away from Max's grip and put one hand on the small of Max's back. "This way," he said, guiding the trembling man down the steps and across the front of the congregation as the next reader took the podium behind him.

Max whispered, his voice conspiratorial, "There's a door this side, too. Just keep walking. I saw what you put in your pocket. Let's go home and I can show you where it's written about Tom."

"I'm not going home with you, Dad," Ben said. They had reached their pew; Smitty stood beside Max, Lindquist right behind. Ben met eyes with them, realizing that they knew his father's crimes. They were here on Tom's bidding to keep Max's fists from striking again. He put Max in their hands, walked to the far end of the pew, entered there and stood beside Donna. The reading over, the congregation stood to sing and as Ben watched them, all of Annapolis gathered beneath the dome, blessed by the light of the little heaven that had come to hover so meaningfully above him here. In his handgrip on the pew he felt again the thunder of the music. One by one, those he knew turned to him singing, and smiled, their eyes telling him that they knew about his suffering, that they had with one voice objected and now welcomed him home.

Ben reached to his inner pocket for the diary. He took out Admiral Johnson's letter, too, and tucked it in the back. He had been reading Katie's turmoil over her legal separation. Her heart was torn; how to maintain a relationship with Max's mother, how to keep Max safely involved with his child, how to try to reach Max, her longing for him to be transformed as she felt she was being changed. She was ill, trying to hide recurrent bladder infections from Uncle Gregen and Aunt Sibilla who were burdened with their own ill and aging parents. Then her pregnancy's wonders dominated the narrative.

In the chapel around him, a soloist sang the haunting "Gesù, Bambino." Ben bent his head to read that they were visiting Ella when Katie's labor started, when the first snowflakes fell. She had not expected him for two more weeks and attributed her odd feelings to the excitement of having Tom and Laurie visit for the Columbus Day holiday. But labor turned precipitous, as furious and unrelenting as the blizzard outside, and by the time Katie knew that her time had come, the roads were filling with drifting snow still flying on hard winds.

The little town's two ambulances were stuck on Route 17, seeking injured motorists. Gregen himself, taking the train home from the airport, arrived just in time to find Tom standing behind Katie, supporting her shoulders, counting during her contractions, "One…two…three…breathe now, the baby needs air…four…five…six…hold on now," Tom coached. "Wait for your Uncle Gregen to wash his hands…" The diary said that Laurie extended both hands to support his emerging head, while with tender skill, Gregen applied counter pressure to ease his shoulders out, but life's relentless strength rushed him and he slipped into Laurie out-stretched hands.

Katie described the moment when she first held him. She wrote that her strength was spent, but her heart exhilarated and eager for him. When she stretched out her hands, arms shaking from the rush of birth, Tom's arms encircled her shoulders. With his hands he held up her elbows, giving her arms his own strength to receive the child that Gregen and Laurie placed into her outstretched hands. An image formed in Ben's mind of the moment when those eight hands held him up in quick triumph—he came to them alive, breathing, eyes awakening, reaching arms and fingers, all of him still gleaming with the salt water of life.

Over and over he read, and on and on he studied the scribbled story as the chaplain spoke his careful sermon. Relentlessly down the row, Max hissed in whisper to get his attention. Ben kept reading:

> I have discovered that the hospital chaplain called the Marine Corps Commandant a week ago when they thought I was sure to die. So my estranged husband had to be forced to come to see me as I lay dying. But I improved. Max will to be home at the end of next week. Our baby will be nearly six weeks old by then.
>
> Sometime in the vague clouds of my illness, I realized that since I am the only one who knows the capacity of Max's anger, I had better put my stipulations about the baby's care and future in writing. I have a feeling, that when Max sees this gorgeous child, he will be compelled with desire and will want to possess him as he did me. The child looks like me, but with a beauty of spirit, an elegance that I imagine he caught from the spiritual and practical care given him by Laurie and Tom. This deep beauty is recognizable in their sons and it comes from love. Just as in my absence Laurie fed and nurtured my son, so also in Max's disregard, Tom filled the office of love and became the baby's true father. I will never regret my relationship with Max because it helped to bring me this child (who, as my sole heir, I have decided to name Thomas Benedetto Hunter), but I do not wish my son's heart ever once to feel the panic his father's touch will cause.

Ben sat up, drew an audible breath. His father's whispered call was squelched by Smitty and Lindquist; Ben's ears sounded with fierce emotion. He flipped the book to the back cover where he'd stuck Admiral Johnson's letter. He felt inside it and found the small, waxy paper he expected. Ben felt the raised seal and the shivers scurried up his arms to his ears. The words were small and faint, but issued in the State of New Jersey, it certified that a boy was born on his birthday to Katrine Marie Hunter. The father was named as expected and true, Maximillian James Hunter.

Another soloist sang, the lights dimmed and Ben stared at the proof of his father's lies, the sleight of hand used so easily with him blinded as he had been by hope and loyalty. Ben read the official document again and again. There was shuffling, ushers passing offering trays. Ben took out his wallet and put the birth certificate in behind his driver's license. When he moved to replace his wallet, he saw a couple of pieces of paper float out of the diary to the kneeler. In his peripheral vision, he saw both Max and Gran flick out hands to get them, but Donna, closest to Ben, retrieved them quickly and put them in his hands. One looked like the remainder of the article he'd found on Thanksgiving. The other was a photograph.

An icy draft swept along the stone floor of the chapel and despite the soloist's volume, Ben could hear the wind driving clumps of snow and ice against the tall windows above him. In his clutched hand the paper fluttered. He opened the diary and fitted the newspaper against the part of the article that still clung to the staples in the last page. From his right hand pocket, he took out his own journal and flipped to the pages he'd written around Thanksgiving. Stuck in there was the headline to this article. Ben fit it against the other two fragments, the story complete at his fingertips.

The chapel went dark and the tones of "Silent Night" sounded gold and true from the organ pipes. In the dim light Ben peered at the photograph. It showed a smiling woman with three children. He recognized young Peter's earnest face, baby Joe's unmistakable grin and dimple. The woman held a baby wrapped in a blue and yellow quilted blanket. The blanket's pattern of triangles was familiar. The motion in the chapel distracted him. Around him people fumbled with their candles. Keith, reaching across Donna, tapped Ben's arm with a candle until Ben took it absently in hand. Peering at the photograph, Ben noticed two things at once. He saw, as if in a mirror, the baby's eye was his own with its wide, keyhole-shaped notch; he saw that this woman's eyes were likewise divided by malformed pupils and looked as blue as his own damaged eyes now shimmering with quick tears.

"Oh," he whispered in the darkness. "It's you."

He looked up again, blinking back the tears. Around him his friends and neighbors awaited the ushers bringing them light. Ben saw their shadowed faces, solemn, expectant, sure they had come to witness his coming to know. Glancing at his mother's picture, he knew a surge of love for her, a feeling of deep familiarity that had risen in him at her distinct voice speaking in those penned words. Her winsome face, her contemplative expression, her smile, her struggles—these elusive qualities were what had made her concrete to him. Those who sat closer to Ben saw his head bent in tears of grief, saw his shoulders shake once, twice in silent sobs. So lately identified, so briefly real to him, so recently loved, he did not have to read the article that lay under his hand to know that it said his mother had died there on the corner of East Crescent Avenue and Franklin Turnpike.

Tears splashed on his wrist in a fury of grief and light. Three people had died in the accident. Gregen's Sibilla died trying to report Max's crime. Certainly the other driver had died or Max's horrible secret would sooner have been known. The third was his mother. She had died, he realized from the description at his hand, trying to leap from the car. In a wildly hopeful gesture, she meant to catch up what his father had thrown away. She had died trying to snatch him from the trajectory toward death that his father had willed for his life.

He touched the torn newspaper article, eyes catching words through the swimming tears.

> Captain Thomas C. MacBride, USMC, of Annapolis, Maryland, rescued the infant when he stopped at the accident scene. "I heard the baby crying and saw him going under so I picked him up," MacBride told police.

He found me in the puddle. Ben recalled the look of astonished joy, now fully justified, that met him always in Tom's eyes. Behind the paper he felt padding and touched underneath. Stapled there was a torn fragment of the quilt in the photograph. He compared them, holding the photograph up to it, then touched the seams with his finger and remembered doing so to lull himself to sleep when he was young. Ben noticed a small paper label, Gregen's handwriting recognizable. Ben lifted the fragment and it came off the book into his hand. Gregen's label identified it as the piece torn off when Tom lifted him from the water to safety, the edges too ragged to be sewn back into the little quilt that had comforted him when he had been small and suddenly motherless.

Ben slid his mother's journal into his pocket. The last pages were letters to him. These he would read and treasure in the days to come. He looked up and moved his head to see Laurie. She was watching for him and smiled her yearning smile. Cara rested on her shoulder and Ben saw again his blanket's pattern repeated in miniature, in pink, wrapped around the baby. *Bien sur*, he told himself. It was the signature of Eight Hands Around. Blazoned on the paper bags that daily held his lunch, she had also made a flag of it and hung this from her wide front porch to fly out over Annapolis to beckon him. The blanket had given him threadbare comfort, but Tom and Laurie had taken the memory of its soft, humble beauty and made a home for him here beneath that banner, a home that they had filled with everything he loved—a home irresistible to him.

Beside him, a scuffling noise startled him from his reverie. His father was leaning past Gran, nearly stepping on Keith while Donna and Tim tried to flatten themselves back against the pew. Max held his lit and dripping candle out to Ben. Rapidly and with an odd detachment, Ben saw the shape of his own hands in Max's, saw the muscled curve of the thigh, the exact length as his. He saw the wide foot so like his own, but kicking back now at Smitty who was reaching to restrain Max. Ben knew he would not allow his own foot, made in his father's express image, to kick in vicious temper. Like Tom, like his mother, he might feel an impulse, but would choose to rule it.

Inside Ben his spirit breathed.

But Max wiggled, rebuffing Smitty, slapping shamelessly at the hands that tried to impose dignity upon him. Max held out his candle and whispered hoarsely, "Ben! Ben!" his hand shaking so badly that the wax splayed on the hymnals. Beside him Gran also held out her candle to Ben, mouthing the words, "Please, give me your journal. Think about this."

Lindquist had come around the front of the pew and was reaching for Max's candle when Ben called him. "Major," he whispered. Ben took his own journal and pressed it into Lindquist's hand. "Could you see that the admiral gets this, please?"

Lindquist nodded solemnly. "Absolutely," he said.

Ben turned from the hands thrust at him, turned from the protests hissed to him. He gripped the rail that held him in that pew and felt once more the quiet tremors of the holy song moving through the chapel into the very wood of the pews like a heartbeat to fingers. Across the chapel, the light grew down the rows. One by one, each candle was lit until Ben saw a string of lights leading across the room to the pew that held the MacBrides. His own grandmother had said it, though in spite, still true. "Biological parenthood is so random." The truth of his belonging had been pictured at his uncommon birth.

Gregen lit Tom's candle, Joe tipped his candle into Tom's flame. Joe looked up, met Ben's eyes. Leaning on his hand, Ben vaulted over the pew railing. The row tangent to his looked up and as one man, sat back. They made room for Ben and ushered him along the row as he begged them excuse him in his nearly headlong rush to get to Tom, whose confession of the deeper, spiritual responsibility he felt for Ben stood clearly true in the darkened room. And to a boy like Ben, who knew now that he was more than a physical being, who had learned just this hour that the ineffable qualities last like gold, to this boy, this sort of fatherhood seemed beautiful.

Friends, neighbors, Tom's colleagues, Ben's peers leaned back to make way, held their candles up high above their heads to light his path, and between breaths of the song, they whispered encouragement to him, helping him pass through, hands like fond uncles or aunts patting his waist and shoulders.

Tom was waiting for him. Ben stumbled out of the row and Tom held out his candle, leaning forward, his other hand extended, welcoming. Ben stood before Tom, suddenly shy, and saw the candlelight's glow in an orb around Tom's hand. At the railing he dipped his dead wick to light it in the flickering flame that Tom held out to him.

Ben took the bit of torn blanket from his mother's journal and wrapped it around the base of the candle. He held the delicate light up for the MacBrides to see. In a moment they were over the pew, out of the row in a tight circle around him. Eight hands reached to hold him, candles held aloft shone down on their overjoyed faces. The truth came clear: one father had cast him away, but another took him up again.

"Can I have a ride home, Coach?" Ben said. "I'm too hungry to run."

Epilogue

In the MacBrides' living room, warm from the fireplace's light glowing red-orange and fragrant with the melting smell of a dozen flickering candles, Ben sat between Tom and Laurie watching everybody gather to await midnight's coming. Uncle Gregen held Cara in his arms and showed her the twinkling lights on the Christmas tree. Tommy rushed into the room with a big plate of cookies and Peter followed carrying a tray with cups of steaming chocolate. Joe sat down at the piano and played the Christmas songs they called for as Bonnie Jean sang along.

Laurie chose the biggest cup from the tray and put it into Ben's hands; he stirred the cream into his chocolate and lifted the spoon to his lips. His senses were awake and tingling to the laughing sounds of their music, the mellow beauty of Bonnie Jean's shining eyes, the tumult of patchwork quilts tossed on the back of the chair, Peter's bold still-life paintings framed on the walls amidst prints of faded maps and ancient drawings of angels with wings as bright as the fire that burned now bright and brighter.

Now Gregen took Cara to stand before the fireplace, holding her up so she could coo at the kindly, winking Santa on the mantle. In the quiet between songs, Gregen read her the names embroidered on the stockings hung there until he came to the last one, nameless and unused. When he touched it, Laurie said, "Oh, I made that years ago for Ben...hoping." She reached her hand out. "Toss it to me, Uncle Gregen, please. I'll embroider Ben's name on it now."

When he put it in her hand, she reached inside where she'd left a threaded needle and slid it through the fabric. Indicating Cara's car seat left empty beside the table, Peter said, "I remember a baby in a seat like that, right next to Joe. That must have been you, Ben. I called you 'Baby.'"

"You called him 'Ours Baby.' Ben wasn't officially named yet."

"That's right!" Peter said. "Ours Baby and Joe."

Ben confided, "My mother wrote that she wanted to name me Thomas Benedetto."

"It's a great name," Bonnie Jean said.

"Thomas. That's cool," Tommy said. "Just like me and Dad."

"And Benedetto, after your Uncle *Benedetto* Gregen," Laurie added, smiling.

Gregen nodded. "My grandfather—your great-great-grandfather—was also named Benedetto. It is a name that has been in our family for generations."

Looking at Tom, Ben said, "Did you know what...she wanted to name me, when you were up there in Hillside?"

"Neither Laurie nor I knew that then. Your mother...*Katie* must have written that while she was in the hospital."

"I didn't see that much of Katie those weeks," Laurie said. "I was so busy taking care of you and Pete and Joe."

"Laurie stayed with us at Apple Tree Farm," Gregen said, "to care for you."

"I came up on weekends. I have a picture," Tom said, digging his wallet out of his pocket and from between Peter and Joe's pictures, he pulled out the faded, folded photograph. The MacBrides crowded around to see.

"You were *so* cute," Bonnie Jean said.

"You were eight days old," Tom said. "That's me holding you. You can just see my chin, but that's me."

Ben could see that it was Tom: the way he held his arms with the baby cradled in the bend of the elbow, the gesture of the broad, tanned hands—this he had seen a hundred times in his care for his own children. And Ben thought that Tom still wore the shirt shown in the picture—a kind of a yellow checked thing.

Joe said, "Isn't that the same shirt you had on this morning?"

"I love that shirt. It's still in good shape."

Laurie rolled her eyes and the MacBrides giggled.

"See, Ben, when your mom had to be hospitalized for her kidney infection, you were frantic when she wasn't there. You refused to take a bottle—refused water, formula, everything—and screamed so hard your whole body was quaking. And you kept it up for hours. I finally got the bright idea of giving you a bath to calm you down."

"You mean since he was too young to go for a run," Joe teased.

"You have to understand how much Ben screamed," Laurie said. "No sleeping."

Gregen, with Cara asleep now on his shoulder, leaned over to see the photograph. "I suggested a wet nurse, of course."

"The bath did distract you from thinking about your mother and feeling upset about being offered a bottle. Then Laurie was able to coax you to nurse."

"*What* did you say?"

"Aw, you don't mean..." Joe said.

"Mama?" Bonnie Jean asked.

"Yes. That's right. Laurie fed you for about a month."

Ben turned to her, wide-eyed. "Like—you mean—"

778

With a shrug, Laurie rocked her needle into the stocking fabric and said, "You refused any kind of bottle or anything that goes *in* a bottle—"

Tom interrupted, "We tried spoon feeding, tried dipping your pacifier in formula and offering that—"

"It is a perfectly sensible alternative," Gregen said, "and also kind."

"You protested a little, because you knew Laurie wasn't your mom, but she held you there and then put Joe across her lap so he could nurse on the other side."

"Both of us?"

"It's done all the time with twins," Laurie said pulling the thread taut.

"Joe was five months older and already a champ and I think he cheered you on."

"Yeah, Joe," Peter said, elbowing his brother.

"Having him there, kind of holding you in, you probably felt secure," Tom said, looking at Ben, his eyes careful and sympathetic.

Joe and Ben looked at each other and said, "Freaky." Laughter tiptoed among them.

"That's when we all fell in love with you," Laurie said, knotting the gold thread with one deft motion. "And because Tom knew your cry, he found you the day of the accident."

"Yes, of course," Gregen said. "Tom was beside you seconds after he opened his door. I had not even stopped the car."

"My window was open and I heard you. Screaming. Furious. So I looked toward the sound and you were on your back, struggling in this"— he gestured with his arms to show the dimensions—"pothole at the side of the road. It was fairly deep—I'd say about ten inches deep and wide. All the rain we'd had that week melted the snow left from the blizzard and it was full of water. If we'd stopped a few feet closer, we would have hit the puddle." Tom shook his head, chills rising on the tanned skin of his neck, his hands and forearms to where his sleeves were rolled.

"And it's a good thing you were crying," Laurie said, "because you went under. Tom saw you sink under and if he hadn't heard you—and seen where you were…"

"Holy sh—sugar," Joe said.

"That's the drowning kid story, isn't it, Dad?" Tommy asked.

Peter breathed in awe, "Dad, man. Way to keep a secret."

Bonnie Jean said, "So, the puddle cushioned his fall, right? And *he* lived."

Tom looked at his daughter, eyes shining. "I am grateful. I'll be grateful forever."

"You both—" Ben whispered, "did—all that—for me?"

"You were hungry," Tom said.

"You were wet and cold," Laurie whispered.

"Does all this stuff about Mama feeding you make you our *brother*?" Tommy whispered.

"*No*," Bonnie Jean said. "Of *course not!*"

"It's food," Joe said, "not genetic material."

And Gregen, standing behind Joe, nodded. Watching them, heart full, Ben could not speak.

"He's part of our family," Tom said.

"There's no standard way to define his connection to us, so—" Peter said.

"But it means he's ours," Tommy said.

"That's right," Tom said. "He's ours." Ben's eyes flooded and he saw them all in a shimmer of water and light. They moved in close around him, Gregen and all the tenderhearted MacBrides, crying and hugging him as he clung to Laurie, burying his face in her neck; he drank in her scent, the feel of her sturdy arms holding him, believing in her love, because this warmth was so typical of her and her scent now so reasonably familiar. Ben cried hard from a deep down place and he had no sense of time passing. The MacBrides stayed close to him, each with fingertips touching him; they prayed for him, taking turns, praying again, until sorrow had gone and the room was filled with their whispered wonder, with their hopes and desires softly stated while the radiant fire coals dwindled smaller than the roots of the sputtering, sleepy candles lingering faithfully nearby.

Ben brushed his teeth that night standing between Peter and Joe so close that their elbows bumped and they had to angle their shoulders to spit in the sink. Peter draped an arm around Ben's shoulders and smiled at their reflection in the mirror. "We should have grown up like this," Joe said, his mouth full of foam as he gestured with his toothbrush. Ben's heart stirred at the sight of the trio that should have been; he understood now why Joe had always been able to speak his obscured thoughts. Not blood brothers, their connection—born of sympathy, nurtured by generosity—lived in the heart and mind and felt more real to Ben.

"Use the mouthwash," Joe said, thunking the bottle down with a challenging look to Peter first, then Ben. Peter took a swig from the bottle and handed it to Ben.

Joe pumped the liquid around in his mouth, puffing out his cheeks. Ben poked Joe's side and he spit in a burst that sprayed the mirror and sink. Above their laughter, Ben heard Tom call from the next room. "Wipe that up!" and Peter gave the mirror a cursory swipe with his hand and whispered to Ben, "He's everywhere. Never forget that."

Crowding through the bathroom doorway together, Peter and Joe took him into their room that was the bluish color of the bay and busy with shelves of trophies and books, bulletin boards and posters on the walls. Between the sturdy wooden beds, under the window, a bed had been made for Ben.

Laurie turned down the puffy cover on his bed. "I know you boys are too old for tucking in," she said, laughing at herself, "but Dad and I haven't outgrown it yet."

Tom took the pillow and set it down, with a gesture toward the bed. "It's just a trundle we keep under Joe's bed, but it's nice and soft and it's yours—"

Ben stared at it. "Coach."

Tom patted the bed. Laurie held up the corner of the covers like the door of a tent. In Ben went, sinking deep into the fluffy softness that cushioned all his angles and sore places with a cool smoothness. Tom pulled the cover up to his chin and Ben moved his palm across the bed and the softness whispered answered prayers to him. He watched Tom and Laurie unfold a bright quilt. Each took a corner; orange and gold, green and blue, crimson and brown flashed as they shook it above him like a bird's wing outspreading. Tom smoothed the quilt out over the duvet as if fastening down the cloud blanket to keep Ben safely there.

"I owe you *my life*," Ben vowed in a whisper.

"Then give it to God." Tom said.

"How do you *do* that?" Ben asked, looking up to see Tom's answer in his eyes.

"You start by asking that question."

BLESSING HOUSE PRESS

Blessing House Press presents works that explore the importance of community, compassion, creativity and beauty in showing God's love to a world of frail and faulty people. Believing that unique voices should be heard, Blessing House Press offers thoughtful works that explore important ideas and invite readers to hope. To read a Blessing House book is to enter a vivid, unforgettable world where, despite the trauma of life, beautiful things happen.

Solomon's Puzzle is Blessing House Press' debut novel.

FOR MORE INFORMATION:
www.solomonspuzzle.com
blessinghousepress@gmail.com